BY THE AUTHOR

STARK SECURITY
shattered with you
shadows of you-short story
broken with you
ruined with you

THE STARK SAGA
novels
release me
claim me
complete me
anchor me
lost with me

novellas
take me
have me
play my game
seduce me
unwrap me

deepest kiss
entice me
hold me
please me
indulge me

For all of JK's Stark World and other titles,
please visit www.jkenner.com

Praise for J. Kenner's Novels

"*Shattered With You* is a sultry little page turner that comes brimming with scorching passion, edge of your seat action, and heart-wrenching emotion." *Reds Romance Reviews*

"J. Kenner is an exceptional storyteller. The drama, tension, and heat were perfect." *About That Story*

"PERFECT for fans of *Fifty Shades of Grey* and *Bared to You*. *Release Me* is a powerful and erotic romance novel." *Reading, Eating & Dreaming Blog*

"I will admit, I am in the 'I loved *Fifty Shades*' camp, but after reading *Release Me*, Mr. Grey only scratches the surface compared to Damien Stark." *Cocktails and Books Blog*

"It is not often when a book is so amazingly well-written that I find it hard to even begin to accurately describe it . . . " *Romancebookworm's Reviews*

"With her sophisticated prose, Kenner created a love story that had the perfect blend of lust, passion, sexual tension, raw emotions and love." - Michelle, Four Chicks Flipping Pages

STARK
SECURITY
COLLECTION

NEW YORK TIMES BESTSELLING AUTHOR

J. KENNER

M&O

Cover design by Michele Catalano, Catalano Creative
Cover images by Annie Ray/Passion Pages
ISBN: 978-1-949925-94-4
Published by Martini & Olive Books
v-2020-4-29P

SHATTERED WITH YOU

SHATTERED
WITH YOU
J. KENNER
NEW YORK TIMES BESTSELLING AUTHOR

CONTENTS

PREFACE

I know I shouldn't want him.

I wish I didn't crave him.

With every day that passes, I pray that the sweet throb of yearning will dim. And yet it doesn't.

Awake, I can feed the pain. Can fall back into those memories that cut as deep as a knife. Passion erased. Love eradicated.

Before, there'd been a man who wanted me. After, only a scorch mark remained, like a shadow burned into the ground from a nuclear explosion.

Awake, I can hold onto my anger.

But in my dreams, I always surrender.

I tell myself I'm better off without him. But I need him. His skills. His help.

I have no options left. He is the place where desire and fear meet. And all I can do is pray that I don't shatter like glass under the weight of my regrets.

1

BUILT IN 1931, the historic Hollywood Terrace Hotel once reigned supreme as the place to see and be seen along the famous boulevard. But time wreaked its revenge, and like the fading beauty of Golden Age starlets, the Art Deco palace fell into disrepair as flappers gave way to hippies and Baby Boomers, all of whom were overrun by Millennials who watched as the twentieth century rolled inexorably into the twenty-first.

For the first decade of the new millennium, the once majestic icon stood faded and broken. The exterior stucco dulled to a lifeless gray. Windows soiled and cracked. The famous gardens overrun with vermin and weeds.

The interior fared no better. Mold grew around leaky pipes. Rats scurried the halls, surrendering only to the feral cats who claimed the dark spaces as their own. Carpets rotted. Wallpaper peeled. And a fine dust covered every surface like a blanket of neglect.

With the determination of a beleaguered prizefighter, the building fought to stay upright despite the repeated blows of weather, earthquakes, and the monotonous parade of progress marked by shiny new storefronts. When yellow tape emblazoned with *Condemned* and *Do Not Cross* appeared across the etched glass doors, the locals were certain that the final blow had been landed.

Then Scott Lassiter rode to the rescue, and it turned out that the story of the Hollywood Terrace wasn't a boxing movie after all. It was a makeover. *My Fair Lady* for the bedraggled hotel.

The international real estate developer pulled out all the stops, remaking The Hollywood Terrace into the gem it had been almost a century before. He turned the mezzanine conference rooms into his private suite of offices, and claimed the entire top floor as his stunning penthouse residence, complete with an indoor pool and a formal ballroom.

Everyone who was anyone attended the grand reopening five years ago, and Lassiter was feted by the town's movers and shakers as a hero. A miracle worker. A true citizen, devoted to preserving the history that had put this corner of Southern California on the map when those first pioneers with cameras had hustled to the land of manna and sunshine.

That party had made headlines across the globe, the Hollywood connection and the many stars on the guest list making the story too delicious to ignore.

Tonight's party was even more lush. Dozens upon dozens of guests filled the meticulously restored Art Deco ballroom with its bold colors and geometric designs. The combined incomes of the well-heeled, international guests made a Hollywood star's bankroll look like a teenager's allowance. Rare champagne vintages flowed in fountains of pure silver. The women glided over the marble floors in formal gowns designed to accentuate assets of the non-gemstone variety. And any man in a suit that cost less than twenty-five grand was obviously a poser.

And yet despite the beautiful people floating on clouds of money-soaked power, there was no press in the ballroom for this soirée. No photographers clicking away for sexy images to post on Page Six or Instagram. On the contrary, this party was an intimate affair conducted in Lassiter's own private fiefdom.

And only a *very* select and very exclusive clientele had been invited.

Stark Security operative Quincy Radcliffe was not on the guest list. Not officially, anyway. That, however, didn't stop him from signaling a passing waiter and snagging a scotch and soda.

He sipped it slowly, his dispassionate gaze studying the cadre of tailored men and coiffed women who moved in and out of Lassiter's orbit, as if they were coming to pay tribute to a god.

Blind fools.

All they saw was Lassiter's money and power. They had no idea that their host's hefty bank account had been generated less by his real estate portfolio and more by the percentage he took from money laundering and protection schemes.

Scott Lassiter was a manipulative prick whose sharp talons reached deep into the criminal underground. And someday it would be Quince's pleasure to pull the rug firmly out from under the feckless tosser, then ensure that Lassiter abandoned his plush penthouse for a different view. The kind with dozens of iron bars.

That, however, wasn't on tonight's agenda. For the time being, Lassiter was the lesser of two evils, and if everything went as planned, the pathetic wanker would be an unknowing conduit to the sex-trafficking, sub-human monster who was at the core of tonight's mission: *Corbu. Marius Corbu.*

"Incredible, isn't he?"

The breathy voice came from a brown-eyed blonde with long, straight hair that hung to the middle of her back and a soft fringe of bangs that brushed her perfectly arched brows. She wore a filmy gold dress and make-up so expertly applied it seemed invisible except for the dark liner that shaped her wide eyes and lipstick so red he couldn't help think of ripe cherries.

"You're referring to our host, Mr. Lassiter?"

She giggled and sloshed her champagne as she struggled to clap her hands. "O.M.G.,"—she actually said *O.M.G.*—"You're British."

"Bloody hell. Am I really?"

She laughed again. "And funny, too. No. What's that word? *Droll.* You're very droll." She cocked her head, studying him. He knew what she saw. Dark hair, a lean face, and deep-set gray eyes. He wore an Ermenegildo Zegna bespoke suit that cost more than his car, and according to his partner Denise, he looked "fabulously fuckable."

The blonde apparently agreed, because he saw the exact moment that her gaze shifted from amused to predatory. "I like a funny man." Her voice was low. Sultry. "A man who laughs probably does other interesting things with his mouth, too." She tilted her head provocatively. "I'm Desiree. What's your name?"

"Canton," he said, giving her his mission alias as a hedge fund manager based in Hong Kong. "Robert Canton."

She eased toward him, the dress shifting from opaque to sheer as she stepped into a puddle of light. She was entirely bare under the flimsy gown, and he felt his body tighten in reflex, but not desire. Slowly, she ran her fingers over the lapel of his jacket, then continued the downward motion until she was cupping his cock, hard now because, after all, he wasn't dead. Nor was he surprised. This party was about sex, after all. Paid, kinky, anonymous sex. And God knew he wasn't immune to the charms of a beautiful woman.

She pressed her free hand to his shoulder as she leaned in to whisper. "Well, I'm all yours, Mr. Canton. However you want me, all the way until the sun comes up." She nipped at his earlobe, and he thought how easy it would be. She'd be willing to do bloody well anything—that was the point of tonight's little meet-and-greet. And damned if he didn't need to take the edge off.

Some operations were harder than others, and this one was a right pisser. It had gotten into his head. Worse, it had gotten into his blood. And it burned there like a slow poison. Or more accurately like a fuse. Let it burn too long, and he'd explode. The dark memories would win out, the monster would grab control, and–

Bloody hell.

"Oooh, I think that's a yes." She started to slowly stroke him. "I've never fucked an English guy, and I promise you I'm worth it. Please tell me you haven't given some other girl your key."

He produced a thin smile, then slowly moved her hand off his crotch. "Sorry, love. I'm sure you'd give me a right proper ride, but my key's already spoken for."

"Maybe not," the female voice said into his ear. It was Denise, and she was currently on the roof across the street. And also in his ear. Listening to absolutely everything since their coms were on VOX. *"I can't get the transmitter arm to lock in place. I'm going to have to stay up here and position it manually."*

"Bloody hell."

"What?" Desiree asked.

"It's just a pisser that you won't be in my bed tonight. But rules are rules." And the rules of this party mirrored the old suburban key parties of the sixties and seventies. Bottom line—a man claimed a woman with a key, she went to his room, and he spent the night enjoying her, as Desiree had said, any way he wanted until the sun came up.

The beauty of the party from the perspective of the men was that every woman was a sure thing because each and every female was a high class call girl who was well-paid by Lassiter to attend. Denise included, although to be fair, it was her alias—Candy—who was getting that nice pay day.

As for the men, they each paid Lassiter a hefty sum, supposedly for a room at the hotel. In reality, the payment assured the privilege of finding a Miss Right willing to satisfy any and all kinks, fetishes, and predilections. As a bonus, they each enjoyed the smug satisfaction of buying sex without actually paying for sex.

Quince didn't need a woman in his room. He needed a partner to act as a lookout and keep the small signal booster in perfect alignment with both the transmitter and Lassiter's computer. The transmitter that Denny was battling on the nearby roof wouldn't do a damn bit of good if the signal wasn't captured in his room on the fourth floor, then boosted down to where Quince would be hacking Lassiter's computer on the mezzanine level.

And while Desiree might be willing to fulfill his every kinky fantasy, he doubted that she would regard helping him hack into Lassiter's system as a genuine fetish. Besides, she'd already wandered off in search of another key master.

Easy come, easy go.

"You realize this is a problem," he murmured, lifting his

glass to hide the slight movement of his lips, then taking a long swallow because he damn sure needed it.

"No, really? I'm so glad you're here to explain things to me."

He swallowed a laugh. "Temper, temper."

"You can't tell, but I'm flipping you off."

"I'd expect nothing less." He crossed to the window so that he could talk more easily, keeping an eye on the guests in the reflection as he pretended to study Hollywood below. Denny was out there, perched atop an old department store that had been converted to office space.

"Fuck it. I'm going to use a strip of duct tape to get as close to dead-on perfect as I can. I can get back pronto. You need me in that room."

He did, dammit. But they also needed certainty with regard to the transmission. This mission was the pivotal point in a joint EU and Spanish task force operation to take down Corbu and his international sex-trafficking operation. Stark Security had been hired to handle this one critical piece of the puzzle. A single, limited mission to get in, obtain and decrypt Lassiter's contact files, then pass along the contact protocol for Corbu to the task force.

Fail and Stark Security would lose its growing reputation in the international intelligence community. More important, thousands of innocent lives were at stake, and the window of opportunity was tight. As they said at America's NASA, failure was not an option.

"I'm coming to you." He knew damn well she was more than competent, but he had to try. "Maybe I can secure the arm."

"There's not enough time. I have to capture the signal in fifteen minutes and you need to be in position in twenty. Blow the window and we're fucked."

He pulled out the antique Patek Philippe pocket watch

that had once belonged to the father he'd barely known. Exceptionally crafted, it still kept perfect time, though its accuracy had little to do with why Quince wore it religiously. Almost superstitiously.

The Patek Philippe was a reminder of the past, a warning against the future.

It would never lead him astray, and right then it told him that Denny was right.

Bollocks.

"All right," he said. "Get over here." It was a huge risk, but the powerful transmitter was designed to allow for the transmission and reception of the massive data packets necessary for the cutting edge decryption software hosted back at the SSA. With luck, Denny's rigged up anchor would allow the transmitter to capture and relay enough of the signal to the booster in Quincy's hotel room. That device worked much like a WiFi router, and it would send the signal out into the interior of the hotel, where it would hit the tech that Quince would be using to hack into Lassiter's system.

For that to work, however, the transmitter's signal had to hit the booster with dead-on accuracy. Anything less, and the booster would be relaying garbage to Quince, not the high-end hacking software created by Stark Applied Technology. Not an ideal situation, but they had no choice.

He turned back to face the room. He needed to know where Lassiter was so that he could slip down to his assigned room on the fourth floor without being noticed. *There.*

Lassiter was standing in a group of five men and two women, his hand low on a slim brunette's back. Reddish-brown hair fell down to her shoulders, her smooth skin revealed in the low-cut dress that came close to revealing the crack of her perfect, heart-shaped ass. There was something so familiar about her...

He brushed the thought away as irrelevant. "All right. I've spotted Lassiter. I'm heading—"

Then she turned, and he saw her face.

He froze. He absolutely fucking froze.

Eliza? Surely it couldn't be Eliza.

"*Quince?*" Denny's voice was tight. "*Is it Lassiter? Is he suspicious?*"

"Not Lassiter. A ghost."

"*What?*"

Because she had to be a ghost. The woman with mahogany hair and sky-blue eyes. The woman whose dimple had once made his heart flip.

The woman he'd cherished. Whose scent still lingered in his dreams.

The woman he'd loved more passionately than he'd believed possible. And who now surely hated him more than he could imagine.

There was no way that woman could be at a party like this. No way at all.

Could she?

Dear God, what had she gotten herself wrapped up in?

Without conscious decision, he moved toward her, his long strides eating up the distance as Denny chattered in his ear. "*What's going on? Dammit, I'm on my way. Rendezvous at the room in four minutes.*"

He knew he should turn around. There was too damn much riding on this mission. The lives and freedom of so many innocents who'd become ensnared in the Romanian kingpin's sex trafficking confederation. Thousands upon thousands of tormented victims, including one innocent, terrified thirteen-year-old girl.

Her abduction was the trigger that had pushed the EU task force into immediate action. The daughter of the Prince Regent of one of Europe's smaller monarchy's, the princess had been abducted during a school trip. Her father had gone to the task force's leader, a classmate from Eaton, and essentially opened up the monarchy's massive coffers to fund whatever it took to get the girl back and shut down Corbu's operation.

Quince shuddered as the image of another teen girl flashed in his head. *Shelley.* Her trusting eyes. Her choking sobs. And his own screams of terror and helplessness as fiery pain ripped through him and the world collapsed around him.

And in that moment, he knew what he had to do.

"Stay on the roof," he ordered Denny.

"What? But—"

"Trust me. I've got it covered."

He'd been too damn weak to save Shelley.

He'd failed her. Hell, he'd failed himself.

He damn well wasn't going to fail again.

Even if that meant pulling Eliza Tucker into this buggered-up scheme.

2

HE'S TOUCHING ME. This too-polished, too-twisted, smarmy son-of-a-bitch actually has his hand on the small of my back, his thumb rubbing the bare skin at the base of my spine. It's intimate. It's possessive. It's revolting.

It's my own damn fault.

I'm the one who shoved my tits into this too-tight dress. I'm the one who caught Scott Lassiter's eye. And now it looks like I'm the one who's going to have to endure a night in bed with him if I don't want to risk blowing my cover.

My cover.

The irony isn't lost on me. For my entire life, my sister Emma has been my protector. A brilliant, strong, vengeful angel standing between me and the dangers of the world. Didn't matter if it was mean teachers, street thugs, or our own monstrous prick of a father, she was always right there, doing whatever she had to in order to keep me safe.

And now here I am, stuck in the middle of a situation I don't fully understand as I pretend to be my sister. Or, more accurately, as I pretend to be my sister pretending to be a call girl.

Thank goodness I've spent over a decade working as a semi-struggling actress. Sliding in and out of roles. Commercials, community theater, the occasional bit on a soap opera, and a few small parts in films shot in New York.

I've never tried to land a recurring television role or a long-contract run on or off Broadway. It just doesn't appeal. I want success, sure. It's just that there's something compelling about variety. After all, the more I can get lost in someone else's life, the less I have to examine my own.

All of which makes me an excellent chameleon. Which is probably the only reason that no one is pointing a finger at me à la *Invasion of the Body Snatchers* and screaming that I'm a fraud who doesn't belong here.

Because I don't. I really don't.

And when Emma finds out that I'm not only impersonating her but that I'm putting myself in danger, she's going to be royally pissed. But that's okay. Pissed means she's alive. And all things considered, I want her ranting and raving and furious. Because the alternative is too horrible to even contemplate.

I draw a deep breath. My worries about Emma have been a constant for a full twenty-four hours, ever since I realized she was missing. But I need to push them down, because I have more immediate problems. Like how I'm going to extricate myself from this perv who's decided that I belong to him tonight. Because every minute I'm trapped with Scott Lassiter is another minute I don't have answers.

I shift slightly and glance around the room, wondering who my contact is supposed to be. According to Emma's partner, a few days before she disappeared, an anonymous source had reached out to Emma. He called himself Mr. X and promised her information about a case she was working. All she had to do was meet him at this party.

"They couldn't grab a booth at McDonalds?" I'd asked.

A wide grin had split Lorenzo's ruddy face. He'd run a hand over his head, pushing a tuft of hair to one side to reveal his growing bald spot. "Pretty sure that wasn't on the table, baby girl."

I crossed my arms and cocked my head in response to the endearment, but he brushed me off. I've known Lorenzo since I was nine and he was a beat cop in Venice Beach who'd looked the other way when he caught Emma and me sleeping in an abandoned car.

All Lorenzo knew was that Emma had been working on one of her pro bono cases. After over a decade working for the government, she'd gone out as a full-time private investigator a few years ago. Her passion is helping runaways and other endangered kids, and Lorenzo told me that she'd stumbled across some sort of exploitation conspiracy that was organized in forums hosted on the dark web.

"I'm guessing Mr. X is in deep, but wants out," Lorenzo had said.

"So he contacted Emma and set a meet," I guessed. "But before it could happen, the real baddies also realized she was poking around in the forum. Somehow they figured out her identity and grabbed her."

"That's what it looks like to me."

My chest tightened as I forced out the next words. "Did they—do you think they killed her?"

"I hope not," he'd said, his basset hound eyes profoundly sad.

"I have to go to the police."

"And what would they do? For starters, they'd tell you to wait. Her apartment is relatively neat—"

"Someone was in it." I was sure about that.

"*You* say. But it's not ransacked. You say things are out of place, but that doesn't necessarily mean foul play. All you know is that she's gone and you don't know where. But she's a grown woman. She could have left on a whim. Gone off with a man. Decided to take up fly-fishing."

"She always tells me where she's going. We don't keep secrets." I think of the things she's told me that she should have held close. Dangerous things if anyone found out.

No. She wouldn't keep something important from me.

"Last I heard, you were supposed to be on some cruise ship," Lorenzo says when I point that out. "She said you'd told her not to bother calling, but that you'd check in from various ports."

I grimaced. All true. Except that I never even had the chance to set sail.

I'd landed a role in a shipboard musical. Three full months at sea visiting a variety of ports. Three months of one and two week excursions, a different set of passengers on every journey. Ninety full days with no one from my past, and no one who would be part of my future. The job had sounded like heaven, and I'd jumped all over it.

But then the cruise line cancelled the show entirely, replacing the large-cast musical with a single stand-up comedian. Budget cuts. Which left me not only out of work, but at loose ends.

Which was why I'd decided to fly to LA to visit my sister.

Emma, however, was gone.

"She would have sent an email if she decided to take a last minute vacation," I told Lorenzo. "You know she would." Emma and I are more than just sisters. She practically raised me. And it had been the two of us against the world ever since that horrible day when she'd pulled me from the house that was never, *ever* a home.

Lorenzo had nodded sagely. "I know it. You know it. The

cops don't. You need more if you want help. *We* need more. You think I'm not worried? This is Emma we're talking about. She's like a daughter to me. You both are."

"You really think this Mr. X knows something?"

"I think he's the only lead we have. I'd go if I could, but I don't think I can pull off a low-cut evening gown."

He was right. I knew it. And not just about how he'd look in drag.

I either went to the meeting or I let time slip away until the cops might legitimately get interested.

Put it that way, and there was no question. Emma was in trouble, and that was all that mattered to me. Because at the end of the day, *she's* all that matters to me. Well, her and Lorenzo. They're all I have. All I've ever had.

Once upon a time, I thought there might be someone else. Dark and edgy, sweet and sensual, Quincy Radcliffe had an intensity that had drawn me to him and a strength that had held me close. In his arms, I'd felt safer than I had since I'd left Emma and Los Angeles. I'd opened the steel cage around my heart and invited him inside.

We were together for almost three months, and in that time I let my guard down completely. I let myself love him, and I thought he loved me, too.

I'll never make that mistake again.

He ripped me apart. Shattered my soul from the inside out.

He'd made me love him. And I can't forgive him for that.

But I have to thank him, too. Because I learned my lesson that spring in London. I'd thought that maybe I could change. That perhaps the wall I'd built and the masks I put on didn't have to be permanent. That I could chip away at those barriers and try to let someone else inside.

Quince made me want to try. He made me hope.

And when he betrayed me ... well, he taught me that I needed those walls. They were what kept me safe.

Now Emma lives inside the walls. Lorenzo, too.

Just them. Only them.

They're all I have, and that's why I'm here in the Art Deco elegance of the Hollywood Terrace penthouse ballroom.

It's why I followed Mr. X's detailed instructions for the meet. Why I'm pretending to be one of the many call girls hired for the evening. And why in addition to my slinky black dress, I'm wearing a red ribbon as a bracelet, just as instructed. The point is to signal to Mr. X that I'm the anonymous BAB, the alias Emma was using in the forum.

It stands for Bad Ass Bitch, though I'm probably the only one in the world who knows that. Right now, I don't feel particularly bad ass. I wish I did. Because a bad ass bitch could probably figure out a way to disengage herself from the man who seems determined to keep me at his side.

Then again, I'm supposed to be in character. A call girl named Bunny. And girls like Bunny aren't bad asses. On the contrary, girls like Bunny drop to their knees or spread their legs on command. I understand Bunnies, so I'm not exactly stretching my acting chops tonight.

Maybe if my name for the night was Amber or Domino or Serena. If I had a riding crop instead of a red ribbon. Maybe then I could put on a show. Really step out of myself and pull on the BAB persona.

But I don't. I can't.

Just as well, I think. Because from what I can tell, this is a party full of Bunnies. Not Serenas.

In other words, I've stepped into a world that is run entirely and completely by men. Rich, powerful, controlling men. With dark and dangerous appetites.

Oh, Emma. What did you stumble into?

I've been asking myself that question ever since Lassiter zeroed in on me, which happened the moment I'd entered the penthouse. At first, I'd thought it was because he saw through my cover. Later, when he commented on my unusual bracelet, I breathed a sigh of relief, assuming that he was Mr. X. Soon enough, though, I realized that he just wanted me naked.

Now, I'm stuck with him when I need to be mingling. I need to be reaching for drinks on waiters' trays, making sure I flash the red ribbon enough that Mr. X can't miss it. At the same time, it's very clear that female autonomy is not the buzzword for the day, and that if Lassiter wants me at his side, then I'm stuck there until he deigns to set me free.

Fuck.

"Actually, I'm already in progress on similar remodels in Chicago, Houston, and Manhattan," Lassiter is saying to some billionaire mucky-muck with a thick Italian accent who'd asked if Lassiter was planning to expand his "business model." Since I'm disgusted by the whole scenario, I tune him out, only to jump when I hear my name. Or, rather, when I hear my hooker name.

"—like Bunny here."

"I'm sorry, what?"

Lassiter smiles indulgently, then squeezes my ass. I refrain from slapping him, since that would definitely be out of character. "I was telling Mr. Scutari that all of the women at my soirées are delightful, but there are a few who have a rare quality. A stunning allure." He brushes my hair behind my ear, and I have to force myself to smile instead of flinch. Not that I'm a shiny, pure little angel. Far, far from it. But there are men who can have me in their bed and men who can't.

Lassiter lives deep in *can't* territory. And right now I'm praying that Mr. X finds me soon. I'd even be okay with a massive earthquake hitting LA. Anything to keep Lassiter from presenting me with his key and aiming me toward his room. Because I'm pretty sure that the only reason he hasn't keyed me yet is that he's the host, and he has to wait until all his guests have selected their girls.

I expect him to continue waxing poetic about the quality of the merchandise, but instead the conversation shifts to international finance. As if this is an average cocktail party and I'm his dutiful, doting girlfriend.

The whole thing is very surreal, and with every moment that passes, I'm afraid that coming here was a mistake. I'm not any closer to finding Emma, and as the night drags on the chances of ending up in Lassiter's bed are increasing. I'd known that was a risk, of course. But I'd assumed that Mr. X would find me, then we'd go to his room, purportedly for sexy shenanigans, but really for an intensive, clandestine discussion of what happened to my sister and how we can help her.

So where the hell is he?

I punctuate the thought by twisting around to survey the room. Lassiter's hand stays possessively on my back, and I force myself not to grimace. I'm so focused on not jerking my body out from under his touch that I can barely take in the room around me.

Which explains why I don't immediately register the man stalking toward us, his long stride eating up the ground as he crosses the length of the ballroom.

Quincy Radcliffe.

The man who left me. Who broke my heart.

My mouth goes dry, my blood running hot through my body.

My palm tingles with the desire to slap him. And when I see those deep gray eyes lock onto mine, I silently scream out a warning begging him not to say my name.

That's when it hits me.

That's when the pieces fall together.

Quincy Radcliffe is the reason I'm here. My Quincy is Mr. X.

So what the hell am I going to do now?

3

I watch his face as he approaches, searching for some hint of pain. Some shadow of regret.

There's nothing, though. His face might as well be carved out of stone, his gray eyes forged in steel. He doesn't waver. His expression is carefully blank. If I didn't know better, I'd think he didn't recognize me at all.

But he does, of course.

For three glorious months, Quincy Radcliffe had been my everything. My champion. My knight. He'd stood at my side and battled my demons, and I'd surrendered to him completely, shedding my fears and, yes, even nurturing my hopes.

He was my love. My heart.

The man whose smile had teased me and whose body aroused me. The man with whom I'd shared my secrets and my tears.

He knew me better than any man ever had, and he cut me more deeply than any man ever could.

I want to rip my arm away from Lassiter. I want to sprint

out of this room on these nail-point heels. I want to forget everything—Quincy, Emma, Mr. X.

Most of all, I want to escape myself and my memories.

But I can't. And as I stand there gawping at the gorgeous bastard who is advancing toward me, the floor opens up, and suddenly I'm hurtling more than four years into the past ... and into the memories of the man who destroyed me.

———

It was my last full day in the UK, and despite the September chill and the light drizzle, I walked the short distance from my tiny, eclectic flat in Soho to the Waterstones bookstore at Picadilly Circus. I wanted to buy a novel. Something uniquely British that wouldn't be published in the States for at least a few more months. And I wanted to go upstairs and enjoy afternoon tea by the window while I savored the first chapter. Then I'd silently close the book and tuck it away to finish on my flight back to Manhattan.

To be honest, I couldn't wait to get on that plane and escape this cramped island, so small that my memories had no place to go, and so they clung to me. Weighing me down.

Back home, I'd be able to shake them off. Banish them. *Go west, damn memories!* But here...

Here in this ancient city, it felt like he was everywhere. And all I wanted to do was escape the foolish, horrible pull that Quincy Radcliffe still had over me.

How quickly things change, right? Because when I'd arrived six months prior, I'd been giddy at the thought of living in the UK for half a year. I'd come to London to join the cast of a unique improv company that performed modern riffs on favorite Shakespeare plays. The thought of playing a different role each night had made my heart soar and my creativity sing. The run was supposed to be five months, and afterwards, I'd spend a month sightseeing before heading back to Manhattan where I'd already lined up a small role as a murder victim in the upcoming season of a popular television show.

But that's not how things panned out. The show closed after one week, which meant I was in a foreign country with no income. I considered going home—I didn't have immediate work lined up there, either, but auditioning in New York was at least a familiar process. Plus, I knew all the best temp agencies.

Emma had come to my rescue, as usual. She reminded me that I'd flat-swapped. Which meant that I didn't have a home to return to, since a British author was currently in my apartment, using the time to finish his latest project. "You've already got the flat in London," she'd said. "All you need is spending money."

Since she knew I wouldn't take her cash as sisterly charity, she offered me the long-distance job of organizing her and Lorenzo's online files. It was a little bit of a gimme, but not entirely. Both Emma and Lorenzo lacked the organizational gene. They could scan, download, or type information into a computer, but then it just stayed there like a dead fish stinking up their hard drive. My job was to shove all those rotten fish heads into tidy little digital folders. Hard for them, easy for me.

Which meant that I was gainfully employed in London with a job that took very little effort and left me with all the time in the world to explore the city, pretending I was a Londoner. Or maybe a runaway heiress. Or a travel photographer. God knew I took enough shots with my ancient Canon.

And, in fact, it was the camera that introduced me to Quincy.

It was an unusually warm day in March, my tenth day in London, and my twenty-fourth birthday. Since I had no one in town to celebrate with, I spent the day wandering London with my camera. Around lunchtime, I was taking photos of the ducks in Hyde Park—because you can't have too many cute duck photos—and I'd been backing up slowly as I tried to adjust the composition. At the same time, Quincy had been walking down the path toward me, sipping a coffee and talking into his phone. He looked down as I stepped back, and *boom*, his white-starched shirt was drenched in black coffee.

"Bloody buggering hell," he snapped, then went immediately contrite as I turned around, completely and totally mortified. "Oh, bloody fuck, I'm sorry."

"No, no. It was my fault. I was ... well, actually, I blame the ducks."

"Ah, I thought they might be up to something. They look a bit shady around the eyes."

I nodded sagely, ridiculously pleased that such a ruggedly handsome man shared my sense of humor. "And you see how they're just meandering around now, pretending to be all innocent? But we know. We can see their devious little duck natures hiding right beneath the soft, feathery surface."

I was kidding, of course. Except maybe I wasn't. There's far too much darkness buried just below eye level. I should know. I've watched the shadows rise up more times than I like to think about.

I started to brush away my words, to add something light to the conversation so he would only see the joke and not get an inadvertent peek into something deeper. But then I saw his eyes, and I stumbled. And that's when I knew he understood. This was a man who'd stood at the threshold and looked into the abyss, too.

I shook myself—it was a ridiculous thought. "Anyway, right. I should let you get going. You probably want to change that shirt. Actually, I should have it cleaned for you."

"Shall I take it off, then? Hand it over to you, and we can meet here again tomorrow?"

"I—" He was teasing; I was certain of it. And yet my senses kicked into overdrive as I imagined him unbuttoning his shirt, stepping closer to give it to me. The scent of him. The frisson of awareness as our hands brushed. And then the anticipation as he leaned closer and—

I took a firm step backward. "Maybe I should just write down my number and you can call me with the bill?"

"Why don't you let me buy you lunch and we'll call it even."

"Oh. Well—wait. I think you've got that backward."

His smile shot straight through me, warming me from the inside. "No," he said. "I didn't."

"Oh." I rarely date. I'd had my share of one-night stands, though. Bar pickups. Friend fix-ups.

Most of the time, those encounters were just fine. Nothing special, but more entertaining than an evening with a battery-operated boyfriend.

It was the next morning that was always the kicker. Because no matter how energetic that romp in the sheets might have been, it was never quite right. Never quite what I needed. What I craved.

And what I knew I shouldn't want.

The next morning was always an awkward, silent, stumbling hell. Stilted conversation and that too-familiar tightening in my chest, because the bottom line was that I didn't know how to tell Mr. Last Night that he really hadn't gotten it done.

Not that this coffee-soaked stranger was inviting me into his bed. At least not overtly. But there was an electricity between us that was already snapping and crackling. Go with him, and I was certain that the afternoon would lead into evening, and the evening would lead to sexy hijinks.

Did I want that? Another attempt to find a guy who filled that hole inside me? Another futile fuck and then the disappointment of slinking away unsatisfied? Because I was *always* unsatisfied.

Part of me liked it that way, because if I ever did find a guy who touched those secret, hidden desires, I'd have to finally acknowledge those dark needs that had teased me since puberty. But that wasn't a place I wanted to go. Because that was the place that reminded me of *him*. That reminded me that his blood flowed in my veins, and that at my core lay something very, very bad.

I stifled a shiver, hugging myself as I looked up at this smiling stranger with the stormy eyes. Better to just push him away now and be done with it. At least then I could go home and enjoy the delicious fantasy of the man and avoid altogether the disappointing reality.

That was the plan, anyway. The execution turned out to be a lot harder.

His gaze bore down on me. "I'm not quite certain if I should take your silence as a yes or a no."

"Sorry." I stifled a wince. "I appreciate the offer. Really. But I probably shouldn't."

He said nothing for a moment, just looked at me with

those dark, penetrating eyes. Then he took a single step toward me so that he was close enough that I could reach out and touch him. Close enough that I caught the scent of musk and male hidden under the overpowering aroma of coffee.

A charged silence hung between us, broken only by the low quacking of the ducks. My breath came shallow, and I could feel my pulse beating in my throat. And the longer his eyes stayed on me, the more an unexpected heat built between my thighs.

Really shouldn't, indeed.

When he finally spoke, there was no disappointment in his voice. Just a low, even tone that suggested that nothing ever ruffled him. And that he was used to getting what he wanted.

"Are you saying no because you're afraid of what will happen between us? Or are you more afraid that nothing will happen at all?"

"I—"

That's all I managed before the words caught in my throat and my mind turned to mush. My senses were on overdrive, and every warning bell in my head was going off. This was the kind of guy who could get under my skin. This was the kind of guy I should run from.

Finally, I gathered my wits enough to answer. "Those are my only two choices?" I lifted my brow in what I hoped was a haughty gesture. "I think you're being awfully presumptuous."

"I'm not. But I also have rules, and one is that I never argue if a woman says no. So tell me, Eliza. Are you declining my invitation to lunch?"

"I—wait. How do you know my name?"

His eyes dipped toward the ground where I'd dropped my camera bag. *Eliza T.* Right there on the top, along with an email address to help the bag find its way home to me in case it got lost.

"Right." I shoved my hands in my pockets, not entirely sure why I was still here. Hadn't I already assessed this guy? Didn't I already know he was dangerous?

But maybe a little danger was exactly what I needed.

No. Don't go there, Eliza. Do not go there.

"What's your name?" I asked, taking that first tiny mental step in the absolute wrong direction.

"If we're parting ways, I hardly think that matters." He reached out, and I was surprised to find my hand rising to meet his. "Will you tell me something?"

"Maybe."

His thumb lightly stroked my skin, sending shockwaves of pleasure coursing through me, teasing that already growing ache at my core. "Why are you hesitating when you clearly want me—"

I sucked in air, irritated by his presumption. And by the truth of it.

"—to take you to lunch."

"Oh."

He cocked his head, the corner of his mouth twitching. I felt my cheeks burn. Obviously, he knew exactly what I'd been thinking. "Don't shy away from what you want," he said, his voice soft but commanding, full of a quality I couldn't define but that I knew I craved, even as it scared me.

"Say yes," he continued. "I promise, you won't regret it."

"I don't usually go out with strangers I meet in the park." My suddenly dry mouth made my voice rough.

"I like being an exception."

I looked him up and down, and I had to grin. "Yeah. I bet you do. Fair enough, Mr. Mystery. But I'm buying lunch."

"Not a problem," he said with the kind of sexy grin designed to make a woman melt. "I'll buy breakfast."

I tilted my head, making a show of looking him up and down. "In that case, I think you better tell me your name."

4

IT WAS QUINCY. Quincy Radcliffe, which seemed so very British to me. But not in a clichéd stuffy way. Quincy had more of a sexy, James Bond vibe.

"I like it," I announced. "It suits you."

"Most of my friends call me Quince," he said.

"Really? You seem like a two syllable kind of guy."

He eyed me sideways as we continued walking through the park toward the street, though I wasn't sure which street. Hyde Park is huge, and I'd managed to get completely turned around.

When we finally escaped paradise for the hustle and bustle of cars and cabs and buses, I turned in a circle, trying to get my bearings. No luck. "In case you hadn't guessed, I'm not from around here. Any suggestions on where to feed you? And don't even try to talk me out of paying."

"What makes you think I'd do that?"

"There's a chivalrous look about you."

"You have something against chivalry?"

"Let's just say I like a little bad in my boy." *Oh my God, where had that come from?* It wasn't true at all. I was fishing in the nice guy pool, and I was certain that eventually I'd catch one who wasn't lacking. Who'd satisfy me in a way that didn't touch the scary shadows in my soul.

Bottom line? I needed a guy who was way the hell and gone from my father. Which meant I *definitely* didn't need a bad boy.

He paused on the sidewalk, and I turned back to see what had caught his eye, only to realize that it was me.

"What?" I asked, suddenly antsy under his attention, like I'd walked through a charged electrical field.

His smile was slow and easy, the kind that reached his eyes and suggested that he knew a secret.

"Quincy," I demanded. "What?"

"Nothing," he said in voice that telegraphed the opposite. "I just think that you're a woman with a lot of layers, Eliza T. And I'm going to enjoy peeling away each and every one of them."

"Presumptuous, much?" I spoke archly, but it was just for show. That electrical sizzle had ramped up, making the tiny hairs on my arms stand up and the back of my neck prickle. Right then, a little peeling sounded just fine by me.

For a moment we simply looked at each other until, finally, I cleared my throat and looked away.

"No," he said.

I turned back. "No?"

He reached out, and my breath caught as he gently ran the pad of his thumb along my jaw. "No, I'm not being presumptuous."

"Oh." My cheeks burned, and not from the bright spring day. "I—um, I still have absolutely no idea where to eat around here."

His hand left my jaw, leaving a warm spot on my skin that suddenly consumed every ounce of my attention. Or it did until I felt that same hand at my lower back, the pressure just enough to guide me down the sidewalk. I realized I was grinning like a fool, and I looked down at the ground to hide my goofy expression. I wasn't entirely sure what was going on here, but I couldn't deny that I liked it.

As I'd insisted, I did buy him lunch, and although I hadn't planned on a full-on formal dining experience, the cute little pub in Mayfair he guided us to was significantly less posh than I'd intended, especially considering we ended up at the take-out window.

"Was your shirt so cheap that you think it would be unfair for me to shell out for a full meal?" I knew it wasn't cheap, of course. When you grow up watching your sister pull off complicated cons just to score a room for the night, you learn a bit about the wardrobe habits of the rich and successful. From what I could tell, Mr. Quincy Radcliffe was either a very experienced con, or he came from money.

Note the *came from*. Not *new money*. And yeah, there's a difference. A newly monied man might have been polite about the soiled shirt, but he would have still been irritated. And he certainly wouldn't still be wearing it, the brown stain across his chest like a beacon declaring his—or my—clumsiness.

"First of all," Quincy said, "some of London's best food comes from pubs. And second, I'm going to guess that you've never had a Scotch egg."

I wrinkled my nose. "I'm more of a wine girl."

He just chuckled, then held up two fingers to the man at the window. "Trust me," he said, as I shelled out very few pounds in exchange for two little paper boats. In each sat what appeared to be a giant hush puppy surrounded by sweet potato fries.

I looked at the meal dubiously, then followed him to one of the outdoor tables. "Do I get a hint?"

"A hard boiled egg, sausage, bread crumbs. And it's deep-fried. Need I say more?"

"Not to me." I wouldn't call myself a foodie, but I'm definitely a girl who likes to eat. Which explains why I also like to work out. Although *like* might be a slight exaggeration.

I used a little plastic knife to cut through the breading to reveal exactly what he'd described. An egg nestled in a delicious layer of sausage-y goodness. I cut a piece off, used the toss-away fork to spear it, and then bit into what had to be a tiny niblet from heaven.

"Holy wow." I covered my mouth with my napkin—my best first date manners—and looked up at him. "You are an amazing human being for turning me on to these."

"I'm very glad to hear it." His mouth twitched.

"Don't even say it." I could hear the laughter in my voice, because I knew *exactly* where he was going.

"Say what? That I'm very happy to have turned you on? I wouldn't dream of being so forward."

"Mmm." I took another bite, and wisely decided to stay silent. An easy plan to stick to since the food was delicious and my mouth was fully occupied.

Despite his earlier tease that he'd buy breakfast, I'd expected him to make his escape. Probably he'd tell me he needed to get home and change before an evening meeting. Because clearly this was a guy who worked in the private sector. But he never even hinted that he wanted to get away from me. On the contrary, when I told him that I'd only been in London for a little over a week, he suggested one of the hop-on/hop-off double-decker tour buses. And because I'm a total geek about that kind of thing, I accepted immediately.

It was only when we were settled next to each other on a small bench seat at the top of the bus that the import of his offer hit me. Somehow, our chance encounter in the park had morphed into an actual date.

I really needed to remember to thank those ducks.

Despite a decent guide who spoke to us from the front of the bus, I learned nothing about the city. Instead, I spent the next hour flirting with the man beside me. Sharing details about our lives and cracking the occasional stupid joke.

"Actress," he said, when I refused to tell him what I did and ordered him to guess.

"You're good. Most people I've chatted up over here think I'm a grad student."

"I spend a lot of time watching people."

"Is that part of the job description for an international financial consultant?" I'd gone first in the guess-my-job game. I'd guessed that he was in the corporate world, but he'd narrowed down the specifics for me.

He shook his head. "No. Let's just say it's one of my special skills."

"So lay it out. What marks me as a woman of stage and screen?"

"For one thing, the prop." He glanced down at my camera bag, then back up at me, the certainty reflected in his face both impressing and scaring me. No one but Emma had ever seen me quite so clearly.

"Prop?" I tried to keep my voice nonchalant, but I don't think I succeeded. "I like to take pictures, that's all."

He nodded, as if encouraging me to talk, and despite telling myself that I was going to shift the conversation around to him, I heard myself saying, "I'm lousy at it. Snapshots, sure. But anything that resembles actual art? Or skilled photography? Really *not* me."

"But you enjoy it."

I shook my head slowly, trying to find the right words. "I enjoy the idea of it. The camera gives me an excuse to go places. To just walk and look."

"Why do you need an excuse?"

I shifted on the warm leather seat. "I don't, I guess. But I like being someone."

The corners of his mouth turned down, and I could see that he was thinking about my words. Analyzing them. Probably seeing more than I'd intended him to. That seemed to be Quincy's special skill.

I expected him to eventually offer a platitude. Something along the lines of, "Everybody's somebody," or some equally facile bullshit.

But what he said was, "Is it really that much better to have a role than to be yourself?"

"I—" I sat back in the seat, my focus on our guide and not on the man beside me.

"Eliza?"

I told myself I didn't want to answer. That he was digging too deep for someone I barely knew. But that mental lecture was for nothing, because it *felt* like I knew him, and before I even realized I was speaking, I heard myself saying, "I guess I've never been very good at being me."

Considering how ridiculously cryptic that was, I expected a moment of silence preceding a snappy change of subject. Instead, he said, "What are you hiding from?"

The question surprised me so much, it stole my words, so that all I could do was sit there and wonder about this enigmatic man who saw so much. More, in fact, than I wanted him to see.

An awkward silence hung between us. I considered not answering at all, but I was enjoying our time together and didn't want to put him off. At the same time, I didn't want to tell him the truth. Or maybe I didn't really know the truth.

Finally, I lifted a shoulder and simply said, "Isn't everyone hiding from something?"

He pursed his lips, as if he was truly considering the question. Then he nodded. "In my experience, yes. I'd have to say that's true."

I leaned sideways, butting my shoulder against his. "Lots of clients hiding their funds? The deep, dirty, and mysterious world of high finance?"

"Something like that," he said, in the kind of voice that made me think that my joke had more truth in it than I'd intended.

I wanted to ask him more, but I wasn't sure if I should. I felt a connection to this guy, yes, but I didn't trust it. Not yet. What if it was just the euphoria of meeting a nice, good-looking guy on a lovely spring day? What if he wasn't feeling the connection, too?

I thought he was, but—

Screeeeeeech!

My thoughts were rudely cut off by a burst of feedback from the guide's microphone. "Sorry," the guide said. "But at least it woke you all up, because we're about to enter one of London's poshest neighborhoods. Even if you don't recognize the politicians' and executives' names, I'm sure you've heard of Madonna, one of the most famous former residents in this ritzy part of London. Can you guess some others?"

As other guests in the group started to shout out the names of celebrities, I turned my attention back to Quincy. "So how often do you do this?"

"This?"

"Invite tourists you've stumbled upon to ride the double decker bus."

"Would you believe me if I said this was my first time?"

I started to laugh, but something about his tone stopped me. "Actually, yeah." I flashed a shy smile, and I'm really not that shy a person. "Yeah, I think I would."

Our eyes met, and if we'd been in a movie, that was where the couple's theme would have started, low at first and then building to a dramatic kiss, probably with Big Ben in the background and the sun setting so that the sky was ablaze in orange.

I was so lost in the fantasy that I was surprised when he broke the mood and said softly, "This is where I grew up."

"London? I assumed as much, though I guess anywhere in the UK would—oh, wait." I cocked my head, then looked around at the stunning homes, like something out of an incredible movie. Or at least a fun one. Like the über-posh townhome where the British version of Lindsey Lohan lived in *The Parent Trap*. "You mean *here* here?"

"Just down this road, actually."

"Wow." I grinned. Apparently I'd been right about that whole *came from money thing*. "Which house?"

He hesitated, then started to point in the direction of a stately white home when the guide, who'd paused to field celebrity guesses, began to speak again. "But it's not all celebrities and high-flying business moguls. This neighborhood has a dark side, too."

"Oooh," I said, in the same voice I'd used for a campy horror movie. "Now we're getting to the real gossip." I expected Quincy to crack a smile, and when he didn't, I sat back, a little embarrassed by his less than enthusiastic reception to my sometimes warped sense of humor.

"Take the house to my left—number 806. It looks like your typical high-end home. A lovely place, you'd think, to raise a family. To be a child, carefree and young."

I frowned, because number 806 was the mansion that I thought Quincy had indicated.

"But this home—which became famous as the site of the murder of heiress Emily Radcliffe—hosts a dark history with a sad cast of characters. A terrified little boy. A mother, killed in her effort to protect him. A father who disappeared into the wind, only to be found assassinated within the year, and revealed as a traitor to both Britain *and* to the foreign power he'd so blithely and secretly served."

Beside me, Quincy stiffened, his shoulders back and his face unreadable. I didn't know if I should, but I couldn't stop myself. I reached over, and I twined my fingers with his. At first, his hand was a dead weight. Then his fingers gently curled around mine.

"It's a hop-on/hop-off bus," I said quietly. "Why didn't we get off before we turned in here? Surely you knew they'd mention it."

"Everyone has a story, Eliza. As an actress, you must know that."

"Maybe," I agreed. "But not everyone shares their stories so easily."

"You're the first person who's learned that about me in a long, long time. Not since Dallas. My friend," he clarified. "Not the city. And I told him a lifetime ago."

"Oh." Part of me wanted to ask why he let me learn this dark fact about him. Sure, the guide mentioned the name Radcliffe, but that's hardly an unusual name. If he hadn't started to point to the house—if he hadn't reacted when the guide told the story—I doubt I would have guessed.

I didn't ask why, though. Instead, I heard myself saying, "I'm sorry about your dad. My father—well, he wasn't a good man either." And wasn't that the understatement of the year?

"I'm sorry."

"I don't want to say it was the same—it wasn't. It was bad." I licked my lips, forcing myself to just talk and not to remember. "But it was different. He—well, it doesn't matter. I just ... I guess I just wanted you to know that I understand at least a little."

The bus had maneuvered to a stop, and several of our co-riders were getting off. Quince glanced at me, and though he didn't say a word, we rose together and headed for the stairs in the front. When we reached the sidewalk, we didn't talk about either of our fathers again, but that didn't matter. Something fundamental had changed. At first, the connection between us had been like lighting. Fast and surprising and a little bit dangerous. Now, it felt warm and steady, like a softly glowing ember that had the power to ignite into flame.

He took my hand silently, and I fell in step beside him. We walked out of the neighborhood, twisting and turning on small residential streets, narrow lanes lined with shops, and around a few fenced neighborhood gardens. The sun was beginning to creep lower, and we walked through more shadows cast by the many trees that lined the neighborhoods, their leaves dappling the late afternoon light.

We walked for over an hour, talking about everything and nothing. The kind of conversation that flows easily among old friends. And it really did feel as if I'd known him forever, as if the pain in both of our pasts had forged a bond between us. As if I hadn't come to London for a job at all, but to see this man.

After a while, we realized that it had been hours since we'd had lunch, if a single Scotch egg and fries could be considered lunch. I had no idea where we were, but Quincy quickly surveyed the area, announced that we were at

Marble Arch, and that we'd managed to return very near to where we left the park. "If you don't mind a walk, I know a great little Indian food place just over that way."

"I'd do pretty much anything for great Indian food," I told him.

"I'll keep that in mind," he countered, and there was no mistaking the suggestive tease in his voice.

"Good," I said boldly. Because, yeah, this whole day had been good. *He* was good. For that matter, *we* were pretty damn good.

Dinner was good, too. We ordered almost every curry on the menu and shared them all. We also shared a bottle of wine. Okay, two bottles of wine. And it's fair to say that I drank most of it. Because I knew what would come next. I knew he'd come to my apartment. I knew we'd get naked. I knew it would be fabulous.

And I also knew that by morning this would all be over. Because it always was.

"You're frowning. Tired of me already?"

I had to laugh. Only a confident man would ask a question like that, and I already knew that Quincy was a confident man. I liked that. It attracted me. Hell, it aroused me.

But I knew damn well it wouldn't be enough to satisfy me, even though I wished otherwise with all my heart and soul. I wanted him. Right at that moment I craved him. Just watching him eat—the smooth motions as he lifted a fork. The small sounds of pleasure when he tasted a particularly satisfying dish. The heat in his eyes when he offered me a fork full of something delicious, as if it wasn't the fork I was closing my lips around, but something so much more intimate.

Oh, yeah...

I wanted him.

At the same time, I didn't want it to end. And wouldn't that be an awkward conversation? *So, listen, Quincy. I'm pretty much so desperate for you that I'd do anything you asked, but the thing is that I know as soon as we do it'll all be over, so I think I'd rather skip all that. Maybe we can just play chess?*

Yeah, not so much.

He chuckled, and I realized that I'd just allowed a crazy gap of silence after he suggested I was tired of him. Definitely not earning stellar date points tonight.

"Sorry. I think I'm getting tired. Or tipsy. Or both. This is a lot of wine on top of a lot of walking."

He reached across the table and took my hand, and wild bolts of anticipation shot through me. In that moment, I knew I had to be the mega slut of the year to want him so much even though I knew that would be the end of it. But I couldn't help it. I wanted him. I wanted to feel his lips on me, his cock inside me. I wanted to be surrounded by his scent and lose myself to the sweet surrender of the wine as he whispered naughty things to me and then did every one of those things to my body. I wanted to fall asleep in his arms, and wake up with him beside me. I wanted a night of bliss. A night of passion.

A night so incredibly transcendent that even though it would be the last time, I could hold onto it forever, a delicious memory to spice up my fantasies and keep me warm at night.

He lifted a hand to signal for the check. "I think it's time we get you home."

"Yes, please." My pulse pounded in my throat. Hell, it pounded between my thighs. With each moment that passed, I was more and more turned on. I blamed the wine —it's definitely my aphrodisiac of choice—but those lovely grapes weren't entirely responsible for this sweet longing. On the contrary, that was all the man.

A man who took my hand and very gingerly helped me down the narrow stairs to the street, where he hailed a cab. "I'll have to remember you're a cheap drunk," he said, his hand sliding down to cup my bottom. I bit my lower lip and leaned into it, then moaned with satisfaction as he nuzzled my neck. "That's valuable information to store away."

"If that's the kind of information you want, I'll tell you anything. Just don't stop doing that."

"Ah, but I have to. Your chariot awaits."

He stepped around me, leaving me bereft from the sudden lack of contact. He opened the door like a perfect gentleman, then stepped back, as if to close it, rather than sliding in beside me.

"Are you getting in on the other side? I can slide over."

"You're going home alone," he said, and my entire body went cold from the giant bucket of rejection he'd just dumped all over me.

"I—what? Why?" I frowned. "I thought you were buying me breakfast. I thought we were going to—" I closed my mouth because under the circumstances I really wasn't going there.

"You thought I was going home with you. That I was going to kiss you. That I was going to pull you so close your breasts were crushed against me, and your ass was tight in my hands."

"I—Quincy..." I shot a mortified look at the driver, who was sitting like stone, his hands glued to the steering wheel as he looked straight ahead.

"Hmm," Quincy said, then leaned over and handed the driver a ten-pound note. "Sorry to keep you waiting. This should cover the inconvenience." And then, as if the delay was the only thing odd about this situation, he turned back to me and said, "That would be my very great pleasure, Eliza."

"But. Wait. What?" I wasn't sure if it was the wine or the shock, but he was making no sense.

He put a hand on the roof and leaned in. "You're dangerous, Eliza. You and me, we're a lot alike."

"That's bad?"

"I told you. It's dangerous."

"Oh. I see." I swallowed. And told myself not to cry. I didn't know him well enough to cry. Which begged the question of why tears were pooling in my eyes. "Well, it was —I mean, I had a nice day. Thank you. It, ah, it was really nice to meet you." *Bastard.*

His mouth twitched, and for a moment I feared I'd said that out loud. "Is that a brush off?"

"What, no. Wait—I thought *you* were brushing *me* off."

"Do you want me to?" Again with that tiny smile.

"No, and you're teasing me. What the hell, Quince?" At that, he laughed outright.

"Now I know."

"What?"

"If you and I spend much time together—and I certainly hope that we will—when you call me Quince it's because I'm in trouble."

I tilted my head and crossed my arms in a display of irritation. And I *was* irritated. But I was also hopelessly, giddily relieved. "Fine. You're in trouble. Don't scare me like that. You acted like you just wanted to send me on my way."

"I'll tell you what I want," he said, bending lower and speaking softer. But not so soft the driver couldn't hear.

"I don't just want to go home with you. I don't simply

want to fuck you. I want to claim you, Eliza. I want you to surrender completely. To give me your trust entirely."

"I don't understand. I don't know what that means."

"I think you do. I want control." He brushed my lips with the pad of his free hand. "To take you how I want you. In the back of a cab like this. In your bed. Tied down. On your knees. I'll give you pleasure, Eliza. More than you can imagine or have experienced."

"You can't know that."

"I can, and I do." He hesitated a moment, his eyes burning into me. "I can't promise to save you from whatever darkness is inside you—only you can do that. But there are shadows in your eyes, and I want to be the one to bring back some light."

I tried to speak, but I couldn't. His words... His promises...

Was this really happening?

"I don't understand."

"Then let me make it perfectly clear. I want you. All of you. Not just a body in my bed. I want your trust, but not blindly. I will earn it. I can promise you that. And in exchange, the power over your pleasure belongs to me. It's a responsibility I will cherish. And that you will enjoy. Surrender, Eliza, and let the layers fall away."

My mouth had gone entirely dry, and though I knew I shouldn't look, I could see the driver's wide-eyed, open-mouthed reflection in the rearview mirror. I told myself to get out of the cab. To put a stop to this unexpected and entirely inappropriate proclamation.

But I didn't.

Instead, I asked, "Why?"

He smiled. That's when he knew he had me. And I

couldn't even rally against his smugness because, dammit, he was right.

"Why?" I repeated, because right then, that was the only control I had.

"Because that's what I want. And I think we both know that it's what you need. Isn't it, love?"

"I—I barely know you."

"We both know that's not really true."

I opened my mouth to respond, but he pressed a finger over my lips and continued.

"I want every thing I said. I do. But not now. Not tonight when you're drunk and aroused and flattered and vulnerable. All I want from you tonight is to think about it."

"To think about it?" I sounded like a parrot and hated myself for it.

"Tomorrow," he said. "The offer for breakfast still stands." He nodded toward a small cafe at the end of the block. "If you want what I'm proposing, then meet me there at ten. I'll buy you that breakfast, and then we'll go from there."

"And if I don't?"

"I'll be disappointed, but I'll respect your decision." He leaned forward and kissed me on the cheek. "Good night, Eliza. I hope to see you tomorrow."

His words tormented me through the night. Making me ache with need. And also making me tremble with fear at the thought of being at his mercy. Not fear of him. Not fear that he would hurt me. But at the realization that what he was describing was the very thing that I'd been craving.

I went to him, of course. How could I not? He'd said I had the power to walk away, that the decision was mine. But it wasn't. Not really. He'd claimed me with his words. His touch. His promises. And so we had breakfast. And then, dear God, we had so much more.

———

Those sweet and bitter memories wash over me as I stand in The Hollywood Terrace's ornate ballroom and watch as Quincy Radcliffe walks toward me. The man to whom I once gave my heart and my soul, my submission and my trust. The man who, for three months in London, was my entire world.

I'd revealed so much to him. Secrets. Hopes. My deepest fears, my most horrible memories.

I'd told him things that only Emma knew, shared all the shadows of my past.

I'd opened my heart, and he'd challenged me. Pushed me. Protected me.

He'd taken me in hand, and he'd peeled away the layers, just as he promised he would. He'd revealed desires and needs I'd kept buried, and in his arms I felt more like myself than I ever thought possible.

He'd loved me. He'd cherished me.

At least that's what I thought.

Because once he'd truly captured me—once I was so in love with him that it felt like I'd been filled with light—he shattered me completely.

He left.

Just up and walked away, taking my heart and my soul with him.

And the son-of-a-bitch never once looked back.

So what the hell can he possibly know about Emma's disappearance?

5

"*TRUST YOU?*" Denny's words rattled in Quince's brain as he closed the distance between him and Eliza. *"Hell, yeah, I trust you. But I still want to know what you're up to."*

"So demanding," he murmured.

"Dammit, Quince. I'm your partner, not some nosy neighbor."

He put a hand over his mouth as if stifling a yawn. "I've located an ally."

That wasn't exactly true. Once upon a time, Eliza Tucker would have done anything for him. But things had changed. Hell, he'd been the one who changed them.

He knew he'd hurt her, and God knew it had ripped him up inside. Everything he'd suffered—every horror that he'd endured during those ten torturous weeks had felt like nothing compared to the pain in his heart when he realized that he couldn't go back to her. Couldn't even say goodbye for fear he'd—

No.

Now wasn't the time, not when he was working to a tight window. Not when Denny and the task force were waiting.

And certainly not when the life of a thirteen-year-old girl hung in the balance.

Eliza might hate him—most of the time, he hated himself—but she *would* help him. He'd make sure of it.

He drew a breath, forcing his mind back to the present as he closed off those dark memories, locking them up tight inside the hidden corners of his mind. Over the years, he'd become an expert at pushing away the hell he'd endured. Or, at least, he told himself that he had. Considering how often the past seemed to haunt him lately, he couldn't help but wonder if those walls were starting to crack.

"An ally? Who the hell—"

"Not now." The words were terse, his lips barely moving. He was closer now, and Eliza had noticed him. From the Arctic ice in those deep blue eyes, he knew he'd been right; this wasn't going to be a warm and welcoming reunion.

Then again, under the circumstances, any greeting milder than castration counted as a win. God knew he deserved a hell of a lot worse.

"Mr. Canton!" Lassiter unpeeled his right hand from Eliza's back, then held it out to Quince for a firm handshake. "You have the look of a man who's enjoying himself."

Quince flashed his most charming smile. "You assured me that this would be a spectacular party. My compliments. For the event, for this stunning renovation, and," he added as he deliberately turned toward Eliza, "for the spectacular ornamentation."

"You have good taste," Lassiter said. "I'd say she's among the loveliest of the flowers decorating the room."

Quince knew the role he was supposed to play. With deliberate slowness, he let his eyes roam over her, as if inspecting the merchandise. When he reached her face, he allowed himself a hint of a smile, like a satisfied customer.

She didn't smile back, and he was surprised at the wave of loss that crested over him. During their time in London, he'd come to rely on that cockeyed smile, as dependable as the rising sun. She'd see him across a room, and her lips would curve in greeting, her dimple flashing and her eyes sparkling with an invitation that was impossible to ignore.

Considering the situation, he shouldn't have expected to see any sort of light in her eyes. But while reason knew that, his heart was less astute.

He willed his features to stay bland, fearing that his disappointment would show on his face. Damn, but he wished he didn't still want her so much. Didn't still crave those wonderfully sweet days they spent exploring London—and the wickedly sensual nights they passed exploring each other.

He wanted to hold onto those memories. Wanted to wrap himself in them when the nightmares came. But how could he when they were so inextricably intertwined with pain? The bloody, brutal, fucking pain that he battled down every goddamn day. It had changed him. Tainted him.

He'd walked away so that he wouldn't soil her, too, and he'd sworn to himself it would be a clean break for both of them.

And yet here he was, standing in front of her, about to demand help from the one woman in the world who truly—and deservedly—hated him.

Beside him, Lassiter cleared his throat, and Quince realized that he was still staring at Eliza.

He turned to his host, his demeanor casual. As if he couldn't be bothered about anyone else's comfort or expectations. "Since she's with you, I assume she has yet to be keyed by one of the guests?"

He spoke matter-of-factly, and only to Lassiter. Eliza was

chattel tonight, and although that simple reality burned a hole in his gut, there wasn't a damn thing he could do about it right then.

"Ah, I'm afraid I've been keeping Bunny occupied," Lassiter said, which Quincy understood as his claim on Eliza. Lassiter couldn't key her outright—he was the host, after all. But he could subtly suggest that if Quince disrupted his plans for the girl, then Lassiter would ensure that Robert Canton's name was conveniently dropped from future guest lists.

As far as Quince could tell, it was working. In just the time it had taken to cross the room, he'd noticed at least three of the guests stealing hungry glances her way. And one, a broad-shouldered man with a goatee and short ginger curls, hadn't taken his eyes off Eliza.

Fortunately for Quince, this was a one-time gig. He stepped toward her, then took her wrist, using the tip of his forefinger to trace the red ribbon she'd tied there. *Why had she worn it? Coincidence? Probably. But maybe there was a tiny bit of affection still lingering beneath the hatred? A sign that while she hadn't forgiven him, there might be a few lingering memories that she cherished?*

After a moment, she tugged her hand away. She met his eyes, silently daring him to call out her bad behavior.

"She and I have met before," he said, speaking again to Lassiter and not Eliza. "London, perhaps. No, it was Paris. Tell me, Scott. Do you know Sir Jonathan Semple?"

Lassiter's face showed that he did, and Quince wasn't surprised. Semple was an entitled British prick who had spent his life bouncing from party to party, spending his massive inheritance on drink and women. And he had a tendency to buy his friends' loyalty by buying them women.

Quince had infiltrated one of Semple's parties during his

time at MI6, but that was long before he'd met Eliza. The mention of Semple's name to Lassiter was nothing more than camouflage.

He and Eliza had gone to Paris, though. One Friday on a lark they'd popped over to St. Pancras station, bought two same-day tickets, and taken the Chunnel to Paris. They'd found a small hotel on *la Rive Gauche*, and had wiled away a weekend both in bed and wandering the streets and shops of the City of Lights.

Because she said it was the memories that mattered, she'd turned down all the gifts he'd offered her except for a bundle of roses and a hardbound copy of *Le Petit Prince.* "Emma used to read it to me," she'd told him. "I've always wanted to learn enough French to read it in the original language."

As for the roses, they'd stayed in the hotel room until they returned to London, when they'd left the still-lovely blooms for the maid. But he'd taken the ribbon that had bound the stems and tied it around her wrist. He hadn't known why at the time, other than some primal need to mark her as his own. She'd declined his offer of a Cartier diamond and sapphire bracelet, and he assumed she'd laugh at the ribbon, then take it off once they left for the train station.

But she kept it. For that matter, she wore it continuously.

She'd even been wearing it on that day he'd gone to see her. The day she didn't know about.

He'd watched her from across the street, and his heart had wrenched at the sight of her. He'd almost approached her. But how could he? He'd never again be the man in Paris who gave red ribbons. That man might have been a bit damaged and rough around the edges, but at his core, he was whole.

The man who'd watched her in silence was broken. Inside and out. And the shards of his soul would cut her to pieces.

He'd watched, hidden in the shadows. He'd mourned what might have been.

Then he'd left.

And when he finally reached the tiny, antiseptic government dorm that had become his temporary home, he'd wept.

Today, he didn't have the luxury of turning away. Didn't matter if it would hurt either one of them, he and Denny needed help. The princess needed help. Every one of Corbu's tormented victims needed help.

And Eliza was the only one he could turn to.

"You and Bunny crossed paths at one of Semple's parties?" Lassiter said. "What a stunning coincidence."

"Small world." Quince put on his most charming smile. "At the time I believe she was hopping all over the continent. If I recall, she was well worth the, ah, time I spent spent with her." He rubbed his fingers together to suggest her very steep price. But of course neither Robert Canton nor Lassiter would be so uncouth as to talk about a call girl's price out loud.

As Lassiter watched with a frown, Quince took Eliza's hand, forcing himself not to react to the visceral memory that washed over him merely from the feel of her warm, smooth skin. "It's a pleasure to see you again, Bunny."

Eliza's expression never changed, but she turned her hand over and opened it, so that Lassiter could see the ornate brass key now resting on her palm. "I'm a creature of habit," Quince said. "Once I find something I enjoy, I claim it for my own."

"A very wise policy, Mr. Canton." Lassiter seemed to be

talking through his teeth, his desire for Eliza warring with his duties as a host.

Eventually, duty won out. "Go with Mr. Canton, Bunny." He gave her a pat on the rump, and Quince fought the urge to land a right hook on his jaw. "Make sure he enjoys himself this evening."

"Of course, Mr. Lassiter." Her voice was as smooth as he remembered, strong and musical. A good voice for the stage, and he wondered what had happened to her acting career. He'd checked on her over the years, and he knew she worked steadily. So why was she now performing sex acts for strange men instead of Shakespeare? The question sat heavy in his gut, especially considering everything he knew about her. Was she here merely as a practical solution to some unmanageable debt? Or was there a darker need lingering under the surface? Some void she was desperately, foolishly trying to fill?

He wanted to know. Hell, he wanted to help.

But now wasn't the time. "With me," he said, relieved when she came easily, almost eagerly.

"So what do you have to tell me," she whispered, as soon as they were out of earshot.

Tell her? Tell her what?

What he was doing there? Why he'd left her?

A thousand possible questions burned in his brain, but he didn't have time to examine any of them. Right then, all that mattered was getting her to his room and getting her hands in position on that relay.

"Sounds like you're on the move," Denny whispered in his ear. *"Cough to confirm."*

He coughed.

"I'll expect to hear from you in three. Get to the room."

He didn't bother acknowledging again. But he did pick

up his speed. Eliza's heels clicked beside him. "Qui—I mean, *Robert.*"

"We'll talk in my room." They'd reached the elevator where several groping couples waited for the car to arrive. He slid an arm around her waist and for a moment he was lost in the memory of her soft curves. Of the way they'd once fit together so perfectly, as if they were two halves of a whole.

Then she stiffened and the illusion shattered. Now, he was all ragged edges and missing pieces. Maybe they'd fit once, but they could never again.

The doors opened and they followed the other couples into the mirrored interior of the elevator car. He saw them reflected back at him. Men falling into lust. Women dialing up the heat. For these ladies, he knew, it was all about the payday. But you couldn't tell from the images in the mirror. Each and every one was putting on an award winning performance—and not a single person in the car was paying any attention at all to him and Eliza.

And thank God for that.

The car descended to the fourth floor, and they got off, along with two other couples who turned in the opposite direction. Quince kept a firm hand at Eliza's waist, afraid she'd say or do something to attract attention, but she moved in step with him, cooperating fully. By all appearances she was just as keen to get to the room as he was. She wanted an explanation, of course. And he'd give her one— he owed her that.

But it would come after they'd completed the mission. Call it incentive. Hell, call it payment.

Whatever it took, he'd promise it. Because one quick glance at the analog face of the Patek Philippe confirmed what he already knew—they were running out of time.

The lights from the city illuminated the hallway, streaming in through a floor-to-ceiling window framed by an ornate, geometric carving. A similar window stood in his room opposite the king sized bed. And that window was handy for two reasons. One, it had provided Denny with access to the fire escape that led to street level, allowing her to slink across Hollywood Boulevard to the opposite office building. The original plan had been that she'd set up the transmitter, then return to this room and operate the relay, adjusting for any variation in the alignment so that the signal coming through the window was fully captured, then relayed into the building's interior. And Lassiter's office.

Now, of course, she had to keep the transmitter steady. Eliza would have to take over the role of middleman, making sure the relay's indicator stayed in the green zone so that he could do his job downstairs.

Hell of a risk, but he had no choice.

At the room, he pulled out the flat, hotel-style card key. The brass key Quince had given Eliza was only for show—he'd tried it out of curiosity and learned that not only did it not unlock the door, but that the door couldn't be unlocked from the inside without the card key. Apparently the men who'd come expecting companionship for the night required assurance that their companion wouldn't be taking her leave before they were done with her.

Quince used the card key and opened the door, ushering Eliza in before him.

The second the door closed behind them, she whipped around. "Why did you insist on the red ribbon? You couldn't have possibly known it was me. Did you know it was Emma?"

He stared at her, trying—and failing—to make sense of her words. All he understood was *Emma*. But he didn't know what tonight's party or the ribbon had to do with her sister. And right then, he didn't have time to find out.

"Eliza, I don't—"

"*No.*" She thrust her hands up and out, landing them hard on his chest. The move was so completely unexpected that he didn't have time to compensate, and he stumbled back, then landed against the door with a *thud*.

"What the bloody hell do—"

"Goddammit, Quincy! Don't you dare play games with me."

"*She's Eliza?*" The shock in Denny's voice reverberated through his head. Of all of his friends, Denny was the only one in whom he'd confided about his past. About Eliza. And about what had happened. Not everything—God, he barely let himself remember everything—but he'd told her enough. And he knew her well enough to know she had to be both curious and sympathetic.

Mostly, though, she'd be worried about the mission.

A thought that was borne out by her next comment. "*Put it away for later, Q. The clock's ticking.*"

"I know," he snarled.

"Then talk to me," Eliza pressed, talking over his thoughts and Denny's curse in his ear. "You're the one who contacted me, dammit."

"Fuck." He ground out the word at the same time he grabbed Eliza's wrist. In one swift motion, he whipped her around, so that they'd completely changed positions. Now she was against the door and he was the one blocking her.

He had one hand on her wrist, pressed tight above her head. The other he had cupped over her elbow, which was also firm against the door. In that position, there were only inches between them. They were intimately close, and he could feel her heat—her fury—burning through him.

He was a full head taller than her, and he looked down into her fiery upturned face. Her eyes burned like a blue flame, and he could practically see the wheels in her mind turning.

"Let. Me. Go."

He ignored her. "I don't know why you're here. I don't know why you think I know something about your sister. I do know that you hate me, and I can't say that I blame you." He saw the flicker in her eyes and the shadow on her face. He ignored it. "We can talk. I'll help you if I can. But right now you're going to help me. It's not a question. It's not a request. I'm running out of time, and I need you."

She spat in his face.

She actually, truly, spat in his face.

"Six minutes. You have six minutes to get into the office and online."

Shit. Two floors below and he had to break into the office and then boot up the computer.

"I'm really sorry about this, Eliza."

Her eyes widened as her mouth parted, either to spit again or to ask what he meant.

He didn't take the time to find out which. "But I need your help."

"What—" she began, but her question was cut off as he tugged her away from the door, and in one smooth motion spun her around and tossed her onto the bed. She yelped and started to rise, but he didn't give her the chance.

He moved fast, getting onto the bed and straddling her waist before she even had time to react. Then he leaned forward, drew a pair of fluffy pink handcuffs out of the bedside table, and said very simply, "Trust me."

6

"WHAT THE HELL, QUINCY!" He's holding fuzzy pink handcuffs in one hand and reaching for my arm with the other.
With one quick, efficient movement, he snaps the cuff
around my left wrist. "Trust you?" I kick, trying to dislodge
him, but his knees are tight at my waist, like I'm a bucking
bronco and he's a rodeo star. "I tried that, remember? And it
didn't work out too well for me."

He's holding onto the free end of the cuff as he leans
toward one of the metal bars that make up this party theme-
compatible headboard. His hips rise a bit as he stretches,
and I take advantage by bouncing my ass on the bed, then
thrusting up, trying to dislodge him.

It doesn't work. All it does is upset his balance so that he
falls on top of me, crushing my breasts as he knocks the
wind out of me.

For one moment, he hovers over me, his lips slightly
parted as his breath comes hard and fast. His eyes are locked
on mine, his pupils dilated. I can see his pulse beating at his
temple, and I can smell his cologne. That's what does it.
That's what finally makes my muscles go slack in surrender

—that familiar scent that I'd once associated with feeling safe and warm and loved.

"Quincy," I whisper, at the same time I hear a sharp, distinctive, *click,* and he sits back, once against straddling my hips in a position that would be intimate if it weren't so damned infuriating.

Dammit, dammit, *dammit.*

I yank my arm, wincing when I can't pull it down from over my head. "I swear to God, Quincy, I'm going to—"

"—do exactly what I say," he finishes. "Because I don't have time to argue or explain."

He reaches for my other hand, and I completely lose my shit. I kick and scream and writhe and practically growl at him. I'm not *scared* so much as confused and pissed and frustrated. I came to find a clue about Emma's disappearance. I didn't bargain on Quincy, and seeing him has thrown me completely off balance.

Despite my contortions, he grabs hold of my wrist. I wasn't a match for him when I was completely free, and since I'm now attached to the bed, my resistance is both lame and futile. I'm quite certain there's another set of cuffs in that drawer, and that pretty soon I'll be spread-eagled across this damn bed.

The thought sends a shiver of anticipation running through me, and that—more than anything Quincy has done tonight—is what really pisses me off.

"I swear to God, if you cuff my right hand to the bed you better intend to leave me here forever, because I will rip your balls off with my teeth."

"How remarkably innovative," he says mildly. "And I'm not cuffing you."

That surprising statement is punctuated by him taking something about the size of a cell phone out of his pocket and thrusting it into my right hand. He curls my fingers around it, then holds them in place. My thumb's on a toggle button, and I'm staring at a small screen with a single vibrating needle. The needle's intersecting a line that's red on both sides and green in the middle. Right now, it's moving toward the red.

"Push down," he says. "Keep the needle in the green."

"Why should I do anything you say?"

"Eliza, please." He presses a gentle kiss to my forehead, the gesture so surprising that my control slips, and I feel tears prick my eyes. "If our time in London meant anything, then do this one thing for me."

I want to ask why. I want to ask what the hell this is about. I want to ask—oh, hell. The whole thing is so damn strange I don't even know what I want to ask. All I know for sure is that I don't know anything at all. Except that I'm pretty sure he doesn't know a thing about Emma.

He's off the bed and practically sprinting toward the door.

"You're *leaving* me?"

He brushes a hand over his ear, then mutters a curse. "I'm out of time. Remember, keep it in the green. There's a little girl's life at stake, El. And she doesn't have an Emma watching over her like you did. Just do this."

Before I can catch my breath, he's gone, and I'm left tied to a bed and holding the freaky gizmo as the needle wavers toward the red.

For a fraction of a second I allow myself the fantasy of hurling the device across the room.

I don't do it.

I have no idea what Quincy's in the middle of, and I damn sure don't trust him. But as I lie there cuffed to the bed, I realize one vital thing—I believe him.

I know one more thing, too. I never really knew Quincy Radcliffe. Because the man who cuffed me to this bed and bolted out of this room isn't a financial consultant. Not now. Probably not ever.

I spent three glorious months in a foreign country falling in love with a man who was a ghost. Who didn't really exist. And for the life of me, I can't decide if that makes me feel better or worse.

———

I'm not wearing a watch, and there's no clock in the room, so I don't know how much time passes as I toggle and adjust, toggle and adjust. It's hardly a difficult chore, but I give it my all, not only because Quincy said it was important, but also because the minute adjustments occupy my mind, leaving only a tiny bit of mental background space in which to wonder about what he's doing and who he really is.

I've zeroed in on the big picture, of course. He's either law enforcement or intelligence, that much would probably be obvious to anyone, but to me it's like a big, red beacon of *duh*. After all, my sister was scary-deep in the intelligence world for over a decade, and a PI for even longer. First as her government cover, and then as a legit, full-time job after she left the agency.

I've even worked part time in her office, running skip-traces on her computer, filing documents, and typing client reports for both her and Lorenzo.

So, yeah. I know the signs. And they're flashing neon where Quincy is concerned.

Then again, maybe he's a master thief who tossed in the bit about the teenager because he has a talent for the con.

If that's the case, I can go back to hating him.

If he's a spook ... well, then I have to wonder if that's what he was doing back in London. And if so, is that why he disappeared? Some botched up mission?

It makes sense, and I like it better than the alternative theory that he simply tired of me and walked away.

But that begs the question of why he didn't come back to me when he came back to London.

Because I know he returned. I saw him. The day before I returned to Manhattan I'd been at loose ends. Part of me was desperate to get home and away from the memories that lurked around every corner. Another part wanted to hold on tight to my time with Quincy. I still couldn't quite believe that he'd really just up and disappeared. One day, he'd been touching me intimately and telling me that he loved me. The next, he was gone.

It didn't make sense. The man I knew—the man in whom I'd confided my deepest secrets and most intimate desires—couldn't be the kind of man who could cut me so deeply. On the contrary, my months with Quincy had been like a balm to my soul. He'd not only healed me, he'd helped me discover parts of myself that I'd kept buried since childhood, and I couldn't wrap my head around his betrayal. Because if he'd truly left me—if he'd actually, purposefully walked away with no contact and no explanation—then that's exactly what it was. A betrayal of the most brutal kind.

He'd left on a Friday for what was supposed to be a quick weekend trip. "I have to play nice with the client. Handhold a bit and play the social game." I'd nodded my understanding. Networking is a huge part of acting; I assumed it was the same in the corporate world, too. I'd expected him back on Monday, but didn't start getting worried until Tuesday. He hadn't called or texted while he was away, but that was easy to justify. He was busy.

International rates were expensive. They'd gone into rural China where cell service is spotty.

Those were all the justifications that ran through my head on Tuesday and Wednesday. By Thursday I was dialing Emma for reassurance, then hanging up before it rang and telling myself I was being a baby. By Friday, I was officially nervous, and I let the call to my sister ring through. She told me not to worry. It was probably nothing and he'd come home with apologies and presents. That soothed me over the weekend, but by Monday I was a wreck.

I tried to hold off calling. I told myself he'd gotten sick. He was catching up at work. He was in Switzerland counting the money in a private numbered account. Probably not accurate, but since I had no idea what his job actually entailed it was the best I could come up with. But it wasn't good enough, and I called his office at eight o'clock sharp.

He'd given me his card after our first actual date—the one that had started with breakfast and lasted a full thirty-six hours. "In case you ever need someone experienced in financing multinational corporations."

"Oh, I'll definitely keep it handy then," I'd said, then tucked it neatly into my back pocket. I hadn't needed it since then. Why would I when we'd been together almost constantly from that moment on?

I'd so thoroughly convinced myself that he must still be out of the country—*had I gotten the dates wrong?*—that I actually apologized when the receptionist answered the phone.

"I hate to bother you—and I know he's probably still in China—but I'm trying to reach Quincy Radcliffe. Is he—"

"One moment please." The crisp, efficient female voice was followed in short order by soothing classical hold music. Which was good. Because her reaction had surprised me. And, yeah, I needed to be soothed.

What did it mean? That he was right there at his desk? That he'd flirted with her that morning? That we only dated for three months and even though that time had been magical, I needed to get over myself?

"This is Andrew Donovan. How can I help you? Hello?"

"I—what? Oh." I blinked, only then realizing that I'd lowered the phone. I pushed the button to switch to the speaker. "I'm here. Sorry. I'm trying to reach Quincy Radcliffe."

"Who's calling, please?"

"My name's Eliza Tucker. I'm his—I mean, we were sort of dating, and then he went on a business trip and—" I broke off, feeling suddenly foolish, then cleared my throat. "I just haven't heard from him, and I'm a little worried."

"I see. Yes, well I'm sorry to tell you that Mr. Radcliffe decided to transfer to our Taipei office."

My knees turned to liquid and I slid down the wall. "I see." I didn't see. I couldn't see a single freaking thing. "Um, can you give me his new work number? I've tried his cell, but—"

"I'm sorry, but all client calls are being routed through our switchboard."

"Oh, well, that's fine. You can just route me that way. What time is it in Taipei?"

"I'm afraid we can only forward client calls."

"But I—"

"I'm sorry we couldn't be of more help."

"But—"

"Have a good day, Ms. Tucker."

And then he hung up, which is when I threw my phone across the room, shattering the damn thing.

I didn't care. I was too numb to care.

And for three days, all I did was sleep.

On the fourth day I told myself that something really massive must have gone down at work. He was battling for his career, and of course calling me got pushed to the back burner. But we were pushing on two weeks, and surely he'd left a voice mail by now.

Which, of course, I couldn't check because of my phone.

Getting a replacement was a bit of a production because I wasn't in the good old U.S. of A., but Emma and DHL helped, and soon a replacement phone fully loaded with my account info arrived at my London flat. By that time, I'd learned how to check voicemail remotely—there was nothing—but I was holding out hope that a half dozen text messages would pop up the moment I had a signal.

Nada.

I wasn't really surprised. My computer receives messages, too. And Quincy knew my email address.

That's when I went back to bed. A nest lined with pillows, quilts, five remotes, and a variety of crisps and biscuits, even though I was craving chips and cookies.

For the record, I was done with London. Done with Quince. Done with men.

And I would have gotten my ass right back to Manhattan if I'd had a place to go. Since I didn't, I wallowed, alternating between sleep, action movies—*no* romances—and junk food.

Three days later, I woke up to Emma stroking my hair. "You need a shower," she'd said.

"Great to see you, too." I shoved myself up on my elbows and blinked. She'd turned on the lights, and I grimaced as a million tiny pins started poking at my eyeballs. "How'd you get in?"

Her brows rose, and I waved the question away. "Forget I asked that." Emma started working on her B&E skills when I was four and she was eleven. That was the year our father started locking us in the utility room. To say she has mad skills now is an understatement. Emma has lots of skills. Most of which I'm not supposed to know about. She swore me to secrecy the day everything changed for us. The day her murder arrest went *poof* and she got a scholarship to Pepperdine.

My sister's life is like something out of an action movie, but to me, she's always just been Emma. Sister, mom, friend. There's nothing we won't do for each other, and tops of that list is that we don't spill secrets.

"You didn't have to come," I said.

"Don't be stupid." And then my sister did exactly what she'd done for my entire life. She pulled me out of hell. She protected me. And she made me strong again.

So strong, that for my remaining months in London, I convinced myself that Quincy hadn't destroyed me. That our time together had been a fun dalliance, but that's all. Sexual exploration, a few hundred mind-blowing orgasms, and a new level of self-awareness for yours truly.

It wasn't a travesty that he'd disappeared. Soon enough I would have zipped off back to the States anyway. On the contrary, it was convenient. No unpleasant goodbyes. No trying to squeeze a square vacation romance into a round life hole.

That, at least, was the mantra I repeated daily, and as my time in London drew to a close, I even started to believe it.

At least until that last day when I got it into my head to walk by his office.

I remember sighing as I went into the lobby with no real purpose other than to rest my feet. I sat there, scrolling through my phone, and when I'd looked up, there he was.

Not that he'd seen me. No, he was in the lobby coffee shop, undoubtedly ordering a double espresso, something he did every day and which I told him was completely un-British. Weren't Brits supposed to be all about the tea?

I started to push off the bench—*he was here. He was back.*

But then the real truth of the matter hit me. *He was here —but he hadn't called me. Hadn't left a message. Hadn't done a single, goddamn thing.*

Maybe he had a family tucked away and maybe he didn't. Maybe he was based in Taipei now and maybe he wasn't.

I didn't know. I told myself I didn't care.

Because the bottom line was that Quincy Radcliffe had walked away. And when he'd come back, he hadn't returned to me.

———

The click of the lock yanks me from my memories, and my eyes cut to the door as I exhale with relief. I want to pass off the responsibility for this gadget, and then I want to get out of here, away from Quincy and the brutal memories that keep assaulting me.

Most important, I need to get back to square one. Because if Quincy isn't Mr. X, then that means that Mr. X never showed up at the party, and I'm no closer to finding my sister.

"Finally," I say as the door begins to move. "Take your gizmo and—"

He steps inside, and I snap my mouth closed.

It's not Quincy.

This man has short, curly red hair. His face is too large and his eyes too small. He wears glasses that sit on a bulbous nose, and his lips are unnaturally pale, so when he speaks, it's almost as if a hole is opening up in his face.

He speaks now, and I instinctively scoot backward until my back is pressed against the headboard, my cuffed arm twisting awkwardly as my free hand clutches the gadget for dear life.

"You're a hard woman to find."

He's such an unattractive man, that his pleasant, almost gentle voice surprises me into speech. "I—I didn't know you were looking for me."

Even as I say the words, I realize my mistake. I'd noticed him watching me at the party, but paid him little mind. After all, he never approached me and never commented on the ribbon tied to my wrist. I assumed he was just a guest sussing out the possibilities.

"You," I say, sparing a look at the gizmo and toggling the switch down to edge the needle further into the green. "You're Mr. X." I relax a little. After all, this is the man I'd come to meet. "Why didn't you come to me? We could have—"

My words are cut off by my scream as he leaps onto the bed, yanks my hair back, and presses the blade of a knife against my throat. I go completely still, completely cold. His face is right in front of mine, and I don't see anything human in his eyes.

I hear a small mewling noise and realize it's coming from me.

"*Where is she?*"

I open my mouth, but it's too dry to speak. I don't know what I'd say anyway. He can't be talking about Emma. He thinks *I'm* Emma. Doesn't he?

His thumb presses tight against my jugular. "I could just as easily push down with this blade. Do you understand?"

I'm too afraid that a nod will slice my throat, and I can't find my voice. I manage a strangled sound that he takes as an affirmative.

"I'm glad we understand each other. The girl, you fucking bitch. Where did you hide the girl?"

That's when it clicks. *Quincy's thirteen-year-old.* That's who he's looking for.

And not only do I have no clue where she is, I'm terribly afraid that I've just destroyed Quincy's chance to protect her. Because in my terror at being attacked at knifepoint, I'd managed to lose the gadget.

I squeeze my right hand as if it will magically appear, but there's only air. I whimper, terrified for me and also horribly guilty about that girl. I know what it's like to be young and afraid. Emma had been there to protect me, just as Quincy's trying to protect this girl. And I went and screwed it up for him.

"Where?"

I start to speak, but I can't tell him that I don't know, and I'm too scared to concoct a lie. All I can manage to do is gape at him and whimper an incomprehensible medley of "I, uh, I—"

"Stupid cunt," Mr. X snarls as he takes the knife from my neck and, before I can even breathe a sigh of relief, drags it from my neck to the slit at my thigh, slicing my dress in one easy motion, then pulling it wide, so that I'm naked except for my tiny thong panties.

The tip of the knife must have grazed my skin, because I see small dots of blood gathering in a line from my cleavage all the way down to my belly button. I hadn't felt pain in the moment, but now the wound begins to sting and tears prick my eyes. I'm terrified and lost and entirely at this bastard's mercy. I want to scream for Quincy—for anybody—but I know that if I do, it will be the last sound I make.

Futilely, I tug on my cuffed arm as I throw my free arm over my breasts to shield myself. I try to pull up my legs so that I can curl up into a ball, but he's sitting just above my knees as he moves the knife slowly back and forth above the band of my thong.

"Please." My voice is shaking. "Please don't."

"Don't?" He lifts the blade. "But why not? It's a party, isn't it? And you're all soft and pretty." As he talks, he's creeping up my body until his face is over my breasts. I could thrust my hand up and punch him—I'm certain of it. I was even in a movie once where I did that very thing. In the movie I knocked out the bad guy and got away.

I'm thinking that won't happen here.

"Move your arm, bitch."

I shake my head and keep my arm protectively over my breasts.

"Have it your way," he says. "You want to stay that way, then fine by me. But remember it was your choice." His eyes meet mine, and all I see is a man who's dead inside. "You move and you'll regret it."

And then, as I fight to stay absolutely still, he zips the razor sharp edge of the blade along the underside of my breast.

I whimper, more in fear than the pain, because it's happened so fast I haven't even registered the pain yet.

"Shut your mouth, you cunt. I barely nicked you. But next time, I'll slice the whole titty off."

"No. Please, no." My eyes and throat are full of tears, my body sharp with pain and fear. "Please, please no."

"Then talk you useless whore. Where'd you stash the little bitch?"

"She's in ... she's in..." I don't have to work to make my voice tremble; I'm already terrified. Especially since I don't know what to tell him, and all I can do is buy time and hope that if he believes I know where the girl is, that he won't kill me right this very second.

"*Now.*"

I yelp as he rests the knife blade against my nipple, then I scrunch my eyes closed and cry out inside my head to my sister. *I'm sorry, I'm sorry. I'm so, so sorry.*

I failed her. I failed me. And I'm all out of options.

The mattress shifts, and I gasp as the knife clips the underside of my chin. "Talk. Now. Or else I skewer you."

I'm dead, and I know it.

I never expected the end to come like this.

Except it didn't. It hasn't.

With a jolt, I realize that the pressure against my chin is gone, as is Mr. X's weight on top of me.

More than that, I feel the lingering sting of the slice under my breasts, the pain ratcheting up with each breath and beat of my heart. Not something I'd usually celebrate, but surely if I were dead there'd be no pain at all.

I giggle, and a voice in my head tells me I'm in shock. The voice is probably right. This really isn't a giggling kind of scenario. And, in fact, I swallow the next bubble of laughter when I open my eyes and see Quincy beside the bed, his arm around Mr. X's throat in what looks to be the kind of hold that could easily snap a neck.

And you know what? I'm perfectly okay with that.

But instead of falling down dead, Mr. X thrusts his body backward so that Quincy is shoved against the dresser near the now-closed door. The impact makes Quincy loosen his grip, and Mr. X breaks free. Immediately, he lunges, leading with the knife. Even I can tell that was a mistake. Quincy knocks it free with a sideways swipe of his arm, and at the same time his leg lashes out to slam into Mr. X's kneecap.

Mr. X lets out a wild howl, then stumbles toward the door. He yanks it open, then slams past a wide-eyed blonde in a sheer black dress over what looks like a black unitard.

"Fuck!" She bends over and pulls off a black-heeled sandal, then hurls it down the hall in the direction Mr. X disappeared. At the same time, Quincy races out the door and disappears from view, his cry of, *Check her!* lingering in the air.

Immediately, the blonde is in the doorway. Her eyes skim over the room and over me. She's clearly a professional, because her only reaction is a pair of slightly widened eyes. Outside the room, I hear glass shatter. She must hear it, too, but she doesn't react. Her attention is entirely on me, and she rushes to my side, then sits carefully beside me on the bed.

"I'm Denise," she says, pressing her hand gently to my forehead. "I'm going to help you."

I nod, in shock. I'm lying on top of the spread, and I'm grateful when she reaches over me and tugs the free half over my exposed body. She's searching the drawer for the handcuff key when Quincy enters. He takes one look at me, and I watch the emotions play over his face. Fear, then fury, then something soft and tender.

Then absolutely nothing at all.

"He went through the window."

Denise looks up at him. "What? He jumped?"

"Not exactly."

I see that register on her face, and she nods. "Any activity from the other rooms on the floor?"

"Not so far. Party's shut down and everyone's snug in their rooms."

Denise nods. "At least in that regard we seem to have caught a break."

"Did you," I begin, but my throat is so dry, I have to clear it. They both look at me when I begin again. "I dropped the thing. When he came in."

The damn tears start up again, and Quincy comes to sit by my side, then gently takes my hand.

"I didn't mean to," I say. "Did I—I mean, is it okay? Will the girl be okay?"

His expression never changes, but nods. "You did good. We got what we came for thanks to you."

I nod, relieved. My eyes are so heavy. Intellectually, I know it's the shock. I need to sleep. But I don't want to stay here. "I want to go home," I murmur.

"I'm all for getting out of here, too," Quincy says.

"No argument from me." Denise crosses to the window, then grimaces. "I need to go down. See if he survived."

She starts to lift the sash, then looks from me to Quincy, then back to me again. "On second thought, maybe you should go." She's clearly speaking to Quincy—I'm hardly in a position to go anywhere—but she's looking at me. And right away I understand that she knows at least some of our story. For all I know, she knows more of the real story of Quincy and Eliza than I do.

"I'm not leaving her."

"Quince." Her voice is as firm as his, and I decide in that second that I like this woman. She reminds me of Emma.

"It's okay."

They both turn to look at me, and I realize that my voice is so low and so raw that they probably couldn't even make out my words. I lick my lips and try again. "Quincy can stay."

She nods and raises the windowpane, and for the first time I realize she's planning to leave that way. I must look confused, because she says, "Fire escape."

"Send me a status on our red-haired friend when you hit ground level. I'll get her out of here and signal you when we're clear."

"Will do." She starts to pull the shift-style dress over her head, leaving her clad in skintight black.

"What the hell, Denny?"

She tosses it to him. "She'll need it."

She's right. It's thin and black and won't cover anything, but technically I'll be dressed. And at a party like this, no one will think twice if I walk down to the lobby in it.

By the time Quincy brings the dress to me, she's gone.

He sits on the edge of the bed, then takes my free hand. His grip is firm but gentle. As soothing as his proximity. I don't know what's going on here tonight, not really, but in this tiny bubble of time, I'm grateful that he's with me.

He gently pushes my hair back off my face. "How badly are you hurt?" His voice is even. No nonsense. Like a doctor. And for some reason, that soothes me even more.

As he speaks, he pulls the cuff key out of his pocket and leans over me, reaching for my right wrist. The position puts his face in front of mine, his chest brushing against the spread that now covers my bare breasts. It's oddly intimate, the memories of him mixing with my lingering fear and the way that he is now so sweetly tending to me.

"Eliza?"

I have to rewind the conversation to remember his question. "Oh. Um, I don't think I need stitches. He—ah, he cut my dress off. And he—" I turn my face away.

"He cut you?" He sits up quickly, his voice sharp. My wrist is free now, and I use my right hand to massage it. For a moment, I don't even notice that his abrupt motion caused the spread to shift off me, exposing my bare hip and the side of my breast.

I start to tug it back, but he stills my hand, and as he does the side of his hand brushes my bare hip and I tremble in response to the sweet, horrible, visceral memory that washes over me, culminating in a wave of regret and longing so powerful I almost curl up into myself.

If he notices, he doesn't react. "Let me see what he did to you."

I shake my head and hold the spread in place.

"Eliza. I need to see. I need to know if you need stitches."

"I'm fine."

"No, love, you're not."

I close my eyes. "Don't call me that." I hear the break in my voice and hate myself. "Please."

When I open my eyes, he's looking at me, his gray eyes stormy. "I'm so damn sorry."

"Now isn't the time."

He stands, then shoves his hands into his pockets. "I suppose it isn't. But dammit, Eliza, it's my fault this happened to you. Please. I need to be sure you're okay."

For a moment, he just looks at me. I want to ask him about our past. I want to ask what the hell he's doing here. I want to ask about Emma, even though I'm pretty sure he knows nothing about her, and about the little girl. I need to tell him why I came here tonight. That Emma is missing, and that the man who attacked me had set up a meeting through a message board. I need to tell him that Mr. X asked about the little girl, and I don't understand why.

Somehow, Quincy is tied into the same thing that Emma was investigating. Which means he can help me find her. Which means I need him.

But I don't tell him any of that. Instead, I say, "It's not your fault, and I don't think I need stitches. But I definitely need some Band-Aids."

And then, because I really do understand that he needs to see for himself, I bite my lower lip, then carefully readjust the bedspread to reveal the incision at the lower part of my breast as well as the long, thin trail of blood from my breast-bone to my bellybutton.

"Eliza. Oh, Christ, baby, no." He drops to the edge of the bed, and in that moment he looks as exhausted as I feel.

"Is it that bad?"

He shakes his head. "Yes. No. You don't need stitches." Slowly, his finger traces the curve of my breast, not touching the cut, but near it. His finger is warm, and I bite my lower lip, but I don't tell him to stop. Right or wrong, I want his touch. Not intimately. Not sexually. But so help me, I want to be tended to. I want to be taken care of. I want answers and my sister and peace. I've fallen down the rabbit hole of a nightmare, and I don't have the slightest idea how to claw my way out again.

And right now, the only thing that's keeping me anchored is the touch and attention of this man who once destroyed me.

7

RAGE BURNED THROUGH HIM. A cold, hard fury at himself for pulling her into this, and at the red-haired man for torturing her for something that she wasn't even part of.

He'd walked away from her in order to keep her safe and whole. And now, because of him, she'd been scared, tortured, and mutilated.

He clenched a fist at his side, fighting against the monster now rising in his chest. A beast that fed on his anger, his helplessness. That he had to battle back if he was going to be any help to her at all.

Slowly, he unfurled his hand, letting himself feel every motion, assuring himself that he was in control. That it was *him* in this room with her. Quincy James Radcliffe. That he was here. That he was present. And that no one—not him, not the red-haired man, not anyone—would hurt her.

"Quincy?"

He drew in a breath, then gently cupped her cheek. Her blue eyes locked on his, and he saw the trust reflected back at him. Despite every way he'd hurt her, she wasn't running.

Maybe she should...

He pushed the thought away as foolish. As dangerous as they might be together, until he got her the hell away from The Terrace, he was keeping her close.

"I'm on the ground," Denny said. *"Subject terminated. Witness called it in, so we'll have company soon. I'll catch you at HQ."*

"Roger that."

Eliza lifted a brow, and he just shrugged. He'd fill her in later. Right now, he was more concerned with her wounds. Gently, he ran his finger over the long scrape marks on her belly. Lines and dots, like Morse code.

She bit her lower lip, wincing slightly, but she didn't flinch. "I'm so sorry," he said, even though the words were nothing but hollow platitudes.

"It's not that bad. At least the bleeding's stopped. And considering I was expecting to be dead, I'm perfectly fine with the pain." She grimaced as she pushed herself up onto her elbows, sucking in air. "Okay, maybe *fine* isn't entirely accurate."

"We'll find you some pain killers. First, we need to get out of here." He'd always intended to exit the building after downloading Lassiter's files, but now it was even more of a necessity. Once the police or a witness identified the window from which Red fell, they'd surely come inside and start knocking on doors.

He studied Eliza with a frown. "Do they know your real name?"

She shook her head.

"Good." He nodded, indicating Denny's dress. "Do you need help putting it on?"

Her cheeks flushed, and she dropped her gaze. "I—no. I can manage it. Can you, um..."

He stood and turned away from her, facing the window.

As he did, he realized that he could see a partial reflection in the raised pane. A gentleman would divert his eyes. He watched. Once upon a time, he'd believed he could be a gentleman. Now, he knew better.

She stood gingerly, as if it hurt to move, which he knew it did. He thought of the shallow cuts that had once covered his chest and abdomen, along with his inner thighs. The wounds were no longer open; instead he was marked by a web of thin, white scars. The skin had long ago knitted, the pain only a brutal memory. But that didn't mean he was healed. Far from it.

He pressed his fingers to his temples, and forced the memories back, focusing instead on the reflection of the woman who had once belonged to him.

She moved slowly, and the motion of raising the dress over her head accentuated her small waist and perfect breasts. She had an athletic frame. Long and lean and lovely. Some men might consider her breasts too small, but they'd be wrong. He'd tasted those breasts, held their weight in his hands. He recalled one time in particular when he'd dragged his teeth over her erect nipple. It was as if he'd lit a firecracker inside her. Her ankles and wrists had been bound to the bed, and she'd arched up, her body practically vibrating with pleasure as she moaned his name and begged him for more. For everything.

He'd slid his hand under her skirt, his fingers teasing their way inside her soaked panties. She'd bucked against him, fucking his hand like a wild thing, and then begged for his cock. He'd denied her, of course. Made her wait until she was so hungry for him she could barely breathe. Then he'd buried himself in her, his fingers squeezing her nipples as he watched passion and euphoria rise on her face as he took her to the limit and she exploded in his arms, her loud cries pushing him over the edge along with her.

That same memory had threatened to burst free earlier, when he'd pulled out the cuff and attached her to the bed. He'd pushed it brutally away, both because he needed to focus on the job and because he had no business remembering. Not when he could no longer have her. There was no point to self-flagellation, after all. It didn't even faze his demons.

Now, though...

Now he realized that he was either a shamefully weak man or a fucking masochist, because even though he knew that he couldn't ever have Eliza in his bed again, he'd still opened the floodgates to his memories, and now his cock was straining against his trousers, on high alert from the enticing, delicious, erotic images flooding his brain.

"Okay," she said as he heard the first wail of sirens approaching the building. "I'm dressed. Not that it makes much difference in this outfit..."

He focused on the carpet, drawing deep breaths before he turned around. It wouldn't do for her to see just how much her presence—and his memories—had affected him. But as soon as he saw her standing there in the sheer black shift, her nipples hard against the thin material and her tiny, flesh-colored thong barely covering her sweet pussy, his cock sprang to attention all over again.

She met his eyes, then crossed her arms over her chest.

Damn. "Sorry, love. The dress suits you."

She rolled her eyes, but at the same time, some of the tension dropped away. "Are we ready?" She took a step toward the door.

"Not that way."

She turned, her brow furrowed. "Teleportation?"

"Funny. The fire escape."

He expected her to protest, and he had all the reasons why they couldn't go out the front lined up and ready to go. Most important, avoiding the authorities.

As for reason number two, that stemmed from the fact that he'd just hacked Lassiter's computer system and now held in his pocket a flash drive with stolen information that he was quite certain Lassiter would kill for. Probably Lassiter had yet to discover the breach. But that wasn't a gamble Quince was willing to make, especially not with Eliza in his care. So any exit that reduced the chance of stumbling over Lassiter, the better.

Eliza didn't argue. She just nodded and stepped toward the window, then hitched the dress up to mid-thigh, giving him an enticing view as she hooked her leg over the sash.

He frowned at her bare feet. "Shoes?"

She glanced down at the impractical heels she'd left on the floor. "I can't climb in them."

True enough; the fire escape was constructed with a metal grating, and the heels would sink right through. Still, they needed to look like a couple out for the evening once they hit street level. He took one more look at her, the dress even more sheer now that it was backlit by the city's ambient light.

"Here," he said, shrugging out of his suit jacket and handing it to her. Then he bent and picked up the shoes. "I'll carry them. We'll need to blend."

She drew in a breath, squared her shoulders, and didn't protest.

Considering the nightmare he'd dragged her into, she was being quite compliant. He had no idea how she'd ended up at this party, but he could assume. Her acting career had stalled. She needed cash. One of her friends moonlighted as an escort and told her about these parties where a girl could earn enough in a night to last her six months. It had been too tempting to pass up, and Eliza had turned into the real-life version of Denny's alias—a struggling actress resorting to selling herself to make ends meet.

And didn't that just break his heart?

As far as Quincy was concerned, a woman could make a living however she wanted. In theory, he had no problems with sex as a commercial transaction. So long as the person getting paid was entering into the arrangement fully of his or her own free will, then the details of what went on in the bedroom—including activities or payments—were nobody else's business.

But Eliza wasn't just anybody. She was *his*, dammit.

The thought hit him like a sledgehammer, and he shook himself as he mentally backtracked. Because she wasn't his. Not anymore. She hadn't been for a long, long time.

But just because he no longer had a claim on her, didn't mean he no longer understood her or cared about her. He *knew* her, dammit. Her heart and soul; her fears and doubts.

She'd told him how she'd grown up. The abusive father. The protective big sister. The months living the streets. She'd witnessed the kind of perversions that no little girl should ever have to deal with, and yes, her past had scarred her.

But it hadn't destroyed her.

He knew that; he'd seen it. Hell, he'd helped her discover what she needed to feel whole. For Eliza, sex had always been about the connection. The surrender.

The trust.

The Eliza he knew would have to be truly desperate to sell herself to a stranger.

And yes, he'd taken her places she'd never gone. Pushed

her limits. Claimed her submission. And together they'd lost themselves in shared ecstasy. But the road they'd traveled had been paved with trust. With passion. And, yes, with love.

A love that he'd betrayed, goddammit, but that was hardly the point now.

No, the real bottom line was that she had no business being at a party like this, and the thought of her naked and bound in another man's bed made him want to punch something.

It didn't matter if he'd walked away—didn't matter if he could never claim her again—didn't matter that he had no right to judge her or to help her. All he knew was that she didn't belong in a place like this. Didn't deserve to be touched by a man who only wanted to get off. Who saw her only as a tool for the satisfaction of his cock. Who only wanted—

"—now?"

He snapped to attention. "What?"

"I said, are we going now?"

"Sorry." He tapped his ear, feeling only slightly guilty about the suggestion of a lie. "I was listening."

"Did she say if it's clear?"

He made a non-committal noise, then pointed up. "We're going over. Up to the roof, down to the back alley. Everyone will be in front with Red, so we're going the other way."

She didn't argue or complain. Instead, she just slipped out the window in her bare feet, her small body lost inside his jacket.

He followed her up the ladder to the roof, staying a few steps below in case she stumbled, a position that gave him an enticing view of her ass peeking out from under the hem of his jacket. He swallowed, told himself he'd be better off looking at the small of her back, and soldiered on.

Once they reached the flat, gravel-topped roof, he took her hand and they hunched down as they crossed, staying mostly in the shadows thrown by the smattering of utility boxes and access sheds that dotted the roof.

When they reached the far side, he peered down, making sure no one was on the ground looking back up at them. Then he helped her over the edge and onto the ladder that led down to the highest platform of the fire escape. Thank goodness Lassiter had kept the building's original features. So many remodels did away with the external fire escapes.

Within five minutes, they'd reached the alley, and he held her steady as she slipped on her shoes. Another five minutes and they'd reached Hawthorne, the street that ran parallel to Hollywood Boulevard.

"Do you have a cell phone?"

She shook her head. "A friend dropped me at the hotel. I thought it was better not to bring anything personal." She met his eyes. "I wanted to be anonymous."

He nodded, assuming that *friend* was code for *Madam.* He considered asking her if it was money or something else that had brought her tonight, then told himself it was no longer his business. Instead, he pulled out his own phone, intending to summon an Uber once they'd reached the intersection of Hawthorne and La Brea. "I'll get you home. I'm sorry to have dragged you into this mess. I don't know how Red got wind of what Denny and I were doing, but—"

"Quincy—"

"No, wait. There's more I need to say. I know tonight was a freak occurrence. But even so, this kind of thing isn't safe.

Some of the men who come to parties like this ... Eliza, they aren't—"

"Like you?" Her brows rose as she stopped at an intersection. "Are you telling me that the kind of men who come to parties stocked with call girls might actually hurt me?" Her voice rose as if in indignation.

He allowed himself a mental sigh of relief, pleased that she understood. "That's exactly what I'm saying."

She crossed her arms over her chest, her eyes practically burning through him. "But you'd never hurt me, would you, Quincy? You'd never dream of ripping my heart out or tearing my soul to shreds."

His gut twisted, both from the truth of her words and the fact that he'd walked right into that. "Eliza, that's not what I—"

"Fuck. You." She started walking, her heels clicking on the pavement.

He caught up with her, then took her elbow and tugged her to a stop. "If you need money, I'll help you. But this kind of party—come on, love, you know it's a bloody awful mistake."

She nodded slowly, and he hoped she was considering her words. He assumed she'd either tell him to go to hell or she'd agree to his offer. But he definitely wasn't expecting her question. "Tell me about the girl."

"The girl? Denny?"

She rolled her eyes. "No. I think I've got that. You work with her. You might be sleeping with her—that part I'm not sure of."

"No, I—"

"I'm talking about the thirteen-year-old. The girl you said needed my help, remember? The reason I had to hold that receiver thingie."

"Do you think I made that up?"

"I think she's missing."

He stopped, shocked by her words.

A moment later, she stopped, too, then turned back to look at him. "So I guess I'm right."

"Walk me through it, Eliza. Every little thing you think you know."

She bit her lower lip, clearly considering her words. "Red wasn't in that room because of whatever you and Denny were doing."

"What are you—"

"He was there because of me."

He took a step back, her words hitting him with the force of a slap. "You? Why on earth do you think that?"

She flashed a wry smile as she held up her wrist, still decorated with a simple red ribbon. "Freaky coincidence, huh? But he's the one who picked the ribbon as the way to identify me. Or, Emma, really. I kind of showed up in her place."

"Emma was supposed to be at the party?"

"Not like that. She was coming in undercover. For a meeting."

He nodded, remembering that Emma had worked as a PI. "She was on a case? And you're telling me that ribbon was a signal?"

"Exactly."

"Then why were you there instead of Emma? And what does any of this have to do with Ariana's disappearance?"

"That's the teenager? I don't know how any of it ties together. All I know is that I snuck in because Emma's gone missing, and the message about the meet and the ribbon was the only clue I had."

She blinked, and for the first time since she'd climbed

through the fire escape, he saw her control start to slip. "I don't understand what's going on—really I don't. But that red-haired bastard thought I was Emma. And he asked me where the girl was. That's all he wanted to know."

She met his eyes, hers scared but defiant. "Which means I need your help. Because your missing girl must somehow be connected to my missing sister, and—"

"—that means I'm not sending you home after all. Instead, you're coming with me."

8

"*You're coming with me.*"

Those delicious, familiar words rumble through me as I climb into the backseat of the Uber that's pulled up beside us, then slide over to make room for Quincy. I hug myself as I watch him get in next to me, but I'm not seeing the man as he is now, in his fine tailored suit. Instead, I see his hard, lean body in jeans that hug his perfect ass and tight thighs. I see a pale gray Henley under a black leather jacket instead of a starched white shirt. I see a man whose hard eyes appraise me and whose appreciative smile warms me.

I see the Quincy of that first morning when I'd made up my mind to meet him, and as this Los Angeles ride share pulls away from the curb and the man from tonight sits silently beside me, I let myself drift back to London and into those memories of the man from before...

I'd spent most of the night after he'd put me in the London cab telling myself that I wasn't going to meet him that next morning. Our time exploring the city together had been incredible, sure, but the man was too arrogant. Too unpredictable. I'd expected to spend the night with him, and he'd turned that expectation on its ear. Teasing me instead of satisfying me, and making arrogant assumptions about what I wanted. And how could he possibly know what I craved when I hadn't even figured it out for myself?

Better to chalk it up as one of those incredible tourist experiences. Something a brochure would headline *An Encounter With a Native*. But definitely not something that needed to go any further.

Those were the things I'd told myself, anyway. I even used my stern and reasonable voice. And yet when morning rolled around, I found myself showering and dressing, and then taking the tube back to Marble Arch and winding my way down the London streets to the little cafe that he'd pointed out.

With every step I told myself that I would leave *if*.

If he wasn't there, I'd turn around and go shopping.

If he said that he knew I would come, I'd tell him I only came to let him know that I wasn't giving him the satisfaction.

If he even hinted that I'd come only because his raw sensual promises had enticed and aroused me, then I would turn on my heel and go. I was intrigued, true. But no way was I going to trust my body to a man who would so cavalierly toss my curiosity and desire back in my face.

The first *if* was negated when I walked through the door. Even though I arrived a full ten minutes early, he was already sitting in the third booth, positioned so that he faced the door. And the moment I stepped over the threshold, I saw the smile light his eyes. He stood, then lifted a hand to signal me over, making no attempt to hide his pleasure.

"I was hoping you'd come. I was afraid I'd scared you off."

Poof. There went the second *if*, evaporating into a cloud of smoke.

"You might have made me a little nervous," I admitted, sliding into the booth. "But not scared."

"I'm sorry about the nerves, but I'm very glad you came. I had a good time yesterday. I hope you did, too."

"Very much," I said, realizing that he'd thoroughly annihilated all of my excuses. I was stuck there by my own rules, and perfectly happy about that.

The cafe served American-style pancakes, and I ordered a stack of chocolate chip, black coffee, and a side of bacon. I was starving and ate the entire thing, which is not something I'd normally do on a date, as I don't want to come off as a human vacuum. But the taste of home was too good to pass up, and honestly I was so lost in the conversation I didn't even realize how much I'd eaten until the waitress took away my empty plate.

"How much have you played tourist during your time in the city?"

"Not much," I told him. I'd already explained yesterday about the show closing and my unexpected freedom.

"That's what I thought." He tilted his head. "I hope you're free all day. There are so many things I want to show you."

If I wasn't already prepared to spend a full day with him, the heat in his voice would have prompted me to clear my day completely. He took me all around London on the back of his Ducati, which was, frankly, the perfect way to see the town.

"Do you mind?" he'd asked, passing me a spare helmet. "I can hire a car if you'd rather."

"Are you kidding? This is fine." I meant it, too. I've known how to drive a motorcycle since I was twelve, though Emma almost always took the controls. It was our primary mode of transportation until she was old enough to get a license. Nobody bothered us on the bike, even when she was too young. It was as if we were invisible. Which was probably why she continued to ride it for so long, only really using the car when she had something to carry or a passenger. Or when she was on a stakeout. It's hard to hunker down for the long haul on a bike.

All of which meant that I was more than happy to slide onto the bike behind him. And, frankly, the feel of my inner thighs against his hips wasn't a bad way to spend the day at all. In fact, as the day went on and my body rubbed against his and the motorcycle revved beneath me, my thoughts drifted more and more to the naughty promises he'd made last night. His promise to claim me. Pleasure me. To make me surrender.

I wanted that. And the more I thought about it the more my body thrummed with anticipation.

And yet the hours kept ticking by, without even a passionate kiss to suggest that there was anything more on the agenda.

We rode all over town, with Quincy showing me his favorite open air markets, then taking me to some stables near Hyde Park where we saddled two horses and went exploring. Or, rather, I explored. He knew exactly where he was going, as it turned out that he owned the horses.

"I love riding out here, but I rarely take the time," he told me as we took a break to sit by a pond and have some wine and cheese that he'd asked one of the stablehands to prepare. He took my hand, his thumb lightly stroking my skin in a way that shot fire through my entire body. "I'm very glad we came today."

When he spoke, he looked straight at me, as if I was the only thing that mattered in the entire world. It was a nice feeling, and a rare one. And the truth was that Quincy had a way of always making me feel like that.

He somehow arranged a private tour of the Tower of London, including the Crown Jewels—"connections," he told me, making me suitably impressed—and it wasn't until the evening approached that he took me to his place. That same house that we'd seen on the bus tour. Only Quincy, it turned out, had converted the backyard servant's cottage into his private residence.

"I thought we'd order a light supper for delivery," he said, as he helped me off the bike.

"Um, sure," I said, as I followed him inside the charming residence. In truth, I'd thoroughly enjoyed spending the day with him, but it hadn't panned out the way I'd been expecting. From what he'd said the previous night, I'd anticipated some sort of fantasy encounter like a scene from a sexy late-night cable show.

As if he could read my mind, he bent to my ear and whispered, "Foreplay. The motorcycle especially, don't you think? All that power vibrating between your legs?"

My mouth went completely dry, and he flashed a mischievous grin, took my hand, and led me to the living room. "Wine?" he asked as I settled onto the sofa. His voice and attitude were perfectly casual, as if he hadn't just made perfectly clear that he knew exactly where my thoughts had been all afternoon.

I nodded, and he brought me a glass of red. I drank it,

welcoming the buzz and barely even tasting the grape. All I wanted was for him to kiss me.

And finally, thank God, he did.

He didn't ask. He simply set his glass down, then took mine from my fingers and set it on the table, too. Then he leaned in and closed his mouth over mine, and I just about melted from the pleasure of his lips on mine, his tongue teasing and demanding entrance. He buried his fingers in my hair and pulled me closer, taking the kiss deeper and wilder, as if he'd been thinking about nothing else all day, and now he couldn't get his fill. God knew I couldn't either.

Then his hands were at my waist and he was pulling me onto his lap. I was wearing thin black leggings, and I could easily feel his erection through his jeans, and the knowledge that he was as turned on as I was only made me more excited. I ground against him, letting the sweet sensations build as he deepened the kiss, one hand still holding my head steady and the other cupping my breast.

I lost myself in that kiss, in the feel of him. In the tremors of pleasure that coursed through me, more intense than anything I'd ever felt before.

"Take off your clothes and get on the bed," he said, and I froze, my hips going still in the midst of grinding myself to my own climax.

"What?"

He leaned back, putting space between us as he cupped both my breasts, his thumb and forefingers teasing the nipples that were straining against my lacy bra.

"I—"

"Do you trust me?"

I licked my lips, but I nodded. I *did* trust him.

"Then go. Naked," he said, as if I'd forgotten. "On your back. Your legs spread." He looked me up and down, and the heat in his eyes almost made me come right then. "And I want to see you touching yourself when I walk into that room."

I swallowed, not at all sure I liked this. Being on display. It was too much. And I didn't want those harsh memories rising.

"I don't think I—"

He brushed his thumb over my lower lip. "You can say no, Eliza. You can always say no."

"I can?" For some insane reason, that simple statement was a revelation to me. I'd never been able to say no with *him*. And Emma sure as hell hadn't been able to either. Did he mean it? My gaze dipped down to the very obvious bulge in his jeans. As if reading my mind, Quincy chuckled. "I promise, I'll survive. There are plenty of other options. Or we can just watch television."

He pulled me close, then kissed me sweetly. "I want to touch you," he whispered. "I want to take you places you've never gone, and I want to make you explode as you scream my name. But I don't want any of that unless you do. Whatever you want, Eliza. All you have to do is decide."

I drew a breath, then nodded. "Okay," I said, then started to turn toward the bedroom.

"Wait."

For a moment, fear bubbled inside me, and I was afraid that I'd hesitated too long and he'd changed his mind.

"Do you know what a safe word is?"

"I—kind of."

"It's another way of saying no. A better way, with no confusion. What's your safe word, Eliza? Something you wouldn't normally say in bed. Something you can remember."

"Ducks," I said, thinking of the first moment I'd met him. "Ducklings."

It was silly, but from his smile and nod, I could tell that he approved.

"Go on," he said, and with those two words, his entire demeanor changed. Where only moments before he'd been warm and careful and instructive, now he seemed dark and sensual and a little dangerous. But not scary. My fear had entirely disappeared.

I did as he asked and got undressed.

Naked and with my heart pounding, I climbed onto the bed. And though I started out wildly embarrassed, once I closed my eyes and imagined Quincy watching me, I actually got into touching myself. So much that by the time I heard his footsteps and his soft command to keep my eyes shut, my body was already sparking with the precursor to an amazing orgasm.

"Beautiful," he murmured, and I felt the bed shift under his weight as he sat on the edge of the mattress. Then he gently lifted my hands and I gasped in surprise, almost opening my eyes when I felt him put velcro padded cuffs around my wrists.

"Quincy..."

I heard the tension in my voice, and he must have as well, because he whispered, "Shhh. It's okay. Keep your eyes closed." And then, as if to ensure that I did, he slipped a blindfold over my eyes.

Without conscious thought, I pulled my legs together, as if my body was trying to claim some amount of modesty in response to the fact that I couldn't move my legs. "Oh, no, love. None of that."

I whimpered, then bit my lower lip, but he showed no pity. Instead, he moved down to my ankles, binding me fully to the bed, my body forming an X. Honestly, I was glad for the blindfold. I don't know that I could have stood the embarrassment of seeing the way he looked at me, even though the tone of his voice and the words he spoke told me that he both liked the way I looked and that he was very turned on.

I'd never done anything like this before, and I got lost in the slow, delicious sensuality of his touch. First teasing me with a feather, then tormenting me with an ice cube. But those touches were nothing compared to an actual vibrator that created such a riot of sensations that I writhed and strained against my bonds, trying desperately to close my legs as my body both rebelled and rejoiced from a harsh pleasure so intense it bordered on pain.

With expert skill, he teased me, taking me close to orgasm and then pulling back until I was teetering on the edge and begging for release. Only then did he continue his erotic assault with his own fingers and mouth, as I shamelessly bucked against him, craving a control that he'd forbidden and begging for the feel of him inside me.

When I finally came—when he finally *let* me—the force of the orgasm was overwhelming, more than I'd ever experienced as every cell in my body seemed to turn inside out until I was nothing more than a limp, satisfied shell of a woman.

"You're amazing," he whispered, his hands stroking me as he moved along my body and down to my ankles and wrists. Gently, he released me so that I could curl up beside him. "Do you have any idea how incredible it is to watch you? To see you writhe in pleasure from my touch?"

I couldn't answer; I was too spent. But I molded my body to his, my face tucked in against his neck, and murmured something about being lost in heaven.

His low laughter rumbled through me, and he pulled me close, then stroked my hair as I floated somewhere above the earth until finally—*finally*—I came enough back to myself to form coherent sentences.

"I thought I would hate it," I murmured, then gathered enough strength to prop myself up so that I could see his face. "I thought I'd cry out the safe word in the first few minutes."

His forehead creased, and I knew that I'd worried him. That he understood that I wasn't talking like a woman who simply hadn't ever played these kinds of sex games before. But instead like a woman with secrets.

Gently, he brushed my cheek. "Eliza, love. What is it you haven't told me?"

I knew I should have said something before, but even as nervous as I was, I'd wanted to be with him. To experience everything he had to give. And I hadn't wanted him to back away, believing that I was too fragile.

But when we were all relaxed after, I did tell him. Even more, I wanted to.

I wanted him to understand my hesitations. And—God help me—I wanted to share that deepest, darkest piece of me.

So I told him. I told him about my father.

About the horrible things he did to Emma. The things he did to me.

True, we weren't tied up. No wrist cuffs or ankle restraints. But we still couldn't get away. Our father had all the power.

It was horrible, and I told Quincy all of it.

And then, as he brushed away my tears, I confessed that I thought it would be like that with him. "I thought I'd feel trapped. Used." I ducked my head, embarrassed. "But it wasn't like that at all."

For a moment, he simply looked at me, and I thought that I'd blown it. That I should have just kept my mouth shut. "You thought you'd be helpless," he said. "The way you were with him?"

I nodded as he hooked his arm under my shoulders and propped me up while he used his free hand to point out the window. "I know a bit about that," he said. "Do you see that window?"

I nodded.

"That was my parents' bedroom. The night those men came in—the ones who had the vendetta against my father—I was seven years old. I'd been playing on the foot of the bed while my mother read a book. She shoved me under the bed and told me not to come out for anything. I was flat on my belly and shaking with terror and there wasn't a bloody thing I could do."

He turned to face me. "So I understand helpless. It's when you have no control. When it's ripped from you. Like me with those men when I had no chance in hell of protecting my mother. And you with your father, when you were powerless to do a goddamn thing."

I blinked away the tears that had pooled in my eyes.

"With your father, you had control ripped away from you. With me, you have all the control."

"I don't understand."

"You gave control to me, El. *You* did that. You had the power to stop at any moment. You gave me your trust. And that was your gift to me. You surrendered control. I didn't steal it. Do you get it?"

"Yeah." I thought about it, then grinned as I rolled on top of him. "Want to try it again?"

He laughed, but he didn't turn me down. And, honestly, I could have spent the rest of my months in London in bed with him. At that point, I was addicted.

As it turned out, we explored the city as much as we explored each other. Quincy made me feel free. Confident. Most of all, he made me feel loved, and every day we grew closer, as we learned each other's boundaries. We pushed each other's limits sexually, and I discovered things about myself that I'd never known. We played and experimented and laughed, and through him I learned that I truly enjoyed sex. That it wasn't something to be endured, but something to be shared.

Maybe I would have eventually discovered that on my own, but that wasn't the point. Because with Quincy, I'd fallen in love.

I would have stayed forever if he'd let me, and for those three months, I truly believed that he would.

I never expected that his love for me was an illusion. That our days together were nothing more than a fantasy, something ephemeral that could be swept away on a whim, or flicked out of existence like a rabbit on the wrong end of a magician's wand.

But that's what happened. And soon enough our storybook romance ended, and I was thrust rudely out into the cold, bitter embrace of reality.

And now here I am, tossed into the backseat of a car zipping through Los Angeles with the man who threw me away.

And all I can think is that this time I will not trust him. This time, I know that he lies.

9

"ANYTHING?" Quincy asks, as he paces along a row of computers. They're all dormant, a 3D rendition of the SSA logo tumbling across the otherwise quiet screens. All except for the one where Denny sits, now wearing black track pants and a white tank top—both also with the SSA logo.

"Yes, I've cracked the case," she says, without looking up. An incomprehensible string of numbers and letters pour across the screen like a reverse waterfall, moving so quickly it almost makes me dizzy.

Denny looks back over her shoulder at Quincy. "The butler did it."

I laugh, and Quincy turns the scowl he'd aimed at her in my direction.

"Seriously, Q. It's encrypted, remember? And you only walked through the door ten minutes ago. I'm good, but give a girl some space."

Quincy catches my eye, clearly frustrated. As for me, I have a total girl crush on his partner.

I've pulled my hair back into a ponytail and am dressed similarly to Denny, the outfit provided by the fitness room of the Stark Security Agency. According to Quincy, it's a relatively new venture, part of the broad universe of billionaire Damien Stark.

The same Damien Stark who—even though it's three in the morning—is in the glass-enclosed conference room on a speaker call with another man who, unlike Stark, I've never seen in the tabloids. He has hair the color of mine, and a no-nonsense smile. Quincy identified him as Ryan Hunter, the head of the SSA, and promised he'd introduce me to both men when they were off the call.

There'd been another man in the office when we arrived, too. Liam Foster. A tall black man with military bearing, a rock-solid build, and kind eyes that looked like they'd kept a lot of secrets. He'd taken my key and gone off to Emma's condo. Not only to retrieve the phone that I'm desperate to check, but also because I'd told Quincy that Lorenzo and I disagreed about whether someone had poked around in Emma's things. Quincy assured me that if anyone could clock the signs of an intruder, it would be Liam.

I glance at the digital clock on the far wall and consider calling Lorenzo again. But I've already called twice. Once in the Uber using Quincy's phone, and once from a landline in the fitness center. Both times had rolled to voicemail.

I'm frustrated, but not too concerned. True, Lorenzo knew that I was going undercover to the party, but he also knew that I might have to play the role of party girl all night in order to maintain my cover. I'd seen the disapproval in his eyes when he'd hit that realization, but to his credit, he didn't try to talk me out of it. Other than Emma, no one knows me better than Lorenzo, and he knows that there are no limits to what I'll do for my sister.

So while he knew I might not check in until morning, I also expected him to be glued to his phone. But considering it's almost four in the morning, I should probably cut him some slack. He probably fell asleep. And despite all the stereotypes about law enforcement types being constantly aware, Lorenzo sleeps like the dead.

He wakes at six every morning, so I'll call him then. In the meantime, I watch Denny's fingers fly across the keyboard as I try to figure out what she's doing. Since I haven't got a clue, I quickly tire of that activity. I find Quince at a nearby workstation. He's wearing half-frame reading glasses that make him look both intellectual and ridiculously sexy, and he's scowling at something on the screen.

I consider going and peering over his shoulder, but decide against it. My relief and gratitude at being saved from Red's knife has already started to melt away, once again exposing all my raw edges where Quincy Radcliffe is concerned. And here—in this fancy office in front of these strangers—is really not where I want to get into it.

Instead, I cross the giant room to the western-facing wall of windows. This building is located at the center of a new Santa Monica office park called The Domino. According to Quincy, the SSA takes up four floors, with this first floor serving as home base for analysts and the IT staff, which explains the rows and rows of computer-topped workstations.

This wall is made entirely of one-way glass, and I stand there now and look out at a tranquil garden area, obviously designed as a respite from all the craziness going on around it.

Because of the lighting, I can see Quincy's reflection as he approaches me. He slides his hands into the pockets of his trousers. He hasn't changed clothes, and while I look like a sloppy student who rolled out of bed for class, he looks like a master of the universe.

The disparity pisses me off, which isn't fair, but I'm bone-tired and no closer to finding my sister than I was before. Only now instead of being on my own and befuddled I'm surrounded by gazillions of dollars in tech and befuddled.

That doesn't make me feel better.

As if that weren't enough to be going on with, I've spent the last few hours with a man I once loved who it turns out I never really knew. And I'm not sure if that's his fault for keeping secrets or mine for being so ridiculously naive.

His eyes meet mine in the glass. "How are you hanging in there?"

"Fine. Who doesn't like to be tossed down the rabbit hole?"

A single brow arches, and my heart twists painfully. It's a trademark Quincy affectation, and one that used to make me melt. Now, I just want to slap him. "What?" I demand.

"Seems to me you walked into the warren of your own free will."

"The party, you mean?"

He nods, and on that point I have to agree. Possibly not the smartest of decisions, especially when I factor Red into the equation and the fact that he seemed to want me—or at least Emma—dead. But I wasn't thinking about that. "I meant you," I tell him. "The rabbit hole of you."

I turn so that I'm looking at him rather than his reflection. "The slippery slope of realizing that the man I spent three months with—the man who I confessed my love to—the man who fucking walked out on me—was never the man I thought he was. Sucks for me, right?"

He doesn't react. Of course he doesn't. Quincy always did have one hell of a poker face.

I yank the ponytail holder off my hair, just for something

to do with my hands, and my hair spills over my shoulders. "This isn't a new venture, is it? You didn't suddenly get tired of the world of high finance and decide to leap into the wide and exciting world of private intelligence. Did you?"

"No," he says. "I didn't."

"No," I repeat. "Score one for me. Let's see how I do on the bonus round, because I'm thinking that the closest you ever got to high finance was your family's net worth. I'm thinking that before you worked here, you worked for the government. British, obviously, so I bet you were with MI6. Or, I don't know, whatever private paramilitary organizations hang out around London."

"Hang out?"

I cock my head and cross my arms. "I lay all that on you, and the only response you have is to criticize my word choice?"

"Go on."

I make a show of raising my brows. "What? There's more? Or are you talking about the fact that you were in intelligence even back when we were together? Because I'd bet money that you were. And I'll even double down and say that it was some mission that called you away. What I don't get is why the hell you stayed away. Because honestly, Quince, I really don't know how I surv—*shit.*"

He says nothing, just watches my face. And there is no way I am confessing the depths of my pain. No way at all.

Instead, I roll my shoulders back and focus on his face. "I was in love with you."

He swallows, but his expression doesn't change. For a moment, he is silent, then he says simply, "And now?"

I consider lying, but what would be the point. "Now? Now I kind of hate you."

I exhale, feeling a little better since that is off my chest. I don't look at his face. Instead, I turn and walk toward Denny, then slide into the chair next to her.

She glances sideways at me, and I have the feeling that she understands more than she's letting on. For the first time, I wonder about her relationship with Quincy. Are they work partners? Or is there more going on between them?

Considering I just told Quince that I hate him, I probably shouldn't care one way or the other. But, of course, I do.

I clear my throat and nod at the computer screen. "I'm confused," I confess. "I thought I had to hold that gadget so that some sort of decryption software could get beamed down to Quincy. But if that's the case, then what are you decrypting now?"

She glances toward Quincy, who's watching us from the window, and I see him nod, giving permission to bring me into the loop.

"That software got us past the system security and also instituted a high speed cloning program."

"So you stole his database, but it's still encrypted?"

"Pretty much."

I frown. "But you can decrypt it, right?"

"Me personally? No. But fortunately I work with some of the best geniuses Mr. Stark's money can buy."

"So why did you steal it? What's on there, and who hired you?"

She runs her fingers through her fine, blond hair. "I'm pretty sure that's above your pay-grade."

I let out a frustrated sigh. "Fine. How long is it going to take? I'm only here because our problems overlap, and I want to know if that thing's holding information about my sister."

"Well, that's the million dollar question. And the reason

we took the clone with us instead of hanging around. Could be five more minutes. Could be five months."

"It won't be five months," Quincy says, joining us. "My friend Noah ran the team who developed that fine piece of software. It'll work fast. You can count on it." He cocked his head toward the conference room. "Come on. They're off the call. I'll introduce you."

I've met a lot of celebrities over the years. It comes with the territory when you do as many random roles as I have. But I've never met someone like Damien Stark. He's tall and lean, and I remember that he used to be a professional tennis player before reinventing himself as one of the wealthiest men in the world. He has dark hair and fascinating dual colored eyes—one black and the other amber. He projects a commanding manner that should be intimidating but isn't.

"Ms. Tucker," Stark says, extending his hand. "I apologize for keeping you waiting. Quincy, nice work in the field."

"Except that database still isn't decrypted," I say, because I'm so used to speaking my mind with Lorenzo and Emma that I forgot to turn on my filter.

"Denny will have that remedied by the time we're finished here," Ryan Hunter says. "I think Damien was talking about you. Didn't our red-headed friend come close to gutting you?"

"Oh." I realize that Quincy must have tapped out an update to the team during our ride from Hollywood to Santa Monica. Frankly, I'm flattered that Stark and Hunter think of me as anything other than someone who could have potentially gunked up their mission. But I do take his point, and I turn to Quincy with an apologetic smile. "Did I say thanks?"

Amusement lights his eyes. "You're welcome."

Ryan nods, then indicates the nearby chairs. I sit, grateful to be moving past the introductions. On the whole, Hunter seems more approachable than Stark, but at the same time, I think that's a facade. According to Quincy, Ryan's the big cheese at the SSA, which means part of his job is to get close. To watch. Right now, he's watching me, and I wonder what those blue eyes see in me.

I have a feeling both of these men make friends slowly, but when they do, they're loyal to a fault. It's a quality I admire, and which reminds me of Emma.

Looking at these three men now seated around the table, it's like I'm an extra in a movie featuring three A-list guys. They're that gorgeous. At the same time, all three seem like real people, with rough edges and a core of steel inside. Nothing airbrushed about them at all.

Between the three of them, Quincy is the most real to me. But even he seems a little rough around the edges. As if he isn't quite tame. I'd seen hints of that in London, but now it's more obvious. A dark watchfulness. The sense that he's on the hunt.

Whatever it is, there's even more of an edge to him now, and I think that's partly why I've felt safe, even on what has been one of the most horrible nights of my life.

But safety with Quincy is dangerous, too. Because while I'm happy to not be dead from Red's blade, I'm terrified of knocking down the wall I built around my heart to keep Quincy Radcliffe out.

"—and then maybe a quick rundown? Eliza?"

I jump, embarrassed to realize that Ryan Hunter is talking to me and I've completely zoned out. "I'm sorry. It's been a really long day." True, but that's not the reason my mind was elsewhere. "What did you say?"

"Sorry. I know you're exhausted, but obviously our interests overlap. Quince gave us the short version of why you were at The Terrace. Could you fill in the gaps?"

I lean back in my chair. "Well, that depends." I look between him and Damien Stark, wondering at the extent of my moxie. "Are you going to tell me why you were hacking Scott Lassiter's system? Because, color me naive, but I'm pretty sure that's not legal."

"Bloody hell, Eliza." Quincy's voice is sharp. Frustrated.

I glare at him. "Excuse me for wanting to understand the level of shit I've stepped in the middle of."

"Ryan just wants to know—"

"No," Ryan says. "It's okay." He looks to Stark, who slides seamlessly into the conversation.

"Are you familiar with the name Marius Corbu?"

I frown, then shake my head. "Should I be?"

"Probably not. He's the leader of a Romania-based sex trafficking ring."

"Oh." I sit back in my chair. I'm not shocked. On the contrary, the pieces are starting to fall into place. "Go on."

"The ring's been in operation for over a decade, sometimes taking hits from law enforcement, but mostly flying under the radar. Or over it, depending on your perspective."

"Like the mafia."

He nods.

"Most of the victims are from underdeveloped countries. People trying to make a better life."

"I know. Lots of Nigerian refugees get sucked in." I know more than I want about sex trafficking since Emma spent so much of her time in intelligence fighting an essentially unwinnable fight.

"There's a European Union task force that's zeroing in on some of the key players, and so far it's done a good job. But Corbu is the holy grail, and he's a tough man to find. So

Stark Security was commissioned to aid the task force by recovering a contact protocol for Corbu."

"At the party? But that doesn't—*oh.*"

Quincy nods, obviously realizing I've caught up. "Apparently Corbu is among Lassiter's clients. Whether Lassiter knows about Corbu's role in the operation is anyone's guess. From what we know, he's just your average scumbag with extortion, prostitution, and drug trafficking lining his bag of tricks. Worth going after, but right now he can lead us to bigger fish."

"Like Corbu," I say. "Because if Corbu's a client, then Lassiter must have some way to contact him."

"Exactly," Ryan says. "And our intel suggests that Lassiter keeps all client contact information on his highly encrypted hard drive."

"Which we now have," Stark adds.

"So this is all part of a sting," I say. "You get the protocol, then you contact Corbu, then—"

"Not us," Ryan says. "But presumably that's what the task force agents intend. As soon as Denny pulls the protocol off that disk and we transmit to the EU, the SSA's role in this operation is officially over."

"Okay," I say. "But what does that have to do with the thirteen year old girl that Quincy mentioned? She's got to be the same girl that Red mentioned, right?"

"We think so," Ryan says.

"Who is she?"

"Princess Ariana of Eustancia. And she was recently taken."

I feel my eyes go wide. "A princess? Seriously? Of what country?"

"Eustancia," Stark says.

"It's a small but incredibly wealthy monarchy tucked in

near Switzerland and Italy," Quincy adds. I've never heard of it, but I believe him. "The task force isn't sure why Corbu would risk exposure by snatching someone so high profile," he continues, "but the sources are confident."

"And Stark Security is working the kidnapping, too?" I can hear the incredulity in my voice and hope that they're not offended. "But seriously, doesn't Europe have, oh, law enforcement?"

"Actually, we have nothing to do with the princess," Ryan says, sliding into the conversation. "Or we didn't until we got your intel."

"My intel," I repeat, looking at Quince. "You mean the fact that Red asked me about the girl?"

"So far, it's the only real lead."

"But he may not have even been talking about this princess."

"True," Stark says, "but the Regent is willing to take the gamble. He wants us to pursue the lead. And since I'm acquainted with him and his brother, we're taking the assignment."

"Oh." The closest I've ever come to royalty is meeting Queen Latifah when I had two lines in one of her movies. That and watching the changing of the guard outside of Buckingham Palace with Quincy. So right then, I'm a little in awe.

A hint of a smile touches Stark's lips, and I'm certain he's read my reaction perfectly. "Obviously, we need your help."

"I hate to be the bearer of bad news, but I've told you everything I know. I'm not sure how much more help I can be."

Ryan leans back in his chair. "Why were you at The Terrace?"

"You know why. I'm trying to figure out what happened

to my sister." He already knows that, of course. I'd told Quincy everything in the Uber, and he already relayed it all to Ryan and Stark.

"The same sister that Red thinks knows about the girl?"

I nod.

"And we all assume that this girl is Princess Ariana?"

Again, I nod.

Ryan spreads his hands in a *there you have it* gesture. "Seems to me that we need to find your sister. And to do that, we need your help."

"And Eliza," Quincy adds gently, "I think you need our help, too."

I'm surprised by the amount of relief that courses through me. Lorenzo's smart, and I know he's just as worried as I am, but his resources are nothing compared to what's in this room. "Yeah," I whisper as Denny taps on the glass door. "I really think I do."

Ryan signals her to enter and she practically bounces into the room. "Got it," she says. "Am I amazing or what?"

"Your skills never fail to awe and inspire," Quincy says dryly. In reply she grins and buffs her nails on her chest.

"He's just jealous of my awesomeness," she tells me conspiratorially. I nod and force a smile as I realize that right then, I'm a little jealous, too.

The teasing doesn't faze Quincy, who steers me out of the conference room so that Stark, Ryan, and Denny can call the task force commander with Corbu's contact protocol.

As we exit the conference room, I see Liam coming in through the main door. He raises a hand in greeting, and we meet him halfway, the three of us grabbing chairs from the nearby computer stations. "Well, you were right," he tells me. "Somebody was in her place."

"I knew it," I say. "Lorenzo said I was just being paranoid, but I know Emma." I tilt my head, studying him. "You are as good as advertised. But how can you be sure?"

He holds out his phone. It's open to his photos, and I gasp when I see the first one. It's Emma's apartment, but it looks like a tornado has ripped through the place. "I'm thinking they came back after Red took a tumble," he says, as I nod numbly. "Also, your phone is missing. They may think it's Emma's."

"*Shit.*" The curse slips out, but it's heartfelt. My life is on that phone which, fortunately, is backed up to the cloud. It's locked, but if we're really dealing with international organized crime, I'm betting they can hack it. Which means that if they didn't already have Emma's email address and phone number, they do now. And if she sent me any messages, they have that as well.

"What if she messaged me?" I ask Quincy. "They'll know where she is. Hell, they can pretend to be me. And, oh, *fuck.* I have that location app that lets you find your friends. If she has her phone, they'll know exactly where she is."

Quincy takes my hand, and that tiny show of support strengthens me. "She's smart," he reminds me. "You've told me so a hundred times. Right now, you just need to take care of your phone."

He's right. I don't think there's anything on there that would cause me trouble—I don't have banking apps and I don't use my phone to pay for things—but even so, I swivel toward a computer. I need to log on and wipe the thing remotely, and I need to do it right now.

Quincy's way ahead of me, and he's already logging in and navigating to the iCloud site. I look around to figure out how to wipe my phone, then realize I can track Emma's phone from here. I click, the screen changes to a map, and I wait for the little dot that represents my sister to pop up.

Nothing.

"She wiped her phone, too," Quincy says. "Either that or she turned it off."

"Which means that she probably didn't contact you. At least not from her phone," Liam adds. "Probably not from her regular email address, either. Assuming she's as smart as you both say."

I nod slowly, relieved. Then I lean over and wipe my phone as well. It takes some time—the computer is determined to make sure I *really* want to remotely delete all my information—but soon enough, it's all gone.

I lean back, suddenly overwhelmed by the impact of what I've just done. Because for the first time in my entire life, I'm completely disconnected from my sister.

Beside me, Quincy takes my hand. "It will be okay," he says gently.

Once upon a time, I would have believed him, taking comfort in his words.

Now, though?

Now, I'm just scared. And even with Quincy beside me, I feel very, very alone.

10

Quincy's Santa Monica condo is smaller than I expected, and at the same time it suits him perfectly. There's a small entrance hall with a coat closet on the right and a galley-style kitchen on the left. The kitchen boasts a pass-through bar that opens into the living area, the far side of which is made up of a sliding glass patio door which can be closed even more thoroughly by a garage-style metal door that's currently in the up position. A dim porch light illuminates the patio, allowing me to see the cushioned metal chair and lounger that take up the small space.

Impeccably tidy, the condo is sparsely furnished with contemporary furniture in various shades of gray and black. A wall unit dominates one wall, the cubbies filled with an impressive stereo system, dozens upon dozens of vinyl albums and CDs, and what must be hundreds of hardback books ranging from well-known classics to historical nonfiction to loads of modern spy thrillers.

I don't see a television, and I'm not surprised. The Quincy I knew only watched television for the news, and then on a small set that he kept in his massive bathroom and turned on while he shaved. I wonder if that's still his routine, or if he's switched to getting all of his news from some app on his phone.

What does surprise me is the punching bag by the patio door. Not one of those little speed bags, but the kind that is huge and probably weighs more than I do.

It's not that Quincy doesn't keep in shape—unless things have changed, he's solid muscle under that suit, with a broad repertoire of martial arts skills. Before, I'd believed his interest in taekwondo, karate, and all the other disciplines stemmed from his childhood and his mother's murder. Now, I think it's bigger than that, and his array of skills is tied to his intelligence work. More, I have a feeling that despite being British, his skill set is way more Liam Neeson than James Bond.

Still, London Quincy wouldn't have had exercise equipment in his living space, and I wonder what it means that the bag takes up such a prominent corner. It's as if I'm getting a peek into the current life of this man I once knew so well, but I don't have the benefit of explanatory footnotes.

There are other hints as to the man he's become. Like, the cluster of framed photographs on the display table behind his couch. I recognize one as his mother; it's a photo that used to be in his London home. Another shows him and a pseudo-celebrity, Dallas Sykes, a well-known New York playboy dubbed "The King of Fuck," who'd been even more in the public eye after his affair with his adopted sister went viral.

I glance sideways at Quincy, but he offers no explanation, and I don't ask. I would never have guessed that Quincy would be friends with a guy like Sykes, but then again, there are all sorts of things I don't know about Quincy Radcliffe.

That simple reality makes me sad, and I push the thought out of my mind and start to turn away from the table. I stop, though, when a small photo on the end catches my eye. A smiling woman holding up a stuffed bear, a carnival shooting booth in blurry focus behind her.

Denny.

Immediately, I feel hot. No, cold. I'm honestly not sure, other than I don't like my reaction. Hell, I don't like that I'm reacting at all, because what do I care anymore what Quincy does in his personal life or who he does it with?

I tell myself to just walk away. Instead, I glance up and find Quincy looking back at me. "I didn't realize you and Denny were together." I keep my voice bright. Chipper.

I feel like a fucking hypocrite, but no way am I letting him see that this peek into his life hurts me. Because it shouldn't hurt me; I shouldn't care at all.

"You didn't?" His brow furrows, and I suppose for good reason. I mean, they definitely had a rhythm going at the party. He must think I'm blind. "For about eight months now."

"Oh. She's great. I like her a lot."

"As do I. And now that she's getting back in the field more—"

He cuts himself off sharply, his head cocked as he studies me. Slowly, the corner of his mouth curls up, and I see his eyes sparkle with amusement.

"What?" I hear the wariness in my voice and wonder what I'm missing.

"She's my partner, El. That's all she's ever been. And even if she were single, that's all she'd ever be."

"Oh." And then the import of his words hit me. *Oh.*

He takes a step toward me, so that he's close enough now that he could reach out and touch me.

He doesn't.

I don't move either. I just stand there like a fool, looking up at him and kicking myself for revealing way, way more than I'd intended.

"I haven't been involved with anyone since you." His voice is soft. Soothing.

"Oh." I'm having a hard time breathing, and the air between us crackles. He takes another step, and now he's close enough that I can smell the scent of his cologne, still lingering despite being up all night. His eyes are locked on mine, but I don't have a clue what he's thinking. My breath stutters, and in that moment, I am certain that he will kiss me. But whether I'll melt against him or slap his face, I have no idea.

I don't have the chance to find out. Because in the end he does neither. Instead, he points behind me. "The bedroom is in there."

"I can't take your room. I'll sleep on the couch."

"No," he says. "My house. My rules. And that means that tonight, you're in my bed."

"Oh. Right." My cheeks burn even though I have nothing to be embarrassed about.

I pause in the doorway, then turn to face him. "I should have taken Mr. Stark up on his offer of a room at the Stark Century Hotel."

"I'd still be sleeping on sofa. If you think I'd leave you alone tonight, you're crazy."

"Technically, it's morning. And Denny would have stayed with me."

He looks me straight in the eye. "Probably. But I want you here with me."

My heart does a little flip-flop number, the reaction pissing me off, because he has no right to make me feel this way. No right at all.

I backtrack my way into the kitchen, then help myself to a bottle of sparkling water from the fridge. "Why," I say with my back to him.

He doesn't answer, and I turn to find him standing just a few feet away, only the breakfast bar separating us.

"Quincy, why?"

"Because you've gotten caught up in something bigger than you anticipated. Because you don't understand all of what's going on, and no—do not even argue with me. You don't, and the reason I know you don't is because neither do I. You're in deep now, Eliza. And until I know you're safe, I'm not letting you out of my sight."

"Because that's your job," I say, unable to keep the tinge of dark sarcasm out of my voice.

His expression doesn't change at all, and throughout his silence, he keeps his eyes locked on mine. I see no reaction. None at all.

"Yes," he finally says. "It's my job."

Bastard.

I take a long swallow of water to camouflage my roiling emotions, then leave the small kitchen. I give him a wide berth as I return to the open bedroom door. "When you said I could stay here, I assumed there'd be two bedrooms. It seems small for you."

He glances around the tiny condo. "It's big enough for me. And it's only a rental. A friend owns it, and it suits my needs. And it's not that much smaller than my place in Manhattan."

"New York? You live in New York?"

"I did. Before I accepted Ryan and Damien's offer to join

the SSA full time, I worked for a small organization based in the Hamptons. Moonlighted, actually. Most of the time I was with Deliverance I was still on the MI6 payroll." He casually lifts a shoulder. "When Deliverance disbanded. I considered retiring altogether, but decided to come here instead. Liam made the same decision."

"I see," I say, though I have a feeling he's only hitting the surface details. Not that I care much. I've locked onto the bigger picture. "Did you know I was still living in New York, too?"

He nods, and I swallow the hard knot that suddenly fills my throat. Not that his admission changes anything. But somehow the thought of him ignoring me from all the way across the Atlantic was easier to handle than the knowledge that he ignored me from only a few cross-town blocks.

I lift my chin as I return to the bedroom. "Good night, Quincy." I pause on the threshold, then look back over my shoulder. "Do you have any idea how long it took me to get over you?"

It's a lie, of course. I'm not over him at all, no matter how many lies I tell myself.

"I'm sorry."

"I'm sure you are. So what?"

He doesn't answer; what could he say?

I head into the bedroom and sit on the edge of the bed as he moves closer, hovering at the threshold, as if he's waiting for me to dismiss him.

I don't.

"Someday, you have to tell me why," I say. "I deserve to know."

I think I see a spark of emotion fire in those stormy gray eyes. "Maybe you do," he says evenly. "But I think we both know that in this life, you don't always get the things that you deserve."

Then he reaches for the switch and turns out the light before gently pulling the door closed, leaving me alone in the dark with my memories. And my regrets.

11

"HERE," Emma whispers, shoving Mister Wellington into my arms. "No matter what, you pretend to be asleep, okay? And you keep your back to the room and your face up against Mister Wellington's fur. You don't roll over, and you don't look. Promise?"

I nod, pulling the stuffed bear close.

"Say it," she orders. "It's only a real promise if you say it out loud."

I take my thumb out of my mouth and whisper, "I p-omise." I've just lost my first tooth, and I'm having trouble pronouncing my R's.

Emma—a grown-up with all her teeth to prove it—frowns as she looks at me. I can tell she's not satisfied, but she doesn't say anything else. She just nods, then climbs into bed with me.

There are two twin-size beds in our dank, windowless room, but we never sleep apart. We're only apart when he comes in, and that's never a time for sleeping. That's only a time for pretending to sleep. For me, anyway. Emma has to be awake. He says he wants her eyes open. He says he wants her to watch while he touches himself that way.

I never look. I don't want to, but even if I did, I wouldn't. I trust Emma, and if she tells me to keep my eyes closed, I do. Because I know that she'll always take care of me. I know because she tells me so every day. And because she tells me she loves me, too. She's the only one who does. And she's the only one I love.

Certainly not him. I hate him. If I knew how to hurt him, I would, but I know I'm too little. Even Emma's too little, and she's fourteen.

Sometimes I wish our mother was here, but most of the time I don't. I know better than to believe in wishes, because they never come true.

I don't remember her, anyway, but Emma says she loved us. She says that our mother hated him, too, but that she wouldn't have left us alone with him on purpose. Not ever. She says it's his fault that she died, but nobody knows that. And she says that it will be okay. That she'll take care of both of us. That even though we miss our mommy, we don't need one. That she can be our mommy. And that someday, we'll get away from him.

She just doesn't know when.

"Go on now," she urges, then shoves a lock of red hair out of her face. It's thick and wavy and I think she looks like a movie star. He likes it, too, and she says that she'd cut it off if she could, but it would make him angry. But she doesn't because it's not good when he's angry. Besides, she said our mommy loved her hair. She'd sit with Emma for hours and brush it. Emma tells me that's what she thinks about whenever he runs his fingers through her hair. She imagines our mommy and tries to block him out.

I know there's something different about tonight, but I don't know what. I already know that I'm supposed to always keep my eyes closed and never, ever look when he's in the room. So I don't know why Emma keeps reminding me today. She's acting weird, and I'm scared, but I don't want to tell her, cuz then she'll *feel bad. So I just keep my face pressed up against Mister Wellington and my thumb in my mouth. Emma climbs in behind me and hugs me close, and I try really, really hard to go to sleep.*

I can't, though.

I just lie there, breathing dusty bear fur and listening to the wind outside, making the limbs on the big tree rattle and scrape against the side of the house. It's spooky, but Emma's with me, holding me while I hold Mister Wellington, so I'm not too scared. Not of the house or the tree.

I'll be scared later, because I know he's coming.

And then he does. The heavy footsteps. That rough, wet cough.

I hear the jangle of the key in the lock, and then the creak of the door as it opens. I screw my eyes shut tighter and I fist my hands in Mister Wellington's fur. Emma's arms tighten around me, and I can hear her breathing. Then I feel his hand on my hip, and I smell his sour breath near my ear.

"Your turn, girlie-girl."

I freeze, then I remember Emma making me promise to pretend to be asleep no matter what. I tell myself I'm as still as a rock, I'm dreaming, I'm not moving at all.

"Is that so, you little bitch? Faking it, are you? We'll see about that."

Huge hands grab me around the waist, and I scream and scream and scream until the hands are gone and Emma is on top of me yelling and yelling, and I can't understand what she's saying until suddenly she's gone, and I look up to see her skinny body flying through the air to land on the other bed.

He reaches for me again, but she hollers, "No! Me! Leave Eliza alone. I'll do anything. I swear."

Slowly, I feel him move away, until I can finally breathe the air again.

"Anything?" he says, in a voice from my nightmares. "Well, I think we can make that work out just fine."

A tight arm hauls me up by the waist and plops me back down. "Open your eyes, girlie. Or it won't be good for you and it'll be even worse for your slut of a sister."

I make whimpering sounds, and I hear Emma's wet, raw whisper saying, "It's okay, Eliza. I think you have to. I think we both do."

He makes me watch. Every night he makes me sit up in bed and hug Mister Wellington tight and watch the nasty things he does to my sister. One hundred and fifty-seven times. I count them, then mark them in pencil on the wall after he leaves and while Emma washes off in the little bathtub in the corner of our closet of a room.

One hundred and fifty-seven times before Emma figures out what to do. Before she saves us.

Or at least, before she tries.

She picks the lock of that tiny room, and she leads the way down the stairs. We move slowly, careful not to let the floorboards creak.

And I can see the front door ahead of us. It's open, and outside there's sun and clouds and a perfect day. Right there.

We're close. So very, very close.

That's when Emma's scream rips the air. When I see her fly past me down the stairs, tumbling into a broken pile of limbs and flesh and blood on the tiles below.

I turn away, horrified, and see him behind me. His bloodshot eyes. His crusty skin.

His lips curve into a hideous smile, and as I try to run, he grabs my arm and yanks me to him, then puts his mouth next to my ear as his hand slides down between my legs.

"You're next," he says, and I scream and I scream and I scream.

I wake in terror, my father's arms tight around me.

I can't get loose. I shake and I kick and I scream, but I—

"Eliza. Eliza, hush. It's okay. He's not here. You're safe. I've got you."

Quincy.

I relax, and the strong arms surrounding me loosen a bit.

"It's okay." His voice is gentle. Soothing, and I press my face against his chest and breathe deep, my hands clutching tight to his shirt. One breath in, one breath out as Quincy gently strokes my hair, his touch as calming as his familiar scent.

"I'm sorry." My words are muffled, but I don't want to move. My heartbeat has slowed, and I feel safe now in his arms. "I'm sorry," I repeat, my chest aching from the terror that had so recently pounded through me.

"Oh, love, no. There's nothing to be sorry about." There's sympathy in his voice and understanding, and I melt just a little more.

"Do you want to tell me? Was it your father?"

Until Quincy, I'd never told anyone about my father. And I've never told anyone since.

Neither has Emma. Not even Lorenzo, who we both love and trust. Some things you have to hold painfully close, because they're too dangerous to let out into the world.

I told Quincy because I loved him. Because he saw the scars on my soul and wanted to help me heal.

I trusted him. I guess maybe I still do, because I nod as his arms tighten around me. Then I take a deep breath, close my eyes, and try to describe the horror.

"He had me. He was dragging me back, and Emma was

gone. He—he killed her. And I was all alone and I didn't know how to fight him, and—"

"Shhh." His lips brush my forehead, the touch gentle and sweet and achingly familiar. "It's okay. I'm here."

"Are you?" I know I shouldn't, but I tilt my head up, wanting what I shouldn't want, craving what I wish I didn't need. Quincy is the only man who knows my secret past. The only one who has ever been able to tame my demons, and oh, dear Lord, I need him now. I want to slide under, to surrender completely, and let him take me to all those familiar places where I used to lose myself in his arms.

I want to bring the past back, and even if I can't have forever I want right now. And in this moment, I don't even hate myself for craving him so desperately.

His eyes meet mine, and I see the storm brewing. That familiar intensity, that controlled wildness, like a tempest in a bottle.

"Eliza," he says, though what I hear is, *no.*

"Just one kiss," I beg. "You owe me that much."

He doesn't answer, but my palm is pressed to his chest, and I feel the pounding of his heart. I feel his breath on my face and the heat of his skin against mine. I don't know what happened to us, and I have no illusions that anything will ever be like it was again. But right now, I need to bring the past back. I need to get lost in sweet memories, not in horrible, twisted ones.

I want Quincy, dammit, and I reach up, sliding my fingers through his coarse, dark hair. I'm never this bold, but I've spent more than four years craving something I couldn't have. I've been starving, and I didn't even know it.

He doesn't resist as I tug his head toward me, and I'm ridiculously grateful. I crave his lips, his touch. My desire for him is as strong as it was all those years ago in London, and

I'm not sure my ego would survive if he didn't at least want me a little.

The air is charged between us, and I'm certain that I'm not imagining his desire. He wants this as much as I do, and that knowledge emboldens me. I brush my lips over his, a sweet, tentative touch. But I want so much more. I want what we had. His body pressed on top of me, his hands around my wrists, holding me still. The hard tension in his muscles as he takes what he wants, leaving me to surrender to the pure pleasure of being his.

I want that again. To be his. To belong. To *feel*.

I want it, yes, but right now, I will take whatever I can get, and if that is one single kiss then I'll hold it close and cherish it forever. *Just please, please, touch me now...!*

The words pound through my head as I tease his lips, willing him to open to me. I don't know what drew him away from me in London, and right now, I don't care. Those days don't exist. They don't matter. All I have is this moment and my nightmare and Quincy. I need him. I need him to erase the horror.

"Please," I whisper. "I'm begging you."

I don't know if it's my words or my touch, but the dam breaks. His fingers slide into my hair as he holds my head steady. His mouth devours mine, tongue and teeth clashing as he takes and takes, and in the process is giving me exactly what I've been begging for.

We've been sitting awkwardly on the bed, my body twisted to face him. But now, he takes me by the shoulders, and I gasp as he pushes me back so that I'm lying on the bed. Before I can catch my breath, he's on top of me, one hand on my breast as he holds me steady and claims my mouth with his. I whimper, opening to him, my fingers clutching at his hair as I pull him closer, as if I can capture him in this moment and bring him back to me.

My heart pounds, my body fires, and a desperate heat settles between my thighs. "Please," I beg, and when I hear his soft murmur of, *Eliza*, I know he's back. Maybe not forever, but in this moment he's mine, and, I—

"*I'm sorry, El.*"

In the time it takes me to process his words, he's on the other side of the room. His eyes are wild, his breath coming hard. He looks like a man standing on a window ledge trying to convince himself not to jump.

I sit up, confused and embarrassed as I pull the sheet up over the thin tank top and panties that I'm wearing. "Quincy, what are you—"

"I can't." The words are heavy, and his expression impenetrably sad. "I'm sorry," he says. "I'm so goddamn sorry."

"But—"

He lifts a hand and shakes his head. "I'm sorry, Eliza," he says again, looking me square in the eye. "I do want you, but—"

I frown, and force myself not to press him. Clearly he *doesn't* want me. He hasn't wanted me for a long time.

"You should get dressed," he says. "We can get you a new phone on the way to the office."

I nod, too numb to talk, and he leaves the room, pulling the door closed behind him.

I pull my knees up to my chest, then hug them tight as I draw long, deep breaths. Light streams into the room, and as I sit there and force myself not to cry, I see the photos framed on the top of the dresser across the room. There's something familiar about them, and I frown, then crawl to the end of the bed for a better look.

I gasp, because these are photos of me. Standing beside the fountain near Buckingham Palace. Feeding the ducks beside the Serpentine. Sitting on the grass in Paris, the Eiffel Tower rising up in the distance. And one that a stranger took for us—me and Quincy holding hands in Montmartre, all of Paris spread out below us like a postcard.

He kept them.

I hug myself, hope rising. But the more I think about it, the more hope fades. Because even though it's clear that he still wants me, it's equally clear that he's determined to stay far, far away.

12

BLAM! Quince landed another punch to the center of the bag, then followed with a jab and a swift left hook. He hadn't bothered with tape or gloves, and he'd been going at it with his bare hands since he'd heard Eliza turn on the shower. Christ, but he wanted her, and he'd almost let himself believe he could have her. But no—dammit, *no*.

He should never have touched her. She'd been through so damn much, and she deserved so much more than a man who'd inevitably hurt her. It didn't matter how much he longed for her, he should have never opened that door.

But he had, and now the memories were pushing through. The dark humiliation, the searing pain. The terror. And the remorse.

Pow! Smack! Pow!

Again and again, over and over. As if he just needed to find the right combination of jabs and punches so that he could propel himself back into the past. Then maybe he'd have a chance to stop them. To start all over again.

Maybe she wouldn't be dead.

Maybe the bastards would never have—*No*.

He sucked in air, forcing his arms to keep moving. Faster and faster until his muscles ached and his knuckles bled. Harder and faster, as if he could force the memories out with the blood, and then, maybe, he'd be whole again.

A fantasy. A goddamn, fucking fantasy, and he was too old for fairy stories. He'd seen too much to believe that the good always won out in the end. He of all people knew better. The good were punished. The good lost everything.

And there wasn't a goddamn thing he could do about it. *Fuck.*

One final punch, and he bent over, his hands on his knees as he sucked in air, exhausted. Physically and emotionally.

"Does it help?"

He froze, her soft voice seeming to lock him in to place. After a moment, he turned to see Eliza standing there. She was wearing the SSA track pants she'd borrowed last night, but the shirt was one of his. A threadbare Manchester United T-shirt he'd had for over a decade.

She tugged on the hem. "I slept in the tank top, so I borrowed this. It was sitting folded in a laundry basket, so I assumed it was clean. Do you mind?"

As far as he was concerned, the shirt had never looked better. "Yes. I mean, yes, it's clean. And no, I don't mind."

A hint of a smile touched her lips, and she nodded. He recalled how many times she'd helped herself to his T-shirts during their months together. Eliza was the kind of girl who would happily dress to the nines out in the world, but inside the house she was happiest in his old pajama bottoms and T-shirts. He'd happily shared his wardrobe, thinking she'd never looked sexier than when she wore his clothes. Except, perhaps, when she was out of them.

"Did it?"

He realized she'd asked him something. "I'm sorry, what?"

She nodded toward the bag as she headed into the kitchen. "I don't think you heard me the first time. I was asking again if it helps."

He studied her, wondering if she understood the full depth of the question. "Yes. And no." It was the simplest and truest answer. But he knew it wasn't nearly enough. Considering the way she studied him as she helped herself to a cup of coffee, she knew it, too, and he held his breath, waiting for her to ask him again about what happened in London. To press until he told her about the monster inside. The beast he had to constantly battle back down.

She didn't, though, and he told himself he was relieved.

But that was just one more of the lies he told himself.

———

"Okay," Denny said, as Quince and Eliza looked over her shoulder. "You should be all good to go." She passed the new iPhone to Eliza, who looked at it dubiously.

"I'm okay to use it? Even though they had it? My emails and everything?"

"We wiped your phone and logged you out of any apps that were already running. I just changed your ID, and I checked to make sure you're not logged on anywhere else. I put your apps back on, too. So, yeah, it should all be pretty seamless."

Eliza bit her lower lip and looked up at Quince. "It's really okay to use?"

Denny laughed. "Oh, yeah. I see how I rank. Trust the guy you used to sleep with instead."

Quince cringed as Eliza twisted her head to look between him and Denny, her mouth curving into a frown.

If Denny noticed, she didn't say anything. Just rattled on with, "I swear, you're good to go. But I have a filter set up. If your ID or email address end up logged in to any other device, I'll get pinged." She lifted a shoulder casually. "Just to be sure."

Eliza nodded. "Okay. That should work. I don't want to get a new cell number or new email address. Because what if Emma is trying to reach me?"

Quince caught her eye. "If she already emailed or messaged you and they deleted it, then emptied the trash, you're out of luck. But Denny just changed your passwords to your Apple and Gmail accounts. Anything new, they won't see."

She looked between the two of them. "Okay, then. I trust you."

It was a throwaway comment, but it settled in Quince's heart in a way that felt both nice and a little bit dangerous.

"What now?" she asked.

"Briefing in five," Denny said. She indicated the cavernous room now filled with over a dozen analysts manning their computer stations. "I'm waiting for a few reports, and then we're meeting in the conference room with Ryan and Liam."

"Anyone else assigned to the team?" Quince asked.

Denny shook her head. "Just us chickens. Trevor and Leah are in New York. And Winston's in Hong Kong." The organization was still new, and Ryan was very selective. Which meant that the SSA still boasted only a handful of active field agents. "If we need more manpower, you know Ryan will pull someone else over from the dark side for a temporary assignment."

"The dark side?" Eliza repeated. "What do you mean?"

"Denny used to work security at Stark International," Quince explained. "And Ryan used to be the head honcho over there. Still is, technically, though he's been kicked up the ladder. Day to day falls to someone else now, and Ryan oversees the daily grind here."

"But if we need manpower, it's a good picking ground," Denny added. She stood, her hands resting on the top of her monitor. "Anytime this year would be good, Mario. Just saying."

"Sending it now, boss," the skinny analyst on the far side of the room said.

"That should be the last of the reports," Denny said to him and Eliza. "And just in time."

Quincy turned in the direction she was looking, and saw Ryan enter the conference room. The three of them followed, and a moment later, Liam joined them, sliding into one of the padded chairs with a broad grin.

"Let me guess," Quincy said. "They put Pepsi back in the vending machine."

"Funny man," Liam said, then turned to Eliza with a conspiratorial gleam in his eye. "Sometimes it's best to just ignore him."

"Believe me, I know." She tossed a grin his way, and Quincy's chest tightened. For a moment, it felt like old times, the way it used to be so easy between the two of them.

"So what have you got?" Ryan asked.

"Just got off the phone with Enrique Castille," Liam said, referring to the head of the EU task force. "They're using the information you two retrieved to set up the sting to contact Corbu. It's going down tonight. With luck, he'll be in custody by tomorrow evening."

"Excellent," Quincy said.

"Good work, you two." Ryan nodded to Quince and Denny.

"I'll be more impressed with us once we find Emma and the princess," Quince said.

"I sent an email just now," Eliza said. "But I doubt she'll answer it even if she gets it. She's too careful. My whole life she's told me that in a pinch you can't communicate through regular channels."

"Pretty intense philosophy for a private investigator," Liam said, voicing what Quince was thinking.

"She's thorough." Eliza's eyes dipped to the tabletop, a reaction that probably slipped under everyone else's radar but caught Quince's attention. It was, after all, Eliza's most obvious tell, both at the poker table and in her daily life. Any fib, and she lowered her gaze.

Which made him wonder what secret she was keeping about Emma.

"We're getting ahead of ourselves," Ryan said, leaning back in his chair and looking at each of them in turn. "Right now, we're assuming that Emma has the princess with her. But we're basing that assumption on a mountain of circumstantial evidence. Are we getting any closer to finding actual proof? Figure out how those two got together—*if* they got together—and we may have a better chance of figuring out where they are."

Eliza leaned forward, looking around Quince so that she could focus on Denny. "Did those usernames I gave you last night help?"

Before they'd left, she and Denny had made a list of possible usernames that Emma might have utilized while navigating the dark web.

"Afraid not," Denny said. "But we knew it was a long shot."

"What was?" Liam asked.

"We were hoping that Emma had gone into the dark web forums with a username that Eliza knows. That way we'd have a better chance of following her trail."

"I texted Lorenzo right after Denny fixed up my phone and told him to call me. But he hasn't yet. He might know the password, but I doubt it. That's not the kind of thing Emma would think about sharing."

"It's okay. I've got another lead," Denny said. "Since I couldn't get in as Emma, I made up my own username and went in. We know she was looking into sex trafficking, so I followed those kinds of rabbit trails."

Quince heard the enthusiasm in her voice and smiled. "And since you're telling us all this, I'm guessing one of those trails led somewhere?"

"The Perlmutter Hotel in Pasadena. And one guess who owns it."

"Scott Lassiter?" Eliza guessed.

Denny tapped her nose. "Got it in one. And it gets better. The chatter was about an auction for extremely high quality merchandise."

Eliza's eyes went wide, and Quince saw her shiver. He reached over and took her hand, then gave it a gentle squeeze. She and Emma hadn't been trafficked, but God knew they'd been abused. And none of this could be easy on her.

She squeezed back. And she didn't let go.

Across the table, Ryan pushed away from the table and stood. "Obviously, we're all thinking that the princess was the merchandise in question. And I have to say, I think that's a solid bet."

Eliza frowned. "So that would mean that Emma learned the truth and got her out before the auction took place?"

She tilted her head, her forehead furrowed in thought. "So she's poking around online, trying to get information on sex trafficking and stuff. And Mr. X sets her up. Tells her to meet him at Lassiter's party. Probably says he can be a source."

"Probably plans to kill her," Denny added, picking up the thread. "She's poking around where she doesn't belong."

"But then she learns about the auction," Eliza continues. "I have no idea how she gets the princess away, though."

"For now, we assume that she does," Quince put in. "Obviously, she has more important things on her mind than making the meeting with Mr. X."

"But since I don't know that, when I'm trying to find my sister and that's my only lead, I decide to go in her place."

Liam nodded thoughtfully. "And Mr. X is pretty damn surprised to see you there, but considers it a great opportunity to find out where the princess is, because—for some reason—he's convinced that you took her."

"But why would Emma be the only suspect?" Eliza asked.

Quince released her hand as he pushed back his chair, spurred to action by the force of his realization. "There's video," he said. "Somewhere, there's surveillance footage." He smiled at Eliza. "And that footage shows you taking the princess away."

13

"Me?" I gape at him, my jaw literally hanging open until I realize what I'm doing and give myself a solid mental shake. "Quincy, what the hell are you talking about? I didn't steal a princess? I can't even imagine the steps that would go into stealing a princess."

"Maybe not, but Emma could, couldn't she?"

I nod. "Well, yes. I mean, it's not out of the realm of possibility. That's sort of the assumption we've been going on. But you said *I'm* on the video."

"Let me put that another way. The video shows someone who looks like you. And Eliza, love, you two do look an awful lot alike."

"Not really. She's four inches taller than me and her hair is red. Plus, she's almost a D-cup, and I'm really not," I add, glancing down at my chest to accentuate the point.

"I've seen the proof. Remember the photo of you two on the Santa Monica Pier. Black and white, and your hair looked almost the same color. She was taller for sure, but in those silly sweatshirts you were wearing, bra size was a mystery. And in a video, she would have been alone. No way to tell how tall she was without a point of comparison."

I continue to gape at him, trying to make sense of what he's saying. Denny seems to get it, though. She leans forward, her blond hair hanging like a curtain around her face. "You're saying Emma got away with the princess, and that somewhere there's surveillance footage which shows the whole thing?"

"That's what I'm saying," Quincy says, and as their words sink in, I realize I don't really have an argument.

"Too bad we can't ask Red if we're right," Denny adds. "But I should hear back about the fingerprints soon."

Both Quincy and I turn to look at her. "You didn't tell me you got fingerprints."

She grins. "I was right there checking his pulse and playing concerned citizen. It was the least I could do."

"You're really good," I say.

She wrinkles her nose with pleasure. "I know."

Quincy ignores our banter. Instead, he pushes back from the table and starts to pace. "Assuming we're right, then that means that Emma figured out where they were holding the princess, managed to get there, get around security, and get the girl free. Again," he says with a sideways glance at me, "that's impressive for a PI."

I lift a shoulder. "We ran away when she was fifteen. You learn a lot of survival tricks being on your own that young."

"It's got to be the Perlmutter," Liam says, and we all look in his direction. "The odds are good that Emma was operating with much of the same information that we have. That would lead her to the Perlmutter. It's owned by Lassiter, who we already know is into some dicey shit."

"But he's never been on the radar for something as egregious as sex trafficking," Ryan adds.

"Maybe he got in over his head," Quincy says. "But Liam's correct. The Perlmutter is our best bet. Not only is it our only bloody lead, but it's also got a basement."

"Quince is right," Ryan says. "I remember Jackson talking about it once."

It takes me a second, but I remember that Jackson Steele, the architect famous for designing the Winn Building in Manhattan is also Damien Stark's brother. Not to mention the architect for The Domino.

"He said the Perlmutter was unusual for Southern California because it has a basement and a sub-basement. It was a bank before it was a hotel, and apparently that's where the vaults were. He and Damien thought about buying the property at one time. Considering Lassiter signed on the dotted line, I guess they changed their minds."

"A sub-basement would make an interesting stage for the auction of extremely high-quality merchandise," Liam commented, using the language that Denny had run across in the forums.

"Yes," Ryan says, "it would."

"I'll get Mario on it," Denny says. "If he can't hack into the security feed, then it can't be done. But if it did show Emma stealing away with our girl, then I bet I'm going to find that large chunks of time are missing."

"Check traffic cams, ATMs, private security feeds," Quincy suggests. "We're just looking for confirmation at this point."

She nods.

"As for Lassiter, I think it's time we had a little chat."

"He may be a pawn in all this," Ryan says. "His parties at The Terrace are an open secret and technically legal. A bit risky to add sex slave auctions to his repertoire. Especially at this level. The kidnapping of a princess won't exactly fly under the radar."

"He hardly has clean hands," Denny notes. "That disk we got is a blueprint to money laundering and blackmail. Enough to put him away for a good long time."

Quincy nods. "So we talk to him, find out what he knows about Emma or the princess, if anything, and then turn him over to the authorities. Ollie?"

My head is spinning watching them talk and plan a mile-a-minute. Granted, I've seen Emma in full-on investigative mode, but it's been a while. It's invigorating, but it's also exhausting.

I lean over and whisper to Quincy, "Who's Ollie?"

Apparently, I'm a louder whisperer than I realize, because Ryan explains that Orlando McKee is a good friend of Damien's wife, Nikki. A former lawyer, he's now with the FBI. "Should be a solid feather in his cap. And if we bring Lassiter in now, then there's less chance he'll discover the breach of his disk and report it back to Corbu."

"Liam and I will go talk to him," Quincy says. "And by talk, I mean bring him back here and into holding."

Liam grins. "Sounds about right. And then, my friend, I think you should be the one to do the talking."

Quincy shifts so that he's looking right at me. Heat spirals through me, so vibrant that for a moment I can't even breathe. Suddenly, it's as if no years have passed at all. I know exactly what he's thinking. I know that he's remembering the way Lassiter had his hands on me. The way he'd sidled up next to me, and tried to claim me.

"Oh, yes," Quincy says, leaning back in his chair. "I think we'll have a jolly good talk."

14

"MAKE A RIGHT HERE, and then a left at the light," I tell Denny. It's just past noon, and we're in Venice Beach. I'd texted Lorenzo to tell him we were on our way, and he'd responded immediately with a *Thank God, girlie. You've taken ten years off my life.*

Considering he hadn't called, texted me, or emailed me —at least not according to my shiny new phone—I thought that was a tad melodramatic, but I'd been so nervous about the party at The Terrace that maybe I'd gotten my wires crossed. For all I know, the standard protocol for an operative walking into a sex party while pretending to be a call girl is to contact her handler post haste, and under no circumstances does said handler contact the girl.

At any rate, I'd see him soon, and I was ridiculously happy about that.

"So how much does Lorenzo know about you and Quincy? I don't want to put my foot in it." She flashes me a grin. "I have a talent for doing that."

I frown as I consider the question and all of its implications. "Nothing, really. Just that we dated in London a while back. And he dumped me." Lorenzo is like a dad to me, but there are some things that parents don't need to know. "Um, how much do you know?"

She lifts a shoulder then lets it drop.

I'm not entirely sure how to interpret that, but my best guess would be *everything.* I frown. "Um, Quincy told me—I mean, are you two involved?" Quincy said they weren't, and I want to believe him. But I'm not entirely on board the Quincy-Trust Train.

Denny hits the brakes harder than necessary and I jerk forward at a red light. "Oh, crap, no. Never. And don't be mad. We've been working together for a while now, and we've gotten to be really good friends. He—well, he's been through a lot of shit, you know. So he gets my moods."

"Moods?"

She shoots me a sideways glance as she pulls into the intersection. "There's this situation with my husband," she says. "It's been a little rough."

"Oh. I'm sorry. Are you—I mean—" I shut up, because I assume that she's talking about a separation or a divorce, but I don't quite know how to phrase the question.

For a second, she looks confused. Then her eyes go wide. "Oh, no. No, no. I—we're happy. We're just apart. Really, really, really apart."

She sighs loudly, and I don't understand any more than I did a few moments before.

"He's a field agent. Off-the-books, high-level operative that I can't talk about because if I did, they'd hunt us down and kill us."

"Good plan." I clear my throat. "I guess he's away a lot."

"Going on three years now." She glances sideways at me. "It kind of sucks."

"But you can FaceTime and Skype and email and stuff, right?"

She shakes her head.

"Not a word? Not anything?"

For a moment, she says nothing. Then she lifts a shoulder as she veers right, following my gestured instructions, which are totally unnecessary since the GPS screen is showing every turn. "That pretty much sums it up."

"I'm so sorry."

"I'm not looking for pity, really. I'm just telling you that Q and I kind of bonded. Being so long away from the people we love."

I sit back, my chest so tight it's suddenly hard to breathe.

"It ripped him up, you know." Her voice is gentle, but I don't find it soothing.

"*Stop.*" The word is out before I can call it back. "Do you think you're helping? If it hurt him so much, he shouldn't have fucking left in the first place."

"Oh, God, I'm sorry. I—"

"Do you know?" I turn violently in the seat so that I'm facing her straight on. "Do you know where he was? What happened to him? Do you know if there is one shred of a reason that I can hold up against the wound he left in my heart to staunch the flow of blood? Because if you do, then tell me. Otherwise, please, just shut up, because it hurts too damn much."

Tears prick my eyes, and I scrunch them shut as I slam myself back against the seat and pull my knees up to my chest. *I will not cry. I will not cry.*

But I'm so afraid I'm going to lose that battle because between losing Emma and finding Quincy I am completely raw inside.

"I'm so sorry. And my timing sucks, too. But we're here,"

she says, at the same time that the GPS announces that we've arrived at our destination.

She passes me a tissue. "Do you want to wait a bit?"

I shake my head, hating that she has to tend to me. I need to be focusing on Emma, not on Quincy. Do that, and maybe I can keep my shit together. I push the door open. "No. Let's go."

Once I'm out of the car, I can't get to the front door of Double-T Investigations fast enough. Tate and Tucker, for Lorenzo and Emma. Not the catchiest name, but they never seem to lack for business. Part of that is because Emma gets so many referrals from her friends in intelligence. Lorenzo just thinks it's because of their growing and stellar reputation.

The building itself is a plain office in a strip center located on a street that runs straight to the ocean. Not that you can see the Pacific where we are. On the roof, you can sometimes see a patch of blue if the sky isn't hazy, but that's about it. Not every corner of Venice Beach is as advertised. But it's home, and the office is owned outright by my sister, who made the first payment back when she was only sixteen years old. Life tried to squash her, but Emma kicked its ass. She's tough that way. And that's why I know she's got to be okay. Because after everything we've survived, I absolutely can't lose her now.

Denny and I have just about reached the door when it bursts open and Marissa races toward me. Just shy of twenty, Lorenzo's only niece started working for the firm about six months ago when her stepfather announced that she needed to understand the value of a dollar. Considering she's decked out entirely in designer clothes, I'm thinking the lesson is getting lost and her salary is going to Nordstrom.

"Eliza! Thank goodness, Uncle Lorenzo was so worried about you last night."

"Was not," the gruff voice says from the doorway. He winks at me. "I know she can handle herself." His bushy brows move as he squints at Denny. "And who the hell are you?"

"Denny," she says easily. "I'm going out on a limb and saying that you're Lorenzo."

"Smart girl," Lorenzo says to me. He cocks his head, ushering us inside. It's basically one giant room with four giant office-salvage desks for Lorenzo, Emma, Marissa, and anyone else who needs a workspace.

I hoist myself up onto the spare as Denny drops into one of the guest chairs. Marissa sits cross-legged on top of hers, and Lorenzo settles in behind his desk, his elbows propped on the laminate surface.

He points at me. "I know you didn't take your phone to The Terrace, but why the devil didn't you text me back this morning? Not that I was worried," he adds, shooting a narrowed-eye glance at Marissa. "I just wanted an update."

I meet Denny's eyes, and she fields that one. "Her phone was stolen. Sounds like they deleted anything that came in before we were able to wipe it."

"Great," I say, wondering what else I've missed ... and what personal info they now have on me.

"Stolen?"

"Out of Emma's apartment," I explain. And then, because it's all so complicated, I start at the beginning and give him a rundown of everything that's happened. Including Quincy.

"The lousy little prick?" Marissa asks, her eyes widening when Lorenzo zings a rubber band her way. "What? That's what Emma called him. He's the guy you dated in London, right? And he totally dumped you."

"Doesn't mean you say he's a prick out loud," Lorenzo says. "Didn't my sister teach you manners?"

"Sorry."

"'Course, you're right," Lorenzo says. "Anybody hurts one of my girls, they go on my shortlist. I don't care if this Quincy Radcliffe is the queen's right-hand man. He hurt my Eliza. That makes him a prick."

In the chair beside me, Denny shifts uncomfortably.

"He's helping me find Emma," I say. "So is Denny. They're friends."

"But for the record, you're right," Denny says. "And Quince would agree. He's beat himself up a lot for what happened in London. He didn't mean to hurt Eliza."

"Well, then he's a prick *and* an idiot. What did he expect? Congratulations and a parade?"

Denny grimaces. "Well, for the record, he's on-board now. Looking for Emma, I mean. And so am I."

"Why?" Lorenzo asks, shifting his attention from Denny to me.

I'm taken aback. "Why is he helping?" I don't know how to answer that. To make amends? Because he still cares about me? Because Emma's disappearance overlaps his own case?

I only know for certain that the last one is true, and that's the one I can't tell Lorenzo.

"Why is he involved at all?" Lorenzo asks. "The man's a banker. Or that's what Emma told me."

"You must have misunderstood," Denny says easily. "Quincy works in corporate private security. When he and Eliza met, that's what he was doing for an international investment firm."

"Right," I say, eagerly adopting the lie. "And it doesn't matter anyway, you guys. All that matters now is finding Emma."

I want to tell him about The Perlmutter Hotel and the princess, but everyone from Quincy to Ryan had drilled into me that I couldn't share. I'd gotten there on my own, of course. Basic rule of thumb: when an EU task force and missing royalty are part of the equation, you have to keep the details to yourself.

"Have you heard from her?" I'm sure the answer will be no, but instead, he breaks into a broad smile. "What?" I demand. "When? And why didn't you say earlier?"

"I'm saying now. Marissa got a text from her a little bit ago. At least, we assume it was her."

"We don't have a clue what it means," Marissa adds.

"Okay," I say. "Tell me."

Marissa holds out he phone, and I hop off the desk to go get it. I read the cryptic text, then look between him and Marissa. "What the hell?"

"I know," Lorenzo says. "Doesn't make a bit of goddamn sense."

I read the words once again, making sure to keep my expression blank. Because it makes perfect sense to me, and right now all I want is to get the hell out of here and go find my sister.

15

Tell my friend who talks to the animals not to drive angry, but to circle the wagons.

QUINCE SCOWLED at the screen as he read the text for the third time. No luck. It still didn't magically translate into something that made even the tiniest bit of sense. For a moment, he wished that Denny hadn't already headed back to HQ. She was always handy when faced with a puzzle.

Finally, he shook his head. "All right. I give up. Which one of you is going to interpret?"

"They don't get it, either," Eliza said, then pointed a finger at Marissa, a lanky college-aged girl with a habit of twirling her hair around her forefinger. "You should, though," Eliza said. "You've been there, after all. Twice."

"Dammit, where?" Lorenzo asked.

Quince had arrived fifteen minutes ago, after Denny had called and told him to get his butt to Venice Beach. Since

things with Lassiter had gone far swifter than he'd anticipated, he'd been able to come right away.

For the first ten minutes after Quince arrived, Lorenzo
had offered him a perpetual scowl. Now, at least, he seemed
more wrapped up in the mystery and less in vetting Quince.

"The ranch," Eliza said, as if that should make sense to
everybody. Though judging from the loud exhalations and
chorus of, *oh, of course,* it finally did make sense to both
Lorenzo and his niece.

"Explain, please," Quince said, a little frustrated at being
the only one in the dark.

"My friend who talks to the animals..." She trailed off
with an expectant glance toward Marissa.

"That's Eliza," Marissa said. "Emma's talking about
Eliza."

Quince looked to Lorenzo and was happy to see the
older man looked equally gormless.

Marissa rolled her eyes and sighed. "Talks to the
animals, right? Dr. Doolittle. I mean, hello? The guy's even
British. You should totally get it."

"Well, I'm not British and I still don't get it," Lorenzo
growled.

"Dr. Dolittle. *Eliza* Doolittle. *My Fair Lady,* right? And
her name is Eliza."

From where she perched on the desk, Eliza lifted her
shoulders and nodded. "Yeah, that part refers to me."

"I'll take it on faith," Quince said. Maybe it was a sister
thing. "What about driving angry?"

"Not sure about the angry part," Eliza said. "But drive
means just what it sounds like. I'm thinking angry means
driving fast. So she's saying that we don't have to hurry.
Because clearly she's hidden away safe somewhere."

He nodded. "Go on."

"Circle the wagons means the station wagon," Marissa said. "Because that's how we'd get there. In that hideous old station wagon Emma had. And there's a circle of stones near the front of the house," she added as an afterthought. "We pretended it was a fort."

"See?" Eliza said, but to Marissa, not him. "It was easy. Why didn't you get it right away?"

Marissa's shoulders hunched. "Dunno."

Eliza turned to Quince. "Clear as mud?"

"It's about the most buggered up message I've ever run across. But, yes, it makes sense now that you've translated it. Assuming you know where this place is."

She laughed, and her whole face lit up. For the first time since he'd seen her at The Terrace, he saw no hint of worry when he looked at her. As far as she was concerned, her brilliant, self-reliant sister had made a clean break.

He wasn't as optimistic, but there was no way in hell he'd say something that would erase that expression of joy.

"Of course I do. It's our ranch house."

A chill shot up his spine. "*Our*. As in you and Emma own it?" That meant property records. And that meant they could be tracked. Odds were good Corbu's people were already there, coded message or not. "We need to get going."

"We do," she said. "But not because of what you're thinking. It's not in my name or Emma's. It's not even in our father's name."

"But it's yours? As in it belongs to you?"

She nodded.

"Then you can explain all that on the way."

"I've got a cooler in the back and some sodas and chips you can take," Lorenzo said. "Sleeping bags, too, in case you need them." He pointed to the women. "You two go pack up his car. I want to talk to the boy."

Eliza flashed an encouraging smile as Quincy stepped toward Eliza, feeling more like *a boy* than he could ever remember being. "Yes, sir?"

"I don't know what happened between you two in London. And I don't know what's going on with you now. No," he held up a hand. "Not my business. I just want you to know that that girl and her sister are like daughters to me. You hurt her—you hurt either of them—and I will hunt you down like a rabid dog and kill you with my bare hands." He narrowed his eyes, his bushy brows coming to a point over his nose. "We understand each other?"

"Yes, sir," Quince said. "We understand each other just fine." He gave Lorenzo a nod, then stepped toward the door. He paused, then looked back. "For the record, sir. I think she's lucky to have you."

Then he stepped out the door without looking back.

In the small parking lot in front of the agency, Marissa was slamming the back hatch shut of his black Range Rover. "You're all set. Sweet car. Even if it is humongous."

By the passenger door, Eliza rolled her eyes. "Marissa's aiming for a Ferrari."

"I was supposed to get one for my twentieth birthday, but then Daddy Dearest went and got my mom all uptight about privilege and responsibility and stuff. I mean, come on. *He* has two Ferraris plus a Porsche."

"Yeah, you have it rough." Eliza gave the girl a hug, then climbed into the car.

"You'll keep us posted?" Marissa asked him as she trotted back onto the sidewalk.

"Absolutely."

"Cool. Find Emma, okay. This whole situation blows."

He slid in the car, and repeated the assessment to Eliza.

"Well, she's not wrong," Eliza says. "It does blow. You want to get on the 10, by the way."

"Interesting kid," he commented as he pulled out into traffic.

"She's okay. A little confused about where she fits in the world." At his questioning glance, she continued. "Her mom is Lorenzo's sister. And they grew up in Inglewood, so not exactly rolling in money, you know? Single mom, got into acting. She ended up doing bit parts, then got a sitcom, then got a small movie role as a hooker who gets murdered after she has an affair with a cop."

"I think I saw that. Wasn't the cop that actor, what's his name? Huge star? John something?"

"That's him. They got married when Marissa was fifteen. So she goes from near poverty to having a stepfather who could probably buy Australia."

"And this is a problem?"

"I guess it is when mom and stepdad want to make sure she understands the value of a dollar."

"Ah. Frustrated youth."

"Like I said, she's a good kid. But according to Emma, she's been picking up more and more hours at the agency. I figure she's trying to prove she's responsible. Either that or earn enough to go shopping with her friends, who all have cash, of course." She shifted in the seat, tucking a leg up underneath her. "I guess she's like a cross between you and me. Started out as poor as dirt like me, but ended up pretty well off, like you."

"Except I had access to my money."

"True. Must be frustrating. Still, I've known her most of my life. She'll figure it out. Most people do."

He frowned. "Do what?"

"Figure it out," she said. "Life throws shit your way, you

roll in it, get dirty and pissed off, but then you clean up and deal."

He shot her a sideways glance. "Is that what you do?"

"About most things, I think. But with you ... I don't think I ever managed to quite clean you off of me."

"I'm not sure I like the analogy."

She sat back, slipped off her shoes, and put her feet on his dashboard. "I'm not sure I meant you to."

He said nothing—honestly, he deserved that—and he didn't protest when she reached over and flipped on the radio. "You're going to take the 101 to the north," she said, leaning back and closing her eyes as classic rock poured out in stereo around them. "We're heading all the way up to San Luis Obispo."

For over three hours, The Doors, The Beatles, AC/DC, Aerosmith, and Queen blared out of the speakers, and Eliza managed to sleep through it all. Not that he was surprised. He remembered how she slept like the dead, wrapped naked in a sheet as he began his morning. For the first week, he'd tiptoed around the house. He was a naturally early riser and didn't want to disturb her, especially since he tended to keep her up so very late.

After a week of that, though, he learned not to bother. In fact, he soon fell into the habit of drinking coffee and listening to the news on the radio in bed, just for the pleasure of feeling her curled up beside him.

He missed that—hell, he missed her. But he knew damn well he couldn't have her. Not any more. Not after—

The sharp, musical chime of his phone yanked him from his increasingly maudlin thoughts, and he glanced automatically toward Eliza who, of course, wouldn't awaken unless hell was freezing over.

He punched the button to answer through the onboard

system, and grinned as Liam's deep voice filled the car. The two of them had worked a lot of jobs together, and Quince was glad his friend had signed on with Stark. "Got your text. What's the story with this ranch?"

"Eliza tells me that it belonged to her grandfather—a hunting cabin. And he sold it to some land mogul who was buying up ranch land in the area and all around the cabin. He didn't want to sell, though, so the mogul made a side-deal with him. The family could have free access and use of the cabin for fifty years. But it's just a handshake deal with a signed agreement locked in the mogul's safe. Anyone checking the deed records would only see the rancher's name."

"In that case, it sounds like a safe enough place to hole up," Liam said.

"Sounds like. But you and I both know how often things that sound fine go south."

Liam chuckled, but not with humor. "You got that right."

"Speaking of going south, things didn't go too well for Lassiter today." The smarmy bastard had been easy pickings for Ryan and Liam, who'd delivered him back to Quince at HQ. "How's our houseguest feeling this afternoon?"

Quince had acquired many skills during his time with MI6, but the one that had proved to be the most useful was his interrogation repertoire. In fairness, MI6 had only introduced him to the art. Quince had honed his own techniques, refined his own tools, and mixed his own pharmaceutical aids.

When he'd first been trained, he'd found some of the methods distasteful and had been somewhat reluctant to put them to use. But he'd been green in those days. As soon as he crawled deep into the underbelly of the criminal world and saw the level of treachery and pure evil, his reservations had evaporated. And after he'd been tied to the victim's chair himself, he'd realized that he'd go to whatever lengths were necessary to put the scum away and protect the innocent.

"I've said it before and will say it again, you are one scary motherfucker in a room," Liam said. "Lassiter's just now realizing how much he told you, and he is beyond pissed at himself."

"The man wasn't even a fair test of my skill. He's a spineless little worm who doesn't give a damn about the consequences so long as it makes him a buck." It had been easy enough to wring information from Lassiter. He knew that his hotel was being used for a private sale, and though he hadn't been told outright, he suspected that a young girl named Ariana was on the block. After pushing the issue for a solid hour, Quince had been convinced that Lassiter didn't realize the girl was royalty. "At least we know the princess is really away."

She'd been put up in a room and assigned a guard, and all Lassiter knew was that somehow she'd gotten out. Quince and the rest of the team assumed that it was Emma who had managed that feat, but as everyone knew the danger of making assumptions, they were still working to confirm that.

And since the process of extricating information about the girl had been so damn easy, Quince had taken the time to dig deep into the data buried in Lassiter's hard drive.

"Stark's brought his friend Ollie in for a conversation," Liam said. "Sounds like the FBI's going to take a nice long look at Scott Lassiter's books. Those feds are pretty damn touchy about things like blackmail and money laundering."

"That's what I hear," Quince said, biting back a grin.

They ended the call with Quince's promise to report in

once they reached the ranch. Eliza was still asleep, but he needed coffee and the Range Rover needed gas, so he pulled into a petrol station and killed the engine, leaving her to her coma as he went in for sustenance.

"So you got Lassiter," she said, as soon as they were underway again.

He shot her a sideways glance. "You were awake for all that?"

She yawned and sat up straighter, then noticed the coffee in her cup holder. "Tell me that's for me and I'll love you forever."

His mouth went dry as her eyes went wide.

"Sorry, I didn't mean—*Fuck*. I'm still half-asleep."

"Figure of speech. No worries. And yes, it's yours. I got some biscuits, too," he said, nodding at the box of short-bread cookies on the console between them.

She snatched the box and fumbled it open, but whether she really wanted the biscuits or was just covering her faux pas, he didn't know. "And, yeah," she said. "Sort of. It was like you were having a conversation in my dream. It was all very surreal. Did I hear that the princess escaped? With Emma?"

"Escaped, yes. With Emma? That's unconfirmed, but assumed."

"Well, that's our job, right?" Eliza said. "Yours and mine. To hit the cabin and confirm that my sister has her?"

"Denny's on it, too. She's searching for surveillance video that catches your sister on camera. We won't really need that if we find Emma herself, but—"

"We will," she said firmly, then leaned back and put her bare feet up on the dash again. Her toes, he noticed, were painted pink. They were damn cute toes.

After a moment, she turned to look at him, her head cocked and her mouth curved down into a frown.

He glanced her direction. "Problem?"

"Like I said—surreal."

He ran the conversation through his head, but it didn't translate any better the second time around. "Come again?"

"You. Me. Here on a road trip. I never expected to see you again, much less be together. Even if we are only together by virtue of proximity."

"Ah." He kept his eyes on the road and drew a breath. Then he turned enough to see her and addressed the very large pink elephant in the room. "I never told you I was sorry."

"No, you didn't. Are you sorry?"

"Of course I am."

"Hmm."

He frowned. "That's it? Just *hmmm*."

"I guess ... I don't know. You probably didn't apologize because it was pointless. You figured you'd never see me again, so why bother."

"That wasn't why," he said sharply. Her words were like a knife, and he regretted opening the damn door in the first place. Or had she opened it? He wasn't entirely sure.

He waited for her to ask what the real reason was, but she stayed silent, and her indifference, marked by the lingering silence, hurt more than he'd believed possible, especially after so much time.

The miles ticked by. Two. Four. After six, she spoke, her voice unbearably soft. "I called your office, you know. They told me you'd transferred to Taipei. Just had an urge to pull up stakes and settle in Asia, as one does."

"I shouldn't have—"

"I know you came back to London." The words were flat, no-nonsense, and entirely lacking emotion.

"What?" He'd heard her perfectly well.

"I saw you."

He sucked in air but had a hell of a time catching his breath. "I'm so sorry."

"Well, at least you can now say that you apologized."

"Eliza—"

"No. It's fine. It's more than fine. I mean, I survived, right? For awhile I didn't think I would. Honestly, Q, I was so in love with you it was overwhelming. Those three months? They felt like three lifetimes, and all I wanted was more. Then it was gone—*poof*—and I didn't understand. I was terrified something had happened to you. Then I was angry. Then I thought it was me. There was something wrong with me."

"No." He reached for her, but she flinched away.

"But it wasn't me. It was you." She drew a loud breath. "You're the one who fucked up, Quincy. We had something great, and you blew it. *You.*" For a moment, silence lingered. "I just wanted to make sure you knew that."

"Yes," he said. "I know it all too well."

16

"RIGHT THERE," I say, pointing to an overgrown dirt road off to the right.

"You're sure?"

I smack my foot against the dashboard in frustration because, no, I'm not sure. I haven't been here in ages. Probably not since Emma and I brought Marissa camping for her eleventh birthday.

"It's been almost a decade since I've been here," I snap. "And I was always a passenger, never a driver. So no, I'm not sure. Do *you* want to play navigator?"

He lifts his hands off the steering wheel as if in a gesture of surrender.

I deflate. "Sorry. I'm worried and I'm frustrated and— wait, that's not the turn after all. It's the next cut-off."

He glances at me, but says nothing. I see the question in his eyes, though. *Can I get us there?*

"Really," I assure him. "See the red X on the boulder? It's faded, but you can still make it out? Emma let me spray that. I was eight. Maybe nine. She did it to mark the turn. I'd totally forgotten."

Right then, I'm thankful for my sister's foresight. Because this ranch covers over six hundred acres, and the cabin is tucked in somewhere in the middle. Without landmarks, the odds of finding it are slim. And while that makes it an excellent hiding place, I'm fast-approaching my breaking point; I really, *really* need to find Emma and assure myself that she's okay.

"Still looking familiar?" Quincy asks after we've followed the winding road for what seems like forever.

I hesitate, not wanting to admit that nothing looks the same at all. Why would it? It's all mostly trees and shrubs and those things are constantly growing. Except—

Yes.

"We're almost there," I say, pointing to a dead tree split straight down the middle. A victim of lightning, and I guess the owners never thought it was worth ripping the tree's corpse out of the ground. "We'll crest a small hill, and then the cabin is in a little valley. There," I add gleefully, pointing to the dirt road that winds up a mound that barely qualifies as a hill but is sufficient to block the view of what lies beyond.

I practically vibrate in my seat as we climb the hill. I have fantasies that Emma will be out in front, her hand shading her eyes from the late afternoon sun.

That's not what I see.

Instead of joy, I'm rocked with fear. My stomach clenches, and I hear myself screaming for Quincy to stop the car, because I have to get out before I throw up from the horrible sight in front of me.

The cabin.

Except it's not. Not anymore. Now it's just the charred, still smoldering remains of a few support beams and pieces of the roof. Around it, the ground is also burned, the vegetation nothing more than ash.

I have a vague sense of throwing open the door. Of my feet pounding the ground. Of singeing my knees and hands as I fall to the ground, and then of Quincy's strong arms around me, pulling me back and holding me close as I sob against his chest.

"She got away," I whisper as Quincy folds me into his strong arms. "They must have gotten away."

Quincy says nothing, and after a moment I look up, then follow the direction of his gaze.

Her Jeep. Only now it's nothing more than a burned out shell.

My knees go out, and I fall to the ground, only Quincy's continuing grip keeping me from landing with a hard thud.

He crouches beside me, then pulls me close so that my face is buried in his chest and my tears are soaking his shirt. Gently, he strokes my hair, and I try to catch my breath. Try to *think.*

"We'll find her," he says, and I pull back, needing to see his face.

"You think they took them," I say, as tiny sprigs of hope poke up through the darkness that has filled me.

"Don't you?"

Slowly, I nod. Because of course they would take them. They want the princess—she's a commodity. And as for Emma ... well, she'd be worth a lot if they could manage to sell her. Which I'm quite certain they wouldn't. At the very least, they'd want to question her. To find out what she knows about the scope of their organization—and who she's told.

"Yes." I nod. "Yes, of course they'd want to take them

both alive." I pull back, away from his embrace. It's too comforting, and I don't want to rely on what I can't have. Besides, it's hard to think straight in Quincy's arms.

I start to stand, then pause. "How did they find them? Even if they intercepted that text, they couldn't possibly have decoded it. Could they?"

From his frown, I can tell that the question bothers him, too. "No, I can't imagine they could. It's possible they tracked her from the hotel. Or they embedded some sort of tracker in the princess. I don't know, but it's definitely disturbing. Right now, though, our problem is the opposite. If we want to recover your sister and the princess, we need to be the ones tracking them."

"Right," I say. "How?"

He gently kisses the top of my head, the touch simple and casual, and I'm far too aware of it. Then he stands and pulls out his phone. I close my eyes and try to think as I hear him say, "Ryan, it's me. What's the chance of calling in a few favors for satellite surveillance?"

As Quincy plays the role of super-spy, I start to walk the circumference of the burn zone. Something doesn't feel right, but then again, nothing about this situation feels right. Add to that the destruction of this one place from my childhood that actually has a few happy memories attached, and it's a wonder I can focus on anything at all.

Not that the cabin had been a happy retreat when our dad was alive. He'd lock us in the cellar while he went hunting, supposedly so we wouldn't go wandering around and accidentally get lost or shot, but Emma said it was because he was a controlling bastard who needed to always know just where to find us.

He made us sleep down there, too, but only when he

wanted us *that* way. That's when Emma would get the bed and he'd tell me I had to sit on the wooden chair. I had to watch, he'd say. So that I'd know what to expect when it was my turn.

I tremble with the memory, grateful that the bastard is dead. Grateful that Emma got us the hell away from him.

And absolutely terrified that something horrible has happened to her. Something even more horrible than our father.

I jump as Quincy rests a hand on my shoulder, his touch yanking me back to the present. "Are you okay?"

"My father used to bring us here," I tell him.

He says nothing, just moves behind me, then wraps his arms around my waist. "And after that?"

"After?"

"You and Emma came by yourselves, didn't you? You toasted marshmallows under the stars. You walked to the stream. You used that old Canon of yours to take pictures of butterflies. And you brought Marissa here and made it a retreat for your real family. Not a cage built by a monster."

I close my eyes, both amazed and grateful that he gets it. "We never toasted marshmallows," I say, smiling a little. "Emma was afraid we'd burn the place down if we lit a campfire." I make an ironic noise in my throat. "Guess she saw that coming."

"But you're right," I add, as I turn in his arms, then lean back so that I can face him. "We did make it more of a home. Especially that vile cellar. We bought gallons and gallons of white paint, and we did all the walls. We even cleaned out the drainage tunnel so that we could get rid of the mildew smell before—*Oh.*"

I step back so quickly I almost fall.

"El?"

"The tunnel. Oh, holy crap, I forgot about the tunnel."

"What are you—"

But I'm off and running, Quincy right at my heels.

Emma called it a drainage tunnel because any water that collected in the cellar after a rain always dribbled off in that direction. But the truth was that we didn't know what the tunnel's real purpose was. From what we'd learned, the cabin wasn't the first structure on that site. We'd found what appeared to be a stone foundation a dozen or so yards away one time when we planted a vegetable garden, and Emma said it was probably a house, and that our tunnel may have been part of it.

We never tried to figure out the *why* of the tunnel, but we did follow it once. A horrible, claustrophobic experience that had me in tears by the end because the tunnel narrowed so much, it tore the sleeves of my shirt where my shoulders scraped the wall. I wanted to turn back, but I also didn't want to crawl backward, and Emma gently urged me on, telling me it would surely get better.

It did—because we finally came to the end. A small cave in a cliff-face overlooking a fast-moving stream.

That's my destination when I take off running, and when I reach the spot on the cliff above the cave, I lie on my belly and lean over. "Emma! Ariana! Are you there?"

Quincy catches up to me and pulls me to my feet. "What the hell?"

"The drainage tunnel." I point down. "That's where it lets out."

I can tell right away he gets it, and a few minutes later he's on his stomach, watching as I carefully follow the chiseled toeholds that Emma put in place over the course of years. I wiggle inside the small cave, then use my new phone as a flashlight.

"Anything?" he asks, as I sink to my knees in relief. Because there, on the stone wall is a message for me. All it says is *Alive*.

But that's enough.

17

It's late by the time we finally leave the ranch. We're both exhausted, emotionally and physically, and I'm really not looking forward to another long drive.

Even so, I'm surprised when Quincy pulls into a charming boutique hotel on Avila Beach, only about thirty minutes away from the cabin. I twist in my seat. "You're kidding, right?"

He draws a breath as he turns to look at me. "We're both exhausted and uncomfortable, Eliza," he says gently. "We need food and we need sleep. Tomorrow, we'll head back to LA."

I want to tell him that crashing here won't do a thing for my comfort level. Where Quincy is concerned, the only thing that will make me comfortable is curling up against him. Feeling his strong arm around my shoulders and letting his heartbeat fall into a pattern with mine. Because as much as I appreciate that he's helping me find my sister, being around him is hurting my heart.

Part of me wants to tell him so. To just say flat out that I want to keep driving so I can go home. But the truth is that here or there won't matter. Because even in LA, he'll insist on staying with me. I crashed Lassiter's party. Red died after a fight in my room. And I helped Denny and Quincy steal data. Emma may be my top priority—and the princess may be at the top of Quincy's list—but no matter what, he'll say that I'm in danger, too. And he'll stick to me like glue.

"We can stay," I say. "But I want to eat at the patio restaurant. Not room service." The weather is perfect, the ocean is beautiful. And the sunset is sure to be stunning. The only thing that would make it better would be if this were a date. But I figure three out of four is better than nothing.

Since we don't have luggage—something the barely pubescent desk clerk seems to find amusing—we head straight for the restaurant. And, because I need it, I order a bottle of wine. Red, because that's my favorite. Pinot Noir, because that's Quincy's.

"Are we going to find them?" I fire off the question as soon as the waiter pours our wine and drops off a basket of bread. I'm not in the mood for small talk or coddling, and I take a long swallow of the wine, enjoying the tingle on my throat and anticipating the sweet lightheadedness that I know will follow. I've eaten nothing but shortbread cookies all day. I just want to eat my salad, drink my wine, fall asleep, and not dream a thing.

That, at least, is what I tell myself. Because what I *really* want to do isn't something I'm ever going to get to do again. And I want to do it with the man sitting across from me.

I draw a breath, gather myself, and study his face.

To his credit, he doesn't shy from my question or my steady gaze. "Yes," he says simply. "We'll find them."

"Good answer. Now explain to me why it's the truth and not bullshit."

"Because I'm not willing to accept failure, and because I don't bullshit."

I lean back in the seat and take a long sip of wine. "Clearly you're talking about work. Because as far as relationships are concerned, failure and bullshit are pretty much your stock in trade."

He pushes his chair back and stands. "I can only apologize so many times, Eliza, before it starts to sound redundant."

"You really think we've hit that point?" My heart is pounding. Part of me wants to call back the words. I just want to have dinner. I just want peace.

The other part wants to yell and scream and rant. I want to toss my wine in his face and smash the glass on the floor. I want to hear an explanation, not an apology. Because I don't give a crap that he's sorry. Everybody's sorry about something. I want to know *why*.

I want to know what the hell I did wrong.

I watch, baffled, as he seems to melt back into the chair, then reaches for my hand. "Oh, Eliza, love. You didn't do anything wrong. Not a single bloody thing."

Oh, hell. "I said that out loud?"

The corner of his mouth twitches. In London, I was always saying things I didn't mean to. Usually comments on how ridiculously hot he looked or how much I wanted to be having sex instead of doing whatever else we happened to be doing. I was always mortified. He thought it was adorable. So adorable that the sex part usually came true.

That's probably why I never tried too hard to control that little quirk...

Now, though, I really am embarrassed, and as my cheeks burn, his hand tightens around my fingers.

"Don't," I whisper.

"Don't what?"

Gently I pull my hand out of his. "Don't touch me. It—I'd just rather you didn't touch me."

We're not together. I know that. He doesn't want to be together. I get it. But my body still reacts to him, and just the simple brush of his fingers against my palm sends shock-waves to my core.

I'm glad we have a suite—and I'm glad he's giving me the bedroom—because I already know that I'm going to fall asleep tonight with my hand between my legs. Pathetic, perhaps, but at this point, I really don't care. After London, I thought I'd never see Quincy Radcliffe again. Under the circumstances, I think I'm entitled to a little pathos and a few self-induced orgasms.

He sucks in air and nods. "Of course. Whatever you want."

"But that's not true either, is it?"

He doesn't answer, and I can't really blame him. I'm pretty sure I've crossed the line from wounded to bitchy. I take another sip of wine to center myself. Then—what the hell—I finish the glass and pour myself another. As I do, I notice that he's finished as well, and I silently applaud. Misery loves company, after all, and I refill his glass, too.

Our food arrives, and we eat in silence as the sun sinks slowly toward the horizon. It is breathtakingly beautiful, and my chest swells with awe. In that moment, I feel the same sense of hope and wonder and possibility as I used to feel with Quincy. And the fact that I've lost that is so unbearably sad that I blurt out a question I swore I would never, ever ask.

"Did you ever really love me at all?"

I see the pain slash across his face before he looks down at his empty plate. The echo of my question fades, and my heart twists with the knowledge that he's not even going to give me the satisfaction of answering.

Then he lifts his head, his eyes steady on mine. "How can you even ask that? Of course I loved you. I never stopped loving you."

My heart skips a beat, and I can't seem to catch my breath. I swallow, then blink as I look away, trying desperately not to cry. "Then why?"

"Please," he says. "Please don't ask me that."

I want to do just that, but the waiter arrives, and Quincy asks for the check. He signs it to the room, then stands, not asking if I'm ready. I'm not, of course, but I follow obediently, fully intending to get into this once we reach the room. *He loves me.* If he loves me, then we can make this work. And I don't understand why he doesn't see that.

"We need to talk about this," I say the moment the suite door closes behind us. But Quincy just shakes his head.

"We're both tired. I'm going to take a quick shower and then the bedroom's all yours."

"Quincy, please. We—"

"Tomorrow," he says. "I'll be a captive audience for more than three hours." He turns and heads for the bathroom, leaving me standing in the living area, wondering what the hell to do now.

I'm not ready to end this. I can't just leave it be until tomorrow when he's regrouped and pulled back even more. The man just told me he loves me. The same man who walked away from me without so much as a "see you later."

As far as I'm concerned, I don't owe him anything, and certainly not polite acquiescence to his request that I simply put this conversation on hold.

On the contrary, he played dirty in London. I can play dirty right now.

And even though I'm terrified that I might be crossing a line I can't come back from, I strip off my clothes as I walk toward the bathroom, then I turn the knob, push open the door, and step from the carpet onto the slick, cool tile.

The shower is huge and enclosed in glass. He's facing the back wall and the shower head, and doesn't see me, and for the moment I enjoy the view of his well-muscled back and his tight ass as he tilts his head back and lets the water pound his face.

He has a mole on his left side just above his hipbone and seeing it now, I can imagine the feel of it under my fingers. How many times have I touched his skin and lazily stroked that very spot as we lay together in bed after we made love?

I want that again. That intimacy. It's not even that I want sex, though I won't deny the way my body craves him now, or the building heat between my thighs. But that's not the core of it. I miss our closeness. The sweet touches. The long talks into the night. The way he always knew how to draw me close and make me feel safe.

I swallow, ridiculously sad, and for one tiny moment I almost back out of the room because I'm terrified that if I walk to him and he pushes me away again, that I really won't survive the loss.

But I'm not surviving now, am I?

I've been in limbo since London. Mourning the loss of him. Not moving on.

Maybe it's wrong to push him, but he was wrong to leave the way he did.

I need closure. I need to know if there's still the slightest chance for us.

I need to either take a step toward putting the pieces of our life back together, or I need him to finish the work he started and destroy me completely. One way or another, it's time for a new beginning, and the first step is to cross this bathroom.

Squaring my shoulders, I do just that. He still hasn't turned, which makes it easier, although I'm surprised he doesn't know I'm there. Quincy is always so aware of his surroundings.

I pause just outside the shower and take a breath for courage. Then I reach for the handle on the glass door.

I see his body straighten as I tug it open. I freeze, then tell myself that I've already crossed the Rubicon. No point stopping now.

"I hoped you were going to change your mind," he says, with his back still to me. And I realize that, of course, he knew I was there all along.

"I almost did," I admit. "But I think we're worth taking the leap." I ease up behind him and slide my arms around his waist.

"I didn't want to have to push you away," he says.

"Well, you don't actually have to." I press my lips to his shoulder blade, my hands lightly stroking his lower abs. "Free will and all that. It's a thing."

I don't see him smile, and I don't hear him chuckle. But there is a slight quiver in his muscles that I think might be a laugh, and I silently rejoice.

"I wish you hadn't come in here."

I take a risk and slowly slide my hand down, then smile when I discover that he's hard. "Really? You don't seem displeased."

This time, I know I hear him chuckle. "I'm human, Eliza. I never said I don't want you. But I can't have you."

A wave of frustration washes over me, and I have to work to keep it out of my voice. "Yes, you can. I'm right here."

I ease around his body, needing to face him. "Talk to me,

Quincy. Tell me what happened, and then maybe I can understand. But instead you just shut down on me. Like dropping one of those giant metal doors. *Boom*, and you were gone. Do you know how much that hurts?"

I'm looking at his face, and I see him wince. He gets it—I'm certain of it. He knows he's hurt me.

And he wants me.

But he's not giving an inch.

I just don't get it.

"Is it me?" This time, there's no keeping the frustration out of my voice. "Or have you just decided to be celibate?" He makes a sound that's almost like a laugh, and a hot blade of jealousy slices through me. "Oh, great. So you've slept with other women since you walked. I guess it really is just me." *Fucker.* It takes all my willpower not to say that last bit out loud.

"Slept with, no. Fucked, yes."

Stupid, stupid tears sting my eyes. "Why not me?"

His expression is so tender that the tears almost spill down my cheeks, and I'm grateful we're in the shower, where maybe he won't see.

Gently, he cups my face. "Because you matter."

I shake my head, not sure if I'm confused or angry or sad. All I know is that this isn't right. "You once told me you'd protect me. Do you remember? You pointed out your mother's bedroom and you told me the story." I remember it all. How she'd shoved him under the bed. How he'd wanted to come out and fight for her but he was too scared. And how later he swore he'd never let that happen again.

"Didn't I live up to that promise?" His words are harsh, and I know I touched a nerve. "Didn't I get you out of The Terrace?"

"You did, yes. But that doesn't make it better. Because

you're the one who hurt me, Quincy. You hurt me when you walked away."

I see the anger flare across his face, but it's banked quickly, fading into acceptance as he slowly nods. And then I see regret.

"Do you think I don't know that? Do you think I don't hate myself every single day?"

"Then why?" I shiver, but not from the water. It's still pounding hot, filling the room with steam. No, I'm shivering in fear, because I have no idea what his answer will be, but I'm certain I won't like it.

He starts to open his mouth and I think he's going to tell me. But then he lashes out, his fist landing so hard on the glass wall that I'm surprised it doesn't shatter.

I gape, not sure if I'm scared of his temper or pleased to have gotten a reaction. I don't have time to decide, though, because suddenly he has me by the shoulders. He pushes my back up against the wall and pins me there, his eyes wild as he looms over me. "Don't you get it? I can't be the man you need."

"I'm not asking for forever," I lie. "Just right now. Don't *you* get it?" Boldly, I cup his erection. "And right now, I think you're up to the task."

For a moment, we just stare at each other, both of us breathing hard. Then he swoops down, captures my mouth, and kisses me long and deep.

It's heaven and hell all at the same time. This is what I've wanted. What I've craved. And I fear that it's going to evaporate far too quickly. But, dammit, I'm going to take what I can now and screw the consequences.

With that as my mantra, I lock my arms around his neck, then practically climb him until my back is balanced against the wall but my legs are tight around his waist.

He turns the shower control, cutting off the water, then maneuvers us out of the bathroom and to the bed. We're both still wet, but I don't care. I'm not letting go of him for anything. Not until he drops me onto the bed, then closes his mouth over my breast.

I moan and arch up as he sucks hard, sending sparks of electricity shooting from my nipple down to my core. As if the thread is visible, he follows it down my body, tracing the path with his lips until he finally buries his face between my legs, his tongue working all sorts of magic as his fingers slide deep inside me, and I rock my hips, wanting so much more. Wanting everything.

When he starts to kiss his way back up my body, I know what's coming—what we both want—and I tremble in anticipation and desire. I reach up, stretching my arms above my head, waiting for him to grab my wrists. To hold me down and take me hard. Or to flip me over and spank me before sinking himself deep inside me.

And yet he does none of those things.

His mouth teases me and his hands stroke me, and it all feels delicious and wonderful. I'm not complaining, but at the same time, I want to fall back into the past. I want the Quincy who possessed me. Who forced me to surrender. Who let me slide down into my own desire and lose myself safely in those dark places. Because I need that right now. With Emma missing and fear nipping at me, I need him to push me to the edge. I need to know I can go there, that he will be with me, and that I can get back okay.

But he doesn't. He knows me so damn well—has always known exactly what I need—and yet he just doesn't go there.

Instead he keeps me on my back and he rides me hard, and yes, it feels amazing even if it is a little tame. I hook my legs around him and cup my hands on his ass, urging him deeper and harder. Until, finally, the friction of our bodies sends me spiraling over the edge and I explode, my body clenching tight around him until he follows me right over into the stratosphere.

It's incredible. Mind-blowing. And not nearly enough...

Stifling a sigh, I twine my fingers in his hair. He slides up my body, then pulls me close. I start to speak, though I'm not entirely sure what I intend to say. It doesn't matter, because he puts a finger over my lips, shushing me.

"You won the war, love. Give me this small victory. Just let me hold you. Just let me fall asleep with you in my arms."

Since that's hardly a difficult demand, I agree and snuggle close, feeling safe and loved for the first time in a long time.

I drift, half in and out of sleep, until I'm rocked into full wakefulness by the man tossing and turning beside me.

I shift, propping myself on an elbow, then gently lay a hand to his chest to coax him out of his dream.

But before I can even wrap my head around what's happening, he's grabbed my wrist and is hurling me out of bed. I hear my own scream echo in the room as he slams me against the wall, knocking the wind out of me.

I try to catch my breath, but now it's impossible, because his hand is at my throat, and I'm starting to feel dizzy and terrified and completely confused.

Frantic, I thrust my knee up and manage to catch him in the balls. He howls and opens his eyes, but it's clear that he's locked in a nightmare and doesn't see me. But at least his hand is no longer at my throat. And as he starts to reach for me again, I do the only thing I can think of. I scream, "Duck! Duckling! Duck!" at the top of my lungs, and hope to hell the old safe word gets through to him.

18

Duck! Duckling! Duck!

The words burst into his head, past the red haze of memory, and Quince stumbled backward, horrified to realize that he was looming over Eliza, who looked terrified.

This was it. This was why he'd left. Why he'd been right to stay away. The Berlin mission had destroyed him. He'd lost Shelley. He'd lost himself.

And even though they hadn't taken her from him, he'd lost Eliza, too.

He sucked in air, his mind a mess of wild thoughts and violent emotions. God, he should have known better than to touch her. He'd been a bloody fool to think it would be okay. To think he could ever have any sort of chance again.

They'd broken him well and good, and he'd do well to bloody remember it.

"Quincy?" She reached for him, her gesture tentative and her expression wary. Smart girl. "It's okay. You're awake now. Everything's fine."

He made a raw noise—everything was a long way from fine—then backed away from her, shaking his head. He opened his mouth, as if there were words he could say to explain, but of course there weren't. He was broken, and that was obvious enough just looking at him. What could he possibly add?

He lifted his hands, as if warding off her compassion. Blocking that confused, concerned expression, he turned, saw his jeans folded over the back of a chair, and tugged them on. He didn't bother with a shirt. Didn't bother with shoes. He just went out onto the back patio, opened the little metal gate, and followed the path down to the sea.

The sky was clear, the almost-full moon hanging low in the sky, its reflected light illuminating the froth on the tumbling waves. He stood at the edge, letting the frigid water of the Pacific slosh over his bare feet. For a moment, he allowed himself the fantasy that he could walk out into the waters. That he could swim toward the horizon until exhaustion pulled him under, and he would drop down, down, down, only to rise up again in triumph, cleansed of all the evil he'd witnessed. The horrors that clung to him like blood, staining and tainting him.

But he didn't have time for foolish fantasies, and he knew damn well that the blood on his hands could never be washed off. And so he clasped his arms around his bare chest to ward off the chill, and started walking along the shore, for no other reason than to clear his head and induce exhaustion. So that maybe, with luck, when he got back to the room he could creep in without waking Eliza, lie down on the couch, and sleep.

Of course it didn't work out that way. He should have known she wouldn't make it that easy. And there wasn't a damn thing he could do to avoid her, because she was sitting on a blanket on the sand right smack in the middle of the path he needed to walk to get back to their room.

"You should be asleep," he said, standing at the edge of her blanket.

She held his shirt up to him, and he took it gratefully. "So should you." She nodded at the space on the blanket next to her. "We should talk."

"I'm tired. I just want to go in."

"Sit," she said. "You owe me that."

"For attacking you." It wasn't a question.

She flinched. "No. Duh. For walking out on me. For leaving me in the dark for years. For not trusting me to help you the way you helped me." She crossed her arms over her chest. "Seriously? That's what you think of me? That I'd toss you aside because of a nightmare?"

He didn't answer. But he did sit down.

To her credit, she didn't push him. She didn't even look at him. She just sat with her knees pulled up to her chest and a second blanket around her shoulders. She reached out with her left hand and took his right, and though his first instinct was to pull away, he didn't. He wanted her touch, the comfort of knowing she was there with him. That she didn't hate him for what happened. And the reassurance that he hadn't scared her away.

He didn't want her to know what had happened in Berlin, but at the same time he wanted to tell her. He missed her so bloody much. Maybe if he'd never seen her again he could have lived with the hole in his gut. But he had. She'd stood there in The Terrace Hotel and he'd seen her and everything had changed.

Him, most of all.

"Quincy?" She started to twist at the waist, obviously intending to check on him.

"No," he said. "Stay the way you are. Give me a minute."

To her credit, she did as he asked. And though he never

would have thought it possible, he heard himself start talking.

"You've probably figured out that I've never worked in high finance. And while I've been to Hong Kong, China, and Taipei many times, I didn't go that summer." He paused, but she didn't interrupt, and she didn't turn to look at him. He drew in a breath, grateful, and continued. "Instead, I was tasked with a quick and easy escort job. A favor for a key asset in Berlin. Nothing more. Very low risk. No espionage component. Just a trip like any other trip. At the time I was on the payroll of both MI6 and Deliverance, but I was on vacation from both, and enjoying myself very much."

She ducked her head, and he saw the hint of a smile. He hooked a finger under her chin and tilted her face up to look at him. "You were the best part of that down time."

She smiled, then started to turn away again.

"No. It's okay," he said, and closed his hand more tightly around hers. "At any rate, like I said, it was supposed to be a nothing gig. The girl had been traveling with friends, who turned out to be more into partying than she was. She called her father to come get her in London and take her back home, but he was in Hong Kong. So he called my boss and asked for a favor. All I needed to do was get her home to Berlin."

"I'm guessing it didn't go well."

"No. It really didn't." He drew in a breath, trying to think how to lay it all out quickly and simply. He wanted to tell her, but he didn't want to dwell on it. And once it was out and the air was clear, he wanted to go to bed and hope to hell he didn't dream.

"We were ambushed," he said quickly, just to get it out. "Grabbed and taken to an abandoned warehouse. Five men. I'd never seen any of them before. Or, at least, I didn't think that I had. Turns out I saw their ankles when I was seven years old."

He saw her throat move as she swallowed. "Your mother's murder?"

"I guess they weren't satisfied with killing her and my father. They wanted to take out the entire family. But more than that, they wanted to torture us, too." He stood up, because he couldn't sit still and tell the rest. "They started with Shelley," he said, his back to her, and his eyes on the ocean. "One simple job. Get the girl back home to Berlin." His voice hitched, tears clogging his throat. "I told her I'd keep her safe. They took me out with a tranq gun. I woke up tied to a wall, bare ass naked. And Shelley was in a chair in front of me. Arms tied. Ankles tied. Still dressed. They'd combed her hair. Said they wanted her to look pretty for me."

He turned his head, just enough to look over his shoulder to see her horrified expression. "They took pictures of her. Polaroids. Just let them fall there on the warehouse floor. Then they aimed a gun at her face and told her she was going to die. But if she begged me, maybe I'd save her."

"Oh, God." Her words were soft, barely audible, but they cut through his heart.

"She was only sixteen. And, yeah, she begged. And every cry, every plea ate away at my soul. I swear to God, I died that day, too."

"They shot her."

He turned back to the ocean, dark and infinite. "Right between the eyes."

"They let you go?"

He made a scoffing noise. "They raped me." His voice was flat, emotionless. "Over and over."

When he looked at her again, he saw that she looked numb. Just like he felt.

"How did you get away?"

He twined his fingers behind his neck and closed his eyes, for just this once letting the memories flow. "Part of my training included drug resistance. Sometimes, they'd drug me and untie me. Guess they figured it made ripping into me that much more special. They dosed me, but they didn't want me completely unconscious because where was the fun in that. One time, they didn't use quite enough. On anybody else, it would have been plenty. But I had some resistance. They touched me, and I exploded. After that initial burst, I don't remember any of it. Just a red haze in my head, the smell of blood, and the sounds of their screams."

She had her knees up against her chest and she was hugging them tight, her eyes wide, her mouth open in horror.

"When I got my senses back, they were all dead, scattered and bloody across the floor. Five sprawled and bloody corpses. I left them there on the floor of that warehouse. I got out. Got to our Berlin safe house and radioed for assistance, then passed out. When I came to, I gave them the coordinates, but the bodies were gone. I was in the hospital for weeks. Then I went back to London for physical therapy. I think I'd been back about two weeks when you saw me, but I saw you before that."

Her head shot up, her brow furrowed. "What? Where?"

"You were with that friend of yours. The thin woman with the curly black hair. You introduced us once at the theater, and—"

"Right. Alicia. I went out to lunch with her a few times after you—well, we hung out a bit."

"I couldn't do it," he said simply. "You were laughing. You

looked happy. And I was in a dark place, craving revenge. Not sleeping because of night terrors. And I couldn't—" He cut himself off with a shake of his head.

"What?"

"Sexually. Emotionally." He shook his head, rubbing his temples. "I wasn't in a good place. I'm still not."

He watched the play of emotions over her face and was certain she was trying to think of some argument. Some magic words to make it all better when there was no magic to be had.

"Sometimes I think I'm cursed," he said. "My mother. My father. Then me."

"No," she said simply, and he just scoffed, then held up his wrist, showing her the Patek Philippe.

"Did I ever tell you why I wear this? It's a compass," he continued when she shook her head.

"It's not just a watch?"

"I mean that it guides me. It was my father's, you know. They let me go through his things after they found his body. The watch was a gift to him from the royal family. He betrayed them. The country. So the watch became my compass. I wear it to remember that I have to keep a tight rein on myself. To always think before I act." He drew a breath. "I didn't do that tonight, and I'm sorry."

"You were trapped in a nightmare."

"I should never have taken you to bed in the first place."

She stood up, took a single step toward him. "You didn't hurt me. You snapped out of it."

Her words blossomed inside of him, like a tiny seed of hope. But he didn't trust it. Instead, he said, "I've missed you."

A small smile touched her lips. "I'm ridiculously glad it's not just me."

"I've missed you," he repeated. "And touching you felt so damn good. But I don't know how to make this work."

"Can we try?"

Inside him, the monster curled. Cold guilt and red rage. "I don't know."

"It wasn't your fault. You know that, right? Not what happened to Shelley. Not what happened to you."

"I know," he said simply. "But knowing really isn't enough."

19

"Is everything okay between you two?"

Startled, I look up from where I'm sitting with my feet in the shallow end of Damien Stark's pool. Denny is standing above me looking down, her green eyes reflecting the concern in her voice.

"What? Me and Quincy? Of course." I'm speaking forcefully, as if adding strength to my words will make them true. "What on earth makes you ask?"

Denny shakes her head. "Just a feeling." She kicks off her sandals then sits beside me, dangling her feet in the crystal clear water as well. "I've gotten to know him pretty well, and he just seems off today. You, too."

"You don't know me well enough to know if I'm off."

Denny points a finger at me. "True. We should get to know each other better."

I laugh. "Today may not be the best time for that. They'll all be back soon."

The entire team from Stark Security—including, by default, yours truly—has gathered at Mr. Stark's incredible house in Malibu for an impromptu welcome reception for Prince Michel of Eustancia, Princess Ariana's uncle and the National Security Director for the small country. He'd arrived in Malibu with a small cadre of bodyguards while his intelligence team remained in their suite of rooms at the Stark Century Hotel with Liam Foster there as the SSA liaison.

At the moment, the prince and most of the other guests are in Mr. Stark's massive, underground garage. Apparently Prince Michel is as much of a classic car aficionado as Damien Stark.

"For that matter," I continue, "I'm not sure today's the best day to talk about my relationship with Quincy at all. I mean, we really should be focusing on the princess."

Denny shakes her head. "A little free advice? I promise it's worth more than I'm charging you."

"Um, okay."

"You can't think like that. Not if you're going to survive in this business."

"I'm an actress. I'm not actually in this business."

Denny rolls her eyes and kicks, sending droplets of water flying. "Fine. I'll rephrase. If you're going to manage to have a life with someone in this business you need to learn that you can't wait for things to be calm. Because things will never be calm."

She blinks, and I realize that she's fighting tears. "Denny?"

"Sorry." She sniffles, then rubs her face with the palms of her hands. "Sorry, sometimes I'm perfectly fine and then, *poof*, I'm not. But that's kind of the point. I'd give anything to have Mason here. To talk about things we left unsaid. To just have a *life*. I took that for granted before—well, before his mission. And now there's been no word for so long, and I'm starting to wonder if I'll ever have the chance to say all the things we left unsaid."

I take her hand and squeeze it. "You will." It's a stupid thing to say, because I don't know that at all. But I want to believe it. And right then, I think it's what she needs to hear.

She pulls her feet up onto the deck. "Sorry about that. I didn't mean to get all maudlin."

I think about all the years without Quincy. "I get it. Really."

"Good. So talk to him. There's something real between you two. Don't let that get lost in all the noise." She exhales loudly. "God, I sound like someone's interfering grand-mother. But I just—I guess I figure if I earn enough relation-ship Karma, then the universe has to send him back to me."

I have no idea what to say to that, so I just reach over, squeeze her hand, and say, "Thanks."

She lifts a shoulder. "If I'm meddling, just tell me to shut up. But Quince is like a brother to me, and I really like you. I just want to see you two crazy kids work it out."

I laugh. "I really like you, too," I say, which is a total understatement. I hesitate, biting my lower lip as I look at Denny. Then I decide I have nothing to lose and bite the bullet. "How much do you know? About Quincy's past, I mean."

"Ah, well, I could ask you the same thing."

I grin. "But I asked first."

"Fine. But this is just between us girls, right? If I acciden-tally tell you something you don't know, you didn't hear it from me. And you know that I'm only talking to you because it's for his own good. And because, well, wine and gossip."

"Scout's honor," I say, then cross myself.

"I think you got that part wrong, but whatever." She scrunches up her mouth as if considering her words, then says, "Do you know about his dad?"

"Yeah. And his mom. And that he still owns the house—or he did back when we were together in London."

"Then you know that eats at him. His dad. Not being able to save his mom."

Again, I nod.

"There's something else, too. Something big that messed him up back when he was still working with MI6 and Deliverance. You've met Dallas, right?" The latter seems like a non-sequitur, and it takes me a minute to remember that Dallas Sykes is Quincy's friend who founded Deliverance, which I've recently learned is now a defunct vigilante-para-military kind of organization that existed primarily to locate and rescue kidnapped children.

"Not yet," I say. "But I've seen pictures of him in the tabloids. Isn't he here?"

She nods. "He and Stark are friends, and I guess he also knows the Prince Regent—Ariana's dad. Dallas is like the playboy of the western world. Or he was until he got married. Anyway, not important. I was just saying that something happened back then. Something really bad, I think, but I don't know the details."

Since she doesn't know anything, I'm not sure why she's telling me this. My confusion must show, because she adds, "I asked him once if he wanted the name of my counselor—I see him sometimes when it gets too hard, dealing with Mason being away."

"Oh." I sit up, interested. "Did he?"

"No, and he didn't tell me why not. But I think it was because he was living and breathing work, so he never cared enough about getting his personal shit together." She climbs to her feet, then lifts a shoulder as she looks down at me. "I think he might care enough now."

I grin, ridiculously warmed by her words.

"It's a party, and I'm having a drink," she tells me, in a tone that suggests it's time to leave serious topics behind. "Want one?"

"No thanks. Later." Right then I'm thinking about what she said. Or, rather, I'm thinking about Quincy and what happened to him. About what I know that Denise doesn't.

And about what Quincy and I didn't say this morning on the drive back to LA from San Luis Obispo.

He'd slept on the couch last night, which I suppose was to be expected, but I'd hoped that we would talk more on the drive. He clearly has demons to exorcise, and I wanted to help. But he'd been mostly silent, and when he did speak, it wasn't about last night's revelations—or his trip to the dark side—at all.

Instead, we'd talked about Emma and the princess and the details of the investigation. We'd both wondered how her pursuers had found the cabin. The place was completely off the grid, and yet the bad guys had made it there before us. And not by much, considering that the ground had still been smoldering when we arrived.

"Even if they somehow hacked her phone, there's no way they could have interpreted that message. I mean, even Marissa didn't get it, and she's been to the place."

"It's possible they have surveillance on her," Quincy had said. "If they worked fast after she took Ariana, they may have managed a tail."

"Then why not grab them sooner?"

"I don't know," he'd admitted, the truth of that statement frustrating us both.

I frowned, another question occurring to me. "Why ping

Marissa?" I asked. "Why wouldn't Emma text me? Actually, never mind. She thinks I'm on that cruise."

"Even if she didn't, she might not text you. My guess is she wanted to keep her baby sister out of it."

I made a scoffing noise, but I knew he was right. "Did you ever hear back about the satellite?" He'd called somebody from the ranch, and I had a fantasy that even now NASA had a giant space laser pointed at the bad guys.

"Unfortunately, that's a dead end. There were no satellites tasked over that location, and no way to re-task one quickly enough to be any use to us. And as for traffic cameras, we have analysts reviewing feeds from the area, but this isn't Los Angeles, and there aren't as many cameras set up."

"Great." I'd slunk back in my seat, disappointed.

"At least we know about the truck."

I nod, because that's something. About half an hour before we arrived on site, the owners of the ranch house called the local police to report that their Ford F-150 pickup truck had been stolen right out of the driveway. "But Emma's too smart to keep it for long. Which means that unless a cop or a camera pick them up soon, that clue will be useless."

"True," he'd said. "But at least we know they got off the ranch."

I'd nodded, because that was something, and we'd spent the rest of the ride in silence with Quincy thinking God only knows what, and me having long conversations in my head about what happened to him and how to deal with it, and how if he'd just let me help him, we could get through it together.

In my head, it worked out great.

In the car, I said nothing as classic rock blared all the way back to Los Angeles.

We made a pit stop at Quincy's apartment to change clothes, then headed to Malibu, having gotten Ryan's message about Prince Michel while we were en route.

Since Emma's place had been ransacked, until all this was resolved, I was to be Quincy's permanent houseguest. I did tell him that I was sure I could bunk with Denise if he'd rather. Considering how much last night had freaked him out, I thought he might prefer me gone.

"No," he'd said, and that one simple word had elevated my mood for half the journey.

Now, I hear chatter from inside the house and realize that the group must be returning from the garage. I stand, wanting to get a drink before the whole crowd rushes the bar.

I ask for a martini, then watch as the college-aged bartender expertly mixes it. It occurs to me that he must have been vetted—he's at a billionaire's house serving drinks to royalty—and I wonder if he does this kind of thing a lot or if he's jumping up and down inside, desperate to get back to his friends and tell the story.

"You look amused," Nikki Stark says as I step away from the bar with my drink. "I hope that means you're having a good time."

Damien's wife is beautiful in a girl-next-door kind of way. I know there was a ton of gossip about her and her famous husband back in the day, but to be honest I didn't follow it at the time. Now, I don't really want to track it down. I like her too much, and I hate the thought that she'd been dragged through the tabloids, especially since I've seen first-hand what a great couple they are.

Another woman joins us, looping an arm around Nikki's shoulder as she sticks her other hand out to me. I take it, a little bit intimidated, not just by her manner but by the fact that she is stunning. Like, leading lady stunning. And the more that I think about it, the more I think I may have seen her on television.

"I'm so sorry I'm late," she says. "I had to skip out on work, but I couldn't miss this." She leans forward conspiratorially. "I mean, *royalty*. Honestly, Nicholas, you've come up in the world." She hip-checks Nikki, who shakes her head, clearly bemused. "*James*, I'd like you to meet Eliza Tucker. Her sister—"

"—is the PI who rescued the princess from sex traffickers. I swear I want the story. Can you imagine what a coup it would be to do that interview and air it live?"

"Not the time, James," Nikki says.

"Sorry. It's not. I'm Jamie Archer by the way. Well, Jamie Hunter, but I still use Archer professionally."

"*Oh*. Hi." It all falls into place now that I realize she's Ryan's wife.

"Jamie and I have been friends since forever," Nikki explains. "Don't worry. She grows on you."

"Like mold," Jamie says dryly, and I laugh. I like both of them a lot. "Oh, here come the menfolk."

Nikki shakes her head, looking like an exasperated mom, an expression I assume she has down since she and Damien have two little girls, both of whom are apparently staying with their aunt and uncle so as to be out of the way during the party.

As for menfolk, Jamie got that right. In addition to Quincy, I see Damien, Ryan, Prince Michel, two bodyguards, Dallas Sykes, and a man I was earlier introduced to as the FBI agent, Ollie McKee. He'd told Quincy and me that Lassiter was not only in custody, but that he was cooperating fully. It's amazing what the carrot of a minimum security Federal pen will do when the punishment someone is staring at is hard time with the likes of murderers and mafia types.

I assume that the guys are simply coming to join me, Nikki, and Jamie for casual conversation and refreshed drinks. So I'm unprepared when the prince pulls ahead of the pack, marches straight toward me, and says, "You. Tell me about this woman who has absconded with my niece."

"Absconded?" I repeat, looking from the prince to Quincy and then back to the prince. "Excuse me?"

Damien steps forward, then turns and makes the smallest of bows. "I'm sure Prince Michel misspoke. I imagine the word he was looking for was rescued."

The prince crosses his arms. I get the impression he's not corrected often.

He doesn't apologize, but focuses again on me. "She is your sister?"

I nod. "Yes."

"I understand there was a fire. That she kept my niece safe."

"Yes, sir."

"Why has she not made contact again?"

I glance to Quincy, but answer truthfully. "I don't know."

"Where would she go next?"

"I don't know that either."

"Why should I trust that this ... woman ... can keep my niece safe?"

I prickle at his tone and his implications. "I don't think you have much choice, *sir*, considering we don't know where they are."

His eyes narrow, and I'm sure I've angered him, but I can't say I care. I don't like him. And now I feel even sorrier for Ariana. I hope her father's a nicer guy.

The prince stares me down, and then surprises me by

nodding his head, just slightly. "You will accept my apologies. I am concerned for my niece's welfare. We owe your sister a great debt, of course. I simply fear that the longer they stay on their own, the more likely whoever is pursuing them will catch up. I would appreciate, Miss Tucker, if you could reassure me as to your sister's ability to keep my niece safe."

"Oh." Okay, I like him better. "Emma's a survivor, sir. She pretty much raised me. She's taken every martial arts class imaginable, and she's absolutely brilliant. She's been working as a private investigator her entire adult life. And she's very good with kids. She'll take care of the princess, sir. And she'll also keep the poor girl from getting too scared."

I hope he doesn't ask more. I don't know why I didn't mention that Emma worked in intelligence for years. After all, *this* guy must be in intelligence if he's the director of security for his entire country. For that matter, he may already know about Emma. I consider that, fighting the urge to frown. Does he know I'm lying? Or if he does know Emma's secret, would he just assume that I'm in the dark?

I don't know. And all my meandering thoughts have done is reiterate that I am really not cut out for espionage. I can play a spy on television, but that's as far as I want to go with danger and intrigue.

I smile at the prince, hoping it looks natural, then focus on Quincy. Not because he can help me, but because it calms me just to know he's there.

Finally the prince gives another crisp nod. "Thank you for your honesty. I am relieved to know my niece is in good hands."

Ryan had stepped back from the group to check a message on his phone. Now he steps to the front and addresses the prince. "Your highness, we've received word that Marius Corbu is in custody. With luck, we'll know by the end of the day which of his lieutenants kidnapped your niece."

20

"So give," Dallas said as he followed Quince down the path toward Damien's private tennis court. "What's on your mind? By the way, I like Eliza. She's stunning, too. Just like you said, what, three, almost four years ago?"

"Closer to five," Quince said, then sat at the end of one of the lounge chairs set up along the perimeter of the court. Dallas pulled over a folding chair, straddled it like a teenager, and crossed his arms atop the backrest as he regarded Quince, those deep green eyes seeming to see all Quince's secrets.

He and Dallas had been best friends since they were kids at St. Anthony's, a prestigious boarding school just outside of London. Quince had gone there because his guardian found it easier to pack him up and ship him off. And Dallas had been sent all the way from the States because his father was convinced he needed to get his shit together.

They'd been at St. Anthony's, in fact, when Dallas and his sister, Jane, had been kidnapped. Quince had even witnessed the abduction and hadn't been able to do a goddamn thing to stop it.

As an adult, he realized that any attempt would have gotten him killed. As a kid, he'd felt the weight of guilt for years. And though Quince never learned all the gory details, his friend had confided in him enough that Quince knew that Dallas had been tortured. Brutally. Sexually. Emotionally. And that knowledge had only made Quince's guilt that much heavier to bear.

That was one of the reasons why, when Dallas used his inherited billions to found Deliverance, Quince had signed on without question, his only caveat being that he wouldn't betray MI6 by going behind its back. His father had been duplicitous, but Quince sure as hell wouldn't be.

Because of the possibility for additional intel, his handler had agreed, and a complex dual identity had been born, with Quince being one hundred percent loyal to two different entities. With the exception of national security, he fully shared intel. The only thing he didn't share with Dallas, in fact, was what happened during the Berlin mission. He'd told his friend only that it had gone south, he'd been injured, and that he needed to take some time off from Deliverance.

The truth was, he hadn't wanted to burden Dallas with his pain. His friend had already been through so damn much.

But now...

Well, now he looked at Dallas and saw a man who had his shit together with a beautiful wife and a baby on the way. And damned if Quince didn't want to understand how Dallas had pulled himself out of the dark.

"How's Jane?" Quince asked. "I'm sorry she couldn't make it. It's been too long."

Dallas practically lit up. "She's great. Frustrated as hell since the doctor has her on bed rest, but she's a trooper."

"Tell her I said hello."

Dallas shifted his arms so that he could rest his chin on his fist. "I will," he said slowly. "So what happened to you and retirement? For a while there, you were thinking of quitting this crazy lifestyle. Stark make you an offer you couldn't refuse?"

"Pretty much," Quince admitted. "And I did leave MI6. Easier not to have two masters. Mostly I realized I like what I do. And it needs to be done." He'd thought about Shelley. About all the victims he'd helped over the years. And he'd realized he didn't want to leave that behind. The job was hard, but it was also the light that battled the darkness in him. And that, when it got bad, helped to hold back the monster that lived inside him.

"Glad to hear it. You're too good at what you do to sit around doing jigsaw puzzles."

"Well, yes, that was my retirement plan."

Dallas cocked his head. "Are we done now?"

"Done?"

"With the bullshit small talk. Not that I mind catching up with you, but I don't really think chitchat was what you had in mind when you asked me to take a walk."

"No," Quince said. He stood, then shoved his hands in his pockets. "Honestly, I was wondering about Jane."

Dallas's brow furrowed. "Jane?"

"Did it help? Being with her, I mean. Did it help keep the memories away, or did it just make it that much worse."

For a full minute, Dallas said nothing. Then he simply said, "Berlin. Motherfucker, what did they do to you in Berlin?"

Quince sat, his head in his hands, then looked up at his friend. "Did she help?"

"You should have told me back then. Christ, man. Why go through that alone?"

Quince didn't answer. There wasn't a bloody thing he could say at that point. And after a moment, Dallas nodded and stood, taking a few steps and then returning, as if he had to move a bit or go crazy.

"It helped," he finally said, then made a scoffing sound. "Of course, getting together at all was the first hurdle. There are a few complications when you're in love with your sibling." He paused in front of Quince, his head tilted as he studied his friend. "But that was the key. We love each other. Do you love Eliza?"

"Yes," Quince said, realizing how pathetic it was that he was telling Dallas that fundamental truth before telling the woman herself.

"And her? She loves you back?"

"She does." He knew it. He'd always known it. And as far as he was concerned, the fact that she loved him was a minor miracle.

"Well, that's the key. But it's not a magic pill. You have to talk with her. You have to actually communicate. Scary stuff, right?"

Quince chuckled. "You could say that."

Dallas flashed his famous grin, the one that had been on the cover of dozens of magazines over the years. "Speak of the devil," he said, looking over Quince's shoulder.

Quince turned, saw her walking toward them, and felt the warm swell of pleasure curl through him. It was love, all right. For better or worse, Eliza was in his heart.

"Nikki said she saw you two head this direction."

"Do you need me?" He stood.

"Always," she quipped, then turned to look at Dallas, too. "Actually, I was hoping to talk to both of you."

"Fair enough," Dallas said, taking his perch on the chair again as Quince gestured for her to sit on the chaise.

"I, um, well, the truth is I wasn't entirely honest with the prince."

Quince met Dallas's eyes, and saw his own wariness reflected back at him. "Okay," he said slowly. "How so?"

"When he asked about Emma and why she's qualified to take care of Ariana, to keep the princess safe. Well, everything I told him was true. It just wasn't the whole truth." She grimaced. "I just—well, it wasn't my place to say, but there might be a problem." She looked between the two of them. "So I'm going to tell you."

Quince held out his hand, and she took it, flashing him a small, trusting smile as she did so.

"You can tell us anything," he said. "We'll keep your confidence, and we'll deal with it." He looked up at Dallas, who nodded consent. "So what's going on?"

She drew a breath, then said, "We ran away when Emma was fifteen. She—well, she pushed our father down the stairs. We honestly thought he was dead, and we ran. And then we lived on the street for years, bumming rooms in some really dicey neighborhoods, and Emma would do whatever she had to in order to provide for us. I was still pretty little."

Her shoulders rose and fell as she took a breath and looked between them again, as if to see if they were shocked. She must have been okay with what she saw in their faces, because she continued. "Like I said, she did whatever she needed to make sure we were safe, and when she was eighteen, she—well, she killed someone. It was justified, I swear. He would have killed both of us without even blinking. But the cops tagged her, and she had a pretty stuffed juvie record at that point and, I don't know, I guess they wanted to make an example." Her voice broke, and a tear trickled down her cheek.

She squeezed Quince's hand so hard he thought she'd crush his fingers. "They were going for the death penalty. And then, suddenly, all the charges went away. Her lawyer told me it was an evidentiary technicality, and I believed him. I was only eleven, and I was so happy that they weren't taking my sister. But it wasn't a technicality. She didn't have to tell me the truth—she wasn't supposed to tell me—but we've never kept secrets from each other. Not ever."

"They recruited her," Quince said, his voice little more than a whisper.

She nodded. "A black-ops group. Government, but buried deep. I think it's funded by NSC money, but I've never been clear. I just know that they trained her and they paid her well. We had a house. A real life. And she really liked the work, too. It was totally Emma, you know?"

"That's how she became a PI," Dallas guessed. "That was her cover?"

"Exactly. Anyway, she did it for years. Mostly jobs in the US, but some foreign work, too, though she turned those assignments down until I was old enough to take care of myself."

"You said she did it for years," Quince said. "So she quit?"

"A while back. She still does the odd freelance assignment, but she's legitimately a PI now."

"Why are you telling us this?" Dallas asked.

"Because I don't get it. She's on her own. She stumbled across a scheme to auction off a princess to a slavery ring.

The bad guys got really close to her, and she's on the run. And the only one she contacts is Marissa?"

"Why didn't she reach out to some of her old contacts?" Quince said, following her train of thought.

"Exactly. Even if you were completely out of the game, you'd still know how to reach people to help if you were in a jam, wouldn't you?"

He nodded. "No doubt."

"It's a good question," Dallas said slowly, clearly turning it over in his mind. "And I can only think of one reason that makes sense."

"Someone in the intelligence community is on the bad side of this thing," Quince said.

"Exactly." Eliza sat on the chaise, looking relieved to no longer be shouldering this burden alone. "I didn't want to tell the prince unless I was sure."

"Agreed," Dallas said.

Quince nodded. "I'll talk to Ryan and we'll see if we can narrow down a lead, then we can go to him with some solid information."

She sat beside him, then brushed a kiss over his cheek. "Thank you. Thank you both," she added to Dallas.

"No kiss for me?"

"Careful," Quince said as Dallas and Eliza both laughed. He shook his head, bemused. "Since we're discussing Emma's contacts, I'm not sure that she made the right choice reaching out to Marissa."

"Why not?"

"The timing, for one thing. Someone got to that cabin before we did, but the only one who had that message was Marissa."

"But she didn't translate it," Eliza said. "I did."

"And you were surprised she hadn't already managed

that," Quince reminded her. "What if she had? What if she sent the location ahead well before we arrived? You said she's hard up for cash."

"No." Eliza shook her head. "No way. I've known that girl since she was tiny, and Lorenzo is like a father to me. There is no way she would sell us out because her stepfather's being stingy with her allowance."

"People have done even more for less," Dallas said.

"I know her," Eliza said. "You two don't."

"El, think about it."

"I am," she snapped. "Are you? Because not everyone betrays people who are important to them, Quincy. Not everyone is your father."

He flinched, but held his ground. "If it wasn't her, then how did they know about the cabin?"

"I don't know. Somehow."

He held her gaze, and she melted a bit. "I don't do this for a living. How does anyone in this business get information?"

"A bug," Dallas said, and Quincy nodded slowly.

"Possible. We talked. We loaded up the car. They would have only had a short lead, but that fits with the facts."

"See?"

He almost smiled. She looked so earnest. Instead, he pulled out his phone and called the office. "Mario," he said when the young analyst answered. "I need you to get an electronics team to Emma's PI agency. Do a sweep for bugs and call me back."

He wrapped up the call and passed her the phone. "Let Lorenzo know they're coming. Tell him it's just routine."

"Thanks," she said, but to him it sounded like, "I love you."

And that felt pretty damn good.

21

QUINCY'S PHONE rings as we walk into his condo, and he answers it before the second ring, then gives me a quick nod to signal that it's the office. "Thanks, Mario. Right. That's brilliant. You'll handle it? What? Oh, well that's too bad, but I appreciate the heads-up."

I frown. The only reason Mario would be calling is to tell Quincy about the bug search at Lorenzo's. And from this side of the conversation it doesn't sound good. I still can't believe that Marissa is selling information about Emma to sex traffickers, though. That goes against everything I know about her, and I tell Quincy as much the moment he ends the call.

"What?" For a moment he looks confused. Then he grins, pulls me to him, and kisses my forehead. "You were right, love. The place was teeming with bugs. The sweepers left them in place and informed Lorenzo and Marissa. We'd rather the bad guys not know we're onto them yet."

"Oh, right. Good. But then what was too bad?"

"Red's fingerprints," he says. "Turns out there weren't any." He wiggles his own hand. "Acid."

I cringe.

"So that's a dead end, but at least we know there won't be any more leaks about Emma's location through her office."

"Which really isn't a problem," I say, "since we don't have any idea where she got off to."

"Hey." I'm still in his arms, and he tilts my chin up so that I'm looking right at him. "I'm proud of you, love. You pushed for what you believed in, and you're loyal to your friends. I should have listened to you."

"Thanks," I say, ridiculously pleased with his praise. "I appreciate that, but you were doing your job. And part of that job is to be suspicious. Besides, you did listen. That's how they found the bugs."

"Right you are," he says. "We make a great team."

He leads me to one of the bar stools then goes around and enters the kitchen. "Wine?"

"Yes, please." I feel the need to celebrate.

He pours for both of us, then passes me my glass as he leans on the counter across from me. "I listened to more than your suspicions about the bugs," he tells me. "I was listening last night, too."

My chest tightens with a hope I'm afraid to let blossom. "Last night?"

"When you asked if we could try. If we could try to deal with my rages or night terrors or whatever the hell you call the bloody things. If we could try to make it work between us."

I swallow, my fingers so tight on my wine glass I'm surprised I haven't snapped the stem. "You said you didn't know." My voice is little more than a whisper, and I'm afraid to let myself hope.

"I do know. We can try," he says, moving out of the kitchen and circling the bar. He stops in front of me, then twists my stool so I'm facing him. "And we can make it happen. Together."

I hear my pulse beat in my ear. "How?"

The corner of his mouth twitches. "Oh, you want to do the work? I think counseling's on the list. And communication." He brushes my cheek, and I realize that he's wiping away a tear. "Baby steps, okay?"

I nod, too happy to form words.

"I want to get past this," he says. "I want to get past this rage and this darkness so I can be with you. Really be with you. I love you, Eliza. I've loved you for a very long time."

"Quincy, oh God." My voice is thick with tears. "I like hearing that."

"Just hearing?" There's a tease in his voice as his hands slide down to my waist. "I can show you, too."

"Can you?" I hook my arms around his neck and my legs around his waist as he lifts me, cupping my bottom as he carries me to the bedroom. I laugh, then squeal as he tosses me onto the bed, then follows, caging me beneath him, his mouth attacking mine.

"Eliza," he murmurs, as his hands roam over me, and we tug and pull and twist until we're both naked and touching, with lips and hands and a wild passion that makes me laugh with joy and pull him close.

"You feel so good," I tell him. "Oh, God, *that* feels so good."

His hands are roaming all over me. Sliding over my breasts, slipping between my legs. I arch up into his touch, then cry out when his mouth closes over my breast and his teeth scrape my nipple as his fingers slide deep inside me.

I want to surrender completely to him. I crave the sensation of being completely overwhelmed, unable to do anything except fall deep into a sensual assault. But I bite my lip and say nothing. How can I when this feels so good and so right, and I can't risk destroying this moment? Can't risk drawing out the darkness.

And what does it matter, anyway? Because I *am* surrendering. To his touch. To his kisses. To our own shared passion. Baby steps, right? And eventually we'll get there. Back where we were before. Until then, I let myself go, reveling in the knowledge that it's my time to take what I want. "Roll over," I whisper, pushing him as I speak as if in illustration.

His brow rises in amusement, and then with heat once he's on his back and I'm straddling him. I work kisses down his chest, then lower and lower until I take him in my mouth, enjoying the power I'm claiming. But I don't just want the taste of him. I want him inside me. I want the connection, the heat. I lean forward, losing myself in a long, slow kiss before rolling on a condom, then lowering my hips until I'm riding him, and the sensation of being filled by this man I love is almost too much to bear.

"Eliza."

My name sounds like a prayer, and I tremble, arching back as his hands cup my hips, then tighten at my waist as I rock against him. The sensation is so sweet, better still when he slips one of those hands between our bodies and uses his finger to tease my clit. I bite my lower lip, and I'm so close to exploding, and I know that he is, too. And I want it—that final thrust, that brilliant explosion—even while at the same time I never want this feeling to end.

"Eliza, love. Eliza, *fuck,* it's the office."

Only then do I hear the chirp of his phone. A unique ring tone that I understand is the SSA. "Bastards," I mutter, then slide up his body, curling against him as he answers. "Right," he says, sitting up and leaning against the headboard. "And we believe him? The Raven? You're serious? All right. Send them over."

He ends the call and slips the phone back onto the nightstand. "Sorry."

"No, it's okay. Disappointing, sure, but—anyway, was that Ryan? What did he say?"

"Corbu swears he had nothing to do with taking the princess. He says he wouldn't be that much of a damn fool, but he's certain he knows which of his lieutenants would be. He says the man's reckless, he put Corbu's enterprise in danger, and Corbu wants to take him down. He says he'll share information in exchange for clemency."

"Information?"

"His code name. His photo."

"Raven," I say, and he nods. "And the photo?"

"Apparently, it's coming," he says, right as his phone chirps again. I crawl over him to retrieve it, laughing as he smacks my ass lightly.

"Be good," I say.

"You're sure that's what you want?"

I scowl at him, but inside I'm cheering. This is sweet and easy and playful, and I think that maybe we're going to be able to conquer that damn, fucking beast that set up residency in the man I love.

His phone is locked, of course, so I pass it to him, then scoot beside him so we can both see the image. It's a bit blurry, but the guy in the picture is identifiable enough. He's standing in a doorway, his face almost full on to the camera. He has a strong jaw and chin, deep-set eyes, and thick dark eyebrows. He looks Italian. Frankly, he's damn good looking, which seems unfair to me considering we know he's evil.

"Right out of central casting as the sexy bad guy," I say,

expecting Quincy's laughter. Instead, when I look at him, he's pale as a ghost. "Quincy? Quince, what is it?"

He doesn't answer. Instead he hurls his phone across the room, where it shatters against the wall.

I scramble off the bed, taking the top sheet with me without even consciously thinking about it. I just need to be covered. "What?" I say. "Talk to me."

I'm watching him, wary of the rage that overtook him at the beach. But there's no rage right now. All I see is cold calculation.

When he looks at me, his eyes are flat. Emotionless. It's like he's crumbled into himself, and I have no idea what's going on.

"Who's in the picture?" I ask, my voice level and gentle and very afraid.

"A ghost," he says. "A ghost from Berlin. The ghost of a man I killed."

22

RAGE AND FEAR and pain and darkness. They burned inside him, eating him up from the inside out.

Right then, he wanted the monster to rise. Wanted it to consume him. To sniff out the Raven so that Quince could reach down his gullet and rip him apart.

But the monster didn't come.

Half blind, he got out of bed then pulled on his clothes. He didn't know where he was going, he just knew what he was going to do.

He was going to find the bloody prick and he was going to slit his throat.

"*Quince. Quincy. Goddammit, Quincy, look at me.*"

He looked. Through the red haze of memory, he looked at her. And he shook his head. "No."

"The hell you say." She was standing as straight as a soldier, her naked body wrapped in a sheet. She was warm and beautiful and perfect, and in that moment he was certain that he should never have drawn her in again. Never let her get close. Because now they were going to be hurt all over again.

Hurt.

The Raven was going to hurt, too. Quincy would kill him —hell, yeah. But he'd make him suffer first. The monster that lived inside him? For the sake of the Raven, Quincy would happily free the beast.

Except it didn't come. He was too damn numb, and the beast was trapped behind a wall of shock.

"*Quincy.*"

He just shook his head. "I was a bloody fool, wasn't I? Thinking that it had all ended. That I could get past it and you and I could frolic through the world in search of a happy ending. Bollocks to that."

"What are you talking about?"

"I said we could try? How? This is my life. My legacy. And I'll be damned if I'm going to drag you into my torture chamber. I'm not that bloody selfish."

He was talking in circles and he knew it, but dammit he loved her. Couldn't she see that he was cursed? Tormented as a child. Tortured as an adult. And now the ghost of bloody Christmas Past was back to haunt him all over again. It never stopped. He'd never be free of the monster, and she deserved a hell of a lot better than what he could give her. Because until the Raven was dead, he had nothing inside him to give. He had to strip down to the core. Rely on his training.

He had to become a hunter.

He had to finish what he thought he'd already accomplished. Because so long as the Raven was still alive, Quincy would always be a little bit dead inside.

He turned and looked at her again, knowing that he had to apologize, to explain. And damned if she didn't slap his face.

"*Stop it.* Just stop it."

The words burst out of her, harsh and angry. But she didn't cry. She stared him down, her face strong and fierce. "I know you're freaked. I know you're in shock. But you need to focus, Quincy. Because I'm not the problem. In fact, right now, I'm the solution to your problem."

He frowned at her, completely confused. "What are you talking about?"

"If this guy really is still alive—if he's the one who kidnapped the princess—then he's looking for Emma and Ariana right now. So are we. You want to destroy this guy, then we have to set a trap."

The churning in his gut started to calm, and he looked at her, deathly still. "Go on."

"We get them first. We get to Emma and the princess, and then we let him know we have them. A trap."

"He'll never fall for it. He'll know we don't have them, and—"

"No." She shook her head, cutting him off. "No, you're not listening. We get them. Really get them."

He started pacing, feeling more like himself as he worked this problem. "Eliza, you're missing the bigger picture. We don't have them. And we don't know how to get them."

"Yeah," she said with a very smug smile. "I do."

He gaped at her, certain he'd misunderstood. "What are you talking about, love? We've been looking for them for days. Now you know where they are?"

"No, but I know how to find out. It's so obvious I can't believe I didn't see it before."

As far as he was concerned, it wasn't obvious at all, and he told her so.

"It's in the first message she left us. Or that she left Marissa. Remember? *Tell my friend who talks to the animals not to drive angry, but to circle the wagons.* I assumed that the *angry* just meant that we didn't have to drive fast. That we weren't in a hurry."

"Go on."

"I was wrong. Angry Words."

He just shook his head.

"It's one of those phone games. It's a game you play on your phone against other people. It's like Scrabble, but you get extra points if you use curse words. So, you know, *angry words.*"

"I know you're going somewhere with this, but I'm still not seeing it." He was, however, feeling more centered. Calmer. And even though he didn't see how it was going to play out, he could see the beginnings of a path. More than that, his promise to her was starting to seem less foolish. *We can try.* Maybe they could.

Maybe they'd even succeed.

She smiled at him, and that seed of optimism bloomed even more. "Come here," she said, pulling out her phone. "I'll show you."

He watched as she opened the app, then logged out. "I don't know Marissa's username, and in case he's got Emma's phone, I don't want to use my regular account. So I'm going to create a new name and then send her a friend request. Hopefully she'll realize it's me."

"What are you going to use?"

She grinned at him. "Mister Wellington."

It took him a second, but then he remembered the bear she'd had as a child. She created the profile, found Emma's username, and sent the request. They waited, but nothing happened.

"If she's not online, it could take a while." She frowned.

"It's not that late, though. I can't imagine she's asleep. She never—"

Ping!

She met his eyes, and he felt his heart pound in his chest. On screen, there was a picture of linked hands and the words, "Friends Forever."

"Now I can message her."

"And he won't know?"

"He'd have to be logged in as her, have the app open, and be looking at notifications. Even so, I want to be vague."

She typed, *We've got an Angry Words club going. Better chance of winning when u play in a group. Join us? Just need ur location. Playing in person is more fun.*

She showed him the screen. "You think?"

"Give it a try."

He watched as she pressed her lips together, then pressed the button to send the message. They waited. And waited.

And waited.

"She thinks it's a trap," he said.

"Maybe. I need to send her something so that she—"

Ping!

They both stared down at the message: *RL. Have a glass on me.*

Frustration burned through him. "What? Is that her way of telling us to fuck off?" But then he saw that Eliza was grinning.

"Come on," she said. "I know exactly where she is."

————

Exactly turned out to be not exactly true.

"She doesn't know the address," he told Ryan as they

raced from Los Angeles to Redlands, a small town about an hour outside the city at the base of the San Bernardino Mountains. "But she's dead right about the plan." She was in the passenger seat, and he smiled at her, then reached over to squeeze her hand.

"I was only eight," she clarified. "We lived there for about two weeks when we were on the move. But it was an abandoned winery. And there aren't that many in Redlands. It's not really wine country."

"So Emma and the princess are holed up in this winery," Ryan clarified. "We're going to locate and extricate, get them safely back to HQ, and set a trap for the Raven."

"That about sums it up," Quincy said.

"We're doing research now, trying to locate abandoned vineyards. Each team will take a different location. Denise and Liam, Prince Michel and his team. I'll come out to be on site and I'll arrange for extra manpower from the Stark International security force. Keep communications open. And if you see any sign of the Raven or anything suspicious, radio in."

"Roger that."

He ended the call then turned to Eliza. "Anything?"

She was on her phone, poking around on a tourist site. "There's a pretty famous abandoned vineyard, but Emma wouldn't go there. It would be off the grid. Probably not even on the web, or very difficult to find if it is.

"And you don't have a clue."

"Even if I did, the town's changed. More houses, fewer orange groves. Nothing stays the same except—*oh.* There was a graveyard. I played in it. Graveyards stay. And if you walked in through the gate, you were facing the mountains. Which doesn't narrow it down a lot, but—"

"—every little bit helps. See what you can find."

She poked around on her phone some more, then squealed in victory. "Take the next exit, like you're going to Lake Arrowhead. Then you're going to turn left after a few blocks."

While he followed her directions, she called it in, giving Ryan the location of the vineyard they'd be checking so that the other teams wouldn't overlap.

It took another ten minutes of cruising residential streets and weaving down a few dirt roads, but they finally found the graveyard. The vineyard itself had been developed, turned into small, box-like houses. But the sales office still stood, broken and dilapidated, on a large plot of undeveloped land.

The property was gated, but someone had cut through the chain. Emma, most likely, and they pushed open the gate, then drove through slowly.

"Familiar?" He turned to look at Eliza, who was gazing out the window as if she were lost in time.

"Yeah." He could hear the awe in her voice. "It's all coming back. There are huge wine cellars under the house. Like a rabbit warren. I used to explore, and Emma would get so nervous because she couldn't find me. I got locked in one of the cellars once. They have these iron doors—I guess so that the owners could store the high end wines there—and I pulled it shut. It locked automatically. Emma never did find a key."

"How'd you get out?"

"Turns out you could get out, but not in. There was a hidden latch camouflaged in the stone. I found it accidentally. That was the only time Emma ever spanked me. She was so furious."

"More like frantic, I bet."

"True."

After a few more minutes, they found the stone patio that marked where the cellars used to be. "There was a building here before," she said, toeing the ground as they walked around. "It looks like it burned."

"Here's the entrance." He'd found a set of stairs that seemingly led straight into the earth. That, however, was an optical illusion, and once they actually started down, the path turned into a concrete tunnel that led the way into a series of concrete and stone storage rooms. A rabbit warren, just as she'd described.

"She must be down here," Eliza said, her mouth curving into a frown. "Should we split up?"

"Absolutely not." He was already worried about having dragged her into the crossfire, but under the circumstances he hadn't had much choice. But if anything happened to her...

She paused, reaching out to grab his arm. "Did you hear that?"

He cocked his head. "What?"

"Behind us. I thought I heard—"

But he didn't hear what she thought, because instead he heard a throaty female voice saying, "Eliza?"

"Emma!" She ran forward, Quincy at her heels, then launched herself into one of the small cellars. He was a few steps behind, saw her disappear from his sight, and felt his heart skip a beat.

He caught up to her, then relaxed. She was safe in the cave-like room, her arms wrapped around a woman who looked like a slightly older version of Eliza with red hair instead of Eliza's muted chestnut.

They were clutching each other as a petite blonde teenager sat on a wine barrel, her eyes wide and a small smile on her pretty face. A few other barrels were scattered throughout the room, along with a pile of empty wine bottles on the far side of the cellar.

After a moment, Eliza turned to him, her face streaked with tears. "We found them," she said, and he couldn't help but laugh. "Yes," he said, "we did."

"I'm Emma," the redhead said, extending her hand.

"I figured. I'm Quince." She had a firm handshake and a bright smile.

"Yeah, I figured that out, too." Her clothes were dusty and lived in, her face drawn with exhaustion. Even so, she was lovely. And her bright smile erased some of his worries.

She crossed to the girl and took her hand. "This is Princess Ariana."

Quince bowed. "It is a pleasure, your majesty."

The girl smiled brightly, then looked to Eliza, who curtsied. "You're a difficult young woman to find."

"Your sister has been taking good care of me." She spoke with heavily accented English and great composure. "But I would like to see my father now."

"Do you know who did this to you?"

She started to answer, then sat up straight, her eyes going wide.

Quincy turned to see Prince Michel hurrying into the room. "Ariana! Thank God you are safe. Dear girl, your father and I have been so worried."

He took a step into the room, and as he did, the little girl opened her mouth and screamed.

But Quince didn't know if she was afraid of her uncle or the man behind him.

The all-too-familiar man who'd just fired the Glock, straight into the back of the Eustancian prince's head.

23

I HEAR someone screaming and realize it's me.

The world is exploding around me, nothing making sense at all. Except it is. It's like one of those moments in the movies where everything slows down and you can catch all the details. Or like the way survivors describe car wrecks. Everything's crystal clear, but you're not able to stop any of it.

This is exactly like a car wreck. And as it all happens, every tiny detail makes sense. A horrible, awful kind of sense that, maybe, we should have seen coming.

The guy with the gun now pointed at Quincy is the Raven—that's easy enough to figure out since I'd been looking at his picture only hours ago.

And the Raven is one of the men who tortured Quincy. A man Quincy thought he'd killed but who had, somehow, survived.

"I suggest you remove your weapon, Mr. Radcliffe. Because if you don't, I'll put a bullet through your pretty little girlfriend's brain."

My mouth goes dry; I'm certain he means it. And while I

wish I was brave enough to tell Quincy not to comply, I'm
not. I stay silent. I don't want to die. Not right then; not like
that.

Quincy's wearing a plain white T-shirt and it's obvious
he has no shoulder harness. But he does have a small gun in
a holster inside the waistband of his jeans. Slowly, he takes
it out, then squats to put it on the ground.

"Kick it over here."

He kicks it, but the gun slides right past the Raven,
coming to a stop only when it hits the far wall.

"Overshot," Quincy says. "Sorry about that."

The Raven takes a menacing step toward him, and
Quincy glances down at the prince's body. "Why?"

The Raven shrugs. "He was losing his nerve." His words
are slow and thick in my head, as if they were carved in
syrup. "His own idea to punish his bastard of a brother, and
he starts to get sloppy. He would have given himself away
eventually. I did him a favor."

He's looking at Ariana as he speaks, and I think that I
may be the only one in the room who sees Quincy leap. I
want to scream at him to stop, because the Raven still has a
gun, but the words stick in my throat. I'm too afraid that the
Raven will react to my scream, and if he fires it will be
because of my warning.

And then Quincy tackles him, and the gun goes flying.

Immediately, Emma bursts into action. She grabs
Ariana's wrist and yanks her off the barrel, then sprints for
the door. The Raven manages to get free of Quincy and dives
for the gun, and I realize that it's right by my foot. I kick it,
hard, and it slides across the floor.

For a moment, I cheer my victory. But that's premature,
because the Raven launched himself at it, and just as Emma

reaches the door, he reaches the gun. He fires, and Emma goes down, and I scream.

It's her thigh, and I see the pain on her face as she hobbles toward the door, she and Ariana locked together as they try to move toward freedom.

The Raven lifts the gun to fire again, but Quincy lands a solid kick, knocking the gun out of his hand and sending it sliding across the floor and into a drain, dropping so far down it seems to take forever to hit the ground.

Quincy attacks, but the Raven counters and they both tumble, giving Emma and Ariana time to get out of the room.

"Go!" Quincy calls. "Shut the door!"

Emma stumbles, sickeningly pale. But her gaze finds me. The Raven is on top of Quincy, pushing himself up to his knees. There's clearly no way I can beat the Raven to the door, and so I tell her to shut the door and call for help. She stumbles again, and Ariana grabs her, then kicks the door firmly closed.

The bottom of the door is solid, and that means I can no longer see them. All I can do is pray that Ariana gets Emma outside and that there's a medic to treat her.

In the meantime, I have to fight.

For a moment, everything seems to freeze. Then the world snaps back into real time and I go from feeling like an observer to being very much in the middle of all of this. And completely terrified.

Except it turns out that my terror isn't complete after all. Because there's still room for more, something I find out when Quincy catches my eye. He starts to stand and the Raven lashes out with a hard, fast kick, connecting with Quincy's head and sending him tumbling back to the ground. I wait for him to get up, but he doesn't move.

That's it. He's unconscious—and, honestly, I'm terrified that he's dead, but I can't dwell on that question because the Raven is now coming toward me. Walking slowly and with menace. I've worked on plenty of action movies and this isn't the way it's supposed to happen. Trained spies who are the good guys don't get taken out with one blow. Evil bad guys do not get to win.

But apparently life doesn't imitate art, and I'm left to wonder how—if the Raven managed to knock out Quincy—I'm going to have any chance at all.

I've got only one option—get the hell out. And if I'm going to get to the hidden latch, I have to cross almost the entire cellar without the Raven grabbing me. Even then it's not ideal, because either the Raven will manage to escape with me, or else I'll end up locking him in with Quincy. But if I'm free I can help. Inside, I'm just a victim that Quincy will try to protect. Assuming he ever wakes up.

Please, please wake up.

I glance around, plotting the best course. I decide to race to the side and grab a wine bottle to use as a weapon, then make a run for the hidden latch. He'll know where it is, of course, but I don't see a way around that. And I need to get out. I need to check on Emma. I need to get help for Quincy. And if I stay in here, I know damn well I'll end up dead. Or worse.

Before I can talk myself out of it, I bolt toward the cluster of wine bottles. I smash one, turning the raw end into a weapon. I don't know why I expected that to slow him down. He charges me anyway, and I hurl my broken bottle, hitting him but not slowing him at all.

I reach for more, practically losing my mind as I throw bottle after bottle at him. He dodges them, and they shatter on the floor. He barely slows, and when I finally have had enough and make a break for the door, he dives for me, grabs me around the waist, and sends us both tumbling to the ground.

I thrust my hands out automatically to break my fall, and then scream in pain as I land on dozens of shards of glass that cut deep welts into my hands.

"Bitch," he says, and before I can even react, his arm is around my neck and I'm struggling to breath as he drags me across the room. I kick, but each kick is weaker than the next one, and soon the world turns grayer and grayer until it's nothing more than a deep curtain of black, and my last, lingering thought is that I haven't said goodbye to Emma or Quince.

24

QUINCE FELL in and out of consciousness as the world shifted and moved, and his battered body screamed in protest. His mind was fuzzy, but he realized that he was being dragged across the floor, the broken glass beneath him tearing into his skin. His wrists were bound behind his back, and as he tested the bonds and felt the sharp edge of hard plastic, he realized that he'd been bound with cable ties. He struggled, but it was no use. The ties held fast.

The Raven grunted, hunched over with his hands under Quince's arms as he pulled him, leaving Quince's useless hands to drag. Or maybe not so useless.

He clutched at the debris on the ground as it slipped by, taking care not to show his pleasure when his fingers caught a shard of glass.

He hoped it would be enough.

He hoped the Raven wouldn't notice it.

When they reached the far side of the cellar, the Raven dumped him, then stood up and stretched. Quince groaned, intentionally loud, and he pressed the shard into the indention where the floor met the wall.

In front of him, the Raven crouched. "You should have killed me right the first time. Because now it's not only you I'm going to fuck with, it's your girlfriend. Pretty thing. But I don't think she's going to look quite so pretty when she's dead."

"You even think about touching her, and I'll kill you," Quince promised.

The Raven pressed his fingers to his mouth. "Oh! Too late! That's all I'm thinking about. How I'm going to do it. How I'm going to make it hurt. I'll probably fuck her, too. Just because I can. But don't worry—I'll let you watch."

Quince hauled back and spit in his face.

The Raven wiped it away impassively. "Not very nice. I'll remember that when your turn comes. And it will come. I won't kill you fast. Not even close."

"They'll find us here," Eliza said, her voice groggy, but at least Quince knew that she'd come to. "You won't get away with it."

"Don't be stupid," he said. "I'm part of the team, remember? And this vineyard is off the grid. Going to take them a while to find it. Plenty of time for your sister to bleed out. For you two to die. And for me to be the last victim of his highness. Pity he snapped like that. Jealous of his brother. Decided to sell his niece. Then had to take us all out to cover his crimes. I only barely survived."

He pressed a hand to his ear. "What's that? You say that Ariana knows the truth? She does. She saw me kill her uncle, the man who arranged for her sale. Lots of witnesses to back that up. And then she saw me defend myself. Of course she was scared, poor little thing. But I wasn't going to hurt her. I was trying to rescue her."

"Bullshit," Eliza said, and Quince felt a surge of pride. She was a fighter, that's for damn sure.

"That's not very nice." He stood and walked to her, scooping up a piece of glass along the way. "I think you need a lesson in manners."

Quince saw the fear in her eyes and struggled to rise, but his legs were tied together as well. He could only watch, helpless, as the Raven cut off her shirt and then, very slowly, started to make shallow cuts along her belly.

He heard her whimper, and the sound almost killed him, but he stayed silent, watching as she squeezed her eyes shut, his fingers grappling for his own piece of glass. Twisting it in his grip. Then scraping it like a saw over the ties that bound his wrists.

There was no way to accomplish the feat without slicing his own skin, and he bit the inside of his cheek in defense against the rising, raw pain. He worked as fast as he could, but carefully, too. It was one thing to draw blood, but if he accidentally cut his wrist too deep, he'd be no help to anyone, much less Eliza.

Again and again he sawed at the zip-tie. And again and again the Raven taunted Eliza.

Almost there, love. He wanted to scream the words. Wanted to tell her that he would never even think about leaving her again. That he was wrong to think he had to do this first. Fight this battle. Wage war against the pain he'd suffered and the dark inside him.

On the contrary, she was what gave him the strength to get through it. Now, in the horror of this prison. And every day, when the memories rose.

His only regret was realizing that truth now, when he might never get the chance to tell her. Show her.

No.

He'd get free. He'd kill the Raven. And they'd walk out of this room together.

He just had to keep going.

"So pretty," the Raven said, stepping back from Eliza's body so that Quince could see the red lines that crisscrossed her abdomen. Her eyes were on his, and he could see the pain. But also strength. *Good girl*, he thought. *Just hold on a little longer.*

"Should I fuck her now?" the Raven asked. "Or should I carve my name on her face? Hard decisions, but I think I'll fuck her. And I think you need to watch."

On the wall, Eliza struggled. Quince did the same, the reaction instinctive. But as he fisted his hands and lashed out, he felt the snap as the ties he'd been sawing broke from the force of his violent response.

He allowed himself a second to rejoice before returning to reality. Because his legs were still bound and he couldn't cut those ties without giving himself away. Which left him at a decided disadvantage.

Unless...

He started to scoot along the wall, trying to remember where the gun had landed. Across the room, Eliza had her eyes screwed shut as the Raven dragged a shard of glass down to her sex. *Christ, was he going to mutilate her?*

"I'll fucking kill you," he said, just to get the tosser's attention.

It worked. The prick turned, glowered at him, then opened his eyes in surprise. Quince still had his hands behind him, but he'd inched down the wall. And the Raven had to know his destination.

"Not too bright are you? Grab a gun with your hands tied like that and you'll probably shoot your own ass off. Not to worry. I'll save you from temptation."

He stepped away from Eliza—thank God—and started toward Quince. "Naughty, naughty."

Quincy waited. He was weak and sore and battered, and that meant he couldn't be sure of his aim. He needed to be dead-on. Which meant he had to risk waiting.

One step toward him, then another. The Raven flashed that vile smile. Silently promising Quince unendurable pain.

"I'll just get that gun out of your way. Don't want you playing with naughty toys, do we?"

He bent over as he came closer, and as he did, Quince thrust out his arm, his fingers closing over the handle of his small Ruger. He twisted, aimed, and got off three to the chest.

If the whole situation wasn't so horrible, the expression on the Raven's face as he fell forward would have been comical. Blood pumped out of him as his heart pounded out its last few beats. Then the Raven stilled, his blood spreading.

The bloody bastard was dead.

As fast as he could, Quince used his shard of glass to cut through the ties around his ankles, calling out to Eliza as he did, telling her he'd be right there.

He pulled his phone free and saw that there was no signal, which meant the team couldn't track them. Hopefully Emma was okay. With luck, she'd gotten clear of the cellar and even now Ryan and the others were arriving with a full medical team.

But he couldn't worry about that now. Right then all he wanted was to get Eliza free. And he stumbled to where the Raven had bound her to a built-in wine rack, then gently cut the zip-ties to release her. Her wounds weren't deep, and he rejoiced in that one small blessing as he peeled off his shirt and then carefully covered her.

"I love you," she said, her voice slurred with exhaustion

but her words filling his heart to bursting. "I'm so damn tired."

"Shock," he told her. "It's okay. I've got you. And Eliza, love, I promise, I'm never letting you go again."

EPILOGUE

QUINCE WOKE to sound of children laughing and the feel of a naked woman in his arms. Slowly, he slid his hand over her waist and hip, careful not to touch her injured belly.

Eliza sighed and wriggled against him. "Nice way to wake up," she murmured. "Will be even nicer when I can move without pain."

"You'll get there," he said. "We both will."

He sat up, intending to go relax by the pool with some coffee. Stark and Nikki had insisted that Emma, Ariana, Eliza, and Quince stay on the property overnight, along with the doctor he'd brought in to treat them. Emma and Ariana had stayed in the actual house, while Quince and Eliza had been given the guest house.

Now, they both dressed quickly and headed to the pool where Ariana was in the water with the Starks' daughters, Lara and Anne. Emma was by the pool, her thigh thoroughly bandaged and a promise from the doctor that she would make a full recovery.

Ryan had ordered a full briefing that morning, and

Denny was already present. Liam was probably inside, as he was perpetually prompt.

"I'm going to go get a coffee," Eliza said. "Bring you one?"

"I'll get it for you," he said.

"Nope. I can manage. It's the least I can do for my hero." She bent over and kissed him, long and slow, then pulled back with a grin. "Once I'm healed I can do more than that, too."

He laughed. "Fair enough. For now, it's coffee and kisses."

While she went inside, he sat down by Denny, who shot him a bright smile.

"I'm so glad you two are together," she said. "You were meant to be, you know."

"I do," he said. "And I'm determined not to blow it. We're even doing counseling. First session next Thursday."

"Good for you. I'm really happy for you."

He believed her, but he couldn't ignore her melancholy tone. He pressed his hand over hers. "Are you okay?"

She blinked quickly, then nodded. "Just melancholy. I love you, and you're one of my best friends, so don't take this the wrong way, but I miss Mason so much, and right now I'm so goddamn jealous I can't see straight."

"I'm sorry, Denny. I wish I could give him back to you."

She nodded. "I know." She twisted around and pointed toward the door where Eliza was emerging with a tray. "Looks like she brought coffee for everyone. You should give her a hand."

He recognized it as a dismissal, and did as she suggested.

"Is Denny okay?" Eliza asked as he took the tray.

"Lonely," he said, and saw the compassion on her face.

She smiled up at him. "Just goes to show you. We can never take anything for granted."

"Never," he said. "That's a promise."

She followed him as he took the tray to the table beside Emma, then they settled in two of the empty chairs beside her in the shade of the patio umbrella.

"When do you leave?" he asked. Despite her injury, Emma had insisted on escorting Ariana home that afternoon, on temporary assignment to the SSA.

"Not for a few more hours. It's nice to just chill after yesterday."

"That it is. Still, if you feel the need for a little more excitement in your life…"

He let it hang out there; he knew that Ryan had already talked to Emma about recruiting her.

She laughed. "You people are relentless."

"Maybe we just know talent when we see it. You'd make a great team member."

"I'm not really a team player." She shot a glance toward her sister. "But if I were, this would be a pretty good place."

Behind them, he heard Denny's phone ring, and she stood up, then crossed to the far side of the patio to take the call.

A few moments later, she returned, looking more than a little shell-shocked.

Eliza stood, going immediately to her side. "Denny? What's wrong?"

"That was Colonel Seagrave," she said, her voice thin. Shocked. "Mason's boss."

She lifted her face, her eyes not quite focused as she looked around the group. "Mason's back," she said. "And he doesn't have a clue who he is."

The End

SHADOWS OF YOU

SHADOWS
OF YOU
J. KENNER
NEW YORK TIMES BESTSELLING AUTHOR

CONTENTS

A NOTE FROM JK

This story first appeared in an anthology that I participated in with several other authors. The *Be Mine* anthology was only for our newsletter subscribers and included entirely original content.

At the time, I had no more plans for Mason and Denny (who had a "walk on" role in *Lost With Me* and, later, *Damien*), but I fell so in love with the characters that their story spoke to me, and I knew that they had to be a big part of Stark Security.

You can read their story now in, *Broken With You* (the next part in this anthology), without reading this prequel ... but why would you? So just keep flipping pages!

XXOO
   JK

1

I GAPE at the closed circuit image on my terminal, completely flabbergasted by the extent of my assigned agent-candidate's idiocy. "Left! I said *left*."

I stare at the screen, then I throw up my hands in surrender as Agent Idiot turns to the right. "*Left*," I repeat into the microphone. "Your *other* left."

He immediately corrects, which is more than I can say for some of the applicants I've tested, and continues through the course. When he gets to the ordnance area, I pull off my headset and lean back in my chair, glad to be passing him off to another unfortunate operations manager.

"A little frustrated?"

The male voice is smooth and deep, and I turn in my chair to find myself staring at my immediate boss, Ryan Hunter, the Security Chief for Stark International. He's tall and lean with chestnut hair and patient blue eyes. More patient than my green ones, I fear. Especially today.

"Sometimes I wonder where you find these candidates."

"That's why we call it an evaluation." I hear the humor

in his voice, and I sigh loudly as he pulls out the chair at the empty station beside mine. He sits, his elbows on his knees as he looks earnestly at me.

"What are you doing, Denise?"

I've worked for Ryan for years, and we've become good friends. I adore his wife, and I know that they're both genuine, caring, talented people. Honestly, I couldn't have found a better place to work.

But that doesn't mean I want to be coddled. Especially not today when I'm feeling particularly raw.

"I'm just doing my job, Mr. Hunter."

One of his brows rises almost imperceptibly. He's no fool. He knows he's treading on dangerous ground. But Ryan doesn't pull his punches where his friends are concerned. And as much as I want to just go home and sleep straight through this horrible night, I know he's not letting me out of here until he says his piece.

"You should be in the field," he says. "Not operating a desk. Not putting agent candidates through their paces." Stark International has a private security force, the highest level being the newly formed Stark Security, which is where I'm currently assigned. At all levels of the organization, though, the security officers are called agents. And with Ryan at the helm and Damien Stark overseeing the entire organization, the team is at least as well-trained as any government operative.

I should know. I used to be one of those government operatives before I signed on for field work at Stark International. But that feels like a lifetime ago.

"I like what I'm doing," I say, unable to silence the defensive note in my voice. "We both know how burnt out on field work I became. And this way I can—"

"What?"

I shake my head. "Nothing. Have a life. A normal schedule."

"Review confidential files? Tap into international resources? Monitor communications channels?"

I swallow, but say nothing. Just hold my body stiff. I didn't realize he knew how much I've been using—and abusing—corporate resources.

He watches me, then sighs. "Dammit, Denny," he says, calling me by the same nickname that Mason used to use. "Why didn't you just come talk to me?"

I lift a shoulder. How can I tell him that I'm drowning. It's been two years. Two long, lonely years since my husband went on a deep cover assignment. I haven't heard a word since the day he walked away. Not a postcard. Not a phone call. Not a single rose on my birthday. Just days upon days of empty, lonely hours. And today is one of the hardest days of the year. Not only Valentine's Day, but also our anniversary.

"I don't even know if he's dead or alive."

My voice is so low that I'm not even sure Ryan hears me. But he takes my hands in his, then leans forward earnestly, looking me in the eye. "We tried to find him."

"What? Who?"

"Damien and I. We used all our resources. Put out feelers to every government agency we could contact. Reached out to mercenary organizations, anyone and everyone. I'd hoped he'd get wind. Figure out a way to reach out to you. I'm sorry, but we didn't hear a word back." He exhales, and I hear genuine regret in his voice. "We all know you're hurting, Denise. And we're all your friends."

I lick my lips, fighting back tears. I'm not going to cry in front of my boss. That is just not happening.

"You know you're not happy in this work. He wouldn't want you stuck at a desk. It's not you."

I lift a shoulder. "Honestly, I don't know. Maybe it's the me I've become. But I can't think about it now. Not today of all days."

"I'm sorry."

I nod, knowing he means it. I try to conjure a smile, but it's just not in me. "Thank you," I say. "Tell Jamie I said hi. Do you guys have big plans for Valentine's Day?"

"We're using a company limo to go down to La Jolla for dinner. But I'll be back at work tomorrow. I better not see you. You need to take a day off."

I make a face, but I also nod. I can see he's serious.

He passes me an envelope. "And here. From Damien and me."

I frown, confused. "What is it?"

He just cocks his head.

"Sorry. Stupid question." I rip open the envelope and find a hotel card key with a room number scrawled across it with a Sharpie.

"The penthouse," he says, looking up. The agent monitoring station is deep in a sub-basement of the Stark Century Hotel, forty-six floors above us.

"I don't understand."

"We thought you needed to be pampered. Actually, it was Jamie and Nikki's idea," he adds, referring to his and Damien's respective wives. He glances at his watch. "You should get up there if you want some time to yourself before the appointment."

"Appointment?"

"At seven. According to the girls, a massage is just the thing to help you relax. I hope they're right."

Despite myself, I smile. If I can't have Mason, I can at least lose myself in a good, hard, relaxing massage. And then I can fall asleep watching a sappy movie on the big screen knowing that, at the very least, I'm blessed enough to have some truly incredible friends.

2

Despite working in the basement for years, I've never actually been in the penthouse, and when I step through the double doors, I gasp. I'm facing a wall of floor to ceiling windows, the lights of the city stretching out toward the dark, moon-dappled Pacific beyond.

It's as if I'm floating in a calm, dark world, and already I feel more at peace. I want Mason desperately. I miss the man who was—*is*—husband, lover, and friend. But he has uncommon skills, and I know that he's doing important work. That doesn't make it better, not really. But maybe it makes it easier to bear. And the fact that I have friends holding me up when times get tough …

Well, that definitely helps. As do the roses that fill the room, their beauty and their scent making me smile. They are everywhere. Vases on the table tops, and petals on the bed and floating on the surface of the already drawn bath.

There are even petals on a silver tray on which sits a chilled bottle of Pinot Grigio, my favorite.

I'm definitely feeling pampered.

The only thing that would make it better would be

Mason beside me. And since that's not happening, I may as well enjoy myself.

I pour a glass of wine, then glance at my watch as I explore the suite. It's almost seven, so I don't have much time before my massage. But as I wander through the spacious, well-appointed rooms, I consider my options for the rest of the night. There's a television over the deep tub as well as one mounted opposite the bed. So the question is, do I watch in a bubble bath or snuggled up in the soft cotton sheets?

And, of course, the bigger question of sweet romance or soft-core porn. Because if I let my mind wander to Mason while I'm getting my massage, I just might be in the mood for the latter.

A girl gets lonely after two years, and I'm not the type to stray. Not as long as I believe he's out there and that he's coming back to me.

I take a sip and sigh.

Maybe I'll mix it up. A bath and an orgasm. Then bed and a sweet movie as I fall into my dreams.

I'm thinking that actually sounds pretty good when the doorbell chimes. I hurry that direction, and open the door to a fifty-something woman in a severe white uniform. "I'm Melisse," she says. "I'm here to get you prepped."

My brows rise. *Prepped*? It sounds like a surgical procedure. And when she rolls in a high-tech looking massage table, I wonder if maybe I've misunderstood what Ryan and the gang planned. "Trust me. The Master is the best. You will be very relaxed."

"The Master? I'm not sure this is—"

"Trust me," she says firmly. "There is no pressure. You can terminate the session at any time." She finishes setting up the table, then spreads the sheet over the top.

"Should I go change?"

"In a minute," she says, passing me a spa robe from a duffel she brought with her. "The massage package that was selected for you is the sensory immersion experience. So when you return, we'll put on your aromatherapy blindfold."

"Blindfold?" I've spent too many years in intelligence. I'm not sure that I like the idea of being naked under a sheet and blindfolded. Even if it is for an incredible massage experience.

"Please. Mrs. Stark and Mrs. Hunter selected this package. I assure you, it is a favorite."

I take a deep breath, then nod. I trust Nikki and Jamie completely. If they say this is the way to experience a massage, then who am I to argue?

Melisse hands me the robe, then nods toward the bathroom. Dutifully, I head in that direction. I strip, slide on the fluffy robe, take a deep breath, and return. The last time I had a really good massage was from Mason, who has the best hands of anyone I know. We'll see if this Master can top him.

Melissa turns to give me privacy, and I climb onto the table and cover myself with a sheet. She adjusts it, then ties the blindfold over my eyes. I can't say I like the sensation of being so vulnerable, but I take calming breaths and remind myself that this encounter was orchestrated by my friends.

I hear a tap on the door, followed by Melisse's footsteps heading that direction. The soft exchange of a conversation, and then the heavier tread of a man's footsteps.

"Melisse?"

I feel the pressure of a large hand on my back through the sheet, and then the brush of air as it's pulled down, exposing my back and shoulders. "Shh," a man says. "Melisse is gone."

My breath freezes in my throat. I know that voice. Oh, God, I *know* that voice.

"Mason?" His name is barely more than breath. I must be wrong. Surely I'm wrong. But he doesn't correct me. And when his large hands spread out on my shoulders, a rush of memories overwhelms me, so palpable I'm surprised I don't pass out.

I lift an arm, determined to rip off the blindfold, but he holds it down. "No."

"Please. Please," I beg. "I have to see you. It is you. Isn't it?"

"Relax. Just relax." He takes my arm and moves it to the edge of the wide massage table. Before I realize what's happening, he's cuffed my wrist to the bed. I struggle, but he's too quick, and soon my other wrist is bound as well.

"I'm sorry," he says. "The blindfold is important, and I can't risk you removing it. But if you don't like it, I can unstrap you and leave. It's up to you."

"Is it really you? Your voice. Please tell me. Mason, is it you?" I hear the desperation in my voice. The growing need. I want to know, and yet I also understand. If it is him, he must have learned of Ryan and Damien's efforts to locate him. He couldn't come officially, and so he came surreptitiously. I've worked in intelligence long enough to know that he could have learned of the massage gift and twisted the appointment around to his advantage. It wouldn't be hard at all

If it is him, he's breaking all sorts of rules to be here.

And if it's not him ... well, maybe just for tonight, I need to believe the fantasy.

I draw in a breath. "I don't want you to go."

"Good," he says, and then focuses those miraculous fingers on the tight muscles of my back, working and kneading. Warming me. Exciting me.

Lower and lower his hands go, until he's so close that I'm certain he's going to trail his fingertip down the crack of my ass. He doesn't, though. Instead, he comes just close enough to tease, then moves down the table to my ankles.

I gasp when he ties them to the table as well. "What are you doing? I can't take off the blindfold with my toes."

He slides his hands up my body, then brushes his mouth against my ear. "You're beautiful," he says. "I want you open for me. I want to see you when I touch you. I want to watch your cunt. I want to see your arousal. I want you wet for me, and I want to know that you want me, too. That you crave me. Crave *this*."

I swallow, telling myself again that this must be Mason. But damn me, part of me doesn't care. I'm too aroused by his touch and his raw, evocative words. And too lost in the fantasy. Even if he's only a shadow of my memory, a manifestation of my desire, I want the touch he's offering.

I feel a tear trickle down my cheek. Sweet and melancholy. I miss being touched like this. I want Mason, yes. But I *need* this.

Slowly, he strokes me. Warm hands moving over my calves. Fingertips teasing my inner thighs. My body responds. My sex throbbing. I know I'm wet. Desperate. And when his fingers gently part my folds, I gasp with both surprise and pleasure.

He slips a finger inside me, then another and another. He fills me with slow, sensual thrusts, then teases my clit with one hand as he traces a path from my pussy to my ass, making me writhe with desire, longing for a rough touch along with the sweet caresses.

"Please," I beg. I shouldn't want it. I don't even really know that it's him. But I do. I want him inside me. I want to feel the weight of him above me and his cock filling me. I want his mouth on my breast, his teeth scraping my nipple. I want the man, the fantasy, the sensation. I want to lose myself in pleasure. And so help me, I'm not too proud to beg.

"I shouldn't," he says. "It's too risky."

"What is?"

"You. Seeing me. It's not safe."

I bite my lip, trying to make sense of those words. Is he in disguise? Has he changed his appearance? Is he no longer dark-haired with deep-set brown eyes accenting a face highlighted with a cleft chin? It would make sense. How else could he get so close without anyone recognizing him? And how better to stay deep undercover for two years, getting lost from even the likes of Damien Stark's exhaustive resources.

"Plastic surgery?" I ask, and am not surprised when he stays silent.

"I need your word," he says. "The blindfold stays on."

"Yes." *It is him. It must be him.*

He moves quickly to release my wrists and ankles, and I think that he must be as eager as I am. I'm true to my word, and I don't touch the blindfold as he gently lifts me, then carries me to the bedroom. I'm not expecting it, but he ties my wrists to the headboard, and when I murmur a protest, he says only, "It's for your protection as well as mine. If you see me—if they find out—then you're a liability."

I want to ask what he means. I want details of what he's doing. But the questions don't come. They leave my head like so much fluff as his mouth closes over mine, and we kiss, hot and wild and with such familiar abandon that my doubts fade almost entirely away. *This must be Mason. It must. It must.*

"Dear God, you taste like Heaven," he says. "Like sweet memories and warm chocolate."

I laugh, because isn't that just the kind of thing Mason would say?

But the laugher dies in my throat as his mouth closes over my breast. His teeth scraping my nipple, making me arch up toward him. "That's it, baby. Tell me what you want."

"Fuck me," I say boldly. "Please, I want you inside me."

His fingers cup my sex, thrusting slowly in and out. "Like this?"

I shake my head. "I want your cock. Please, Mason. I want to feel you explode in me."

Thank God I don't have to beg. I hear the rustle of material as he strips, then the weight of him above me. His cock rubs against my belly and I writhe against him, anxious. "Please. Now. Hard." I haven't been fucked in years, and I want it wild. I want to be taken. I want the full fantasy that this night is giving me.

He understands—when hasn't Mason understood me? —and I feel the pressure of his cock against my entrance, then the sharp sweet pain as he thrusts inside, forcing my body to yield to him.

I cry out, and as he moves rhythmically inside me, he muffles my cries with his mouth.

I wrap my legs around him, using my muscles to push him in harder, deeper, until I don't know where he ends and I begin. All I know is that right now, in this moment at least, he *is* Mason. He has to be. Because no one but my husband could make me feel this good.

I'm unprepared for the force of the orgasm when it

finally takes me. I arch up, my muscles squeezing him tight so that he explodes inside me. Finally, my body goes slack, the tension easing out of me as every muscles turns soft and heavy.

"That was perfect," I say, as he spoons against me.

"*You're* perfect," he replies, and I smile sleepily as I snuggle my back against his chest. Gently, he strokes my arm. "Sleep now."

I don't want to, but I can't fight the heaviness in my eyes. "Will you be here when I wake up?"

He kisses my shoulder, but he doesn't answer, and I know that means he'll be gone.

I want to beg him to stay. I want to tell him we can run away. Hide somewhere. Be together.

I want to ask him if this fantasy was real. If *he* is real.

But I don't. I'm too tired. Fading too fast.

And maybe, just maybe, I'm afraid of the answer.

3

As I'd both feared and expected, I wake alone.

I explore the penthouse, but he's not there, and the massage table is gone, along with the robe and other paraphernalia.

There's nothing left but my memory. That, and a single rose on the dining table, laying across a sheet of white paper.

The note is written in block printing, and I can't tell if it's Mason's handwriting or not.

But I smile as I read the note:

 Lovely Denny,

Thank you for the night. For fueling my heart with new memories. For reminding me that there are things to live for and fight for. Things that burn hotter than a shooting star and last longer than eternity.

We will, I think, see each other again, though I cannot say when or where. But I will hold onto last night and the pleasure we shared.

Don't look for me. Don't try to find me. Don't ask questions to which you don't truly want the answers.

For the time being, last night was enough.

Yours,

The Master

I pick up the note and press it against my heart, holding the memories close. I think he was Mason, the man who always spoke to me of stars and eternity. I hope he was. But in the end, it doesn't matter. The man—The Master—gave me back hope, along with a fresh taste of joy.

And for now, I think, that is enough.

———

Keep reading! There's more to Denny and Mason's story!

BROKEN WITH YOU

BROKEN
WITH **YOU**
J. KENNER
NEW YORK TIMES BESTSELLING AUTHOR

CONTENTS

PREFACE

Faith is a tricky thing. Faith in people. In the universe.

Faith that at the end of the day, the power of good will overcome the power of evil.

I've managed to keep that faith through my entire life, even when the world was battering me like a raft on a stormy sea. Loss, pain, heartache—through it all, I somehow managed to hold tight to my unflappable optimism.

But that was before.

Now ... well, now is harder.

Now, I stare down loss and loneliness on a daily basis. Now, I look back over the last two years and wonder how I've managed to survive without him.

Now, I fear that he's never coming home. The man I love. The husband I need.

I know I must stay positive. I understand that I should keep hoping.

"Have faith," they all say, and I try. I really do.

But the truth is that my faith in the universe disappeared along with my husband.

And I'm terrified that I've lost both forever.

1

Darkness.

For an eternity, that's all there was. Just darkness. A void. An empty hole where nothing existed. Not even him, whoever the hell he was.

There was comfort in the dark. As if he was wrapped in a womb. Safe now. Not like before.

Before?

Strands of emotion, the precursors of thought, twisted inside him. There'd been pain in the before time. So much pain. Like fire in his gut. Like glass in his eyes.

How long had he suffered, his mind screaming, his body so exhausted that death would have been a welcome relief?

He didn't know. For that matter, maybe death *had* come to release him. Or maybe none of it had happened yet, and his pain wasn't a memory but a forewarning.

He didn't know. He was simply *there*—no longer attached to time, to space, to anything. He was free. Not hot or cold. Neither happy nor sad. He was secure in the comfort of simply being, and it seemed as though he could stay that way, safe and warm and content—for all eternity.

Except...

Except there was something hidden beneath the calm acceptance of this new reality.

Something important. Something urgent.

A secret? A task?

It was right there, at the edge of his memory, but every time he grasped for it, it slipped away. He shouldn't— couldn't—let it go. But how could he follow? How could he leave this safe, warm place?

He longed to stay forever. Secure and comfortable and free.

And yet at the same time he didn't. He wanted more. He wanted...

He didn't know what.

He just knew that something was nagging at him. Something he missed. Something he craved.

Her.

A shock of awareness cut through him, along with a jolt of something he recognized as fear. And loss. And regret.

Mischievous green eyes flashed in his mind's eye. Warm laughter teased him even as soft strands of golden-blond hair brushed against his skin.

She was his—and he yearned for her with a longing so intense it bordered on pain. Urgency roiled within him. Danger. Terror. Those dark secrets that he needed to—

No!

Oh God oh God oh God, please no.

His body—his *being*—lurched, trying to reach her. Trying to battle back the horror that was looming, coming faster and faster. But he couldn't see it. He couldn't fight it. All he could do was sink into the whirlpool of disconnected, incomprehensible voices and images that were suddenly swirling around him, thick and fast and hot.

Where is it?

You might as well tell us?

Nothing to go home to. Nothing at all.

But there was. *She* was there. His life. His woman.

He had to get back to her.

Back? There's nothing for you back there. She's dead. I fucked her, then I killed her.

His body burst apart from the force of his scream, but the relentless, horrible words wouldn't stop.

Do you know why she's dead? Because you went to her. You told some useless cunt our secrets.

Beep-beep!

We had to punish you. Had to show you that we can always get to you.

His mind was spinning, trying to remember. To see her. To feel her.

To save her.

Remember, dammit. Remember the roadrunner. They can't kill the roadrunner.

But he couldn't move. Couldn't think. Couldn't do anything but exist in this cold, dark limbo as more voices assaulted him.

It's all your fault.

Your friend? I was never your friend.

It's not a tunnel. Just a black hole painted on rock.

32355 5-null 717

That won't help you anymore. Not anymore, you wily sonofabitch.

You think he's the only one? Damn naive considering your reputation.

Guess you're not made of brick or stone after all, are you fucker?

Beep-beep.

Wily? Maybe once, but you're not wily anymore.

Again and again, the flat, emotionless voices pounded against him as he struggled to find himself. To understand. But there was nothing. Only the words and the nonsensical images of numbers floating against a black background as a variety of tones beeped in his head.

32355 5-null 717

Beep-beep!

Most of all, there was fear. A cold, harsh terror that ran through him like ice, freezing his blood, making his skin prickle.

His blood? His skin?

Slowly, realization came. He was returning. Heading back from wherever he'd gone. Going back to the pain. The hell.

Mostly, though, he was going back to her...

————

The first thing he noticed when he woke was the cold. An icy blast from a wall mounted air-conditioner. An ancient unit with white plastic strings streaming from it, flapping in the frigid air.

He sat up, realized he was naked, and pulled the dingy, gray sheet up to his hips. There was no blanket, and the thin sheet did little to relieve the chill. His palms stung as he clutched the sheet, and when he looked down at them, he saw that the heels of both hands were abraded, as if he'd fallen onto something rough, like asphalt or gravel.

Maybe he'd been in an accident? Thrown from a car? A motorcycle?

He didn't know.

Squinting against a violent headache, he let his gaze

sweep over the rest of the room, looking for—what?

Something, anything, that would tell him where he was and what had happened to him.

And, most of all, who in God's name *he* was.

Because right then, he didn't have a clue.

A cold shaft of panic impaled him, and he fought against it, determined not to lose his shit. Not when control, reason, and observation were all he had going for him.

Observation first.

He cast his gaze around the room. A pair of threadbare jeans hung over the back of a straight-back desk chair. He stood, planning to walk toward them, but was forced to clutch the bedside table as his head dipped and swam.

What the hell was wrong with him? Had he gone on a bender? Been involved in a drunk driving incident?

He didn't remember, but he didn't think so. He didn't think he was a man who'd drink to excess.

Was he?

Christ, what the hell was going on?

He drew in a breath and ordered himself to be calm, not actually believing he'd get anywhere with such nonsense. But to his surprise, it worked. As if something in him was programmed to focus. As if this was just one more problem he could tackle.

Hell, yeah, he could.

He took another step, relieved when the room seemed to spin a bit less this time. He hadn't passed out drunk—he was certain of it. Considering his vertigo and queasiness, that would actually be a reasonable guess, but the evidence suggested otherwise. There was no smell to his breath. No fuzzy sensation on his tongue. He hadn't vomited that he could tell, and he didn't need to. He didn't need to piss, either.

Without any evidence that he was lost in the mother of all hangovers, he moved methodically on to the next option. But after running his fingers through his short hair and over his scalp, he found no bumps or abrasions.

So not a head injury. *Strike two.*

He thought of his red, raw hands. Something more sinister, then?

He shivered a bit, certain he was right. He didn't know why he was so sure, but at the moment he didn't know much of anything. If intuition was knocking, then he'd damn well open the door.

He continued to the chair, but didn't stop. He just ran the tips of his fingers over the filthy denim. He glanced at the dust that attached to his fingertips, but since he had no explanation, he pushed the questions away. His head was clearing, and he needed to focus on what he did know. Solid facts based on his surroundings, not to mention any memories those facts might provoke.

He'd start with himself.

The bathroom door was ajar and he stepped over the threshold into a small but surprisingly clean bathroom with a porcelain basin on four thin chrome legs, a fiberglass bathtub with a clear plastic shower curtain, and a toilet with a dingy brown mineral stain at the waterline.

The only mirror hung above the sink. A fogged-up piece of shit glass with a long crack marking off one corner. But it was large and mounted in a way that tilted down, so that he could see his head and his hips at the same time. And if he backed up, he could see even more.

He looked, his dark brown eyes taking in the image reflected back at him. His left brow was broken by a scar—probably a knife wound—but a quick check confirmed that his vision was fine in both eyes. The question of why someone had come at his face with a knife was one that would have to wait.

He focused next on his body as a whole. His chest and abs were rock hard, but laced with scars, most white, but some still slightly pink. None tender, though, and he assumed that even the newest was several months old.

The same couldn't be said of his neck, where five fresh, circular scars rose from his skin in a jagged line down from under his jaw to his collarbone. Cigar burns, maybe?

He filed the possibility away to contemplate later. This was a time for inspection, not for opining about why someone would hold a lit cigar against his flesh.

Still, he had to acknowledge that the wounds didn't hurt, despite two of them clearly bordering on infection. Which meant that he was in shock or someone had drugged him and the effects still lingered.

He didn't know, but he assumed the latter. Especially considering the odd, frenetic quality of those dreams he couldn't quite recapture.

Once again, he mentally filed the question and returned to his assessment.

He guessed himself to be about thirty-seven years old, and since he had the kind of body a man only got by working out regularly, that gave him a solid bit of information about himself. From his position facing the mirror, he could see that he had a tribal band tattooed on his left arm and something else inked on his right, though he was at the wrong angle to make out the design. He didn't bother turning for a better view. All in good time, and right then he needed to be as methodical as possible. Anything detail could be a clue to his identity. Any wound or bruise might bring back a flood of memories.

His dark hair was short, but still long enough to be

sleep-tousled. An ungroomed beard suggested he hadn't picked up a razor in ages, and that lined up with his sense that he'd been passed out for days.

He turned his attention to his hands. Notwithstanding the scrapes, they were strong, and his fingers were calloused. He wore no wedding ring and had no tan line suggesting that a ring had once been there. That thought made him pause, as a glint of green eyes and golden hair flashed in his mind. *His dream.*

Was she real? A girlfriend? Sister?

Was she in danger?

In the dream, someone had been speaking to him, saying vile things about a woman. But who?

Try as he might, he couldn't recall the dream. Damn frustrating, but it would come back eventually. And he had more than enough to worry about at the moment.

Drawing in a breath, he continued his self-inventory. His teeth were white and mostly even, so he'd probably had money for braces as a kid. But his nose was crooked, and he guessed it had been broken more than once. Possibly sports, possibly fights.

Considering the scars that decorated his chest, abs, and eyebrow, his money was on fights.

He turned sideways, and once the tattoo came into view, the crisscross of scars over his body made more sense. It was a skull wearing a green beret on what looked like a coat of arms. The words *de oppresso liber* filled the space at the bottom. He recognized it, though he didn't remember the circumstances around him getting it.

The Special Forces motto.

So he was a soldier. Or he had been. And though he didn't remember one minute of combat, knowing that he was part of that brotherhood gave him some comfort. And it proved what he already felt in his gut—that he could take care of himself, no matter what the world threw at him next.

Based on the man he saw in the mirror, it seemed that the world abused him regularly.

Christ. What had he been into? And who the fuck was he?

A wave of panic crested over him and for a moment he let it sweep him away. He let himself wallow in fear and self-pity, losing himself in the black hole of his mind.

And then he turned that shit off. He had more pressing things to do than wallow. He didn't have a memory? Fine. That was his starting point.

So, first question: what did his lack of memory tell him?

That something had happened to him.

Okay, but what?

Best guess—trauma. Either physical or emotional.

As for which, he didn't care. For the moment, the question was academic. Either way, he was dealing with the same blank slate.

The situation stank, but God knew it could be a hell of a lot worse. He'd once watched a movie about a guy with no short term memory at all. He'd had to tattoo himself to hold on to facts. Great flick—*Memento*, it was called.

And goddamned if he didn't remember *that*. He had some memories, at least. He remembered the names of the planets and the months of the year. He knew how to read. And he remembered that Luke Skywalker was Darth Vader's son.

He didn't have a fucking clue what the names of the elements on the Periodic Table were, but at least he remembered there *was* a Periodic Table. And he had a feeling he'd never known the elements, anyway.

So his mind worked. To a point.

His name, his age, his background? As for *those* facts, he

was completely at a loss. But he'd get it back, damn right he would.

And if he didn't ... well, he'd coped with shit situations before. Not that he could remember any of them, but there was a certainty in his gut and the evidence was on his body. He might not know who he was, but he damn well knew *what* he was. And he wasn't the kind of man who curled up into a fucking ball and whimpered.

A sharp rap sounded on the door, and he spun around, his right hand crossing over to his left side as he reached for a holstered weapon.

For a moment, he froze in that position. Then he slowly pulled his hand back and repeated the motion, a smile breaking across his face.

Muscle memory. Three cheers for muscle memory.

A key rattled in the lock, and he sprinted across the room and practically threw himself against the door before whoever was rattling that key could enter.

"Who is it?" His voice came out raspy, as if he hadn't spoken in months. He coughed, then tried again. "Who's there?"

"Housekeeping. I clean room, yes?"

He shifted, then peered through the peephole at the wisp of a woman standing next to a rolling cart. Behind her, a battered Toyota was parked in front of the door. His?

He didn't know.

All he knew was that she wasn't coming in. "It's fine," he said. "I've got everything I need."

Not the truth, but not exactly a lie, either. He had air in his lungs and a beating heart, didn't he?

"Okey-dokey, mister," she said, then pushed on toward the next room. He stayed at the peephole, his attention now on the Toyota's plates. California.

Frowning, he returned to the desk, then grabbed the jeans and shook them, sending dust flurries into the air and a pair of navy blue boxer briefs tumbling to the floor. He scooped them up, sniffed them, then shrugged and put them on, following the underwear with the jeans.

In addition to being filthy, the jeans were a mess. Ripped at the knees and not in a way that was fashionable. More like he'd taken a nasty fall.

He looked at his palms, looked at his knees, and as he did, he remembered. Not everything. Not his life. Not even his name.

But it was something.

Darkness. And motion.

He was blindfolded in some sort of moving vehicle, probably a cargo truck, his ankles tied together and his hands tight behind his back. He was listening, trying to gather as much information as possible, but there was nothing. Just heat and motion. And that was all he knew. Literally, all. It was as if he had been born into that moment, fully adult, and into that truck. There were things he remembered, yes. But not him. *Whoever he was, he'd just popped into existence. A blank slate. An empty jar.*

But he was aware now...

The truck bumped and rattled—and then it screeched to a stop.

A door rumbled up, and light seeped in around the edges of his blindfold. Strong hands grabbed him, pulling him to his feet and making him stumble forward. He was standing—he must have been right about it being a cargo truck—and then he heard the sound of a blade slicing through cord. His ankles were freed first, then his wrists. And before he could react, the truck started to move.

At the same time, someone shoved him from behind, and he

fell onto the rough, hot asphalt, his hands thrust out to break his fall.

He turned, yanking off the blindfold and squinting into the sun, as someone in a black T-shirt and jeans rolled the truck door down from the inside as the vehicle peeled away, careening down the deserted highway toward the horizon.

In the motel room, his memories flooded back. Nothing before the truck, but now he recalled the feel of the road beneath his hands, the sun beating down on him as he walked for miles, the relief of finally coming across this shitty little godsend of a motel.

He'd stumbled into the office, found a hundred and fifty dollars in his pocket, and bought six bottles of water, five cans of mixed nuts, and three Hershey's bars. Then he'd booked a room for two nights.

That left him with just over thirty dollars, which he remembered shoving back into his jeans.

He'd had no identification, but the woman behind the counter hadn't seemed to care. He'd registered as Jack Sawyer. He couldn't remember his name—or anything about his own life from before the ride in the truck—but he did remember the television show, *Lost*, and he'd claimed those two characters' names for his own.

Now here he was, Jack Sawyer, in a shitty motel with no memory at all. His whole goddamn world was this tiny room and these filthy clothes. And wasn't that a happy notion?

He shook his head, tamping down on the fear and frustration that was returning. Yes, it sucked, but at least he was alive. And he was going to stay that way.

Resolved, he tugged on the T-shirt. Originally white, the shirt was now a dingy gray with sweat stains under the arms and at the back of the collar.

A pair of dark brown loafers peeked out from under the desk, and he shoved his feet into them, unable to find any socks. At the same time, he patted himself down, his hands searching the pockets of the jeans and the seams, just in case there was something sewn in. But he found nothing except the thirty-three dollars he'd received in change and a room key with 107 etched on it.

Finding no help on his own person, he searched the desk and bureau drawers, but the drawers were empty except for a Bible, a Book of Mormon, a black pen, and a takeout menu for a pizza place in Victorville, California.

His stomach growled, and he started to reach for the phone to order something, then decided against it. Thirty dollars wouldn't last long. Better to stick with what was in the room.

He popped nuts as he paced, analyzing his next steps. His fevered dreams still lingered, but the words had no more clarity than they'd had while he was sleeping. Less, even. In his dreams, he'd felt trapped, but not confused. Now, the strange words and threats and cartoon references were just nonsense, the numbers even more so.

Without anything else to write on, he pulled out the menu, then scribbled what he remembered: *32355 5-null 717*

Presumably, the word "null" meant zero, so he crossed out what he wrote and started over: *32355 50 717*

Still nonsense, and he scowled at the numbers and their refusal to provide him any information whatsoever.

But, fine. The numbers meant nothing to him? Then he'd start somewhere else. He knew that something had happened to him, and after that mysterious interlude, he'd been blindfolded and bound, pushed from a truck in the desert heat, and abandoned.

Not a scenario he wished to repeat, and since he had no

idea whether his captors had truly abandoned him, he intended to be ready if they returned.

In other words, he needed a weapon.

He could splinter a drawer and use a length of wood, but he had a feeling the nice lady in the office would frown on that. Instead, he returned to the bathroom, then tugged the key out of his pocket. He shoved the end between the mirror's frame and the glass in the lower right corner, then gently pried. As he'd hoped, the crack was both long and deep, and as he increased the gap between the frame and the mirror, he was able to pop it out, an icicle-shaped piece of the mirror, about five inches long.

Just what he needed. Because he sure as hell didn't know what to expect when he walked out the door.

He wrapped one raw edge in toilet paper, forming a makeshift handle, then shoved the whole thing deep in the pocket of his jeans as he crossed to the door. He opened it slowly, then stepped hard into a wall of heat.

The sidewalk was clear on both sides, and only a few empty cars dotted the parking area as heat shimmers rose off the asphalt. The world was a fucking inferno, but all things considered, that seemed apropos. Hadn't he been tossed right out of the frying pan and into the fire?

A sign that looked like it hadn't been updated since the fifties sat perched atop vertical steel poles and identified the rundown little motel as the Stay-A-While Motor Inn. Hopefully that was only a suggestion, because he wanted to get out of there sooner rather than later.

He walked down the sidewalk toward the sign, passing the pastel colored doors along the way. Green, room 106. Blue, room 105. Yellow, room 104.

This path was familiar, and there was some comfort in that.

At the same time, having the full extent of his remembered life marked by the Easter egg colors of a half dozen doors wasn't exactly enough to have him jumping for joy.

The same woman was in the office. About sixty with Lucille Ball hair—he remembered *I Love Lucy!*

She smiled at him from behind a counter. "Well, you're looking much better today. Got yourself some sleep, I guess?"

"I did," he said, then cleared his throat as he glanced around the room. "You got a bus schedule?"

She shook her head. "Sorry, no. Where you heading?"

"Just meandering," he said, as if he was Jack Reacher, and it was perfectly normal to wander aimlessly around the country.

"Well, let me see if I can find a schedule online for you." She inched toward a computer that looked to be older than he was, but stopped midway down the counter to answer the phone as she rummaged through a drawer.

He cocked his head, his hand sliding into his pocket as his senses went on high alert.

The phone.

He relaxed.

Of course. He should have realized immediately. The numbers. They were a phone number. 323-555-0717.

"Oh, good, I found it," she said after ending the call. She pulled a crumpled brochure from a drawer. "So the Greyhound station's not too far away. That what you're looking for? Or did you want local routes?"

"Greyhound," he said, thinking of the 323 area code. "I need to make a phone call. And then I think I'll head to Los Angeles."

"Friends there?"

"I guess I'll find out."

2

BACK IN HIS ROOM, Jack sat at the edge of the bed, the old-fashioned keypad phone in his lap as he held onto the handset, which was tethered to the base by the curlicue cord.

He didn't know who, if anyone, would be at the other end of that number. The only thing he knew for certain was that he knew nothing else. He was a blank slate with this one, scribbled note on it.

So dial the fucking phone, Jack.

He lifted his hand, then hesitated. What if it was a trap? A memory deliberately put into his mind.

But to what end?

Refuse to call, and he denied them the satisfaction of seeing their plan succeed.

But what if there was no plan? What if they were done with him, and they'd tossed him out onto the highway with no memories and no resources, fully expecting that was the last they'd see of Jack Sawyer, or of the man who'd come before?

Then again, if they'd wanted him dead, why not just kill him? Why stuff cash in his pocket and leave him alive?

If he refused to dial, he might be screwing them, but he'd definitely be screwing himself.

And, goddammit, right then the possibility of finding even the smallest clue about the man he was before outweighed every other consideration. A trap? Maybe. But he'd survived worse. Or, at least, he'd probably survived worse. He was a scarred-up, badass member of the Special Forces. Or so he assumed. At a minimum, he should be able to make a phone call without triggering Armageddon.

In his hand, the dial tone changed to a squawking wail. He tapped the switch hook, tucked the handset between his ear and his shoulder, and dialed the number that had been running through his head.

On the other end, the phone rang twice before an efficient male voice came on the line. "Monrovia Travel Adventures. Are you a client?"

"Ah, yeah."

"Your user name, please."

He hung up. Wrong fucking number. Either that or he'd misremembered the number.

Frustrated, he stood and paced and re-ran the nonsensical dream through his mind again. Nonsensical being the operative word. Cartoons and disembodied voices and random phrases and numbers that wouldn't make sense to anyone.

Except...

With a frown, he turned and looked at the phone. Maybe they did make sense. In the world of Ethan Hunt and Jason Bourne, those nonsense phrases might make a lot of sense.

Not that he was Bourne, but maybe ... just maybe...

He dialed again, and this time the call was answered by a woman. When she asked for his username, he took a shot in the dark, having parsed through all the nonsense in his head to find the most likely handle.

"Road Runner," he said, hoping to hell he was right.

For a moment, there was only silence. Then her voice returned, curt and crisp. "Hold, please."

He held, his gut churning. He wasn't sure what he'd just done, but he was certain that he'd set wheels in motion. But whether that was a good thing or a bad thing, he really didn't know.

The line clicked, and this time the speaker was male. "Pass phrase?"

He started to speak, his posture straightening as if he was reporting for duty. As if this was a familiar routine. At one time, he assumed, it had been.

Today, he didn't have a clue.

"Pass phrase?"

"I'm sorry, I—"

"Please state your name, your location."

"Victorville," he said. "I need to speak to someone in charge. It's urgent."

For a moment, there was silence. "This office utilizes certain protocols. This call will be terminated in five, four—"

"*Wait.* Something's happened. I can't tell you the pass phrase because I can't remember it. I've been drugged or brainwashed, or I don't know. Just let me speak to your superior."

Silence.

Mountains and mountains of silence.

Then, "I'm sorry, sir. Protocol requires that—"

"Wile E. Coyote! Looney Tunes! Beep-beep!" He

sounded like an idiot. "Shit, I don't know. Who is this? Who am I calling?"

"Hold, please."

The dispassionate voice disappeared, replaced by a rhythmic ticking in lieu of hold music. For what felt like an eternity, he simply held the line.

He was about to give up and start the process all over again when he heard a series of clicks followed by a gravelly voice saying, "Good God, Road Runner. Where are you? What's your status?"

He started to answer. He actually started to open his mouth and spill everything to the man with concern in his voice. Then rational thought returned, and he said, "Why don't we start with who you are."

Silence. Just long enough to be noticeable. He'd surprised the guy. Good. Jack was getting tired of being the only one behind the curve.

"I'm Colonel Anderson Seagrave. And right now, I'm the only one willing to trust you." The words were stern, but not hostile.

"Because I didn't know the pass phrase."

"Didn't you?"

Good point. He must have rattled off the correct one—or at least come close enough to pique this colonel's curiosity.

"No," he said, figuring it was better to be all in or all out. "I took an educated guess."

"I see." The voice had tightened, and when he spoke again, Jack heard a dangerous edge. "And how exactly did you manage to get so well-educated?"

"You mean did I beat the shit out of someone to learn the secret handshake?" He knew he was being ballsy, but this guy was a colonel. That meant military, the government, some sort of heavy shit. And no way was Jack strolling into that environment like some meek little lost puppy. He'd lost ninety-nine percent of himself; he was damn well going to cling to that final one percent like grim, fucking death.

"Something like that," Seagrave said. "So you tell me—are you the Road Runner? Or have you just poked around in his mind?"

Jack closed his eyes, then pinched the bridge of his nose between his thumb and forefinger. Moment of truth time. Hopefully, this wouldn't prove to be the biggest mistake of his life.

The good news, at least, was that he couldn't recall any bigger mistakes to compare it with.

"Truth?"

"In this business, that would be nice for a change."

"Fine, then maybe you can tell me who and what I am. Because I haven't got a goddamn clue."

He waited, anticipating an explosive response. A series of verbal slaps to put him in his place for playing such stupid games with someone who was obviously well positioned in the intelligence community. Jack may not know his pass phrase, but he knew the hallmarks of a covert intelligence operation that managed agents in the field.

Whether he was still a soldier or not, he was certain that he was some sort of intelligence officer. What he didn't know was if this guy was a friend or someone who'd screw him over six ways from Sunday.

"Can you?" he demanded, as the silence lingered—and this time he was certain it was a tactic. "Can you tell me who the hell I am?"

"I think so," Seagrave said. "I may even know what happened to you. Some of it, anyway."

"I'm all ears."

"Hmm. Have you been calling yourself something?"

"Not for long," he admitted. "As far as I can tell, my world began when I woke up a few hours ago. With a little bit of a prologue before that. The exciting kind with a mystery thrown in."

"A mystery?"

"I've been calling myself Jack," he said, ignoring Seagrave's unstated request for the details of Jack's ignominious dive from the back of the truck. "Jack Sawyer."

Seagrave burst out laughing, and the sound was so real —and so damn familiar—that Jack found himself chuckling, too.

"Why doesn't that surprise me?" Seagrave asked.

"Under the circumstances, I'm the wrong one to ask." He was getting pretty quick with amnesia-laced repartee.

"You were a huge fan of *Lost* back in the day. Used to watch it with—"

"With?"

"Me," Seagrave said, though Jack was certain he heard a lie in the man's voice. "We'd drink beer and watch the absurdity."

"So we were friends."

"I hope we still are."

"Then tell me who I am."

"I can't do that. Not right now."

Jack tensed. "Why not."

"Because you might not be my friend anymore. And if that's the case, I don't want to give you anything more to work with."

"Fuck." At some point he'd stood without realizing it and started pacing. Now, he sat. "We need to meet. Face to face. I need to see you to know if I trust you. And apparently you need the same thing."

"Where are you?"

"Doesn't matter. Just tell me where to go in LA and I'll meet you."

"Better if we extract you and bring you in."

"Not going to happen," Jack said.

"Why not?"

"Because right now, I'm a man with no friends. I don't know who I am or who did this to me. So you tell me straight—do you really think that I would trust you with my location?"

"I'm sorry, Jack. And you're right. I never thought you'd give me your address."

As Seagrave spoke, a steady *thump-thump* filled the air, and the cardboard walls of the tiny motel room started to shake.

"Christ," Jack whispered. "What have you done?"

"I swear no one will harm you. Just let them take you in."

He didn't bother answering. Just ended the call, his mind whirring. His hand went to the swathed end of the mirror shard, and he clutched it tight, ready to slice or stab.

But that was a pipe dream. He could already tell from the increasing volume that this wasn't one lone helicopter. These were military choppers, and his best guess was at least five of them. Probably two in the parking lot, one in the air, and two behind his room.

One bit of a broken mirror and his scathing wit were hardly going to hold them at bay. Which meant he had a choice. He could cower in the room and try to fight them off, or he could open the door, walk out onto the sidewalk, and accept the next step of what was turning into a most unusual adventure.

3

SO HERE'S the salient fact of the day: I, Denise Ellen Marshall Walker, am a horrible person.

Or at least a very screwed up one.

I must be, right? Because here I am soaking up the sunshine in one of the most posh backyards in all of California, and instead of thinking, *wow, lucky me to have such amazing friends and colleagues,* I'm seething with envy.

Not about the house, although no one could blame me for that. After all, this is Damien Stark's Malibu property, and that man does nothing half-assed. I can't prove it, but I'm ninety percent sure he imported the sunshine along with the patio's gorgeous Italian flagstones.

But no, it's not real estate that's turning me the color of Elphaba. Instead, it's my partner, Quince, and his girlfriend, Eliza, who are holding hands and looking like they could eat each other up. And why not? They've finally gotten back together after an interlude long enough for dinosaurs to evolve all the way to extinction. But am I happy for them?

Oh, please. Of course, I am. I'm screwed up, but I'm not a bitch.

I *am* happy for them.

I'm also sick with jealousy, and hating myself because of it. But the simple truth is that I don't have the patience to wait for another era to pass. I want my husband back. I haven't seen Mason in over two years. Not since he left on a deep-cover assignment, and I miss him so much that sometimes I'm afraid I'm going to curl up and die just from the pain of my loneliness.

I'm pushing through, though. My friends help. My work helps. And my certainty that he's out there—that he still wants and misses me—helps, too.

But none of that helps enough to dull the knife-edge of jealousy when I witness a happy reunion.

And today, I'm pretty much drowning in a sea of happy.

If it were just Quince and Eliza, maybe I wouldn't be such a basket case. But the point of this day is to celebrate the successful wrap-up of a Stark Security case, along with the impending reunion of a European princess with her extremely relieved royal father.

The Stark Security Agency is a relatively new division of Stark International, a huge conglomerate owned by former tennis player turned entrepreneurial billionaire Damien Stark and operated by Ryan Hunter, who used to head up Stark International's corporate security.

Formed after Stark's youngest daughter was kidnapped, the SSA is staffed by some serious badasses, most of whom left other law enforcement or intelligence jobs because they believe in Stark's mandate of providing help where it's needed, no matter how big or small the job.

I'm one of those badasses now, having left my covert government job a while back. I'm not feeling particularly tough right now, though. Instead, I'm moody and lonely and jealous. Because everyone else is celebrating, and I just feel lost.

Really not one of my finer moments, and I force myself to look away in case either Eliza or Quince notices my melancholy expression and it puts a damper on their happiness.

Frankly, it's a good decision, because once I shift my attention to the pool, it becomes much harder to remain melancholy. Not when dark-haired little Lara Stark is splashing water on her giggling younger sister, all while the recently rescued princess tries half-heartedly to interest both Stark girls in the colorful pool noodles.

From the opposite side of the pool, Eliza's sister, Emma, is watching the girls as well, a smile crinkling the corners of her eyes. She's in a tank top and shorts, her thigh tightly bandaged after yesterday's battle.

Only yesterday.

Honestly, it already seems so far away, and the despicable truth is that I want another case. And soon. Even though that means that there's someone in trouble. I want it, because without it, I don't know how I can keep my thoughts from wandering back to Mason, or my heart from breaking into pieces all over again.

Damn. I wipe my damp eyes and hope no one notices. I really should have worn my sunglasses...

The thought still lingers when I realize that Quince is coming my way. I'm desperately in love with my husband, but that doesn't mean I don't appreciate a good-looking man, and Quince definitely qualifies. He's British, which is really neither here nor there, but that awesome accent definitely adds to the appeal of his dark, lean looks. He has an edgy, dangerous air, but at his core, he's one of the kindest men I know. And the most loyal.

Most of all, he's completely smitten with Eliza. Honestly, it's kind of adorable.

As he approaches, I look past him for her, then realize that she's disappeared. Probably inside the house where Nikki, Damien, and the rest of this morning's crew have gone for coffee and a buffet-style breakfast.

"So, we did it," he says as he sits on the edge of my chaise.

"You and Eliza?" I quip as I scoot over to make room for him. "I should hope so, the way you two have been making puppy dog eyes at each other for the last few days."

"Funny girl," he retorts, but he's grinning so I know that he doesn't mind me teasing him. He knows perfectly well that I adore Eliza and think they make a terrific couple. "I want to hear it straight from you."

"Hear what?" I'm genuinely confused.

"That you and I make a great team, and you're going to stay in the field and not decide this was a one-off and go back to riding a computer."

I make a scoffing noise, as if he's saying the most ridiculous thing. But he's not. After all, that's what I'd done right before we met. I'd been so morose at Mason's long absence that I'd left my government assignment and taken Ryan up on his offer to recruit me over to his security team. But I'd refused field assignments.

Quince is the one who convinced me to get back in the field. We worked a bit together during the Stark kidnapping investigation and hit it off, probably because both of us were walking around under the same dark cloud. Whatever the reason, we ended up as friends, and the assignment that we just wrapped marked our first official job as partners.

"No way you're getting rid of me now," I tell him honestly.

His brows rise. "Now?"

"Sure." I flash a mischievous smile. "Now that you're with Eliza. That means I have someone I can gossip to about all your annoying habits."

"Ah, well, then I guess it's lucky that there's not a single bloody thing about me that's annoying."

"Yeah," I say, deadpan. "Lucky."

We share a grin, and then I reach out and put my hand over his, which is resting on the chaise cushion. "I'm so glad you two are together," I tell him sincerely. "You were meant to be, you know."

"I do," he said. "And I'm determined not to blow it. We're even doing counseling. First session next Thursday."

"Good for you," I say, wondering if maybe I should try that, too. Maybe I could learn how to fill this cavern that's growing in my soul. I shake the thought away; this moment isn't about me.

He shifts his hand so that he can close his fingers around mine and gives them a gentle squeeze. "Can you tell me what's wrong?"

Such a simple question, but it's said with so much genuine concern that my eyes water, and I have to blink away tears. "Just melancholy. I love you, and you're one of my best friends, so don't take this the wrong way, but I'm so goddamn jealous I can't see straight."

"I'm sorry, Denny. I wish I could give him back to you."

"I know," I say with a nod, and even though Quince has always called me by the nickname that Mason tagged me with, this morning, that name makes me want to burst into tears.

Over Quince's shoulder, I see Eliza step through the open doorway, a tray full of coffee cups in her hands. I point toward her, suddenly desperate for a few moments alone.

"Looks like she brought coffee for everyone. You should give her a hand."

"I'll bring you a cup."

I shake my head as he stands, and his brows rise in surprise because he knows damn well I'm addicted to the stuff. "I think I caught a bug. My stomach's been rebelling when I have coffee on an empty stomach. I'll grab some food soon," I say before he can offer to bring me that as well.

"Fair enough," he says, obviously hearing my underlying plea that he leave. Most of the time I'm doing just fine—truly. But today, with the celebration and the love and—

I sniff and blink and will myself not to cry as I watch him stride toward Eliza, and my breath hitches at the way she lights up upon seeing him.

I swallow. Must. Stop. This.

Seriously, I have got to stop feeling sorry for myself. But, dammit, I don't know what's happened to him. I don't know if he's safe. I don't even know if he's alive, although surely I'd feel the pain in my heart if he'd already left this world.

The only thing I know—or think I know—is that four months ago, I thought—

"Born in the USA..."

My phone's ringtone is both loud and totally unexpected —because that particular Springsteen song is assigned to my former boss, Colonel Anderson Seagrave. I snatch my phone up eagerly, then answer with a mix of hope and trepidation. Because Seagrave is still Mason's boss.

"Have you heard anything?" I ask without preamble. I know it's not his assistant making the call. Anderson's a busy man, but he wouldn't do that to me; he knows too well that I'm desperate for news about my husband.

"Denise." He clears his throat. "We need to talk."

———

"Where is he?" I see no sign of my husband as I peer into what looks like a nice studio apartment, but is really a secure, government hospital room. The walls are painted a soothing beige, made even calmer by framed landscape paintings that are artfully arranged on the walls.

"He'll be back soon," Seagrave assures me, but all I can do is shake my head. Mason might come back into the room, but he won't really be back. Not if what Seagrave told me on the phone is true.

"This will be hard for you to hear," he'd said, and my body had turned to ice.

"He's dead." I was sure of it. Seagrave's the commander of the Western Division of the ultra-secret Sensitive Operations Command. He's a good man, but highly placed. And he doesn't have time to call about routine matters.

"No, no," Seagrave's rebuttal spilled out, breaking through the rising hum in my ears. "He's alive. But he's lost his memory."

I made a strangled sound, then immediately looked down at the flagstone patio, not wanting Quince or anyone else at the party to notice my expression. "His—what? What exactly do you mean?"

"He doesn't know who he is. He doesn't know who I am."

"And me?" My heart was pounding so hard I could barely hear his response.

"I'm sorry, Agent Marshall," he'd said, the reference to my professional title obviously intended to shore me up emotionally. "But he doesn't know you, either."

I don't remember ending the call. I don't remember talking to anyone, but I must have, because Quince and Eliza drove me into downtown Los Angeles.

I'd managed to gather myself during the drive, but I'm still in shock. Slightly queasy. Cold, despite Quince loaning me an oversized sweat jacket that he'd found in the back of his immaculate black Range Rover.

Most of all, I'm in denial.

Because despite what Seagrave told me about Mason remembering nothing about his life or me, I'm absolutely, one hundred percent certain that the moment he sees me, it will all flood back. Maybe not work. But me. Him. *Us.*

Considering what he and I share—the intensity of our relationship, the strength of our bond—how could any other result be possible?

And yet doubt still niggles at my soul...

Now, I draw a deep breath and focus on the room that has been my husband's home for almost a week. I'm still angry that Seagrave didn't contact me right away, but those emotions will get me nowhere, and I've pushed them out of sight, hidden them in the trash can of my mind where I store all useless facts.

Instead, I let my gaze play hopscotch around the room, wishing that he were in there at this moment. But all I see are the furnishings. A dresser, a small writing desk, a kitchenette, a bed. The IV rack and monitors mark the only clue that this room is anything out of the ordinary.

That, and this window made of one-way glass. From Mason's perspective, it's a full-length mirror next to the bathroom. I wonder if Mason remembers enough about his past life and career to realize that's total bullshit.

The thought makes me frown, and I glance at Seagrave. He's looking into the room, too, but he must feel my eyes on him because he tilts his head up, then wheels himself slightly backward so that we can face each other more directly.

He's in his mid-forties with an easy smile and dark hair that's already graying at the temples. I don't know how he lost the use of his legs, but I heard through the grapevine that it wasn't in battle, though he's seen more than his share of action.

He's efficient, fair, and a natural leader. I would have happily worked under him forever had it not been for Mason's disappearance. I'd wanted to head up an extraction team. Seagrave not only flatly refused to authorize the mission, but also denied me any lead or clue as to Mason's whereabouts. Continent. Country. City. I had no clue where to start, which meant that even a vigilante-style extraction would have been impossible.

I respected his decision—truly. But I resented it, too. And as the months dragged on, I couldn't stay with the SOC. Not with my fears and memories beating down on me every damn day.

"How are you doing?" he asks me now.

"Stupid question," I mutter.

"Is it?"

I shrug, wishing that Quince and Eliza were still with me. But this is an authorized personnel only situation, and they have no connection with my former government job.

"You were one of my best agents, Denise. And you handled everything I threw at you. You'll get through this, too."

I look away from him, because I think we may have just found my limit. Because I'm not handling this well at all. Instead of facing reality, I'm clinging to the scenario I've been playing out in my head. Me walking into that room. Mason standing politely, his head cocked in that way he has when he's trying to work out a puzzle. For a terrifying moment, his expression will be blank. Then a smile will spread across his face and sunshine will fill those chestnut eyes. "Denny," he'll say, as I slide into his arms. "Christ, Denny, I thought I'd lost both of us." "Never," I'll whisper. "I'll always see you home."

That's what I want. That's what I'm imagining.

But I know it's not real.

I spent too many years working the tough cases. I've seen too many horrors, and over the years my skin has gotten too thick. The optimism I clung to as a child has been chipped away, replaced by a dark reality where every happily ever after comes with a price.

And now I'm terrified that this is the price Mason and I are paying for our years of bliss.

From the speakers mounted above us, I hear a click as the bathroom door inside the room opens. Mason steps out, absolutely and completely nude. Seagrave immediately spins his chair around, as if to give Mason privacy, but I stay as I am, looking over Seagrave's head at my husband, a slow burn of anger rising at the unfamiliar scars that now mar his beautiful skin.

I don't know what happened to him, but if I ever find out who did that, I'll kill them with my bare hands, I swear to God.

"Did they break any bones?" My voice is low, but even.

"His nose. His arm. Recent, but healed by the time we acquired him."

"Acquired," I repeat. Not rescued. Not recovered. Not exfiltrated. In other words, Seagrave still sees Mason as a risk.

I get that. I understand his reasoning and his fear. But he's not right. He can't be right, because that would be the final blow that absolutely destroys me.

"No head injuries," he continues, his voice bland. "That's

not the cause of his memory loss."

"I wasn't even thinking about that. I was just—"

I sigh, overwhelmed by the sight of him and the situation. But no matter how horrible everything is, that is my husband in there. *Mason*. The dark hair that appears so thick and coarse, but is as soft as silk to my fingers. Those deep-set eyes that can steal my breath with a single glance. His rugged face highlighted by the slight, kissable cleft in his chin.

And his body. Tall and muscular and vibrant and *mine*. *We'll get past this. Somehow, I'm going to get him back.*

As if he can hear my thoughts, Mason turns and walks toward the mirror. Toward *me*. He stops in front of it, completely naked, his head tilted slightly down so that our eyes meet, though I know he can't see me. My pulse kicks up, and I let my gaze roam over every delicious inch of him, soaking him up like candy.

"That's Mason," I whisper, my attention focused especially on the tribal band tattoo on his left arm. Mason doesn't like rings—not since he saw his cousin's finger get ripped off after the seventeen-year-old got his hand caught in construction equipment during a summer job. Instead of a ring to symbolize our marriage, he'd chosen to get a tattoo. I'd considered doing the same, but in the end, I'd gone with my platinum band.

I press my palm against the glass and sigh. "He may not realize it, but that's definitely Mason."

Seagrave's back is still to the glass, so I can easily see the way his forehead creases as he studies me. "If you're about to give me a run down on specific physical attributes, don't bother. I've gotten a full report from the med team already."

I smirk. "I definitely recognize every inch," I say, choosing not to comment on the spider web of scars that make me want to weep. "But that wasn't what I meant. I'm saying that he's Mason. With Mason's habits. His—I don't know— *programming*."

"Programming?"

I shake my head quickly. "I don't mean he's gone all *Manchurian Candidate* on us. I just mean that people develop certain patterns over a lifetime. He hasn't forgotten those. Even if he's forgotten where they came from. That has to be a good sign, right?"

"He walked naked into a room that he may well believe is private. So what? Tell me what exactly that means to you."

"Defiance," I say, grinning at my bare-naked husband still standing in front of the mirror, looking hard at us even though I know that all he sees is himself. "We both know he understands what that mirror is—don't try to tell me you think otherwise. So that's one clue. Here's another—Mason never leaves the bathroom naked. He always wears a towel or dresses in the bathroom."

That, in fact, is a quirk that I've always found unfortunate since the man has an incredible body. But he shared a room with his sister until he was fourteen and now the towel habit is deeply ingrained. He's broken pattern only twice in our marriage—our wedding night and the night before he left on this mission. Mostly because I'd cajoled him into—and out of—the shower with me.

Not that I'm going to share those details with Seagrave.

"But he's *not* Mason," Seagrave says. "That's the point. That's why he's breaking pattern. No towel. No old habits."

"Maybe. Or maybe this is his way of flipping you the bird."

I watch as Seagrave's mouth curves into a frown. He spins the chair, then stares at Mason, who's still standing in front of the mirror. "He knows we're here. And so he's purposely acting against instinct, knowing full well I'd be watching."

At first, I think he's mocking my theory. Then I realize he means it. "You agree with me."

"That he knows we're behind the mirror and that he is, as you say, flipping us off? Yes. I do." Seagrave's shoulders rise and fall. "But as to whether he's in defiance of the habit of the towel, too ... well, that I can't be sure of."

I shrug. "Fair enough," I say. "It's enough that I'm certain."

I think about what he's just said. "Why do you say he knows about the mirror?"

"We weren't twiddling our thumbs in the days before I called you. We've been doing a series of tests and interviews. He recognized his Special Forces tattoo. He admits to a level of familiarity regarding intelligence work, though no specific assignments."

"Familiarity," I repeat. "Like habits. Behavior."

"Yes."

"So he knows he's an agent. A spy."

"Or that he was. But what we didn't know—and what he couldn't tell us—was if he'd been compromised."

I feel the blood rush to my face. "Brainwashing. Triggers." I think about my *Manchurian Candidate* quip and wish I'd said nothing. The idea that some enemy of the state or vile mobster brainwashed my husband to blow a gasket when he sees a particular pattern or hears a trigger phrase or verse ... well, the possibility is too horrible to even think about.

"No," Seagrave says gently. "He's undergone hours of testing and interviews with Dr. Tam, and we've reached almost one hundred percent confidence that he hasn't been compromised that way."

I nod slowly. I trust the SOC's staff psychiatrist, but in the intelligence world, nothing ever reaches one hundred percent certainty.

"I want to see him now," I say simply.

"I'm not sure that's a good idea today."

"You've run your tests. You've run your evaluations. You've had him for over four days. It's time to open a window for him to his actual life."

"I don't disagree."

For a moment, I'm confused. Then I exhale loudly. "Right. This isn't about him. You think I can't handle it. You think it's going to break me if I walk into that room and he doesn't know who I am."

"Won't it?"

"No," I lie, but I can see on his face that he doesn't believe me. I can't get angry about that, though, since I'm not sure I believe it myself.

"I told you on the phone this was an informational visit only," he continues.

"Please, Anderson," I say, feeling a hot tear trace a path down my cheek. "I need this. I need to go in there. I need to see my husband."

I watch his face. The way his shoulders dip slightly. Anderson Seagrave is a good man, and I know he's only trying to protect me. But I'm done in. At this point, every moment I'm not in that room with Mason is hell. And when I see Seagrave nod, I know he's finally realized that, too.

"All right, Denise," he says. "You have ten minutes."

I start to protest, but he lifts a finger, reminding me that he's the one calling the shots here.

"Ten minutes," he repeats. "And there are a few conditions as well."

4

_____

I PAUSE OUTSIDE THE DOOR, trying to gather myself. I press my hand over my queasy stomach and try to will my nerves under control. I don't completely succeed, but I'm also not willing to wait any longer. With a deep breath for courage, I reach out and rap on the door.

Almost immediately, Mason's voice filters through the speaker system. "What the fuck, Seagrave? You know damn well I can't let you in."

I mentally kick myself, then tap in the code, wait for the locking mechanism to disengage, and push the door open. I step inside, then freeze when I see him, forcing myself not to whimper with the anguish that washes over me.

His back is to me, and I catch sight of the black band of his briefs peeking out from the waistband. He's pulling on a shirt, and I watch as the muscles in his back ripple, the urge to touch him—to hold him—so powerful that it's almost painful.

It had been hard enough to view this medieval nightmare of crisscrossing scars through the one-way glass. Now, the sight has completely broken me, and I have to fight the urge to sob on his behalf. I want to hold him close and soothe him, and I crave the caress of his breath against my ear as he whispers softly, promising me that we'll get through this together.

Most of all, I want to release my fears and lose myself in the arms of the husband who loved me.

But that's not the man I'm looking at.

Not anymore. Maybe not ever again...

Oh, God.

"Are you okay?"

I look up, only in that moment realizing that I've shifted my attention to the floor in an unconscious effort to hide my tear-filled eyes. I sniff and manage a wobbly smile. He's looking at me with such tenderness and concern that I truly can't wrap my head around the fact that this man doesn't know me.

With a mental curse, I wipe it away. I'm better trained than this. But my reaction isn't about work. It's about my husband. It's about Mason Walker. Who likes to jog with me on the beach at sunset and spend lazy summer mornings in bed sharing a carafe of coffee as we watch old film noir movies or big budget fantasy flicks.

But now they tell me he doesn't remember any of that.

It's bullshit. It *has* to be bullshit. Because despite the years of training. Despite having actually taken a bullet not once, but twice. Despite having some serious covert creds, I can't wrap my head around the words Seagrave kept pounding into me. That the man on the other side of this room is going to look me straight in the eye and not have a clue who I am.

That can't be right. He has to know me, because that's the only version of reality that my fragile heart is willing to accept. Seagrave has to be wrong, and I take a step toward

Mason, certain that any second now I'll see the polite confusion on his face shift into loving relief.

He'll whisper my name, his voice thick with tears, and then he'll sprint across the room and pull me against him with such force that we'll both fall to the ground, holding each other as we sob with relief and joy.

That, of course, doesn't happen.

Instead, he grabs a box of tissues from the dresser and walks toward me, extending the container like a peace offering. I'm left handed, so when I reach for the tissue, my simple platinum wedding band gleams under the fluorescent lights.

I see his eyes dip to it before returning to my face. *This is it*, I think. *This is the trigger that restores his memory.*

"I'm going out on a limb and guessing that we know each other," he says, shattering my hope. "Or knew. I'm still a little uncertain about which is more grammatically correct under the circumstances." His mouth curves into an ironic smile and I laugh despite myself. Then I want to cry all over again, because Mason could always make me laugh with his stupid, random jokes.

A fresh tear trickles down my cheek, as if determined to completely eradicate that tiny bubble of levity, but I manage to hold the smile. "Yeah," I say, as I study his face for any sign of recognition. "We know each other."

"Present tense. I like it." I watch his gaze flick over me. "You look like someone I want in my present and not just in my past."

"Do I?" My voice is strangled, and it's all I can do to get the question out without crying. "Do you have any idea who I am?" All I want in that moment is for him to throw me a bone. Some tiny hint of recognition. Some flash of reaction in those deep brown eyes I know so well.

But there's nothing.

Nothing except a calm assessment, an apologetic shake of his head, and then the flat, emotionless gaze of a man trained to hide all expression. "I don't. I'm sorry. But if we're playing the elimination game, I can rule out Seagrave, Dr. Tam, and a few of the med techs."

"That's a start," I say, trying to keep my voice light.

"After that, I'm at a loss. But maybe there are a few things I know."

A flicker of hope tickles in my chest, like a tiny bird fluttering its wings. "What do you mean?"

"We must have been close."

I nod, mute.

He grins, like a little boy who's just won a cookie. As he moves to sit on the edge of the bed, he gestures for me to take the single chair by the small table, I do, grateful to sit.

"I've spent the last few days studying every inch of my face, and I don't see a resemblance between us," he says. "Which means we're not relatives, right?"

"No," I whisper. "No shared blood at all." I swallow, then force a smile. "Is that all?"

"I'm just getting started." His grin lights his face in a way that I hadn't seen while watching through the window. *That's for me*, I think. *If nothing else, I've brought him a tiny hint of joy.*

I relax a bit, returning the grin. "Enlighten me."

"You're married," he says, as I realize that my thumb has been caressing my ring. "Which means you're not my girlfriend." His gaze skims over me, quick but thorough. Then he flashes a familiar half-smile, the one that makes his hidden dimple pop into view. "Of course, we could be having an affair..."

For a moment, the possibility hangs in the air, heavy

with the memory of his body on top of mine, his eyes seeing straight into my soul. At least that's what pops into my head. I have no idea what he's thinking.

I really wish I did.

"Do you think we are?" I ask, pleased that my voice betrays no emotion. Thank God for government training. "Having an affair?"

He hesitates before answering, his eyes never leaving my face. "No."

"Oh?" My voice stays level, reflecting none of my insecurities. *Doesn't he find me attractive? What happened to our connection? That spark that had flared the very first time we met?* "Why not?"

His gaze dips to my ring finger. "Because I'm not the type of guy who sleeps with a married woman. And I doubt I was even when I knew my name. Plus, I know you aren't the kind to cheat."

"You know that?" I raise my brows. "How?"

"Your ring."

At first I don't understand. Then I realize that I've been fiddling with it constantly. Rubbing it with my thumb. Spinning it. Touching it in some way or another.

It's not just a ring. It's a symbol. It's my way back to Mason.

And the irony is that the man sitting in front of me doesn't even have a clue.

"A woman so completely focused on the symbol of her marriage wouldn't cheat."

I'm not sure I agree with that as a blanket statement, but he's right about me. So I simply nod. "You still haven't said how we know each other. You've said we're close and we're not sleeping together. So far, you're two for two. But what about the rest?"

He holds up a finger. "I'm close with your husband, right?"

"Well, not anymore," I say, both deflecting the question and broadening his grin.

"You make a good point." He leans forward, his elbows on his knees and his chin resting on two steepled fingers. It's a completely classic Mason pose, and I have to work to hold my stiff smile in place.

"Was I close with your husband?"

I nod slowly. "That would be a fair statement."

"Fair, but not entirely accurate?"

"Are we playing Twenty Questions now?"

He laughs, but the sound is hollow. "At the moment, my life *is* a game of Twenty Questions."

I nod, conceding the point. "Correct. Fair, but not entirely accurate."

"All right. That means he and I weren't partners, were we?"

"No, you weren't."

"Which means that you and I were."

I lurch back, my mouth opening in surprise. "How did you work that out?"

"So, I'm right. Good. If I was wrong I was going to have to rethink everything."

"I'm serious," I press. "How did you know?" Does he remember that part of our life? Is he seeing little flashes of our first few years together? I swallow, trying not to be too hopeful. But if he's started to remember that, what else might he remember?

"I'll trade you. Tell me my name, and I'll tell you how."

It would be so easy. All I have to do is spit it out.

Granted, the moment I do, agents will burst in through the door and drag me off to military prison. Probably. And even if that doesn't happen, I'll have completely destroyed Seagrave's trust in me. Which isn't something I can live with. I respect the man too much.

Not only that, but I've been trying to foster a working relationship between the SSA and Seagrave's operation. Go against his direct orders and that will never happen. And Seagrave was crystal clear with his instructions—I can't tell Mason his name. I can't tell him our relationship. I *can* tell him that we worked in the field as partners. But that's as far as I'm allowed to take it.

I'm not crazy about the parameters, but I would have agreed to anything to get through that door. Now that I'm in, I'm not going to risk being dragged out again.

"I take it by your silence that you're not going to tell me," he says. "It's okay. I didn't really expect that you would."

"If it helps, I was debating. But I'm pretty sure I'd end up chained in the dungeon for the next decade if I spill. And I just started re-watching *Game of Thrones*. It would suck to have to stop midway through season one."

Mason and I watched the show together until he went away, and I search his eyes for a flicker of recognition, but I don't see a thing. My shoulders droop with disappointment, but maybe it's for the best. According to Seagrave, Dr. Tam insisted that any specific reference to his name, his relationship to me, or any past assignment runs the risk of short-circuiting his brain, which could end up blocking the information for good.

"She explained it with medical speak and a fifty page brief," Seagrave had added when he gave me the rundown. "But that's about what it amounts to. Something traumatic happened, and we're assuming that event is tied to his discovery of key information that could lead to us shutting down that terrorist cell once and for all. We can't risk burying that information forever."

Maybe not. But at the moment, I care a hell of a lot more about Mason than I do about a terrorist cell. But only in my heart. My training is too ingrained, and no way would I compromise the country's security or undermine all the work that Mason did while he was gone.

So instead of telling him his name, I volley the question back to him. "What are you calling yourself?"

"Jack Sawyer. It amused Seagrave. I guess it amuses you, too," he adds, obviously noticing my grin.

"You always were a fan of *Lost*. Do you remember the show?"

"I do. Life on that freakish island seems more real at the moment than my own." He stands, then goes and gets a cup of coffee from the Keurig in the corner of the room. "Want?"

I nod, and a few moments later he brings me a Styrofoam cup filled with the magical elixir. Our fingers brush as I take it, and an unexpected shock of awareness ricochets through me at this first contact in what feels like forever.

I tense, hoping he doesn't notice, and at the same time delighting in the flood of memories that even this slight contact with him revives.

Mason—no, I need to call him Jack—returns to the bed and sits again, slowly sipping his coffee. As far as I can tell, he's completely unaffected by the brush of skin against skin.

"Your turn," he says, and it takes me a second to realize he wants to know my name.

"Denise. Denise Marshall." I've always used my maiden name professionally, so it easily rolls off my tongue, even though what I want is to tell him that my name is Denise Marshall Walker, and why the hell doesn't he remember that?

"And your husband?"

I hesitate only a second. Then I look him straight in the eye. "Mason. Mason Walker."

For a moment, the name hangs in the silence. Then he says, "Is he dead?"

I'm unable to hold back the small, strangled noise that escapes my lips. "He—he's been gone a long time."

He nods sympathetically, and I'm terribly afraid he's going to ask me a more probing question. One I really can't answer. So I fire my own question off first. "How did you know we were partners? You still haven't told me."

"Well, apparently I'm a hot shit intelligence officer."

It's the right thing to say, as a laugh bubbles out of me, lightening the mood. "Can't argue with that, but I still want to know your reasoning."

"I was close to him, but you said we weren't partners. If we'd been just run-of-the-mill friends he wouldn't know about my work."

"Not everyone in intelligence works undercover."

"But I did. Or at least, I'm playing the odds and saying I did." He sweeps his arm, indicating the room. "If not, all this seems like overkill."

Since I can't argue with that, I don't. "How do you know that he was aware of your work?"

"A guess, honestly. But you know. And if I wasn't Mason's partner, the next best guess to get you into this room is that you're in intelligence too, and that—"

"—we're partners. Yeah. I get it."

And I do. It's cold, hard reasoning, which has always been one of Mason's strong suits. Right now, though, he's reasoned me right out of his arms and into another's. I'm his friend. His colleague. His partner.

But I'm not his lover, and I'm not his wife.

He's erased me. Somehow, his mind really has erased me along with everything else, and there's not a damn thing I can do about it.

I can't wrap my arms around him and weep. I can't twine my fingers through his hair as my mouth finds his.

I can't kiss him back to reality as if I'm a fairy tale princess and he's a prince trapped in a hundred year sleep.

I can't even tell him the truth.

All I can do is cry, but I'm not even allowed to do that.

"You have to hold it together," Seagrave had said. "You're a professional, Agent Marshall. If I let you walk into that room, I expect you to behave like one."

The memory whips through my head, and I draw in a resigned breath as I once again focus all my attention on Mason.

Correction: Jack.

He's Jack Sawyer. I'm Denise Marshall. And never the twain shall meet.

"How long have you been in the private sector?" he asks, interrupting my pity party and making me look up sharply.

"How do you know I am?"

"Because if we were still partners, you would have popped into my cell before now. You're still in the business, though. Just more on the civilian side of things."

"Guess you really are a hot shit intelligence officer."

"I know something else, too," he says with a grin. "We made a damn good team."

"You don't know that."

"Sure I do," he says. "I don't remember it, but I feel it. We were good together, weren't we, Denise?"

"Yeah." My voice catches. "We made one hell of an awesome team."

5

_____

"That's about the saddest thing I've ever heard," my friend Cass says, glancing up from where she's doing the final touches on a wrist tattoo of a single domino with four dots on one side of the tile and two on the other.

I've just finished telling her and Sylvia—who's getting the ink— that I saw my husband this afternoon, and he didn't have even an iota of an inkling of a clue that I'm his wife.

"Believe me," I say. "I know."

"Are you supposed to be telling us this?" Cass adds. "Isn't this one of those situations where you can tell us, but then you have to kill us?"

"Yes," I say, looking from her to Sylvia. "As soon as you finish Syl's wrist, I'm going to take you both out."

"Well, hell," Syl says with a put-upon sigh. "What's the point of getting a new tattoo if I don't have time to show it to anyone?"

"That's true," Cass says. "Whacking us would be just plain rude."

I exhale loudly and flop down into the big leather

armchair that's been tucked in this corner of Totally Tattoo for all the years I've known Cass. I keep my expression bland, but inside I'm grinning. I knew my friends would make me feel better. "Fine. You live. But that means you both owe me a drink." I glance at the kitty cat clock with the swishing tail. "As soon as the big hand gets to the twelve, I expect my due compensation."

"I can't believe I'm saying this, but I'll have to take a rain check." Syl offers me an apologetic smile. "I'm so sorry I can't stay. Because honestly, Denny, if anyone deserves a drink today, it's you."

"I won't argue with that," I say. "And I forgive you. Big plans?"

Her huge smile is answer enough. It lights up her face and makes her eyes twinkle. She wears her hair short, like Audrey Hepburn in *Sabrina*, and the style complements her elfin face.

"We're dropping the kids off with Nikki and Damien for the week," she tells me. "Then Jackson and I are heading to the airport."

"That's right," Cass says. "The museum dedication in Reykjavik, right?"

Syl nods. "I've never been to Iceland, and Jackson's giving a speech and getting an award. It should be a fabulous week."

A world-famous architect, Jackson Steele is also Damien's half-brother. And Sylvia, in addition to being Jackson's wife, is a high-level exec with Stark Real Estate Development.

Considering I now work for the Stark Security Agency, I find it completely ironic that I met Sylvia through Cass and not through Damien. Especially since Cass isn't a billionaire, doesn't work for any Stark subsidiary, and doesn't know squat about the intelligence community.

On the contrary, Cass is just Cass—one of the best tattoo artists I've ever met, which isn't saying much since I still haven't summoned the nerve to get a tattoo. But back when Mason got his tribal band, I did a ton of research on local parlors and learned that Totally Tattoo is one of the best.

The studio's been around for over three decades, and Cass has been working at the place in various capacities since she was a kid. Back then, her dad ran it. And from what she tells me, she and Syl met when they were teenagers, hit it off, and have been lifelong besties.

When Mason and I came in, the plan was for us to get matching ink. After watching the process with Mason, though, I'd chickened out. I may be a badass in the espionage world, but that doesn't mean I want to voluntarily get stabbed with a zillion little needles.

Cass took my wishy-washiness in stride, which was probably the second thing about her that impressed me. The first, of course, was her looks. With her ever-changing hair—today it's dark with pink tips—her brilliant green eyes, and the magnificent tattoo of an exotic bird that marks her shoulder, Cass has always been exceptional.

Since I felt guilty for bailing on my ink and leaving Cass with a big gap at the end of her Friday calendar, Mason and I took her out for a beer. After that, we started hanging out a lot. Me, Mason, Cass, and her girlfriend, Siobhan.

That's part of why I feel no guilt for sharing Mason's secrets. I know Cass loves him, too. Not like I do, but our friendship is strong, and when that first month without Mason dragged into two, five, ten, it was to Cass's house that I'd go when I needed a reality check or a shoulder to cry on.

That shoulder is the reason I came here today instead of

going straight to my house in Silver Lake. I need a hug. I need to talk. I need...

Honestly, I need Mason. But since that isn't going to happen, a friend is the next best thing, which is exactly what I tell her when we're finally settled at Blacklist, the Venice Beach bar just a few blocks from Cass's shop.

"The bottom line is that I couldn't bring myself to go straight home," I tell her as I sniff my bourbon at the long oak bar, then push it away. "I didn't want to walk into that house without him, which is stupid, since I've been going home to an empty house for over two years now."

"But before it was empty because he was away working, but you knew that he was wishing he was there with you. And that made it important." She traces her finger thoughtfully along the rim of her wine glass. "Because it belonged to both of you."

"It still belongs to both of us," I say defensively.

"I know," Cass says gently. "But it's hard to be in a place after the meaning changes." She looks down at her wine, her head tilted so that her hair falls in a curtain of curls, partially shielding her face. I expect her to brush it back, and I frown when she doesn't.

"Cass?"

She takes a sip of wine, shakes her head, and tucks her hair behind her ear. What she doesn't do is look straight at me, and in that moment my gut twists and I realize I'm the worst friend ever.

"What happened?" I say. "Is Siobhan going to be stuck in Chicago longer than you thought?" After organizing a few successful fine arts exhibitions in the LA area, Siobhan got invited to work on a touring show, and she's been traveling for months. The last I heard, she was in Chicago for the final three-week run.

I assume Cass is just missing her, so I'm unprepared when she lifts her head, meets my eyes, and says flatly. "She's staying."

"Staying? So, what? She wants you to move to Chicago?"

"No," Cass says. "She doesn't want me there at all. I'm pretty sure Anthony doesn't want me there either."

"Anthony." The name comes out flat, and I say nothing else. I don't have to. I know where this is leading.

"At least Siobhan will finally make her dad happy. He hated when she dumped her boyfriend and came back to me."

That was before my time, but I've heard about how Cass and Siobhan had split up, then got back together. But from what Sylvia told me, those two were meant to be, and Siobhan's return had been both a happy surprise and inevitable.

"Does Syl know?"

Cass shakes her head. "She knows that I've been irritated with how little Siobhan was checking in, but I just wrote that off to her being so busy. This is a new development—yesterday, actually. At least from my perspective. Apparently from Siobhan and Anthony's point of view, it's been almost four months in the making." She shrugs. "I thought about telling Syl at lunch today, but I didn't want to drop all this on her right before she heads to Iceland."

I get that. The news hit me with the force of an anvil, and Syl has known Siobhan for years—and witnessed their first break-up and reconciliation. She's going to be knocked sideways second only to Cass herself.

I take her hand and squeeze. "I'm so sorry."

"I appreciate that, but I really didn't mean for this outing to be about me. After all, if we're comparing pain, I'm going to say that you win."

I'm not entirely sure that's true. As much as it hurts for

Mason not to know me, I can't even imagine how horrible I'd feel if he'd willingly walked away from me. At least this way, I know that it wasn't his decision.

"True," Cass says when I tell her that. "But I still think it's worse for you. I could fly to Chicago if I wanted. Put up a fight. You can't. Because even if you tell him who you are, he doesn't remember it. So there's no solid ground for the two of you to stand on. From his perspective, it would be like you were arguing about some characters in a TV show. Vaguely familiar, but nothing to do with him." She lifts a shoulder apologetically. "At least if Siobhan and I have it out, we both know what the stakes are."

I let her words flow over me, then nod. "You're right. I'm definitely the one getting screwed here."

She laughs, as I'd hoped. And even though I meant what I said one hundred percent, I laugh, too.

"Of all the things I imagined when we got married, this was never on my radar. I mean, I thought about when we would have kids. And what we would do if we retired. I worried I couldn't handle it if he got sent out on assignment with another woman. You know, the usual stuff. But it never once occurred to me that I'd be totally erased from his life. It's—it's like being hollow, and I can't wrap my head around it."

"And it's worse because you can't tell him."

I nod, then reach for my drink before remembering I don't want it.

"What?"

"Just not in the mood for alcohol, I guess."

"Here, take my water." She pushes it to me. "But that wasn't what I meant. There's something else on your mind."

I shake my head, part of me not wanting to talk about it,

and the other part not knowing how to put what I'm feeling into words.

"You thought he would know," she says softly. "That he would snap back when he saw you. You thought it would be like a fairy tale, and you'd step into the secret cave and rescue the wounded prince."

"You make me sound like a fool."

She flashes a sad little smile. "I don't mean to. I think I'd feel the same way. Anybody would. What you're going through—it's not exactly normal."

"Maybe I just did it wrong," I quip. "I mean, in the fairy tales, it's always a kiss that works the magic."

Beside me, Cass grins. "Maybe you should try that."

"I wish I had the nerve," I admit. "But I have a feeling Seagrave doesn't share my romantic streak. I'd end up getting banned from the SOC, and Mason would be confused—possibly turned on—but none the wiser."

"I'm sorry," she says, all levity evaporating from her voice.

"Thanks." The real truth is that I don't know what to do with myself now. Despite my rather hairy childhood, I've always believed that things would turn out all right. That my father abandoning me and my mom wasn't an omen. That —just like my mother told me—if I kept a positive outlook, everything would be okay. I just had to keep the faith.

And so I did. Even when cancer settled into her bones. Even when she died despite promising that she'd never leave me. That she'd fight it, and she'd win.

Even with all her promises, she lost the battle. But I still clung to that stupid, fucking optimism. I'd kept the faith, and when Mason came into my life, I truly believed that he was my reward.

But now he's gone, too. And I can't seem to wrap my

head around the randomness of the world. Like it's nothing more than a game of chance. Dice or cards or...

I frown, turning to Cass as I remember Sylvia's tattoo. The domino wasn't the first—far from it. In fact, the first time we went to the beach together, I was surprised to see how many she had. "Memories," she'd told me after I commented on her ink. "And a bit of therapy. A map of triumphs and milestones that I hold close."

"What was the point of the domino?" I ask Cass, then realize I know the answer as soon as the question leaves my mouth. "Because of the business center," I answer.

The Domino is a relatively new business park in Santa Monica. Specifically, it's a co-development between Stark Real Estate and Steele Development, which means that Jackson and Sylvia worked on it together. And I can't blame her for wanting to memorialize that in ink.

In fact, the more I think about it, the more I think that it's a very good idea. And despite my aversion to tiny needles, I shift on the bar stool to face Cass directly. "Can we go now?" I ask. "There's something I want you to do for me."

6

_____

His dreams had been filled with a green-eyed beauty, and Jack woke with her still on his mind. And he hated himself for it.

He'd dreamed of the soft brush of her blond hair against his bare chest. The gentle pressure of her full lips against his skin. The flash in her feline eyes as she'd tilted her head up, then practically purred as she eased down his body, her soft hands exploring his skin, her generous mouth doing such extraordinary things before she straddled his hips and rode him all the way to heaven.

He'd awakened worn out and sated, the memory of her scent clinging to him as tightly as the hot, twisted bed sheets.

He tried to tell himself that his dream lover had been an anonymous girl. A fantasy woman. The blond-haired, green-eyed siren of his earlier dream in the hotel. But it wasn't. The woman who'd so sweetly tormented him in the night wasn't an ephemeral fantasy. She was Denise Marshall. And he had no business allowing her into his dreams, much less fantasizing about her lips on his cock.

She was his former partner. A professional, just like he supposedly was, although damned if he could remember any aspects of his career. And she wasn't just his partner; she was another man's wife. A man who was gone.

A man she wanted back.

He'd stood right here in this room and assured her that he was honorable. That he would never take what belonged to another man. That he would respect her pain and loss.

And all of that was bullshit, because damned if he didn't fuck her in his dream.

Yesterday, he hadn't known what kind of man he was. Not really. How could he have?

Today, he knew.

"Perhaps you're being too hard on yourself," Dr. Tam said when he met her in therapy later that morning. She wore a plain gray suit, her shirt buttoned up to her neck. Her dark hair was cut short, revealing small ears that contrasted the lovely, huge eyes that hid behind the large, plastic frames of her glasses.

He guessed her to be in her late fifties, and he knew from Seagrave that in addition to her work with field agents, she conducted independent research and was a frequent lecturer at medical schools around the globe.

Jack didn't care about any of that. If she could peel back the curtain to reveal his memories, she was useful. Her credentials were just so much noise.

"Fantasy is an important aspect of life," she continued, her eyes never leaving his face. "An important part of being human."

"I already knew I was human," he told her dryly. "Now I know I'm an asshole, too."

"Because you made love to a woman in a dream?"

"Fine," he said. "You're right. I'm making too much of it."

The words were a lie, of course. He didn't know why, but Denise Marshall had gotten under his skin. She was a constant in his thoughts, so much that she felt like a talisman. As if her kiss could restore him. As if the only way he could find peace was in her arms.

It was bullshit, and he knew it. She was beautiful and he was lost. Lost in the world. In his own head. And he didn't need Dr. Tam to tell him that he was clinging to her as a connection to his past. His former partner. His friend. He'd elevated her in his mind and turned her into something she wasn't.

He got it. He didn't need therapy to explain it.

And he damn sure didn't need to share it.

He dragged his fingers through his hair. "Look, I'm sorry. But like I said, you're right. I'm drowning in self-pity, but we both know I'm not exactly sure-footed here. My entire world is inside this building. My little prison. This tiny room. Seagrave's office. At least he has a view."

The room that was his new home had no view; just that damn mirror through which Seagrave and Tam and everyone else could watch him as if he was a goddamn hamster in a cage. And this office he was in now, while cozy with its walls of bookshelves and comfortable chairs and sofas, was nothing more than a disguised surgery center—where Dr. Tam used her words instead of knives to cut into his brain.

Only Seagrave's office had a view. Not a lovely one—just a few rooftops and downtown structures. But at least there was sunshine.

"The accommodations are a bit bland," she said. "But you understand why, I assume?"

"Less stimulation in my environment, more stimulation

in my head." He leaned back in the overstuffed armchair. "That's the theory, anyway. I think it's bullshit."

Her brows rose over the tops of her tortoise-shell frames. "Oh?"

"How the hell can I recover my life if I can't experience my life?"

"We've had this discussion, Agent Sawyer."

He made a scoffing noise that she must have heard, but she continued without missing a beat.

"We don't know if your memory loss was due to physical trauma, mental trauma, or a combination of both. We don't know if your memory was intentionally wiped, perhaps through drug manipulation or hypnosis. In short, we don't know anything except that you were a key player in an important investigation. You discovered something both urgent and dangerous. You signaled that you would be making contact with key intel, and three weeks later you called Colonel Seagrave from a hotel in Victorville, seemingly with no memory of yourself, the information, or what had happened to you."

"Seemingly?"

"Surely you can understand why we must proceed with caution."

He did, of course. Grudgingly he nodded. He understood everything she was saying, but that didn't make it any easier. He'd been inside these walls for over a week now. It had been days since he'd seen Denise Marshall. In person, anyway. God knew she'd been showing up in his head regularly enough.

And it had been less than twenty-four hours since they'd told him he'd made contact, warning about an urgent threat. He disagreed with their rationale for waiting, but there wasn't a goddamn thing he could do about it. He was a prisoner here. A mind for them to probe. An unknown entity with no name, no resources, and nowhere else to go.

In other words, he was at their mercy.

The thought was not a pleasant one.

"You have a job, you know," Dr. Tam said, studying him with those intelligent eyes.

"Do I?"

"You're not a prisoner, Jack. You're an asset."

"If I'm an asset, the world is fucked." The fact that he said it with a smirk didn't mean he believed it any less.

"I want to talk about what you do remember. A truck you said."

"You know what I said. We've been over this multiple times."

"You recall being thrown out of a truck. You don't remember the face of whoever tossed you. You aren't even sure if the person was male."

"I remember movement. I remember the impact when I hit the street. I remember the sting in my palms and the needle stabs to my eyes when I blinked from the sun. I remember a black shirt and the impression that it was a man standing in that open cargo door. I remember all of that, but I'm not sure about a single fact."

"But you did walk, and you did end up in a motel in Victorville. That's verifiable."

"Has anyone here been able to locate the truck? Traffic cameras? Any satellites that happened to be taking snapshots? Any cars that passed me who called in a sighting of some battered man walking down the road?"

"If we'd found anything, we would have told you."

"Would you?" He dug his fingers into the padded armrests. "You haven't even told me what agency this is. I'm going on faith that this is a government operation. Well, faith and observation."

"Faith?"

"Apparently I worked for you. For this. I don't like to think I was working for the bad guys."

"We could be an independent organization of good guys."

"Possible. But there was a paystub on your desk yesterday—old fashioned, by the way. Most people just get an email. But clearly government issue."

She almost laughed, and he liked her more in that moment. "The funds are direct deposited. But I haven't gone paperless. I file the stubs. I suppose that makes you right. I'm old-fashioned."

"Convenient for me. As for Seagrave, there are quite a number of military commendations hanging on his walls. I doubt a man with that much cred with the military would chuck it all to go private."

"You're in the main office of the Western Division of the Sensitive Operations Command. The SOC is a covert, off-the-books paramilitary and intelligence organization that operates independently with oversight from the NSC."

"You're telling me just like that? I thought you didn't want me to have details about my life."

"I want you to trust me, Agent Sawyer. I need you to trust me—and Colonel Seagrave—to give you what you need. And to guide you as we think best."

"In other words, you just tossed me a bone."

"And you caught it." She smiled at him, easy and friendly, and the tension that had been building inside him dissipated a bit. He didn't understand her approach or agree with her choices, but he wasn't a shrink. At least, he didn't think he was. And for the moment, at least, he would trust her.

He spread his hands. "Alright. Go for it. Ask me questions. Get into my head. Do your worst."

"How about we both do our best?"

He nodded. One crisp tilt of his head.

"I'd like to go back to the truck. You've told me everything you recall?"

He closed his eyes and let it all play back. "I could smell exhaust. I was bounced around. The truck had a roll-up door. And there were at least two people, because the truck pulled away as the guy who tossed me was still standing in the cargo area."

"And your first memory?"

"The motion. Swaying. My hands tied behind my back. My ankles bound. My back aching from trying to stay seated. I was on a bench of some sort. You already know all of this."

"You remember nothing prior to that? Nothing before the motion of the truck?"

"No."

"So what does that tell you?"

"Not much, but it raises a hell of a lot of questions."

"Such as?"

He drew in a breath, then met her eyes. "The biggest, of course, is whether the memory is real."

She tilted her head. "You think it might have been planted?"

"I think I don't know you people any better than I know myself."

She surprised him by smiling broadly. "And now, Agent Sawyer, you're beginning to live up to your reputation. Yes, that is a risk. It's also possible that older memories are resurfacing." She reached for a remote and clicked on a wall-mounted television.

He turned, frowning as the screen popped on, revealing a mission report with all names redacted.

"That report's over a decade old," he said, skimming the paragraphs that summarized a mission in which the reporting agent had been held captive, then tossed from the back of a cargo van. "I filed this?"

"You did."

"So you're saying that I might be pulling up old memories. Dumping them into the present?"

"It's a possibility we can't overlook."

"Then how did I end up here? Like this?" He held out his hands, still red from the fading abrasions.

"Escape. Given up for dead and left at the side of the road. We may never know."

"We won't unless I remember. Why won't you help me remember?"

"Agent Sawyer, we've discussed—" She cut herself off with a shake of her head. "Jack." She began again, more gently. "I know it's difficult, but you need to trust me. Telling you your past runs the risk of destroying that past. We must approach our work in small increments. Otherwise we risk burying your secrets permanently."

He sat up straighter. "And if that's a risk I'm willing to take?"

She leaned back in her chair, studying him. Then she seemed to make a decision. She reached for her tablet, tapped the screen a few times, and a new image popped onto the television screen. A video of a man. He was sitting on his knees rocking back and forth. "And then," he said. "And then and then and then."

The video changed. Another man, this one sitting on the edge of a cot, staring blankly into space, a smile on his face.

Another. A man playing chess against himself, muttering. "That's all he does," Dr. Tam says. "He plays chess. I think he's trying to work it out. That somewhere inside his mind, he thinks that if he can beat himself, he'll get out of his own head. But if you're playing yourself, you can't beat yourself."

Jack felt cold. "Who are these men?"

"They could be you."

He swallowed. "Agents you pushed. Who were force fed memories."

"I didn't push them," she said. "I would have advised against that course. They were sent to me afterwards, with the hope that I could help. But I can't."

"Oh, God." His gut clenched.

"I can tell you this much—you are an agent of this organization, and you took an oath upon joining. This risk is not yours to take. Your memory and your mental health are under my protection, and that is a responsibility I take very seriously even if you do not."

He nodded slowly, hating what she was saying but also realizing he was in no position to argue. "Okay, but at least tell me what you can. How did I make contact? Was I working undercover? How long had I been in place? Do we have other assets in the field?"

He knew all the questions to ask. He knew how the job worked. He knew what he did as an agent. He just didn't know what he'd actually *done*.

And right at that moment, he felt more frustrated than he'd ever felt in his life.

At least as far as he could remember...

"I want answers."

"So do we all," she said. "That's why you're here. That's why we're having these talks. So that I can guide you. So that we can take it slowly and not miss anything. Not bury anything."

"What if I don't want to go slowly?"

"You were a good agent once. You valued the mission over self. Over family."

"I'm not the same person I was. Aren't you the one telling me so?"

"I'm the one trying to help you find that self again." She looked at him over the rim of her glasses. "Are you telling me that's no longer your code?"

He wanted to say yes, that was exactly what he was telling her. He wanted to demand that she do anything and everything to excavate his damn memories, and fuck the risks.

But he said nothing. She was right. He couldn't— wouldn't—risk burying whatever dark secrets he'd stored away.

"We'll do it your way," he said. "But I can't live like this. You want me to remember my life? Then I need to be allowed to live it."

He watched, his heart pounding, as she nodded slowly. "I don't disagree. I can speak to Colonel Seagrave. But I think we both know that you can't return to active duty. Until we know what's hidden in that head of yours, your clearance won't be reinstated. The issues SOC agents deal with are far too sensitive."

She was right, of course. And when he insisted that she let him put the issue to Colonel Seagrave himself, the older man simply repeated the doctor's concerns.

"You may have literally just fallen off the turnip truck, but you're not completely ignorant of how we work,"

Seagrave told him when Jack was escorted to the older man's office. "As much as I need what's in your head to protect national security, I can't risk that same security by letting a man without a memory run around like a loose cannon."

Jack nodded, then took a sip of the coffee Seagrave had offered him. "You're right, of course," he said. "But what about matters not related to national security?"

For a moment, older man simply studied him. Then he put down his coffee cup, leaned back in his chair, steepled his fingers beneath his chin and asked, "What exactly did you have in mind?"

7

RYAN HUNTER SITS at the head of the conference table, his fingers dancing over a keyboard as he skims a screen, then lifts his face and surveys the table. Lean, with chestnut brown hair and commanding blue eyes, Ryan is a natural leader. "Where do we stand, Noble? Your team ready to go?"

A lanky man, Winston Noble's wind-worn face speaks of the West Texas plains where he used to work as the sheriff before moving to California for reasons that I still don't know, and don't intend to ask. Not after seeing the haunted look in his eyes whenever his past is mentioned. He has a slow, easy way about him, and his thick Texas twang disguises a sharp intellect. Winston's a man that no one sees coming. More than that, he's one hell of a nice guy and an excellent leader. One I'd serve under without hesitation.

"I'd like to join the team," I say, swallowing the bite of dry toast I'd been nibbling on. The daughter of a Chinese diplomat was snatched during a family vacation in Washington, DC. The call came in at six this morning. It's eight now, and Winston's crew is wheels-up at nine. Under the internal rules of the SSA, Quince and I are both still on

Local Assignment Status for another thirty-six hours, a policy designed to ensure that agents recover sufficiently following a rigorous mission.

I'm hoping that Ryan will overlook that fact. Because knowing that Mason is back in LA and holed up in an SOC observation room where I can't see him without command level approval from Seagrave is absolutely messing with my head.

I've barely slept for the last two nights, and when I do, I dream of my husband. I rub my wrist where Mason's newly tattooed name is hidden under the cuff of my starched, white button down. I'd thought the permanent reminder would act as a talisman and give me some peace. So far, it hasn't helped.

I want him back so desperately, but the truth is that even if he walked into the room this very second, he still wouldn't be Mason. He'd be Jack Sawyer. And I'm having a hell of a time dealing with that. More, honestly, than I would have expected, but the stress is taking a toll on my stomach, and I've been waking up queasy and unsettled.

Thus my breakfast of dry toast and apple juice instead of my usual black coffee and a power bar.

From the end of the table, Ryan meets my eyes, his gaze sympathetic but firm. "You're needed here, Denise. Besides, Winston and Leah are set to go. And Trevor is already on the ground in DC."

I start to argue, but across the table, Leah gently shakes her head. I worked with Leah on Stark International's security team before moving over to the more specialized and elite SSA. And while I really want to flip her the bird and snap that she doesn't have any right to tell me when to back off a mission, I also know that she's right. So is Ryan. So are they all.

Because the only reason I want to go to DC is to run away from my own hollow heart. But that's not something I can escape from anyway.

"Good luck," I say instead. "You have me here for tech support if you need it."

"When don't we need you, darlin'?" Winston asks. "You're the computer whisperer, aren't you?" He grins and the room laughs, including me. I worked in the field with Mason for years, and more recently with Quince. But what I really love is squeezing information out of bits and bytes.

"Go on," Ryan says, dismissing Winston and his team with a nod of his head. He turns his attention to Liam and Quince. "You've got your assignments. Any issues?"

"Any other day I'd complain that reviewing surveillance tapes is bloody boring," Quince says. "But under the circumstances, I'm content with a nine-to-five assignment."

Ryan grins. "Enjoy your evenings while you have them."

Quince glances at me. I know exactly how his evening will be going. At home with Eliza. I roll my eyes in response to his wink, hoping he can't tell that underneath my happiness for him, I'm a jealous, lonely mess.

"Foster?" Ryan turns his attention to Liam, a tall black man with a solid build, military bearing, and a dry sense of humor.

Originally from New York, Liam Foster came to the SSA from his post as the head of security for the Sykes chain of department stores. A pedigree that I thought was ludicrous until I learned that the security job was only a blind. Legitimate work, yes, but hardly his focus. And definitely not the line on his resume that landed him at the SSA.

I should have known there was more to him from the first moment I met him. After all, a department store gig wasn't exactly the kind of job that hardened a man. And despite his kind nature, Liam is definitely hard. Turns out that Liam served in the military for years. And after that he was second in command of Deliverance, a once-secret vigilante organization that tracked down kidnap victims, mostly children, and did whatever was necessary to rescue the victims and bring the perpetrators to justice.

He's smart, competent, and loyal, and we've become good friends.

"I'm set. Got a meeting during B-shift," he adds. The SSA operates on a twenty-four hour schedule, with teams of agents reporting every three hours. "I'll be on the job after that."

Ryan nods assent as Liam packs up his things. He and his team are working a standard protection detail for a rising pop star whose manager insists she needs protection despite the star's protests.

He pauses at the door, then turns back to me, one thick finger aimed my direction. I sit up straighter, wondering what the hell I've done to draw his fire, but all he does is smile gently, nod, and head out the door.

"He's right," Ryan says, when the door clicks closed.

"About what? He didn't say a word."

Neither does Ryan. I roll my eyes. "It's like having a bucket full of older brothers."

Ryan chuckles. "I'm not sure Leah and the other women will appreciate that."

"Siblings," I say. "For an only child, I'm surrounded by siblings." I don't add that it's nice. Odd, but nice.

I take another bite of my toast, my queasiness finally starting to fade. "I'm going to go review Winston's mission specs," I say as I begin to gather my things. "I can start setting up some parameters, maybe even get some additional intel by the time they land in DC."

I stand, but Ryan motions me back down. "That's a good idea, but we need to talk about Cerise Sinclair."

I settle back into my chair. "Did something happen?"

In her early twenties, Cerise Sinclair is one of Los Angeles's pretty faces who grew up with money, has a trust fund as a cushion, and pays her daily bills off the income from being a social media influencer. A year ago, she bought a cozy little house in the Hollywood Hills without giving a thought to security. She has three vacant lots surrounding her, all with steep terrain, but not so unfriendly that a determined stalker couldn't walk there. And considering how much of her personal life she shares on social media—and how often she shares those details in only a bikini—she's collected quite a few ardent followers. Some of whom seem to think her posts are something akin to foreplay.

Before Quince and I dove headlong into the search for Eliza's sister and a missing princess, I'd consulted with Cerise on the installation of a security system for the property. The system is top notch and, as far as I know, hasn't registered any breaches to the home's perimeter.

Ryan shakes his head. "There've been no attempts to enter the residence, but Cerise asked if you could swing by. She didn't say why, but..."

He trails off, but I understand. Cerise may be a little high-maintenance, but she's both a client and one of Ryan's personal acquaintances, having come to the SSA via Ryan's wife, Jamie, who had interviewed Cerise a while back for a television news segment about the growing popularity of social media.

I glance at my watch. "I can go now and then devote the rest of the day to getting through my backlog and doing research for Winston's team."

Ryan's phone vibrates on the table, and he glances down

as I start to stand. "She's in San Diego for the day, and asked that you come this evening," he says as he taps out a quick reply to the incoming text. "Just as well. I want you to take a partner with you."

I settle back into my chair, studying him. "To go to Cerise's? Why?"

"New man on the team. Might as well ease him in."

"Ease him in? Since when is this the kind of operation that eases anybody in?" Though relatively new, the SSA has already developed a reputation for complex jobs, many with international components. We're not a training facility.

Ryan ignores me, instead pushing the button on the desk's console that shifts the conference room's status from locked to open. The light above the door clicks to green and I watch as Damien Stark pulls open the door and steps in, all strength and command and poise. He's flanked by Seagrave and Mason, with Quince and Liam bringing up the rear.

I glance at Ryan, realize my mouth is hanging open, and shut it. I turn my attention to Quince. We've worked together enough now that I've gotten good at reading his face. But he looks as confused as I do, and I realize that Damien must have asked him and Liam to join the meeting, probably figuring I needed a buffer.

I'm just not sure what exactly I need buffering from.

"Denise," Mason says, his too-familiar smile both delighting me and making tears prick my eyes. He steps toward me, his hand extended. "It's really good to see you again."

I take his hand automatically, realizing in that instant that except for a light brush when he passed me coffee, it's the first time we've touched since his return, and I have to force myself not to squeeze tight and tug him closer. On the contrary, I gently pull my hand free, my heart pounding in my chest as my whole body sings, begging for more than this simple brush of hand over hand.

"New?" he asks, as I slide my now-free hand into the pocket of my jacket. I must look confused, because he nods toward the pocket. "Your wrist," he says. "The tattoo."

Without thinking, I pull my hand out of my pocket. The cuff has pushed up and is gripping my forearm, revealing my wrist and the single word inked in Cass's clean, simple font: MASON.

"I'm sorry," he adds, and I shake my head in confusion. "You didn't have that when we met. I can't help but think I said something that made you sad."

"I—" I swallow and try again. "It wasn't anything you said. Where Mason's concerned, I'm always sad. I just realized that I wanted a tangible reminder."

"One of Denise's good friends is a tattoo artist," Damien explains, then gestures for us all to take our seats.

I remain standing, my attention alternating between Damien and Ryan. "Can I speak to you two outside before we get started?" My smile is so sweet it's a wonder everyone in the room doesn't develop diabetes. "I was just about to update Ryan on a crisis that's developed in the Michelson matter."

There is no Michelson matter, but to both men's credit, they simply nod. Damien stands, then gestures for the door.

I'm about to step that direction when Mason also rises. "Wait a moment. Please."

His attention is entirely on me, and I feel his gaze burning through me, sending a tumble of emotions roiling through me. I want so badly to be with this man, and yet I'm afraid I'll reveal too much to him and make things worse.

I'm furious with Damien and Ryan for putting me in this

position. Seagrave, too, and that bastard hasn't even said a word. He's just sitting there like some chess master moving us around as if we were pieces on a board.

Mason's the only one I'm not irritated with, even though he's the one who frustrates me the most, since he's the one around whom I must watch myself, putting on my Academy Award winning performance when all I want to do is hold him close and tell him the truth.

I say none of that, of course. Instead, I look to Mason and say, very simply, "What is it?"

"If there really is a Michelson case that needs your attention, then by all means, don't let me stop you."

I start to take a step toward the door.

"But if you just want to get your two bosses past that door so that you can rip them new assholes, then you're about to attack the wrong people."

I stop moving, cross my arms, and stare at the stranger who is my husband.

"I arranged this," he says. "If it makes you uncomfortable, please don't blame Mr. Stark or Mr. Hunter. Or Colonel Seagrave, for that matter."

Beside him, Seagrave grunts, but says nothing else.

"Go on."

"You know that Dr. Tam thinks that any direct revelations as to my past might be detrimental to my ability to pull out my memories, especially the memories of my last mission. Which, I'm beginning to realize, was an even more crucial assignment than I'd originally believed."

He says the last with an eye to Seagrave. I knew nothing about his mission other than how long it took him away from me. But I did know how much the government trusted my husband and his skills, so learning that the mission was key comes as no shock.

He looks at me as if waiting for me to ask a question. I don't. I just twirl my hand in a *get on with it* gesture.

The corner of his mouth twitches, and I feel a pang in my heart, because this is an all too familiar scene. Mason going on about something at length when I'm already caught up, and me impatiently urging him to wrap it up.

"If the SOC wants my memories but can't give me the canvas on which to paint them, then it makes sense that I should go back out in the field. Step as much into my old life as possible."

"Work with me, you mean." The words both excite and terrify me. "I'm not sure how much that would help. It's been years since we worked as partners."

He nods. "I know. But right now, you're the best connection I've got."

I look helplessly at Liam and Quince, both of whom look sympathetic, but offer no practical help. As for Seagrave, his expression remains entirely blank.

"You approve of this? You and Dr. Tam? You're not afraid that Ma—the man he was before Jack Sawyer won't get buried?" I hold Seagrave's eyes, certain he understands my question: *If I do this, am I going to lose any hope of getting my husband back?*

"We think our Mr. Sawyer might have a point," Seagrave says.

"And you two?" I say, turning to Damien and Ryan, who know full well what this will do to me.

"Even if he's forgotten who he is, he still has skills," Ryan says slowly. "The man will be an asset."

"And working together may well be therapeutic," Damien adds, and I know damn well he means that it might be therapeutic for me as much as for Mason.

"I realize it's strange," Mason—*Jack*—says. "I even know

it's going to be awkward for you. I don't have any excuse. All I can tell you is that I'm selfish. I want my life back, and I will go to the mat with all of you to get this chance. Denise," he says softly, "please help me."

I draw in a strangled breath, then look at the ground so he won't see my tears. I'm better than this. I'm not some emotional twit who cries all the time. But apparently where Mason is concerned, I am.

"Why me? Why not just return to the field?"

"Because we were partners," he says. "And because I trust you."

I shouldn't have asked. His words are too hard to hear. But they also drive home the simple truth that I'm all out of objections. More than that, I want this. As dangerous as it is to my heart and as hard as it will be not to accidentally reveal too much of our past, I want this chance to once again work with my husband.

"Okay."

His brows lift in surprise. "Okay? Really?"

"Do you want me to reconsider?"

He laughs and shakes his head as I glance over at Quince who's grinning. We sound, I'm sure, like a quarreling couple.

"We'll go see Cerise Sinclair together this evening. In the meantime, I can give you the file to read." I frown. "I was going to run some errands before meeting Cerise. I can pick you up. Are you going to be staying in your room at the SOC?"

"Yes," Seagraves says.

"Absolutely not," Jack says. He faces Seagrave dead-on. "I'll check in regularly. I'll report to Dr. Tam daily. But you will not hold me prisoner. And if you don't like it, you're going to have to arrest me or kill me."

I hold my breath until Seagrave nods. "Where will you stay?"

For a moment, I actually consider offering him our house. Fortunately, Liam jumps in before I make that ridiculous mistake. "He can stay with me. Assuming you don't mind the beach?"

I watch as Jack's face light's up. We bought property inland because it was the only way to afford a house big enough to raise the family we eventually wanted. But my husband loves the beach.

"No problem. I've always wanted to live by the beach." He grins at all of us. "Or, at least, I think I have."

8

———

"Nice place," Jack said, standing at the windowed back wall of Liam's beachfront condo. The condo sparkled and still had that new car smell that signified either fresh construction or a recent remodel.

"It's been around since the nineties," Liam said when Jack asked the question. "Most of the units were remodeled at least a decade ago. But this one was owned by an elderly woman who lived with her six cats—and no, I'm not exaggerating. When she passed away, the family didn't want to bother with it—they live in Idaho—and they put it on the market without any updates. Got a few nibbles but everyone haggled. I made a cash offer, then had Jackson draw up some plans. Then I hired Syl to act as a contractor, and the rest is history."

He shrugged and grinned, looking pleased with himself. "Got it reappraised after the remodel, and even with my outlay of cash, I'm still in the black. That plus an ocean view. I consider it a win."

"Not bad," Jack said. "Syl and Jackson?" He almost hesitated to ask the question. Probably someone he should remember.

"Jackson Steele. He's a pretty famous architect. Ring any bells?"

"Not even a tingle."

"Jackson's Damien's half-brother. He designed The Domino, actually."

"*That* I remember. The business park where the SSA is located. Was in the news for a few years while it was in development, right?"

Liam nodded. "I'm impressed," he said as he headed into the kitchen. "Coffee?"

"Thanks. Black is good." He moved to the back wall composed of glass sliders. "It's weird what I remember. I know who's president. I remember the oceans and continents, and I know the plot of at least a half dozen *Star Wars* movies."

Liam laughed. "Not surprised. Denise is a huge *Star Wars* fan."

Jack frowned, then looked back over his shoulder, and saw a flicker of something cross over Liam's face. Like he was irritated with himself.

"Denise? So, she and I saw a lot of the movies together?"

"You were partners," Liam said evenly, his attention on the coffee pot. "And you both like action movies and fantasy."

"Huh." Jack turned back toward the ocean, wondering what it was about Liam's response that made him feel so off. Like he should remember something. Like maybe he wasn't as honorable a guy as he liked to think and he'd taken his partner to the movies, not simply as casual friends, but for the pleasure of sitting next to her in the dark, their fingers brushing over the popcorn.

Fucking hell...

"Were Denise and I—"

From over the pass-through bar, Liam looked at him, his expression bland. "Say again?"

"Nothing. Just wondering if we worked well together."

"I never worked with the two of you, but from what she says, you guys made a great team."

He nodded, pleased that he'd managed to divert his own misstep before Liam noticed. And irritated that his thoughts had zeroed in on Denise Marshall with such laser-like intensity. Not because she was his partner, but, damn him, because he craved her.

There. He said it. Maybe not out loud, but he'd voiced the words in his head. Words he'd been dancing around since the first moment she'd walked into his little cell of a room at the SOC. And now here he was, about to start working in close proximity to her.

All of which made him a fucking idiot, because the part of his body that he needed to kick-start was the memory centers of his brain. Not his damn cock. And the last thing he wanted to do was insult her or the memory of her husband.

If he was a better man, he would have stayed away. Not approached Seagrave with his plan to spur his memory at all. But he couldn't deny that spending time with her had been at least as appealing as the possibility of sparking his memory. And definitely more certain.

He sighed, looking out over the Pacific. "Sometimes I wonder if I forgot myself because I'm just that much of an asshole."

Liam frowned. "Come again?"

He waved the words away. "Sorry. Pity party. Ignore me."

"Yeah, well, if anyone deserves one, it's you." He stepped

out from behind the counter with two mugs and handed one to Jack.

"Thanks. And thanks for letting me stay here. You sure I'm not putting you out? Wife? Girlfriend?"

"Just me." There was a hard edge to Liam's voice. The kind of edge that hinted at secrets. And had Jack shifting the conversation. He might be curious, but he wasn't about to piss off his host. Especially not since he hoped that host would grow into a friend.

Liam cleared his throat. "Let's get you settled, then I need to head back for my team meeting. Denise is picking you up this evening right?"

Jack nodded, then held up the duffel that contained all his belongings in the world. "I'd like to own more than one pair of jeans and an extra pair of skivvies. Thought I'd grab an Uber and pull out the shiny new ID and credit card Seagrave arranged for me. That is, if you don't mind giving me a spare key."

"It's a keypad lock," Liam said, telling him the code. "And no need for a ride share. You can handle a bike?"

"Let me guess. A Harley?"

"If that's your poison. There's one in the garage. A Ducati, too, along with a few other beauties. Keys are on the hook by the fridge. But don't touch the Bonneville. I just finished restoring her, and I always take the inaugural ride."

Jack's grin stretched so wide his cheeks hurt. "Liam, my man, I think I'm going to like crashing here."

————

He didn't need much. Considering he had no closet of his own, Jack only intended to buy the bare minimum. A clean pair of jeans without rips in the knees. A couple of decent T-shirts so he didn't look like he'd raided his grandfather's closet. Figure of speech, that. He didn't even know if he had a grandfather.

Shoes. A razor. A toothbrush.

Nothing but the essentials. Get in, get out, get back to Liam's and do a little prep work on Cerise Sinclair, thanks to Ryan agreeing to shoot the encrypted files to the spare laptop Liam had left for him. Not strictly necessary—Ryan had assured him the matter was simple enough that Denise could brief him on the way—but Jack didn't intend to slack. If he was on the team, he was doing the job.

Besides, Denise had already seen him at his worst. He wanted her to know that he was also sharp, efficient, and always prepared.

He remembered that there was a mall in Century City, an unremarkable memory for most people, but one that had him fighting the urge to do a victory dance. It turned out to be of the Pyrrhic variety, however, because he quickly learned how much he hated shopping. The only point was to acquire clothes and other necessities, and yet as far as he could tell, the stores wanted to make the process a multi-media experience.

And if one more rail thin woman asked to spray him with some new cologne that she assured him was manly, he feared he'd have to break something.

He ended up escaping with a single pair of jeans, a gray Henley, a sport coat, shoes, and a package of underwear. After that, he hit a drugstore for bathroom essentials. As he was heading toward the checkout, he passed a display of condoms—and immediately his mind filled with images of Denise Marshall. Not X-rated. Not even NC-17. But definitely a strong R-rating.

He was in so goddamn much trouble.

He drew a deep breath, told himself that he had bigger things to worry about than getting laid, lectured himself on the importance of being a professional, and then got the hell away from the display as fast as he possibly could.

By the time the doorbell rang at six that evening, he'd cleaned up, changed, reviewed the Sinclair file, and resisted the urge to plug Denise and Mason's names into Google.

For a while, anyway.

He'd originally justified the urge by telling himself that she knew a hell of a lot more about him than he knew about her. But that was bullshit, of course. What he really wanted was to see what made her tick. *Who* made her tick.

He wanted to find out about Mason—and he wanted to find out almost as much as he didn't want to be the kind of asshole who'd do that.

So he'd backed away from the computer.

And then, dammit, he'd come to terms with the thought of being a prick. He'd run five searches and he didn't find a thing. Not one single thing. Not a name. Not a picture. Not a half-assed remark in someone else's Twitter stream.

Nothing.

So he ran more. Looked deeper. Harder.

Crickets. Not even a hint.

Which mean that Mason had been a ghost. A high-level operative who was placed in key, long-term, undercover missions. The kind of guy who, for every one of him, there were at least fifty other agents parked at computers across the world whose job entailed nothing more than making sure he was completely erased from the web, the deep web, the dark web, and all the layers in-between.

More than that, it meant that Mason could still be alive.

He frowned, trying to remember his earlier conversation

with Denise. She still wore his ring, and she'd told him
—*what?*

Not that her husband was dead. All Denise had said was
that he'd been gone for a very long time. Jack had assumed
the rest.

With a sigh, he leaned back in his chair, and once again
condemned himself as a prick. He'd just learned that his
partner's husband—a man who by all accounts had been his
friend—might well be alive. He should be happy. He should
be scheming ways to learn the truth, even if it pissed off
Seagrave and the rest of them. Because God knew Jack
didn't have anything to lose at this point.

He should be doing anything other sitting there numb
and feeling like a little boy who just learned that Christmas
was canceled.

Asshole.

Yeah, that's right. He needed to just own it. He was a
fucked-up, horny, prick who hadn't been laid in God knew
how long. He met a woman he was attracted to—a woman
who turned out to be off-limits—and that fact offended his
apparently Neanderthal sensibilities.

Well, too bad for him.

Because in the grand scheme of things, he had a lot
more important things to worry about. Like, oh, who he was
and what he'd been working on. Everything else could wait,
and if that meant he took two cold showers a day, then so
be it.

For that matter, he should probably take one right now...

Ding!

He frowned, the sharp chime of the doorbell reminding
him that he was all out of time. "Coming!" he called before
stopping by the bathroom to splash some cold water on his
face.

Then he hurried down the stairs, only to stop short when he saw her standing in the entrance hall.

"Sorry," she said. "I was already inside by the time I realized you'd probably said *coming*, not *come in*."

"It's all good," he said. "I'd offer you something to eat or drink, but it's not my kitchen, not my food."

"No worries." Her grin lit up her eyes making them spark like green flame. Christ, but she was lovely. "But if you need a tour of Liam's kitchen, I'm happy to walk you through."

A nip of jealousy grabbed hold of him, like some irritating little mongrel he couldn't shake loose. "You hang out here a lot?"

"I'm the plant and fish girl." She laughed, obviously in response to his expression. "I stay here when Liam's out of town. I like walking on the beach. And I'm not all that crazy about my house anymore." She met his eyes, then looked away quickly, as if she didn't want him to see her secrets.

"The house you shared with Mason."

"We never got around to fixing it up. And it's lonely without—him."

He had the impression she'd been about to say something else, though he couldn't imagine what. "And that ties in to plants and fish how?"

"You obviously haven't seen Liam's room. Come on."

She took the stairs two at a time, passing the open door to his bedroom, and continuing up to the master bedroom that took up the entire third floor. The minute he stepped through the door, he understood what she meant. Small potted plants dotted the room, but it was the outdoors that truly drew his attention. The balcony was covered with greenery. Not in an overbearing way, but in a way that made the outdoor space welcoming and pleasant for anyone who wanted to sit out there and watch the surf.

He thought of Liam—big, muscular Liam—sitting at the small metal table sipping coffee, and had to grin.

"Bet if you had to guess what was on his balcony you would have gone with a weight bench and a punching bag."

"Pretty much," he agreed. "And the fish?"

"Oh, the fish are especially cool." She cocked her head, and then led him into the huge master bath, where one entire wall was a giant seawater fish tank filled with stunning, colorful sea life.

"That's incredible."

"I know, right? When I stay here to plant and fish-sit, I sleep in the guest room. But I told Liam that he had to let me use the master bath. It's just too fun."

"Jackson Steele did this?"

"Liam told you about the remodel? Yeah. I keep thinking I'll ask Jackson to come up with something equally awesome for my house. But then..." She didn't shrug, but her overly casual smile worked equally as well as a dismissal.

He didn't take the bait. "You didn't want to work on the house alone."

She turned back toward the fish, and for a moment, he thought she wasn't going to answer. He was about to apologize for pushing too hard, when she said very softly. "No. No, I was wa—"

"Waiting for Mason to come home? He's alive, isn't he?"

She'd shifted, returning her attention to him. "I never said he was dead."

"But you knew I'd think it. And for awhile, I think you believed it."

Her brow furrowed as she studied him. "What makes you say that?"

"You looked so haunted when you'd said he'd been gone a long time. Anyway, it doesn't matter. The point is that he's not dead, is he?"

"No." Her throat moved as she swallowed. "He's not."

"I'm glad for you." He meant the words. He had no desire to hurt her. But they still left him hollow. "He was on an undercover assignment, right? Deep cover?"

"How do you know that?"

"A guess, but clearly a good one. If he was in deep cover, how can you be sure he's alive? Has he made contact?"

She drew in a breath, then looked him straight in the eyes. "Yes," she said. "Twice. And you know enough about that world to know I shouldn't be talking about it. Which means this conversation is done."

"Fair enough."

She glanced at her phone, then frowned. "We need to hurry if we're going to meet Cerise on time."

"Want me to drive?" He still had the Ducati's key in his pocket, and now he dangled it. He was teasing, of course. He knew damn well they'd take her car.

Which was why her delighted laugh and eager nod threw him completely off guard. So off that he couldn't prevent the words that burst into his head, terrifying in their truth—*Damn, but he could fall hard for this woman.*

9

"I FORGOT about the hills and curves," I shout as I cling to Mason—*Jack!*—while he expertly navigates the Hollywood Hills. "Take your next left, then an immediate right."

He may have lost his memory, but he hasn't lost his skill on a bike, and I'd be lying if I said I wasn't enjoying this chance to hold onto my husband. His well-muscled body fits perfectly against mine, and I keep my arms tight around him, my chin resting on his shoulder as we sail over streets carved from these tree-covered hills.

Cerise's house sits at the rise of one of the steepest hills, and I press my thighs more firmly against Jack's hips, holding on as we creep up the hill at an obscene angle. Her place is lovely—three levels of stucco and wood with an incredible view of Universal Studios and the valley beyond—but access is a challenge, and this isn't a route I'd want to navigate daily.

Nor is it a home I'd want if I was worrying about stalkers. It may be hard to get to, but it's also hard to leave. Her road is a dead end, and her only neighbor is an elderly man who spent his youth working on television sitcoms.

The three lots that surround her property are for sale, but so far no buyer has been interested in tackling the engineering nightmare that comes with building on such steep lots, particularly with the hassle of getting equipment up these narrow streets.

"Still," Jack says when I run all of that by him, "that's one hell of a view."

He's right. And for a moment we stand at the side of the road in front of the bike, looking past the house to the view beyond. "Some consolation for living up here," I say. "All the same, I think I'd choose the beach."

"Or your place?"

I frown. I love my house—I do. But I love a vision of it that may never come to fruition. And that's not something I want to talk about with Jack. Especially not with Jack.

Instead, I divert the conversation, lifting a shoulder and saying simply, "Neither hills nor beach. I'm a sad example of a real estate maven."

"I don't think you're a sad example of anything." There's something soft and familiar in his voice, and I turn without thinking to face him, then draw in a tight breath at the look in his eye. A familiar glint of humor and passion. The kind of look that was usually followed by a swift tug on my arm to pull me close, a firm grip on my ass, and the kind of hot kiss that would melt me right into bed.

I swallow a strangled gasp and yank my gaze away, suddenly fascinated with the cuff of my jeans.

"Denise, I—"

The rumble and squeak of the rising garage door cuts off his words, and I silently thank Cerise for her ill-timed appearance. She's standing inside the garage, and she bends down to slip under the door, then waves at us.

The wind has caught her silky, black hair, and she

pushes a wild curl out of her eyes. "What on earth are you doing out here? I saw you pull up and got tired of waiting. Your bike?" she asks, eyeing Mason in a way that makes my girl parts sit up and start growling.

"Cerise," I say, forcing myself to be polite, "this is Jack Sawyer, my new partner. I wanted to introduce you and let him take a peek at the equipment. And we both want to hear whatever it is you wanted to talk about. Ryan was rather vague."

"Oh, sure." She hugs herself and flashes an extremely photogenic smile at Jack. I tense, forcing myself not to sidle next to him and hook my arm possessively through his.

"Are you having trouble with the system?" I ask as she leads us inside through the garage.

"Not really," she says with a small frown. "I don't think to check the video that often, but since the feed goes direct to your monitoring station, I feel pretty confident." She looks over her shoulder as we move down the back hall toward the main living area. "I know setting me up was small potatoes for Stark Security, but it's made me feel a lot safer knowing your staff monitors the feed."

"That's the point," I say. She's right, of course. For the most part, the SSA takes on high-end assignments. But Damien's always been adamant about the SSA being service-oriented. Which is why we also provide basic security service for celebrities at events and home security for anyone who walks through the door and can afford the equipment and monthly fee. And a few people who can't, if Damien or Ryan approve the cost, as I've seen them do for a number of near-destitute women who were being harassed by their ex-husbands or boyfriends.

"No one's been too obnoxious in person," Cerise continues, "but some of the online comments…" She trails off, her nose wrinkling.

"I get it," I assure her. I'm not online much, but I have a very good imagination. "So, all in all you feel safe up here? You're pretty isolated."

"That's part of what I like," she says. "I really do love this place. That's why—" She cuts herself off with a shake of her head. "I'm probably just being paranoid."

"It's usually someone who thinks they're paranoid who gets kicked in the nuts," Jack says.

"Well, then I'm safe," Cerise quips, making me laugh.

"What do you think you're being paranoid about?" Jack asks.

She drags her finger through her hair. "I saw someone last night, way down the hill. But he was just out of camera range. I checked the feed, and it cut off before the dip. Right there," she adds, pointing down. "It's not even my property, which is why I figure I shouldn't worry about it. Probably a homeless person. Or maybe the owner was walking the property. Thinking about clearing brush or something. The sun was behind the hills, but it wasn't pitch black yet."

"Maybe," I say. I don't mention that the lot is currently owned by the bank. So there's no owner who could be wandering it at night.

"Peter said it was probably a coyote and not a man at all," she adds, a blush rising on her fair skin. "But he said I should call you if that would make me feel better."

I grin, amused. "Peter?"

Her whole face lights up at the question. "He's fabulous. We've been seeing each other on and off for a while, but now…" She trails off and sighs happily. "Well, I think he wants to get serious."

"That's great," I say. "Congratulations."

"Thanks." She hooks a thumb toward the kitchen. "Do you want some wine? I'd just opened a bottle before you got here."

We agree, and she returns a moment later with three glasses hung by the stems in one hand and a bottle of red in the other.

"To you and Peter," I say after she pours.

"And to tightening up your camera array," Jack adds.

"Oh, I almost forgot," she says after taking a long sip. "I'm meeting Peter tonight at Westerfield's. I told him all about how you worked with me to get the house security set up, and how I feel so much safer now, and we thought it would be fun if you came, too." She looks at Jack. "Even better now that you'll have a date."

"Ah, well..." Jack looks at me, his expression decidedly uncomfortable. My stomach does that unpleasant flipping thing again, but why wouldn't I be a little nauseous at the realization that my own husband is disgusted by the idea of going out with me?

I stiffen as I say, "I don't think we—"

"Of course, we'll come," Jack says, talking boldly over me. "We'd be thrilled."

10

I PARTED ways with Jack after we returned to Liam's so that I could go home and change. Now, I arrive at the West Hollywood club alone. The line, as always, is down the block, but mine is one of the names permanently on the VIP list—a perk of working for Damien Stark, who owns the popular hotspot. Not that he comes often anymore. With two little girls, I don't think he and Nikki frequent the club scene.

I step inside, then pause, letting the music wash over me. I glance around for Jack, but don't see him. I do, however, catch sight of Cass. With a grin, I head that direction.

"Hey, stranger," I say, letting her pull me into a hug. "Am I interrupting a date?" I look around for a girl who might be with Cass, hoping that she's moving on after the bullshit with Siobhan. But she shakes her head and gives me *the look*.

"I'm not even playing the field," she says. "I only came for the awesome company."

"So this isn't a coincidence?" At the same time I ask the question, Quince and Eliza approach, and I actually clap my hands, delighted.

Quince is carrying two drinks, one of which he passes to Cass before hooking his free arm around my shoulders and giving me a squeeze.

"Hell of a way to start the weekend, eh?" His British accent is more pronounced than usual, so I figure this isn't his first drink of the evening.

I look between the three of them. "This isn't a coincidence, right? Not that I'm complaining."

"Cerise called," Cass says simply. "Said she'd invited you and Jack and that I should come down, too. Then she asked me to invite Syl and Jamie and their guys, but obviously Syl's already left the country."

"So Jamie and Ryan are coming?"

"That would be big, fat no."

She's grinning when she says it, and I narrow my eyes, wondering at the joke. "Well?" I prod.

"Oh, right. Jamie's exact quote was that she already had Ryan naked, and that while we were all a lot of fun, he was better."

I slam my hands over my ears in mock horror. "I did *not* need to hear that about my boss."

"You asked," Cass says.

"And I should have known better," I admit. I love Jamie, but the woman has no filter at all. "Where's Cerise?"

"Around here somewhere," Quince says. "She's got her boyfriend with her, so you might check dark corners."

Beside him, Eliza gives him an elbow nudge.

"What?" he asks. "You know I'm right."

Cass laughs, then points at Quince and Eliza while still talking to me. "I didn't know they'd be here. So I consider them a perk. And a comedy show, too. All rolled into one."

"Funny girl," Quince says, making Cass grin.

Quince drags over an extra chair, and we all squeeze in

around the small cocktail table. Cass slides her drink my direction. "Want to share until we can get a waiter's attention?"

I take it, ready to start Friday right, but just the smell of the whiskey makes my stomach roll, and I decide to stick with water, hoping that whatever bug has taken up residence in my stomach gets bored and moves out quickly.

Still, probably best to stay sober, especially since Jack should be here soon.

As if he's reading my mind, Quince says, "How are you coping?"

I shrug. "I disarmed a nuclear weapon once. Did you know that?"

He shakes his head.

"That was easier."

"Denny..."

I manage a half-smile, feeling even more sorry for myself at the sound of my name on his lips. Not that I mind Quince adopting the nickname. But it was Mason who first started calling me Denny, and his are the lips I want to hear it from.

Beside Quince, Eliza leans forward. "I'm so sorry you have to deal with this."

"I appreciate that," I say, and I mean it. But at the same time I don't want to talk about how hard it is. Because that just makes it harder.

In an effort to deflect the attention off me—and because I'm legitimately curious—I ask if they've heard from Emma. Eliza's sister was at the center of the case Quince and I just wrapped. Now she's in Europe, returning a kidnapped princess to her monarch father.

"I talked to her this morning," Eliza says. "So far, the trip's gone smoothly."

"Has she decided what she's going to do?" Emma's a

private investigator with a seriously badass covert ops background. Basically, my job is as boring as alphabetizing an old-fashioned card catalog compared to some of the stuff Emma has handled in the course of her career.

Which means she'd be a hell of an asset to the SSA, and I really hope she decides to come on board.

Meanwhile, I look around for my not-covert, not-badass client, and finally see her talking with a guy on the far side of the room. They're in shadows, so I can't see his face, but something about him looks familiar. I'm about to stand up and go talk with them when I catch sight of Jack heading my way from the other side of the room. And, of course, the sight of him erases every other thought from my head.

I'm not even exaggerating. Nor am I surprised.

The first time I saw Mason, I'd been walking into an NSC briefing at the Pentagon. A room full of the most powerful people in the country, including me, newly-anointed to go out into the world to fight terrorism at its root.

But did I act the part of the well-trained badass?

Well, actually, I did. That's where the "well-trained" part comes in. Because the moment I saw Mason sitting at that table, all rational thought left my head. Suddenly, I was just a girl in high school crushing on the cute guy. The smart guy. The clever guy. *The perfect guy.*

And when I found out that he felt the same way about me...

Well, for Mason and me, there was no slow burn. We were combustible from the first moment we were together. And it kills me—absolutely slays me—that he can walk so casually across this club, sidle up to me, and say nothing more engaging than, "Fancy meeting you here."

Honestly, it's not even that cute a line.

Where's the man who could make me come with a heated look?

Who'd tug me into a dark corner for stolen kisses or even naughtier moments?

The man who could shut that all down during a mission, then release every trapped desire the moment we wrapped, fucking me for hours in our bed until we were both exhausted and sated?

I want that man back as much as I want the guy who'd drink wine with me on the sofa while we watched reruns of *Firefly*. The guy who'd bore me to tears spending hours in Home Depot comparing paint colors for the bathroom. The guy who knew how to grill a steak better than any five star chef.

In other words, I want my husband. Mason, not Jack. The man who remembers he loves me. The man with whom I'd shared a life. A history. The man who knew my secrets and my fears, my hopes and desires.

But Mason is gone, and it's Jack standing beside me. Jack with whom I have to play a role, when all I want is to go home and cry.

"Denise?" He's peering at me, his brow furrowed. "You okay?"

"Tired," I say. "And sober. I've got a stomach bug or something and alcohol is not sitting well."

He flashes a grin, revealing his dimple. "That is a tragedy. How about I take the edge off and—"

We don't get to the *and.*

Instead, we're interrupted by the arrival of Cerise and her companion.

He isn't in the shadows now—in fact the whole club fills with wild, flashing lights. The beams bounce with the music as they crisscross the dance floor, illuminating every inch of his all-too familiar face.

"Peter," I squeal as I throw myself into his outstretched arms.

"Denise!" He hugs me tight, then pushes me away so that his hands are on my shoulders and I'm grinning up at him like an idiot. "I had no idea you were in LA."

"Same," I say. "This is amazing."

"I'm sorry," Cerise says. "You know each other?"

Peter and I exchange glances. And with perfect timing, we look back at Cerise. "Nope," we say, then start laughing all over again.

11

I'M STILL GRINNING when Jack approaches, but my smile fades when I see the way he's rubbing his temples. Peter's hand rests on my shoulder, and I slip out from under his touch, then approach Jack, lightly brushing his arm as I try to read the expression in his eyes. "Are you okay?"

He gives a little half-shake of his head, his expression one of mild annoyance. Not at me, I don't think, but at his own discomfort. "I think it's the damn lights. They started flashing, and it's like needles to my eyes."

"You're not prone to migraines," I say.

"Aren't I?"

I bite back a wince, realizing how close I came to giving away too much. But it's reasonable that I'd know if my partner suffered from migraines. Still, I need to be more careful.

Now, though, I just shrug. "Not that I've seen before."

"Probably a symptom," he says. "My already battered brain doesn't like the crazy disco lights."

"Trust me," I say dryly. "It's not just you. Welcome to Friday at a club." I sweep my arm out to encompass the entire room, noticing as I do that Cerise has moved a few feet away and is laughing with a group of women I've never met before.

"Speaking of welcome," Peter says, waving for Jack's attention. "It's great to see you again, M—"

"*Jack*," I say firmly, speaking loudly on top of Peter before he can announce Mason's real name. "Jack, this is Peter."

"Am I missing the joke?" Peter asks, looking between the two of us.

"Jack's having a little trouble with his memory."

"Which is the polite way of saying that I'm a blank slate," he puts in. "And we're sharing this information why?"

"It's okay. Peter and I worked together for about a year in Washington before I moved over to the SOC."

"Obviously, I don't remember you," Jack says. "Sorry about that."

Peter shakes his head. "No worries. I would say your little problem is an occupational hazard, but the truth is that I haven't seen this before. Heard of it. But I always assumed the stories were urban legend."

"A story they tell about bad little agents?" Jack quips, making Peter laugh.

"Is that what you were?"

Jack shrugs. "How the hell do I know?"

Peter chuckles. "I see you kept your sense of humor."

"Did we work together, too?"

Peter shakes his head. "No. We only met the one time when you two got m—"

"Medals of commendation," I interrupt, shooting Peter a sharp glance, in response to which he looks sufficiently contrite. We don't actually have any medals of commendation, and even if we did I don't know why Peter would have come to the ceremony. But thankfully Jack doesn't seem interested in the point. Or in Peter or I for that matter. On the contrary, he's looking at something across the room, his brow furrowed as if in confusion.

"The lights still?" There's no laser light show at the moment, but there is a colorful disco ball that's casting moving circles of light on the walls and floor.

"Mind if I borrow Denise for a second?" Jack says, to which Peter shrugs and says he'll go freshen his drink.

"What's going on?" I ask, waving off Cass who's started to head in our direction.

"I'm not sure." He nods toward the dance floor. "When the lights started, I thought I saw…"

"What?"

He shakes his head. "I don't know. A face."

"A face?"

He meets my eyes. "A face."

"We're in a club. There are a lot of faces."

"I don't know why it struck me. I can't even find it again in the crowd. I'm not even sure if it was a man or a woman, much less real. Maybe it was just a shadow. A mirage in the dark."

"But you don't think so." It's a statement, not a question.

"I think it's a memory. I think there's someone here with us that I remember. Or that my mind is trying to remember."

"From your past? Or from your mission?" I'm assuming the latter. And I'm trying not to let my feelings get hurt because he's semi-remembered a shadowy face before he remembered his wife.

"From my torture," he says flatly. "I saw that face, and my blood ran cold."

My hurt feelings are pushed away by guilt, and I take his

hand. "We'll find him. We'll find him," I repeat, "and we'll get some answers."

"I'm going to make a few rounds through the club, then I'm going to head back to Liam's. I know tomorrow's Saturday, but I'd like to work. Maybe go over some of our old files. See if that triggers any new memories. Okay?"

"Of course. Meet you in the office around ten?"

"I'll be there," he says, then slips into the dark.

I stand there for a moment, letting the beat of the music pound through me. I want to follow him. I want to take his shoulders and look into his eyes and tell him everything.

But I can't. And I hate how impotent I feel.

I turn with a sigh, intending to go to the bar for a tonic and lime. Instead, I find Peter behind me. "You okay?"

"Sure. Where's Cerise?"

"Ladies' room." He holds out his hand. "Dance?"

I shake my head. "Not in the mood."

"A pity. I am."

"I'm sure Cerise will be up for it when she gets back. I like her a lot," I tell Peter. "But she doesn't seem to be your type."

"That's because you were always my type."

I mentally kick myself. I should never have opened that door. Peter and I worked in the same field office and got along great. But the times we partnered for a mission together, I was never at my best. I could feel the attraction rolling off him. And while Mason's interest in me never got in the way of our work, it was a distraction with Peter. The difference, of course, was that I wasn't in love with Peter, and so I didn't trust him the way you trust a true partner. And Mason always was a true partner, even before we became involved.

"Peter..."

He holds his hands out in surrender. "I know. Just friends. Don't worry. I'm over you. I'm just stating a fact. And Cerise is a doll. I really do adore her."

"I'm glad to hear it. She's not just a client. She's a friend."

"So why aren't you telling him the truth?"

It's a total flip in the conversation, but I follow his thread easily. "You know I can't give you details. Let's just say it's protocol."

He nods, then steps back, his eyes looking me up and down. I'm wearing jeans and a plain white tank top, and the heat in Peter's eyes is the kind I want to see in Jack's.

His gaze stops at my wrist, where Mason's name has been recently inked. "Who does he think that is?"

I draw in a shaky breath. "My husband. Who may or may not be dead."

"Makes it rough for you, doesn't it?"

This time, I can't follow his thoughts, because everything about my life and Mason is rough right now. "What do you mean?"

"I saw the way he looked at you. Guy's hot for you. And looks to me like you want him, too."

I swallow. "Where are you going with this?"

"Same place you are—nowhere. Because you're too honorable a woman to cheat on your husband. Which means that you can't cheat with your husband. No matter how much you want to." He's got about six inches on me, and he uses the tip of his finger to tilt my chin up. He locks his gaze with mine and flashes a wicked grin. "Or are you planning to fuck him anyway?"

With effort, I resist the urge to reach up and slap his face. Instead, I say, "This is why you and I never got together. I prefer my men with a bit of character."

"What can I say? You bring out the worst in me."

"Try to keep it inside," I say, then turn and walk away. I don't see Quince or Eliza, but Cass is laughing with a cute blonde by the bar. I catch her eye, then point toward the door. She lifts her hand to her ear in a "call me" gesture, and I nod. I'll give her a buzz tomorrow. Right now, I'm heading home.

On the sidewalk, I lean against a signpost as I tap my phone and order an Uber. It's five minutes away, and I take a moment to close my eyes, draw a breath, and enjoy the sounds of the night.

The cool steel of a blade presses against my throat and my eyes fly open. I stay perfectly still, trying not to breathe, and cursing myself for inexplicably dropping my guard.

Whoever is holding the knife is behind me. About my height, and his hand doesn't shake, so it's clear he knows how to handle a knife.

When he leans in close to my ear, I catch the smell of jalapeños and tequila, and I make a note to have one of the tech team pull the receipts from Westerfield's and use the security feed to match them with patrons. Maybe I'll get lucky.

"I'm not the only one who can get to you," the man whispers. "Keep that in mind. Tell him he needs to remember. If he wants you to stay safe—to stay alive—he needs to give back what he took. Tell him."

"Who?"

"Cunt," he says, and I gasp as the knife presses harder. There will be a thin line of blood on my neck, I'm certain of it. "You know who." But then, as if he wants to be sure there's no confusion, he whispers, "Mason Walker. You tell him. You tell him you're a dead woman walking unless he comes through."

Something hard smacks my head, knocking me forward

at the same time he yanks the knife away. An instant later, he shoves the back of my neck and I fall to my knees as a black Lexus squeals to a halt, and he turns just enough for me to see greasy hair, bushy eyebrows, and a bulbous nose. Then he leaps in. The car races away down Sunset Boulevard, the Arkansas plate undoubtedly stolen.

I stumble to my feet at the same time my Uber arrives, and I climb in, draw a breath, and pull out my phone.

12

It was almost three in the morning, and Jack still hadn't made it back to Liam's place. He'd left Westerfield's intending to return to the Malibu condo, but instead he'd let the bike take him where it wanted to go.

Or, more accurately, where his subconscious wanted to go.

He assumed he'd lived in LA before they'd stolen his memory, but no one had specifically told him that. Hell, no one had told him shit. And even though he knew the reasons, it was still damn hard to stomach.

So he drove the streets of Los Angeles County, praying that some spark of familiarity would strike him.

He recognized a lot of things. Malls. Restaurants. Tourist attractions. He remembered The Getty Center and the Santa Monica Pier, the MOCA downtown, and Rodeo Drive in Beverly Hills.

He didn't wander the hiking trails off Laurel Canyon, but he had a feeling that if he did, he'd remember every twist and turn. And when he closed his eyes he could almost remember the swell of music bursting from the Hollywood Bowl amphitheater.

Goddammit, he wanted his mind back. His life back.

Unbidden, Denise popped into his thoughts, and he swerved the bike onto one of the Mulholland Drive turnouts, killed the engine, and let his head fall down to rest on the handlebars.

There it was—a living, breathing reason why he had to get his memory back, and sooner rather than later. Because damned if he didn't want her. If he hadn't wanted her from the first moment he'd seen her. And the hunger for her was only getting stronger with each passing minute.

He'd stood in that club tonight surrounded by beautiful women in revealing dresses and low-cut shirts, and he hadn't felt the slightest twinge of interest. Then he saw Denise in her simple jeans and plain white tank top and he'd just about lost his shit. The way the denim hugged the curve of her ass. The way the white of the tank contrasted her tan skin. The hint of bra he could see when she bent to put her drink on the table. The sweet curve of her lips when she smiled at him.

His fingers had itched to touch her, and he'd closed his eyes and imagined what every silky inch of her body would feel like against his fingers, his lips, his cock.

And when he'd seen her with Peter ... well, that had really fueled the fire.

God, he was an asshole.

She trusted him as her partner. She was helping him pull his life back together. Most of all, she belonged to another man. And yet there he was, fantasizing about getting her naked and beneath him.

No. He drew in a breath and sat up straight. *No, that wasn't entirely true.* He wanted her—damned if he didn't—

but not just physically. He wanted to be with her. Wanted to talk with her, walk with her. Laugh at silly things and soothe her through the sad ones.

He didn't know if this was new or if he'd been enthralled by her for months. All he knew was that whatever barriers had held him back before seemed to be crumbling.

Most of all, he knew that if he wasn't careful, this uncontrollable infatuation would be the death knell of a friendship that he cherished.

A wave of exhaustion overtook him, and he yawned deeply, then pulled out his phone to check the time, only then realizing that he'd turned the thing off in the club and forgot to turn it back on. What was the point considering he'd been with Denny, and barely even knew half a dozen other people?

Even so, he switched it back on. Almost immediately it emitted a cacophony of buzzes and pings signaling missed texts and phone calls.

He glanced at the screen, saw that almost all the calls and messages came from Liam, and started to dial his host back, feeling like an ass for making Liam worry about his whereabouts.

The call hadn't even connected before headlights appeared behind him. He ended the call, then turned, squinting into the lights from an SUV that he couldn't identify in the glare. The door opened, and a mountain of a man stepped out.

Jack didn't have a weapon, but he flipped on the bike's ignition, prepared to speed away if he needed to.

The man walked forward, his back to the SUV's headlights so that his face was in shadows. "Christ, Jack. What the fuck have you been doing?"

Liam.

"I tried calling, but your phone's off. I had to log into the tracker I keep on the Ducati. I've been tailing you for almost an hour. What the hell are you doing riding in circles around the damn city?"

Jack dismounted, trying to process everything Liam was saying. "I should have called—sorry. I just needed a ride in the fresh air to blow out some of the shit floating around in my head."

"I hear you, and normally I wouldn't play babysitter, but Denise was freaked when she couldn't get a hold of you, so I—"

"Wait. What?" He took a step toward Liam. "What happened? Why was she calling? Why was she freaked?"

"Somebody attacked her outside the club. A man, she says. She's fine," he added quickly, holding up a hand to forestall Jack's burst of terror and fury. "But she said it might have been your face?" He shook his head. "She didn't explain, but she did say that you'd understand. And that the bastard told her that you needed to remember. That you needed to return what you took. Ring any bells?"

"Not a goddamn one." And now Jack was kicking himself for not trying harder to track the Face down in the club.

"Well, I told her I'd find you."

"I need to go to her."

Liam took a step toward him. "No, she's asleep. As soon as the bike pinged on the tracking map, I called. Said I'd catch up to you and that she should get some sleep. I finally got her to agree—she sounded bone tired—and she said she'd see you at the office at ten."

Jack nodded slowly, considering. "Fine. Then I'll show up at her house at eight."

"Jack..."

"Best I can do, man. May as well not even bother arguing."

Liam chuckled. "Fine. I'll let Denise shoot you down. God knows she's capable."

"Hey," Jack said. "Thanks for running me to ground. Sorry to lead you all over the city. I had a lot of thinking to do."

"No surprise there. Just glad I found you."

"How'd your job go tonight? Security for Ellie Love, right? I heard on the radio that the concert was a sell-out. I like a few of her songs. She as good live as they say?"

Liam shook his head, looking a little frazzled. Jack didn't know him well, but he had a feeling that frazzled wasn't a usual state for Liam. "For such a tiny woman, she's got some serious pipes. And one hell of a lot of talent. She's also a royal pain in the ass with some serious attitude, but as it's SSA policy not to speak ill of a client, you didn't hear it from me."

Jack chuckled. "Sorry about that."

Liam shook his head, looking both amused and exasperated. "Honestly, man, I still don't know what to think of her, and I didn't see a damn thing that suggested a threat, so I don't know what game she or her manager was playing. But the woman's like a damn force of nature, and woe to anybody who tries to get her to do something she doesn't want to do. But at least it's over. A one-night gig and the cord was cut. I don't expect she'll be back in LA until she puts out her next album."

"And maybe then she'll hire some other security company."

Liam's teeth shone in the moonlight with his smile. "We can hope." He pointed at the bike. "Stay out as long as you want, but keep your damn phone on, okay?"

"Deal," Jack said, then waited until Liam and his SUV disappeared over the hill.

Then he dialed the phone, feeling absolutely no guilt when a groggy voice answered with a sleepy, "Hello?"

"It's Jack," he said. "How soon can you meet me?"

———

Despite seeing him at four in the morning, Dr. Tam looked completely awake and perfectly put together. Jack had to give her props; she hadn't protested when he'd insisted on the early morning emergency session.

Then again, he had a sneaking suspicion that he might be the most pressing unanswered question at the SOC at the moment, so helping him was in everyone's best interest.

"So this man, this face, triggered a reaction," Dr. Tam commented. "But you don't have any specific memory?"

"None. And I need to know where I've seen him. I need to figure out who he is. Name. Location. Anything. This fucker attacked Denise and he's going to do more unless I reveal something I don't even remember. So, dammit, make me remember. Use hypnosis if you need to."

Dr. Tam leaned forward, her elbows on her knees. "Jack, we've talked about this. Walking you through your memories—something you reported or something we can find in hypnosis—is dangerous. We could literally short-circuit your memory centers. You've seen the videos."

"I saw. But I've also poked around online, and despite what happened to those men, the technique has a high success rate."

"You poked around online?" Her brows rose above her glasses. "You managed to log into the government's confidential files regarding memory work and treatment with affected intelligence officers? Because my guess is that you're looking at bullshit articles that your phone pulled up with Google. I know you're good at your job, Mr. Sawyer, and with time, I'm sure you could find the right files. But you haven't found them yet, or you'd know I'm telling you the truth."

She was right, of course. And while he wanted to shout curses and demand she do anything and everything to make him whole, he wasn't quite that rash. "All right. Then explain to me the difference. Why is someone like me who's trained to control their mind, reactions, and emotions more susceptible to melting down than some traveling salesmen whose mind got wiped after his car went over a bridge?"

"You just answered your own question."

He shook his head. "I guess I'm not as smart as you think I am. Spell it out for me."

She took off her glasses and rubbed the bridge of her nose. "You may not remember it, but your training was quite extensive. You learned how to withstand torture, both physical and mental. And because of your affiliation with the SOC, that training went further and deeper than most of our intelligence officers ever experience."

"And that's good, right?"

"Of course. But no program can render you entirely immune to torture. At some point, you reach a limit. You reached yours, Mr. Sawyer. For purposes of this discussion, we'll say you snapped."

He swallowed, hating that his own failure to hold it together had led to this condition. "Go on."

"In our salesman, that snap happened much sooner. He barely fought it at all. The bad guy—in this case the accident and nature—didn't have to torture him too much before he reached his limit. To make the concept visual, we'll say that he sunk three inches into the hole."

"I'm listening."

"In contrast, you fought and fought and by the time you snapped, you were six feet under. His little hole is easy to climb out of. Yours, not so much. You try, and you end up pulling more dirt down on top of you. If you don't climb out slowly and methodically, you'll end up buried alive. Do it right, and you can find yourself on the green, hugging all those memories close." She looked hard at his face, staring him down. "Don't bury yourself."

"So, what are you saying? I shouldn't even try? Shouldn't talk to people I used to know or go places I used to visit?"

She shook her head. "No, no. I'm not saying that. But you have to move with care. Go too fast or dive to deep and—"

"What?"

"You'll feel it. When I say you could lose those memories forever, it's not just a psychological break, there's a physical one, too. You can burst a vessel, damage a lobe. You could end up with a migraine that keeps you down for a few days or fried synapses that put you in a catatonic state for the rest of your life. It's not an exact science, Jack. And the bottom line is that you were on that mission for a reason. We need to know what you know. And we can't risk losing all that intel forever."

He nodded, recalling the headache that had come on so unexpectedly at the club. Wasn't that about the time he first noticed the face? Had that memory been pounding hard to get back in?

"Tell me you understand," Dr. Tam demanded. "And promise me you won't be reckless."

"I understand. And I don't know myself well enough to know if I'm the reckless sort."

"Jack…"

He stood and shrugged. "I'm not going to let them hurt her."

"That's a noble outcome," she said. "But protect her with your brawn, Agent Sawyer. And keep your mind intact."

————

He was free of Dr. Tam and on his way to Denise's house by five-thirty. He'd been up all night, and was too exhausted to think straight, so he decided to wait an hour before waking her for the conversation about their work and his mind.

Unfortunately, it was hard to nap on a motorcycle, and she had no furniture on her front porch.

Undeterred, he slipped through the gate and into the backyard, pleased that it wasn't any trouble to do so, and also irritated that someone with a job where she saw all types of nastiness in the world didn't bother to lock her back gate. Or the glass and screen door of her patio sunroom, he added a few moments later.

At least the door between the patio and the kitchen was locked tight. He considered picking the lock—both to judge the level of security and to prove that he at least remembered *that*—but he was too damn tired. So instead he moved to the eastern wall, laid down on a lounge chair with forest green cushions, closed his eyes, and drifted off almost immediately.

The next thing he knew, the sun was spilling over him, a gentle hand was on his shoulder, and when he opened his eyes he was looking into Denny's beautiful face.

"Denny," he murmured, and heard her gasp in response.

He pushed himself up onto an elbow. "You okay?"

"I—yes. What are you doing out here, anyway? You

should have just knocked. Or let yourself in." She grinned. "We both know you could have, even with my alarm system."

He sat up, matching her grin and relieved that she didn't seem annoyed that he'd camped out on her patio. "I was completely wiped, and I didn't see the point in bothering you, especially when this patio's perfectly comfortable."

"All right." She'd been standing beside him. Now she settled herself on the cushion by his legs as he sat up to give her more room. "That explains why you crashed on the patio. Now tell my why you came here at all."

"I need you to walk me through our missions. Hell, our lives. How we started working together. What you know about my background before the SOC. Any details of the last job I was on. Introduce me to our sources. Pull files so I can review mission briefs. Arrange meetings with mutual friends. Start from the first thing you know about me and take me step by step through to today."

He rattled the words off, afraid that if he paused at all she'd shut him down. She didn't. But she did stand and move to window, her back to him, the morning breeze through the screen catching the loose waves of her golden hair.

"Denny?" He frowned, noticing that he'd called her by the nickname. He liked it, though. It felt right. "Denny," he repeated. "Are you listening? I need you to do this for me."

"Why? What changed? I thought you were supposed to take it slowly."

"I saw Dr. Tam this morning." Not a lie. "And I need to jumpstart my memory." Also not a lie. Not technically, anyway.

She turned around, her arms crossed in front of her chest, and studied him. "You talked to Liam."

"I'm not going to put you at risk because my mind is Swiss cheese."

"I'm not a civilian. I can take care of myself."

"Not disagreeing. But even if some asshole hadn't attacked you, we still need to know what's trapped in my head."

She nodded slowly, as if considering. "So you want to move faster. Amp up our efforts to get the memory ball rolling. Not just put you back into your life, but sit down and tell you specific stories about your past and hope it all sticks."

"Exactly. Essentially what we've been doing, but kicked up a notch. Before, it was almost academic. They'd dumped me like garbage, but where was the rush? Now, we know there's something in my head they want. Which means I caught wind of something specific they're up to. We need to know what. And the sooner the better."

She crossed the patio to him, then stood right in front of him. She bent, cupped his face, then kissed him ever-so-gently on the mouth.

Then she pulled back, a sad little smile touching her lips as she said, very simply, "No."

13

I SHOULDN'T HAVE KISSED him.

I don't know what the hell I was thinking, but I know that I absolutely shouldn't have kissed him. It was just an innocent peck. A friendly touch. But, dammit, it opened a door I should have kept firmly shut.

Now, my lips tingle from the memory. I can still recall his scent. Can still hear the way he drew in a sharp breath in surprise at my boldness.

Most of all, I want more. Want *him*.

It's as if I struck a match and now my whole body is on fire, every hormone buzzing and humming. My nipples are tight. My skin so sensitive. I flipped a switch that I had no right to touch, but the truth is that I don't regret it at all.

I'd felt so helpless after Seagrave's call had awakened me. The colonel had given me the entire rundown of Mason's meeting with Dr. Tam. And knowing that Mason intended to take such extreme risks because he was worried about me, was like getting a hard punch to my gut.

"He stormed out," Seagrave had told me. "I imagine he

needed time to think, but I don't like leaving him alone that long."

Neither did I, and the relief that had washed over me when I found him here at our house—right where he belongs—was like sunshine blooming inside me.

He was Mason in that moment, not Jack. He was my husband, asleep in our home, his focus on protecting me.

And then he'd called me Denny, and it had taken all of my strength not to cry.

It was all too much, and I'd needed that one, tiny kiss to ground me.

Still, I shouldn't have done it. I shouldn't have opened that door.

Now, I lean against the kitchen counter and draw a breath, gathering myself. In front of me, the coffee maker's automatic timer triggers, and I hear the gurgle and hiss as it starts to brew.

Behind me, I hear Mason open the door.

"No?" He says the word as if no time at all has passed. As if I haven't wandered down long roads in my mind, only to come back here to my kitchen and my problems. "You can't just shut me down with a no."

"Yeah, I can." I draw a breath and then turn to face him. His expression of determined frustration is so familiar that I almost laugh. I really do know this man so well. "You want to dig deep into your past? Peachy keen. But you can't do it alone because, hello, you don't remember your past. So, yeah, I can say no. And that's exactly what I'm saying."

"Then I'll find someone else." He takes a step toward me. His jeans are dusty, his T-shirt wrinkled. His jaw is shadowed with stubble and his hair goes every which direction. He looks tired and irritated and amazing, and all I want to do is pull him into my arms, kiss him, and tell him to shut up about doing stupid things.

"No," I repeat. "You won't."

"Why the hell not?"

He's only inches away, his eyes boring into mine as if he can read the answer on my soul. I reach up without thinking and cup his face, his stubble scratchy against my palm. I see the spark flare in his eyes, and I draw in a breath, feeling it —*fighting it*—too.

"I know what could happen," I tell him gently. "Seagrave's call woke me up and he told me everything."

He starts to turn away, but I lift my other hand and hold him in place, my gaze never wavering. "It's amazing that you would take that risk for me, but I won't let you. I won't let you risk losing yourself."

"That's not your decision to make."

"And," I add, ignoring him, "I can't handle the thought of losing you that way. I've already lost most of you. Don't steal the rest from me because of some bullshit sense of chivalry."

For a moment, we just look at each other, the air thick between us. Then he takes a step back. I lower my hands, releasing his face.

He reaches out and, very gently, runs the tip of his finger over the thin, red cut that the Face's blade left on my neck. "I don't like seeing you in danger."

"I'm not crazy about it either, but it comes with the job description."

He sighs, then sits in his usual spot at our breakfast table. "This whole situation is fucked up."

"No argument from me." I sit across from him, just like I have for so many mornings. "Thank you," I say.

His brow furrows. "For what?"

"For being willing to take such a huge risk for me. Just

because I won't let you go through with it doesn't mean I don't appreciate it."

His mouth curves into a wry grin. "You're welcome," he says, then stands up and heads to the coffee maker. I stay seated, thinking about another risk he took about four months ago on Valentine's Day, our anniversary. A day when he broke cover to come to me, knowing how desperately I was missing him.

Not that he ever admitted that it was him. And not that I saw him. Our reunion had rules, and one was that I was blindfolded.

But I know my husband's body. His touch.

And I know that it was him who made love to me that night. That one magical respite in a sea of days and months and years apart.

"You're smiling," he says as he returns to the table with coffee for both of us.

"Why shouldn't I be? It's a lovely day, and I woke up to find one of my favorite people on my patio."

He laughs. "I don't know, Denny. Sounds like you're too easy to please."

"Denny," I repeat as I lift my coffee cup. I look at him over the rim. "Mason used to call me that. He was about the only one who would until Quince decided to take it up."

I shouldn't be telling him this. It's edging too close to the truth. But I can't seem to help myself.

"Does it bother you?"

I press my lips together in an effort to battle back the tears that threaten. Then I shake my head. "No."

Almost as a diversion, I lift the cup to my lips, breathing in the coffee scent I usually love, but I realize I don't want it and put the cup back down.

After a moment, I notice that Mason's staring at me, his

brow furrowed. *Jack*, I remind myself. But it's getting harder and harder to remember.

"What?" I ask as he continues to study me.

"Coffee."

My brows rise. "Yes. Good call. What was your first clue? The smell? Or the glass container of grounds sitting next to the machine?"

He ignores my sarcasm, and when he speaks, his voice is low and a little unsteady. "I remember," he says. "I remember you and coffee. Always a cup in your hand. Always making jokes about needing your caffeine hit."

I sit back, my body going cold as my stomach churns.

He cocks his head, looking at me. "You haven't taken even one sip. Are you feeling okay?"

I ignore the question. "You remember? You're not just piecing together things you've seen since you showed up at the SSA?"

"I don't kn—" He cuts himself off, and I watch as a violent shiver cuts through him. He's looking down at the table, his hands tightening on the edge. When he lifts his face, there's triumph in his eyes. "I remember."

A shock of joy cuts through me and my throat goes dry. "Everything?" My voice is raspy, my entire being on edge.

He shakes his head, the triumph fading, and I feel like a total heel. "No. No, not everything. Hardly anything, I suppose."

I reach across the table and take his hand, squeezing hard. "That's okay," I say. "You remember coffee. And me. I think that's a hell of a good start."

His mouth twitches, then curves into a smile. "Yeah," he says. "I suppose it is."

"So you remember my coffee habit. What about yours?"

For a second, he looks blank. Then his face clears. "I

don't have one. Not a habit, anyway. I drink a single cup in the morning, then I switch to smoothies. Greens and protein. I make them myself..." He trails off, shifting in his chair as his gaze locks onto the Vitamix that sits near the coffee maker. He frowns, and for a moment I wonder if he's putting it together. If he's realizing that he's Mason. That he's my husband.

But he just frowns and says, "A contraption like that. Every morning. Right?"

I shrug, trying to look nonchalant. "As far as I know."

"Okay. Good. This is good. What else?"

"We're not going to push, remember?"

"That wasn't a push," he says. "That was a memory. A real, live, fucking memory."

I get up and take my coffee to the sink, then dump it. My back's to him, and I allow myself a bright smile and a silent sigh of relief. Maybe his memory really will come back. Maybe—

"Hey."

I whirl around to find him right behind me. Immediately, my pulse kicks up, and I pray he doesn't notice.

"What's up with that?" he asks, nodding toward the sink.

"What do you mean?"

"I remember coffee and so you dump it?"

He's teasing, I know, but I feel unreasonably defensive anyway. "I'm not changing my habit because I want to mess with your head."

He lifts his hands in supplication. "Sorry. Didn't mean to—"

"No, I'm the one who's sorry. I've got some sort of stomach bug, and it's been lingering. I shouldn't have snapped. Feeling bad is making me moody." I take a deep breath, willing myself to feel better. "It'll pass," I add. "It always does."

Something important flits into my mind, then flits right back out again. A thought. Something I should heed. But damned if I can lock onto it.

Frustrated, I shake my head, then focus on Mason. "Listen," I say, "I have an idea."

He takes a step back, his hands sliding into the pockets of his jeans. "I'm listening."

"I'm not going to tell you stories about the past like I'm some modern version of Homer," I begin.

"But?"

I roll my eyes, but I'm secretly delighted by the interruption. Because that's exactly how Mason would interrupt.

"*But*," I continue, "you and I did a lot of stuff together, even outside work. And I'm thinking maybe we should cover some of that ground. See if it trips any memories."

"You mean play hooky today." His smile lights his face, and I match it.

"That's exactly what I mean."

"Lead the way."

"Really?" I plan to start with the beach, and I know that lunch will be on the agenda. One of the places that Mason and I haunted regularly. I take a quick look at Jack, then frown. "You look like you slept in your clothes."

"That would be because I did."

I smirk. "Do you want something else to wear?"

"Do you have something?"

"You and Mason are about the same size," I say casually. "You can borrow whatever you want."

He stays still for a moment, and I begin to fear that I've somehow gone too far. But then he nods and smiles. "Let me borrow the shower, too, and we have a deal."

14

———

"You remember how to ride a bike well enough," I say, as we both bring our bicycles to a stop. We've been riding for the last hour, first on the Venice Beach bike path, and then through the cute little neighborhoods of the coastal LA-area town.

"Let's walk for a bit," he says. "I saw someplace I want to check out."

"Someplace you remember?"

"Maybe."

I'd been about to suggest food, but since his plan sounds promising, I decide to ignore my growling stomach, appeasing it with only a long swig of water from my bottle. The bikes are ours—not that Mason realizes that he's riding his own bike—and we brought them here from Silver Lake on the rack that's a semi-permanent fixture on the back of my Highlander.

Now, we lock them back onto the car, and I follow Mason's lead as he weaves us back toward Windward, one of the main streets that runs perpendicular to the ocean.

He twists and turns and obviously knows where he's

going. I'm honestly not paying that much attention. Instead, I'm lost in my thoughts, wondering how he can remember his way around a town but not his wife.

Which is why I'm completely blown away when he stops at a corner, points down the street, and says, "There. We passed it earlier, and I want to go in."

He's pointing at Totally Tattoo.

"Do you remember that place?" My mouth is so dry it's hard to get the question out.

"Honestly? I'm not sure. I think so. I thought we could go in and ask them if that's where I got this." He taps the tribal band below the sleeve of the Grateful Dead T-shirt he "borrowed" from Mason.

I follow him toward the shop, forcing myself not to cross my fingers. I want so bad for it all to flood back. Maybe it's foolish, but I can't help but think that if he just finds the right key, all of his memories will ease back into their proper little boxes.

Could our wedding tattoo be that key?

All the chairs in the parlor are full, but Cass herself isn't doing anyone's art. Instead, she's sitting at the counter, her laptop open and a scowl on her face.

"What a warm and welcoming look for those of us entering the shop," I say with a laugh.

"Hey, you two," she says, glancing up. Her hair has streaks of magenta today, and she's wearing it in a ponytail, probably to keep it out of her way as she works.

"Bookkeeping?" I ask.

"The devil's work," she says. "I'm absolutely sure of it." She smiles at Mason, and I hope she remembers that for the time being, he's Jack. "Did you have fun at Westerfield's?"

"I did," he says, his eyes cutting to me. As for Cass, her gaze shifts between Jack and me, and she looks a little too much like a girl with a secret. Honestly, I love Cass, but it's a good thing she doesn't work in my profession.

"I didn't realize this was your place," Jack says. "Denny told you about my memory?"

Cass's eyes widen as she looks at me, obviously unsure if she's allowed to be in the know. I nod, and she visibly exhales. "Yeah. No offense, but it's like something in a movie."

"I suppose this is the town for it," he says. "I was wondering what you know about this." He taps the tattoo, and once again Cass looks to me.

Jack laughs. "Never mind. Got my answer."

"Oh, shit. I'm sorry," she says to me. "Was I not supposed to say anything?"

"You didn't say anything," Jack points out.

"It's fine," I tell her. "Jack remembered your storefront and thought this might be where he got the tattoo. It's fine that you confirmed, but you can't tell him anything else about it." I look at her hard, willing her to understand. "It's important that all the memories come from him. No prompting."

"Sure. Right. I've totally got it."

"I just want to know when you—" Jack begins, but I cut him off with a shake of my head.

"No," I say. "Take a seat, soak up the atmosphere, meditate if you want to. But nobody is going to just plop facts in your lap. Okay?"

He doesn't answer, but he does walk to a display wall and start looking at photos of some of the ink the shop's turned out.

"Can I talk to you for a sec?" Cass asks me. "You're okay for a bit, right, Jack?"

"I'll be here," he says wryly. "Lost in my memories."

I roll my eyes and follow her into the back storeroom.

"What's up?" I ask, expecting to hear a blow by blow of her evening with the cute blonde she was talking to at Westerfield's.

Instead, she says, "Are you ever planning on telling me? I mean, I get that you didn't want to talk about it before, what with him being gone. But now that he's back and he can't even know ... I guess I just figured you'd need someone to talk to."

My stomach twists, but I'm not sure if it's nausea or dread. "What are you talking about?" But even as I ask the question, I know.

Cass leans forward. "Seriously?"

"I can't be." I shake my head. "I can't possibly be pregnant."

"Wait. Whoa. Back up. You really didn't think about it before? And yes you can. Four months ago, remember? He was here. With you. On Valentine's Day." Her brow furrows. "Are you telling me you've had your period since then? Because if that's the case, then maybe you're just sick, and—"

"I haven't," I say, feeling like the world's biggest fool. "I never got them regularly, and I'm on the pill so I never thought about it."

"And I'm guessing you weren't that careful about the pill, what with Mason being gone."

I nod. "And I don't keep track on a calendar because why bother? It's not like I've had sex in forever."

"Except for Valentine's Day." She takes my hands. "Is this good or bad?"

I look up into her blurry face and realize I'm crying. I pull one hand free and wipe my tears, then suck in a watery breath. "Good," I say. "Of course it's good. Mason's child. But—"

"You can't tell him."

I shake my head. "I can't tell Mason because he doesn't know he's Mason. And I can't tell Jack because he knows how long Mason's been gone." I choke out an ironic laugh. "I don't want him to think I cheated on my husband."

"I'm sorry."

"It's kind of a mess."

"But a good mess," she says, pulling me into a hug as I nod. "You should take a test just to be sure."

"I will. But I'm sure." Now that we've said it out loud, I don't know how I could have been so blind for so long. I can only assume that my subconscious didn't want to think about being pregnant without Mason here to go through it with me. Denial. Big time.

And now that he is here ... well, part of me still wants to ignore it while another part of me wants to sing with joy.

"Ready to go out and face him?" she asks. "Or do you want to sneak out the back and I can say you were kidnapped by fairies?"

"A nice offer, but I'll go with door number one." I draw a breath, square my shoulders, and head back out.

"What do you think?" he says, pointing to a picture of a guy with a shaved head and a tattoo of a tree going up the back of his neck to burst into leaves on his scalp. "Is it me?"

It's kind of cool in theory. But Mason, it's not.

"Come on," I say, taking his hand as he grins. "I want an ice cream and a walk in the surf."

He glances over at Cass. "How do I say no to that?"

"I don't think you do," she says. She wiggles her fingers in a goodbye gesture, then adds, "If you remember more about getting the band and want to ask me questions, you know where to find me. And don't worry," she adds to me, "I won't tell any more than I'm supposed to."

I nod. But I don't know if she's talking about the tattoo, the baby, or both.

"Is this something else we use to do," Jack asks later as we walk through the surf. I have my shoes in one hand. The other swings beside me, and more than once it's bumped Jack's free hand. It feels flirty, like we're on a date. And under the circumstances, I like the way I feel a little more than I should.

Which, of course, is totally unfair. He's my husband. I'm supposed to be able to hold his hand and romp in the surf. I'm supposed to be able to tell him about our baby. I'm supposed to be able to stop and kiss him. I'm supposed to be able to say, "I love you."

But I can't. Not yet.

And today especially, that breaks my heart.

"Are you okay?"

I realize I've slowed down and have fallen behind him.

"Yeah. I am. Sorry. I've just been thinking."

"Me too." He tilts his head inland. "Can I buy you dinner?"

"Sure." It occurs to me that Seagrave must have set up a full Jack Sawyer identity, which would include Jack Sawyer credit cards and bank accounts. I hadn't thought about it before, and those aren't the kind of details that usually escape me.

What do they call it? Baby brain?

We walk silently to Blacklist, a restaurant Mason and I frequent when we're in the area. Usually, we sit at one of the sidewalk tables, but today he leads me inside to a small table in a dark corner.

We order, then sit in an awkward silence until the waiter

returns with our food. Cheese fries to share, a sparkling water for me, and a beer for Jack. He takes a sip, looking like a man seeking liquid courage, then puts his glass down.

"What's going on?" I ask, hearing trepidation in my own voice.

"We need to talk," he says, and I wonder if he overheard Cass and me talking about the baby. And about who he really is.

For a moment, I'm giddy. Because if that's the case, then Dr. Tam was wrong. He had the truth dumped on him, and his brain is just fine.

Then he says, "I know you loved your husband," and my little fantasy goes *poof*, replaced by my hard, sharp-edged, strange reality.

"I did," I say. "I do."

"Of course. I didn't mean to suggest—" He cuts off the words. "My point is that I know that. And I'd never try to suggest that you don't love Mason or that you should try to get over him."

I frown, not understanding where he's going with this.

"I should probably just keep my mouth shut, but we know I have to get my memory back, right?"

I nod.

"And that means I have to look at all my memories."

"Jack, I'm really not following you."

He sighs. "Look, I don't want to make you uncomfortable. I don't want to ruin our friendship. I'm asking you this because we *are* friends. Because even if this is something you want to leave behind, I trust you to give me an honest answer, okay?"

"You're kind of freaking me out."

"Okay?" he repeats, and I nod.

"Yes. Of course. Okay."

He draws a breath, then looks down at his hands where he's been ripping his napkin into tiny shreds. I still have no idea what he's going to say, but I definitely know that he's nervous.

"Before when we worked together—even when Mason was around—was there ... I mean, were we ... oh, hell. Were we having an affair?"

I'd been about to take a sip of my water. Now I freeze, the glass suspended there. Slowly, I return it to the table. "Why do you ask that?"

He sighs. "Vague memories. The way Cass looked between us—as if there was more connection than just partners. The way I see you looking at me sometimes. The clothes in your closet that fit me and don't feel like another man's clothes. The Vitamix that makes me wonder if I left it at your house to make my mornings easier. The way I knew where you were going to sit at the breakfast table. The way—"

"Okay. I get it."

"—the way your kiss this morning felt like—"

"Like what?" I whisper when he cuts himself off, leaving silence hanging between us.

He hesitates, his focus on the napkin shreds. Then he lifts his eyes to mine. "Like coming home."

"Jack, I—" I take a long sip of water, then stand, my mind racing. "Excuse me," I say, then hurry to the ladies' room before he can stop me.

In the small space, I clutch the counter and lean forward, staring at myself in the mirror as his question swirls through my mind. Literally, the answer is no, because I've never cheated on my husband, and Jack ... Mason, whoever he is, wouldn't ever betray a friend. And I don't want him thinking that he's the kind of man that would.

But the core of his question—the *are we together* part—well, the answer to that is yes.

Except I can't tell him so without risking destroying him. Literally destroying him, since, "Why no, honey, we're not having an affair because we're married," is exactly the kind of memory trigger that Dr. Tam is certain would set off a horrible chain reaction.

Bottom line, I have to lie. I have to tell this man I love and am desperately attracted to that I don't want him. That I've never wanted him. Because he's Jack and I'm married to Mason, and neither of those men are the type who would cheat with their partner or a friend's wife.

With a sigh, I press my hand over my belly. "Your mommy is a mess," I say. "And Daddy's not doing too great either."

I draw in a breath for courage, open the door, and step out into the dark alcove that separates the dining area from the kitchen and restrooms.

I don't see him until he says, "Denny." Then I turn and find him in the farthest corner. And, because I'm a fool, I go to him.

I start to speak, but before I can utter a word, he takes my wrist and pulls me close. I only have time to gasp before his arm is wrapped tight around my waist and his mouth closes over mine. And, damn me, I can't help it. I melt into his embrace. My mouth opens to his and our kiss is deep and hot and oh, so wild.

It's everything I want, everything I need, and I feel the surge of our connection pulsing through me. I want him so badly. Want to feel his hands on my breasts, between my legs. I want to feel him moving inside me, making me wild and wet. I want to forget everything except the reality of his touch, and when I explode, I want to return to a world where my husband knows me and himself.

But that won't happen, and it's the memory of that truth that has me pulling away.

"Jack, please, we—"

"I remembered something else, too," he says, gently brushing my hair out of my face. "I remembered making love to you."

A lump of tears sticks in my throat, and all I can do is shake my head helplessly. I don't know what to say. I don't know what to do.

And so I take the coward's way out, and bolt.

I pause at the entrance to the dining room and look back. "I can't," I say, a sob stuck in my throat. "And I'm sorry, but you're going to have to find your own way home."

15

I'M A WRECK. A sniveling, teary-eyed mess who clearly doesn't know what she wants and is utterly incapable of navigating a personal crisis.

I also should never have gotten behind the wheel of my car, and it's only by some miracle that I got home safe and sound, because God knows my mind wasn't on the road, and I could barely see through the tears that kept leaking from my eyes.

I made it, though. And I'd burst into the house, raced to my bedroom, threw off my clothes, and slid all the way under the covers. My plan was to sleep through the rest of the summer and on into Christmas. Then, like a groundhog, I'd peek out and decide if it was safe to emerge.

Of course, I hadn't factored in little things like eating and giving birth. All I wanted to do was sleep off my misery like a horrible hangover.

He wanted me. I wanted him.

And I couldn't have him.

Why?

Why, why, why?

The question keeps circling in my mind, and the more it bounces around in my head, the more I lose sight of the answer. I know I'd had reasons to walk away, but what were they?

That I don't want to cheat on my husband? That one is laughable. Mason is my husband, no matter what his name.

That I don't want him to see me as a woman willing to cheat? Maybe, but to what end? I've never been unfaithful, and under the circumstances, Jack can hardly think ill of me.

That I don't want Jack to see himself as the kind of man who could seduce a married woman, a co-worker, a friend? Maybe, but again, to what end? If his memory comes back, he'll understand. And if he never remembers his past? Well, in that case there won't be any danger of a visit from a cuckolded husband.

Every reason I consider and shoot down makes me feel foolish for walking away from him. Foolish and empty, because damned if I don't crave him so much I feel hollow.

And yet...

I close my eyes and let the truth wash over me—I want him, and yet I run. But I don't understand what it is I'm afraid of.

I toss and turn in the bed, but I can't sleep for even an hour, much less until Christmas. Annoyed, I slip out from between the sheets, tug on my bathrobe, and pad barefoot into the kitchen.

Coffee, wine, and whiskey are all out of the question, so I settle for hot chocolate. I haven't made it in ages, but I have milk and a tin of real cocoa that I bought last winter. I even have some whipped topping in the fridge, left over from a recent craving for ice cream with bananas and caramel. A craving that had seemed inexplicable at the time, but now makes perfect sense.

I stir the chocolate into the milk, then wait until it just starts to bubble around the edges. Then I pour it into the huge Disneyland mug that Mason bought on our first and only trip to the park. I add a squirt of whipped cream, put the mug on the table, and then head to the pantry in the hopes that I have a package of Oreos. Honestly, I should have planned my descent into self-pity better.

As it turns out, my quest is successful. Shocking, really, since without Mason in the house, my shopping list doesn't usually include sweets. But I've been shopping on autopilot lately, and apparently the little dude or dudette growing inside me is making some of my choices.

"Good job," I say, patting my belly with one hand and carrying the Oreos with the other. "What are we going to tell your daddy, and when are we going to tell him?"

Excellent questions, and not ones I feel like contemplating at the moment. Because unless Mason miraculously gets his memory back, I know that the first thing I have to do is set a meeting with Seagrave and Dr. Tam. I want Mason—or Jack—to know his child. But I don't want to fry his mind while telling him the truth. And the idea of him being Uncle Jack instead of Daddy just doesn't seem fair.

Frustrated, I break open an Oreo, then eat the un-iced half as I wait for the cocoa to cool. I'm just about to lift the mug for a tiny test sip when a rap on the kitchen door makes me jump.

I hurry to the wall switch, flip on the light for the covered patio, and find Mason standing on the other side of the kitchen door, peering at me through one of the six panes of glass he'd installed himself.

I should tell him to go away; I'm too raw to do this tonight.

I should, but I don't.

Instead, I open the door, greeting him with, "What the hell are you doing sneaking in through back patio again?"

"I wasn't sneaking, I swear."

"Most people arrive in the front."

"Your lights were off. I wanted to see if you were still up, and I figured if the lights were off back here I'd leave you a note on the porch. But the light was on, and there you were, and so I came in."

"You shouldn't have," I say, suddenly very aware that I have nothing on under my robe. "And I shouldn't have let you in."

"Maybe not. But since you did…" He trails off, his head tilted a bit to the side and a cocky grin dancing on his mouth.

I shouldn't take the bait, but I do. "What?" I demand as I tighten my sash.

"Since you did, the least you can do is share your Oreos."

Mason, I think, feeling both delighted and a little weak in the knees.

I stand up straighter, and keep my expression stern. "That seems awfully extreme. I mean, we're talking Oreos. There are some sacrifices a woman shouldn't be expected to make." I allow myself a slow grin, and he smiles back.

"I promise I'll make it up to you with the pleasure of my company."

"Sit," I say. "I'll get you some cocoa. Unless you'd rather have bourbon?" Bourbon and Oreos is Mason's favorite late night snack. I've always thought it's a bizarre combination, but he swears by it.

Now, I watch his face, but see nothing other than an adventurous acceptance. "I'm game. Will you join me?"

I shake my head. "It's a cocoa night for me. But for you..." I trail off as I grab a bottle of Knob Creek from one of the lower cabinets. I put it on the table, bring him a glass, and watch as he slams a shot back.

I lift my brows. "It's supposed to be savored with the cookies."

"I'll do that, too. I needed a bit of fortification for what I need to say."

"Oh." I pull out my chair and sit down. "So we're to that part already."

He takes another sip, this time pairing it with an Oreo. "That really is remarkably good," he says, then stands up again. "And completely beside the point." He draws in a breath. "I should never have followed you in the restaurant. And I definitely shouldn't have kissed you. I probably shouldn't have even asked you if there was ever a thing between us. I pushed boundaries. I made you uncomfortable. And I'm sorry. Truly sorry. It won't happen again."

"Oh." This isn't at all what I expected, and I want to say something else, but I honestly don't know what, and an awkward silence hangs between us, all the more awkward because I've never for a moment felt uncomfortable around Mason.

"Right." He clears his throat. "Well, I should get back to Malibu. Liam's going to start to wonder if I forgot the way there along with everything else."

He turns to leave, and as I watch him go, it hits me, and I know what it is I'm afraid of. That he's going to disappear from me just like my father did. Like my mother did. And, yes, like Mason did.

My father walked away, but Mom didn't want to leave

me. She hadn't been given a choice. Neither had Mason. One day he was here, and the next he was gone. He's back now—not whole, not yet—but he's *here*.

And my deepest, darkest fear is that he's going to disappear all over again. Losing him once almost killed me. Twice will do me in.

So there it is, the reason I don't want to get close now. It's not because of Dr. Tam's rules about his memory or any misplaced notions of fidelity as applied to amnesia victims. It's because I'm protecting my heart.

But in that moment, I realize how much more I'll lose by not going for it. Even if it's only a month, a week, a day's worth of memories, that will be that much more to keep for our baby. Even if he forgets everything. Even if he disappears for another two years, I'll have a little bit more of him than I did before.

But oh, dear God, I hope to hell he doesn't disappear.

He pauses at the kitchen door, then turns back with an apologetic smile. "Thanks for the snack. I'll see you at work tomorrow. And I'll behave myself from now on."

I just stare, by mouth literally gaping open, stuck in that horrible place between what I want and what I fear. But then he pulls open the door and leaves the bright kitchen for the patio, and I can't stand it any longer.

I race after him and grab his hand before he can push open the screen door that leads into the backyard. "Wait!"

He stops. "Denny?"

"I can't," I say. "I can't let you walk away. Not knowing that you might end up staying away forever."

Confusion washes over his face. "I don't know what you're—"

"Dammit, Jack," I say, untying the sash on my robe and then shrugging it off my shoulders. I stand there naked, my heart pounding in my chest as I watch his face, illuminated now only by the light from the kitchen seeping out through the windows. "Just touch me."

"Denny." His voice is thick with a desire so familiar I don't know if I want to cry or celebrate. "Dear Christ, you're beautiful."

"Look all you want," I say, taking his hand once again and this time putting it on my breast. "But you have to be touching me, too."

"I like your terms," he says, his eyes on mine as his thumb brushes my hard nipple, sending rocket flares of need coursing through me. I make a whimpering sound, and bite my lower lip, fighting the urge to beg him to kiss me. I want that kiss, yes, but mostly I want the pleasure of losing myself as Mason explores my body for the zillionth—and the first—time.

He doesn't disappoint.

"Close your eyes," he whispers, and I do as he says. He continues to tease my nipple with his thumb, adding his other hand as well, so that both my breasts are getting his full attention. Then I feel his lips brush my temple, followed by the whisper of breath against my ear before his tongue traces the curve. I shiver in response, biting my lower lip.

He chuckles, the sound soft and low, then kisses his way down my jaw before brushing his lips over mine. "That's my job," he murmurs, before kissing me so sweetly, the gentle pressure turning demanding when he pulls away, his teeth tugging on my bottom lip and sending a coil of heat all the way through my body, from my greedy mouth all the way to my pussy.

I whimper, then shift my stance, spreading my legs and relishing the sensation of the air between my thighs. I'm wet and needy, and I'm craving his fingers, his mouth. He's

taking his damn time, though, and so far he hasn't even
ventured south of my breasts.

"Jack...please."

"Please, what?"

"Touch me," I beg.

"I am touching you." His lips move against my ear as he
talks. "I want to hear what you want." As he speaks, one
hand slides down, moving south on my belly. "Tell me how
to touch you, Denny. Tell me what you like."

"This," I say, and I've never spoken truer words. I'm
opening up after a long hibernation. I'm back in my
husband's arms, and I don't even care that he doesn't know
it. He's bringing me back to life, just like a princess in a fairy
tale. "This," I repeat. "I want all of this. And more."

"Me, too." His voice is a growl. Rough. Edgy. And I know
that he's as desperate as I am.

"Denny," he says as he drops to his knees. "I have to taste
you."

I tremble, overwhelmed with desire as his hands cup my
thighs, and he slowly eases them up until his thumbs are
teasing the tender skin between my sex and my legs. He tilts
his head up and meets my eyes just long enough for me to
see the hunger on his face. Then he gently strokes my clit
with his tongue, sending shockwaves of pleasure rushing
through me, so intense it's a wonder my legs don't collapse
beneath me.

I whimper when he pauses, then suck in a sharp breath
when he orders, "Play with your nipples."

My body tightens in response. Mason isn't usually this
demanding, but I like it. I want to arouse him as deeply as
he's aroused me. I want to hear what he wants, share his
fantasies. Hell, I want to *be* his fantasy.

I want to surrender to his every whim, and that's why I

eagerly tease and pinch my nipples as he laves my clit with his tongue, his hands cupping my ass as he holds me firmly in place.

I could stay like that forever, but Mason changes the game. His hand on my rear shifts, and he slides it between my ass cheeks, then further still until his fingertips find my core. I'm incredibly wet, and he thrusts inside me as I grind against him, craving every pleasure and sensation that he is giving me.

Too soon, he pulls his hand away, then teases his wet fingertip along my perineum before stroking the tight muscle of my ass. I gasp at the unfamiliar sensation, but I can't deny that it feels fucking incredible.

"You like that." It's a statement, not a question.

"Yes. God, yes."

But it's as if my admission is a indictment, because he stops. I whimper, and he stands, his expression teasing and devious. "I like the look on your face," he tells me. "As if you want to beg, but don't want to give me the satisfaction."

"I'll beg," I say. "I'll do anything you want me to."

"I like the sound of that," he says, then kisses me hard and deep. It's a wild kiss, all tongue and teeth and violent demand.

When he pulls away, we're both breathing hard. "You should beg. You should tell me everything you want, every naughty thought, every wild fantasy. Because all I want is to satisfy you. To feel you surrender. To hear you scream. I want to make you explode, Denny. And then I want to do it all over again."

I stroke his face, his stubble rough against my palm. "Who are you?" I whisper.

Mason's not shy in bed—not by a long shot. But this intensity is so much more. I don't know if it's because of our time apart or his new boldness, but I've never been so turned on in my life, and every one of his touches sends shivers through me.

He smiles in response to my question. "I'm the man who's making love to you."

"Yes," I say. "Oh, yes, you are."

He takes my hand and tugs me to the small sofa under the windows that look into the kitchen. He sits, then holds up a hand to stop me when I start to go toward him. "Wait. I want to see you."

"I'm hard to miss. I'm right in front of you and very naked."

His mouth twitches. "Touch yourself."

My pulse kicks up, and a delicious heat settles more firmly between my legs. "What?"

"You heard me." He moves his hand to his cock, stroking it through the denim of his jeans. Even from where I stand, I can tell how hard he is. And I can feel how wet I am.

"Denny," he says. "I want to watch."

It's such a simple statement compared to the intensity of his gaze, and I find I can neither protest nor resist. He wants to watch, and damned if I don't want to perform. Want to feel his eyes on me as I play with my clit. Want to watch the motion of his hand quicken on his thick cock as I thrust a finger in my pussy, then suck my sex-slicked finger.

I want wildness. Fantasy. Desire.

I don't know. Maybe I want to make up for lost time.

Mostly, I just want Mason, and as he watches, I close my eyes and slowly slide my hand down, then start to tease my hard, slick clit.

"Baby," he murmurs, the need in his voice so intense it sounds as though it's laced with pain.

I'm wet—so wet—and it's all because of him. I slip my

fingers inside myself, and as I do, he tells me to open my eyes. I comply, and the passion on his face rocks through me, the precursor to a wild explosion.

He sees it and I watch as his hand tightens on his straining cock.

"Take off your clothes," I say.

"Why?"

"Because it's my turn. Because I want you."

He doesn't make a move, so I climb onto his lap, straddling him, then rub myself over the bulge in the denim.

I whimper, and he laughs. "I like watching you."

"Yeah? Would you like fucking me, too?"

He doesn't answer aloud, but he unbuttons his fly, then slowly takes his cock out. He's huge and hard, and I stroke myself over the length of him as he groans, then closes his eyes and tilts his head back as he holds my rear and guides my movements.

He's harder than I've ever seen him, and tonight we've been wilder than ever before. "What are we doing?" I ask, as I continue to rock my hips and he teases my rear with his forefinger. "We've never—"

"What?"

I gasp as his finger explores me more intimately, my whole body craving him, wanting to be filled by him.

"This," I say when I can force out the words. "Everything."

"So I was right. You. Me. The past. We did have a thing. This isn't our first time."

I swallow, trapped in my own obfuscation. "You know it isn't. And please, please, right now I just want—"

"Tell me."

"I want you inside me. Please, Jack. Please fuck me."

"I don't have a condom," he says, breathing hard.

"It's okay," I say. "It'll be fine. Just please, don't stop."

I start to shift, rising up so that I'm no longer riding his shaft. I want the head. I want all of him inside me.

"Denny, I don't think—"

"I'm on the pill," I say, which isn't technically accurate anymore, but he's also not going to get me any more pregnant than I already am.

"Denny..." He looks into my eyes, his gentle and sad. "We can't risk it. I'm not worried about a baby—"

"Then what?"

"I don't know what they did to me. I don't know what *I* did. And I won't risk you—"

I kiss him, then smile when I pull away and look into his confused eyes. "It's okay," I assure him. "Seagrave and his team did every test imaginable on you. You're clean, I promise."

I think that will reassure him, but he looks even more confused. "Why on earth would they tell you that?"

Because as your wife they thought I might want to know.

"We're partners."

"Yes, but that doesn't—"

"Jack," I say firmly. "Do you want to debate privacy policy at the SOC, or do you want to fuck me?"

Shock flickers in his eyes, changing swiftly to amusement.

"Trust me, sweetheart, debating is the last thing on my mind."

"I'm very glad to hear it."

He cups my neck, then pulls my face down for a hard kiss, with tongue and teeth and heat, and so wild and deep it's almost fucking. But not close enough, because what I want is Mason. My body is on fire, craving release. Needing satisfaction.

"I can't wait any longer," I tell him.

"Me either."

I bite my lower lip, then shift my hips until I feel the head of his cock against my core. His hands are on my hips, and I let him maneuver me, lifting and lowering me as he teases himself and me, barely slipping inside me, then pulling out, then repeating again in a maddening ritual that has me going absolutely crazy.

Him, too. I can tell from his face. From the ecstasy etched on his features.

"More," he demands, releasing my hips and giving me full control. I take it greedily, impaling myself over and over again as my body tightens, every atom in me pulling together, readying for a wild explosion.

Tighter and tighter, faster and faster.

Inside me, Mason's close, too. He's as tight as a spring, and I want to explode with him. I want us to come together, to be together. I want—

The world shatters around me.

I rock back, my body on fire, my husband's name on my lips. "Mason! Oh, God, Mason!"

And then I realize what I've done.

His body goes tense as my eyes fly open in shock and embarrassment. "Jack," I say. "I didn't mean—"

He stands up, then tugs on his jeans as I wince, feeling like an absolute shit.

"I'm sorry," I say as he shakes his head, then reaches down, grabs my robe, and tosses it to me.

"No, I'm the one who's sorry." He drags his fingers through his hair as I slide the robe on and pull it tightly closed. "I can't be what you need. I can't be a stand-in for your husband."

I shake my head. "You're not. I swear you're not. It just slipped out. It didn't mean anything—"

"Dammit, Denny, it meant everything."

Hot tears spill down my cheeks, because it's happening just as I feared. I'm losing him all over again. "Please," I whisper, but he just shakes his head.

"I don't want to be the kind of man who cheats on a friend. And you're not the kind of woman who cheats on her husband. I don't know what kind of madness grabbed us before, but—"

He cuts himself off, his brow furrowing as he lifts his face to mine, a wild, almost feral look in his eyes. "You're not the kind of woman who cheats," he repeats, then reaches out for my left hand so quickly that I gasp with shock. "Not you," he says, rubbing the pad of his thumb over the platinum band the way I do when I'm lost in thought.

He draws in a stuttering breath, then squares his shoulders as he looks straight at me. "You didn't cheat tonight, did you?"

Fear and joy war for space in my heart. Is he saying what I think he's saying? "Jack, I don't—"

He presses a finger to my lips and shakes his head. "I'm not Jack," he says. "I'm your husband. I'm Mason."

16

He was Mason.

Mason Walker, not Jack Sawyer.

Mason Walker, former Special Forces soldier turned covert operative for the Sensitive Operations Command. Not that he remembered any of that. But he knew it was true. Just as he knew that he was married to Denise Marshall. *Denny.* The woman who'd made his heart stop from the first moment he'd seen her inside that goddamn little cell at the SOC.

The same woman who was looking at him now as if he were a lit fuse, and any moment he would burst apart. He stifled a wince. Considering the state of some of the amnesia victims Dr. Tam had showed him, he supposed that wasn't an unreasonable fear. Right now, though, he felt fine. All he wanted was his life back.

He drew in a breath. "This is our house? We own it together?"

Her eyes widened a bit, but she nodded.

"When did we buy it?"

"I don't think I should just tell you—"

"Yes," he said stepping closer to her. "You should."

"Dr. Tam said—"

"No." He shook his head. "I know the risk. I know the concern. But my head feels fine."

She shook her head, and a single tear spilled down her cheek, making his heart crack open. "I can't," she said in a voice clogged with tears. "I get that you're angry with me, but I'm so goddamn happy to have you back. *You*. And I can't risk that. I just can't."

Oh, God, she was killing him.

"I'm not angry with you," he said, using his forefinger to tilt her chin up. "I'm relieved. Confused. Thrilled. Awed."

"Awed?"

"That you belong to me. That the woman I've fantasized about since the first moment I saw her actually belongs to me."

"It was hell having you gone," she whispered. "I'm used to missions, but that one went long, and I didn't hear anything and…" She trailed off with a shudder. "It was hell," she repeated. "And then you came back, and … well, that was hell, too. I was so thrilled to know that you were alive. Thrilled to have you with me again. But it was a whole new level of hell, Mason. It really was."

She sniffled, then brushed tears away with her fingertips before using the sleeve of her robe to wipe her nose. "Sorry. I'm kind of a mess. I'm exhausted and, well, let's just say it's been an unusual day."

"It definitely has."

He took her hand. "Come with me."

He led her inside, a throbbing need building inside him. Not sexual—not entirely. But demanding and urgent.

"This is our kitchen?"

"Such that it is," she said. "We got new appliances because you like—*liked*—to cook. But the countertops and new floors and all that..." She trailed off with a shrug.

"You were waiting for me to come back."

"We wanted to do it together, the way we'd done the back porch. Room by room, a year or so of weekends. And then we'd have a new house by our anniversary." Her voice cracked as she spoke.

"I'm sorry."

She shook her head vehemently. "No. Don't be. We both love our work. I still do, even with everything that's happened. And despite leaving the SOC to move over to Stark. What we both do, it's important. You may not remember what you were doing, but I promise you it was something vital. And we bought this house knowing that anything could happen. We could get transferred to another country. We could end up on a long-term undercover assignment. One of us could get whacked on the head and end up with amnesia." She said the last with a sad little laugh, but he couldn't bring himself to smile in return.

She cleared her throat. "Anyway, the point is that we knew the risks. And we knew that we might never be able to settle down like civilians. This part?" She swept her hand to encompass the room, the house. "The part where I couldn't deal? That was all on me." Her lips twitched with humor. "I guess I loved you even more than I realized."

He moved closer, then cupped her chin and gently tilted her face up. Then he kissed her. Just a gentle brush of lips on lips, but it set him on fire, and when he stepped back he was breathing hard. And he knew exactly what he wanted. Her. His life. *Everything*.

"We'll finish the house," he said. "We'll finish it together. We can start tomorrow."

Something bright shone in her eyes. "Really?"

"It belongs to me, too."

"Right. Of course. It does." Her voice was soft. Breathy.

"So do you."

"I do."

The words—a vow—sliced through him, hot and demanding.

"Take off your robe," he said, barely able to hear his own voice over the pounding of his pulse in his ears.

"What?"

"You heard me." He moved closer, knowing he was pushing limits, but also knowing that he had to. That it was right here and right now that would either make this shadow life real for him, or leave him outside the glass looking in.

She was breathing hard, her lips slightly parted as she studied him, as if trying to read his mind.

"You're my wife, aren't you? You belong to me as much as this house? This furniture?" He reached for the loose end of the sash. "Love, honor, *obey.*"

She met his eyes, hers sparkling with mischief. "Actually, we left the obey part out of our vows."

"And if I want it back in?"

Her brows rose. "Do you?"

"Do I want to know that this is still real to you? Me? This marriage? Do I want to know—truly know—that you belong to me, wholly and completely? Do I want to know that there is nothing you won't do if I ask, just as there is nothing I won't do for you? Yes, wife. I want that."

She didn't answer him, not in so many words, but the color rose on her face and she was breathing hard when she closed her hand over his and tugged the sash loose. She moved her shoulders, and the robe slithered to the ground, leaving him holding only a white cloth sash in his hand, dangling down to where it was tethered to a puddle of crisp, white terrycloth.

He dropped the sash.

For a moment, he simply stood there, taking in every inch of her. Before, she'd been a woman he desired. But that desire had been mixed with guilt. He'd not only coveted another man's wife, he'd pulled out his cock and fucked her.

Except he hadn't.

The woman he'd craved was his. His woman. His partner, his friend.

His wife.

His life.

Wasn't that the way it was supposed to work? And in his case, it was more true than usual, since the sum total of his known life was so small. But Denny was at the heart of it, and he had the feeling she always had been, even when his life was as wide as the world.

"I love you," she said. She stood naked and unabashed in front of him. "God, Mason, I love you so much."

The words warmed him. Centered him.

He supposed that to another man in his position they might be terrifying. But not him. Not with her. Denise Marshall was saying those words to him, and even though his mind had been erased, he felt like the luckiest man in the world.

"Upstairs," he said. "I want you in our bedroom."

For a moment, she didn't move. Then a smile lit her face. "Yes, sir," she said, then walked out of the sunroom ahead of him.

He followed, enjoying the view of her heart-shaped ass and the way her hips swayed.

His, he thought, and still couldn't quite believe it.

When he got to the bedroom, he found her on the bed, ankles crossed, arms stretched wide. "Like a feast for me," he said.

"Oh, I think I'll enjoy it, too."

"Wife," he said, then drew in a breath. "My beautiful wife."

As he watched, her cheeks turned rosy from her pleased blush.

"Husband," she countered, holding out her hand. "Will you make love to me?"

"Oh, yes," he promised, climbing onto the bed. But first he wanted to explore every inch of her. Wanted to listen to her breathing quicken as his fingertips traced her skin. As his lips tasted every inch. As he discovered a smattering of freckles on her shoulder and a diamond-shaped birthmark that seemed to float right over the indentation between her torso and her thigh.

She had a kissable dent at the base of her neck, and it also was her most ticklish point. And when he ran his forefinger under the arch of her foot, she just about leaped off the bed.

"You're extraordinary," he said finally, though he wasn't through exploring her. Hell, he'd probably never be through. Right then, though, he wanted more. He wanted to kiss her. To lose himself inside her. And then, after they'd both exploded in each other's arms, they'd drift off to sleep together.

That's what he wanted, he thought, as his cock slipped deep into her tight, hot core. What he craved, he thought as he moved inside her, their bodies joined. One heart, one soul. One memory.

Her. Them.

In that moment, that was all there was.

And the true miracle of the moment was that he knew without a shadow of a doubt, that she felt the same way, too.

17

I WAKE to find Mason beside me, propped on an elbow as he looks down on me, his expression so tender it almost hurts my heart.

"Good morning, wife," he says, and I smile and snuggle close in response.

"Can we just stay like this for a week or two? Surely the universe owes us that much."

"Sounds good to me," he says, his fingertip gently stroking my bare arm. "I'm not ashamed to say I'm exhausted. It takes a lot out of a man to be deflowered by his wife."

I burst out laughing. "Deflowered. You? Hardly."

He sits up, pulling me up with him. "Ah, ah. No arguing. Especially when I'm right. That was the first time for me, after all. At least as far as I can recall."

I grin, because he's right. And then, inexplicably, I start to cry.

Or maybe not so inexplicable. Baby hormones, after all.

But all the hormones are doing is stealing my self-control. The worry and fears are real. As are my tears.

"Hey," he says, pulling me to him. "Hey, we're going to be just fine."

I suck in a ragged breath. "Are we?" I ask, and then kick myself because I don't want to have this conversation right now. And yet it looks like we're going to be having this conversation. Right now.

"What do you mean?"

"I just—it's just—Oh, hell, Mason. You're here, and I love you, and I'm your wife, and from my perspective, that's all amazing."

I mean every word, but I'm going to have to bite the bullet and reveal a little bit more of my heart if I don't want Mason to think I'm a crazy person.

He scoots back so that he's leaning against the headboard. I shift, too, so that I'm sitting cross-legged in front of him, the sheet pulled up to cover me since I feel so damn exposed.

"Denny," he says, his voice tense. "What's going on?"

"I'm just afraid," I say.

"That I won't get my memory back?"

I nod. "And that you can't—come on, Mason. You don't remember me. You don't remember yourself. You're here in this bed because you're my husband, but what if you're not the same person now? What if you don't want to be here?"

What if you don't want a baby when you don't even remember its mother?

I push the thought away.

"I'm sorry," I say. "You have so much to deal with and now I dump this on you, but—"

"You're afraid," he says simply as he reaches out to hold my hands. "Of course you are. Your husband came back and he doesn't even know you."

I make a harsh sound. "Yeah. That about sums it up."

He scoots closer, pulling me toward him as he does so that our hips touch and I can lean into his outstretched arms.

"I'm sorry," I say again. "This shouldn't be about me. Not after everything you've—"

"The hell it shouldn't." His lips brush my forehead. "Here's the thing, though. We made a vow to each other, right? For better or for worse? Are you saying we should bolt just because we're skirting up against the worst?"

"I don't know," I say, honestly. "People leave. They leave all the damn time."

"I'm not leaving." His voice is hard. Intense. A statement and a promise. "Hell, even with amnesia, I came back. And here's something else—I do love you. And I expect that will deepen over time."

"You don't even know me."

"I know your core. Your heart. I know I like what I've seen. I know that I trust my gut, and so far it seems to me that Mason Walker is a pretty decent guy."

I grin. "He is."

"And he loved you. Which makes me pretty sure I love you, too. Or I will. Right now, it might just be all about the sex."

Now he's teasing me. "The sex is definitely worth sticking around for," I say, meeting his smile.

"Definitely." He taps the end of my nose, something the old Mason used to do, and happy butterflies dance in my soul. "Did you know I remember movies?" he asks. "A lot of movies."

"Um..." I have no idea where that came from. "I knew about TV shows. I mean, you remember *Lost*."

"And I remember *When Harry Met Sally*. All those real life interviews. One of them was an arranged marriage, and they did just fine. So why can't we? I mean, if we want to?"

And there it is. He's just voiced the heart of what's terrifying me. "Do you want to?"

"Oh, yes," he says, and there is no denying the depth of passion in his voice. Or in his kiss when he bends and kisses me ever so sweetly. "Don't ever doubt that I love you. Not now. Not ever."

I bite my lower lip as I nod. "Okay. Don't ever make me doubt it."

"Deal." He tugs my sheet down and gently cups my breasts. "In fact, I'll go one better," he adds as slowly slides one hand down my belly. "How about I show you?"

———

"Feeling better?" he asks me, two orgasms later.

I nod, then roll over onto my stomach. I prop myself up on my elbows and just look at him, this man I missed so much. Who has, miraculously, come back to me. And who means to stay.

I still need to tell him about the baby, obviously, but I don't feel any guilt about waiting. He's had a lot of reality thrown at him in the last few days, and it's not like I'm going to go into labor this afternoon.

Plus, I need to talk to Seagrave and Dr. Tam. I got pregnant when Mason snuck back to me during his operation. And that's a pretty intense memory. If I tell him, are we risking blowing the circuits in his mind?

I don't know, but I'm not about to do anything that puts Mason at risk. Which means the baby and I are in a holding pattern for now.

Meanwhile, I have a job, and he's still supposed to be

shadowing me at work. If that kick-starts his memory, then all the better.

"We should get up," I say. "We're supposed to be at work. Chasing bad guys. Filing reports. Getting the details from Liam about his concert prima donna."

"And yet I'm not racing for the shower." He runs his fingers lazily over my bare arm. "Was I always such a rule breaker?"

"You were a soldier, so no."

He smirks. "Amnesia agrees with me."

I laugh, which changes quickly to a moan as he flips me over, then straddles me, his mouth closing hard over mine. "Again?" I bite his lip. "You're an insatiable rule breaker."

"Is this a problem for you?"

"Really not," I say, and wrap my arms around his neck right as his phone chimes.

He scowls as he rolls toward the side table. "Only a handful of people have that number, and I probably shouldn't ignore any of them. Sawyer," he says, as he presses the button to start a speaker call.

"You want to tell me why my bike is parked outside Denise's house?" It's Liam's voice, and I sit bolt upright, feeling as guilty as a student caught kissing in the janitor's closet.

"Because we're still in bed. And naked."

There's a pause, then Liam says, "Probably more information than I needed," and I try very hard not to laugh.

"Turns out she's my wife."

I hear Liam's sharp intake of breath. "You remember?"

"Actually, no. Not a goddamn thing. But apparently it's true. And right now, I'm enjoying being blissfully ignorant. Or I was, until you interrupted."

Liam sighs. "Definitely TMI."

"You outside?" Mason asks. "Because you could have just knocked."

"Got worried. Just in case you forgot who you were again. Would be a shame to lose such a nice bike."

"On the contrary, I'm feeling remarkably self-aware."

"Uh-huh. Ryan says to get your asses to the office."

He winks at me. "Apparently we're in trouble with teacher."

"We're on our way," I shout over him, then smack him in the shoulder as he laughs and ends the call. "I think we shocked him," I say.

"I doubt that."

I shrug. "I don't know. I adore Liam, but I'm not sure he dates. I don't think I've ever heard him talk about going out with anybody." Then again, he's best friends with Dallas Sykes, so I doubt anything could shock Liam.

"Maybe he has a secret lover tucked away somewhere. And maybe," he adds as he tugs me out of bed, "I don't want to talk about Liam while I have you naked in the shower."

18

"You have your memory back," Ryan said, clapping Mason on the back as he slid into a chair next to Denny. "That's incredible. How the hell did it happen?"

"Apparently through the wildfire of rumors," Mason said, his gaze landing on Liam. "I said I knew my name. That's about it."

Liam leaned back in his chair, clearly unperturbed. "It's a start."

"How'd you remember it?" Quince asked.

Mason bit back a smile as he recalled how Denny had screamed his name in bed. Beside him, Denny scrolled through her text messages with her left hand as her right closed over his thigh. Her fingers dug deep into his flesh in a not so subtle warning.

"Just something Denny said." He smiled at the team. "It just clicked."

He pressed his hand over hers before she could pull it away, wanting to keep the contact.

"Here's hoping for more pieces of the puzzle," Ryan said. "As for today's briefing, we need—"

"I'm sorry," Denny said, sliding her chair back and tugging her hand free. He was on his feet, too, pushed into action by the worry etched on her face.

"I just got a ping on Cerise's system. Someone's on her property right now."

"Go," Ryan said. "Check in later."

They both nodded assent, and hurried to the garage. They'd come on Liam's bike, which turned out to be fortuitous considering the early morning snarl of traffic. "I'm going to get me one of these," Mason said as they dismounted at Cerise's house, where an LAPD patrol car was already parked.

This time, Cerise didn't step out to greet them, and when they knocked on the front door, a shadow passed over the peephole before the lock clicked and the door opened. At the same time, a car skidded to a halt in front of the house, and Denny spun. Her hand, Mason noted, was on her weapon.

"I hoped you'd beat me here," Peter said as he sprinted for the door. "Tell me the system notified you directly, and you're not here because Cerise called you, terrified, like she called me."

"The system," Denise assured him. "And it called the police, too."

"They're in the backyard," Cerise said, biting her lower lip as she stood on her front patio. "Two cops. But the guy was already gone."

"You have the feed?" Peter asked Denny.

She nodded. "I can download it to my phone. But it'll be clearer on Cerise's monitoring system. Can we go inside?"

"Huh? Oh, yes. Of course." Cerise stepped back in, then signaled for them all to follow.

The system was set up to play the feed through Cerise's

home entertainment center, and Mason watched as Denny turned on the television, selected the proper input, then rewound the video.

"I'm putting it at forty seconds prior to the time-stamp on the alert I received," she said. "Let's see what was happening then."

"Definitely an improvement on coverage," Mason said as the image filled the screen. "No more blind spots. And see? Right there. Movement in that bush."

"I see it," Denny said, moving to stand beside him.

"See!" Cerise squealed the word, then pointed to the shadow of a man as he crawled up the steep incline of the lot behind her house. The sun hung low in the sky, and the vegetation made the area even darker. But as he moved up the hill, more light found him, and the man's features became clearer.

Denny stood beside Mason, their arms brushing as they studied the feed. So he both felt and heard her shocked reaction when the man looked up, and the camera caught him. *The Face.*

Cerise's intruder was the man from the club. More important, he was the man who attacked Denny, who gave her the long, thin injury over which she now pressed her hand.

Behind him, Peter was talking to Cerise. "Do you know him? Is he the same man you saw before?"

Mason was only half-listening. How could he hear over the rage that was bubbling up inside him?

He turned, then met Denny's gaze. She didn't look scared. On the contrary, she looked furious.

And he knew in that moment they were thinking the same thing. They were going to find the Face—and then they were going to do whatever was necessary to figure out what the fuck was going on.

———

It took some time to get Cerise settled. She didn't want to leave her home, but she also didn't want to be alone, and Peter assured her he'd stay the night. Or as long as she needed.

"We're going to assign a team to stay outside the property, too," Denny said. "They'll either act as a deterrent or they'll be first responders if he comes back."

Cerise nodded. "Thanks. I think that would make me feel better. At least for a few days."

"Go open a bottle of wine," Peter suggested with a hug. "I'm going to walk Denise and Jack out."

At the end of the sidewalk, his gentle demeanor changed to one of hardened fury. "The minute I find out who's fucking with her—"

He cut himself off, then drew in a breath as he looked between the two of them. "Who is that asshole, and what's going on?"

"A good question," Denny said, her face all hard lines and grim determination. She met Mason's eyes. "We're going to find out."

"Find out?" Peter's brow rose. "Dammit, Denise, I saw your face. You two know something. You've seen him before. Who is he?"

She started to reply, but Mason jumped in first. "When we know, you'll know."

Peter studied Mason's face, then nodded. "Fine. Good." He sighed. "I want her feeling safe." He pointed between the two of them. "Call me."

As soon as he disappeared back into the house, Denny raised a brow. "I've worked with him. He's a solid agent."

"Doesn't mean we need to pull him into this loop. It's not his rodeo," he added when she raised a brow. "And I don't think Mr. Face has a damn thing to do with Cerise."

She nodded. "I was thinking the same thing. It was one thing for you to notice him at the club. I mean, maybe his face was familiar because you saw him walking down the road as we were driving up, and it had nothing to do with your amnesia at all."

"But..." He tapped his own throat.

"Yeah. Exactly. The assault on me."

"So this guy's been stalking Cerise in order to keep an eye on you or get your attention," Mason said, turning the possibility over in his mind.

"More than that. Maybe he wants *your* attention. The message he gave me was for you."

He let that sit awhile and then shook his head. "Except Cerise's first incident was before I was on the team. It doesn't make sense."

She exhaled. "Then we keep poking around until it does."

"Agreed. At least we have a photo now."

"I already texted a screenshot to Ryan. He's got the tech team on it. With luck, we'll get a hit by tonight. If not, we can call in a favor with Seagrave."

"Good," he said, not at all surprised that she'd already forwarded the image. He may not remember his past with his wife, but he knew her now. And he knew that she was a rock solid agent.

"Back to the office?"

He shook his head. "Let's work from home. I want to get settled." He watched her face as he spoke, both relieved and thrilled when her initial confusion shifted to understanding and, thank God, delight.

"You're moving in." Her bright smile rivaled the California sun.

"It's traditional to live with one's wife." He hesitated, hoping he hadn't assumed too much. "If that's okay?"

"Don't be an ass." Her eyes danced. "I'd kiss you right now, but I don't want to be unprofessional."

He glanced over his shoulder, noting that the two uniformed officers were returning to their car.

"I'll happily take a rain check." He indicated the bike. "I'll drop you off at home, then go leave the bike at Liam's, grab my tiny duffel of personal possessions, and catch a rideshare back to your place."

"Better idea. I'll get a ride with the officers, and you meet me at the house with your stuff. It'll save time. Liam's that way," she said, pointing vaguely toward the coast, then turning and indicating the opposite direction. "And that's us."

"Fair enough." He ran his finger along the line of her jaw. "I know you're going to want to work when I get there, so I'm telling you right now—I get an hour. Free and clear. And entire hour at my complete discretion."

"Is that right? And what happens in that hour, Mr. Walker?"

"Well, last night I studied your body and learned so many ways to satisfy it. Considering my memory problems, I thought I should see just how well I recall exactly what you like…"

19

As MY TWO cop chauffeurs argue about the thematic similarities in Marvel and Star Wars films, I lose myself in more immediate concerns. Specifically, Cerise and the Face and the mystery of what Mason is supposed to remember. Important enough to attack me on the street, but even such a bold move can't produce results. Not when the information is locked away tight, with no way to get it out.

No way that's safe, anyway.

I frown, thinking about what Seagrave told me. That trying to prime the pump by telling Mason what he's done in the past could permanently injure him. And then my frown deepens as I wonder how in the name of hell I'm supposed to explain getting pregnant.

The patrol car pulls to a stop in front of my house, and I hop out, thanking them for both the ride and the entertaining film discussion. The driver chuckles, and I wave as the car pulls away from the curb.

Instead of going inside, I head to the detached garage that sits at the end of our long driveway. Having lived alone for a while, I've gotten in the habit of eating out or ordering in. Mason was the cook in our family. I was the one who would make a meal of cheese and Ritz crackers if that was the quickest thing to grab.

Tonight, I want to make dinner together. Which is why I get in the car, back out carefully, making sure our neighbor's little girl hasn't left her trike halfway in our driveway, and head down the road to the nearby Ralph's.

Since I'm not a whiz in the kitchen, it takes me a while to navigate the store, which is frustrating as I want to beat Mason back so that I'm there when he arrives. Soon enough, though, I'm clutching two canvas bags with steaks, potatoes, fresh broccoli, and a rather pricey bottle of wine. Plus vanilla ice cream and Chips Ahoy cookies, a sentimental favorite from our early days.

I put the bags on the floorboard, amazed to realize I'm humming. I don't think I've randomly started humming since Mason went away. And this new sense of peace and happiness only drives home how much I missed him. And at the same time, it reminds of how far we still have to go.

With a frown, I silence my tuneless singing. What if he never remembers? What if this is our new beginning and we're really starting all over again, with no history because he doesn't remember and I'm not allowed to tell him?

I have boxes of souvenirs and thousands of digital photos. And I hate thinking that I won't be able to share those with him—or with our child.

I let out a shaky breath, then drive home in a more somber mood. I ignore the garage and park in the driveway, then cross the lawn with my two bags held in my hands.

My mind is on Mason, and my first thought when I see someone moving on the front porch is that Mason beat me home.

But that thought lasts less than a second, and with my

next breath, I drop my bags and reach for the weapon I have holstered under my jacket. Because that's not Mason—it's the Face.

The groceries cost me time, though, and he has his weapon out before I do, and this time it's a gun, not a knife. I hear the blast at the same time I feel the sting in my chest, right above my breast.

I gasp, my body reeling, then look down, expecting to see a messy bullet wound. Instead, I see the feathered end of a tiny dart.

A tranquilizer gun?

Oh, dear God. The baby...

Cold panic fills me, and I force it under, determined to rely on my training. I turn toward my car, intending to lock myself inside, get my backup weapon, and signal the SSA. Then I'll defend that small space until Mason or someone on the team arrives to shut this fucker down.

Except I can't manage. My brain is trying to operate my legs, but they're not cooperating. In my mind, I'm sprinting. In reality, I'm collapsing onto the thick turf of my front lawn.

I'm face down, unable to see anything, unable to *do* anything. And then I'm being flipped over, a terrifying and odd sensation, as I can't even feel any hands on me. But I can see, and the afternoon sky comes into view above me, blocked only by the ugly visage of the Face looking down on me. A round face with a bulbous nose and rheumy eyes. There's dirt in the crevices of his skin, and I can smell his breath, like rotten fish and onions. He's the stuff of nightmares, and I don't know what he wants with me. Or, for that matter, what he wants with Mason.

Tell him he needs to remember.

He needs to give back what he took.

That's what the Face had said at the club, and it's what

he says again now. I want to scream that I don't understand; that I don't know what he's talking about and neither does Mason. But I can't scream. My throat doesn't work, and even my breathing is slow and laborious.

Am I dying?

"Tell him," the Face whispers before leaning over and doing something on my left. Touching me? I don't know. I can't feel him and I can't move my head to see. "Tell him to look and to see," he adds right before he straightens and stands.

That's when I hear the squeal of brakes, then Mason's voice calling my name as footsteps pound. The Face is standing above me, one foot on either side of my waist.

I can't see Mason, but I know he's there and relief flows through me like wine. He'll catch this bastard. Quince will work his magic with a lie detector, pharmaceuticals, and his other tricks of the trade to get some answers. Everything will be okay.

I just have to hang on long enough.

I have to fight the black that's seeping in around the corners of the world.

"Denny!" Mason shouts again from somewhere off to my left. And then I hear his hard, raw cry of "*No,*" and I watch as the Face jabs a needle into his own neck, then smiles down at me.

But I don't see anything else, because the black has taken me. And the last thing I hear is Mason's anguished cry as he calls my name again and again and again.

20

A TRANQUILIZER? That's it. You're sure?

We're still running tests, but so far the lab results are showing only the tranquilizer in her blood stream. And you can see she's already coming to.

Am I? I recognize Mason and Seagrave's voices, but I'm still a little fuzzy on their meaning. Somebody knocked me out. That much seems clear enough. And—

The Face. And the groceries. And—

Why the hell did he knock her out in the first place? So that she couldn't watch when he killed himself? And what the fuck with the phone?

I blink, the world flashing in and out like someone opening and shutting blinds. What do they mean by killed himself? And what phone?

I open my mouth, then whisper, "Mason."

Or maybe I don't say anything at all, because no one seems to hear me.

Mason, please. We're working on it.

I want the SSA working on this, too. They're her team now. They deserve to be in the loop.

I've already talked with Mr. Stark and Mr. Hunter. An SSA team is being fully briefed.

Relief warms me. I don't know what's going on, but I'm glad my friends are working on it, too.

Look.

That's Mason's voice, and he's close. So close.

"Denny? Denny, it's me. Can you wake up?"

I want to tell him that I am awake. Before, it felt like I was dreaming, but I'm awake now. I just feel so heavy. Even my eyelids are so, so heavy.

"Give her a moment," Seagrave says. "It'll take her some time to swim up out of it."

He's right, and it's a good metaphor. It's as if I'm kicking toward the surface, and I actually gasp as I break through into reality, my eyes fluttering open to find Mason's eyes fixed on me, first full of worry and then shifting to relief.

"Thank God," he says, clutching my hand.

"The Face. He hit me with a tranquilizer?"

"He did." Seagrave rolls his chair beside Mason. "Welcome back."

"Just a tranquilizer. Is it safe?" I think of the baby. Please, please, don't let anything hurt the baby.

"Just a tranquilizer," Seagrave says.

I nod, reassured. I know enough about weapons to not be too worried about a tranquilizer dart. "But why? Did he just want to make a clean getaway after he left the message?"

Mason and Seagrave look at each other. "What message?" Mason asks.

"Same as before," I tell them. "That you have to remember. You have to give back what you took."

Again, they share a look.

"Don't keep me in the dark," I say. My strength is flowing back, the grogginess leaving me. I push myself up until I'm sitting in the hospital bed. Then I look around, for the first time noticing that I'm in Mason's old quarters.

Seagrave nods his head. Just a tiny tilt, but it's enough. Mason focuses on me and says, "There are two things you should know. First, the Face is dead."

"What? Was he trying to escape? Because we needed to talk—"

"Suicide," Mason says. "He injected himself with cyanide."

My mouth drops open, and for a moment I'm dumb-struck. "Why would he do that?"

"One of many questions," Seagrave says, and I look between him and Mason, waiting for him to tell me the rest of the questions. And the answers.

After a moment, Mason lifts a shoulder, looking positively helpless. "He left you a phone. Right in your hand. A smart phone with absolutely nothing on it."

"Oh." I try to process that but it makes no sense. "You tried re-dial? You checked the emails?"

The both just stare at me. Of course they did.

"It's here?" I ask.

Mason points to the side table where what looks like a burner smart phone sits next to a pink plastic jug filled with ice water.

"Can I look?"

He raises a brow, but doesn't protest. I understand I'm being ridiculous; I won't see a thing they didn't. But that knowledge doesn't curtail the urge, and as soon as he puts the phone in my hand, I sigh.

Then I yelp, because the device chirps in my hand.

"What did you do?" Mason says, and I shake my head.

"Nothing. I—look. It's a text message."

They gather close and we read the message together.

The first part is a string of chemical symbols that my poor science can't decipher. I don't need to, though. It's clear enough from the words that follow:

> It's in her blood.
> 72h incubation period.
> Give us the encryption key.
> We'll make her the antidote.
> Reply when you have the key.

My blood.

My blood, my baby. Oh, dear God.

I tell myself it's okay. Maybe this is just a threat. A scare tactic. The SOC team said there was only tranquilizer in my blood, after all.

But I know that's not true. Whatever the toxin is, it's there. The medtechs just weren't looking for it.

Still, so long as I get the antidote in time, the baby and I will be fine.

That's what I tell myself, anyway.

But I don't really know if that's true.

And with the location of the encryption key buried in Mason's head, I don't think I'll ever find out.

———

"He shouldn't be doing this," I say, looking into the conference room through the one-way glass window. Fear burns through me—for myself, for my baby, for Mason.

"He doesn't have a choice," Quince says, putting a hand on my shoulder to stop me from pacing.

"There's always a choice."

"And he's made his," Liam says.

I turn, looking at my friends through tear-filled eyes. "What if it breaks him?"

Neither man answers. They don't have too. Mason loves me. And if the only way to pull the location of this encryption key out of his head is by forcing his memories, then that's what he's going to do. Even though the risk is high. Even though he may forget everything. Or worse.

I think about what Mason has told me. About the videos of other agents who'd been forced to face their hidden memories too early. Men who'd snapped completely.

Please, please don't let that happen to Mason.

On the other side of the conference room, Mason sits in one of the rolling chairs. He's wearing a T-shirt, and a variety of monitoring bands surround his chest and head, all hooked to an array of monitors and a computer that sits in front of Dr. Tam.

Mason's arms are strapped down, and he looks like a prisoner. Someone in for interrogation. And that illusion is bolstered by the two IV drips going into his veins. One drip contains a fast-acting sedative so the doctor can knock him out if he starts to tip over into the danger zone. The other contains a serotonin-like compound that is supposed to keep him calm as he moves through the memory stimulation process.

"Happy thoughts," Dr. Tam had said, with an ironic half-smile. "Think of it as forced happy thoughts."

Not exactly a high-level medical explanation, but I understood what she meant. The amnesia had been induced by some sort of horrific trauma. To pull out the buried memories, Mason had to find his way around that trauma. And that meant not sliding back into the mental state that had surrounded the trauma and instead creating a "happy" back door.

All good in theory. In practice, it sounded pretty damn dicey.

"I can't lose him all over again," I say.

Liam moves to stand beside me at the window. "That's why he's doing it. Because he can't live without you, either. And that's going to happen if we don't get the antidote."

I wipe away a tear and nod. Seventy-two hours. That's the window to get me the antidote. After that, there's no cure, and I'll be dead within a week.

That's what the medical team tells me, anyway. All things considered, I don't have any reason to doubt them.

It's more than just me, of course. The toxin in my blood is something never seen before. It's a national security threat. And even if I were completely healthy, I know that Mason would still be sitting in that chair, ready to sacrifice himself to save the world.

Inside the room, Dr. Tam starts to talk to Mason, her voice calm and level. Since she doesn't actually know what he experienced, she's hypnotized him in the hopes of pulling out those hidden memories more easily. I just hope the memories don't turn out to be dangerous.

She's been fully briefed by Colonel Seagrave, and she starts to describe the mission, the details of which I've never known. Nor have Quince or Liam or any of the Stark team, and I'm grateful to Seagrave for giving everyone clearance. I need my friends' support. And their help.

The job was to infiltrate an international mercenary group known as *La Guerre Rouge* in order to relay back information about its various activities, especially arms and drug trafficking. The insertion was a success, and Mason was able to gain the trust of one of the group's high-ranking commanders who eventually tasked Mason with a secret project that was deep in development.

All of that, the SOC knew from Mason's infrequent reports and dead drops. And as Dr. Tam talks Mason through all of that, his vitals stay normal.

I look at Liam and Quince, trying to hold back my optimism. Because surely this means it's going to be okay. Surely it will turn out that we could have done this straightaway, and that Mason had been left in the dark out of an overabundance of caution.

As I watch, Dr. Tam leads him down the path of memory, and Mason describes the day to day of his job. The horrific things he witnessed, even participated in, in order to establish his cover. I understand the work and what it entails, so I'm not shocked. But I also know that too much living in the underworld can taint a man's blood, and I don't want Mason to go back. Not after this.

I look at Quince, wanting to ask him if he thinks Ryan would recruit Mason into the SSA. But I stop myself from asking. Right now, we just need to get through today.

Finally, Dr. Tam leads Mason up to his last communication. He'd discovered something truly horrific in the works, and he'd signaled that he'd be sending more details. But the details never came. Instead, Jack Sawyer woke up in Victorville.

"Let's start with the truck and work backwards. You remember being thrown out of the truck?"

"Yes."

"Do you remember being put in the truck?"

"No."

The electronic lines on the monitors behind Mason begin to spike. I reach for Quince's hand and hold tight.

"Let's talk about that. Let your mind go back. Who were you with?"

The lines spike more. Mason goes pale.

"Did they say anything before putting you in the truck?"

His body starts to shake, and I hold my breath.

Another question, then another and another, but no answers, and with every question his reaction becomes erratic, his body more strained, until finally Dr. Tam asks him to recall the face of the cell leader with whom he'd become close.

A wild, gut-wrenching scream rips from Mason's throat and he stands up, clutching his head, his face screwed up in pain, as wires and IV tubes flail about, until he drops to the floor, curls up in a ball on the tile, and rocks and whimpers and rocks.

His scream, however, continues to echo—or at least I think it does. After a moment, I realize it's me.

"It's no use," Dr. Tam says into the intercom after she's given him more sedative and helped him back into the chair. "Not right now. I see no signs of permanent damage or regression, but he needs time to recover before we try again."

"She can't try again," I tell Seagrave, who's joined us in the viewing area. "You're not going to get anything and it's going to destroy him."

"That period of time is key," Seagrave says, musing. "Right before they dumped him in Victorville. He learned something. Something dangerous and important. We need to know what that is." He meets my eyes. "And not just because we need to save you. There's more riding on this than the life of one woman, even a woman I trust and admire. And since the toxin in your blood stream is an agent we haven't seen before, we have to assume it's at the heart of a biological weapons attack. We need to know what they're planning, when, and how."

I know all that. Of course I know it.

"We have to try again," Seagrave says flatly. "And we have to keep trying until we get answers. Or we can't try anymore."

21

Mason paced the small suite that the SOC had given to him and Denny for the night, a set of rooms that visiting operatives were permitted to use while on local assignments. Seagrave had smiled when he offered it, calling it a courtesy. After all, the clock was ticking, and both he and Denny needed rest. They didn't need to be driving back to Silver Lake.

That part was true enough. But what Mason also knew was that if they'd said no to the offer, Seagrave would have insisted. The information in Mason's head was too important to let him wander away. Not only that, but while they believed the toxin in Denny's blood was dormant, they still wanted to do regular draws and tests.

Which meant that the suite was more necessity than courtesy.

Even so, it was private, without the monitoring systems set up in the infirmary or the holding cells. And for that courtesy, Mason was grateful. He wanted Denny in his arms. And he wanted their privacy. He wanted them to get lost in each other just in case tonight was the last night they ever could. Or, at least, the last night he'd ever remember.

"I have to tell Dr. Tam to push harder," he said, pausing in front of the table where Denny was reviewing the lab and chemistry reports.

She slammed the laptop shut, obviously frustrated. "I can hack my way into almost any system. I can ferret information out of anything with an electronic brain. But damned if I can figure out the chemistry of whatever they've shoved into my blood."

With a sigh, she dragged her fingers through her hair, then smiled up at him. "Sorry, distracted. What did you say?"

"Dr. Tam. I need to tell her to push harder."

"What? No. We're in this room so we can grab a few hours of rest. So that you can get your strength back. But that doesn't mean she needs to press harder. You started to snap, Mason. Harder, and you will."

"I have to try." He pulled out the chair beside her and sat down. "Seventy-two hour incubation period, and your life is on the line. Do you think I'm going to back off?"

"I think you need to be smart. You push too hard, and you could get lost inside your own head."

"If I don't push, you'll die. Not only that, but they have plans for this toxin. You won't be the only one dead, and we both know it."

She shook her head, but she didn't argue. He knew he was right, and so did she.

"I'm strong," he said gently, standing up and then tugging her into his arms.

She shook her head. "Not strong enough."

He laughed, then wiped away one of her tears. "Thanks for the vote of confidence."

Her lips twitched, but didn't quite turn into a smile. "I can't stand the thought of losing you. Especially not now when—"

She cut herself off with a shake of her head.

"When you've just gotten me back?"

She hesitated, then nodded, and he almost asked her what she wasn't saying. He didn't, though. Instead, he just kissed her. "That's how I feel, too. And I'm willing to do anything to keep you. And, hopefully, come all the way back to you."

"Mason—" She stopped, then slid off his lap and started to pace. "You need to know—"

A hard rap at the door interrupted her, and they both turned that direction.

"Nurse," a deep male voice said, and Denny frowned.

"Come in," she called, then grimaced as she added to Mason, "Time to get stuck again."

A nurse in jeans and a hospital green scrub jacket entered, tossing Denny's chart carelessly onto the table as he prepared the vial. Denny had already taken a seat on the edge of the small sofa in the suite's living area, so he moved to her as Mason hung back at the table.

He'd seen dozens of people have blood drawn, and had himself bled into enough tubes to stock a blood bank. Even so, watching the process ranked low on his list of favorite things, and he looked down instead, his eyes skimming over Denny's chart. He flipped the pages casually, then froze when he reached the doctor's notes.

> Prenatal/Amnio toxin analysis @16weeks:
>   negative
> Maternal toxin: positive

Retest amniotic fluid following 72h inc.
period

He read the note again, then one more time, first with ebullient joy, then with a rising sense of dread and betrayal.

She was pregnant.

He was going to be a father.

But even as those thoughts lifted him up, the reality that surrounded them brought him crashing down. And not the reality of the toxin or his memory. The other reality. The darker reality.

The reality in which his wife who purported to love him had sex with another man sixteen weeks ago.

Who?

The question gnawed at him, the thought of his wife with another man bubbling in his blood like some caustic, toxic poison.

He left the report on the desk and started to pace the room, jealousy and doubt coursing through him. He'd fallen in love with Denny—not just before. Hell, he couldn't even remember before. But *now*. Right here, right now. With her cleverness, her humor, her dedication. And, he'd thought, her loyalty.

Was he not seeing the real woman?

Had there been problems in their marriage before?

Had she believed he was dead, and found solace in another man's arms?

For a moment, he let himself believe that, the theory giving him some peace. Then he remembered what she'd confirmed before the first time they'd made love while he was still Jack. She'd told him that she knew Mason was alive.

She'd known that he—that Mason—was out there in the world.

And she'd still fucked another man.

Goddammit all to hell.

"Are you okay?"

He'd been pacing so fast he was practically jogging. Now he looked around the room in a daze. The nurse was gone, and Denny was standing, her face painted in concern, as if she truly cared at all. As if he wasn't the biggest fool in the world.

"Does it matter to you?"

She blinked. "What? Of course." She took a step toward him. "Mason, what's wrong?"

"I have no memory of our time together before I came back," he said slowly. "No memory of what we had or didn't have. How we loved or didn't love."

"Didn't?" she repeated, her brow furrowed.

"You tell me we were in love, but I don't know. What evidence do I have? What evidence other than the fact that I fell in love with you now. Here."

She licked her lips, looking at him as if he were an old jigsaw puzzle with lots of missing pieces. "I love you, too. Then, and now."

"*Don't.*" The word ripped out of him, and he pointed an accusatory finger at her. "Do not stand there and tell me you love me. Don't lie to me and say that you waited for me, that you missed me and mourned me. Not when it's all a lie. Not when you're carrying another man's child."

She'd been walking toward him, but now she stopped, frozen to the spot, and he knew that he'd hit home. That she hadn't expected the secret to be revealed. And although that was a victory for truth, it damn sure felt like defeat.

"I fell in love with you in the here and now. But I guess that was just Jack. You'd already tossed Mason aside."

She shook her head. "No, you don't—"

"What? Understand? Are you going to explain it to me? I think I understand betrayal well enough."

He wasn't pacing, but he was moving around the room. He didn't want this rage, this fury, but at least it was *his*. He'd felt this way only one other time since he'd awakened in Victorville—when they'd made love. Not fury, then, but a fullness. Real, concrete emotions. Everything else was twinged with a sense of hollowness because he was half a person, his past left behind somewhere. But in her arms, he'd been whole. And now he was whole again as he railed against her betrayal.

How ironic that his love for her both saved and destroyed him.

"Who was it? Quince? Before he met Eliza? Liam? Is that why you love that shower so much?"

Her unreadable expression focused into fury. "Those men are your friends and my colleagues. Don't you dare accuse them that way."

She was right, but he swallowed the apology, not willing to give up any ground, his anger eating away at him, but freeing him as well. Had he lost his shit since Victorville? Was this the first time the wounds had opened and he'd let the bile spill out?

Maybe it was—hell, maybe Denny was getting more than she deserved.

Then he remembered that she was four months pregnant and he'd been gone for over two years, and his rage whipped right back up again.

"Was it Peter? Did you sleep with him?"

"Absolutely not," she said, crossing her arms over her chest and tilting her head to the side. "Are you finished? Do I get to talk? Say anything in my defense?"

She spoke so calmly and evenly, that he could feel his fury deflating. He tried to hold onto it, clinging to it like a life raft. "Are you pregnant?"

"Yup."

"Then I don't know what you could possibly say."

"How about this—you're an idiot."

"I'm a—excuse me?"

"An idiot," she repeated. "One who clearly needed to have the mother of all tantrums because, hello, weight of the world on top of amnesia, so I'm willing to cut you some slack." She screwed up her mouth. "Maybe not for the Liam and Quince comments, though. That pushed the envelope."

"I'm sorry?" The apology came out as a question, not because he wasn't sorry, but because her words and her demeanor were confusing the shit out of him.

"I *am* pregnant, you stupid man. I'm pregnant with your baby."

He just stared at her, because those words didn't—couldn't—make sense.

"I told you," she said. "When you asked if I knew Mason was alive. I told you that he—you—had made contact twice. The second time was now. As Jack, I mean. But the first time —well, that was about four months ago. In February. On—"

"Our anniversary." His voice was barely a whisper. *He remembered his anniversary.* "Valentine's Day."

"You remember? Our wedding? That night?"

He tried to pull it out, but no. All he remembered was February 14. "I remember the date. Like I remember Christmas."

With a sigh, he moved to her, then pulled her into his arms. "I guess that date's important to me. I'm sorry," he added, lifting her hand to his lips and kissing her fingers. "I shouldn't have—"

"No, you shouldn't have." She smiled, then kissed the corner of his mouth. "But under the circumstances I forgive you."

Guilt still clung to him. "I mean it. I'm sorry."

"I know you are. Now shut up, okay? You get a one-time pass. Do something this bone-headed again, and we'll see a different outcome. Okay?"

"Okay." He drew in a breath, the world shiny and new despite all the horror surrounding them. "So we're really having a baby?" Pleasure poured through him. A father— was he really going to be a father?

"We are," she said. "Assuming I survive the next—"

He cut her off with a kiss. "You will," he said firmly. "Don't you dare doubt it."

She met his eyes, the trust he saw there almost enough to melt him. "I don't. But sometimes faith isn't enough. We need a plan. We need information."

"Which is exactly why I need to push harder. Let Dr. Tam go deeper. All these scars on my back. On my neck—I don't know how I got them, but they must be related. They're new. I was tortured. And I stole something. It has to be related."

"Agree."

"Did I have them four months ago?"

She bit her lower lip. "I don't know."

"But I thought—"

"You blindfolded me."

"Did I?"

She smacked him lightly. "Don't look so amused. It was—*Oh!*"

"What?"

"I can't tell you about it. Not now," she added, then grinned at him like a kid with a secret. "But I think telling you with Dr. Tam in the room would be an exceptionally good idea."

22

He could hear their words.

Denny's. Dr. Tam's.

They sounded as if they were above, and he was deep in a well, but he could hear them. That was all that mattered.

He was sedated—he knew that.

He knew that he was hypnotized, too.

Most of all, he knew this was dangerous. Something about the path. Something about how it could all fall out from under him and he'd end up someplace else altogether with no map to get back to himself.

He looked out, and he saw the path. Yes. Dangerous. Mines buried everywhere. Barbed wire on the fences. Snipers hiding behind the rocks.

He had to go slow and be careful.

But he had to go. Because he was going to be a father, and oh, dear God, how incredible was that? He was going to be a daddy, and he had to keep his child safe. Had to protect him from—

From what?

"Was there a meeting?" The voice seemed to come from

inside his head. "Do you remember a meeting where you were told what was going on? You were with them a long time. You must have had their confidence."

He glanced over at the rocks where the snipers hid. Had he ever truly had their confidence? Or had they always had their weapons aimed right at him?

"A toxin," he heard himself saying. His body went tense. *Denny.* She'd been given the toxin.

"And the meeting? Was there a meeting? Or perhaps you stumbled across some information?"

His head started to ache and he felt his body rocking. Had to be careful. Couldn't step on a mine.

"Just a meeting." He knew the voice now—Dr. Tam. "No danger to you at the meeting. You're fine now, just fine. It was a meeting, wasn't it?"

"Yes. They trust me. No barbed wire here. But there's a sniper."

"Deep breaths," the doctor said. "Calm down. The sniper won't hurt you."

"No." He drew a breath. Then another. "I don't know about him. Not yet."

"Who—" Denny's voice.

"Shhh. Later. What did you learn, Agent Walker. What did they tell you about the toxin?"

"All about the economics. That's what Jeremy said. They'd think it was a terrorist act when really it was about getting paid."

"Jeremy?"

"The sniper." His body felt cold. "The pumpkin eater. My ally, only he's not. I don't know that—didn't know that? —but he's not an ally."

He was getting close to the ice. To the danger. "So much wrong there. He's not Jeremy, not my partner." The ice was fire, bleeding into his skull. The pain was creeping up on him. Sharp teeth, long claws. "I need—"

"You're doing fine, Agent Walker. I'm monitoring you. Deep breaths. Good. Take another. I'm keeping you safe. And we're over a month before you returned, remember? Nothing's happened to you yet. Don't worry about Jeremy. Right now he trusts you."

"He has a secret."

"But you don't know it yet, do you? Right now, you're on the garden path. Where does their garden path lead?"

"Death," he said flatly. "Unless there's an antidote, it's death."

He heard a sharp intake of breath at the same time the doctor said, "Unless?"

"They contaminate the population. Infiltrate the fast food market. How much wouldn't the government pay for an antidote? The government, corporations, even individuals? Taint the food at the burger barn or taco shack down the street and the big nasty conglomerate will pay to make the population healthy again?"

He remembered. They'd told him. Wanted him to head up the American cell. The first cell with the first batch of toxin. A demonstration for the rest of the world. If the rest of the world ponied up, no need to infect anyone else. The biggest protection racket in the world.

"Was that when you made contact?"

"No." His voice was like a whimper.

"No? Mason, listen to me. Take a deep breath. Loosen your grip—you're going to draw blood if you dig into your thigh that hard. You're still safe. Listen to my voice. If you haven't made contact yet, you're still a long way from when they will torture you. That's it. That's good. You're doing much better. Are you back on the garden path?"

"Yes." But he knew there were still snipers everywhere.

"What did you do?"

"I infected it. The formula."

"The toxin?"

"The antidote. I didn't have time—couldn't erase it. Couldn't destroy. But a virus. A code. They were afraid— didn't trust their own people. Only one mainframe, one backup. And I was making the trip—coming to investigate supply lines. And I knew I could see her. I could make sure she knew. She'd be my backup in case it all went south."

"Denny? Your wife."

"They didn't know about her. Not then. I went to her. Our anniversary. She couldn't know I was there. Needed deniability."

"You went to her anonymously."

"I—yes." He remembered. Oh, God, he remembered how beautiful she'd looked. How soft her skin had felt. "I had to see her. And I had to give her the code."

"And you did."

"I did."

"And they never knew."

"No. And I went back—I had to go back. There was more to my mission, and I—" His mind filled with red.

"Mason. It's okay. Deep breath."

He sucked in air. Released it. And tried to make his body relax. "Later I learned about Jeremy—that he was the pumkin eater— and when he realized what I knew, he—" His breath was coming in gasps, his lungs like fire. "He didn't kill me. They didn't have the encryption key. Couldn't kill me until they found it."

"You'd hidden it."

"Yes."

"With your wife."

"Yes." An icy calm drifted over him. "They asked me where. They tried to torture it out of me. They came close to getting it. Close to finding it."

"But they didn't. What did you do to keep them from discovering that you'd given it to Denny?"

The cold was peaceful, like fallen snow on a wide open plain.

"I broke."

23

"None of this makes sense," I say as Dr. Tam turns off the music app on her phone, stopping the steady flow of Chopin's *Nocturne*, which she said she'd been using to help make Mason more receptive to hypnosis.

"Why doesn't it make sense?"

I hold Mason's hand as his lids flutter and he comes back to me, opening his eyes as if waking from a nap.

"Because he never gave me anything that night. He barely spoke. And, well, at the time, I didn't even know for certain it was him."

Dr. Tam's brows rise. So do Mason's.

I roll my eyes. "After a point I realized it was you," I say. "Or I convinced myself it was. After all, I didn't think Nikki or Jamie would send me a gigolo. And I was right—it was you," I say. "You just said so."

Dr. Tam still looks about to laugh. I just shake my head, not sure if I should be amused or frustrated. The night had been incredible. A surprise gift of a massage from my friends. A "sensory immersion" experience the attendant had said, then blindfolded me. And then ... well, then there were familiar hands on me and a voice I was certain belonged to my husband. A voice I so desperately wanted to be his...

And it was. *It was.*

"Don't you remember?" I ask now. "Hasn't it all come back? You said you hid the encryption key with me. Can't you remember where?"

But he just shakes his head, looking miserable. "I don't. Dammit, I couldn't find that in my mind. It wasn't there. It just wasn't in my head."

"Probably your subconscious trying to protect Denny. But this is good progress. We can try again tomorrow. Possibly get further."

"And if we don't?" I ask. "I don't have that many tomorrows left."

But Dr. Tam only shakes her head. "He needs rest. I'll be back first thing in the morning."

We both protest some more, but it's no use. Honestly, I'm a little bit relieved. As terrified as I am of this toxin that is threatening me and my child, I still have days left to vanquish it. But one wrong move—one push that's just a little too hard—and I could lose Mason forever.

Mason, however, is genuinely frustrated.

"We can still figure this out," I say. "We just have to try and think like you."

He smirks. "At the moment, you know the old me a lot better than I do. So tell me. What would I have done?"

I exhale, then move into the bedroom of our suite. I climb on the bed and hug a pillow in my lap, my favorite thinking position. "We know it was an encryption key, one you used to give an entire computer system a very bad head cold."

Mason rolls his eyes. "I remember that movie," he says,

the comment making me giddy. Because *Independence Day* was one of our favorite popcorn, wine, and a movie in bed Friday night rituals. The kind of flick we both enjoyed ... but also didn't mind missing if we got distracted.

Right now isn't the time to traipse down that block of memory lane, though, so I keep the focus on our conundrum. "It must have been a physical key, not just a code you memorized."

He nods. "Right. I wouldn't risk something short. Or something written down."

I think about that, then frown. "I suppose you could have written it down. Hang on." I pull up my phone where I keep a photograph of the letter he left for me after that night. "You left me this. But if this was supposed to shout, *Hey Denny, I'm a code*, you failed pretty badly."

He takes the phone, and I read over his shoulder:

Lovely Denny,

Thank you for the night. For fueling my heart with new memories. For reminding me that there are things to live for and fight for. Things that burn hotter than a shooting star and last longer than eternity.

We will, I think, see each other again, though I cannot say when or where. But I will hold onto last night and the pleasure we shared.

Don't look for me. Don't try to find me. Don't ask questions to which you don't truly want the answers.

For the time being, last night was enough.

Yours,
The Master

He makes a scoffing sound. "The Master?"

"Hey, don't look at me. You're the one who wrote it."

"Well, you're right. No code there. What we're looking for is a randomly generated encryption code stored on a disk or a flash drive or something of that ilk. Easy to smuggle out, easy to sneak in."

"Agreed," I say. "What kind of op-tech were you issued?"

He tilts his head to the side and gives me a look until I screw my head back on.

"Right," I say. "You don't remember. Hang on. We can figure this out."

I text Seagrave, expecting him to shoot the answer back to me in the same manner. Instead, there's a rap on our door within two minutes. Mason heads out of the bedroom to answer it, and I stay curled up with my pillow.

"There was a drive in the earpiece of your reading glasses." I can hear Seagrave talking to Mason. "Also a Visa with an embedded drive and a fake ID with the same."

He rolls himself into the bedroom, then comes to a halt at the foot of the bed. Mason follows, then sits beside me on the bed. "Dr. Tam just briefed me," Seagrave says to both of us. "I take it you're trying to put the hours between now and the next session to good use?"

"Damn right," I say.

"Good. I can't fault the doctor for wanting to protect a patient. But..."

"Exactly," Mason says, looking at me with such concern and love it makes my heart flutter.

"Any one of those things could have been left behind in

the hotel," I point out. "It was the penthouse at the Stark Century. Maybe lost and found?"

"It's a long shot, but worth it," Mason says as Seagrave dials his phone. While Seagrave asks Damien to check with the hotel, Mason makes a good point to me.

"I wouldn't just leave it randomly lying around. We know that I left it with you. That's what I said, right?"

"That you'd hidden it with me. Yes."

"You don't live in the penthouse. It doesn't make sense I'd just stick it in a drawer. Did you have luggage?"

"No." I think back. "I'd been working that day. The SSA uses the sub-basement for recruitment and training. I was putting some agent trainees through their paces."

"And?"

"And I was having a shit day," I say. "It was our anniversary. You were gone. I was lonely. Then Ryan told me about the massage that Nikki and Jamie ordered for me, and he sent me up to the penthouse."

"So you had your backpack or a purse or something?"

"A purse. I remember because I'd gone shopping with the girls the previous Saturday and we'd seen all the Valentine's Day displays." I hug the pillow closer. "I guess it was obvious how sad I was."

"Okay. Good. I would have put the key in your purse."

"Except I didn't find a stray credit card or reading glasses or any other drive."

"No new keys hanging on your ring?" Seagrave asks, rejoining our conversation. "Just because those were our op-tech devices, Mason could have used anything."

I get off the bed and find my backpack, then check my keys. Every one is familiar.

I turn back to the men with a shrug.

"How long did you use the purse?"

"Just a few days, honestly," I confess. "It was a nice bag, but I like my backpack."

"Maybe it's still in an interior pocket. Or hidden in the lining."

I nod slowly. That makes a lot of sense, and I look at Seagrave, who frowns. "So we go, right? We go check my closet right now."

"Or I can send an agent to retrieve your purses."

Mason starts to argue, but I cut him off, something else occurring to me. "Why didn't you send it straight to Seagrave?"

He rubs his temples "I don't know. I don't remember. I might never remember." He paces at the foot of the bed. "Maybe I thought it wouldn't be safe? Intercepted? I don't know. But we need to go look."

Seagrave nods. "As I said, tell me where and I'll send a team."

"No. Denny and me. Together."

Seagrave makes a rough noise in his throat. "Not a good idea. I need to keep you safe—Dr. Tam wants back in your head in the morning."

"My head will be right here on my shoulders in the morning."

"And as for Denise, the toxin—"

"Is safe for now," Mason says firmly.

The colonel aims a commanding glance at both of us in turn. "I can keep you here, you know."

"But you won't," I say. "You know we need to look. And you know we're running out of time."

For a moment, I think he's going to disagree. Then he says, "Go. I'll have an agent drive you. But come back with answers."

We don't hesitate, and as our car races toward Silver Lake, I call Damien to check for news from the hotel.

"Sorry. Nothing in the Lost and Found, or the log for that month. I checked the safe and long term storage, as well, in case Mason left it with someone at the front desk. Nothing."

I bite back then urge to curse, thank him, and fill Mason in.

"That just means the answer's at the house."

We drive the rest of the way in silence. Some idea is bouncing around in my mind, but I can't seem to grasp it. And as we go inside, I can only hope that the encryption key will be shoved down in the bottom of my purse, and whatever thought I can't seem to catch won't be important at all.

But there's no key in my purse. Or my backpack.

Or anywhere in the closet.

"There's something," I say. "Something you said or Damien said—I don't know. But something is bugging me, and I can't figure out what."

"Well, you're doing better than me. I don't have any ideas at all, clear or fuzzy."

He heads out of the closet and back into the main area of the master bath. It's a mess, as we'd started to chip away the old tiles before Mason left, and I haven't wanted to tackle it alone.

He holds out a hand, and I take it, then let him pull me close. "We're going to get through this," he says. "And all of this and the rest of the house? We're going to do it together. And when we're all hot and dusty from working, we'll take long soapy showers, watch old movies in bed, and make love."

"Promise?"

He kisses the top of my head. "At least until the baby

comes. Then it will be all four o'clock feedings and dirty diapers."

I laugh, then tilt my head up as fear dries up my humor. "Do you mind?"

He looks completely blank. "Mind?"

"You hardly remember us at all. Now there's going to be a baby, and—"

He kisses me. Hard and fast and so deliciously deep that I'm gasping when he pulls away. "No," he says with so much intensity that I wouldn't dare doubt him. "I don't mind." He strokes my hair. "But let's make sure we get there."

I nod. As much as I want to pretend it doesn't exist, my own blood is a ticking time bomb.

The trouble, of course, is that we don't know where to look next. So we end up in the kitchen. Mason drinking orange juice and me guzzling milk with Hershey's syrup in it, which I never drink, but sounds amazing at the moment.

"The whole thing makes no sense," he says. "I would have told you something. Given you something."

I manage a thin smile. "You gave me a house. A baby. That note."

"Pretty sure I didn't impregnate you with an encryption key," he says. "As for the house, I didn't even manage to help you fix it up before I disappeared on you. And the note..." He shrugs. "Well, looks like that was just a piece of sentimentality."

I toy with my straw. "I still liked getting it. Having it. Something of you to hold on to."

He nods. "I'm sure I knew you'd hold on to it. Which is why it makes sense that I would have used that to communicate. So why didn't I?" He slams back the last of his orange juice. "The least I could have done was told you what color I wanted all the rooms."

I laugh, which is what he intended, of course. But then I freeze, that niggling sense that I know something returning.

"Denny?"

"I think I've got it," I say. "Not exactly, but maybe sort of."

His brow furrows. "I'm listening."

"Earlier, you said the answer's at the house."

"Which is why we're here, and there's no answer."

I push my chair back. "I think there is. Come on."

The house has four bedrooms, and we were using one as command central for the renovations. That's where I take him now. "You wouldn't know that I was going to stop the work," I tell him. "That I couldn't face doing it alone. So you left the key in here. You came while I was at work, and hid it. Then you left me the clue at the hotel."

He looks around at the cans of paint samples and full gallons. At the books of carpet remnants that we were still debating. The boxes of hardwood flooring that still needs to be installed. The tiles, the fixtures, and all the other things that we'd collected but not yet installed or cleared out.

He shakes his head, looking overwhelmed. "I don't know, babe. The odds of us finding it in here. It's small, remember? And that's assuming it's here at all."

"It is," I say, feeling positively giddy. "You told me."

24

"I told you?" Mason stared at his wife, wanting to tell her that she was an optimistic crazy person. He knew better, though. For one, he wouldn't have married a crazy woman who latched onto unsupported optimism. For another, in the short time he'd come to re-know Denny, he'd learned all over again how smart and capable she was.

If she said that he told her, he must have told her. And under the circumstances, the fact that he couldn't remember didn't mean a whole hell of a lot.

"So when exactly did I tell you? And what exactly did I say?"

She reached out and took his hand, then eased close to him for a kiss. "You told me in that brilliant note of yours." Her delighted laugh caught him off guard, washing away the building worry. Maybe they really would get the antidote in time. "Want me to explain how brilliant you were?"

"Yeah," he said. "I really do."

"First of all, calling yourself The Master. Innocuous, right? But it's a clue. Only not the kind you'd see until you saw the other clue. They go together."

He narrowed his eyes. "Now you're just toying with me."

She shook her head and pulled out her phone, then passed it to him, the screen showing an image of the note.

"Burn hotter than a shooting star," she read, looking at the screen with him. "That's another clue. And *last longer than eternity*. Taken together, they lead right over there." She pointed to a shelf in the corner with at least two dozen cans of paint.

He headed over to the shelf and started reading off the paint names. "Moonrise. Nightfall. Shooting Star." He shook his head, still clueless. "They all deal with night?"

"Good guess, but no. *Longer than eternity* is the clue that tells me you're talking about paint." She grinned. "You don't remember, but before you left on assignment, I bitched about how we should have waited to buy the paint until you got back—remember, we never expected you'd be gone so long."

"And I told you that paint's not like eggs." *He remembered.* It was fuzzy, but he remembered.

Her eyes widened, and she nodded slowly. "Yes. You said—"

"—there were so many chemicals in paint that an unopened can would probably last longer than eternity." He pressed his fingertips to his temple and started to idly rub. "Denny, oh my God."

"I know, right? You did this. You sent me a message, and I was too dense to even think about looking for one."

"And when you said that The Master was a clue, it meant that we were talking about colors we picked out for our bedroom?" He said it as a question because he didn't remember, but that seemed to make sense.

She nodded. "And as for *shooting star*..." She pointed to the shelf, where three quart-size cans of off-white trim paint sat in a row. "The walls are going to be a pale, pale blue. You said this would be a perfect complement."

"I don't believe it." His words were barely a whisper. "Whatever we're looking for is in one of those cans."

"Is that a memory or a guess?"

He squeezed her hand. "A guess. But I think it's a good one."

"Me, too."

They looked at the cans together for a moment, then she shrugged and grabbed a flat head screwdriver from a box of tools. "So now we open and dump?"

"That one," he said, pointing to the one closest to him. "See? Looks like one of us cracked the lid."

She nodded, grabbed it off the shelf, then used the screwdriver to pop the lid off. "It's just paint," she said, peering into the can.

He passed her a bucket. "Let's waste some paint, shall we?"

"With pleasure." She upended it, the paint dripped out, and there, in the stream, a small plastic baggie slid out, too, then landed in the bucket with a plop.

He used two fingers to pull it out, and then laid it on a sheet of plastic set up beneath a sawhorse.

"There's another bag inside it," she said, after returning with a damp sponge and wiping off the goo.

Careful not to get paint inside the bag, they opened the seal, then pulled out five nested bags.

"You weren't taking any chances," she said, and he silently agreed.

Finally, they were down to the end, and he held up the small device. "A flash drive."

"Do we need to check it?"

He shook his head, wincing as the low-thud of a headache started to beat behind his eyes. "It's the encryption key. I remember."

———

Mason stared at the map on the burner phone the Face had left with Denny. A pin marked a set of coordinates in East Los Angeles. Then he read aloud the message that made his gut twist. The message that he and Denny had privately discussed for five full minutes before calling the information in to the SOC:

> Send the woman and the key to this location.
> Alone.
> Surveil her, she dies.
> Follow, she dies.
> Disobey, she dies.
> Cooperate, she will be treated and returned.

When he was finished reading, silence hung in the room. Then a voice came over the speaker of Mason's phone.

"And there's no way to reverse-engineer the antidote's formula from that key?" The question was posed by General Montero, a member of the oversight committee responsible for policing the SOC. Mason hadn't been thrilled when Seagrave put him on the line. In Mason's experience, bringing in retired officers tagged with oversight to spec out missions was a universally bad idea.

"No sir," Mason said, hating wasting time going over information again. "I sabotaged their mainframe. I didn't steal the formula. Once they have the key, they can decrypt the formula, manufacture the antidote and vaccine, and sell them to the government and consumers."

"Why haven't they already released the toxin into the food supply?"

"Their plan requires the antidote," he said. As the only SOC agent in the room, he was doing the talking. As far as the General was concerned, Denny was simply a civilian.

"They don't think of themselves as terrorists," he continued. "They're entrepreneurs. They want to create a threat and profit off of providing the solution. And sir, I remember now what the toxin does." He drew in a breath, hating the thought of the toxin biding its time in Denny's blood, a horrific threat hanging over her and their child.

"It destroys tissue, sir," he said, trying to keep his voice even. "Breaks it down completely. Basically, it makes Ebola look like a bad case of the flu."

"Good God." That curse came from Seagrave.

Beside Mason, Denny went pale. He took her hand, and he watched as she drew a breath and straightened her shoulders. She wanted to break down—he was certain of it. And he was equally certain she wasn't going to. The woman was amazing. More than that, she was his.

And he wasn't about to lose her again.

"This organization can't give in to terrorist tactics." Montero's deep voice boomed across the line, firm and authoritative. "As I understand, Agent Marshall has not yet entered the final twenty-four hours prior to infection. That means we have time."

"Begging your pardon, sir, but that means we're lucky. I beg you not to squander this opportunity."

"We won't," he said. "Reply that you accept their demand. Then forward us the coordinates. We'll send a team to intercept their transport. I assure you, we'll obtain the antidote."

"And if you don't? They're going to start shipping out their tainted preservative. It's going to go into commerce. They'll offer the antidote for sale right away, but folks tainted early won't believe. They'll get the antidote too late or not at all. And these bastards are counting on that. They need to make the news. They need a huge scare and bloody, gooey deaths. Because that will drive up the price of the antidote and the vaccine."

"I think you're aware of the skill level of this organization. And for a threat like this, we'll take extraordinary measures to stop the toxin from leaving their facilities."

"And get Denise Marshall killed in the process?" Rage underscored Mason's words.

"Agent Marshall understands that this office must focus on the big picture. If we utilize this opportunity to send in a full team, we can shut them down. This toxin cannot be permitted to enter the chain of commerce. Not with an antidote. Not without an antidote. Not at all."

"Denise Marshall is no longer with the SOC. You're destroying her chance of getting the antidote in time. You're putting a civilian's life at risk and—"

"You have your orders, Agent Walker. Forward the coordinates."

He looked at Denny, and she looked back evenly, her expression flat and emotionless. A agent calling on all her training so as to not give a single thing away.

But they'd talked about this. The risks. The possible outcomes.

They'd talked, and he knew what he had to say now. As

much as he hated what was going to happen, he knew what he had to do.

"I'm sorry, General," Mason said. "We're going to handle this my way."

25

THIS, I think, is a prime example of why I prefer tech work to fieldwork.

Because I would much rather be holed up in windowless room with a computer and some computer-based riddle I had to solve. Or someone whose identity I had to track down. Or even some dumbass game I wanted to code in my spare time.

But, no. Instead I'm standing on a corner in East LA waiting to either get picked up and hauled off to some secret facility or to get shot between the eyes, after which someone will rip the encryption key out of my cold dead hands.

Neither Mason nor I really like this plan, but I'm out of time and the general is an idiot. Seagrave isn't, but his hands are tied. Which means we're going rogue.

Which means I'm following instructions.

Which means I'm a sitting duck.

"We don't have a choice," Mason had said. "We have to get you that antidote and we have to find the facility. But God, it worries me sending you in like this." He'd brushed his hand over my hair, then cupped my cheek. Then he'd shaken his head. "No. We need to rethink. There has to be another way. I can't risk—"

I'd pressed my hand over his. "If we don't risk it, I'm already dead. And so is our child." I'd drawn a breath, gathered my courage, and told him the one fact that I was certain of. "They won't kill me on the street. We both know that. They have to use the encryption key at the facility to make sure it's real. If they kill me early, they know you'll never give them the real thing."

"And once they know it's real?"

I'd shuddered, then I'd met his eyes. "I'm banking on them using me as a test case. Inject the antidote, then test my blood. But they might just kill me. That's why you—"

"I'm tracking you," he'd said. "I'm tracking you, I'm making sure you get inoculated, and I'm getting you out of that place before we destroy the computer, the toxin, the files, and anything else that could ever let them recreate this threat again."

Mason had remembered enough to know that the toxin was only on the one mainframe because of a lack of trust between cells. So the computer that housed both the toxin's formula and the vaccination were standalone machines not connected to the internet. Great for keeping the threat contained, but unfortunately it also meant we couldn't hack in and wipe the thing out.

"I'm not scared," I'd told him right before I'd gotten in my Highlander, the burner phone's map open to guide me. "I know you've got my back."

"I do," he'd promised before kissing me.

I can still taste that kiss on my lips, as well as the lie. Because of course I'm scared.

It's late, almost midnight, and this is not exactly Beverly Hills. There's not much traffic, but what there is notices me.

A number of cars have slowed, and I've been asked several times how much I charge for a blowjob. Apparently I'm camped out on a very entrepreneurial corner.

Ten more minutes pass, and then a van I've seen three times already draws to a stop. The passenger side window rolls down, and I look up—and then gasp when I see Peter looking back at me.

"Oh, good," he says when he sees the expression on my face. "I was afraid you were expecting me, which means that I didn't keep my secret nearly as well as I thought I had."

"I don't—you. Why?"

"We're blocking traffic. Hop on in. We have an antidote to prepare. Wouldn't want you to get all oozy, would we?"

I get in—I don't exactly have a choice—and he pulls back into traffic.

"Here," he says, passing me a blindfold. "Put it on. Can't release you if you know where the facility is, can I?"

I hesitate, but I put it on.

I try to pay attention to the cars twists and turns. Try to make a map in my head. But that's a skill better suited to movies than real life, especially when your captor is chatting with you and making it impossible to focus.

"Give me the burner," he says. "And your phone, too."

I hesitate—Mason can track me through my phone— but I also know I don't have a choice. I pass them over, hear the window roll down, and then back up. The phones, I know, are now smashed somewhere on the side of the road.

I twist my wedding ring nervously, thinking about Mason. Imagining him coming for me.

"A pretty ring," Peter says. "Plain, though. Can't say I think much of Mason's taste."

"I love it."

"Do you? It's shit. Hand it over and we'll give it a toss.

Just like it deserves."

I clutch my right hand tighter over my left.

"Really? You're going to risk your life over white gold?"

"Platinum."

"All the better. Hand it over."

"I just got him back," I say. "You don't get the ring."

There's silence, and then my head is thrown back by the violent smack of a palm against my cheek. "You little bitch. We worked together and I never realized what a little bitch you are. Give. Me. The. Ring."

I try to pull it off, but of course I can't. So I lift my finger to my mouth, suck, and swallow the ring. *Fuck. Him.*

"Oops."

I can practically feel him glaring at me. But I know that he can't kill me. Not until he tests the encryption key.

Doesn't mean he can't hit me again, and I wait for the blow. It doesn't come, though. Instead, he just laughs.

"That's my Denise," he says. "Ballsy as hell."

"I'm not your Denise."

"No, you're Mason's."

I cross my arms over my chest. "I am."

"I told him I fucked you, you know. I told him much you liked it. How you begged for it."

"We *never—*"

"And I told him I killed you. That part was a lie, too. But we might be making it the truth soon enough."

A cold chill settles over me. "You know what happened to him." I remember Mason's headache at Westerfield's. I'd thought it was the lights. Now I'm thinking it was a memory. A memory of Peter.

"You know why he lost his memory."

Peter laughs. "You sweet, naive little girl. Of course I know. He lost it because of me."

26

MASON PACED THE KITCHEN, his phone in hand, his head feeling like it was about to explode. Not because memories were threatening to rip him up. But because he'd lost her.

They'd known that her captor would most likely toss the phone. Unfortunate, but inevitable. Useful, though, because surely he wouldn't look for another tracking device.

And it turned out that his Denny had another device. A brilliant, amazing device. A gizmo so clever it only reinforced his belief that she was one of the best op-tech wizards in the business.

Because she'd installed a tracker in her wedding band.

"It's been my pet project at the SSA for a while now," she'd told him." Watch enough Bond movies, and you want to make the fantasy real."

"And you did?"

She'd nodded, obviously pleased with herself. "I had to hollow out a tiny bit underneath, but the band's wide enough and deep enough, and we've been working on micro-tech. The power supply's the problem, which is why mine is rarely on. You have to constantly recharge for a mission. It only lasts about twelve hours. But it charges fast, so..."

She'd trailed off with a grin, and he'd kiss her again. Just because he had to.

They'd thought the twelve-hour window would be enough, but apparently she'd been wrong about battery duration. Because the phone was offline and the ring was offline ... and that meant his wife was offline.

Goddammit.

He had to find her. They'd agreed that she'd go into the lion's den because she didn't have a choice. Go, and the outcome might be horrible.

Don't go, and the outcome would definitely be dire.

But the plan all along was that he would find her. He would track her. He would save her.

And now he was about to fail her.

The woman he loved. Not just once in his life, but twice over. He couldn't lose her. Lose her, and he might as well let himself get lost inside his own head, in the mishmash of nonsensical memories.

Lose her now, and that might be the only place he could find her again.

With a violent motion, he grabbed his Perrier bottle off the counter and hurled it across the room. It hit a window leading to the sunporch and broke through with a crash, showering glass everywhere.

The sound and destruction should have been satisfying. They weren't. Instead, he just collapsed onto the ground, his back sliding down the cabinetry, his arms encircling his legs. He put his forehead on his knees and waited for the tears. Waited for the darkness, longing for inspiration, but knowing that it wasn't going to come.

He didn't know how long he sat there, praying for either

a plan or oblivion. All he knew was that when he heard the crunch of glass under a shoe, he was on his feet in seconds, a knife from the block in his hand.

"What the fuck happened here?" *Liam*.

"It's a bloody mess, that's what," Quince added. "The situation and the kitchen."

Mason put the knife back on the counter, his pulse returning to normal.

"What are you—"

"We tracked her as far as Ontario." Liam said. "Damn chopper lost her."

Mason looked between the two men, trying to make sense of their words.

"Seagrave called Ryan," Quince explained. "Unofficially, of course."

Mason couldn't help his grin. He knew his friend wouldn't screw them over. Not even when a general was looking over his shoulder.

"Denise rigged a tracker in her wedding ring," Quince continued. "Bloody brilliant, actually, and—"

"I know."

"You remembered?"

"She told me. I was tracking it and her phone. They both went offline."

"On our end, too. Fortunately, we were able to get a chopper in the air before the ring died on us, but the pilot lost them in traffic. Ended up tailing the wrong damn van."

"So she really is lost," Mason said, the hope that had been building in him fading. "All we know is that she's somewhere in the Inland Empire, or she was. Who knows where she'll end up?"

"Hopefully we will," Quince said. "It's a bit of a long

shot, especially with your rather dicey memory, but we might get lucky."

The hope that had died started to flutter. "What are you saying?"

Quince pulled out a chair and sat at the breakfast table. "According to Seagrave, one of the gadgets she was trying to make work back when she was at the SOC was a flash drive that sent out a tracking signal when it was plugged into a power source."

"Like a computer," Liam put in.

"You said *trying*," Mason said.

"She never got it to work. And the tech stayed at the SOC when she moved over to Stark. Probably why she started fiddling with her ring," Quince added. "Anyway, Seagrave says that his team managed to make it work after about a year of trial and error."

"I would have been deep undercover by then."

"You were," Liam said. "But that's why God invented dead drops. The SOC got you one after you relayed that something major was going down."

"Which leaves us with one question," Quince said.

"What's the code?" Mason filled in. "And the answer is, I haven't got a clue. Little bit shallow in the memory department, remember? And even if I did know, how would we log into the tracking system?"

"We know how to do that," Liam said as he pulled open the fridge. "Seagrave sent over the app."

At the table, Quince pulled the app up on his phone and showed Mason. "Alphanumeric. Three letters—the same letters. And then an eight digit number string."

"And you think I set up a code that matched those parameters?"

"Well, we're hoping," Quince said.

"I didn't."

He pulled up the photo app on his phone and slid the image of the letter across the table to Quince. "This led us to the drive. The first paragraph references a specific paint can —seriously. But nothing in there matches the code you're describing. And if there was some other communication, then I don't know—"

He froze, then grabbed the phone back again, using his finger to tap as he counted out letter.

Eight digits later he looked between the two men, grinning broadly. "For a man with no memory, I'm a fucking genius. Gentlemen, let's go save my wife."

27

I'VE TRIED ALL my life to keep my faith. That Pollyanna belief that things will work out, even though so much in my life turned to shit. My father. My mother.

Despite all that, I'd kept a good thought. And the first time I truly broke was when Mason's mission turned from days to years. But even then...

Even then there was some tiny bit of hope inside of me. A small spark of faith that burned in the dark places of my soul.

I'd fed it, nurtured it. And when he returned, I knew that I'd been rewarded for keeping faith alive.

Now though...

Well, now I'm looking at the world through more pragmatic eyes.

I'm locked in a room inside a building inside a city. But I don't know what city, and even if I did, it's not as if I could do anything about it, as I'm cuffed to a metal chair.

My husband is undoubtedly trying to find me, but the tracking device in my phone is useless now, and I'm beginning to fear that the tracking signal emitted by my ring wasn't as strong as I'd hoped. Even if it did make it out of my body, it wasn't intended as a location device inside a concrete building.

And though I've only seen this one room, if it's any indication, this building is one big concrete slab.

In other words, there's really no way for Mason to find me. Which means no one is coming to rescue me.

Maybe if he had all the time in the world to pull traffic camera footage and contact the government to review satellite imagery from the relevant time frames.

But I don't have that kind of time. I'm ticking down toward oblivion.

Because as much as I'd hoped that Peter would give me that antidote, he's made it quite clear that's not going to happen.

So, yeah, my faith is on shaky ground now.

On the other hand, I no longer have anything left to lose. A philosophically freeing thought that does me absolutely no good.

The door on the far side of the room creaks open, and Peter comes in. The room I'm in is cold and windowless, with only the computer, my chair, and its mate. When he steps inside, I feel even colder.

"Hello, Sugarplum," he says cheerfully. "You'll be happy to know the first batch of the antidote has been synthesized, is currently going through the Q&A process, and soon we'll know if we can get this party started."

"You mean taint the food supply," I say.

"And then fix it. For a price."

"And me? When do I get the antidote? Or aren't you a man of your word?"

His eyes widen. "What show have you been watching? Of course I'm not a man of my word. You think I want you running around out in the world? Trust me, we'll all be better off with you dead."

I want to whimper in response to his words. To curl up inside myself. But I don't. I'm too well-trained for that. And that training is all I have to cling to now that faith has fled.

"What happened to you?" I ask as I try to surreptitiously tug on my wrists, cuffed behind me to the chair. But I'm not going anywhere. Maybe if I could do some sort of martial arts flip and break off the back of the chair, but that's really not going to happen. "We were friends once, weren't we? You were sane once."

"I'm sane. More sane than you. Scrimping by on a government salary with the kind of skills you have? How is that sanity?"

I stay silent.

"But you had your virtues. Of course, if you'd slept with me I might be inclined now to treat you better."

"No, you wouldn't."

He grins. "No. I wouldn't."

"And Cerise? You dragged her into this. Why?"

"Even without his memory, I banked on lover boy finding his way back to you. I needed to be close. I watched, learned she was a new friend, saw she could use a security system. Nice girl. Doubt she'll get sick. She's not the type who eats fast food. And as for you..."

He crosses to me, and I shrink back, wanting distance. He crouches in front of me and grins. "You did your part well. After all, you two managed to find the encryption key, didn't you?"

"Who was the man at the club? The one who attacked me and killed himself?"

"Oh, just one of my hired hands."

"Mason recognized him."

"Yes, he used to work in our group. Transport. Errands. That kind of thing. Homeless until we gave him a better life."

I frown, confused. "He stuck himself with cyanide. Why?"

"I gave it to him, of course. Told him he could die the way you're going to, or he could end his suffering before it began. And I told him that I'd provide for his ex-wife and children if he took care of a few teensy tasks before he popped that syringe into his neck." He shrugs. "Everyone has their uses."

I stare at him, horror-struck.

"Oh, don't look at me like that. He was grateful for that syringe. He's seen what that toxin does. And once you're past the incubation period, there's no antidote." He glances at his bare wrist as if he were wearing a watch. "You have a bit of time. But still, tick tock. Tick tock."

"You're despicable."

"Me? Do you know what your husband did? He used a time delayed virus on our computer. So when he went out into the world on his little fucking spree with you, he'd already loaded the virus. But we didn't know. So when he came back, it took a while until we understood what happened. We were all very annoyed. I was very annoyed."

"Good for Mason."

He puts his hands on the arm of my chair and gets right in my face. "You have a choice to make, girlie. You can be polite, and I'll put a bullet in your brain. Or you can be a bitch, and I'll let you and your precious fetus melt away like so much bloody tissue. I'm kind of hoping you'll be a bitch. I do like you—don't get me wrong. But you never should have ended up with a guy like him."

My body goes cold with fear and dread. "I was your partner."

He shrugs. "And I was your husband's good friend Jeremy. Another agent in deep cover—his alias was Jack then, too. Jack Sloane. The man does like his television references."

Alias. Another show Mason and I used to binge.

"He found out you were a double agent," I said. "And he fried your computer. He beat you and you couldn't stand it."

"I don't think you can call it *beating* since I won. He's a mental basket case and his wife is soon to be goo. Kind of a Pyrrhic victory, don't you think?"

"You're a monster."

"Maybe. I did tell him a few lies. And beat the shit out of him. Remember that mission in Aruba? You wore that tiny bikini. So I was able to tell him all about a rather intimate birthmark at the same time I was whipping him. His back's splitting open, and there I was, telling him how I fucked his wife. Then put a bullet in her brain. A lie, but he didn't know. All he knew was that it was his punishment for what he did. For going to you. For telling our secrets to you. And do you know what he did?"

My throat is dry. My body hollow. I don't want to hear any of this.

"He snapped. He's weak and pathetic and he snapped." He grins at me. "It wasn't me. It was you. You were the straw that broke the camel's mind. How does that make you feel?"

I can't get much saliva, but I still manage to spit in his face.

He wipes it away impassively. "And on that note, I'm going to go check on the antidote. Maybe we can work out an arrangement for you to earn it. I wonder as the clock winds down if you'll get down on your knees to save your life. Not to pray, but to suck my cock."

"Bastard."

"Why, thank you."

He leaves, and my shoulders sag as tears start to flow. I can't stop them and I can't wipe my eyes, and I really don't want to give him the satisfaction of seeing me like this.

I close my eyes, breathe, and try to will the tears to stop.

Too late, though. I hear footsteps and realize that he's back already. Probably forgot some scathing, parting insult.

But then he stops, and something in the air shifts. I open my eyes and swallow a cry of joy as Mason hurries to me. He falls to his knees and kisses me even as he curses the handcuffs.

"Dammit, I don't have a key. Quinn's right behind me, though."

"He's here?"

"And Liam and an entire SOC team."

"Oh, thank God. The tracker in the ring worked."

"Actually, no. But the one in the SOC flash drive did. And Seagrave worked some magic and got the general on board. They're securing the lab and—"

"Well, look who the cat dragged in."

The words echo in the room at the same time as a shot rings out. I see Mason's body shake, then realize that the bullet's entered just below his collar bone. He stumbles, then falls, his hand reaching for his weapon. He doesn't make it.

Peter stands in the doorway looking smug. And me? I'm fucking useless. And it's taking all of my effort not to scream and scream and scream.

"She's going to die, you know. But she's got a while before she starts to fall apart. I plan on getting good use out of her before then. I'll let you watch if you're a good boy. And after she's goo, I'll keep you for a pet. Those marks on your backs? That's just the beginning. We're going to have some fun, you and I. Do you remember what we did before? The burns? The whips? Of course you do. I can see it in your face that you remember every lash. Every burn. I'm going to fuck you up even better this time."

He takes another step forward, and on the floor Mason's eyes squint and he grabs his head as he mutters something unintelligible. I cry out, calling his name, but his face contorts with pain, and I think about Dr. Tam's horrible videos of strong agents just like Mason who got lost inside themselves.

"No!" I scream. "Focus. Mason, please, please focus."

But he just rocks and moans to himself as Peter walks closer. Close enough to thrust out a foot and kick Mason's leg. I can see Peter grin. A sick, horrible grin, and I wish to hell I could thrust my leg out and kick him in the balls.

And then—for one horrible, wonderful moment—I think I've done just that. Because there's an explosion and a scream and his crotch is covered with blood. He cries out, falling to the ground, grasping his bloody, mangled balls.

And that's when I realize that Mason was faking it. And now he's on his back, his body braced, and his recently-fired gun still aimed at Peter.

Grimacing, Mason struggles to his feet. "I should kill you right now," he says, "but I think I'd rather see you writhing in pain. I can't inject you with the toxin, but maybe this is the next best thing."

"Fucker." Peter's voice is hollow, but filled with hate.

"I beat you, you bastard," Mason says, swaying slightly. "I don't even have a memory, but I know I beat you."

"The hell you did." He's still on the ground, and he cries

out in pain as he lunges for his fallen weapon. He gets it, lifts it, and I hear a blast—two blasts. And then a scream.

I realize the scream is my own, and that Mason is on the ground. I think at first he's been shot, but then I realize that it was only the recoil of his own gun that knocked him over, weak as he is from his own injury.

This time, the bullet hit Peter in the chest.

And the second shot wasn't from Peter's gun either. That shot came from Liam, who stands now in the doorway, his gun still raised.

Liam's shot went through Peter's throat, and now the man is sprawled on the ground, his position reminding me of the Face, the man to whom he gave a horrible choice.

And as Peter gasps, I can't help but think that he had a choice, too. He made the wrong one, and now he's gasping like a fish and dying as his blood spills from him.

Honestly, I think Peter is getting off easy.

I turn my head, my eyes finding Mason's. He lifts his head and grins weakly, then his eyes roll back and he collapses as I scream for someone to help him.

A second later, Quince races into the room. He crouches beside Mason and puts pressure on the wound. He looks my husband over, then meets my eyes and nods. "He'll be okay."

I sag with relief. "You're late," I say.

"I have the antidote."

"In that case, you're forgiven."

He grins, but doesn't leave Mason until Liam sets me free. Then I fall on the ground beside my husband, whose eyes flutter open.

"It's over," I tell him.

A soft smile touches his lips. "No. It's a new beginning."

28

"HOW IS MASON DOING?" Cerise asks me as I navigate
Damien's back patio with two wine glasses full of Diet Coke.
One for me because I'm on the nine-month no drinking
program. One for Mason because he's still on antibiotics
from the bullet wound. Which, thank goodness, is healing
up just fine. At least that's what the surgeon confirmed
when he removed the stitches today.

"He's doing really great," I tell her, and it's true. I don't
add that he almost convinced me that we should both bail
on this party in our honor. But I reminded him that we
could spend the entire rest of our month off in bed if we
wanted to.

Today, however, is about celebrating with our friends.

"So long as I get you tonight," he'd said. "And every night
after."

It had seemed like a fair trade to me.

Cerise hugs herself. "I can't believe Peter turned out
to be…"

"Evil?" I suggest, when she can't find the word.

She lifts a shoulder. "Pretty much."

"Surprised me, too," I tell her. "But look at it this way—any guy you date next will be a step up."

She laughs. "I like the way you think," she says, then waves to Jamie and Ryan before leaving me to go talk with them.

Quince and Eliza are chatting with Emma, who's already back from Europe. Cass is standing with them, and I can't help but notice the way she's looking at Emma. What I can't tell is if Emma is interested, and I hope that Cass isn't setting herself up for more heartbreak.

When I make my way back to Mason, he's surrounded by Liam, Seagrave, Dr. Tam, and Damien.

"It was what you said about happy thoughts," Mason is telling Dr. Tam. "Or however you put it. Point is, when Peter was trying to get me to fall back into the memories of the torture, I stayed tethered by thinking about Denny. And the baby."

"And I'm very glad you did," Dr. Tam says, smiling over at me.

"Which explains why you didn't regress," Damien says. "But I still haven't heard how you figured out the tracking code for the flash drive."

Mason looks just a little too pleased with himself, but before he can answer, Liam steps in. "Bloody brilliant, as Quince would say. A paragraph with sentences all beginning with the letter D—so that was the triple-letter part. And then right after those three was a paragraph with only with eight words. The number of letters in each of those eight words made up one digit in the eight digit code."

"I was inspired," Mason says, smiling at me.

"An incredible job," Damien says. "And damn good timing."

"Is it true that you've confiscated the toxin?" I ask Seagrave.

"Now, Denise, you know that since you're no longer with the SOC, I can't confirm to you what I just told your husband about how we've ripped the legs out from under that entire cell, shut down the manufacture of the toxin, and taken the leaders into custody."

"Right. I forgot I'm out of the loop now." He and I share a grin as I settle onto the chaise next to Mason, on the side without the injury.

"With luck, Mason will be out of the loop soon, too," Damien says. "When I see an asset, I go after it."

"Do you?" Seagrave asks, but he's looking at Mason.

Mason looks between them. "For the next four weeks, I'm not available to anybody but my wife. So both of you just hold your thoughts."

"Fair enough," Damien says, shifting his attention to Seagrave. "Mason isn't the only new recruit I'm interested in negotiating with."

I watch the colonel's face, wondering. A few weeks ago, I'd have said he'd never leave the SOC. But with the way the general and the oversight committee have been meddling...

Well, who knows?

I catch Mason's eye and we share a knowing look, only to be interrupted by Liam's phone.

He frowns, then steps away to take it. When he comes back a few minutes later, he looks shell-shocked. "That was Ella Love," he says, referring to the pop star he'd been assigned to protect recently. "I need to go."

"What's wrong?" I ask, but he doesn't answer, and I look to Damien, who stands. "I'm going to go check in with Ryan," he says. "He may have spoken with Love's people. In the meantime, Mason, I'm thrilled your shoulder is healing so well. How's your memory?"

Mason shakes his head. "Still Swiss cheese. Honestly, we don't know how much of my past I'll get back."

"I'm so sorry," Damien says. "That must be horribly frustrating."

"It is," Mason agrees. "But it has a few unexpected upsides." He takes my hand, and smiles at me with so much love it almost melts me. "The best is that I get to fall in love with my wife all over again. And how many men get to say that?"

EPILOGUE

Five months later

"OH GOD, OH GOD, OH GOD!"

Mason grimaced as Denny squeezed his hand so hard it was a wonder every one of his bones hadn't shattered. As far as he could tell, giving birth was an endless cycle of pain coming in regularly timed intervals, the purpose of which seemed to be to torment his wife without ever actually producing a baby.

He hated seeing her like this. Hated knowing that he couldn't do anything except be there for her to squeeze and rail against.

"You did this," she said as the contraction passed. "I totally blame you."

"I willingly shoulder the burden," he said, wiping down her forehead as the nurse checked her vitals and cervix. He didn't mention that she could have opted for the drugs, which would have at least lessened the pain he was now shouldering the blame for. Really not the time. Besides, he

understood her reasoning. After being injected with both a
deadly toxin and its untested antidote, she hadn't wanted
any more pharmaceutical products near their unborn child.

He understood. He did.

But he still hated seeing her in pain.

"Oh, Christ, it's starting again."

"The doctor will be here any second," the nurse said.
"It's time."

Mason's heart pounded, the sound of his pulse filling his
head. *It was time.*

The next half hour was a blur of holding Denny's hand,
reminding her to breathe, and swallowing his own awe as he
saw his child's head crowning.

"You have a little boy," the nurse said moments later, and
Mason felt tears prick his eyes as he looked from the tiny,
shiny baby to Denny's beautiful, exhausted, elated face.

"Would you like to cut the cord?"

He almost said no, afraid his hands would shake too
much, but he did, amazed that he was there in that room
with this new life that he helped create.

"You're incredible," he said to Denny, stroking her damp
hair.

"Men always think that. And women have been doing
this forever."

"Incredible," he repeated, then teared up all over again
when the nurse brought his now-clean and swaddled son to
his side.

"Would you like to hold him?"

He nodded, feeling like a bumbling caveman. But then
the little boy was in his arms, his tiny little face scrunched
up and his little fingers grasping. Denny was beside him and
his son was in his arms, and Mason knew that his lost

memories didn't matter any more. Get them back or not, he didn't care.

He had this memory now.

And it was a perfect one.

———

Want to find out what happens to Liam? Be sure to keep reading!

RUINED WITH YOU

RUINED
WITH YOU
J. KENNER
NEW YORK TIMES BESTSELLING AUTHOR

CONTENTS

For Keeana -
thank you so much for your help and support ...
and for putting up with my crazy, partial emails!

PREFACE

I haven't gotten close to anyone for years. How can I, when every conversation is tinged with dread that someone will learn the truth? That my past will come back to haunt me, and that despite all the care I took to disappear, I'll be hauled out of the life I've built and thrust back into hell.

At first, I wore my fear like a cloak, wrapped tight around me for protection. Now it's an innate part of me, as necessary for my survival as blood and oxygen. It is constant. Familiar.

It is the core of the battlements I've constructed to keep myself hidden, and I never once believed that anyone could shatter my defenses.

Then he crashed into my world like a thunderbolt, his strong arms as soothing as his eyes are vexing. Because this is a man who sees things. But the more he breaks through the wall that surrounds me, the more I'm afraid he'll discover my secrets. And that the truth will destroy everything.

1

———

LIAM FOSTER SLIPPED on a pair of aviator glasses, shielding his eyes from the brutal Nevada sun as he stepped out of the private Stark Security jet, all the while trying to convince himself that he hadn't fucked up last week and put his client in danger.

He paused at the top of the stairs, then scanned the executive area of Las Vegas's McCarran International Airport before descending. Not that he anticipated enemy fire, but he'd spent too many years dodging bullets and bad guys to ever break the ingrained habit.

As he set foot on the tarmac, a rising wall of heat engulfed him, as if daring him to keep his suit coat on. It was late afternoon in the summer, and the place was hot as Hades. Liam had been to Vegas more times than he could count, and never under pleasant circumstances. Today wasn't any different, and he silently cursed himself as he tried to pinpoint the exact moment when he'd quit protecting Ellie Love and had instead shoved her into harm's way.

Even now, his mind echoed with the harsh words tossed

at him by Xena Morgan, Love's personal assistant. He'd been at a celebration just a few hours ago, laughing and drinking with his friends over brunch, when his phone had rung. Her name had popped up, and he'd felt that familiar twisting in his gut. Longing tinged with dread. And he was such a goddamn chickenshit that he'd almost let it roll to voice mail. Almost broke his own code by dodging instead of confronting.

But he'd got his act together, and he'd hit the button to connect the call, expecting—well, he still wasn't sure what he'd expected. Not after their last hour on the patio of Ellie's house in the Hollywood Hills, her a little tipsy on wine, him a little drunk on her, and the entire city lit up below them.

He may not have known what to expect on that call, but it damn sure hadn't been the thick, controlled voice that had come across the line, telling him only that Ellie had been attacked during an early morning jog. Xena had spoken with the emotional control of a seasoned police officer, and refused to give him any other details. "*She's okay, and you can hear the whole damn story when you get here, because for some insane reason you're the only one she wants looking into this. Crazy, right? Because you're the one who said there was no legitimate threat. That she was safe.*" Only a slight quiver betrayed her steady tone. "*Maybe I'm naive, but this sure as shit doesn't look like safe to me.*"

"Xena..." The name had barely passed his lips when she handed the phone to her boss, and the rising pop star had said simply, "Haul your ass to Vegas, Foster. I need you on this. You're the only one I trust."

Trust.

He hadn't thought he could feel any worse after Xena's rant. But that one simple word had just about done him in.

With a sigh, he ran his hand over his shaved head. He

didn't take failure lightly—he never had. Somehow, he was going to make this right. Somehow, he was going to deserve that trust.

A space gray Range Rover pulled into view beside the hanger, and Liam walked forward to meet it. The car slowed to a stop in front of him, and the driver, a poised twenty-something with a hint of a beard, started to get out. Liam held up a hand, then opened the back door himself. There were times when rank and position mattered, but this sure as hell wasn't one of them.

"The Starfire, Mr. Foster?" It was a good guess. A Stark International property, the Starfire Resort and Casino was well-equipped to provide support for any Stark Security operation taking place in the Las Vegas area.

"The Delphi, actually. And take me to the performers' entrance. I'm late for a meeting." At least as big as the Starfire, the competing Delphi Casino and Hotel also boasted the Delphi Auditorium, a venue that consistently booked the hottest acts in town.

"Right away, sir."

Liam leaned back, meeting the driver's eyes in the rearview mirror as he settled in. "What's your name?"

"Frederick."

"Summer job?"

Frederick nodded. "Yes, sir. I'm a driver at the Starfire, but I fill in at the front desk when I'm needed. I'll be a sophomore next year. UCLA."

"Did you happen to catch Ellie Love's concert last night?"

His face lit up. "Oh, yeah. It was fuc—I mean fantastic."

"No glitches? Nothing out of the ordinary?"

The kid's brow furrowed, but whether in thought or confusion, Liam wasn't sure. "Well, no. I mean, maybe something backstage, but we sure couldn't tell in the audience."

"Good to know." He'd interview everyone in Ellie's band and crew, plus the on-site employees of the Delphi Auditorium. But unless he missed his guess, the show had gone as smooth as silk, without the slightest hint of trouble. At least until this morning.

"Um—sir? Are the rumors true?"

"What rumors are those?" Liam repeated, knowing exactly what Frederick was talking about.

"My buddy—he's a bellman at the Delphi—and he told me that Ellie—well, Ms. Love—that she was attacked this morning."

"What makes you think I know anything about that?"

"Oh." He could see the kid swallow in the rearview mirror. "I guess—well, you work for Stark Security. And you're going to a meeting at the Delphi Auditorium where Ms. Love's performing tonight. So I just thought, well, you know."

"I know that you'd be an asset in my line of work," Liam said with a chuckle.

"Nah, I just read a lot of thrillers and mysteries. I'm heading for law school."

"A man with a plan. Even better."

His phone chimed with an incoming text, this one from Rye Callahan, Ellie's fiancé and manager, giving Liam the keypad code for the backstage door.

Rehearsal's running long. Feel free to watch or wait in El's dressing room. Will find you.

Liam shot back a thumbs-up, then used the rest of the ride to scroll through his new emails. He smiled at the pictures his friend Dallas Sykes had sent of Jane, his pregnant and bedridden wife. Knowing Jane, Liam was sure she was going out of her mind, but that didn't alter the beatific look on her beautiful face. Considering everything the couple had been through, they deserved this happy ending —and new beginning.

Not for the first time, a wave of unwelcome envy hit him. Dallas and Jane were his closest friends in the world, and he didn't begrudge them one iota of happiness. He told himself he didn't want what they had, but that wasn't true. He did want it. And for a few shining months, he'd had it.

But he knew damn well he'd never have it again.

Fuck.

"Sir?"

He bit back a curse; he hadn't realized he'd spoken aloud. "Nothing," he told Frederick. "Just checking messages."

The rest of his inbox was work-related. Status updates from his team, reports he'd requested, briefings on potential clients and new matters. He shot back a half-dozen answers, including one to Ryan Hunter, the Operating Director of Stark Security and Liam's immediate supervisor, who'd requested status updates on several ongoing matters.

And then there was the message from Quince Radcliffe. Like Liam, Quince had worked for his government before signing up for Deliverance, a now-defunct vigilante group financed and run by Dallas for the purpose of finding, rescuing, and ensuring justice for kidnap victims from around the globe. Also like Liam, he'd joined the Stark Security Agency after Deliverance dissolved.

Both men had wanted to stay in the game, and they believed in the organization's mission statement. Formed after tragedy had struck the home of billionaire Damien Stark, the SSA existed to provide help where it was needed, no matter the size of the job. Moreover, because of the technical input from Stark divisions such as Stark Applied Technology, the organization was at least as well equipped as most government intelligence operations. Probably better.

Liam loved the work. Hell, he lived the work. And he respected the hell out of his colleagues and never withheld information about a case without a reason.

Last week, he'd had a reason.

At the request of Ellie Love, Liam had told no one at Stark Security except Ryan about the absurd outcome of the assignment. But Quince was former MI6 and the guy didn't miss a trick. *Ellie Love*, the message read. *Want to share with the class?*

Liam frowned. *Soon*, he wrote back. The rest of the SSA team deserved to know about the bogus threat in LA last week—and about the fact that this morning's events suggested it wasn't bogus after all. Which meant that Liam had screwed up. He'd cleared the threat in LA and told the entire Ellie Love entourage that it was safe to head on to the next concert venue, and the next and the next.

The case had been open and shut—or so he'd believed. The pop star had been receiving threatening text messages and notes, causing upheaval among her crew. Vague statements about how Ms. Love would "pay," and that she needed to watch her back.

Scary, yes, but it hadn't taken long for Liam to learn that the threats had been a publicity stunt by her over-eager publicist, who'd been determined to get Love as much buzz during her tour as possible.

The publicist had confessed and resigned—fortunately before the threats were leaked on social media. After satisfying himself that the threats were a hoax, Liam had closed the case and promised the embarrassed Ms. Love that he'd file his final report only to those at the SSA who needed to know. As a result, the only people who knew about the fake threats were Ellie Love herself, her now-former publicist, her fiancé, her personal assistant, Liam, and Ryan Hunter.

Bottom line, the threats had been bullshit.

And yet Ms. Love had been attacked that very morning.

So what had he missed? What the fuck had he missed?

Or maybe it was a copycat? Someone jumping into the fray after the stage had been set?

Or even just a random mugging?

He didn't know, but he was going to figure it out. Because no matter what rationalizations and excuses got tossed around, the bottom line was that her assault this morning landed squarely in his domain. And he wasn't going to rest until he found her attacker—and proved to himself that he hadn't screwed up and inadvertently tossed Ellie Love right into her attacker's arms.

2

FROM HIS POSITION in the wings, Liam watched as Ellie Love strutted across the stage in five-inch heels, her tiny, bronzed dynamo of a body bending and twisting to the hip-hop beat as she belted out the lyrics of the show's final song. Considering that morning's attack and the stress she'd been under since the threats started in LA, Liam had to give the rising pop icon her props. If there was anything on her mind other than preparing for tonight's show, he couldn't see it.

She was a professional, through and through. More than that, she was a star.

A narcissistic and obstinate star, but in Liam's experience, that tended to be part and parcel of the celebrity package. And the truth was, he liked her in spite of all those qualities. Or maybe because of them. The daughter of an Irish-born auto-mechanic and a third-generation Latina mother who put herself through nursing school, Ellie was a woman who worked hard, believed in her own talent, and knew what she wanted, which was why her latest album had finally shot her to the top of the charts. And why all eyes in the theater—crew, invited fans, and hotel personnel

—were locked on her during the final moments of the rehearsal.

All eyes except his.

Despite admiring her talent and work ethic, Ellie wasn't the woman who kept drawing his focus. That dubious honor went to the woman directly across the stage from him. The tall, skinny white woman with the cornflower blue eyes. The sharp-tongued blonde who'd spent most of the previous week standing like a damn guard dog between him and Ellie.

As the star's personal assistant, being a wall between Ellie and the world was part of Xena's job description. Considering she was at her boss's side more than Rye, Liam knew she took her job pretty damn seriously. Seriously enough to question everything he did and every command he issued to his team and Love's staff.

On one level, she'd irritated the shit out of him. But she'd also gotten under his skin in ways he hadn't expected, and he'd been relieved to escape when the case finally wrapped. Because despite being a badass security professional who'd traveled all over the globe, spent years in military intelligence, and endured far too many heart-pounding seconds staring down the barrel of some nasty motherfucker's gun, he didn't need extra complications in his life. And though he'd never seen it coming, he learned quickly enough that Xena had the potential to be one hell of a complication, and not just because he was so inexplicably attracted to her, even though she wasn't his type at all.

Assuming that a man who rarely dated and avoided relationships could even say that he had a type. He'd started building that fence years ago, brick by solitary brick, until it was a fortress. And though he'd occasionally breach the wall when temptation or lust or whatever the hell you called it grabbed him by the balls, when he did, he went for women with curves, not Xena's straight lines and hard angles. Plus, she was blond, and blondes had never done a damn thing for him. He'd spent too many nights making inane conversation with overly bleached socialites at the endless stream of parties in the Hamptons that Dallas had dragged him to back when they were both still in their twenties and early thirties.

Hell, if he was going to have inappropriate fantasies about an off-limits woman, it should be Ellie. But no, he'd gone and fixated on a reedy blond girl with a sharp tongue and eyes that seemed to look right through him.

He told himself he didn't know why, but that wasn't entirely true. She was sharp and determined. She spoke little, but when she did it mattered. And her loyalty to Ellie shone like a beacon.

All admirable qualities, but there was more to Xena Morgan, he was sure of it. And it was that mystery that intrigued him. Something raw. Edgy. He didn't know exactly what was buried deep inside her, but he'd seen enough damaged people to know that her soul was at least as scarred as his.

But that didn't make them compatible. On the contrary, that made them combustible.

And that meant that Xena Morgan was a complication he simply didn't need. And the sooner he exorcised her from his thoughts, the better.

A burst of white light flooded the backstage area, and Liam realized with a start that rehearsal had ended. Ellie was leaning against a giant set piece, talking with one of the roadies, and there was no longer anyone standing in the wings opposite him.

Frowning, he started to step onto the stage, then hesitated, wondering if Rye would prefer he go straight to the dressing room. He turned to look for the manager, only to find Xena instead, her head slightly cocked, a knowing smirk playing at the corner of her wide, tempting mouth.

Too tempting, and he thanked his lucky stars and a deep well of self-restraint that he'd kept himself in check despite that final night at Ellie's after-party when they'd stood too close together as the alcohol flowed and the city twinkled below them.

Her hair had been loose, and her soft curls had fluttered in the midnight breeze. Today, those blond strands were pulled back into a severe ponytail, a style that put her face on display.

It was a beautiful face, albeit in an unusual kind of way. The kind of face that probably photographed incredibly well, but in real life seemed a little too sharp, an effect that was softened by a smattering of freckles across her nose and cheeks as well as by her hypnotic blue eyes.

She wore skinny jeans and a white tank top, which clearly revealed that she was about as flat as your average twelve-year-old boy. Even in the flirty black dress she'd worn at Ellie's party, she'd looked delicate. Ephemeral. As if he could break her with nothing more than a hug. He'd imagined her in his arms, their limbs entwined. His black skin in stark contrast to her pale white, so delicate she probably burned if she even thought about the sun. He wanted her under him, her fragile body crushed beneath him, her heart skittering in passion as she surrendered, trusting him not to hurt her despite his power to do exactly that.

She'd wanted him, too; he was certain of it. He'd seen it in her eyes. He'd heard it in her breath. But he'd known damn well that he'd never risk having her, not knowing where it might lead and what demons he might unleash.

He'd learned that lesson the hard way, and he'd been so fucking grateful to drive away that night with only his memories of her to take with him into his bed, despite how much he craved the woman herself.

But now here he was all over again, staring temptation in the face and wondering if she knew.

In front of him, she shifted her weight, then laughed. "Cat got your tongue, Foster? Or do you just not know what to say after such a royal fuck-up?"

He sucked in a breath as a swath of anger cut through him. Apparently, she didn't know the ramblings of his mind. All she saw were his mistakes.

"Good to see you, too, Xena. Let's go see if we can get to the bottom of whatever the hell is going on."

3

THEY ENTERED the dressing room to find Ellie Love seated on a padded stool, her pink-tipped hair pulled back from her face by a matching pink headband and cleansing cream smeared all over her face.

"The fans love the look," she said to their reflection in the mirror, referring to the dramatic makeup that had become her trademark, "but it's hell on my skin." She turned then, aiming her sparkling white smile at Liam. "Hey there, Foster. It's good to see you again."

"Is it?" He crossed to the table to take her outstretched hand, then leaned against the wall as she wiped the creamy residue off with a cloth.

"Hell, yes. Why wouldn't it be?"

Liam frowned, his gaze darting toward Xena, who sat in the chair next to Ellie, her expression flat.

He cleared his throat. "Ellie, I—"

"It's Ella, remember? Ellie is for the stage. Ella is for my friends. And Ms. Love is for everybody else. You, sir, are now a friend. Isn't he?" she added, turning to face Xena.

"Keep your friends close, but your enemies closer?" Xena quipped, causing Ellie—*Ella*—to roll her eyes.

"My assistant aspires to be me. If not on the stage, then in her ability to be a bitch."

"Xena's worried about you," Liam told her, glancing sideways at Xena as the door opened and Ella's fiancé, Rye Callahan, stepped in. "She has reason to be."

"I'm worried, too," Rye said, moving to Ella and putting a hand on her shoulder.

"Exactly," Liam said, with a nod to Rye. "Gordon confessed, and I cleared the case. Next stop on the tour, you're attacked. That shouldn't sit well with anyone."

"It doesn't sit well." Ella pushed back from the dressing table and looked him straight in the eye. "But does that mean it was your fault?"

"It might. Maybe I didn't dig deep enough. Maybe there was a buried threat, and I missed it."

"Well, aren't you the dedicated martyr?"

"Ella..."

"He's right," Xena told her boss. "Gordon obviously had a bigger agenda than his asinine publicity stunt. That whole story about releasing the fake threats to the media? What if it was a blind to cover up a bigger agenda? And Mr. Foster missed it?"

Her words, so damn true, twisted inside Liam. "That's exactly what I've been trying to say," he told Ella, because he couldn't hold his head up if he didn't admit it. He took pride in his work. Hell, his work was his life, and the thought that he'd missed something so important—that his mistake left this woman open for attack—

Ella waved her hand as she stood up, clearly dismissing his runaway thoughts. "Maybe you did and maybe you didn't. I don't know. What I *do* know is that Mr.

Foster did something for me in LA that very few men have managed."

"Whoa there," Rye said, feigning shock. "You're wearing my ring, baby. Do I need to be worried?"

She ran a fingertip from the V-neck of Rye's *Love Hurts* concert tee all the way down to the button fly of his jeans. "Never, *mo chroí.*" They shared a smile, and then she turned her attention back to Liam. "All kidding aside, I was a wreck in Los Angeles with those damn notes and texts. You're the one who got to the bottom with Gordon. You made me feel safe. And now I want to feel safe again."

Without thinking, he glanced toward Xena, who looked right back at him, her expression an unspoken challenge.

He shoved his hands in his pockets and nodded. "All right, then. The attack this morning was either random or it wasn't. It was either related to Gordon's bullshit scam last week, or it wasn't. So let's figure it out."

Ella's bright smile gave her makeup mirror a run for its money. "That's my guy. What do you need to know?"

"Let's start with everything," he said. "And we'll work our way up from there."

"All right then." She frowned at the small couch, currently covered in costumes. "Damn Christy," she muttered, and Liam recalled being introduced to her costume manager. "Xena, pull up some chairs. If she's got those outfits in a particular order, I'll never hear the end of it."

"We're doing this now?" Xena protested. "You have a show in under three hours, and you need to rest and then go over notes with the techs. Shouldn't we wait until morning? Or at least after the show?"

Ella's brow furrowed and her lips pursed as she settled herself on the stool again. She sighed deeply, then leaned forward as if thoughtfully considering a tricky problem. "Who works for who, again? I think one of us is confused."

Liam bit back a grin as Xena scowled, then silently turned toward a stack of folding chairs in the corner. He followed, then grabbed two.

"I can get my own," she said.

"No doubt. These are for Rye and me."

Her eyes narrowed, but she said nothing. Just continued back with the chair for herself, as Liam brought the other two, feeling unreasonably smug after his minor victory.

"Here's the situation as I see it," he said, not letting anyone else have the chance to take the lead. "You two call me and tell me I have to come, which suggests that you think I have some culpability. Neither of you gives me any details on the phone other than that Ella was out for a morning jog and was attacked. How am I doing so far?"

Ella twirled her hand. "Keep going."

"I come here ready to do whatever I can to learn who attacked you, and if necessary to make amends for my failure to properly assess the threat, despite having a full confession and a stack of corroborating evidence taller than I am. Then you announce that you don't think I'm culpable at all—something you didn't mention on the phone—while you," he added, turning from Ella to Xena, "suggest that you've never met anyone less competent."

He opened the flimsy plastic chair and sat, feeling a bit like a giant on a stool made of matchsticks as he turned to face Rye. "And to be honest, I haven't got a clue what you think."

"Well, actually—"

Liam held up his hand. "At this point, it doesn't matter." He stretched out his legs, hoping the chair wouldn't crumple and send him toppling backward. "Just tell me what happened. Not what you think, but what you know."

"Right," Ella said. "Well, I went out for a jog this morning, right after six. The hotel has a nice park area with a track, and I wanted to go while it was cool."

She paused long enough for Liam to nod, then continued. "My picture's all over this town right now—which is great because that's the point of this career—but I didn't want anyone to notice me looking all sweaty and gross. So I took one of the dancer's wigs from wardrobe—"

"Ella!" Xena's voice rose indignantly. "You didn't tell me that."

"It's not a big deal. Liam just wants the details."

"But it is a big deal."

"Why?" Ella asked, and though Liam expected the answer to fly off Xena's obviously irritated lips, instead, she just hung there, like a fly in amber with her lips parted and her brow slightly furrowed. It was only a moment—a brief, odd moment—but then her frown deepened. "Because all those wigs are styled and fitted. Christy's going to have a fit, and I'm going to be the one who gets lectured."

Ella waved the concern away. "Considering my job title, I think I can protect you. Besides, I took it from the swing closet. Just a blond wig that wasn't assigned to any dancer. Seriously, Christy won't notice or care."

Xena leaned back, her arms crossed over her chest. "If you say so."

Liam hesitated, studying Xena as he directed the next question to Ella. "You went out jogging wearing the wig and what? Shorts?"

"Right. One of my concert tees and black running shorts. And I put a ball cap over the wig—the thing didn't fit that well, so I figured the cap would keep it secure."

"A concert cap, or..."

"One of the *Love Hurts* caps. It's all I had, so I grabbed it, and then I headed out. The track is a mile, but it meanders through the park that's part of the Delphi property."

"I'm familiar with it. Where were you attacked?"

"Right past the pond. The trail goes behind some trees and there's a children's play area. It was too early for there to be any kids, and as I rounded the trees, two guys jumped me."

"What were they wearing?"

"Shorts and T-shirts. Plain black, I think. I don't remember a logo. But one of the guys had a tattoo on his upper arm. I couldn't see all of it because of his shirt, but I think it was a snake."

"Had you seen them before?"

"No. I mean, I'm not sure. I used the fitness center entrance to get to the track. I guess they might have been using the equipment or hanging around the juice bar. There were a dozen or so folks in there."

"But you didn't notice anyone follow you outside? And there were no other joggers on the track?"

"I saw two women early on, but nobody else by the time I got to the play area. But to be honest, I had my music on and was in a groove by that time. So I can't say for sure."

Liam nodded, making a mental note to check the hotel's security tapes just in case someone fitting the description did follow Ella out the door. "Go on."

"They—they were behind me, but one of them grabbed my hair—or, rather, the wig. I heard one of them say, 'Guess you didn't see this coming,' and that's when I jerked around, and as I did, the whole wig came off, ball cap and all. Thank God I hadn't taped it on. That would have hurt like a mother."

Beside him, Xena let out a sharp "O*h!*" That was followed by, "I'm—I'm sorry. I just realized. I need to go talk to Tommy. Shit." She jumped to her feet and hurried toward the door. "It's nothing you need to worry about, but if I don't catch him before he's checked the board, it'll be—anyway, I'll meet you on stage. You're going over the new encore with the dancers once more, right?"

She was out the door before Ella even had a chance to answer.

Liam watched the door slam behind her, his thoughts spinning as he turned to Ella. "She okay?"

"Some nonsense with one of the microphones. Nothing that interrupted the show, but I'm sure she just wants to check that everything is good."

He nodded. The explanation made perfect sense, but it didn't sit right. He just couldn't put his finger on the reason why. Yet.

"We do need to hurry," Rye said. "A lot to do before a show."

"What happened after the wig came off?"

"I started to run, but I stumbled. I expected them to grab me, but they didn't. Instead, one of them cursed—I think he was from Jersey—and then they looked at each other. I still hadn't caught enough air to scream when they bolted." She shrugged. "I did, too, but in the opposite direction. Sprinted all the way back to the hotel."

"The wig?"

"I—" She frowned. "I don't know. I don't think they took it. Maybe it's still out there."

"You told hotel security?"

She shook her head. "I called you."

He ran his hand over his head. "We talked about this. You need a full-time security staff."

"Liam's right," Rye said. "Even if it's only one guy. Maybe this guy," he added, hooking his thumb toward Liam.

"Not my gig, but I can recommend good people."

"Not on the table, boys. I'm not hiring a bodyguard to shadow me everyday, and the Delphi provides security during the shows. This was a fluke, right? They were thugs who were trying to mug a random woman and freaked when the wig came off."

"It's a solid theory," Liam agreed, "but I'm not assuming anything." He thought of the way Xena reacted when she heard about the wig. And he thought of how similar in color her hair was to the wig the dancers wore.

"Foster?" Ella pressed. "What are you thinking?"

He shook his head. "Just running through it all. Right now, I'm going to—"

"Hold up there, guy," Rye said. "Whatever you're doing now is fine, but Ella's got a show, and she needs to start preparing."

Born on a Nebraska farm, Rye had washed away any lingering small town innocence, replacing it with a hard-hitting business sense and a cool demeanor. With his total access to Ella, Rye had been at the top of Liam's suspect list last week. But the background check had come back clean, and when Gordon had confessed, Liam had mentally cleared the manager.

Now, though, he intended to take another look. It was probably a random attack—and if so, he could take off the damn hair shirt he'd been wearing since that morning's call —but he wasn't hanging Ella's life on *probably*.

Which meant that right now it was time for Ella to go to work, and for Liam to do the same. Starting with digging deeper into the backgrounds of both Rye Callahan and Xena Morgan.

4

<hr>

Holy crap, holy fuck, holy shit.

I pace the dark hallway in front of the empty sound booth, thankful that Tommy isn't here so that I have time to gather myself, and at the same time hoping he gets here soon so that it doesn't look like I completely fabricated an excuse to leave.

Which I did. Of course I did.

Because I couldn't stay in that room a minute longer without risking absolutely everything. I mean, I was already on edge from seeing Liam Foster, a man I hadn't expected to see again once the tour left for Vegas. A man who, for reasons I haven't been able to fathom, completely rattles me.

And then there was that wig.

My God, that fucking wig.

Why hadn't Ella mentioned that to me? I would never have agreed with her plan to get Foster back if I'd known. I would have said it was a job for hotel security. A random mugging on the property. An attack that surely had nothing to do with who she was.

Because it didn't. It had nothing to do with her at all. And everything to do with me.

Back it off, Xena. Take a deep breath and back it the fuck off.

I try to take my own advice, urging myself to calm down. Telling myself it's a coincidence. Just one of those screwed up, scary, paranoia-inducing coincidences.

After all, it's been six years. Six long, wonderful, horrible years. And even though I know they looked for me during that first year, they never even came close. And that was back when I'd been a complete wreck with no resources, no skills, no support network. Still, they couldn't find me. So why should things suddenly change now when I have a new name and a new look and whole new life to shield me?

Things wouldn't change. They *haven't* changed. There's no reason to think they've found me. No reason to think they're even still looking.

Except that's bullshit.

Of course they're still looking. I know damn well they'll never stop looking. Not men like that. Not ever.

My heart starts to pound, and my head starts to swim. The world is doing that thing where it shifts toward red, and I feel a full-blown panic attack coming on. And right now is really *not* a good time.

I draw a deep breath and order myself to be calm. There's no reason to panic. It's not possible that they've found me. After all, I'm a behind the scenes kind of girl. I'm not a woman who stands out. They'd have to know where to look, and why the hell would they look for me in a pop star's entourage?

They wouldn't. I'm fine. I'm safe.

"Xena?"

I jump a goddamn mile, then turn to Tommy with a sharp cry of, "Jesus!"

"Hey, hey, sorry." He holds up his hands with a friendly smile. Tommy's been in the business since the dawn of time, and I know we're lucky to have him running sound for Ella. But my God, he made my heart stop.

"Didn't mean to scare you," he says, but the words are full of laughter. "Guess you were off in la-la land, huh?"

"Something like that," I admit.

He takes a step closer, and I watch his well-lined face shift into a frown. "What the hell, girl? You look like you ran a mile."

"Just a billion things to do before tonight's show." I flash one of my practiced bright smiles; I'm an expert at looking happy and content when I'm anything but. "I wanted to make sure the short in that backup mic got fixed."

He looks down his nose at me. "Good golly. I didn't even think about doing that."

I ignore the sarcasm. "I know you probably fixed it about thirty seconds after last night's show ended. But it's my job to not assume anything."

"Nice save. Now go tell Ms. Love we're ready for the sound check whenever she is."

I nod, wave, and scurry away, pulling out my mobile phone so I can text Ella and all the backup singers that Tommy's ready for them.

I'm almost to the end of what we call tech alley when I look up and see a man striding down the dim walkway. *Liam Foster.* The few shafts of light hit him only on the left, and with his gorgeous black skin only partially illuminated, broad shoulders, and tailored gray suit coat, he looks like a conqueror emerging from the shadows.

I swallow as panic once again flutters in my chest. But not because I'm afraid of what Liam might do to me. On the contrary, I'm afraid of what he *does* do to me. Because this is a man who has come close to breaking through my defenses. I let down my guard with him once—that stupid, foolish, almost-kiss at Ella's party—but that's not something I can let myself do again. Not now. Not later. Not ever.

And that makes Liam Foster a very, very dangerous man.

I force a smile and lift my hand in a casual wave, ignoring the beads of sweat between my breasts. "Hey, Foster. You looking for Tommy? Or Grant?" I add the second name since we're right by the light booth and Grant is the show's lighting designer.

"You, actually."

"Gee. I'm flattered." I add an edge of sarcasm to my voice. "But maybe we can put a pin in it? I have a lot to do before tonight."

"You think I fucked up."

I cross my arms and tilt my head. "Thanks for the recap. Did you think I'd forgotten?"

"You think I fucked up," he repeats. "Or you did until Ella mentioned the wig."

I swallow, but say nothing.

"Come on, Xena. Why did that shake you up?"

"I really do have work." I try to push past him, but he holds out an arm, blocking my way. "Um, hello, Foster? What the fuck?"

"Please. Just ten minutes. Five." He drops his arm, and I know that if I keep walking he won't stop me.

I should keep walking. I'm stupid not to. But maybe if I say the right things he'll finally back off.

"Thank you," he says, his voice so gentle that for one foolish moment I wonder what it would be like to tell him all my secrets. That, however, is a dangerous urge. Like those people who have to fight a compulsion to jump from high places. I force it down, then meet his eyes. "Fine. What was it you wanted to know?" Like I don't remember what he asked four seconds ago. Like his question isn't completely freaking me out.

Can he tell?

I don't think so; I truly don't. I had years to learn how to hide my feelings, my fears. And I got damn good at it. Hell, I could win an Oscar if it weren't for that whole being in the public eye thing. Because that part really wouldn't work for me.

"The wig, Xena." He's the epitome of patience. "When you learned that part, it freaked you out."

"Freaked me out?" Damn right it freaked me out. "No, it didn't. I was just—hell, I'm not even sure I can put it in words." I'm buying time as I spin my lie. Finally, I take a deep breath, then nod. "Okay, you know what? You're right. It did freak me out. Because it's all so futile, you know?"

I watch his eyes move as he studies me, clearly trying to suss me out.

"The fame thing, I mean. She's worked her ass off for so long reaching for that prize, and it's supposed to be great. I mean, everyone thinks so. And everyone's rooting for her. But then it's like running a gauntlet, because there's always some nutcase. But that's part of the price. For fame I mean. Right?"

He nods, but I can see he doesn't understand. Not too surprising; I'm making this up as I go.

"She tried to circumvent that. She took precautions. She wore a disguise. And she's *still* attacked. So maybe it really was random, like you said. But then that means that no one's safe, right? Or maybe they did know it was her—in which case what's the point of a disguise? You hit that magical celebrity point and you're just screwed? It's totally unfair. And no one can live their life in bubble wrap. So I guess—I guess the whole thing just made me feel terribly sad and worried for her all at the same time."

I lift my shoulders in a *so that's that* gesture, and Liam nods thoughtfully. I work hard to keep my facial expression bland. I think he bought the bullshit I've been selling. Considering I pulled it out of my ass, it sounded pretty good. But that doesn't mean it'll be good enough for the likes of Liam Foster.

"I do understand," he says, taking a single step closer to me. He's strong. I can feel it in the air, and part of me wants to beg him to hold me, just so I can soak up his strength. But I can't be that vulnerable. Not with him. Not with anybody.

"I can only imagine what a shock this morning was after the tension of last week, especially considering how close you and Ella are."

I nod. Even though he doesn't know the entire truth, everything he just said is dead-on. Especially the part about Ella and me. She may be the most high maintenance star in the world, but as far as I'm concerned, that woman is a goddess, and last week, I told him why. Not the entire story, but most of it. And every word I said was true.

But I also left a lot of stuff unspoken.

"Thanks for that," I say.

He tips his head and smiles. A nice smile on a guy who could be scary as shit if he wanted to. I've been around men like that. More than I like to remember, actually, and every one of their slow, dangerous smiles haunts me. So much that I'd spent years seeing a counselor at one of the free clinics in Los Angeles. I'd used a fake name—well, another one—and I'd worn a wig and overly baggy clothes, because you can never be too sure. But I'd gone. And it had even helped. A little. Maybe.

Actually, it must have helped, because Liam's exactly the

kind of man I used to flinch away from. Big. Powerful. Determined. And strong enough to throw me across a room if he wanted to. Or to bruise my arm simply by holding me in place.

The kind of man I normally avoid, even after all this time and all those sessions. But for some reason with Liam, I stepped closer and closer until last week when we were both ready to jump into the flames.

But I can't ever go there again.

"We—" I cut myself off with a shake of my head. "Never mind."

"What?"

"I was just—I was just thinking about Ella," I lie. "Somehow we have to convince her that she needs someone watching her back."

"Agreed," he says, and I'm about to sigh with relief when he adds, "But that's not what you were going to say."

I swallow. "Wasn't it?" I should stay quiet. I should tell him I'm late and just go. Instead, I ask, "What was I going to say?"

He doesn't hesitate, and he doesn't look away. "That it was a mistake." He looks straight at me with such intensity that I can't glance away either. "That we'd both drunk too much, and we both wanted it. But that we're both too professional to cross that line, and that neither of us has any intention of taking it any farther."

Don't we?

Except of course, we don't. Because intentions aren't desires. And while he may be wrong about being drunk, he's one hundred percent on-point about intentions.

I draw in a breath, my eyes still locked on his. "I don't even know what you're talking about."

"Yes," he says. "You do. You know exactly what I'm talking about, because you wanted it as much as I did."

I start to protest, but he continues before I can get out a sound.

"You wanted me to kiss you. Or maybe you wanted to kiss me. I don't think it matters. All that matters is that we both wanted it. Wanted each other. Wanted to get lost for just a moment in that private corner of the patio, with the stars above us and the lights below. To feel lips on lips and skin on skin. To let ourselves go, even if we never spoke of it again."

I'm breathing hard when he takes another step toward me, then lifts my chin with his fingertip. That's when I realize that I'd stopped looking at him and had shifted my focus to the floor. Now, I have no choice but to look at this man. His skin seems to absorb the dim light, making him glow from the inside even as his dark eyes invite me to spiral down with him to someplace warm and wild, and all I can think is that he's a dark angel come to torment me.

When he speaks, it's barely a whisper. "So tell me, Xena. Have I jogged your memory?"

"You've jogged something," I admit. "But we can't. We won't. It's not—it's not what I want." I silently curse, because after what he just admitted, he deserves the truth. "Okay, yeah, maybe I do want it. But I'm not going to have it."

"Do you think I don't understand that?"

"I don't know." My head feels like it's swimming, and I lower my voice, aware of the rising noise as crew and performers enter the venue for the various pre-performance checks. "I thought you understood. But then why are we talking about it? Why are you torturing us both?"

"Everyone has a code." He shrugs. "Part of mine is that I never look away from reality. And that means that I see you.

I see this," he adds, gesturing between us. "I know that I want it. And I know that I'm walking away."

I draw in a breath, unsure what to say.

"Maybe I'm wrong," he says gently, "but I think that's your code, too."

"No," I say, thinking of the past that I've been running from. "Most of the time I'd rather do anything but look."

He leans forward, and I can see the question in his eyes. He's wondering what it is that I don't want to confront, and I want to kick myself for giving so much away. What the hell happened to my shields?

"I believe you," he says. "But here's why we're alike. Whatever it is that's behind you that you don't want to see? You turn to it, Xena. And you look anyway."

The words ricochet through me, full of truth and danger and fear. I swallow, waiting for the other shoe to drop. Afraid he's going to ask what monster is behind me. "I—I should go," I blurt. "They're starting, and I need to be on stage with Ella, and—"

"I know. Go. I'll see you after the show."

"Oh, no. We're not going to—"

"At the after party," he says gently. "In Ella's suite."

"Oh. Right." I'm glad it's dark, because I'm sure I'm blushing. "I'll see you there. I'm looking forward to it," I add recklessly. And, surprisingly, I really am.

He stays where he is, and I walk past him, hurrying toward the stairs that lead down to the auditorium seats and the stage. I've gone about ten feet when I pause and turn back. He's in the same place, his back to me.

"Mr. Foster."

He turns. "Liam."

My lips twitch in what could be called a smile. "Thank you."

It's dark, but I think I see his brow furrow, the tiniest hint that I've confused him. "For what?"

"For not asking questions that I don't want to answer."

"Don't thank me for that. I have a whole list I want to ask you."

"I know," I say. "That's why I'm thanking you. Maybe you do force yourself to confront reality, but you also have restraint. And that's something I admire in a man."

5

Restraint.

Liam frowned as the word rattled around in his head.

He had restraint now; she was right about that. Now, but not always. There was a time when he'd never held back. When he'd worked hard and played hard. A time when he'd let himself fall in love.

That, of course, had been his mistake.

A familiar pain cut through him as he thought about Dion's sweet smile. The way his heart had swelled when she whispered his name, and how his body had fired when she touched him. And he thought about Franklin, the fucker who had stolen that beautiful soul from him. From the whole goddamn world.

They were both gone now. Dion, murdered because Liam had loved her. Franklin, gone because Liam had killed him.

Liam had shown no restraint on that moonless night. Not one goddamn iota of restraint, and it had felt incredible to avenge the death of the woman he loved.

But now...

Well, now he had restraint in spades, at least as far as relationships were concerned. He couldn't get involved. A fling, a night, an encounter to blow off steam— why not? But to give his heart? To hold fast to a woman's love? Considering the life he led, that was far too dangerous. She'd be a target. A weak spot. The wound into which his enemies could rub salt.

After all, a bullet to his brain would only kill him. But a bullet in the head of another woman he loved?

He'd barely survived that first time. A second time would destroy him forever.

With a frustrated sigh, he gave himself a mental shake, forcing his mind back on track. Franklin and Dion were in the past. Right then, he had only one thing to worry about, and that was determining the reason behind Ella's mugging. Who were the perps? Was it random? And if not, then who was the intended victim?

Because despite the carefully crafted story about Xena's deep concern for Ella's well-being and celebrity status, Liam didn't believe a word of it. What he didn't know was why she'd lie. Did she believe that the attackers mistook Ella for her? That seemed the most likely possibility. But that conclusion was based on the evidence before him. The wig. Xena's voice and mannerisms. The fact that the perps bolted when the wig and hat came off.

All the evidence suggested that the perps didn't realize the jogger was Ella. And the reasonable conclusion was that they'd targeted Xena. But Liam knew better than to jump to conclusions, and he couldn't discount the possibility that there was something else going on, but he was standing too close to see the bigger picture.

He sighed, shoving his hands into his pockets. The

bottom line was that he didn't know. But he intended to find out.

He was still standing in the back of the auditorium by the light and sound boards. He glanced over and saw Tommy looking at him, his craggy face scrunched with concern. Not surprising. Ella's entire team was worried. Only a select few knew that Gordon had manufactured last week's intrigue. The rest believed that it was an outside hoax that Liam had forestalled before it spread out to the world.

As for Liam's own team back at Stark Security, he'd gone with the uncomfortable lie that Ellie Love was a high maintenance prima donna and that she and Rye had simply overreacted to a hoax that Liam had shut down. Considering no one at Stark Security knew anyone connected with the show, the subterfuge was simple.

He and Ryan had made peace with the lie, but it still didn't sit well, even though it was in some ways true. Ella really was high maintenance, and she could be an absolute dictator where her show was concerned—a fact that was evidenced right then, because she was on stage, leading her team in a walk-through of the show that involved both praise and a few well-placed curses.

Still, she was fair, and her people seemed to love her. She worked her ass off, and she was beyond dedicated to her team, a fact that had been borne out when she'd insisted that Gordon be protected from his own overeager tendencies.

He lifted a hand to Tommy, waving goodbye, but stopped after only one step toward the brightly marked exit.

Ella *was* loyal, there was no doubt about that. Her team mattered to her.

Xena mattered to her.

And whether Ella wanted to or not, now was the time to

tell him the whole story about the woman who'd risen in the organization to become Ella's friend, confidante, and personal assistant.

He shifted directions, heading not to the door, but down to the stage. He knew he wouldn't get Ella right now, but he could leave a message for her to meet him after the concert.

He didn't see Xena, and he assumed she was probably off enjoying the light meal that he knew had been set up backstage for the performers. But Rye was talking with one of the choreographers, and he went over to him.

"I'm heading to the resort's security office to check the fitness center footage. Can you tell Ella I want to see her in her dressing room after the show?"

"Sure. No problem. Just don't take too much of her time. She'll be wired, and everyone's coming to our suite for the after party."

"I'll be quick. And Rye—I want to talk to her alone."

The other man's eyes widened. "Whoa. Am I in trouble, coach?"

Liam crossed his arms as he studied Rye. "What do you think?"

"That if you think I had something to do with what happened this morning, you are seriously off your rocker. I might beat the shit out of someone I caught messing with my girl, but I'd never lay a hand on her."

"Good to know."

"You're just messing with me, right? I'm not seriously on your radar?"

"Everyone's on my radar." He added a smile. "But you're not pinging too loudly."

"Wow. Well, good to hear it." He chuckled. "Do you know I've never even gotten a speeding ticket? The idea someone would think that I—" He cut himself off with a shake of the head. "Just a little surreal."

Liam started to step away. "You'll tell her?"

"Yeah. Um, there's one other—never mind. I'll let El know."

"What's on your mind?"

Rye shrugged, running his fingers through his tousled dark blond hair.

"It's nothing. Honestly. Just—nothing."

"Rye, your fiancée was attacked, and under the circumstances I'm better equipped to assess what is or is not nothing. So spit it out."

"It's just that I saw you talking with Xena up there, and … hell, I hate to say anything. I might be totally off base."

"Say it anyway."

He exhaled loudly. "Fine. Okay. I did a background check on her."

"When? Today?"

"No, no. Years ago, back when Ella hired her. We'd barely started dating, but I was her manager, and something felt off."

"What did you find?"

He met Liam's eyes. "Not a goddamn thing. Seriously. Nothing. No credit. No property. No anything. I mean, yeah. I found her in the system. We had her social security number. Susan Morgan—no idea why she started calling herself Xena. Anyway, that was it. Born in Idaho. Parents both dead—killed in a car accident. And that's it." He shrugged. "So I told Ella I was concerned. This girl had started working in Ella's house. You know, buying groceries, sorting mail. And I was afraid she was going to scam her. Get her financial info. Whatever."

"So what did Ella say?"

"She told me not to poke around anymore. That there wasn't anything to find, and that Xena'd had a hard life." He shrugged. "I assumed that was code for her being a runaway. What with her parents' accident, she probably got tossed into the system, and it was a bad situation. El's got a big heart, and I figured she wanted to help the girl out."

"But now?"

He exhaled loudly. "Listen, El thinks a lot of Xena. I do, too. She's a great employee. She loves El, I'm sure of it. But I'm worried that maybe there's stuff in her past that's more than just a messed up family life and blowing off a foster home."

Liam didn't disagree, but he kept his expression bland as he said, "Thanks for telling me."

"Sure, sure."

"I still want to see Ella. Tell her I'll come to her dressing room after the show."

"Yeah. I will. Anything you need. I just want her safe."

"That's what I'm here for."

Rye exhaled loudly. "Yeah, you are. No offense, man, but it sucks that you had to come."

Xena's sideways grin popped into Liam's head. "Maybe so, but I'm glad I did. And we will get to the bottom of this."

"Sooner the better. You going to watch the concert? We keep a few front row VIP seats open."

"No, but thanks. I'm heading over to watch security videos. With any luck, maybe I'll spot a mugger."

6

CARLOS MARTINEZ, the head of security for the Delphi Casino and Hotel, was in a meeting, so Liam ended up grabbing dinner—his first meal of the day—in one of the property's many restaurants, then meeting Martinez right about the time Ella was taking the stage.

"Good to see you again," Martinez said, looking up from where he sat in front of a security console, a spot usually reserved for one of the techs. But Liam had worked with Martinez before and wasn't surprised to see that the man was hands-on. A woman had been attacked on his watch, and he wanted to find the perp as much as Liam did.

"You're already reviewing?" Liam asked, peering over his friend's shoulder.

"You mind?"

"Hell, no. The more eyes the better."

Martinez made a scoffing noise. "If she'd reported the attack, we could have had eyes on a live stream. As it is, you know the score. There's no way we can monitor every security feed at all times."

"No one's blaming your team," Liam said. Martinez

knew that, of course. But he'd still take the whole situation very, very personally. "What have you got for me?"

Martinez nodded toward the chair next to him, and Liam sat as the tech on his other side scooted down the console to make room for him. "I've cued it up to where Ms. Love leaves the fitness center to start her run." He maneuvered the controls, and that footage popped onto the screen.

"Nice equipment," Liam said. He'd been the head of security for the entire Sykes Department Store enterprise during the time he'd been moonlighting at Deliverance. The Sykes family had spared no expense in any aspect of their business, but the security system they'd had was a toddler's video recorder compared to this.

"State of the art," Martinez said with as much pride as a new father. "And with cloud storage, we can save our footage indefinitely. We've learned that some women have to talk themselves into reporting bad behavior, and years ago, the evidence was often overwritten." He met Liam's eyes, his own hard. "You see a lot working in this town, and sometimes the hotel guests misinterpret what it means to have a good time. You know what I'm sayin'?"

"Unfortunately, yeah."

As they talked, Martinez stepped through the images. Ella walking through the fitness center. Ella pausing at the juice bar by the exterior door. Ella filling her water bottle. And then Ella exiting through the glass exterior door. And, yes, especially with the cap on, the hair really did look like Xena's.

Of course, Ella was wearing shorts and a tank, which revealed her significant curves. A feature that Xena definitely didn't share, and Liam mentally put a check mark in the *random attack* column.

On screen, Martinez jumped to the point he'd bookmarked from another feed on the jogging trail. "Unfortunately, we don't have complete coverage outside," he said, but he did have enough to confirm Ella's version of the attack.

"Any chance we can get a closer image of this arm?" Liam said, tapping the eraser end of a pencil against the screen. Martinez gave it a shot, but the image never got clearer than a blurry dark splotch.

"Tattoo?" Martinez asked.

"A snake, most likely. Ms. Love said she could only see part of it." He leaned back in the chair, his twined fingers cupping his head. "Show the fitness center footage again. If they were watching her, chances are they were in that room, too."

"Agreed." Martinez pulled up the footage they'd already reviewed, then put the video from the room's second camera on the neighboring monitor. Both covered the open area of the fitness center, but one showed the interior door that led into the heart of the hotel. The other showed the exterior door that led to the track.

With Martinez at one control and Liam at the other, they went frame by frame through the footage, backing up to five minutes before Ella entered and continuing to five minutes after she left.

"This guy," Liam said on their third run through. He tapped the screen again, indicating a stocky man in black shorts and a black tank. He left the treadmill and went to the dispenser to fill his water bottle. Never once did he lift his head.

"Almost like he knows there are cameras," Martinez said, echoing Liam's thoughts.

"Keep watching," Liam said, and as they did, the guy

turned toward the interior door, putting the side of his arm in clear view of the camera. "Bingo," Liam whispered.

"That's a snake, all right. But your boy's exiting into the hotel. And Ella's leaving right now into the great outdoors," he added, pointing to the other monitor that showed activity at the exterior door at the same time-stamp.

Another man in black followed Snake Man, his head also down. "Can you pull up a floor plan?"

"No sweat." Within seconds, Martinez replaced the exterior door cam with a floor plan that showed the layout around the fitness center.

"There," Liam said, pointing to a door a few yards down. "An exterior exit?"

"That it is. The sidewalk leads to the poolside bar. But there's no reason why someone couldn't walk on the grass and catch up with Ms. Love."

"Exactly what I was thinking. I'm also thinking these guys are professionals."

"No face shots."

"None," Liam agreed, frowning as something occurred to him. "Can you run the footage back to when they went through the door?" Like many entrances to hotel fitness centers, the center of the door had an eye-level glass pane. In this case, it was etched with an ornate D for Delphi.

"He turned, didn't he? The one following your snake man?"

Liam nodded. "The door was already swinging shut, and he was in the shadows, but yeah. He did."

"Did he look up?"

"I think so. Let's see if I'm right."

He was—but it wasn't a full victory. Most of the bastard's face was hidden behind the etched D.

"Not sure we're going to get something useful." Martinez frowned as he leaned forward, slowly enlarging the image.

"Can you make a copy for me? If anyone can pull enough information off that image to run it through facial recognition, Mario can." He thought of the young, smart-mouthed analyst who oversaw tech at Stark Security. The kid was always telling everyone he was a genius. Maybe today, he'd prove himself right.

"I'll put it on a shared server. He can pull the feed direct-ly." He manipulated some keys, then pulled up a text message box and typed in a password and a URL. A moment later, Liam's phone pinged. "Send him there. And if he runs into any trouble, give him my phone number. You can log in, too, in case you want to review it on your phone."

"Perfect." Liam pushed his chair back and stood. "I owe you one."

"I'll remember that," Martinez promised. "Always good to bank favors."

Liam was grinning as he left the Delphi's Security Oper-ations Center. He didn't have answers yet, but at least he could report to Ella that he was moving forward. A good thing in its own right, but also a nice buffer to the questions he intended to ask about Xena.

He glanced at his watch, surprised to realize how late it was. The concert would be almost over, and he decided to go straight to the dressing room to wait for Ella and call Mario.

"Foster, my man," Mario said as soon as he answered. "How are things in the land of sex and sin?"

"I'm more concerned about assault, actually."

"I'm listening."

"Where are you? At a computer?"

"How long have we known each other?"

Liam chuckled. "Good point. I need you to manipulate some footage for me."

"Sweet. Are we scamming someone?"

"Not like that. Hang on, let me forward you the text. You may need to use the office computers. I'm assuming we still have a few bells and whistles that you don't have at home?"

"Not many. Ryan's cool with me upgrading my home system so long as the security and firewalls stay top-notch. But not an issue, anyway. I'm at my desk right now. Doing some work for Denny."

Liam frowned. "Denny? She's taking a month off with Mason." An agent with Stark Security from its inception, Denny had spent most of her time on the job mourning the loss of her husband, who'd been gone for years after a mission gone wrong. Recently, he'd resurfaced, but without any memory of Denny, himself, or his past.

Things were solid between the two of them now—thank God—but Liam still couldn't fathom the depths of their anguish ... and the challenges they still faced.

And he certainly didn't understand what Mario had to do with any of it.

"Denny wants to make memories," he explained. "So she's sending me daily images and videos from their travels to compile into an interactive virtual album. Editable—I think she's leaving out the juicy footage—so she can add stuff later."

"Except for you, I've never met anyone better with tech skills than Denny. Why are you doing it and not her?"

"One, I think she'd rather make the memories than record them."

"Point taken."

"And two, I was working remotely from Austin when all

that drama with Mason's return went down. So now I want to help."

"Good for you," Liam said, meaning it. He loved Denny like a sister, and he'd taken a liking to Jack—well, Mason—the moment he met the man. "Anyway, I need you to take a break from your vicarious vacation with them and see if you can rebuild an image. I'm texting you the access info and the timecode for the part I'm interested in."

"Hold on," Mario said, as Liam heard his phone ping in the background. "Oh, yeah. This guy in the window." He let out a low whistle. "Tough one."

"Too tough?"

"I didn't say that. Give me a chance to work my magic. You want to put it through facial recognition, right?"

"That's the goal." Stark Security was fortunate to have many high-level connections that allowed for access to several databases not officially available to civilians. Not that Mario couldn't get through government security, but best to be above-board if possible.

"I'll buzz you as soon as I've got something. It won't be fast, though. Fair warning."

"Whatever you can do, as soon as you can do it," he said as the door opened and Ella stepped in. He waved in greeting as he ended the call with Mario, then smiled at her. "Thanks for letting me invade your space."

"I already told you. Anything you need. I want to know what's going on." She moved past him to sit at the dressing table. "Rye says you were going to look at the security footage. Was it from the fitness center? Did you find anything?"

"Maybe. I'll get back to you."

She squinted, looking ready to argue, but apparently

decided against it. "He also said you wanted to talk to me, and it had to be tonight. Before my after-party."

"I didn't see any profit in waiting."

"I'll admit I'm intrigued. This all feels very espionage-ish. Are you going to interrogate me about my dark past?"

He chuckled, then took a seat on her sofa, no longer covered with costumes. "Unless you're better than Witness Protection at crafting a fake past, I know pretty much all I need to know about you. And while you may have pissed off a few record producers over the years, I don't think any of them would attack you."

"You're saying it was random."

He leaned back, spreading his arms along the top of the sofa. "I think we both know it wasn't."

She'd been looking straight at him, but now her eyes flickered away before returning to his face. "Do we?"

"Don't play games. We're both too old and too smart for that."

She licked her lips. "Then stop trying to trap me and just tell me."

He almost laughed. The woman definitely had his number. "It wasn't random, but it also wasn't about you. It was about Xena." He caught her eyes again, then held them. "But you already knew that, didn't you?"

She lifted her chin, then looked defiantly at Liam. "Not at first. I figured it out after her reaction about the wig. I'm assuming you did, too."

He nodded. "So let's call her in and get some answers." Finally, they were making some progress. And if Xena knew who her attackers were, maybe he could wrap this thing up by morning.

Ella wrinkled her nose. "Well, actually, that's going to be a problem. Xena's gone."

7

THE SOUND of a revving engine startles me awake, and I leap
out of bed, terrified that they've found me. I scramble for
the gun I keep in my purse, then glance at the digital alarm
clock by the bed. Two in the morning.

Shit. I'm in a tiny mountain cottage on a dead-end street
with no other houses. So this really isn't good.

I remind myself that there's no way they can know I'm
here. I came by the craziest route imaginable, and I'm confident that I covered my tracks. There's no car outside to
suggest I'm here, and the interior of the house is completely
dark except for the glowing blue light of the various pieces
of electronic equipment that Ella keeps running even when
the house is closed up.

Besides, it's quiet now. Probably nothing. Just a coincidence. Someone who got lost and was turning around at the
dead end. No big deal.

At least, that's what I tell myself as I tiptoe through the
house in the yoga pants and tank that I'd slept in. Usually, I
sleep naked, but tonight I'd been too nervous, and wanted to
be ready to bolt. I check the doors and carefully peek out

the windows, trying to see something other than shadows from the trees. But there's nothing. No cars, no anything.

I tell myself that's good, and go with my lost driver theory. No big deal and I should just go back to sleep.

Instead, I put on my slip-on sneakers, just in case, then start to do another circuit around Ella's private getaway. A place I know she holds dear, and that I'm so, so grateful she's entrusting to me despite everything.

I've been here twice before, both times after our working relationship turned friendly. Even a little sisterly. I'd loved the place then, with its amazing refurbished bathroom and rustic back patio.

Tonight, I love it even more. It's my hideaway, and considering what I'm hiding from, is it any wonder I'm being paranoid about street sounds?

But is it paranoia if they're really out to get you?

I scowl, and tell myself that no one but Ella knows I'm here. For that matter, only a handful of Ella's closest staff and advisors even know the cabin exists. It's owned by a shell company in a shell company. She wanted a getaway. A real getaway. So she had someone buy it on behalf of a pretend rental company, and she keeps it empty. It's watched over by a caretaker who comes in once a month and whenever she calls to say she's coming.

It's her sanctuary. Her happy place.

I love her for letting me stay here. And all the more for swearing that she understood why I had to leave.

I wipe my eyes with the back of my hand, forcing myself not to cry. I hate that I have to run. That I have to hide. I loved my job, and I feel like I'm letting her down.

I've made the circuit twice now, and I don't see anything that suggests someone is out there. I double-check the alarm, and it's set. I disarm it and then re-arm it, just in case.

That's another reason I love Ella. She told me how to reprogram the system, and even told me not to tell her the code. That way, I'm the only one who knows it. "You'll tell me when you come back," she'd told me.

"What if I don't come back?"

"In that case, we both have bigger things to worry about than dealing with the damn alarm company."

A twig snaps at the back door, and I swallow a yelp. This time I'm certain I'm not imagining things.

With shaking hands, I hold the gun in front of me. "Go away," I call. "I'm armed. And this is private property."

"Xena, it's Liam."

Liam? My pulse picks up tempo, but this time it's not in fear. Relief? Hope?

Or maybe something much more complicated.

I put the gun down on the table by the door. My hands are still shaking, and I'm not taking any chances.

"Xena," he presses. "Open the door."

"How did you find me?"

"You know how," he says, his voice both firm and matter of fact.

I do?

Yes, of course I do. "Ella told you." I hear the accusation in my voice. She promised to keep it a secret. From everyone.

"Ella *sent* me."

What the hell? "Well, I didn't ask her to. And I'm fine. I don't need a babysitter. And I don't—I don't want her in the middle of my problems."

"Considering she was mugged because of your problems, I'd say she already is."

Anger flares inside me, cold and biting. "I mean it. Go away."

I hear him sigh. "Xena, please. Ella's worried about you. I'm worried about you. And I saw your face when she told me about the wig, so I'm pretty damn certain that you're worried about you, too."

I say nothing. He's right, but I'm not going to give him the satisfaction of admitting it.

"Xena, please. It's the middle of the night."

I suck in a breath, punch in the code to disarm the system, then open the door just long enough for him to swoop in. Then I set the code, wait for the green light to show the system's engaged, then turn around and study him.

He's wearing jeans, a black T-shirt, and a sport coat, and he looks just as sexy and commanding as he had in the tailored suit he had on when I saw him last.

Weirdly, that gives me confidence. I wouldn't open that door to just anyone, but a guy this pulled together? A guy that Ella trusts? Well, maybe it wouldn't be so bad having that guy watching my back.

Except, of course, that it might get him killed.

"Xena?" He reaches out and gently strokes my hair.

I flinch away, hugging myself, and he backs off immediately, then says, very gently, "Go sit down."

He nods toward the sofa in the small living room. I take the chair, curling myself up into a ball under the soft, purple blanket.

"What do you want?" he asks, and before I can ask what he means, he's continuing. "Water? Wine? Something harder?"

"Definitely something harder," I say, running my hands over my newly cut hair. "Coffee."

His face lights up with laughter, and I like the sound of it. For such a big guy, he has a very gentle laugh.

"Coffee sounds perfect. I'll be right back."

He leaves, and for a moment I think I should play hostess and follow him. But I don't. Despite telling him to go away not five seconds ago, now I want nothing more than to rest in this overstuffed chair and let Liam take care of me.

I have to fight that urge—I know that. Who knows better than I do the dangers of trusting other people? The only way to stay alive in this world is to watch your own back and not trust other people. And the corollary—let other people into your problems, and they could end up dead. I learned both the hard way, and those are lessons not easily forgotten.

But the truth is, I bent my own rule with Ella. I trusted her the way a wounded puppy trusts a human with a kind scent. I let her tend to me and take care of me, and although I was terrified for those first few months under her roof, my mind finally came to believe what instinct already knew. That she was a good woman who'd never betray me.

I trust her. Which means I can trust Liam. Or I can try to, anyway.

"Cream?" he calls from the kitchen, where I can hear the sound of the Keurig doing its thing.

"Yes, please." I hadn't thought much about the stocked refrigerator and pantry when I first arrived, but now I realize that Ella must have called the caretaker while I was on the road, and I'm grateful for it. I can drink my coffee black, but it's so much more comforting with cream.

He comes back with two huge mugs, hands me one, then sits on the sofa opposite me.

I take a sip, relishing the warmth and the way it gives me strength. "So what now?"

"Now, we talk."

"Right. Okay." I take another sip, but I don't volunteer any more information.

"I like your hair. Had a sudden urge for a change?"

I scowl. I'm not naturally platinum, but I'd been uber-blond for the last three years, hiding myself behind a curtain of long, silvery locks. Now, my hair is chin-length and ebony, still a far cry from my naturally warm, golden tones.

I'd grabbed a bottle of dye from Hair and Makeup before I left Vegas, then used the shower facilities at a truck stop to turn myself into a brunette. As for the cut, I'd popped into a Supercuts in San Bernardino before switching taxis for my trek up the mountain.

I can't say I'm crazy about my new look, but with my naturally pale skin, it suits me, though it's a little bit over-dramatic. I feel like a flapper or a silent film star. But none of that matters; it's not as if I have a photo shoot booked. My only goal is to stay alive.

"It was the hair, wasn't it?" he says. "They thought Ella was you because of the hair."

My instinct is to deny, of course. But I nod. Ella trusts him, so I'll answer truthfully. But I'm not going to volunteer information.

He leans back against the sofa cushions. His dark eyes study me, but I see compassion in them. "What happened, Susan? Who are you running from?"

I go cold at the sound of that name. "I go by Xena now. And I really don't want to talk about it."

"I know you don't. But I need information if I'm going to help you."

My body is tense, my jaw so tight my mouth aches. I draw a deep breath and force myself to relax. "I didn't ask for your help."

"Nonetheless, you have it. Tell me the truth, and I can be

useful. Block me, and I might be a detriment instead of an asset. Is that a risk you want to take?"

"What I want is for you to leave."

He studies me, then stands. "Why?"

I pull the blanket tighter around me. "I don't owe you an explanation. Why do you want to stay? The world's a dangerous place. I'm sure someone else will happily pay Stark Security's hourly rate."

"One, the SSA doesn't charge by the hour. And two, no one is paying me to be here."

I blink, legitimately surprised. "Oh."

"Xena," he says gently. "Tell me your story. Let me help."

I say nothing, my mind whirring as I keep my lips tight together, afraid if I relax for even a second, then all of my secrets will spill out.

I watch as his shoulders slump, and I feel a pang in my gut. I've disappointed him.

"You were a runaway," he says, and since that's close enough to the truth, I nod. "Tell me how you came to work for Ella."

I run the question around in my head, not sure if I should open the door to this man even a crack. But I can't deny that I do need help, even if only to get away, get a new identity, and get settled. Would he do that for me? I'm not sure—how can I be sure?—but if he's really here because Ella asked him to help me, then I think maybe he will.

Even she doesn't know the real truth, but she knows the essence. She knows I was running. She knows I was hiding. She knows I was afraid for my life.

And she knows that I have to go hide again.

"Xena," he presses. "Tell me about the name. How did Xena end up being a nickname for Susan?"

"I can't tell you that without telling you more of the story."

"I don't have anywhere else to be, and I'm not particularly sleepy."

"Me either," I admit. My terror-induced adrenaline rush has faded, but I'm still wide-awake, and not just because of the coffee.

"Then we might as well stay up and talk."

I finish my coffee, then sigh. "Fine. I'm pretty sure I'm not going to get rid of you, so I might as well talk to you."

"I'll take conversation with you anyway I can get it."

I know he's just being agreeable, soothing me like a skittish colt, but I still melt a little under his words.

When I continue to stay silent, he clears his throat. "Why did you run away?"

I lick my lips, debating how much fiction to mix with my facts. "Things were bad," I say simply. "Considering how you grew up, I'm not sure you can really understand that."

I see his eyes widen and know I've surprised him. "What do you know about how I grew up?"

I shrug. "I looked you up before you came to work for Ella in Los Angeles. I knew the SSA had a good rep, but—"

"You look out for her."

I nod.

"Now you've intrigued me. What did you find out?"

"That you grew up in a mansion in Southampton. That your mom was the housekeeper for the Sykes family, you moved there when you were a baby, and you were raised like you were part of the family. Oh, and they have more money than God."

"I haven't actually reviewed God's books lately, but that's probably a fair assessment."

"And I know that Dallas Sykes is your best friend, and

that the family sent you to school with him, at least until he went overseas to boarding school. I know you served in the army and that for years you worked as the head of security for the Sykes Department Store chain."

I watch Liam's chest expand as he draws in a long breath. "So that's all?"

I grin at his flippant tone. "I couldn't find as much recent stuff," I admit. "But somehow you ended up at Stark Security."

"Not a bad bit of research."

"It wasn't too hard. You hang around with the Sykes family, and you can't really stay invisible."

"I suppose that's true."

"And while I can tell you my story, it's not like it matters. It's not like you'll get it at all. I mean, I'm *so* not a Hamptons kind of girl."

"No, you're an Idaho transplant to LA. And your parents are dead, and until Ella you didn't have a support network. I haven't had the chance to dig in, but I'm guessing you were a runaway, probably lived on the streets for a while. Maybe even turned tricks."

My cheeks heat, because he's so far from the truth, but also so very close to it.

"Somewhere along the way, you crossed the wrong person." He tilts his head, as if examining me from another angle. "Maybe drugs, maybe money-laundering, maybe something else. I don't know. But it was big enough that they still want to make sure you stay silent, even after all these years."

He straightens, then leans forward, his elbows on his knees. "How am I doing so far?"

"Good enough to prove my point." My voice is colder than I intend it to be. Deep down, I know he really wants to

help me. But despite my fantasies of having someone at my
side offering aid, I know that can't happen. And he has no
idea what kind of rabbit hole we'd both fall into if I let him.

"Your point?" he asks.

"You can't possibly have a clue about my life."

He studies me for a while, long enough that I start to
squirm under his attention. Finally, he says, "You know
about the Sykes kidnapping?"

I nod. "Dallas Sykes and his sister were kidnapped when
they were teenagers. Around fifteen, I think. They were both
finally released." I don't know a lot about it, actually. My
research was focused on Liam, not the Sykes family. But
Dallas Sykes is a huge celebrity by virtue of his family
money, his playboy heir attitude, and the parties he use to
throw and attend. I've never been much on social media—
and for a long time I couldn't afford a smart phone—but for
a while everyone was calling him The King of Fuck, and it
would have taken superpowers to avoid the gossip entirely.

"They were both my best friends growing up," Liam says.
"Dallas and Jane. They're still my best friends, and I love
them like family. I would do anything for them. They've
endured more than any human should have to endure, and I
don't begrudge them a moment of happiness."

I nod, assuming he's talking about the fact that they're
now married, which is utterly bizarre to me.

"I told Jane to go to Dallas that night."

I shake my head, not following. "What night?"

"Outside of London. The night they were kidnapped.
Dallas was in boarding school, and Jane wanted to talk with
him. She called me before she snuck away from her family
in the city, asking me if she should." He swallows. "I said yes.
And that night, they were both kidnapped."

"I'm so sorry." I lick my lips. "But it's not your fault."

"No, but they were still taken. And they were tortured."

"Tortured?" I repeat.

"Horribly, brutally tortured. The worst you can imagine."

Considering my own history, I can imagine a lot. "Sexually," I whisper. A statement, not a question.

"And there I was safe and sound back in the States, completely oblivious until it was over, then completely impotent after I learned some of the truth. I wanted to make it better. But there wasn't a damn thing I could do for them."

"No." I shake my head. "No, there wouldn't be."

"I joined the Army," he says. "At the time, I didn't even know why. God knows I wasn't from a military family. My father died before I was born. A drug deal gone bad."

"I'm sorry."

"Yeah, well, I'm not. I love my mom, and from what she tells me, my father was bad news. The shooting and the pregnancy pushed her out of the city, and she managed to land a job on the Sykes estate even though she had a baby. I still don't know how, and all she says is that God was looking out for us. But not the point. I ended up in the military."

"Because you felt helpless," I say. "About Dallas and Jane. And maybe even a little about your dad."

"Maybe." He exhales. "Actually, yes."

"Did it help?"

The corner of his mouth curves up just slightly. "No."

"You thought it would."

He nods. "But I learned skills. I formed friendships. The years weren't wasted."

"Maybe not, but you're still chasing that guilt. That helplessness. It's why you work in security."

"That's definitely part of it."

"And the rest of it?" I ask.

"I really do like the work. And I'm good at it. And there are far too many people in the world who need help."

I exhale. He's right about that.

"I'm sorry," I say after a moment. "For you. For your friends." I drop my gaze. "And for being a brat who thinks she's the only one who has a hell-bitch for a guardian angel."

"But you don't," he says, and I look up into those kind, determined eyes. "Not anymore."

My heart skitters in my chest. "Liam…"

I think he's going to press me to allow him to play body-guard. Instead, he changes topics. "How did they find you? Do you know?"

"Ella didn't tell you?"

He shakes his head.

"Those damn super fan invitations." I can see he doesn't understand, so I continue. "Ella's known from the beginning that I was running, and when I told her I wanted to be sure and never be in a photo, she was totally cool with that. Sometimes reporters would ask, you know? Because no one knows a celebrity like their personal assistant. But she'd always tell them that I'm not a public figure and privacy is important and yada yada." I trail off with a shrug.

"But somehow a picture got out there?"

"Oh, yeah." I release a noisy sigh. "You know how we invite fans to the final full rehearsal? Well, we tell them no photography except during the rehearsal performance. Nothing on breaks or behind the scenes. But last week at the LA rehearsal, some clown took a pic when I went on stage during a break to talk to Ella about something that needed to be adjusted before the performance."

"It got posted on social media, and someone saw it."

"Right. And since the attack was in the wake of the

Gordon bullshit, the connection to me wasn't even on Ella's radar."

"But it was on yours. They recognized your face despite changing your hair when you ran."

I nod. "I'm not naturally a blond." I run my fingers through my current strands. "This isn't really me, either."

"Well, so far I've liked all the versions of you." His voice is mild, but I think I see a hint of heat in his eyes.

I look away. "Yeah, well, after the attack, I knew I had to go. So I went to see her before the concert. That was when she showed me the photo on Twitter. Someone had tagged her, and it was just random that she saw it. She usually doesn't pay that much attention to her account. She has a social media team that handles that."

"So she helped you run. Sent you here."

I nod.

"And you're sure they didn't follow you?"

"Positive."

"Tell me how you got here?"

I roll my eyes, but comply. "I took a taxi—cash—to the airport in Vegas, then flew to Burbank. Then I took a taxi to LAX and used a pre-paid debit card that Ella gave me to buy a ticket on one airline to Newark and on another airline to Atlanta. Then I took a taxi to a truck stop in Riverside. That's where I changed my hair. And then another taxi to San Bernardino."

"Why not the bus?"

I shrug. "Faster."

He nods, and I continue. "I took one last taxi up here." I shrug. "If they followed me, I'd call it a miracle."

"I'm impressed."

I don't bother telling him I've had a lot of practice.

"Wait," I say, suddenly alarmed. "Could they have followed you?"

"No." The word is firm. "My route was as random as yours. We're safe."

"Okay." I'm sure my relief is visible.

"Listen, Xena. You're obviously capable, but you're still alone, and we don't know for sure what you're up against. Let me help you. Think of it as an entirely altruistic act."

I shake my head. "No. I appreciate it, but no."

"Why not?"

"Because I don't want you involved. And I don't need you. Don't you get it? They don't know where I am. I'm going to stay here a couple of days to regroup, and then I'm going to disappear again. Another state. Maybe another country. I have money this time. I saved a lot from working with Ella. And she told me to take some cash from the safe in there," I add, pointing to the kitchen. "I'm going to—but only because I plan to pay it back."

He watches me even after I finish talking, studying me like I'm a problem that has to be solved.

"What?" I demand when I can't stand it anymore.

"I'm sorry, but I can't agree to that."

"I'm pretty sure I never asked you to."

"Xena, be realistic. Someone is after you. Let me help you find them. Take them out. Let me help you fix your life so that you can stop running and looking over your shoulder."

The very thought sends cold chills coursing up my spine, and I can feel my heart start to skitter with the precursor to a full-blown panic attack. I tell myself to breathe. To count to ten. And as Liam watches me, I slowly calm down.

"Xena?"

I just shake my head, not quite up to forming words yet. The reality would be horrible enough, but just the *idea* of confronting them terrifies me. I'm not going to tell Liam that. He has no idea how big the monster is. But I do. And I've seen enough scary movies to know that sometimes the only way to survive is to get the hell away from the demon.

"No," I finally say. "I'm sorry, but no."

He doesn't answer, but it doesn't matter. At the end of the day, it's my decision.

After a moment, he stands. "I'm going to raid Ella's bar. Do you want a whiskey? Or wine? I bet she has red. You need sleep, and it might help."

I shake my head. "I don't drink."

His brow furrows. "But that night on Ella's patio…"

"Ella makes sure the parties have non-alcoholic wine for me. It's easier than explaining."

I'm not sure he realizes it, but he takes a step closer to me.

"Funny." That's all he says, but his expression suggests that there's a lot more thought behind the word.

"What?"

"It's just—I thought you were a little drunk that night."

"Oh." And I must be more tired than I realize, because I can't stop what comes out of my mouth next. "You made me feel a little drunk." I meet his eyes, then look down, a tiny smile tugging at my mouth. Why I'm smiling, though, I don't know. God knows I've just revealed more to this man than I ever thought I would. And definitely more than I should.

I bite my lower lip. We'd both stayed in check that night, even though we both wanted so much more. Neither of us had said so, but it was in the air, so thick and potent it's a wonder the other guests didn't notice.

It occurs to me that I won't be seeing him again, because

after tonight he'll be gone, and in a few days, I'll disappear and become someone else. But tonight...

Tonight there's no risk of exposing myself. Of getting in too deep with someone I can't have.

He clears his throat. "Right. Well, I still want that whiskey." He starts to take a step, and before I have time to think about what I'm doing, I reach for his hand.

He stops, turning to look at me, and I pull myself up. He's right there, my hand in his, his other on my back, holding me steady, though how it got there, I really don't know.

That hint of a flame I'd seen earlier in his eyes is a blaze now, and I melt under the heat of it. I want this, dammit. This night. This man. Not because I have no choice. Not because I'm trying to survive.

I want it for me. *Me.*

Because he'll be gone tomorrow, and I'll be on the run. And I want to take this moment with me. Something real and wild to fire my strength. And something warm and tender to soothe my soul.

I see hesitation in his eyes, and I can hear his unspoken words. *We shouldn't.*

"Yes," I whisper. "We should."

For a moment, the world stops turning and the only thing happening in the entire universe is the two of us looking into each other's eyes. Then he groans, and in one bold move pulls me closer and crushes his mouth against mine.

I cling to him, melting against him as I part my lips, welcoming the delicious assault of this kiss I feel all through me, making me tingle all the way to my toes and bringing to life parts of me I thought were dead forever.

All too soon, he pulls away, his questioning eyes searching my face.

"Yes," I whisper, but my word is swallowed by the flash of light that fills the room, the heavy pounding against the wooden front door, and the sharp pain in my arm as Liam yanks me violently down to the floor.

8

A SCREAM SHATTERS THE AIR, and in the same moment that
Liam closes his hand over my mouth, I realize it's coming
from me.

He's looking at me hard, and I nod, hoping he understands that I've gotten myself under control. Slowly, he takes
his hand off my mouth. "It's them," I say, as if he hasn't
already figured that out all on his own. "They must have
followed you."

I hear the accusation in my voice, but I don't care. Damn
him for coming here, and damn Ella for sending him. I love
her for caring, but they're both going to get me killed.

"They didn't follow me," he says. "Believe me when I say
I know how to hide my tracks, and I know how to tell when
I'm being tailed."

"Well, it wasn't me." I have *no* idea why I'm arguing
about this, except that it pisses me off. I was supposed to
have a chance to relax.

"I believe you," he says.

"Then how—"

"Right now, it doesn't matter."

"What was the light?"

"Headlights, I think. Maybe a high power flashlight."

"Why haven't they come in?"

"They must know about the alarm. It's wired to 911?"

I nod. The siren won't disturb neighbors since there are none, but the little police station that serves this part of the San Bernardino Mountains is only one block over. The cops could be here in no time, and they can block the only way off the street even faster than that.

With a start, I realize our intruder—intruders?—must know that.

"Wait here." He stays low as he heads back to the door. He flips the light switch to off, leaving the room illuminated only by the thin blue light of the electronics and the faint glow of moonlight coming in through the windows.

He grabs my tiny Ruger from the table, then comes back to my side. "Do you know how to use this?" he asks when he returns.

I lift a brow. "Point and pull the trigger?"

I can tell from his face that he doesn't appreciate the sarcasm, so I pull back the slide to reveal that there's a round in the chamber, then pop out the magazine before I expel the bullet. I shove the bullet back into the magazine, click the magazine into place, then once again pull the slide back to chamber the round.

"Yeah," I say. "I know how to use it."

He nods, then reaches under his jacket and pulls out a much larger black gun. I think it's a Glock, but wouldn't swear to it. Suddenly, I'm feeling better about our chances.

"Do you trust me to get us out of here?"

"Yes," I say, meaning it wholeheartedly.

He glances around the room, sees the backpack I use as a purse, and asks if I have a compact.

"Um, maybe?" I start to crawl over there but he holds me back, then goes himself, returning with the pack. I rummage through it, find a small gold compact that Ella gave me one Christmas, and pass it to him.

With the compact in his left hand and the pistol in his right, he creeps to the window by the front door as I hold my breath. He uses the compact to look outside, then slowly lowers it. Then he holds up a finger before miming a steering wheel.

One guy and a car. Got it.

I point to the back door, and he goes there next, repeating the process and holding up another finger. *Fuck.*

He comes back to me. "It's too dark to get a good look, but I think they're the same goons from Vegas. Does Ella use some sort of front porch camera? If so, we might have a solid image of his face now."

I shrug.

"I'll find out later," Liam says. "Right now, we need to get out of here, because sooner or later they're going to hack the alarm code or decide to say screw it and come in anyway. They're heavily armed."

I decide not to ask what that means. If they have rocket launchers or automatic weapons, I really don't want to know.

"There's a little cellar under the kitchen," I say. "But it opens up right by the back door."

"Bathroom window?"

"Oh!" How could I forget the bathroom? "Better than that. The wall looks like the side of the house, but it folds back, so that you can actually sit in the jetted tub during the snow. Or take a shower in the outdoors if you're feeling adventurous." It was the one renovation that Ella put in after buying the place, and I think it was freaking brilliant.

"Make sure you have your phone and put on your back-pack. Do you need to grab anything else?"

"I'm good. I've traveled light for years."

He aims a curious look at me, but says nothing other than, "Carry the Ruger and don't accidentally shoot me."

I nod, nervous enough to not smirk at his smart aleck remark. Because unfortunately, he's right about that partic-ular risk.

"Stay low and lead the way."

I nod, then start to scramble that way, not breathing until we're finally inside the small space. Since the entire back wall by the sunken whirlpool tub and rain-style shower opens, there is no window, just a skylight. And that means as soon as we close the door behind us, we can relax. For a second, at least.

"How does it open?" Liam asks.

I stand and step on the wide ledge that runs along the foot of the tub. "This button unlocks it. Then you fold it back and slide it into the wall."

"Noisy?"

I wince. "Not that you'd normally care about. But today..."

He nods, understanding. "Too bad there's not much wind. The sound of the leaves might camouflage it. Doesn't matter. It's our shot, and we're taking it."

I nod in agreement even though I'm nervous as shit.

"The wall opens onto the porch I noticed when I arrived?" he asks. "With the lounge chairs and the fire pit?"

"Right. Once the wall is tucked away, the entire bath-room is an outdoor space." The toilet, thankfully, is in its own tiny room.

He looks around the space, then aims a wry grin at me. "A shame we have to bolt. This bathroom could have been an interesting part of our evening."

Despite my fear, I laugh. "Promise me we'll live to have a rain check."

But he doesn't answer, and for a moment, we simply look at each other. Then he clears his throat and points toward the tub again. "There were stairs on both sides of the patio, right? And about an eight inch drop off the long end?"

"Um, yeah," I say, impressed by his memory.

"What about the alarm. Is it silent? Or does it blare?"

"It blares."

He looks around, then frowns.

"What?"

"No keypad in here to disarm it. We could have you go back into the other room to take care of that, but I think I actually want it to blare—I assume it's loud."

"Apparently. Ella told me not to forget my code because the alarm is earsplitting."

"Okay, okay." He's talking to himself, obviously mulling something. "This can work." He pulls some tissues from a dispenser by the sink, then steps onto the ledge and hands me one. "Rip it up and plug your ears."

"Huh?"

"Trust me," he says, and since I do, I comply without any more questions.

As soon as his own ears are plugged, he looks at my gun, then his own. I know what he's going to say even before he says it. "We can solve this problem right now. They're going to be out of commission for at least a few seconds when the alarm blares. They won't be expecting it. We can take them out before they come after us. And they *will* come after us."

Cold fear washes over me. As much as I want them dead

—as much as I want this nightmare to end—it's too danger-ous. For one, they surely aren't the only two after me. Like cockroaches, if I kill two, four more will replace them.

But more than that, what if I miss and my target takes Liam out? Or me? And if we do get away, then what? We're going to leave Ella to deal with my mess? Bodies in her yard that she'll have to explain?

I shake my head slowly, then tell him all of that. I expect him to argue. To go all hard ass macho on me and tell me it's time to Rambo this shit.

But he doesn't. On the contrary, he nods slowly. "You're right." He rubs his shaved scalp, then sighs. "The fact is, we've only seen two, but there might be more. We're getting out, getting away, and regrouping. You understand?"

I nod. "But what about calling for back-up?" I don't suggest the cops. They'd investigate us as much as the bad guys, and I don't want to be under that microscope. "The SSA. You have guys, right?"

"We're a long way from LA, even by chopper. And pulling in the Sheriff's department would take too long. Unlike in the movies, getting that kind of assistance from law enforcement requires red tape. We could call 911, but I don't think that's a good idea." He meets my eyes. "Do you?"

"No." I swallow. "So how are we getting away?"

"Just stay close. I've got that covered."

I remember the engine that woke me. He must have a car parked among the trees.

"On three," he says. "It's going to be loud. Be ready."

I'm not entirely sure my rubbery legs are going to coop-erate, but I nod anyway.

He counts, and on three, he presses the button and the door unlatches as the blare from the alarm starts to shake the entire house. He shoves the panel aside, grabs my hand,

and races forward, jumping the short distance from the patio to the ground, then sprinting over the undergrowth into the dark, wooded area.

I stumble and fall, and Liam grabs for me. As he does, I catch sight of the guy at the back door, partially illuminated by the moonlight. Unprepared, he's on the ground, struggling to get back to his feet with his hands plastered to his ears.

It worked, I think as Liam tugs me back up and we start running again.

I expect him to take us to the street, but instead we go into the woods, following what I now realize is an overgrown path. There's a hill, and we hurry down it, and I soon realize that we're low enough now that no one in the house or around it can see us. I relax. Slightly.

I start to ask where we're going, but then I see the huge bike parked by a woodpile. He came all the way from Vegas on a bike?

He hurries me onto the motorcycle before getting on in front of me. The guy in the back has stood up now, and I can see him from the saddle. Which means he can see me.

"Hold on," Liam says, his voice tense. And before I've even locked my fingers around him, we're rocketing forward, leaves flying around us as we bounce along the path, then hit the street's asphalt. There's a black car parked in front of the house, and on the porch, a lanky guy in a ball cap turns around, his mouth open in a ridiculous maw.

I see him raise a weapon, and I tense, then scream as a shot rings out, followed by another in quick succession. I breathe deep, expecting pain, then realize that it was Liam doing the shooting. The tires, I assume, but I don't know if he hit them, because we're already careening down twisting mountain roads, and I'm terrified that we're going to wipe out and I'm going to end up dead in a fiery conflagration.

I turn around once, then twice, both times certain I'll see my attackers gaining on us. But there's nothing. No one. Just the dark road disappearing behind us.

We go for what feels like forever, turning down streets, backtracking up the mountain, then going down an alternate route. Circling and twisting until I'm both lost and dizzy and numb from the buzz of the cycle beneath me.

"Stop," I finally shout, my mouth close to the back of his ear. "Please. Please, find a place to stop."

My heart is pounding. My blood burning. I need to move. I need to—I don't even know. But being on this bike is only making it worse.

Soon, he's pulling onto a side road that dips down. I see a wooden sign with the name of a park, but I'm too frazzled to try to read it. He follows a gravel path for at least a quarter mile, then stops the bike in a patch of dirt near a battered picnic table. He gets off, then helps me off.

I tug the tissue from my ears, then bend over, my hands on my knees, and suck in air as he rubs my back and whispers soothing words. "It's okay. It's okay. You're safe. There's no way they followed us. Just breathe. We're fine."

I nod my head. He's right, but it's not enough. I stand, my pulse so loud I can barely hear my thoughts.

"Xen—"

I don't let him finish. Instead, I pull myself up on my toes and capture his mouth in a kiss, long and deep and so wonderfully delicious I feel it reverberate all the way through me.

I pull back, breathing hard, my eyes never leaving his face. His expression is tight, like a spring about to explode.

But whether he's about to kiss me or push me away, I really can't tell.

"We could have died," I whisper, as I slide my hands down to cup his very fine ass. I press against him, his erection hard against me. "We could have died," I repeat. "So don't you dare say no."

9

Xena wrapped herself around him before he could even react, her mouth hot against his. He knew they shouldn't—that they'd regret it in the morning. That *she'd* regret it. But dear Christ, he wanted her. He'd wanted her from the first moment he'd seen her.

That slim body. Those innocent eyes. That kissable, fuckable mouth that even then was warm and wet against his own, her tongue teasing and tempting him, making his already heated blood burn hotter.

Good God, he should hold back. He needed to rein it in and exercise some of that control he was so famous for. But right then they were safe, and she was wild and hot in his arms, and he was breathless and hard and definitely not thinking straight.

She was right—they could have died. And now that the coast was clear, he needed this. They both did. Needed to burn this crazed lust out of their systems, to boil down the adrenaline so they could think again. To push through the fear and the pain.

All of which were just rationalizations to justify taking

her right then, right there, on a damned park bench while her skin glowed in the moonlight.

He stumbled back, then collapsed onto the bench. She gasped, one hand going to the button on his jeans as she climbed onto his lap, her legs on either side of his.

He had one hand at her lower back and the other on her breast. She wasn't wearing a bra, just that sexy black tank top, and he stroked his thumb over her hard nipple as it strained against the material.

She moaned against his mouth, her tongue still warring with his as he hitched the shirt up in the back, then slid his fingers under the waistband of her yoga pants. Her body shook as she drew a shuddering breath, and he cupped one of her ass cheeks, then pulled her closer, so that her body stroked his erection.

Her low, sexy moan teased his senses, and she started to move her hips, the slow, grinding movement making him completely insane. At the same time, the fingers at his fly started tugging down his zipper, while her other hand closed over his, increasing the pressure to her breast as she arched back and ground harder against him.

As her fingers eased into his jeans, she lifted her hips up to free his cock. He shifted long enough to tug his jeans down a bit so that blood would continue to flow, then returned one hand to her breast and rolled that tight, perfect nipple between his thumb and forefinger.

Their mouths were still locked, but she pulled back, her teeth tugging at his lower lip. "We shouldn't do this," she murmured, her voice low and breathy.

"No," he agreed as her hips rose and he took advantage, finding her slick, wet core. "No, we shouldn't," he said, burying two fingers inside her. She bore down on his hand, her head tilted back as she bit her lip and moaned.

"Then let's do it fast. Before we change our minds."

Laughter bubbled up out of him, and she took her hands off him, then started to tug down her yoga pants. "Get these off me."

"Off?"

She grabbed her top and pulled it over her head, then tossed it onto the picnic table behind him.

"Christ, Xena, what are you doing?"

"What *I* want. Please, please, for the first time in forever, just let me do this."

He didn't understand what she meant, but the question evaporated quickly enough as she wriggled out of the pants, managing the whole thing more efficiently than he could have, most likely because he half-believed he was dreaming.

"Touch me," she begged, and when he hesitated, she added, "We're safe. You said so. And if you didn't believe it one hundred percent you never would have let it get this far."

She was right, and he didn't protest when she took his hand and stroked his fingers over her clit. He was so damn hard, and he cupped his hands on her ass as she grabbed his shoulders, using the leverage to lift her hips, then wriggling until she was right over his cock. She settled there, teasing him mercilessly as she looked in his eyes, taking him in bit by bit, making them both crazy, until finally he was buried inside her, and she arched back, begging him to touch her as she rode him like a wild thing.

He cupped one breast and stroked her clit, but he didn't kiss her. He wanted to watch her. The way the moonlight cast shadows on her face. The way her lips parted with passion. The tremors in the tight muscles of her abdomen. And then, when release finally came, the way her entire body trembled and shook as she cried out and pounded a fist against his shoulder.

She was the most alive thing he'd ever held in his arms, and as her core spasmed around him, he exploded inside her. His moans joined hers, their loud cries sending a flock of birds rising out of the trees, their wings black against the night sky.

She collapsed against him, breathing hard. "Thank you," she murmured. "I'm sorry. And thank you."

"Sorry?" He cupped her face and gazed into those shining blue eyes. "Baby, you don't have anything to be sorry about."

A wry smile played at her mouth. "I think I used you."

"I think I liked it." Hell yes, he'd liked it. The way she'd taken control, and the way he'd completely surrendered to the live wire in his arms. It had been beyond delicious, and utterly unexpected.

"Are you okay?"

He realized that he'd closed his eyes, his forehead pressed against hers. He pulled back so that he could see her—then kissed her gently. "I'm fine. You do some crazy things to me."

"Crazy good? Or crazy bad?"

He grinned. "Maybe a little of both," he said, and as he'd hoped, she laughed.

And then he remembered. "*Fuck*."

Her eyes widened. "What? What's wrong?"

"No condom. I'm sorry. I didn't even think. What the hell is wrong with me?"

Her brow furrowed, and he wished he could kick himself in the balls. *Idiot*.

"But you're okay, right? You're clean?

"Yes. God, yes. Of course." He ran his hand over his scalp, still cursing his own stupidity. "I swear."

"I believe you." She brushed her thumb over his lower lip. "You have such a fabulous mouth. You know that, right?"

He caught her hand, then kissed the pad of her thumb. "I'm glad you believe me, but it was still unprotected sex."

"It's okay. I promise. I'm clean, too. Tested and everything." Her voice sliced the air. "And if it's pregnancy you're worried about, well, that won't be a problem either."

"Xena..." He wanted to ask about the knife edge in her tone, but something stopped him. That wasn't a question for now. Not when he was still inhaling her scent and she was still naked in his lap.

She blinked at him, obviously waiting for him to continue.

"Get dressed," he said gently. "We need to find someplace safe for the night. And then tomorrow, we're heading for LA."

10

By the time they left the park, found a crappy motel, and checked in, it was past four in the morning and they had officially crossed the line into a Very Long Day.

Even so, Liam was still wired when he slipped the key into the scuffed lock and pushed open the dingy gray door. The faint scent of mildew lingered under the stronger odor of bleach. He grimaced, but even the tacky room and the unappealing smell couldn't shake the happy out of him. Maybe it was a mistake and maybe it wasn't, but right then, Liam wouldn't have traded the last hour for anything.

The attack before, sure. That he could have lived without. But to hold Xena's naked body in his arms—to feel her shatter around him as her orgasm exploded through her— Christ, he wouldn't trade that memory or that moment for anything. And all he wished right then was that they could have gone to the fucking Ritz instead of the Inland Motor Inn, the sign for which must have been designed in the fifties. And from what he saw as he stepped into the room, neither the furniture nor the carpet had been changed since then.

He said a silent prayer that someone had washed the sheets.

"Welcome to our suite," he said, holding the door open so she could enter.

He saw her nose wrinkle, but when she looked at him, she was smiling. "It's perfect."

"Our definitions of perfect are wildly disparate. But it'll do."

"We paid cash, there's a bed, and there's a door in front of the toilet. Trust me when I say I've seen worse. Much worse."

"Then I pity you," he quipped, then immediately regretted the words. He knew she'd been a runaway. Undoubtedly she really had slept in much worse conditions than this.

"Sorry," he said, but she just laughed.

"It's okay." She took his hand and pulled him the rest of the way in so the door swung shut behind them. She stumbled a little as she headed to the queen size bed.

He lingered to flip the bolt and add the chain, then unholstered his Glock and put it on the bedside table. He placed her Ruger there, too; he'd put it in the bike's storage compartment after they'd bolted from the house, then retrieved it when they'd arrived here.

"Sleep," he ordered. "You're dead on your feet."

She was sitting on the edge of the bed, and now she yawned, as if his words had given her permission. With drooping eyes, she started to wriggle out of her yoga pants, then stopped. "Oh. Sorry. I usually don't sleep in my clothes."

He chuckled. "Fine by me, but don't expect me to keep my hands to myself."

She met his eyes, hers bloodshot with heavy lids, but the

corner of her mouth curved up and she held his gaze as she pulled off the pants, then the tank. Then she held them out to him. "I was going to drop them on the floor, but..." She trailed off, her nose wrinkling with disgust as she looked down at the stained carpet.

He nodded. "Right," he said, then laid her clothes over the back of a chair. By the time he turned to face her again, she was under the covers, her eyes were closed, and her breathing was slow and even. She was either asleep or doing a damn good job of faking it.

He took off his jacket and shirt, then followed with his jeans, leaving only his boxer briefs on. He considered adding them to the chair's decoration, but there was only one bed, and it was going to be hard enough to let her sleep peacefully, even as tired as he was. Because the truth was, their wild coupling in the park had been running in a continuous loop through his mind.

He slid carefully into the bed, his eyes never leaving her. She'd been incredible. Hot. Dangerous. *Fabulous.* And, yes, he wanted more. He wanted to push her to the limit, to go wild with her. He wanted to take control and see all that heat and sensuality bound up in a beautiful package for him. To immerse her in inescapable pleasure even while he pushed himself to his own limits, crossing lines he hadn't stepped over in years.

He'd take her—them both—to the edge. And only when he was certain that she couldn't stand it any longer, would he let the full force of passion consume her, as pure, undiluted pleasure exploded inside her.

Slowly, he brushed his fingertips over her skin, so pale she looked like a doll asleep beside him. He couldn't remember the last time he'd wanted a woman so much...or met a woman who matched him so well. And he wondered if maybe—just maybe—this woman might—

He slammed a door on those thoughts as he felt the tightening in his chest. A low burn of anger and self-loathing. Fear, too, which was ironic considering everything he'd faced in his life. But it was real. And it was inescapable.

With a sigh, he rolled to his back, his head on the pillow as he stared up at the ceiling. He was so damn tired, and he was letting his mind go into forbidden corners. He needed to stay on course. He had a job to do, after all, and sex really wasn't part of it.

His phone was on the table beside his gun, and he reached for it, needing to do one last thing before he could finally sleep. The text to Ella was short: He'd reached Xena, and Ella should call when she got the message. Considering it wasn't yet dawn, he figured he'd get at least an hour of sleep before she replied.

To his surprise, the phone buzzed immediately in his hands.

He stood up, taking the call with a soft, "Ella. I wasn't expecting to hear back so soon."

"I do yoga and meditate before dawn. It's the only time I have. I'd hoped to hear from you last night. You found the cabin okay?"

"Xena and I are safe," he said, to which she replied, "Oh, fuck."

He almost laughed. He'd known from the minute he met her that she was a sharp woman.

"What happened?"

"We had visitors. Not long after I arrived." He gave her the quick version, ending with the motel and skipping the park.

"They followed you." The accusation was clear in her voice.

"I don't think so.

"Xena, then?"

Since he didn't have an answer, he said nothing.

"But you're okay now? They didn't follow you to the motel?"

"No." That much, he was certain of.

"Okay. Good. *Shit.*"

He let her get it out of her system. After a moment, he heard her take a breath. "How's my cabin?"

"I'm going to guess they searched the interior. And you need to send your caretaker—with the cops, just in case, though I doubt they're still around. The bathroom wall is wide open."

"Right. Okay." He gave her props for not asking for more details.

"Do you have front porch cams?"

"Do I—what?"

"Remote security cameras. Sometimes mounted in the doorbell?"

"Oh, yes. Both doors."

"Ella, you just made my morning." He was about to ask her to send him the access information when she texted that exact thing. "You're fabulous. I'll get this to Mario. With any luck, he can pull both faces off those feeds. The image from the fitness center doesn't seem too promising."

"How's Xena doing? Can I talk to her? She must be so scared."

"She's sleeping right now. I'd rather not wake her."

"Oh, God no. She's had a hell of an ordeal." A thickness had entered her voice, and he realized that she'd started to cry. "Do you know what she told me before she left? That she hated being a thorn in my side. That girl has worked for me for over four years now. She's become one of my closest friends. How can she not know that?"

"I think she does. I think that's why it bothers her so much that you're involved in all this."

"I don't even know what all this is. Not really. All this time ... why would her past come back to haunt her after so many years?"

"I don't know either," he said, though he had some ideas. At the core, there had to be something very, very bad. Murder, maybe. Or worse. Because otherwise, Tweedledee and Tweedledum would have stayed hidden. The only reason to come out of the woodwork was if it was very, very important to them that Xena could never, ever cause any trouble.

He glanced at the sleeping woman and sighed. He knew Xena wasn't going to want to talk about it. He also knew that she had to.

"I'm worried about you, too," he told Ella, returning his exhausted mind to the call. "They have their eye on you. And they knew about the cabin. Possibly they followed Xena, but she told me how she covered her tracks, and it was solid."

"Fuck."

"Most likely, nothing will happen. But they know she was your assistant, and once they learn how long she's been with you, they may assume you know where she is."

"Right." She exhaled loudly. "Okay, so what—"

"I'm sending someone. You're probably in the clear, but I don't want to take chances. I'll text his name and information as soon as I confirm he's available." Any of the team at the SSA could do the job, but he wanted Winston Starr. The former West Texas sheriff had an easy manner and serious skills. The best thing about him was that no one ever saw Winston coming.

As soon as he ended the call with Ella, he dialed his friend.

"Do you know what time it is?"

Liam scoffed. "I know you're up. Don't cowboys always rise before the sun?"

"I'd try to find a snappy comeback," Winston drawled, his Texas twang more pronounced than usual. "But you're not worth the effort."

"I didn't really wake you, did I?"

"Hell, no. I'm at the gym. But I haven't had my coffee yet, so I'm in a mood. What do you need?"

"How does an all expense paid trip to Vegas sound?"

"Hong Kong, DC, now Vegas." He chuckled. "When Stark and Ryan convinced me to take this job, I didn't realize I'd be getting so many frequent flier miles, too."

"Got you out of West Texas, didn't it?"

"I got myself out of West Texas, my friend. And as for Vegas, why the hell not?"

They quickly worked through the details, then added Ryan Hunter to the call. As the head of Stark Security, he needed to both be in the loop and sign off on the plan.

Ryan answered on the first ring, wide awake. "Christ," Liam said. "Do none of you sleep?"

"Didn't realize you were such a slacker, Foster."

"I need my beauty rest," Liam quipped, before explaining the situation. Ryan approved, and Winston promised to leave within the hour and text Liam as soon as he was settled with Ella.

"Until we wrap this, I'd like to keep someone on her twenty-four/seven," Liam added, knowing full well what he was asking. The SSA was still a relatively new operation, and the mission statement didn't focus on bodyguard services. Even if it did, the agency simply didn't have the manpower yet, particularly because Ryan and Stark were very selective in who they brought onto the team.

"Pull who you need from the Starfire's security team," Ryan instructed Winston. "And if we hit a snag, we'll figure it out. You coming in today?" The last question was directed at Liam.

"Yeah. We're holed up at the moment. We need to get some sleep, then we'll head back to LA. I'd like the whole team available. Say one o'clock? And I've already got a project for Mario. I'll ping him next and get him working his magic."

Once the call ended, he shot Mario the details of the assignment and the log-on for the cameras, figuring he'd call the kid when he woke up if he didn't find a reply waiting on his phone. Might as well let at least one person sleep until morning.

The kid pinged him back in less than a minute. *On it.*

Liam just shook his head, then laid back and closed his eyes, only to open them moments later when the smell of coffee roused him.

Except it wasn't mere moments later. He'd gone to sleep in the dark, and now light was streaming in through the gap in the cheap, ugly curtains. The aroma was coming from a white paper cup, being held by the beautiful—and once again clothed—woman sitting on the edge of the bed and smiling at him.

"Tell me you didn't walk down to the office."

"Crappy coffee maker. I found it under the bathroom sink."

He pushed himself up and took the cup she offered. She was right; it was crappy coffee. But it was hot and it was caffeinated, and that made it perfect. "What time is it?"

"Just past eight."

He frowned. "We should get going. All the way to LA riding tandem on the Ducati..." He shook his head. "You're going to want a few breaks."

"I'll be fine," she assured him, then looked down at her hands, which were twisting in her lap. "Listen, I'm sorry about jumping you last night."

"Are you? I'm not." The moment the words were out of his mouth he regretted them, fearing that was exactly what she didn't want to hear.

But then he saw the tension leave her shoulders, and heard her soft, breathy, "Oh, thank God," and an unexpected but not unwelcome flood of relief flowed over him, too.

He took her hand in his. "And just so you know, you're stuck with me now. It's an old security agent code. Once a woman jumps you, you're bound to protect her."

"I'm pretty sure that's not a thing."

"It's my thing." He stood up, still holding the half-finished coffee. "Susan," he said, intentionally using her given name to underscore his words, "those men are dangerous, and they're not going to stop. I'm going to help you no matter what. It will be easier if you simply tell me what's going on. The full story. But even if you don't say a word, one way or another, I'll figure it out."

He used the tip of his forefinger to tilt her chin up, then waited until she'd met his eyes. "You're more than just my mission now, and I will keep you safe."

Her lips twitched as if she was fighting a smile. "This time it's personal?"

He held her gaze. "Yes." The word was flat, even, and very true.

She looked away before she reached for his coffee and took a sip. It was an oddly intimate moment, and he couldn't deny that he liked it.

She glanced down at the cup, then handed it back to him with an embarrassed smile. She was still seated on the edge of the bed, and now she put her hands on her knees, her eyes on the floor.

"I don't want to tell you. I haven't even told Ella. Not all of it, anyway."

"Maybe it's time."

"Yeah. Maybe it is."

Her shoulders rose and fell as she drew in two deep breaths. Then she sat up straight, faced him dead on, and said, "First of all, my name isn't Susan."

11

I DON'T WANT to tell him this. I don't want to think about it. I don't want to let any of it into my head.

Except it's never really left my head. I'm twenty-eight years old, and I've been carrying a nightmare around with me for eleven long years. I may have escaped the house of horror I'd been locked in for what felt like a lifetime, but I never escaped the memories.

To his credit, Liam hasn't said a word in response to my revelation that I'm not the woman he thought I was. He's giving me time, which I guess proves what a mess I am if it's that obvious I need a moment to pull my shit together and figure out how the hell I can tell him my story without making it sound like I'm looking for a career writing telenovellas.

Finally, I get into bed, my back against the wall, my knees up, and the covers over me. He hesitates, then sits at the foot of the bed, watching me warily.

"My name's Jenny. Jenny Smith. Seriously," I add, when his brow twitches. "Boring name, and it used to fit my pretty boring life."

"I find it hard to believe you were ever boring," he says, and I roll my eyes.

"I'm from Missouri. My dad had a high school education and managed a convenience store. My mom worked part-time at a day care center. I made average grades, was horribly shy, and dreamt about blossoming one day and becoming a famous actress." I let my shoulders rise and fall. "Like I said, boring."

"I don't know," Liam says. "Sounds normal. And that's not the same thing."

"Maybe, but I spent a lot of time fantasizing about escaping and being discovered. I skipped over the whole auditioning and performing part in those fantasies, of course. But that's the point of fantasies." I shake my head. "God, I was so naive."

"What changed?"

"Everything," I say, then wave away my words. "Sorry. That's actually true, but I'll talk you through it." I don't want to. I don't want to share my humiliation with him, not to mention my fear. But I know he's right. If he's going to help me, he needs to know everything. And the bottom line is that I do want his help.

If it weren't for the attack on Ella in Vegas and us in the cabin, maybe I wouldn't. Maybe I would have been happy to stick with the status quo, living in semi-hiding by riding on Ella's coattails.

I don't know. But now that things have changed, I don't want to go back. I want to get free.

But what scares me the most is that my newfound resolve isn't just because I want to escape the ever-looming threat. It's because of the man. He's given me hope. A glimpse at a real life. I don't mean with him—I won't allow myself to think that boldly—but a future. A real one in the real world, and hopefully I'll find someone to share it with.

"Did I lose you?"

His gentle words pull me back to the moment. "Yeah. Sorry. My mind started wandering."

"You were boring," he says, both prompting me and making me laugh.

"You make fun, but it's true." I draw a breath. "Anyway, when I was a junior, my mom died. Cancer. She'd been feeling bad for a while, but blew it off, thinking she was just tired. By the time she went to the doctor there wasn't anything he could do."

I close my eyes, fighting back my tears. "That was the one part of my life that wasn't boring," I whisper, then look at him. "My parents were great. They loved me and I loved them, and we all actually liked each other, too. And my mom and dad? God, they were so in love it was disgusting. Major PDA, you know. I used to think it was cringe-worthy, but now..."

"Your father must have been a wreck," Liam says gently.

"Understatement." I wipe my runny nose. "That was the beginning of it all, not that me or Daddy knew it at the time. But looking back—I can't even mourn my mom's death without mourning my own life, too. Because burying her set everything in motion."

"How?"

"Daddy spiraled down. I mean, he really went off the rails. I was just starting to think about college. I would have been the first in my family to go. And then one day my dad came home and said that he'd sent in my picture to some modeling agency. He said he knew it wasn't the same as acting, but maybe it was a start."

I look at Liam, expecting him to say something, but he's silent, so I press on, wishing that he'd derailed me.

"He told me that the agency wanted to meet me in person. In New York. He seemed so excited, and I was, too. I mean, *me*. Shy Jenny Smith who was halfway invisible in school."

"It's not unreasonable," Liam says. "You're both stunning and unique, and you definitely have the build and height of a runway model."

"All of which I told myself on the days when I feared that the whole trip would be a waste of time. But they actually paid for the plane ticket. The agency, I mean. And the hotel. And when we got to the office, there were all these posters of models and framed pages from advertisements and it was all so very, very legitimate."

"Except it wasn't."

I lick my suddenly dry lips and hug my knees tighter to my chest. "No." I open my mouth to speak, and then close it again. "I'm sorry," I finally whisper. "It's just that it was—"

"Sex trafficking," he says, and my entire body sags with relief that I don't have to say it out loud or explain or any of that.

"I'm sorry to say I have some knowledge of that," he continues. "I mentioned Dallas and Jane before? Well, their kidnapping wasn't part of a sex trafficking ring, but Dallas started an organization. More of a vigilante group. Deliverance. And part of its mission was to rescue victims of kidnapping, trafficking, anything of that sort."

"You were part of that?"

"I was. I'd still be except that Deliverance doesn't exist as such anymore."

"So you ended up at the SSA?"

"That's about the extent of it. And you? How did you survive?"

I swallow, not wanting to go back to the topic, but knowing I have to. And the small diversion has calmed me down, so that it's easier to talk about.

"They told my dad I had talent and that they were certain I'd be a star. They had an apartment building for their candidates and told him that the board had decided to grant me a scholarship to train as a model—most girls had to pay they said."

"Your father believed them."

"I never blamed him for that. I thought so, too. They were very convincing. And me and my dad were pretty naive." I suck in air. "Right, well, anyway. My dad left that first night and said he'd be back. But he wasn't. And after a while—it was really subtle—they started to suggest that he'd left me there because he didn't love me and didn't want me around after Mom died. And then..."

I pause because I have to swallow, and I realize I'm crying. "They got me hooked on drugs. Pills they forced us to take to get our food. Supposedly appetite suppressants so that we could get model fit, but that was bullshit. And then suddenly my photo shoots were nudes. And my head was swimming all the time. And there were parties and these men, and they'd choose me and touch me and—well, they did things to me."

"You don't have to—"

"Yes. I do. They made me have sex to survive. I had no control over anything. My life. My clothes. Sex. Anything. They'd tie me up and let men use me. Sometimes one. Sometimes many. Sometimes for days on end. Sometime the men would be gentle, but not usually. I was a fucking sex slave, and they were in charge of everything, even down to tying my tubes—I told you I wouldn't get pregnant—and doing that laser hair removal thing on me so they didn't have to worry about getting me waxed. Fuckers."

I've been mostly talking to my knees, but now I look at his face. It's tight; I can see the anger and tension. And a single muscle in his cheek twitches. The sight warms me, because he cares. He genuinely cares, and I blink again, staving off more tears.

"Anyway," I continue. "I tried to escape. We were right in the middle of Manhattan, but I might as well have been on the moon. It was a nightmare. I was high all the time. Or drunk. And I hated it but I was so miserable and lonely that high was better than living in the real world. Especially since they kept telling me that my father left me there because he didn't want to deal with me after my mother died, and if I just made the investors happy my life would change."

"You believed them."

"Not at first. But more and more I started to think it had to be true. And then—oh, God—after about a year they brought me into a room and my dad was there. And he saw me and started crying. He apologized for not knowing what they would do to me. He told me he'd tried and tried to get me out, but they were powerful and he kept hitting walls, and then they grabbed him. He'd been locked up in the same building as me for almost three months, and I didn't even know."

"Jenny…"

"*No.* Please. Xena. Jenny was a fool. A stupid little girl." I look at him defiantly. "I'm Xena now. I'm a goddamn warrior."

"Damn right you are." He takes my hand, then gently squeezes it. "Tell me what happened."

"They told me I was never getting out, and that neither was my father. And then—and then they shot him." I gasp as that horrible memory cuts through me. "And then they brought another girl in. I had no idea why. I was still in shock. And they told me that she wanted out, too. And they shot her as well. I just stood there, completely numb. I didn't do a damn thing."

Tears streak down my cheeks, but I don't wipe them away. "And then the head guy, he looks at me and he says, "How about you, Jenny? Do you want out, too?'"

I force myself to look at Liam then, and I'm so goddamned ashamed. "I couldn't say yes. They gave me an out, but I couldn't say yes. I chose the pain and the degradation and living like that because I couldn't—"

"You chose life." His voice is gentle, and his eyes glisten. "And you were right. Because you did get away."

"I did," I agree. "I figured out ways not to take the pills. To not drink at the parties. I hadn't made enough of an effort before because I didn't care. My dad had thrown me away, after all. But when I learned the truth ... well, I didn't want to be numb anymore."

"You got clean?"

"Not completely when I was in there, but mostly. But after I got out, yeah. I got help in California. Counseling for all the—well, everything. And I started going to AA." My heart is pounding and I'm breathing hard. "I've been clean for years now—no alcohol, no drugs, because they fucking got me addicted and now I can't even enjoy a glass of wine without risking sliding back. I don't think I would—I really don't—but I'm damn sure not going to take the risk. But those assholes had no qualms about stealing every bit of control from me."

"But you did get away. How? For that matter, when?"

"A few days after I turned twenty-one."

His eyes widen. "They had you for four years?"

"Just about. Later, they moved me to a country estate where they held these elaborate sex parties. It was all very surreal."

"How did you get away?"

"I pretended to be docile. And I pretended to be high. They pay less attention to the older girls. We're pretty beaten by then. And so one night I was supposed to entertain this old prick who wanted to walk the grounds. He— well, let's just say he was very nature-oriented. And we were deep in the woods and he had me bent over, and there was a rock, and—" I shrug.

"Christ. Good for you."

I exhale, only then realizing I was afraid he'd chastise me for banging the fucker over the head with a rock.

"I didn't kill him, but he was out cold when I ran. I took his jacket, and my dress was short. So I was mostly invisible in the dark woods. And I worked my way around the house to the side lot where the valets parked the guests' cars. I found an unlocked SUV, got into the back, and waited, terrified someone would find my guy or realize I was gone. But it worked out. The SUV's owner came out with one of the few female guests at these things, and they drove off. Neither of them looked in the back, and she spent the entire drive to Manhattan giving him blowjobs."

"You're pretty damn lucky."

"Don't I know it. It was a huge risk, and I was sure I was done for, but I was desperate, and they didn't catch me, and I ended up in a car park in Manhattan, and suddenly I was free."

Even now, that sounds amazing to say, despite the fact that I was beyond terrified for months after that. Liam asks me how I survived, and I tell him I stole a woman's wallet—something I'm still ashamed of—and she had over five hundred in cash and an ID that was passable enough for me to use. I bought sweats and a T-shirt from a place that was open in Times Square, and hair dye from a Duane Reade. Then I got on a train and went to Pennsylvania. And from there I hitchhiked to Los Angeles.

"And Ella doesn't know any of that?"

I shake my head. "As far as she's concerned, I was a runaway turning tricks in Hollywood. And that's not really a lie, either. I did run away. And I did turn tricks."

"And you survived." He cups my face, then kisses me gently. "Baby, you are an amazing woman."

"No, I'm not. But I guess I am a survivor."

He strokes my hair, my shoulder. It feels nice, as if he's trying to reassure himself that I'm here and I'm whole. As if my story has broken him a little, too.

He asks me questions about the sex scheme. The names of the men, the location of the buildings. I tell him what I can, and he seems to absorb it all.

"But now they've found me," I say with a shrug. "I guess I always knew they would."

"It's good that they did," he says firmly. "Because now we can take them out, and you won't have to worry about them anymore."

"I'm scared." My words are a whisper, and I feel weak even saying them.

"I don't blame you," he says. "But I'm with you now. And just remember what you already told me. You, Xena, are a survivor."

12

A SURVIVOR.

"I am," I say. "But that doesn't mean I want to be. I thought I was past it when I was with Ella. But then one stupid picture, and every horrible thing I did to survive suddenly means nothing anymore."

"It means everything," he says. "Because you did survive. And you have those skills—that grit—to keep you going now."

I screw up my mouth and shrug. "Sometimes it all feels so futile. And random." I reach for the cup and the dregs of cold coffee, but he takes it from my hand with a shake of his head.

"Random how?" he asks, as he goes to the bathroom and fills the coffee maker.

"Do you know how I became Susie Morgan?"

He looks at me over his shoulder. "I've seen some of the world you lived in, Xena. So yeah, I can probably guess."

"Try." I hear the challenge in my voice, because there is no way he'll guess the depths of my shame.

"She was a hooker," he says. "Parents dead. Ran away

from foster care. Ended up turning tricks in the City of Angels. Not an uncommon story, really."

My mouth is dry. He's dead on point.

"How am I doing so far?"

"You cheated."

"Rye told me some—he checked you out years ago. I did a bit more on my way to the cabin. Or I had my team do it. Of course, those are the dry facts. For the rest, I'll have to be a little more creative."

"All right. Go on."

"You met her in LA, somewhere near Hollywood Boulevard. Maybe at a diner. A laundromat. She may have even been the girl who showed you the ropes. Who taught you how to survive without a pimp, because after what you went through, you wouldn't have gone that route."

"No." My voice is thin. "I definitely wouldn't."

He brings me the cup of coffee, and I blow on it before taking a tiny sip.

"I can't guess what happened, but somehow she died. And you assumed her identity, because you needed a clean slate, and you knew she would have wanted to help you."

My eyes are welling up again, but I nod. "She was a user. It was the one thing we fought about. And she got in deep with a dealer—owed him a lot of money. He decided to make an example of her."

"The cops never ID'd her?"

"As far as I know, her body was never found. I got one of those concrete garden marker kits and made one in her honor. Then I buried this goofy stuffed cat she loved and her lucky rabbit's tail." I look at him defiantly. "But I kept her life. She would have wanted me to."

"No argument from me. Did you keep turning tricks?"

I nod. "I didn't like it, but it was like being the CEO of my own business compared to the life I had before. But I also enrolled in school, because I wasn't going to turn tricks forever. I'd have to lay low no matter what job I got—I knew that. But I also knew that if I couldn't have a family, then I at least needed a job where I didn't have to sell myself."

I wait for him to ask why I had to be alone, but instead he tells me the reason.

"Because they'd never stop looking for you. Because your past—your life—could put them at risk."

"Yes," I whisper, hating that basic truth. "No way would I —" My voice breaks, and I force myself to go on. "I saw my father murdered in front of me. And I knew they'd do the same thing to anyone else I cared about. If they found me —*when* they found me—they'd kill everyone I loved in front of me."

I take a deep breath, certain he's going to try to placate me. Tell me that I shouldn't distance myself or that love is worth the risk or some such bullshit.

He looks right at me, but I don't think he sees me at all. And he whispers, "You're right."

The words linger between us, dark and horrible. I fight the urge to ask what's in his head, because I'm certain it's more than just me and my problems. He's seen tragedy, too, and in that moment, I want to hold him. To share what little strength I have. Right then, I think he needs it.

But then he stands, his hands in his pockets, as he goes and looks out that small slit in the curtains. "So you went to school."

I hesitate, wondering if I should push, but I don't. It's not my place, and what would be the point? This man is here to protect me because Ella wants him to. And I want it, too. I want him and his friends and the fucking National Guard if he can arrange it to be on my side. I want him to find out who's after me and I want him to make them go away.

And then I want to disappear again and hope for a few calm years before someone else from my horrific past surfaces again. In my dreams, yes, I might want Liam to disappear with me. But I learned a long time ago that story-books lie, and dreams don't really come true.

He turns to me. "Xena?"

"School. Right, yes." I clear my throat, trying to remember what I was saying. "So, yeah. I had to take the GED, but it wasn't a big deal. I started taking business classes at a community college during the day and turning tricks at night. And I kept going to my AA and NA meetings, and I kept seeing my counselor every week." I meet his eyes dead on. "You might say I had a few issues."

"I'm shocked," he says, making me laugh.

"Yeah, well, I was determined to get it behind me and make something of myself. Make my dad proud, you know?"

"I guess you did. You ended up with a great job working with Ella."

"Oh, man. That was a freaky day. It was my twenty-fourth birthday, and I'd been beat up by a John the night before, so I had this nasty bruise on my cheek."

I point, as if it's still red and swollen. Sometimes I think it should be, the fucker hit me so hard.

"I was in a pissy mood because I'd gotten a shit score on a paper I'd turned in about services for the homeless, and the professor had the audacity to say that I hadn't put in enough research and—" I make a slashing motion with my hand and rein myself in.

"Anyway," I continue, "the point is that I was a mess. But I went to the interview anyway. I figured it was good prac-tice, but I was certain I wouldn't get the job. I'd had no idea who she was when I applied, but after I got the interview, I learned she was this rising pop singer. Nowhere close to where she is now, but she was getting radio play and, well, I figured there was no way in hell she'd hire me."

"But you went anyway."

"Like I said, practice. And, I don't know. I just felt like going."

He grins as he comes to sit on the bed again, only closer this time. "The universe was starting to shift in your favor."

"Maybe so. Anyway, I go in, and she immediately asks about my cheek. I wasn't sure what to say, so I just sort of evaded. Then she asked about school, and since I was steamed about the paper, I told her. She asked me about my research and I went off on her completely."

"She was a stand-in for your professor."

"Big time. I told her I worked on the street and knew what I was talking about, and that I interacted with the homeless daily, and that I'd been homeless for two months when I first moved there, and that if she really wanted to know, my cheek got busted when a John decided to demonstrate his right hook."

"So what happened?"

"She asked me when I could start." I laugh. "At first I thought she wanted to sleep with me—I knew from my research that she'd had girlfriends."

"But nothing there?"

I shake my head, glance at him, then look down at my knees. "Nothing. I like men, even though I haven't slept with that many who, you know, I actually wanted to be with. You're kind of a notable exception."

He reaches out, his hand resting on my covered foot. "I'm flattered."

I look up, then get a little lost in his eyes. In the strength

I see there, and the compassion. I'm spilling all this shit onto him, and I don't see anything reflected back at me that makes me want to curl into myself. I'm the same person to him I was yesterday and the day before. And right then, I really want to kiss him.

"Thank you," I whisper.

"For what?"

I try to wrap my thoughts into words. "For everything I guess. For protecting me. For the way you've touched me." I glance down, no longer meeting his eyes. "For not asking me if I've been tested now that you know my history. I have, you know. Lots." I draw a breath, and look up to see his eyes on me, soft with compassion ... and something more, too. "Anyway, thanks for being a really great guy."

"My pleasure." He smiles as he says it, but his words are underscored with just a tiny bit of heat. Or maybe I'm just hopeful. Or stupid. Because I like this man more than I should. And I want him more than is safe.

He's had it rough, too, I think. More than suffering through a friend's kidnapping and surviving combat. But I don't want to ask. I'm melancholy enough simply from going over my own dark past.

"You and Ella went from employer/employee to genuine friends," he says, and I'm both grateful and frustrated that he hasn't been reading my mind. Because I'm suddenly very aware of the pressure of his hand on my foot. And the fact that he's so close to me on the bed.

I shouldn't feel this way—I know that. And yet I want. I just *want*.

I bite my lower lip, then barrel forward. "You're kind of like Ella."

"It's the hair, isn't it?"

I narrow my eyes, but otherwise ignore the quip. "I just mean that you're the kind of guy that usually scares me."

"Usually?"

I silently curse as he takes his hand off my foot, then smile with relief as he slides a bit closer before reaching over to take my hand, making my pulse kick up its tempo. I like this feeling. This will-we or won't-we. I haven't done this much—the real thing between men and women. I'm not an expert in reading clues or flirting. When a man is forcing or paying, there's really no need for subtlety.

Most of the time I'm terrified of my own emotions. But right now, I want this. Whatever the hell *this* is.

He holds my hand lightly, his fingertips moving over my skin. "Usually," he repeats thoughtfully. "So are you saying I don't scare you?"

I swallow. "If you were paying attention last night, you should know that you don't."

"I'm glad."

I look down at our joined hands. "I'll admit to a bit of nervousness."

His eyes meet mine. "What do you have to be nervous about?"

Everything.

"The fact that you don't scare me." I hear the breathiness in my voice. "That's kind of terrifying."

He tilts his head, but doesn't say anything.

"Don't take this the wrong way, but I want more than to not be scared. I want to trust you, too."

"And you don't?" I can't read anything in his face or his tone. I don't know if I've amused him or offended him, but I rush to reassure and explain anyway.

"On some level, I do. I mean, I'm here with you and my life is in your hands. But that's not really trust."

"Isn't it?"

Once again, I try to read his face, but fail. "No," I confirm. "It's just pragmatism. I don't think I'll ever really trust anyone again. I've gone too long looking over my shoulder."

"And yet there's Ella."

I look at him, and wonder if it's hope that I'm hearing in his voice. Or if that emotion belongs entirely to me.

"Yes," I say. "There's Ella."

"But she's a woman. I'm not a woman, Xena."

"No, you definitely aren't."

"And I would never, ever hurt you."

"I believe you."

He reaches out, then strokes my cheek before sliding his fingers into my hair. "So soft," he murmurs, then brushes my lower lip with his fingertip. "So beautiful."

"Liam," I whisper.

"You don't trust me, but you want me."

"Yes," I say.

"Why?"

"Because you make me feel safe, and I don't mean from whoever is chasing me. I mean in here," I explain, pressing a hand to my heart. "Safe to be me and not what they wanted me to be."

His brow furrows, his expression growing dark.

"I'm sorry," I say quickly. "I don't want to burden you or make you think you're part of a therapy session. Last night was a frenzy, but right now is desire." My words are tumbling out, and I'm not even sure if I'm making sense. "I just want you, Liam. Right now, I think I need you." I lick my lips. "Don't you want me, too?"

He makes a soft scoffing noise. "How can you even ask that? Of course I want you. But I can't have you," he adds as he runs his fingers through my hair. "Not the way I want."

"Sure, you can," I say. "Of course you can."

But he just shakes his head, and it's like a fist squeezing my heart because I'm certain he's saying no. Then he whispers, "You break down all my defenses."

"That's good," I say.

He shakes his head. "No. It isn't."

I sag with disappointment, but before I can argue or ask him to explain, he cups my head, tugs me toward him, and kisses me.

I melt into it, the bed covers dropping as I shift onto my knees and scoot closer toward him.

"No," he says, then eases me back so that I'm flat on the mattress, my body dwarfed beneath his. "Like this."

I melt into the kiss, his lips on mine, his hands roaming over my tank, then easing under the hem as he gently pulls it off me. He tosses it on the chair by the window then closes his mouth on my breast, his tongue doing incredible things to my nipple.

I arch up, wanting more. Expecting the same wicked wildness from last night. A raw, primal passion that I can lose myself in.

But this touch isn't wild. It's contained—as if he's holding back. His touch feels so damn good, but I crave more, and I want to pound on him to let go. To ravage me. To *take* me. To let me feel whatever passion he feels. To be real, because I've never actually had real before.

I want all that, and yet those thoughts and demands fade against the sweetness of his touch. As his teeth lightly graze my nipple. As his hands trace down my belly, then gently tug my yoga pants off and send them flying toward my top.

"Your turn," I murmur, and he nods as I start to tug at his

clothes until he's as naked as I am. "Better," I say, sliding my hand down to find his cock, only to be stymied when he gently pulls it away.

"Put your hands on my back," he says, and I do, relishing the sensations of his muscles moving beneath my touch as he kisses his way down my body, using his own hands to spread my legs even wider as the tip of his tongue finds my clit.

I moan and arch up, trying to wiggle my hips, but he has me held firmly in place, and all I can do is surrender to the glorious sensation. I move one hand from his shoulder to his head, then press him harder against me. I'm rewarded when he shifts from the tiny, teasing movements of his tongue, to laving me completely as his fingers slide inside me, and my hips rock of their own accord in a primal effort to bring this man further and further inside me.

"Yes, yes." The word seems to fill the room, and it takes a second before I realize it's me.

He slides up me again, capturing my mouth as he enters me. It's sweet and gentle and so unexpected. So different from everything I've known. And as he moves inside me, I feel the growing pressure of a coming climax. The tingling on my inner thighs. The tightening of my belly. He murmurs gentle sounds, and I cling to them like a ladder, climbing higher and higher until I'm at the top and have no choice but to fall off and shatter into a million pieces as I break through the blanket of stars below me.

I tremble in his arms, warm and content. Last night in the park had been a wonderful, insane treasure. A celebration of being alive. A testament to my freedom, because God knows I'd never been able to take control like that before.

But this ... for the first time in my life I feel cherished. Adored. Respected.

It's not everything I need in bed—I know that. But what I crave is something I shouldn't want. Something that scares me and makes me fear that I'll never truly get past what happened to me.

I roll over and stroke his face, rough with beard stubble, then trace his lips, soft and swollen from my kisses.

"Thank you," I say, and I sigh as a tiny bit of hope creeps into me. This man is a miracle, and I've never been a woman who believes in miracles.

13

"THIS BATHROOM IS FREAKING AMAZING," Xena said, her voice drifting to Liam from behind the closed door.

He grinned; that was a guest's typical reaction to his master bath, a room that always made him smile. "You've met the fish."

The door opened, and she stood there in a pair of Universal Studios Hollywood sweat pants and a souvenir Santa Monica T-shirt, her freshly washed hair hanging in damp waves around her face. "Fish?" She cocked her head and crossed her arms. "What fish?"

"Funny. I've invited a comedian into my home for a shower and some lunch. What was I thinking?" They'd arrived back in town with time to spare before the meeting at the SSA, and so Liam had brought her to Malibu for food, fresh clothes, and a change of transportation. As much as he loved his bike, he'd happily switch to a car for the rest of the day.

"If that was your idea of humor, I feel very sorry for you." She smiled, and he smiled back, unable to resist the bubble of joy that rose inside him simply from the sight of her looking so comfortable and relaxed.

"Seriously," she continued. "That aquarium is amazing. All those incredible colored fish. And all these plants, too."

"I travel too much to have a dog or a cat, but I like the feeling of having life in the house. It reminds me of home." Though the public areas of the Sykes mansion had regular deliveries of flowers and plants from a local nursery, the wing that he shared with his mother had been filled solely with the flowers and greenery that she tended. He'd missed the scent of the dirt, the coolness of the leaves, and the varied colors of the flowers during his time in the Middle East. And during his years traveling for the department store and Deliverance, he'd only managed to keep a cactus and an aloe vera plant growing in his window.

When he'd started working for the SSA and moved into the condo, he'd made sure that the massive remodel included sufficient windows to provide light for the interior plants. And he'd put enough greenery on the balcony to rival a rain forest.

"Have you named them?"

"The plants?"

"Now you're just messing with me. The fish. Because in case you hadn't noticed, they take up an entire wall in that bathroom."

"Yeah. I'm aware."

"And the shower is glass."

"I'm also clued in to that." He had to fight a smile.

"I just feel that since every one of those fish was checking me out, we're kind of intimate now. I should probably know their names."

"I'll get right on that. In the meantime," he said, moving

to stand in front of her and sliding an arm around her waist, "let's just call them what they are—some very lucky fish."

"That's true," she said. "After all, you shower in there almost every day."

"Sometimes twice a day. It's my favorite room. That and the patio," he added, hooking his thumb over his shoulder to indicate the glass doors that led to the balcony—and the stunning view of the Pacific.

"Oh, really?" Her voice rose with a tease. "Not the bedroom?"

"To be honest, the bedroom's not used for much more than sleeping and reading and blowing off steam."

"Blowing off steam?" Her brows rose with interest. "That sounds like a euphemism for what we did this morning. And last night."

He wanted to say no. To tell her that she was so much more than one of his rare hook-ups. But he honestly didn't know what she was. All he knew for sure was that he wanted to touch her again.

And that she couldn't be his.

So what he said instead was, "As euphemisms go, that's probably fair. But not frequent."

"A selective man." The lightness in her voice sounded a bit forced, and her throat moved as she swallowed. "I'm flattered."

"Listen, Xena—" He cut himself off. What the hell was he supposed to say? That there wasn't anything between them? She knew that. That he wanted her in his bed again? She knew that, too. That a fuck didn't mean a future? Once again, she knew that as well. Moreover, she was already well settled on the no-relationship train.

"What?"

He rubbed his temples. "That euphemism is exactly

what it sounds like. I don't do relationships, and there is no woman in my life. But every once in a while, I want what I want."

Her mouth twisted. "You don't have to be coy with me, you know. I mean, hey, I could probably find you an expert call girl at a really reasonable rate."

"Christ, Xena, I—"

"Sorry. I'm sorry." She ran her fingers through her hair. "I'm tired and I'm hungry and even though we aren't a thing, it still feels really fucked up for you to be telling me that you don't do relationships and don't have a girlfriend. I mean, why lie?"

"What are you talking about?"

She pointed to the pants, then the shirt. "These just happened to be in a drawer? A drawer completely filled with girl-stuff, including a vibrator?"

"A vibrator?" He had to fight a laugh. "Everything in that drawer belongs to Denny." And it would take all his willpower not to give her shit about the vibrator.

"That means nothing to me. You know that, right?"

"She's a friend, and she's with the SSA," he began. "She takes care of my fish and plants when I'm out of town. She stays in the downstairs guest room, but I gave her a drawer up here so she could use the fish shower." He went on to tell her about Denny's husband, Mason, and how he'd come back after being lost to her for so long. "I'm guessing the toy was a pre-Mason thing. Either that or she left it in the drawer to embarrass me if I ever poked around in her stuff."

That, he thought, would be just like Denny. It also fouled up his plans to give her grief.

Well, hell.

"So there's nothing between you two?"

"Pretty sure I just made that clear. I told you. I don't do relationships. And I don't do friends with benefits, either."

"Out of curiosity, what am I?" She leaned against the dresser, studying him openly. "Or are we done, um, blowing off steam?"

"You're a damsel in distress," he said, making her laugh.

"Yeah, I'm *so* the damsel. But the distress part is pretty accurate."

"Exactly. And in the kind of a stressful situation that you're in—that we're both in—blowing off a little steam could be good for both of us."

"Agreed. It's—what's that word?—pragmatic. Or maybe cathartic."

"Could be both."

"We just totally justified fucking again, didn't we?"

"I think we did."

She grinned at him. "Do you know what I want right this very second?"

He lifted his brows and made an attempt to leer at her. "Lunch?"

"God, yes," she said, and he realized that he was having more fun with this woman than he'd had in a very long time.

"How does lasagna sound?"

"Fabulous, considering I haven't had anything since that Snickers we got from the motel vending machine. But I don't think we have time to go out. Do we?"

"Who said anything about going out? Come on." He ushered her out of the bedroom and down the stairs to the kitchen. "I made it the night before I flew to Vegas. It's still fine," he said, pulling a casserole dish of lasagna out of the fridge and sliding two generous pieces onto microwavable plates.

She looked from the lasagna to him and back again. "Seriously?"

"What? I promise it's still good." He popped the first plate into the microwave. "Lasagna will last four, five days as leftovers."

"No, no. I'm sure it's fine," she said. "I'm just impressed." She shrugged. "Of course, I'm a natural in the kitchen, too."

"Yeah?"

"Oh, sure. Pasta, even. My ramen could totally give that piddly-ass lasagna a run for its money."

"And you said you didn't get to do the college thing."

She smirked, then sat on the bar-height stool on the other side of the kitchen island. "Serious question for you."

"Uh-oh."

"Why don't you do relationships?"

He hesitated, then turned to the microwave when it dinged. "Let's just say that you and I are more alike than either of us probably imagined."

His back was to her when he spoke, and when he turned to pass her the plate and a fork, he could see the questions forming on her face and was grateful when she didn't ask him to explain.

He heated up his own serving, and they both dug into the food, her at the bar and him still in the kitchen, eating at the counter. He was going back for a second piece when she mentioned that she'd talked to Ella.

"She called while I was in the bathroom. They can't trace me through my phone, can they?"

"No," he said automatically, then added, "probably not. We'll replace it at the office, just in case." He had no idea how well funded the men after her were, but considering their years of persistence, he assumed there was a large cash pool financing the enterprise. And while the odds were slim, there was at least a theoretical possibility that they could track her when she used her phone. And as far as Liam was concerned, "slim" wasn't good odds at all.

"Okay," she said, and he was grateful she didn't argue. Then again, unlike most clients he'd been tasked with protecting, for Xena the endgame was real, not hypothetical. She knew they would kill her because she'd witnessed them do that very thing to her father. Most people didn't really believe it, even when they were running for their lives.

"—so thank you."

Shit. He grimaced. "Sorry. My mind wandered. What did I do to deserve your thanks?"

"Ella said you sent a guy. Winston? Thanks for watching her back."

"That's what I'm here for. I hope he's bored out of his mind and has nothing to do, but I want him there since they may believe that she knows where you are. And they may try to convince her to tell them."

"She doesn't know. I didn't tell her."

"Good." He took a sip of sparkling water. "Winston texted me, too. Told me that Ella's thrilled he's there, but Rye seems a little on edge."

She took another bite, then swallowed. "I suppose that makes sense. He probably thought with me gone, all would be well." She shrugged. "He's a good manager, and he really does love her, but he's a little overprotective. And I think my sordid past always disturbed him."

"I'm sorry about that. You've been doing a great job for Ella for years. Any hesitations he had should have been alleviated by now."

"And yet, bad guys." She shrugged. "So maybe he was right."

He wanted to argue—to tell her she didn't deserve Rye's

hesitation or condemnation or whatever the hell it was—but she'd already moved on and was thanking him for the food. "It was delicious," she said. "You really made it from scratch?"

"I'm a man of many talents."

"You're an interesting guy, Liam."

"Am I?"

"All these plants thriving. A refrigerator with real food."

"Truly, I am amazing."

She smirked. "You've fed me, clothed me. Fucked me."

"Not exactly a hardship."

"You've taken care of me in every way possible." She smiled, a little shyly. "I really do appreciate it. I know it's a job, and I should be scared out of my mind right now, but I'm not." She indicated the room, the food. "You've made me feel normal. Special, even. So thank you."

"You're welcome, but with talk like that, you're going to completely destroy my reputation as a badass, you know that right?"

"I could be persuaded to keep your secret."

He took both their dishes and slid them into the sink, then leaned back against the refrigerator, facing her. "Could you? And what's your price?"

"We still have some time," she said with a grin. "I thought we could blow off some steam."

14

"So, forgive the fan girl thing, but I really do love Ellie Love's music."

"She's amazing," I agree, unable to take my eyes off of the stunning woman standing in front of me. She's tall and ridiculously beautiful, with coal black hair streaked with pink and purple, and a tiny diamond stud in her nose that catches the sunlight streaming in through the windows in the open area of the Stark Security offices.

But what really draws my focus is the incredible bird tattoo that starts at her shoulder blade and trails down her arm. She's wearing a sleeveless silk top and skinny jeans, and the colorful plumage was the first thing I noticed when Liam ushered me into the room.

"What's it like working for her?"

"Ellie's great," I say honestly, trying to remember this woman's name. "Really. I don't have anything bad to say. Except when she's being a bitch, and then I say it to her face. But honestly, she's hardly ever a bitch."

"You really like her."

"I really do."

"Glad to hear it. Hanging around with Jackson and Damien, I've met a few celebrities. Most are nice, but some are fucking nuts."

"True that." I frown, mentally untangling her words. Damien Stark I've heard of, obviously. A billionaire businessman who used to be a pro tennis player, he's in the news a lot. Plus, his name's on the door, and Liam told me that Stark founded the SSA after his daughter was kidnapped. "Who's Jackson?"

"Stark's half-brother. Jackson Steele. You know his work," she adds. "You're staying with Liam, right? He did the remodel. And this building, too. This whole complex, actually."

"Oh! I have heard of him." The Domino is a high-end business complex in the part of Santa Monica now known as Silicon Beach because it has so many tech companies. There was some controversy about the complex and it was all over the news during construction.

"He's great. And his wife Sylvia and I have been besties since the beginning of time."

I nod, knowing that I won't manage to keep any of this straight. "So what do you do here? It's Cassie, right?" I ask, pleased with myself for finally remembering.

"Cassidy, actually. Cassidy Cunningham. But everyone calls me Cass. And I don't do a thing except occasionally pop by to steal Denny for lunch."

I look around the room, which is ridiculous since I have no idea what Denny looks like. "I thought she was on vacation. Liam told me a horrible story about her husband and amnesia." He's in Ryan Hunter's office, and he'd left me here with Cass, who's doing a great job of entertaining me, but I'm definitely a bit overwhelmed.

"Happy ending, though," she says, still on Mason and

Denny. "And yeah, she's lazing on a beach somewhere. No, today I'm here with Eliza and Emma. We're doing happy hour before girls' night, and I figured I'd come get them."

"Which ones are they?"

"Um, there's Eliza," she says, pointing to a woman with chestnut hair talking with a good-looking guy with a lean face and slightly tousled hair. "Eliza!" she calls. "You ready?"

Eliza gives her a thumbs-up, then kisses the guy. A polite enough kiss for the semi-public setting, but I can still feel the heat beneath it from here.

"And that is Quince," Cass says. "They're a thing."

I laugh. "Figured that out on my own."

"Have fun, love," Quince calls as Eliza approaches us. His voice is deep and rich and deliciously British. "And don't get wankered."

She flashes a flirty smile back over her shoulder to him. "But you like it when I do," she replies with a wink, and I'm absolutely certain I'm missing something.

When she turns back around, she smiles at me and holds out a hand. "Hey, you're Liam's, right?"

"Uh." I take her hand. "Liam's what?"

Her eyes crinkle. "His assignment. Or have I been misinformed?"

"Oh. Right. Yeah. He's doing a stellar job of keeping me alive."

Her head tilts as if she's studying me, and I wonder if I've made some horrible faux pas. Like no gallows humor in the office. But soon enough, her mouth twitches with amusement. "I'm sure he'll stick close," she says, and I actually start to blush. Which is something I haven't done in years.

"Seriously, he's great at what he does. Whatever's going on, he's got your back."

"I know. Do you work with him?"

"Work? Oh, no. I don't work here. I'm an actress. Currently out of work, but I have an audition for a small part in Francesca Muratti's next film," she adds, mentioning an A-list star I've heard of. "So I'm hoping to be gainfully employed again, soon."

"Oh." I frown between her and Cass, neither of whom are actually employed by this place.

Eliza laughs. "I'm only here right now because I'm Quince's girlfriend. God, I love saying that." She shifts her attention to Cass. "We're taking an Uber, right? Because there are three of us, and I'm not riding on the back of either one of your bikes."

Cass rolls her eyes, but Eliza lifts her phone. "Em! I'm calling an Uber now. Come on!"

I turn, and see that she's signaling to a stunning redhead standing with Liam in the doorway of Ryan Hunter's office. Mr. Hunter is there, too—dark hair, blue eyes, and looking at least as good in a suit as Liam does. When he wears one. Right now he's in jeans, which I appreciate since my attire consists of sweats and a tee.

There's another guy with them, too, and since he's holding an open laptop, I'm guessing he's Mario, the tech genius who is trying to get clear facial images of my tormentors.

Liam catches my eye and holds up a finger, indicating he'll be right over, but Emma comes right away. "Sorry, sorry," she says, then, "Oh, hey. You must be Xena."

"That's me," I say, before Eliza and Cass tell me that it was nice to meet me. Emma tells them she'll be along, and I notice the way Cass reaches for her hand, her fingers lightly skimming Emma's before Cass and Eliza head out.

"Nice to meet you," Emma says, as I wonder if she and

Cass are an item. "Sorry about all the shit you're dealing with."

"Thanks. Are you one of the agents here?"

"No, I don't work here," she says, and I'm starting to feel like I'm in a sitcom.

She must notice my expression, because she laughs. "I'm a PI. But I have an offer on the table, and since the SSA frequently works in teams of two, Ryan wanted to talk to me and Liam together.

"I thought Denny worked with Liam."

"Not usually. I think they're just really good friends. Denny and Quince team up a lot, but I guess she'll be with Mason now. At least until the baby benches her for a while. And there's Winston and Leah," she continues, making my head spin. "Between you and me, they need more women here. I know they're actively looking. And I also know they're incredibly selective. I'm flattered, but I also love my job and calling my own shots, and—and all of this is probably very boring to you. Short answer. I don't work here. Yet. Maybe never. I'm still debating."

"Well, good luck deciding."

"Thanks. And it really is great to meet you. I'm sorry it's under such horrible circumstances, but you are in exceptionally good hands."

"Yeah," I say, glancing across the room to find Liam. "I am."

———

"The cameras at her doors are pieces of shit," Mario says. "You should tell her to replace them, stat," he adds, pointing at me.

"On it," I say, while Liam shoots me a *what can you do* look.

"Fortunately," Mario continues, "I have mad skills. A few more passes with my extremely proprietary, no where else to be found, one hundred percent a Sanchez specialty, facial re-generation software, and I should have an image that's clean enough to get us some solid results once we feed it into the facial recognition databases."

"How long until we get a hit from that?" I ask.

Mario shrugs. "That depends on how charitable the system is feeling that day and how lucky you are."

"With my luck, we'll get results sometime around the next millennium."

"With your luck," Liam says firmly, squeezing my hand under the table, "we'll get them tomorrow."

I raise a brow, because clearly he's delusional.

"I'm with Liam," Quince says. "After everything you've been through, you're not only still standing, but you've got a great job with an incredibly generous woman." Because Liam told me I had to, everyone in this room now knows all the details about my truly fucked up life. I know it's necessary, but it doesn't sit well with me.

"Not to mention me watching your back," Liam says, adding a teasing smile.

I shoot him a sideways smirk. "A job I can't go back to and a woman I put in the line of fire."

"Yes," Liam repeats. "But me—and this whole team—watching your back."

"Liam—"

"No," he says, without a hint of humor in his voice. "I mean it. You've survived a hell of a life, Xena. And you have good people helping you now. Ella. Us. Maybe your luck was shit for a while, but it's changing. Help change it more by helping us."

I sag a little, because he's right. "I know. I'm sorry." I look at all of them around the table in turn. Ryan—who told me not to call him Mr. Hunter, Quince, Mario, Trevor, Leah, and, of course, Liam. I know there are a few other new recruits who are on what Ryan calls probationary duties, but this is the team that's helping me—plus Winston. With Liam taking point, of course.

"Thank you," I say. "It really does feel like my luck is changing."

"The short term goal," Liam says to the group, "is to keep Xena safe and catch our two stalkers. Use them to lead us to whoever is pulling their strings. And the longer-term goal is to take down the entire organization, assuming it still exists. Obviously, we're going to need support from law enforce- ment to make that happen, but they should be happy to let us take point early on. Ryan's going to talk with Colonel Seagrave at the SOC to see about getting us additional intel- ligence support, and he's already put a call in to Agent McKee. McKee's with the FBI," he adds to me, "and the SOC is a deep-cover, government intelligence organization. We've worked with both those agencies before."

"Wait, wait." My head is literally spinning. "You're talking an investigation that could take years."

"Possibly," Ryan says. "But if we take them down, it's worth it."

"I can't—" I cut myself off, feeling stupid. I was about to say I can't put my life on hold for years, but my life has already been on hold. Hell, I never got the chance to start my life. And I never will unless I can get this albatross off my back.

I could run, of course. I could leave Liam's house in the

middle of the night and just bolt. Leave the country, manufacture a new identity. A week ago, that's probably what I would have done. But being with Liam—talking with him, touching him—has made me crave a real life all the more. He's opened a door for me, and I think—no, I *know*—that I want to walk through it.

I draw a deep breath and nod. "This is all really overwhelming," I say. "But okay. I just—" I look at Liam, feeling suddenly desperate.

"It's okay," he says. "What?"

"Well, I can't just hang out here forever. And I can't go back to Ella, can I? I mean, that would put her in danger, right? But I have to eat and live somewhere and all that good stuff. And, well, what am I going to do for a job?"

"I think we can work that out," Ryan says. "We're ridiculously low on administrative help at the moment."

"Really?" I look between him and Liam. "I can work here while you guys are doing whatever it is you're doing?"

"According to Ella, you're hardworking, detail-oriented, and efficient. I think we could use that."

I frown, considering his words. "You already thought about this, didn't you?"

"I asked Ryan to call Ella when we were in his office," Liam says.

"Oh." I'm ridiculously pleased that he was so thoughtful. "Thank you."

We share a smile, until I break our connection and look down at my hands.

"First thing," Ryan says, "is to get as much information from you as we can. Locations. Names. I know it's been years, but any details that you can remember."

Across the table, Mario's phone makes a *ka-ching* noise,

like a slot machine paying off. He jumps to his feet, mumbles, "Mainframe," and scurries away.

"Cross your fingers that's something on the facial recognition software," Trevor says dryly. "And not a new profile hit on this week's coolest dating site."

Leah nudges him and mutters, "Stop." Mario, I'm assuming, doesn't date much.

Leah's about my height, with a mass of tight curls. I think her hair is naturally brown, but golden highlights frame her face. She has a strong jaw balanced by oval-shaped black glasses. She's not pretty so much as cute. And from the few minutes I've spent talking to her, I can tell she's super sharp.

According to Liam, she and Trevor and Denny all did security-related work under Ryan at Stark International before Stark Security was formed. And before that, Trevor and Leah worked with him at his own security company, one that Damien Stark bought out years and years ago.

There's an easiness between Trevor and Leah, so it's not hard to believe they've been in the trenches together. And the way they joke around with each other, I thought at first they were dating.

"Trev's gay, so that's a no," Liam told me after we'd arrived at the office but before he went into the meeting. "But his husband walked out a couple of years ago, and they've been rooming together since. So they're definitely close."

"What about Leah? Is she gay, too?"

"I don't think so. Denny mentioned a guy she used to date. Honestly, I don't know. She plays her life pretty close to the vest, and I'm not much for prying."

Now, Ryan pulls the conversation back by focusing on me. "Names?" he repeats. "Details?"

"Right. I don't know many. The customers always used code names."

"That's okay. We're not interested in the clients as much as the players. The big guns and the cogs. Anyone at all."

"I didn't overhear a lot. But the man who—who shot my father. I made it a point to learn his name. It's Noyce. Edward Noyce."

"Excellent," Quince says, then taps something into his phone. "If Mario's at the mainframe, he can start a search. Anyone else?" he asks me.

"I was high all the time. A lot of what's in my head is fuzzy. Surreal. But there was one time I remember, or I think I do. The memory may not even be real."

"Tell us what's in your head," Liam says, putting his hand on mine. "And we'll sort it out from there."

"Right. Sure. Okay." I draw a deep breath, not wanting to fall back into those memories, but knowing that I have to. "There was this one time when everyone in the building was freaking out. Like the world was going to end if everything wasn't perfect. The guy was coming from somewhere in Europe, and he was the big money man. I don't know why I know that, but I think I'm right. Everyone was talking like he was the absolute shit, you know?"

"And you heard his name?" Trevor asks.

"I think so. It was odd. Foreign. So I might be misremembering. But I think they called him Corbu."

Liam's eyes widen, and Quince lets out a low whistle.

"What?" I ask, looking around the table.

"You didn't misremember," Liam says. "And you may have just made this whole case ten times easier."

15

Corbu.

Liam caught Quince's eye, and saw the other man frown. Quince and Eliza had been reunited recently when the SSA had worked with an EU task force in an effort to bring down the infamous kingpin of an international sex trafficking organization. Specifically, the SSA had been tasked with obtaining information about Corbu's operations from a local scumbag, Scott Lassiter. A man that Eliza had also been pursuing, for decidedly different reasons.

"I don't understand," Xena said when Ryan excused himself to go to his office. "What did I say?"

"The magic word," Quince told her. "Corbu's in custody. And that means we have a solid shot at getting some answers."

"Seriously?" This time the question was a whisper, and her hand grasped Liam's, squeezing tight. He squeezed back, relishing the easy familiarity between them.

"Seriously," Liam assured her, then gave her the quick and dirty rundown of the operation.

"So, he's not just sitting in prison somewhere? He's been giving this task force information about all the various cells?"

"The SSA hasn't played a part since his capture," Liam told her. "But my understanding is that he's cooperating. And his various captains around the globe are singing with more force than The Three Tenors."

He had to smile. Sometimes, the system really did work. And this just might be one of those times. And maybe, just maybe, Xena really was about to get lucky.

A door slammed on the far side of the open area, and Mario hurried in, waving a printout. "Am I a genius or what? Why yes, Mario, you are the man. Truly."

By the coffee station, Leah snorted. "I don't know about the man, but you're definitely something."

Mario held his arms out at his sides. "Come on, Leah. You know you want it."

"And yet my feet remain firmly planted."

"Children," Quince chided.

Xena leaned toward Liam. "Are they...?"

"I have no idea." He'd given up on trying to decipher Leah and Mario. Half the time he thought they were flirting. The rest of the time he didn't think about it at all. Bottom line, they'd either end up in bed or at battle stations. So long as they kept doing stellar work, he figured either result was okay.

"Why are you the man?" Xena called out, to which Mario responded with a quick bow. "Because it's in my blood, thank you. Props to the lady who's paying attention."

Liam eyed the techie and cleared his throat.

"Faces," Mario said, dropping the printouts on the desk. "And yes, they're both plugged into the database. So burn some sage, say a prayer, wear your lucky underwear. And maybe we'll get a hit soon."

"I always wear my lucky underwear," Quince said dryly. He glanced at the sheets, then slid them across the table to Xena. "Familiar?"

Liam leaned closer, looking at the images with Xena, impressed with the rendering that Mario was able to coax out of the pixels. Other than from the night at the cabin, he didn't recognize them, though there was no reason he should. But he watched Xena's face, hoping for a sign.

He got none.

"Sorry. If I knew them before, I don't now."

"It's okay," Liam assured her. "You got away years ago, and these guys are foot soldiers. Soldiers change. But they'll lead us back to whoever is pulling their strings, and I have a feeling you'll know who that is."

She hugged herself. "I want to, because I know it'll help. But at the same time, I wish none of it was left in my head."

He put his hand on her back, stroking lightly, wishing that he could do more. But he could, of course. He could do his job. He could find the man who'd sent the goons, and he could take the fucker down. And, dammit, he would.

A moment later, Ryan's office door burst open, and he crossed the room in long strides, his expression unreadable.

"Bad news?" Liam asked.

"Good, actually. Or potentially good. I just got off the phone with Enrique Castille." He turned to Xena. "He's the head of the European Union task force that brought down Corbu."

"And?" Quince pressed.

"They've been busy. Corbu's been singing. Apparently his son was kidnapped by a competitor, and he wants the task force's help getting him back. And taking down his enemy."

Leah leaned forward, her chin resting on her hand. "Which benefits us how?"

"Because every captain has been rounded up. Including Alberto Miro, the asshole who operated the New York cell. His entire organization got caught in the net."

Xena looked between Ryan and Liam, her head moving side to side as if she wasn't quite following. Liam couldn't fault her for that; he wasn't sure where Ryan was going with this either.

"But if the whole organization was caught, who's after me?"

A hard smile crossed Ryan's face. "I said they were all caught in the net. One wiggled free."

"Noyce," Xena breathed, reaching over to take Liam's hand.

"Bingo. He had a shark of an attorney and an alibi for every offense they tried to throw at him, not to mention a history with Miro that his attorney played up."

"He killed my father, and he's walking free?"

Ryan sat on the edge of the conference table beside her. "Apparently his story is that he came to one party without realizing that the girls weren't there consensually. When he learned, he was disgusted and left."

"That's bullshit."

"I know. The task force knows. What they need is proof, and Miro didn't have it to give."

"But there is proof," Liam said, his hand tightening around Xena's. "Xena witnessed him killing her father."

She swallowed audibly. "That's why he wants to kill me."

"And it's why we're going to nail his ass," Liam said,

hating the fact that she was in the crosshairs, but so damned relieved that they now knew why. More importantly they knew who.

They had a target now, and Liam wouldn't rest until the fucker was in custody or dead.

16

"I THINK it's time for you to take a little trip," Ryan says to me. "On paper, anyway."

I look at Liam, alarmed. "What? What does that even mean?"

"It means it's time for Leah to be on point," Liam says. "Unless Ryan has something else in mind."

"Nope, you read me perfectly."

"Ditch and switch?" Leah grins as she winks at me. "I'm game."

"What's that?"

"We want to distract anyone who might have traced you back to LA," Leah says.

"But we were careful," I insist. "There's no way they could have followed us from the cabin."

Ryan slides back into his chair at the head of the table. "Not disagreeing, but even without Liam in the picture, it makes sense you'd come here. You live here, right?"

"Yeah. I rent the garage apartment at Ella's place."

"So if you left the concert because of the attack, the odds

are you'd go home. That's what they'd likely assume, anyway, and we're going to let that play out."

"But I'm not there." I shoot a frantic look at Liam. "I don't want to go back there. If they're watching it—"

"You won't," Liam says calmly. "You're staying with me."

"Tonight," Ryan amends, "she's staying with Emma."

"But—"

He holds up a hand, silencing Liam. "Let me finish."

I glance at Liam, who's looking warily at his boss and friend. But he's letting Ryan continue without argument. For now, anyway.

"Go on," I say.

"I want you to call Ellie. From your phone," he adds, sliding my phone across the table to me. The SSA already gave me another to use while this nightmare is in play, and now I don't even want to touch my old one, in case Noyce and his men really have been tracking me with it. "Not from here. And don't turn it back on yet. Liam can take you to the beach later before he drops you at Emma's. Find a dive where you might have grabbed something to eat, understand?"

I look at Liam and nod.

"Then call Ellie. Thank her for the cabin and tell her what happened—don't mention that you know who's behind it. But tell her that you need to get out of LA since they'll be looking for you there. Tell her you're—"

"Going to Paris?" *With Liam*, I silently add.

I'm being silly, of course. I don't even have a passport, although I bet the SSA could manufacture one for me if need be...

"Seattle," he says.

"Oh. It's not Paris, but that's cool. I've never been there."

"And you aren't going now." Once again, Ryan is making

my head spin. "Tell her you know where you're going to hole up, and you'll call her when you get there. Meanwhile, Liam, you call Ellie, too, and tell her to mention the call and Xena's plans to someone on her staff she'd normally confide in. But to do it near some other crew members. Where she can be overheard."

"Why?" I ask.

"You told me that no one followed you to Ella's cabin," Liam says. "That means someone told them you were there. Which means if they aren't monitoring your phone, hopefully the information that you've left LA will get to them through their mole."

I frown. "There aren't that many people who know about the cabin. Rye, but he'd never hurt Ella, and hurting me would hurt her. Ella's attorney and accountant know, but they're both as sweet as can be. And her producer at the label, but he wasn't there. That's it. That's everybody who knows about it."

"You think," Liam adds, and I don't have a response to that.

"Okay, fine. But why am I going to Seattle? And why are we sending them after me?"

"You're not," Leah says. "That's the point of the ditch and switch. I become you."

I shake my head. "No. No way."

Leah waves a hand. "Oh, please. This is what I do."

"Go around the country pretending to be an ex-prostitute who some dangerous sex traffickers are after? What?" I add, in response to Liam's dark look. "That's what I am."

"No. That's what you were forced to do to survive. And you dug yourself out. You're still digging, and we're here to help you. Let us help you."

"At the risk of her getting whacked?"

"I'll be fine," Leah assures me. "I'll go to Seattle and send her a text from there. From your phone, of course. Then Ella spreads the word on her end."

"Let's record Xena saying she's there with static," Mario suggests. "You can call Ellie and play it, but on the recording she can say she's going to text because the connection is so bad."

Leah nods. "Excellent. That way we'll get them whether they're monitoring phone, text, or Ellie's conversations."

"And then?" I ask Leah.

"And then I buy a return ticket in my own name. I come home, and Xena Morgan stays behind in Seattle."

I glance around the table at all of them. "This will work?"

"It will," Liam says firmly. "All we're doing is buying time and safety."

"What have you got for me?" Quince asks.

"I was hoping you'd go overseas and meet with Enrique in person. The task force does good work, but I want your eyes on their information, and he's willing to let you interrogate some of the men they already have in custody."

"My favorite European pastime—interrogating deviant wankers."

"And if anyone can get more details from a prisoner, it's you," Ryan adds.

"A dubious honor," Quince says. "But true."

I glance at Liam, who nods. I lean back, a little stunned that the seemingly gentle Brit is some sort of master interrogator. Then again, this whole operation stuns me.

"I'll head over tomorrow and take Eliza with me. I've been promising her a trip to London and Paris."

"Nothing like espionage to spice up a girl's vacation," Leah says.

"I bet they'll spice it up other ways, too," Trevor puts in.

Quince grins. "You know what they say about all work and no play."

Leah rolls her eyes. "When do you want me to head out?"

"Tomorrow morning," Ryan says.

"Oh, good. I was afraid you'd say tonight, and I don't want to miss girls' night."

Ryan nods. "Which is why you're not leaving until tomorrow. You're all meeting at Emma's house, right?"

"Yeah, why?"

"Because I want Xena there, too."

"Whoa," Liam says. "She's with me, and while I wouldn't feel emasculated joining girls' night, I don't think the women want me there."

"Which is why it's good that it's at Emma's house. Do you really doubt she'd be safe?"

"Um, hello?" Leah says.

"You're skills are amazing," Ryan says. "Emma's are better. And her house is a fucking fortress."

"Emma?" I ask, wondering what kind of badassery the woman has at her disposal. "She told me she's a PI."

"She's a hell of a lot more than a PI," Liam says, and my imagination churns. "Who else will be there?"

Leah counts the guests off on her fingers. "Me, Emma, Eliza, Cass, Jamie. Maybe Sylvia. With Denny and Nikki out of town, I think that's it."

"I keep telling them to invite me," Trevor says, winking at me. "But so far, no luck."

"Jamie and Eliza will be there," Mario points out to Liam, and I remember someone telling me that Ryan's wife is named Jamie. And I know that Eliza and Quince are together. "If Ryan and Quince aren't shutting this thing down, I think you can assume your girl is safe."

I wait for Liam to deny that I'm 'his girl,' but all he does is nod. "Fine. If they think Xena's in LA, they'll either look for her at her own apartment or mine. It makes sense that she'd be with me since I was with her at the cabin."

"Exactly," Ryan says.

"What's girls' night?" I ask.

"We drink. Talk. Usually watch a movie. Most nights we break up around midnight. But I'm thinking tonight needs to be a slumber party."

"Right," I say, wondering not only what I'm supposed to wear to sleep in, but how the hell I'm supposed to act. I've hung out with Ella before, but I've never done sleepovers. Or girls' nights. Or anything like that. Not ever. Not even in high school.

I reach over and take Liam's hand, squeezing hard. Because right now, the prospect of spending casual time with a group of women scares me even more than Edward Noyce and his well-armed cretins.

———

It takes about forty-seven seconds for my nervousness to fade after Emma welcomes me into her cute little house in Venice Beach. A home which, according to Liam, is a hell of a lot more than the adorable bungalow it appears to be.

"I've done a lot of work," Emma says vaguely when I ask her as much. And although I really want to pry for details, I have a feeling that it's an *I could tell you, but then I'd have to kill you* situation.

I'm the last to arrive, now decked out in a pair of Denny's jeans and my newly washed tank top, and armed with a promise from Liam that we can hit a department store tomorrow. I'd asked to swing by my apartment to get my own clothes, but I hadn't been surprised when he'd quickly shut that suggestion down.

I don't know if Liam told someone that I don't drink, but I'm thrilled to see that in addition to several bottles of wine and an impressive selection of hard liquor, the kitchen island that is currently serving as drinks-central also has a variety of sodas and flavored sparkling waters. I help myself to a raspberry flavored water and follow Emma into the living area. Cass comes over to give me a hug, telling me she's thrilled I'm joining the fun, and I notice that she switches places when she sits back down, leaving a pretty woman with pixie-styled brown hair to go sit by Emma.

Eliza and Leah both wave in greeting, and the pretty woman comes over, introducing herself as Sylvia. "I started coming to these things because of her," she says, pointing to Cass. "It's a nice break from the kids. I love them, but sometimes, you just need adult women."

"I can imagine," I say, although in truth I think I would love to be at home with kids of my own. Such a normal thing, and for so long it was a fantasy I didn't even let myself think about, because it was just too damn painful.

I keep my polite smile on, though, because I don't want to bring the mood down by even hinting that I'm thinking about my past, and if Sylvia notices my moment of melancholy, she's kind enough not to mention it.

"You must be Xena," an absolutely gorgeous raven-haired woman comes from the kitchen, a glass of wine in her hands. "I'm Jamie, Ryan's wife. Sylvia and I go back a few years. Anyway, it's great you could make it. We haven't been doing this for that long, honestly. So you're getting in on the ground floor."

"Cool," I say as I settle in next to Leah, who has scooted over to make a space for me. I mean it, too, only to remember after I've spoken that I may not be hanging around this crowd for long. According to Liam, now that the playing field has narrowed to Noyce, he expects we'll be able to wrap this up and ensure my safety within a pretty reasonable time frame.

I'll still live in LA, of course, and not that far from here in the grand scheme of things, but I doubt that I'd be coming to girls' night. Not without that connection to Liam.

A fresh wave of melancholy washes over me and I have to force a smile as Eliza starts to tell everyone about how she and Quince are heading to Europe tomorrow. "He'll be working during the day, but I'm already planning what museums I want to see. And, of course, we'll have the nights," she adds, batting her eyes and humming innocently as the others laugh.

"I bet he proposes over there," Leah says.

"Oh, I don't think so," Eliza says. "It hasn't been that long."

"You're insane," Emma counters, then glances at the rest of the room. "Raise your hand if you think my sister is insane."

Everyone except me raises their hand. "I don't think I'm qualified," I say, when Emma raises a brow.

"Fair enough. But you," she says to Eliza, "are nuts if you think it hasn't been that long. It's been years. And you know damn well you two are perfect for each other."

"Yes, but that doesn't mean he's going to—"

"He will," Leah says firmly.

"Fine," Eliza says. "But I'll just have to tell him I need time to ponder. Wouldn't want him to think I'm madly in love with him or anything."

They all laugh, and I'm too curious not to ask. "How long have you been together?"

Eliza makes a face. "That is a more complicated question than you know."

"They were all cozy and then motherfucking fate stepped in and pushed them apart," Emma says. "Hell of a journey back together. Like an epic poem by Homer or something."

"Yes," Eliza says dryly. "My relationship with Quince is exactly like *The Odyssey*. You are so weird."

"Am I weird?" Emma asks, directing the question to Cass.

"Very."

"She's right," Eliza says. "Which is probably why I love you so much. And why are we talking about me, anyway?"

"Exactly," Leah says. "We should be talking about men."

"Ahem," Cass says, and everyone laughs again.

"Is Trevor off limits?" Leah asks. "Because I really want to know what we're going to do about him. I mean, he's a terrific roommate, but that boy has been single for far too long."

"Has he brought anybody home?" Eliza asks.

"Nope." Leah raises a shoulder. "He's stayed out all night a couple of times, but when I ask him about it, he just says he stayed with a friend instead of grabbing an Uber. I'm sad for him. He and Jasper were really good together."

"His ex," Jamie says helpfully to me, though I've figured that out on my own.

The evening continues that way for another half hour or so, with the group commenting on the lives and relationships of their friends, including asking Jamie when she and Ryan are going to start a family—"Um, so not ready!"—and someone asking when Nikki and Damien will be back in the country.

Nobody knows—apparently the whole family and their nanny are in Europe, combining a tour of Stark properties and businesses with a family vacation.

"Family vacations and work are not supposed to be on tonight's list of acceptable conversational topics," Sylvia says. "Not when I have kids at home and work spread all over the dining room table."

"Then let's talk sex," Jamie says. "Or bad television. Or sex." She turns to me. "Are you and Liam ... you know?"

Across the room, Sylvia gasps. "Jamie!" She turns to me. "You'll have to forgive her. She has no filters at all."

"Oh, I have filters," Jamie says. "I just usually keep them turned off. More fun that way."

"Um," I say, because I'm really not sure what I should say. I mean, Liam was protecting me. Could he get in trouble if his coworkers learn the truth?

"Well?" Jamie prods, and I wonder if I could conjure a slight case of Ebola and run to the bathroom.

I take the more sane approach and pretend to be clueless. "What makes you think that?"

"Something Leah said earlier. And I saw him walk you in. There was a vibe."

"A vibe?"

"There was definitely a vibe," Eliza says, and Emma and Cass both nod.

"I don't know about that," I say. And then, because I can't help myself, I ask, "Did you pick up a vibe from me or from him?"

Jamie and Sylvia share a grin, my cheeks flame, and everyone starts laughing.

"Busted," Jamie says, and even though she's right, all I

can do is laugh. I've never done this with other women before. Just hung out and talked and kidded each other and had fun. It's nice. And a little dangerous, too, because I know I could really get used to this.

Eliza brings me a fresh water. "Vibe or not, if there is something between you and Liam, I'm glad. He and Quince have been friends for ages, and I know Quince has been hoping he'd get involved with someone again."

"Again?"

She nods, then sits down next to me. "Apparently it was a long time ago. He was involved and I guess it ended badly. Quince doesn't even know the details. It was before—never mind."

"Deliverance?" I ask quietly.

"You know about that? Interesting..."

I don't bother to clarify that he told me in the context of my history and sex trafficking. Instead, I just ask her what happened.

"That's the thing," she says. "I don't know. Neither does Quince. All he knows is that Liam got burned somehow. And that he doesn't do relationships."

"He's not doing one with me, either," I tell her. "In fact, we even talked about the fact that he doesn't."

"And yet there's a vibe," she says, then clinks her glass with mine.

I consider protesting again, but don't. After all, this night is about gossip and girlfriends and having fun. And as far as I'm concerned, fantasizing about Liam is a very fun pastime.

Eventually, the conversation turns more rowdy and someone brings out Cards Against Humanity, which has us roaring. And though I'm not sure how it happens, that game leads into lazing on the floor, sofa, and chairs as we watch

Guardians of the Galaxy, which I've never seen before, and soon I'm laughing so hard I'm crying.

Not because it's that emotional—although considering how silly it is, it does pack an emotional punch—but because this whole night has been so amazing.

And when I eventually do fall asleep on the pullout couch in Emma's loft, with Leah sleeping on a blowup bed beside me, I can't help but think that I could definitely get used to this.

17

FOR THE NEXT FEW DAYS, I live at Liam's side.

I go with him to work, where I scan, file, organize, summarize, and generally make myself useful in this incredibly busy office that definitely does not have enough support staff. It's interesting work, and I enjoy it. Not only because I feel like I'm contributing and not simply sitting back while others protect me, but because I'm working again, and the work is important.

While I'm working, of course Liam is, too. For the last two days, he's been primarily on the phone with Winston or working with Mario on the computer, trying to chase down leads to Noyce's whereabouts.

Unfortunately, there's been little progress on that front, but Liam assures me this is part of the process, and that eventually, I'll be free of the sword hanging over my head.

I believe him, and I'm so grateful for everything he and the SSA have done. But every time he assures me that this will all be over soon, my throat thickens and my chest feels tight. Because once I'm free of that sword, doesn't that mean I'll be freed from Liam's shadow, too?

I should want that. I should want to see my own apartment again. Work my old job. Hang out with Ella.

I should want to be able to move through the world without looking over my shoulder.

And I do. I want it painfully. Desperately.

But I also want Liam.

I'm certain he has no idea of this new direction in my thoughts, and I feel a little guilty about that. But I'm keeping my secret for now.

As far as Liam knows, nothing has changed. I've told him that I don't get involved, and I told him my reasons. If he was paying attention, he knows that I've never wanted to pull someone else into a life with a woman wearing a target on her back.

But Liam is the one working to erase that target. And once he does...

Well, once that target is gone, I guess he can do the math. If he wants to.

And that's the thing that's gnawing at my gut—I don't think he'll want to. He's told me he doesn't do relationships, either, and if what Eliza's told me is true, his words have been borne out in practice. He hasn't been in a relationship since before he and Quince became friends, and from what I can tell, they were both neck deep in Deliverance a long time ago.

"You've been quiet tonight," Liam says as he squeezes his Range Rover into his garage.

"Tired," I say, which isn't actually a lie. "I moved about eight billion boxes from the basement storage area up to Conference Room A so I can start scanning them into the system."

"Eight billion?"

"Slight exaggeration," I say. "And I might have had help.

But it was still tiring. First physically, then mentally. Scanning is not the most exhilarating task in the world. But it does give you time to think."

"Oh?" He kills the engine and looks at me. "What were you thinking about?"

"You," I say truthfully.

"What a coincidence. I spent a lot of time thinking about you today, too."

"I should hope so, considering my ass is your primary investigation at the moment." I frown. "That came out wrong."

"I think it came out exactly right. I definitely need to investigate your ass more thoroughly."

Heat and desire lace his voice, firing my senses and making my skin tingle with a now-familiar need. A craving for him. For this man. For his touch. His scent. His lips. Over the last few nights, I've explored every delicious inch of him, and all I have to do is close my eyes to remember the way he feels inside me.

The memory is sweet, but I'd much rather have the reality, and as soon as we're inside the house, I push him against the wall and close my mouth over his.

"No dinner?" he murmurs when we come up for air.

"Your choice," I answer, then run the tip of my tongue along the curve of his ear. "Leftover meatloaf. Takeout. Or me."

"Well, when you put it that way…"

I squeal as he grabs me by the waist, hauls me over his shoulder, then smacks me lightly on the ass before carrying me upstairs and tossing me into the middle of the unmade bed.

I scoot backwards, laughing, as he gets on the mattress, then crawls toward me on all fours, a dangerous, possessive look in his eyes. "There's nowhere to go," he says as my back presses against the vertical iron bars of the headboard. "And now I'm going to have my feast."

On the last word, he takes hold of my ankles and slides me down the bed. I'm still in the heels and the shift-style dress I'd worn to the office, and the dress doesn't slide with me, leaving my lacy panties exposed as the dress bunches around my waist.

I'm breathing hard as our eyes meet, and I reach up, purposefully grabbing the bars. His gaze is hard and demanding, and I think about that playful smack to my rear. The truth is, I want another. I want to feel his palm against my skin. I want him to take off his belt and use it to lace my wrists to these bars.

Too many times I was helpless with a man I loathed. I want to cleanse that from my past and have my submission be a gift to Liam, not something stolen from me. I want to be claimed. Overwhelmed. But I can't get the words out.

I know that with Liam I should be able to speak freely, but for so many years I wasn't allowed to want anything. And now—now I'm afraid he'll think it's strange, even though I know that spanking and light bondage are about as low on the kink scale as it's possible to get.

I can't bring myself to take the risk. I can't seem to find the words to ask. All I can do is meet his eyes, hoping he can see the desire—the need—in mine.

His lips tease my inner thighs as his finger slips inside my panties, lightly teasing my clit. My pussy clenches with need, and I arch up, silently begging for more until he takes the hint and thrusts two fingers deep inside me. I grind against him, wanting more—everything—then gasp as his mouth continues to roam, finally reaching the lace edge of my panties.

He tugs them aside with a finger, then laves my clit with his tongue while those other two fingers move rhythmically inside me. I buck in response, wanting more. More intensity. More wildness. More Liam.

"Please," I beg. "Liam, please."

"Tell me," he murmurs, his breath on my pussy teasing me as much as the stubble of his beard brushing my tender flesh. "Tell me what you want."

My lips part, and in my mind I spell it out for him. *Tie me up. Bind me. Spank me. Claim me. Take me.*

But it is only the last part that leaves my lips. "Take me," I murmur. "Take me, please."

"Xena, baby. Christ, you drive me crazy." He slides his way up my body, my dress a tangled mess between us. His cock teases my core, and as he pushes my knees up and thrusts slowly into me, his mouth claims mine, his tongue mimicking the movement of his cock until he is filling me completely.

I clutch his back, my fingernails most likely drawing blood, but I don't care. How quickly I've gone from needy to desperate. To wanting what he is giving. To craving nothing but the pure pleasure of this man.

He's on top of me, his huge, muscular body blanketing mine as he thrusts into me, over and over, deeper and harder. I cry out, craving release, craving more as I pull him toward me, wishing we could crawl inside each other so that we would explode together in perfect unison.

And then, oh God, and then the world seems to turn inside out and my body arches up as everything inside me catches fire, and all I can do is burn until I'm nothing but ashes in his arms.

"Was that good?" he asks, holding me close.

"Not even remotely," I say, then feel his laugher reverberate through me. I'm still spinning, still glowing, and the siren's call of sleep is luring me under.

But even as I succumb to pleasure and exhaustion in his arms, I can't escape the tiny pinpricks of regret. Because as much as he took me high, he didn't quite take me *there*.

I want him to claim me.

I want to be *his*.

On so many levels, I want to be his.

But I'm afraid that won't ever be my reality.

I'm a girl who's spent her entire life being disappointed. Who's always gotten the exact opposite of what she wants.

Now I want Liam.

And I'm terrified that history will repeat itself, and in the end, I'm going to lose him forever.

18

I WAKE UP ALONE, but there's a freshly cut rose waiting for me on the bedside table, which makes me smile. There's also a note, and when I read it, my smile grows broader.

Bakery. Back soon. L

In the car yesterday, I'd mentioned to him that I love blueberry muffins with crumbles on top, and he'd immediately shifted course for Upper Crust, a Malibu bakery that he swore had the best muffins in the world. A converted house, it sits on a rocky outcropping and from the drive-through lane, I could see tables out back on a patio overlooking the sea.

Unfortunately, they'd been out of blueberry muffins, so we'd made do with a fresh loaf of bread and some chocolate chip cookies. I'd expected that to be the end of it, and the knowledge that he's making an early morning jaunt for me makes me smile and stretch and hug my pillow, feeling ridiculously special.

I decide to go ahead and shower, as I imagine we'll be heading to the office after we eat, even though it's Saturday. I take longer than I need to, distracted by the multiple jets and the rain-style showerhead—not to mention a few minutes chatting with the fish, some of whom I'm sure are checking me out.

And, yes, part of the reason I linger is the hope that Liam will join me, since I don't imagine he's taken a shower yet. But by the time I'm shampooed, shaved, and scrubbed, he still hasn't slid into this steamy corner of heaven with me. Frowning, I give up, turn off the water, and reach outside the door to retrieve a fluffy towel from the warming rack.

I wrap it around me, then poke my head out of the bathroom door. "Liam?"

I wait, but there's no answer, and I frown as I quickly comb my hair, then do my makeup.

He still hasn't returned by the time I finish, and I'm genuinely starting to worry. I'm actually heading to the bedside table to grab my new phone and call him when it rings, startling me enough that I jump.

His name pops up on the screen, and I sigh with relief, then snap out, "Where on earth are you!" before he can even say a word. "Sorry," I continue, immediately contrite. "It's just that I—"

"It's my fault. I should have called earlier, but you were asleep when I left, and I didn't want to wake you. But it looks like I'll be at least another fifteen minutes, so I wanted to call and let you know I hadn't run off with a gang of pirates."

"Good to know," I say. "But I do think you'd be sexy with a cutlass and an eye patch."

"I'll keep that in mind."

"What's the hold up? Nothing bad happened, did it? No one was following you, or—"

"No, no. Nothing like that."

I exhale with relief. "Did they have to go out and actually pick blueberries?"

He chuckles. "Not that, either, and the bag on the seat beside me is wildly tempting. I'm waiting to enjoy them with you, but I'm man enough to admit that I almost caved once or twice. As for the delay, I'm stuck behind a fender bender, and there's no alternate route. They'll have it cleared soon, I think."

"You weren't in it?"

"Safe and sound but I should have taken the bike. I'd be home with you by now."

"As long as you're in one piece." I say, as I look around the room for my shopping bag from yesterday. "And thank you for going out for me. Sorry it's turned into an ordeal."

"Well, I think you're worth it. But you can thank me however you like when I get back."

The thought sends my imagination flying, and I only snap back to reality when he tells me that he can see the tow truck ahead. "So it won't be long now. I'll see you in—"

"Hang on a sec. Do you know what happened to my shopping bag yesterday?" I'd grabbed a cute pair of white capris and an off-the-shoulder blouse that I planned to wear today. Not to mention a new pair of flats.

"Closet," he says. "Sorry, I wasn't thinking. I tossed it in there with my bag."

"No problem, and thanks. I'll be dressed by the time you get back, so we can have our muffins and head out anytime."

"More's the pity."

"Well, I'm naked right now," I tease, dropping the towel so that I'm not a liar. "You're the one who left me all alone with a bed and a jetted shower."

"Clearly, I'm a fool. See you soon."

I'm still smiling after our mutual goodbyes, and I head to the closet for my bag. There are several in there, and as I grab mine from the floor, I somehow upset the bag behind it, which is sitting on an Army style footlocker. The bag falls to the floor, and I mutter a curse, pulling my own bag out of the closet as I squat to clean up my mess.

It's only when I start to set the fallen bag upright that I get a glimpse of what's in there—and then do a double-take when I see a pair of metal handcuffs.

At first, I think it's something to do with his work. After all, the man chases bad guys. But there's also a coil of silky black rope, another set of cuffs—these lined with fur, and a pair of nipple clamps.

Oh, my, yes.

And even though I know I shouldn't keep snooping in the bag, nothing is going to stop me now. And I become more and more aroused with each new discovery. Vibrators. Massage oil. A silky blindfold. And a sleek leather paddle. These are the accoutrements of the fantasy I want to play out with Liam. The desire I couldn't manage to speak because I didn't know how he would react.

Now, though...

Now I imagine him using everything in that bag with me. *On me.*

And as I hear the garage door start to churn, I tell myself it's time to summon the courage to tell him exactly what I want.

———

"Glad you're there safe and sound," Liam says as he enters the foyer from the garage. He sees me, then holds up his phone, pulling out his earbuds as he switches it to speaker. "What do you think of Seattle?"

"Seems pretty nice," I hear Leah say. "At least what I've

seen from the taxi and out my hotel window. Not that I'm going to slide into tourist mode or anything."

"Anything of substance to report?"

"Actually, yes," she says, and I immediately look to Liam, who raises his eyebrows in a show of both interest and surprise. "I got a call," she says, as if that's supposed to mean something.

Considering the pleased way that Liam says, "Oh, did you?" with a tone of rising interest, I'm assuming that it *does* mean something. I'm just not sure what, and I decide to bite the bullet and display my ignorance.

"Okay, clue me in and explain what you're talking about."

"Someone was checking me—or you—out," she says. "About an hour after I got to the room, I got a call. Some guy with a smarmy voice saying he was with the hotel and was sending up a bottle of wine to me in room 1220 to welcome me to the city. I told him I really appreciated it, but that since I didn't drink he didn't need to make the effort. But that I would love a strawberry waffle in the morning. He told me that could be arranged, and there you go."

I look at Liam and shake my head, not understanding.

"The caller wasn't from the hotel," he says.

"Oh." I'm not sure how he knows that, but I guess that's part of his job. Anyway, Leah confirms what he's said.

"I called down to the front desk and said I'd changed my mind and wanted my complimentary wine after all. The woman assured me that wasn't something they did."

"So they know you're—or rather, *I'm*—there and they have the room number. Good God, Leah, that doesn't sound—"

"Relax. I'm already gone. I left some clothes strewn around

the room and my suitcase open, put the Do Not Disturb sign on, then went down the stairs to the basement and out the employee entrance. Someone will probably deliver a waffle and a bullet tomorrow morning, but I'll be long gone."

"You've arranged for eyes on the hall and a team to take down our man?"

"Not my first time at this rodeo," she says. "Yes. Ryan pulled in a team made up of some security personnel from Stark International Seattle and several men from a civilian SWAT-style team based here that he's worked with before. I'm at Stark Applied Technology right now. We're using one of the conference rooms as base camp."

"You're not heading back to LA?" I ask.

"Not after getting such a solid lead right away. I'll ride this out. And yes, I'll watch my back. Thanks for reminding me."

Liam grins. "Watch your back," he says, and I can practically hear Leah roll her eyes.

They end the call, and Liam looks at me, his smile wide and bright. "Another step closer. This is even better than we'd hoped."

I nod. All we'd expected was to lead them away from LA. Now it looks like we may have actually set a workable trap.

"I have more good news, too," he says, holding up the bag of muffins. "And not just these tasty treats. While I was stuck in traffic, Winston called. He's back in LA, along with Ella and Rye."

"Really?" I follow him to the kitchen.

"I guess they're staying at her place before they head up to San Francisco for another show."

"Of course. Right." I wasn't even thinking. Everyone else would already be on their way to the next gig, but Ella and Rye had intended to take a few days in the cabin. Considering recent events, it makes sense that they're enjoying alone time at Ella's Hollywood Hills house instead. Which also happens to be where my apartment is.

"Could we go see them today? And I can grab some more clothes while we're there."

"Why?" he asks, as he pours us both a cup of coffee. He looks me up and down, his eyes dancing with amusement. "You're not even wearing the clothes you have here."

"True," I say. Despite telling him I needed the bag of clothes, after my discovery, I'd decided to stay in the fluffy robe he'd put out for me this morning. "But eventually, I will have to put on real clothes. Society expects it."

"Damn society," he mutters, shaking his head and making me laugh.

I expect him to say no to the jaunt since they—the infamous *they*—might still be watching the house and my apartment. But to my surprise he agrees, although more for him than for me, as he makes it clear that he wants to talk with Winston some more. He also tells me that Ella or Rye will need to go in and get my stuff—ideally while having a conversation about how they're going to mail my clothing to Seattle for me—and that when we arrive, we're driving into the garage and entering that way once the massive door has closed and hidden us from view.

"In other words, no convertible today."

"No convertible," he confirms, then calls Winston to find out what time will work.

We end up with a plan to meet them at eleven, which leaves enough time to chat and catch up before they have to leave for a meeting with one of Ella's producers.

"Terrific," I say, but I can't help but feel a bit sad. It's been a long time since I've been left out of one of Ella's business meetings. I push it aside, though, then run through a mental map for getting from Liam's condo in Malibu to Ella's house in the Hollywood Hills. I glance at the clock, do some mental math, and decide we have enough time.

"What?" Liam is studying my face, the gleam in his narrowed eyes suggesting he knows exactly what I'm thinking.

"I realize you went to a lot of trouble to get those blueberries," I say, "but I was wondering if we could eat in the car."

His brows rise. "Crumbs in the Beemer? I don't know."

"You have a BMW, too?"

He shrugs. "I like vehicles."

"I guess so."

"You want to tell me for what good reason should I sacrifice my recently detailed car?"

"Oh, no big deal," I say airily. "Just something else I wanted to do before we left ... and I don't think there's time to do both."

"Is that so?"

"Not if we do the first one right."

He takes a step toward me, the humor in his eyes now replaced by a heat that pools in my belly and seeps down between my legs. "Now you've intrigued me," he says. "What do you have in mind?"

I untie the robe, open it, then let it slide down my arms and onto the floor. "Take a guess."

He drops to his knees, his hands cupping my ass and his tongue sliding over my pussy.

I groan, my legs going so weak I probably would have crumpled to the floor if his hands weren't supporting me. "Oh my God, you are a *very* good guesser."

"Just one of my many talents," he says as he rises again, then picks me up so that my breasts are pressed against his chest, my arms are around his neck, and my legs are hooked tight around his waist. He carries me that way to the bed, then tumbles us both onto the mattress.

I meet his eyes and tremble from the desire I see there. I could stay like this for hours, just getting lost in the way he looks at me. Like I'm special. Like I'm the only thing in the world that matters to him.

It's intoxicating. A sensation that is matched only by his actual touch. Which, right now, I desperately crave.

"Finger me," I whisper, and am rewarded with a cocky grin and his fingers dipping slowly inside me.

"A woman who knows what she wants. I like that."

"Funny," I say. "I feel the same way. Tell me what you want. Anything at all."

"I have what I want," he says, his thumb rubbing distracting circles on my clit. "I have you at my mercy."

"I could be more at your mercy," I whisper, my hips moving in response to the incredible way he's firing my senses. "You can do whatever you want with me."

"What I want is to make love to you all morning, but apparently we have an appointment."

And apparently, I'm going to have to be more direct.

I untuck his T-shirt, then unbutton his jeans. I get my hands under the material so I can cup his wonderfully firm ass and pull him close to me as I make my confession. "So, I, um, found my clothes in your closet like you said."

"And yet you're not wearing them."

"Well, we can't move too fast on these things," I quip, earning a laugh. I barrel on. "The thing is, I accidentally spilled another bag. I didn't mean to snoop, but I found—"

"Oh, *fuck.*"

He rolls off me, then props himself up on an arm, facing me, his hand gently stroking my cheek. "I'm sorry," he says.

"Sorry?" I try to process his words, and the only thing I can come up with is that he's had sex with other women. Not exactly a revelation. "It's not like I thought I was the first woman in your bed. I know you blow off steam, remember?"

"Yes, and sometimes I like..." He hesitates, then sits up, two fingers squeezing the bridge of his nose. He looks utterly wrecked, and I have no idea why.

Finally, he speaks, his voice low and even. "I should have put that stuff away. I wasn't thinking. But please know that I understand what you've been through." His voice is calm. The way he might speak to a frantic child. Or a skittish cat. "And I would never, ever ask you to do that."

I stay still, stunned and unsure how to react. How to explain that he has this completely wrong despite his heart being so firmly planted in exactly the right place.

"Liam, I—"

He takes my hand and presses it to his heart. "Xena, baby, I will take care of you, and I want you in my bed. And just because I sometimes need—no, that has nothing to do with you. So long as you're with me, you're in a safe place. I want you to understand that. I would never do anything to trigger those memories, and I am so, so sorry you stumbled across that."

I've clearly thrown him for a loop, and I honestly don't know if I should try to explain or if I should just let this play out and try again later. Considering we need to go soon, later is probably the better option, because I have a feeling that telling this man that even with my history, I want him to cuff me to the bed is going to be a very dicey conversation.

But I do want it. More than that, I need it.

But I need him more.

I swallow, then lick my lips. "It's okay," I say. "Really. I was, um, just embarrassed that I'd run across something so personal. But I'm not upset. Not at all. Truly."

He searches my face, then nods, apparently satisfied. "I want you to trust me," he says.

"I do, I promise." And that's the God's honest truth. I just don't know how to tell him the rest of it.

19

LIAM HAD no idea what the hell he'd been thinking leaving that damn sack of toys in the closet. Except of course that he hadn't been thinking, primarily because he'd forgotten all about the bag and the items inside it.

It had been months since he'd been with a woman that way. Hell, it had been months since he'd been with a woman other than Xena. He'd told her the truth when he'd said that he blew off steam from time to time, but the truth was that since he had no interest in starting a relationship with any of the women who'd shared his bed, he'd become less and less interested in having them in his bed at all.

He'd chalked it up to getting older and having less patience for the tedious repetition that accompanied hook-ups or even casual dating. But that wasn't the real reason. Mostly, he was just over it.

Or he'd thought he was. Because the woman now sitting beside him making small moans of satisfaction as she ate a blueberry muffin—moans that had him wanting to pull the BMW over and make her *really* moan—had snuck up on him and changed the way he looked at everything.

With Xena, he wasn't over it at all. With her, he felt alive again in ways he hadn't felt since Dion. Ways he thought he'd wanted to leave behind forever. But now ... well, now he cherished the way she made him smile and laugh. The way she looked at him with unfettered desire.

She'd opened herself to him about a time in her life that had been beyond horrific. She'd trusted him.

And he'd gone and blown it because he'd cleaned out the drawer of his bedside table a few months ago and never properly put the damn stuff away.

He wanted to fucking kick himself.

"Are you sure you don't want a muffin?" she said. "You look like you could use one."

He drew a calming breath, not wanting to add to the stress he was certain he'd caused her—despite her polite protests to the contrary. "What does someone who could use a muffin look like?"

"Duh," she said. "You."

They'd reached a three-way intersection of the canyon roads leading up to Ella's house, and he looked at her as he waited for an oncoming car to pass, shaking his head in mock exasperation. "Bad joke."

"Oh, no. It was a great joke. You must be misinformed."

"Possibly," he said. "But—" He cut himself off, frowning at the black SUV reflected in the review mirror. Common enough in LA. But had he seen that particular one before, just a few streets back?

"What is it?"

"I'm not sure. Probably a coincidence. But we're taking a different route." He'd intended to go straight, but now he took a sharp right, which had him climbing an unfamiliar street.

He followed the twists and curves until he was certain

they weren't being followed, then he slowed while the Waze App recalibrated and found the quickest route.

He checked repeatedly during the remainder of the drive, but the SUV never appeared behind them again.

"Probably just my paranoia," he said to Winston later, after they were safely in Ella's house. "I didn't even suspect a tail until we were a few miles from Ella's."

"And your windows are tinted," Winston said. "So no chance one of Noyce's random flunkies saw you two and decided to follow."

He said the last with a grin, and Liam responded with a self-deprecating shake of his head. "Yes, I'm sure Noyce has lined the streets with minions in cars just waiting for me to pass."

"Anything's possible," Winston said with equal humor.

"It's her." Liam sighed. "Xena. That woman has me twisted up, and I can't stand the thought of something happening to her because I fucked up."

"You won't fuck up," Winston said. Tall and lanky, with an easy manner and soul-searching eyes, Winston Starr looked the part of the real-life role he used to play. When they'd first met, Liam had been unsure about the value that a former West Texas sheriff could bring to an internationally elite team. But he'd learned soon enough that there was more to Winston than met the eye, and they'd become good friends. One day, he intended to learn about the demons in Winston's past. Until then, he was content to admire the man's work ethic and skills.

They were in the kitchen, and Liam took one of the bottled waters that Ella had left on the counter for him and Winston before she, Rye, and Xena had gone off to the media room to chat. Liam knew they would have preferred to sit on the patio overlooking hills—that same patio where he'd stood with Xena the night he'd been so damn tempted to kiss her. But he was taking no chances with Xena's life. Outside, she was a sitting duck for any of Noyce's assholes with a high-powered rifle. At the very least, anyone with eyes on Ella's house would know that Xena wasn't in Seattle.

It was for that reason that he'd approved the media room rather than the sunny living area. No windows.

And why he'd had Rye and Ella both walk over to the cottage and bring back a bag of clothes for Xena, all the while chatting about how they should see about renting the studio since Xena was moving out of state.

He was just about to tell Winston they should head into the other room and join the others when a text came in from Mario: *Call Me.*

He showed it to Winston, whose brows rose. "Think he got a hit?"

"I think we should find out," Liam said, then started to dial, only to pause as Ella and Rye came into the room, arm in arm.

"Are you two in here eating all my food or discussing all my bad habits?" Ella asked, grinning at them both.

"You have bad habits?" Liam asked, deadpan.

She winked. "Of course. Or don't you follow me on social media?"

He chuckled, and she waved her hand, as if dismissing the banter. "We just came to get popcorn and the two of you," she told them as Rye ducked into the pantry, then emerged with two large, red bags of pre-popped corn, the pantry door still open behind him. "We've already got drinks in the media room fridge. You ready?"

"Just need to return Mario's call," Liam said.

"Does he have news on those two guys?" Rye asked.

"Probably only checking in," Liam said, not wanting to get the manager's hopes up.

"Well, don't be long," Ella said. "We want to start."

"What are we watching?" Liam asked.

"Me, of course. Concert footage. For your entertainment and my edification. If I don't watch every show, how will I know where I can improve?"

She didn't wait for an answer, but turned on her heel and headed back, with Rye right behind her.

"Be there in a minute," Winston called, shooting Liam an amused look.

"We should get her on board at the SSA," he said while he put his phone on speaker and waited for Mario to answer. "That woman knows how to lead a team."

"Got a hit!" Mario shouted out the news without preamble, making Liam flinch, as he hadn't even realized the line had connected.

"Which one?" Liam asked.

"Square jaw. His name's Patrick Weil. Grew up in Jersey, but he lives in Manhattan. One of Seagrave's contacts in the Defense Department called in some favors and got us confirmation."

"Have we got eyes on him?"

"On the address, yes," Mario said. "But not on the man. Confirmation of his location in the city was made twelve minutes ago. An ATM that time-stamped him at that location ninety minutes ago. I sent a team, but he was long gone."

"And his home address?"

"Got a team watching the place," Mario assured him. "Right now, no one's home."

Liam took a long swallow of water, thinking. "Odds are he's still in town, but we can't ignore the possibility that he deliberately used a Manhattan ATM to place him in the city. If he hopped on a bus or a train, he could be long gone by now."

"No argument from me," Mario said. "But this is the best we've got."

"And it's good work," Liam agreed. "I just want this wrapped up. For Xena's sake."

"I get you. And I'll call you if anything happens at his apartment."

"Good. And get in touch with Dallas Sykes, or ask Ryan to. If you need extra manpower, he'll be able to get it to you. And tell Dallas that Xena and I will see him soon."

"You're heading to New York?"

"You know me, Mario. I always go where the action is." He grinned as he ended the call, then met Winston's eyes. "A little progress, at least."

"Always a good thing," Winston said in that slow, easy drawl. "And about time. I haven't learned a thing with Ella and Rye, either here or earlier in Vegas. Well, that's not actually true," he amended. "I learned pretty much everything there is to know about working a concert, but I didn't see a single thing that was suspicious."

"Did you interview the staff?"

"Do I look like I'm new to this game? I did interviews until I thought my ears would fall off. Swept for bugs, the whole nine yards."

"What about doing an electronics sweep here?" Liam asked. He knew it was possible that someone had gotten into the Hollywood Hills house while Ella and Rye were in Vegas and set up electronic surveillance, either audio or video.

Winston shook his head. "Did that, found nothing. But nice of you to double check me."

Liam shot him an apologetic smile.

"Don't worry about me, I don't get my nose out of joint. I know you're trying to cover all bases."

"Mostly I'm just hoping that we'll stumble over something we forgot. Something we missed. I don't know. Maybe I was too quick to assume Gordon's asinine publicity stunt was isolated. Maybe it's actually at the heart of this whole thing."

"So we get eyes on him again. Set up another interview."

Liam nodded. "I will. Although it just doesn't ring for me. But we'll check it anyway." He rubbed his hand over his scalp, then took a long frustrated breath.

"We'll figure it out," Winston assured him. "God knows, I'm invested now too. I'm camping out here with Ella and Rye while they're in town, and then I'm going to head up with them to San Francisco when they finish the tour."

"Are you sure?" Liam asked. "That might be a good time to hand them off to a full service body guard company."

"I'll do that after San Francisco if we don't have this in the bag. But like I said, I want to stick with it. I like them both, and, well..."

"What?" Liam asked, as Winston trailed off.

"Its nothing having to do with your perp. Just those two. My God, he is head over heels for that woman. Reminds me of me back in the day. God, my Linda. I would've done anything for that woman..."

He trailed off again, this time with a melancholy smile lighting his face.

Liam wanted to ask, but he couldn't quite find the words. He knew there'd been a reason that Winston had left West Texas, and he thought that he was seeing a hint of it now.

But that wasn't the only thing that had him holding his tongue. Beneath Winston's pain, there was an undercurrent of something so damn familiar. A kinship between Liam and Winston. And even Rye. A kinship born of loyalty to a woman.

Because with each passing day, Liam felt more and more the same. And as far as Xena was concerned, there was nothing he wouldn't do to keep her safe.

———

"Do you miss it?" Liam glanced over at the woman beside him. They were back in his SUV, driving down the famous stretch of Mulholland Drive that ran along the top of the foothills, separating the west side from the San Fernando Valley.

"Do I miss what?" Xena asked.

"I was watching your face during the concert video," Liam said.

"Don't tell Ella. She'll never let you hear the end of it."

"You can help keep my secrets," Liam said.

She turned in her seat, looking at him, a small shy smile on her lips. "I'll always do that," she said. "You know that, right?"

He did, actually. It was so strange the way that they fit together. The way that she'd simply slid into his life, and fit so perfectly, as if he was one part of a jagged piece of broken pottery and she was the missing piece, and now their rough edges combined to make something perfect and beautiful.

He half laughed, amused by his own flowery thinking. "What?"

He hesitated, wanting to tell her the direction of his

thoughts. Wanting to talk with her and lay out how she made him feel wonderful and confused all at the same time.

Hell, maybe now was the time for that conversation. The famous road was romantic as hell, even in the middle of the afternoon. And he'd enjoy sharing the view with her. "Why don't I find a turnaround and pull over?" he said.

"Why, Mr. Foster. Are you suggesting that we go parking?"

"Maybe I am," he said. "Of course it is the middle of the afternoon."

"I don't have a problem with that if you don't."

He grinned. "Nope. No problem with that at all." He looked around, trying to get his bearings, and was pretty sure there was a turnaround less than a mile away, just past a particularly twisty and narrow section of the road.

They were on a curve at the moment, and when he hit a straightaway, he noticed the vehicle behind them. There had been minimal traffic during the drive so far, and most of the cars had turned off when they hit Laurel Canyon or Beverly Glen, to go down the hill to the west side or into the valley.

As far as he could tell, this one had come up fast behind him out of nowhere. And, he noticed, it was another black SUV, just like the one he'd clocked before they reached Ella's.

He scowled at his rear-view mirror, and released a silent curse. Beside him, Xena shifted. "What is it?" He could hear the nervousness in her voice.

"Hopefully nothing. I just noticed the car behind us." She twisted in her seat, looking through the back window of the BMW. "Is that the same car that was behind us on our way to Ella's?"

Liam grimaced. "Could be. Neither has a front license

plate, but that's not terribly unusual. And from what I can see it's the same model."

"Shit."

"That pretty much sums up my sentiments."

"Can they see us in here?"

"No. The windows are tinted. We can see out easily, but they can't see in."

"Should we let them pass? It might just be a coincidence."

He'd been thinking something along those same lines, but on the narrow road, he didn't want to take a chance if the person behind them was up to no good. And considering the way the last few days had been going—not to mention Xena's entire life—the odds were good that the driver behind them did not have their best intentions at heart.

Making a decision, he turned to her. "Are you strapped in?"

Xena nodded. "Yes, but—"

"Hold that thought," Liam said as he hit the accelerator hard. "And call 911. Just in case I'm right."

The Beemer jumped forward, and he swerved to the left, away from the drop-off that loomed just beyond Xena's side of the car. He could hear her tight gasp beside him, but couldn't take his attention off the road to look at her.

The SUV was closer now, and it made a sharp jut to the right as it accelerated, hitting the driver's side of the BMW near the back tire and shifting the car's ass toward the drop-off.

"Oh my God oh my God oh my God oh my God." Her phone had tumbled to the floorboard, but he could see that she'd made the call, and the phone was automatically sharing its location with emergency services.

He wanted to tell her it would be okay, but he didn't know that it would be. Although he damn sure intended to do everything in his power to make it so. And part of that attempt, unfortunately, meant that she was just going to have to hold on tight and hope that he knew what he was doing, because there was no time for consoling or conversation.

The car shimmied, and Liam realized they'd blown a tire. The SUV had reversed, and was gunning its engine for another slam, and this one would surely send them tumbling over the hill.

There was a guardrail a few feet ahead, and that was what Liam needed. And as the SUV jolted forward, he hit the accelerator, praying that he could cover enough distance before impact. He managed to get close enough that, when the next blow came, the nose of the car rammed the guardrail, stopping them from going over.

But the SUV wasn't giving up, and the driver pounded them again, this time hitting the rear of the Beemer with enough force that the guardrail actually gave way.

Xena's scream filled the car as the sedan started to slide, then jolted to a stop, and Liam realized that part of the now-jutting guardrail had caught the frame.

The SUV wasn't so lucky. The damaged rail had stopped the BMW, but the SUV had hit at an angle and glanced off the rear of his car. The driver had underestimated how much the rear of the car would sway with only the front smashed into the guardrail. It overshot with too much force, and in a cacophony of twisting metal and breaking glass, went tumbling over the drop off to crash into a heap among the trees below.

"Don't move," Liam said to Xena, who was frozen beside him breathing hard.

Around them, sirens blared as emergency vehicles approached.

And it was only when the team had secured the car and safely extracted Xena, that Liam realized he could once again breathe.

20

WE'RE at the site for what feels like forever before the police finally release us and have a patrolman drive us home. But even safe in the backseat of the cop car, my blood is still pounding as I live those last, horrible moments over and over and over.

The driver was the second Vegas attacker, Mouse Face. His real name was Laurence Tesh according to the license they pulled off his body, which may or may not be bullshit. He's one of the men who attacked Ella in Vegas. And he was one of Noyce's men. We've been assuming as much, but today Mario confirmed it.

So that means this horrible dead man who tried to kill us is tied to my past. And that both Liam and I are in danger because of a life I never wanted but can't escape, no matter how hard I try.

That's reality, and it sucks. I want to rail against it. To scream and rant, and then cling tight to something or someone until they set it right.

Automatically, I turn and look at Liam. I'm already holding his hand—we haven't separated since the emergency crew helped us out of the BMW after they stabilized it. For a moment, I just stare, memorizing his features, amazed by how wholly and completely he has become that person in such a short amount of time. The man I want holding me. The person I want comforting me. The lover with whom I want to share my secrets, my hopes, my dreams.

I try to tell myself that it's infatuation or some type of hero awe since he's stepped in to protect me. But I know that isn't true. I've known it, I think, since that first party at Ella's house, the one where we'd both wanted to kiss, but fought the urge.

Today was horrible, but it was also confirmation of just how much this man has come to mean to me. Because as terrified as I was in that car, I was more terrified of losing him.

I suck in a deep breath as tears well in my eyes. Beside me, Liam releases my hand long enough to put his arm around me and pull me closer. And when I rest my head on his shoulder, I almost burst into tears. I'm raw, and I don't know what to do with all these emotions that are going around and around inside me.

I need release—I need *him*.

And right then, what I want more than anything is to be back at his place.

"Xena." His voice is tight, but also gentle. "Are you okay?"

I nod. "That was just—that was just scary." I meet his eyes. "I've seen scary. I've tasted terrified. But the only thing that's messed me up more than tonight was my dad." *Because I lost my dad. And I almost lost you.*

I snuggle closer against him, his body tight and tense, and I know that he is fighting his own battle, too. I've learned how he thinks, and I'm certain that he's feeling guilty. Because even though his specific mission is to keep me safe—and despite spending almost every waking moment with me—he still almost lost me.

Oh, God. He almost lost me. And I almost lost him.

I can't wrap my head around the magnitude of that, and as the cop escorts us to Liam's door, all I can think is that I want him. I want his touch, his mouth, his body. I want all of him, because he's mine—and because he will make me forget.

Best of all, I know he wants it, too, and I'm not surprised when—the moment the door shuts behind us—Liam has me up against the wall, his mouth claiming mine. It's fierce and passionate and I surrender to him, letting myself fall under the spell of his lips, his hands, his touch.

Our kiss is fierce. Fabulous. Teeth clashing, tongues warring, as if this were the ultimate act of connection. As if by kissing me, he is claiming me as his own, marking me as his forever.

And, oh God, I want him to do exactly that. I groan, then suck in air as his hands close over my breasts, teasing my nipples through the thin material of my unpadded bra, then using one hand to unbutton the four tiny buttons that had been holding my blouse closed. He pulls my shirt open, then unfastens the front clasp of my bra to unbind my breasts before his mouth closes over one, his teeth grazing my nipple.

I squirm, unable to stay still from the force of the sensations rising though me, and I move my hands from his shoulders down to his ass, trying to urge him closer.

"No," he says, lifting his head to look at me. I see strength in his eyes along with need and determination. Mostly, though, I see him looking at me. "Arms up," he says, taking me by the wrists and thrusting my hands above my head.

He holds me there, one large hand tight around my overlapping wrists as his other hand explores me. "Close your eyes," he orders, and when I do, his finger strokes me, lightly stroking my cheek before moving lower, taking his time to caress me gently, to tease my nipple, to completely fire my senses, so that by the time he has reached the elastic waistband of the simple skirt I wore today, all I want is for him to rip it off me.

He doesn't. Instead, he hitches it up around my waist, then cups his hand over my pussy, thrusting three fingers inside me so that he has a tight, intimate grip on me. His mouth is on my breast and his other hand is above me, holding my arms firmly above my head.

I struggle, wanting to feel just how completely he has captured me, and as I do, his grip tightens, his mouth moving up to crush mine, his tongue taking me in a wild, erotic demand.

When he breaks the kiss, I am weak, my knees wobbly and my body so overheated, I'm sure that I will melt. "More," I beg.

He steps back, releasing me. "To the bedroom, baby. I promise you more."

I take his hand and slip it back under my skirt, my eyes locked on his. "More," I repeat, and only see confusion in his eyes. "I want you to bring out your bag of toys."

He steps back, releasing me, his head shaking slowly. It's as if I tossed a bucket of cold water all over us, and I desperately hope that I haven't fucked everything up.

"You don't know what you're asking," he says.

"The hell I don't." Anger sparks in me—how dare he presume to know what I need. "You want it—do not even try to say you don't. So why the hell can't you believe that I want it, too?"

"You're sore," he says. "The wreck."

"Yeah, I am," I admit. "But I'd like to be sore from you." I put my hands on his shoulders, moving my body closer. I'm a little afraid that I'm crossing a line, but I'm past the point of caring. "Cuff my wrists," I whisper. "Spank my ass. Give me a bruise that I *want*. Make me stiff in a good way. Dammit, Liam, you want it, too, and for the same reasons."

He tilts his head, his nostrils flaring as if he's fighting some primal urge. *Good*, I think, and press on. "Do you think I don't get it? Do you think I don't understand why you shy away from relationships? Something happened," I say, and see the slice of pain cross his face and disappear, so quick I can almost convince myself that I imagined it.

"The world got out of control and you want to grab it back."

"And you?" His question is hard, almost an accusation. "You were controlled. Forced. Your choices taken away. For years, you were fucking used by those monsters. And now you want me to cuff you?"

"*Yes*." I want to scream the word, as if volume will convince him. "Yes. Cuff me. Blindfold me. Bind my legs. Spank or paddle me." I draw a deep breath, forcing myself to slow my words down. "Whatever you want, Liam. Because I want it, too."

He shakes his head, and I go to him. I press against him, knowing I'm probably pushing too hard, but I no longer care. I'm either going to win or lose, but we're going to finish this.

"I want it," I say gently, "but only from you. Don't you get that? They *took*, dammit. I want to give. You're a strong man, Liam. A powerful one. The kind of man who can make things happen, and I'd be a fool not to know that you're the kind of man who likes to be in control, in and outside of the bedroom."

"I don't need that," he says. "Not like this."

"Of course, you don't. Need isn't the same as desire. And you would never take something you want if you thought it would hurt me." I take his hands. "But please, please understand that your chivalry is misplaced. I want it too. Hell, I crave it."

"Xena, you—"

"Yes, dammit, listen. You want control? Control me. Not because you're forcing me, but because I want to finally, *finally* give someone control rather than having it be ripped from me."

For a moment, he only watches me, and I'm afraid he either doesn't understand or doesn't believe.

Then he meets my eyes and says, "Bedroom."

There's power in that word. Power and demand, and I feel the force of those two simple syllables all through my body.

My knees are weak as I comply, then sit on the foot of the bed. He follows, pausing to lean against the doorframe as his eyes skim over me, his slow, steady gaze making my body tremble with anticipation.

"Take off your clothes," he says. "Then sit back down, legs spread."

My heart pounds in my chest as I comply, already imagining him looking at me, his eyes full of heat, and when I am naked and on the bed, my legs spread so far my inner thighs ache, I'm rewarded by his low groan of satisfaction as well as the way his hand cups his obviously stiff cock.

He moves to the closet, then pulls out the bag. He makes a point of meeting my gaze, then spills out all the toys onto the carpet. I feel my body respond, my nipples going tight as I imagine what he'll do with each toy. What he'll do to me.

"It excites you," he says, and while I hear heat in his voice, I think there is also relief, as if he is only now certain that I'd meant what I said in the hallway.

"Yes, sir," I say, allowing myself the slightest of smiles as I emphasize the last word.

His smile comes easily, and my own wave of relief washes over me as I realize that, yes, we're both finally on the same page.

"What's your safe word," he asks, picking up a blindfold and coming toward me.

I shake my head. "I don't want one."

He lifts a brow. "I don't think—"

"I don't want one," I repeat. "I don't want limits with you. I trust you not to go too far."

For a moment, I think he's going to argue, but then he bends forward and kisses me softly before settling the blindfold on my eyes and tying it just enough so that not even light seeps in under the edges.

I wait for him to ask if it's okay and am thrilled when he doesn't. I want him to claim. To take. I want it because I've given it, and now it's his turn to enjoy what I'm finally— freely—sharing.

"On your knees, baby," he says, his hand at my elbow helping me onto the floor.

I kneel there, listening to him move around the room, then suck in breath as he tugs my arms behind my back, binding my wrists with the padded cuffs before turning his attention to my nipples, his fingers teasing them each in turn as I whimper.

"I'm not asking if you want this," he says. "I'm trusting

that you do. And," he adds, "I'm trusting that you'll tell me if I'm wrong."

I nod, biting my lower lip in anticipation of what I'm sure is coming. Sure enough, moments later, I feel the pressure on my nipples, one after the other. There's pain at first, but then it fades to a nice, deep intensity that seems to stretch like a thread all the way down to my sex.

"Nice," he murmurs, and although I know it's silly, I feel a ridiculous jolt of pride.

I can't see, but I know that he's right in front of me. I can feel his presence, larger than life and wonderfully commanding. And then, as if in confirmation, I hear his hands on his jeans and then the metallic scrape of his zipper followed by the rustle of material.

I make a small, needy noise as heat coils in my belly. I'm wet—I can't touch myself but I can feel the slickness on my inner thighs, and when the tip of his cock brushes my lips, I squeeze my legs together, fighting the urge to come right then as I open my mouth and take him in.

With my hands bound behind my back, I have neither balance nor control. Instead, Liam holds my head, fucking me—*controlling* me—as I submit, reveling in the fact that I am giving this to him. Willingly. Openly. And, more, that he is taking it.

I feel the subtle shifts in his body and am certain that he is close. I expect him to explode in me, but he surprises me, pulling out of my mouth, then taking my arm to tug me to my feet. He turns me around, then pushes me forward until my legs are pressed against the bed. He bends me forward so that my torso is on the mattress and my ass is in the air.

I close my eyes, enjoying the sensation of the bedcover on my clamped nipples. Of the cool air against my heated skin. And of his fingers trailing lightly over my back, then down the crack of my rear until he slips his fingers inside me, his body bending over mine so that the cotton of his shirt brushes my back and his cock rubs my ass as he whispers, "You're incredibly wet." He thrusts his fingers in deeper, then withdraws them, trailing a fingertip lightly over my perineum as I bite my lower lip, lost in a needy, sensual haze. "I like it. Do you?"

"God, yes," I murmur, and he laughs.

"I can tell. Spread your legs, baby."

I do, and he eases off me, lightly smacking my ass with the palm of his hand. I make a low noise in my throat, but press my lips closed. I want more, but I don't want to beg. On the contrary, I want to let him lead this, taking me wherever and however he wants to go.

Thankfully, I soon learn that he wants to go exactly where I do, and he gives my ass another smack, this one harder and followed by his own low moan before he rubs his palm over my skin to soothe me, then slides his hand between my legs to tease my clit.

I wiggle, wanting so much more, and he satisfies me with another spank, then murmurs something about the sweet pink stain marking my pretty pale ass, and how he can't decide if he should keep it pink or go for deep red.

I bite my lip, my breasts aching against the mattress and my sex throbbing with need as he spanks me twice more, then says, "Fuck red. I can't take it anymore."

And then—oh, God, yes—his cock is right there, one hand on my hip and the other sliding between the bed and my body to find my clit as he thrusts into me, fucking me so hard the bed slams against the wall and I think that it's very good that he doesn't share a wall with his neighbor. But that's all I think before passion takes over and I'm incapable of thought. Of anything other than pleasure and sensation and the satisfaction of a spiraling intensity that zooms out to every cell in my body, heating me to boiling as he takes me harder and harder until—finally—I spin up and out, everything inside me ripping apart from my physical body to go whirling off into space, where I finally explode in a fountain of pure pleasure as hot and powerful as a super nova.

I'm breathing hard when I crash back down to earth, and I barely even notice when he gently uncuffs me. He gets onto the bed beside me, and I realize that somehow he'd moved me fully onto the mattress.

"That was insane," I murmur, easing against him. "That was freaking fabulous."

I feel his gentle laughter reverberate through me, and snuggle closer, my hand flat against his chest so that I can feel his heartbeat. For a moment, I simply lie there listening to the sound of our breathing and our hearts beating in the same rhythm. I want to sleep but I'm not tired. I want to know more, I want to know everything. And although I know that Liam does not want to tell me, I push myself up on my elbow and ask very simply, "Will you tell me about her?"

"Who?"

"The woman you loved. The woman who's the reason that you don't do relationships. Did she break your heart?"

For a moment I think he's going to ignore my question and silence hangs heavy between us. When he finally speaks, his voice is so low that I can barely hear him. "No," he says, rolling onto his side. "She's dead. She's dead because of me."

21

I LET his words hang there for at least a minute, then I roll onto my side, spooning against his back. "Tell me the story," I say.

"It's not something I talk about."

"All the more reason. Don't tell it because I'm asking you too. Tell me because you owe it to her to talk about it."

He's quiet, and I press my hand on his bicep, feeling his strength, and I can't help but be struck by the irony that a man this strong can be felled by the weight of horrible memories. But why not? Don't I know better than anyone how the past can affect you?

"It was a long time ago," he says as he turns to face me, his head on the pillow only inches from mine. "But sometimes it feels like yesterday."

A small smile touches his mouth, and it warms me. I'm glad that at least part of this memory brings him a little bit of joy.

"She worked at the makeup department in the Sykes Department Store in London. These were in my early days out of the Army, and I was working a covert job in military intelligence. I had the Sykes job as a cover, though the work was real enough."

I nod, wondering if he understands how much he's sharing with me. How much he's opening up, even though he says he doesn't want to. But I don't say anything. I don't want him to stop talking.

He rolls onto his back, as if he's talking to the ceiling. "Dion was a sweet girl," he says. "Smart, funny, great with the customers. Everybody loved her. She lit up a room when she walked in, and I never heard her say a harsh word to anybody. The moment I met her, I knew I wanted to be around her. Everyone did. She had that kind of personality. I think you would've liked her."

"I bet I would have. What happened?"

"Tragedy. That's always the way it is with these stories, isn't it? There's always tragedy and pain and heartbreak and horror, and it's all a goddamn mess." He pushes himself up so that he's sitting against the headboard. I shift as well, sitting up with my legs crossed, and pulling the blanket up around me so that I'm covered as I face him. "Are you sure you want to hear this?" he asks.

"You know I do."

He nods. "We started going out, first as friends, and then it got serious. I loved her. It boils down to that. We moved in together, bought furniture, and every day she made me smile." He waits as if expecting me to ask a question, but I hold my tongue. This is his story to tell now.

"While that simple, sweet life was going on in our small flat in London, on my off days, I was doing intelligence work, tracking down a man named Anatole Franklin. Definitely not a nice man. He would probably remind you a lot of Noyce."

I shudder simply from the mention of Noyce's name.

"I was getting close to Franklin, and somehow he found out. I don't know how. To this day I have no idea what set him off or how he found out about Dion, but he waited for her outside of the department store, followed her home, and shot her on our front porch stoop." His voice is flat, as if he's giving a police report, and I realize that he's fighting to control the anger and pain.

"Everyone who came by the building saw her splayed out on the stairs as emergency services tried to revive her. They couldn't. She was dead before I got there. I didn't even have a chance to say goodbye."

"Oh God, Liam. I'm so sorry. How did they know it was him?"

"It was a message to me. I knew it was him even before confirmation. But I guess he was afraid that I might miss the point. He made sure he was seen, and there were plenty of witnesses. Three different people identified him from mug shots. But I knew where to find the son of a bitch. He hadn't counted on that."

"What do you mean?"

"I don't think that Franklin realized how close we were on his trail. We knew where he was holed up, we knew what his next move was going to be. He'd been a high placed US official based in the embassy in London, which he'd used as a doorway to other countries we weren't so friendly with. He'd been trading government secrets and he was willing to kill to protect his ass."

"You killed him."

"I did. The government wanted him—badly. They wanted what was in his head. But goddamn it, I didn't care. I was wild with rage, crazed. I forced open his door, raised my weapon, and shot him in the head." He turns now to meet my eyes. "And I don't regret it."

I lick my lips. "What happened?"

"Well, as I'm here, I obviously didn't end up in prison, military or otherwise. He was selling very serious state secrets, after all. And although the government wasn't impressed with my decision to take him out before they were ready, they ended up simply discharging me. Thankfully not dishonorably."

"You were lucky," I say, and he nods.

"My superiors spoke up for me. They knew well enough what I'd been through. And that nothing they could do to me would be worse than what Franklin had already done."

For a moment, I'm quiet. Then I move to sit next to him, leaning against him, wanting to feel his warmth against my body. I take his hand and hold it, our fingers twined. "You know it wasn't your fault, right? You didn't kill her."

"If I hadn't loved her, she would still be alive. He killed her because she was important to me."

If I hadn't loved her...

That's what he's thinking of course, that's why he can't be in a relationship. It's the fear that anyone he gets close to will be taken from him. I understand it. My whole life was taken from me and God knows I'm scared of getting involved too. But I'm hoping that the man sitting next to me will be able to exorcise my demons and clear a path for me to have a normal life and normal relationships.

I don't know if I can be of any help to him, though. All I can do is try to let him see that he has strength enough within himself already to survive whatever life throws at him.

"If I hadn't loved her," he repeats. Then he turns to me, his eyes dark. So dark that they almost scare me. "Please," he says, his voice tight with emotion. "Please don't ask me to love you."

I stay silent, fighting tears. But the truth is, I know that he already does.

22

HE KNEW she didn't truly understand. They were both alike in that they were avoiding relationships, but she was avoiding them because she was the one at risk. He cut himself off because being close to him put others at risk. His job was his life, and his life was dangerous.

"I know what you're thinking," she said.

"Do you?"

"You're thinking that you're a magnet. Not just that you attract women with your amazing charm and incredible looks, but that you're a magnet for pain and for suffering. After what happened to Dion, who could blame you?"

He said nothing. He had already said everything he wanted to say.

"But the truth is, there are a lot of things in this world that are scarier than being in the cross hairs because I'm your girlfriend."

His body tightened at her use of the word girlfriend. But that wasn't someplace they could go.

"Scarier things," he said, trying to lighten the mood. "Like what?"

"Like being without you, dummy." She smiled, as if to underscore that she was teasing. But then she bit her lower lip, drew in a breath, and said, "I'm falling in love with you, you know."

Such simple, common words. Words he hadn't heard for a long time, and that he'd told himself he would never want to hear again.

And he didn't. He shouldn't.

Because those were dangerous words. Those were words that could get a woman killed. And yet at the same time, those gentle, wonderful words lit her from within, making her more beautiful than she already was.

"It's too soon for words like that," he said, wanting to dull the moment. To take away some of its shine. To make it not be something wonderful and precious that he wanted to hold close to his heart.

If she was offended or hurt by his seemingly casual brush-off, there was no sign. She just shook her head gently and said, "No, it's not. It's never too soon for truth. But if you need time to say it back, I understand. In the meantime, I want you to know that I do love you. And nothing you can say or do will flip off that switch inside me."

He searched her face, looking for any hesitation. But all he saw was love. And damned if he didn't have a clue what to do with it.

She yawned, then flashed an apologetic smile as she slid under the covers and curled up against him. "You made a horrible day wonderful," she said. "Now I just want to sleep and pretend like the time between leaving Ella's and walking through this condo's door never happened."

He couldn't argue with that. After almost being killed, there was nothing else he'd needed except her. And they'd made love wildly and with so much feeling, that he felt as if some core part of him had changed forever. But not changed enough to confess something as dangerous as love.

Hell, even knowing the way that she felt about him seemed dangerous. As if she was courting trouble. As if she'd opened a magic box and let all the evil spirits free.

At the same time he couldn't deny the unexpected, amazing truth. Her confession of love had filled him with a sense of warmth unlike anything he had felt in years. It was uplifting and incredible. It was everything he wanted and everything he needed, and it was everything he wanted to run from.

Except that he didn't want to run. Not really. He fit so well with this woman that it felt like a miracle. And the irony of it was that she couldn't be his miracle. Not now; not ever. Because while he might have a reputation as a badass, the one thing he knew would destroy him was losing her.

He could have lost her tonight, and she wasn't even his yet. Not really. And knowing that she might have gone over in the car, that she might have died, that she might have been lost to him forever...

Well, that was something that ate at his soul.

He would protect her. That was the mission. That was what he'd been hired to do.

He would fall in love with her because he couldn't help it.

But in the end, he would leave her, because he had to.

Because the bottom line was that he would do whatever it took to protect the woman he loved. And that included doing something that hurt her.

Beside him, her breathing had slowed. She'd fallen asleep, and he knew that he should do the same. It had been one hell of a long day. Wonderful in many respects, trying in

694 | J. KENNER

so many others. And now he just wanted to slide underneath the covers and let sleep settle over him.

But just as that sweet curtain was about to fall, his own thoughts came back to him—*He would do anything for her. Anything to protect her.*

He bolted out of bed, grabbed his phone, and hurried into the other room so he wouldn't wake her. He dialed, then waited impatiently before Winston picked up the phone.

"I heard about the accident," the Texan said. "You okay? I was going to call earlier but I figured you needed the rest."

"We're both a bit shook up, but no permanent damage. What were you going to call about?"

"The coincidence, my friend. Don't tell me you haven't been thinking about it, too."

"Xena and I being followed so soon after we left Ella's house? And our New York suspect avoiding his very own Manhattan apartment?"

"You read my mind." Liam could hear Winston sigh on the other end of the phone line. "I keep running new checks on this house, thinking maybe I missed a bug, maybe the phone is tapped, but nothing pops."

"I think we need to take a closer look at Rye," Liam said.

"I don't argue with your line of thinking, but I don't see him as our perp. He's too invested in Ella. Either that or he's the world's greatest actor. And I've checked his phone. Calls, text messages, even Facebook posts. So how's he communicating?"

"I don't know. But he's our guy. I'm sure of it. But I'll say his motives are pure."

"What the hell do you mean by that?" Winston asked.

"He's protecting Ella. You said it yourself, he would do anything for her."

"And somewhere along the way, they threatened to hurt her if he didn't help them. You think he's been helping them since the cabin." It wasn't a question, Winston knew exactly what Liam was thinking. "You think he knows where Noyce is."

"I don't think it matters if he knows where Noyce is. All that matters is that he can get Square Jaw to where I'll be. Once I have Square Jaw, I'm sure I can convince him to contact Noyce for me."

Winston snorts. "I'm sure you can. So where are you heading."

"I'm heading to New York, and I want you to make sure Rye knows that. He'll get information to our good friend."

"And if he doesn't?"

"Then we have to decide if we misjudged our buddy Rye. But you and I both know we haven't."

"That's a complicated sting you're constructing. You run it by Ryan? And how do you plan to handle it?"

"I will. And I'm pulling in someone with skills to help me."

"Dallas Sykes," Winston said.

"He'll work with me on this. And I also think that Noyce will come after us himself."

"You mean if Xena is the bait, don't you? Are you willing to take that risk?"

"I'll talk to her about it, of course. But if we don't take the risk, she'll never have a normal life. And I want to end this. I want to see her safe."

And, he thought to himself, he would do whatever it took to make sure that she was.

23

I STEP from the portable staircase into the open door of a private jet. A woman with short golden hair stands there in a white blouse and freshly pressed slacks holding a highball glass with what I think is bourbon and a flute with something that looks sparkly and cool with a piece of fruit in the bottom.

"Good morning, Ms. Morgan. I'm Talia, and I'll be taking care of you and Mr. Foster on the flight. Can I offer you a glass of sparkling water with a hint of raspberry? Or perhaps lime?"

I glance back at Liam, amazed that with everything else he had to arrange to make this trip happen so quickly that he'd thought to tell the staff I wouldn't want alcohol. "Thank you," I say. "I'd love to try it with raspberry."

"My pleasure," she says, handing me the flute. "Sit anywhere, and I'll bring some fruit and cheese after takeoff."

"Right. Thank you." I'm certain I seem overwhelmed by my surroundings, but that's only because I'm overwhelmed by my surroundings.

I step further into the cabin, and then simply pause as I take everything in. As Liam talks to Talia behind me, I take the time to look around the jet. I have no idea what type it is. As far as I know, it is simply a vehicle that flies through the sky and is fancy as hell.

The cylindrical interior is the epitome of comfort, and the furnishings are such to put an airline's first class to shame. Not that I've ever flown first class, but I do watch movies, and so I've seen a lot of airplane interiors. This interior looks like a contemporary furniture showroom with rich wood and soft, supple leather.

In the front there are several individual chairs arranged opposite a tan sofa of the same leather, making the area look like a cozy living room. At the back of the plane I see four chairs grouped together around a table, and I assume that's used as an in-flight work area. I choose the sofa, hoping that Liam takes the seat beside me.

The windows behind me are small, which seems a shame, but I assume that has something to do with air pressure. I'm not afraid of heights, and I wish that one entire wall could be glass so that I could see the world disappearing beneath us.

I turn and look toward the front. Liam is still talking, standing with Talia and a man in uniform who I assume is the pilot. I notice an open folding door that probably serves as a barrier between the crew and us. Since it's open now, I can see what I'm pretty sure is the kitchen area—called the galley, I think—and beyond that I see the cockpit, where another man in uniform is adjusting knobs on a complicated console.

I catch Liam's eye, and he smiles, then hands a clipboard and pen back to Talia, who trades him for the highball glass.

A moment later, he's beside me. "Share your sofa?"

"Not with just anyone," I say, then make a show of looking him up and down. "But you'll do."

He grins, settles in next to me, and takes a sip of his bourbon before taking my hand. I sigh. The circumstances aren't ideal—we're off to trap a bad guy—but other than that, I could get used to this.

"I never thought to ask," he says. "Have you been on a private jet before?"

Considering he knows my history, I understand that he's really asking if I was one of the girls selected to go out into the world and party. Girls taken in private jets to private islands. Girls who wore fancy clothes and tiny bikinis, assuming they were lucky. Girls who often never came back, and while those of us left behind liked to pretend that they were being treated like princesses on tropical islands, we knew it was more likely that they were dead. Or worse.

"They only kept me in New York," I say. "Actually, this is only my second time on a plane at all. Ellie doesn't like to fly, and with the band and the equipment it's easier to go by bus. Now that she's getting huge, though, I think she's going to have to start going the private jet route. Too much time wasted on the road."

"Your second time," Liam says thoughtfully. "You told me Corbu's fake modeling agency paid for your plane ticket, so I'm guessing that was the second time. When was the first?"

"My mom and dad took me to Disneyland when I was five. I know we flew, but I don't remember that part at all. Or Disneyland, really."

"Not at all? That's terribly sad."

"Well, I remember the colors, and I remember princess dresses. They must have made a big impression, because for years I imagined myself in a princess dress." My imagination suddenly conjures me in just such a dress with Liam beside me in black tie and tails.

I look up, feeling a bit ridiculous, and see him smiling enigmatically back at me. I mentally cringe, wondering if he actually read my strange thoughts.

I don't have time to worry about it, though, because a moment later, the captain's voice comes over the intercom, telling us to be sure that we're buckled up for takeoff. Talia sits in the galley in what Liam tells me is called a jump seat.

Soon we're moving, and it feels almost like being in a car until we get to the runway and start to pick up speed. We move faster and faster, and I'm starting to think that nothing is going to happen at all, when I suddenly feel the angle of the plane shift slightly. There's a sensation of something building and building, and then, finally, a sudden, cathartic release.

I look down and realize that I've been squeezing Liam's hand so hard my knuckles are white. He looks at me, his expression both gentle and concerned. "Are you okay?"

I nod and release his hand. "I don't know why I grabbed on so tight. I'm not scared at all. I promise. That was magnificent."

"A little like sex?"

I glance down, weirdly shy, but I agree, and I'm sure he knows it.

A moment later he tilts my chin up and kisses me gently. "Thank you for doing this."

"You don't have to thank me. It's my ass on the line, remember?"

"I know, but we're moving faster than we expected, in a direction that we're not entirely sure about."

"I know." Since Winston and Liam suspect that Rye has been feeding information to Noyce through Mouse Face and

Square Jaw, they decided to set up a sting to grab Square Jaw who, hopefully, can lead us to Noyce. Although, as Trevor mentioned in our pre-departure meeting, it's likely that Noyce has left the country altogether, and the best we'll be able to do is interrogate him—and hopefully use him to track his boss. That wouldn't be the ideal outcome, but I know it's likely. It means I'm a target for longer, of course, but at least I'll still have Liam beside me.

The plan is for Winston to tell Ella that I've gone to New York. He'll say that I'm staying with Liam in his Manhattan apartment while he uses some of his old resources to hope-fully track down more information on Noyce. The hope is that Rye will get the impression that I'll be spending a lot of time alone in Liam's apartment while he's off doing his thing.

Of course, that won't be true. But if the bait works to lure in Square Jaw, aka Patrick Weil, or Noyce, then maybe—just maybe—I'll be able to live a life where I'm not constantly looking over my shoulder.

"And you're sure you're comfortable doing this?" Liam asks me.

I laugh. "Of course, I am. Besides, it's too late now. We're already airborne."

"Well, I could always divert to Paris."

"Sadly, I didn't think to bring my nonexistent passport," I quip. I squeeze his hand. "Seriously, I'm fine, and we need to do this. We need to get it over with. *I* need it to be over."

All of that is true, of course. But my biggest fear is that once this threat is out of my life, Liam will be, too. But I don't have a choice. I have to get free; I have to break these chains so that I can have a life.

He studies me, then finally seems convinced that I mean what I say.

"All right, then. Give me a few minutes to check a couple of things, and then we'll figure out a way to occupy the rest of the trip."

I grin at the thought of what we might figure out, then lean back, thinking about what is in store for us next. The ultimate destination is his apartment, but we're heading first to Long Island to stay overnight with his friend Dallas Sykes in Southampton, along with his very pregnant and bedridden wife Jane, a part of the equation that Rye isn't privy to.

The practical purpose of the detour is to pull in Dallas's help with both information and building a team. But since Liam grew up with both of them, and they are both his best friends, he says he wants me to meet them, along with his mother. I'm flattered and a little heart-fluttery, but I'm trying not to read too much into that, because what I want it to mean is that Liam wants to stay with me even once I'm clear of the threat. But that's not something I can assume—I know his fears, his worries. And I know that I can't convince him not to be afraid. I can only hope he convinces himself.

Since that isn't something I want to think about, I distract myself by flipping through an entertainment magazine until Liam closes his laptop and turns to me.

"All done?" I ask.

"All done," he says, then gets up, says something to Talia, and closes the door between us and the galley.

I raise a brow when he turns back to me. "So, you said you had ideas for occupying the rest of the flight," I prompt.

"I'm full of ideas. We could talk, read, watch a movie ... or I could turn on the Do Not Disturb light and induct you into the mile high club. Your call."

"I love a guy who supports new experiences," I say,

relishing the tingly sense of anticipation spreading through me.

"I'm very glad to hear it." He pushes the button for privacy and returns to the sofa. And as the plane continues to climb, I surrender to what I hope is not one of the very last times I will be with this man.

————

There's a car waiting for us when we land at a private airport somewhere on Long Island. A limo, actually, and Liam tells me that Dallas sent it for us. The driver, a man about Liam's age with bright red hair and a goatee, greets Liam as Mr. Foster and me as Ms. Morgan. He opens the rear door for us with a flourish, his arm indicating that we should get in.

Liam nods at me to go first, then hesitates before joining me. "Good to see you, Roger. But what the hell is up with all the pomp and circumstance?"

I lean forward to see better, and watch as the man's firm shoulders go slack and his expressionless face breaks out into a grin. "Damn, buddy, but I'm glad you're back. I wasn't sure what the protocol was with our guest."

Liam bends over and meets my eyes. "Xena, this is Roger. Roger, Xena. She's... " He hesitates for a moment, then says, "She's with me."

Roger bobs his head, the ginger strands catching the sunlight. "Nice to meet you. Shouldn't take too long to get you to the house. Traffic's light."

He shuts the door, and Liam and I are alone in the back of the limousine. The privacy barrier is up, and I expect that Roger will open it since he and Liam are clearly friends, but he gives us our privacy, and I turn to Liam and ask who the guy is.

"He's exactly who he seems to be," Liam says. "He's one of Dallas's drivers. He also used to do odd jobs for Deliverance. He's a good guy, and he and his family have been working for the Sykes family since we were in elementary school. So I know him well."

We pass quaint shopping areas with coffee shops dotting the sidewalks, and everything has that shiny, polished sheen that comes from money. From there we move into more residential areas, and as we get further and further in, the houses become more and more impressive.

As we drive, Liam points out a few landmarks—restaurants, clubs, the houses of people he knows as well as people he doesn't, but who have a reputation.

The entire area seems to bleed money, and each home feels more and more lush until finally we turn onto a private drive leading up to a stunning multistory mansion that even compared to what I've seen driving through the ritzier areas of LA looks like a residence for a foreign prince.

"This is where you grew up?" I can't help but gawk at this incredible place that rises in front of me like a castle in the middle of a street full of castles. "This is beyond amazing."

"It is," he says. "Not that I realized it when I was a kid. My mother never made a big deal about it. Not about the fact that the house was over-and-above, not about the fact that the Sykes family has more money than the gross national product of many small countries, not about any of it. And certainly not about the fact that we weren't in that income bracket ourselves. She was the help, and I was her son, and that was why we were there."

"She sounds like a great mom. Down to earth."

His eyes warm. "She is. And she never encouraged or discouraged my friendship with Dallas. As far as she was concerned, she was an employee, but I was a guest. And the family saw it that way, too."

The house is even more impressive as we get closer, and I can tell it's larger than I originally thought. "She was *the* housekeeper? That place is huge."

"The head of a team," he clarifies. "Nowadays, she's the only one who lives on site, though. Her and Archie."

"Archie?"

"Butler," he says. "In name, anyway. He was also part of the support for Deliverance. I wish you could meet him, but he took his annual vacation early so he'd be home for Jane's due date."

"What about your mom? Did she know, too? I thought Deliverance was a secret."

"She knows now. She didn't always." He sighs as the car comes to a stop in the drive. "Anyway, this is it. This is my childhood home."

"It's amazing."

"I know it is." I can hear the emotion in his voice, but can't quite place it. A bit of melancholy mixed with pride, maybe. "It's a special place," he says. "But it wasn't until I was older and on my own that I realized what a gift it was to be part of the family."

"Wow," I say as we step through the massive double doors that lead into a stunning entryway full of natural light.

"Impressive, isn't it?" Liam says.

I'm about to agree, when I hear a rich, cultured voice say, "My father intended this room to welcome, impress, and intimidate his guests." The words seem to hover in the air, as if drifting down from the heavens. "Somewhat contradictory goals, I'll admit. But I think he accomplished it. Then again, Eli Sykes is a man who tends to do whatever he sets his mind to."

The voice is coming from the man standing at the top of the ornate wooden stairs. He's tall and lean, and his broad shoulders strain against the simple gray T-shirt he's wearing. His hair is dark brown with hints of blond, as if it's been sun-kissed, and even from this distance I can see his vivid green eyes.

Dallas Sykes. I've seen his photograph on social media and in tabloids for years, but they don't do justice to the man.

"And you aren't?" Liam asks as Dallas strides down the

stairs with the easy gait of a man who is completely at home in his surroundings. Makes sense, I suppose. This is his home, after all.

"I never said I wasn't," Dallas counters. "Then again, I usually go after what I want with less subtlety. Father builds mansions. I take a less metaphorical approach to what I want to accomplish. Right now," he adds with a flash of his famous smile, "I want to meet Xena."

"Oh," I say, a little shaken to be on this man's radar. "Hi." I take his outstretched hand, finding his handshake as firm as one would expect from a man so self-possessed.

"Liam's told me a lot about you."

"Oh," I say again, wondering where my vocabulary skittered off to. I glance at Liam, who just smiles and shrugs.

"Good things," Liam assures me, with a smile that has just enough heat to make me blush, because I'm certain that Dallas has picked up on that, too.

"Listen, Jane is dying to meet you, but she just woke up and asked if we could give her half an hour or so to shake off the sleep. No caffeine on bed rest," he adds with a grim smile to me. "There are a lot of reasons I'll be happy when the baby arrives. Not long now."

"Don't get too eager. She'll probably stay off a while longer if she's breastfeeding."

He nods slightly. "I've thought about that, but I think the trade-off is worth it. A father," he says with so much awe in his voice it almost melts my heart. "Can you believe it?" he asks Liam.

"Hell, no," Liam says, his expression deadpan except for his eyes, which totally give him away. A smile bursts onto his face, as if he just can't hold it in any longer. "Damn, buddy, part of me can't believe you're going to be a father, and the other part can't believe you two waited this long."

"You better believe it," he says. "You're going to be the godfather."

"Damn right I am."

"Are you having a boy or a girl?" I ask.

"That's a question for our doctor," Dallas says. "Although she won't tell you. Strict orders that no one knows until the birth. And that includes me and Jane."

"That's fabulous," I say. "I love that you're doing that."

"Thanks," he says, sounding sincere. "I'll put you in a room with our parents. They think we're insane." He glances at his watch. "I told Jane I'd bring her some herbal tea. Liam, you know where we are. Show Xena around, introduce her to your mom before Helen heads back to the cottage, and by that time Jane should be human again."

Liam nods. "You know I'm going to tell her you said that, right?"

Dallas looks at me. "He always liked her best."

"She's cuter than you are."

"Can't argue with that. Xena," he adds to me, "it's a pleasure. We'll talk more soon."

"Thanks," I say. "It's terrific to meet you."

He heads off, and Liam takes my hand, leading me past the staircase toward the rear of the house. I'm no stranger to luxury—the complex I lived in until I managed to escape was a gilded cage, and the mansions that we were sometimes transported to for parties and events were always ornate, even high-class, if something used for such a perverted purpose can be considered high-class.

This place, however, is different. It's clear that everything is high quality and undoubtedly expensive. It's beautiful and luxurious, but it's also comfortable. It's a home, I realize, and that makes it all the more special.

I tell as much to Liam, trying to put my thoughts into

words and afraid that I'm failing miserably. But he gets it. Maybe I'm doing a better job expressing myself, I think—or maybe he just gets *me*.

Either way, he lifts our joined hands and brushes a kiss over my knuckles, the gesture so offhand that I'm not even sure he realizes that he's doing it.

We meander down long hallways, and I rubberneck, taking in everything as we walk. "What's that?" I ask, noticing clear glass discs mounted just under the ceiling at almost every corner.

"Security system," he says. "The house is equipped with a silent alarm. The discs are unobtrusive, but when the alarm is tripped, the glass flashes blood red. It turns solid red once the system contacts 911, which it does if no one disarms it within ninety seconds."

"That's fast. How far do you have to sprint to disarm it?"

"Not far. We all have the system controls on our phones. Dallas has it on his watch, too."

"So if I run in and out of the house, Dallas's arm is going to buzz? Sounds like a sadistic form of entertainment."

"You're a strange woman."

"A little," I admit.

"And yes," he says, "unless the system's been disarmed for that particular door. The windows are always armed for breakage, and the perimeter of the yard has sensors that turn on video monitoring systems. There's more—with a family this wealthy, there's always more—but the bottom line is that they're safe here. And," he adds as he holds my gaze, "you're safe here, too. I promise."

"I never doubted it," I say honestly. "I was just curious."

"What else are you curious about?"

"Where you're taking me, for one thing. We've been

walking for miles." That's only a slight exaggeration. We've traversed so many hallways I regret not wearing sneakers.

"Almost there," he says as we turn yet another corner and end up in what appears to be a different wing of the house. It's as well appointed, but seems less lived-in. My perception surprises me, and I realize that even though the main part of the house is stunning and expensive and a bit like walking through a museum, it also feels real and homey. This section feels a bit like a hotel. Nice enough, but transient.

I don't think too much about it until he says, "This is it."

I frown. "What?"

"This is where I grew up."

"Really?" I don't mean to sound surprised or, worse, insensitive, but he must hear something in my voice, because he laughs.

"Trust me, it wasn't like this back then. Dallas gave Mom one of the cottages on the property and she moved out of the main house about the time I went into the service. The cottage is nice, don't get me wrong, but this place is home. Although it felt more homey before it was converted to a guest wing."

He gestures to the tiled expanse of hallway. "I rode my bike along here. Jane and Dallas and I built incredible forts down here. And this," he adds, opening the door to a medium-sized room dominated by a four-poster bed, "used to be mine." He shrugs. "Of course, the furniture's changed quite a bit. Originally, I had a bed shaped as a sports car. My mom's Christmas splurge when I turned eight. Later I got a bunk bed, although the only ones who ever slept over were Dallas or Jane. And the walls were covered with movie posters and bookshelves."

I try to imagine his childhood room, and it slowly comes

to life. "What did you look like back then? In elementary school? High school?"

"Elementary school? I was scrawny. Seriously, a skinny thing like you could take me." He grins to show he's kidding.

I roll my eyes. "Let me guess, you were picked on and decided to start working out, and that's how you became this incredible specimen of maleness." I move my hand up and down, indicating his entire body, which as far as I'm concerned is about as perfect as they come.

"Not exactly," he says, and his voice is so heavy that I realize I've struck a nerve.

"I'm sorry. I didn't mean—"

"It was the kidnapping."

I frown, momentarily confused, and then it hits me. "Dallas and Jane," I say. "You felt helpless."

He nods. "And scared. If I'd been there, I would have been no help at all, and probably taken, too. Or killed. So I made myself strong."

I look at him for a moment, my heart breaking for the little boy he used to be. I think of everything he endured, and I think about the choices he made to protect himself and his friends. And I think about what he's now doing to protect me.

"No," I say. "You were already strong. You just worked out so that your muscles could catch up to the man you already were."

I hear his soft inhalation of breath and see a muscle move in his cheek. He swallows, then takes a step toward me. Slowly, he bends to kiss me, as sweet and gentle as butterfly wings. "And that's why I adore you. After everything you've been through, you still see the world with such sweet optimism."

"I see the truth," I say simply. But as I speak, my heart is dancing. Maybe he hasn't said he loves me, but his words come awfully close.

———

"There you are!" Liam's mother stands in the middle of the aromatic kitchen beside a huge work island, her arms held out to welcome Liam's hug. I smile at the way he dwarfs his mother, at least two heads shorter than him, then automatically straighten my posture when she releases him and turns to me. "You must be Xena."

She's got the brightest smile I've ever seen, wide and warm and genuine, and I smile back automatically, then let her pull me into an embrace without even thinking about it, something I rarely do.

She steps back to break the hug but keeps her hands on my upper arms, as if holding me out for inspection. Which, I realize, is exactly what she's doing when she says, "Let's have a look at you."

Since fair is fair, I take the opportunity to study her more closely. She looks to be in her early sixties, with skin slightly darker than Liam's and eyes that are just as expressive. She wears her hair cut short to her scalp, and it's dappled with silver-gray that makes me unexpectedly melancholy when I realize that neither of my parents will ever age in my memory. They will always be young, but in those circumstances, youth isn't a blessing at all.

She wears a pale blue work dress and a white apron, and she's dressed so much like Alice from *The Brady Bunch* that I really do almost cry. Because that was the show that Ella sat me down to watch after I told her my Susan Morgan runaway story. She decided that I hadn't had a normal childhood and that the remedy was a hefty dose of seventies television.

I'm not sure it helped, but it definitely didn't hurt.

Liam had actually told me about the uniform ahead of time. "Dallas and Jane have told her to wear whatever she wants," he'd said. "And Mom says she's doing exactly that. A little old-fashioned, my mother."

So I'd been prepared for the uniform, color and all. Just not for the effect it would have on me.

"You are just as pretty as Liam said you were," Mrs. Foster says, and I glance at Liam, my brows raised.

He lifts his hands in surrender. "Hey, I'm an honest man. I call them as I see them."

"Well, thank you, then," I tell him. "And you, too, Mrs. Foster."

"You call me Helen, sweetie. And you two are just in time. I made a batch of cookies and was about to take some to Jane, but I'll make a tray with enough for the four of you, and you can take it up," she adds to Liam. She turns her attention back to me. "Chocolate chip okay?"

"More than okay." My mouth is already watering.

"Good." She turns to Liam. "One question and then I will say no more. Are you keeping safe?"

"Safer than when I was in combat."

She snorts. "I think that answer should earn me another question, but I'll give you a pass because I love you. You tell Mr. Hunter to make sure you watch your back."

"Yes, ma'am."

She nods, as if that's the end of that, then focuses on me. "Now you tell me about yourself while I make the tray."

"Can I help?"

She shoos me away with a "sit, sit," and I climb onto one

of the stools by the island while Liam comes to stand beside me, his hand on my shoulder.

"Xena's the personal assistant to a pop star," Liam says. "Ever heard of Ellie Love?"

I'm certain the answer will be no, so I'm surprised when she says, "Of course. *Take Time For Me* is a lovely ballad. I confess the faster numbers just aren't my style."

"We were surprised it did so well, but thrilled. It was kind of a breakout for her. Put her on the serious performer map."

She moves about the kitchen as I talk, then pulls a tray out of a rack beneath a cupboard. The cookies are already cooling, and I look around the kitchen as she moves the cookies onto a plate.

The room is spotless and comfortable. It's huge, but still smaller than I would expect for a house this size, and I wonder if some of the connecting rooms are additional prep or staging areas for the inevitable fancy soirees that must have taken place in this house over the years.

On the whole, though, it's a pretty typical kitchen with one prominent exception. One interior wall is covered by shelving that holds cookbooks, spices, a few small appliances, and some dishes. But one section of the shelving is completely missing, replaced instead by an odd cubbyhole.

I'm so curious that I walk over to take a closer look, only to realize that the space isn't "cubby" at all. It's quite large, really. If I were better at yoga, I could fit quite comfortably in what seems to be a large box stuck inside a wall. As it is, I could still fit, I'd just be squeezed a bit. When I notice the gate-style door that is folded into one side, I turn to Helen. "What on earth is this?"

"A dumbwaiter. Haven't you seen one before?"

I have a vague memory of a dumbwaiter featuring in one

of my favorite books as a kid, *Harriet the Spy*. "An elevator for stuff, right? That lets you send things upstairs without having to carry them yourself." I think about the door. "Like a freight elevator for small things."

"That's it exactly."

"There are several in the house," Liam adds. "We used to play in them. Great for hide-and-go-seek. Whoever's It checks out a room, after they leave you use the dumbwaiter to go hide in that room." He grins. "Thank goodness I wasn't claustrophobic."

I laugh, picturing his large frame crammed into a box.

"They are very handy," Helen says, "though we don't use them anymore. I don't think I've used that one since, oh ... since Mr. Eli was in the master bedroom."

"Dallas's father?"

"That's right. He and Ms. Lisa live in the city now, and Dallas and Jane have the master. That's time, always moving forward."

"That's my mom," Liam says with affection. "Always saying profound things."

"Don't you tease your mother, you hear me?"

"Never. I mean every word I say."

He comes over to kiss her cheek, and she gives him a friendly swat with a hot pad.

Helen goes to the windowsill and takes a fresh daisy from a vase full of wildflowers. She trims the stem, opens a cabinet to retrieve a small glass bud vase, then adds it to the tray. "Now, what was I going to ask you? Oh, yes." Her attention is on me. "How did you get a job like that? An assistant to a singer, I mean. Do you need special training? How did you meet her?"

I glance to Liam out of reflex, and he must see panic in my eyes, because he starts to answer. I don't know what he intends to say, but I'm sure it's not either version of the real truth. Not the *she escaped from the life of a sex slave* truth or the *she was a runaway working as a streetwalker* version of the truth.

But I suddenly realize that I don't want to lie to this woman. And I don't think she will judge me harshly for it.

"Ellie rescued me," I blurt before Liam can speak. I see surprise on his face at first, but then I think it's pride.

"Did she? Well, good for her. And for you. What did she rescue you from?"

"Hell," I say simply. And then I tell her my story. All of it. She doesn't move until I'm finished, just watches me with those kind eyes, and once again, I desperately miss my mother.

When I'm finished, she nods and says to Liam. "You take this tray up to Dallas and Jane. I'll send Xena along in a moment."

"Mom..."

"It's alright," I say, and though he studies me for a moment, he doesn't argue.

"Okay," he says, then winks at me. "Don't let her pry out all your secrets."

"I think I just spilled all the secrets I have."

He brushes a kiss on my cheek before going to pick up the tray. "I'll see you upstairs in a few."

As soon as he's gone, Helen tilts her head, studying me. "Now, why on earth would you tell me all of that?"

It's not the question I expected. I anticipated sympathy. A maternal pat on the back. And I stammer a bit as I say, "I don't know."

That gentle smile is back. "Oh, I think you do."

She's right, of course, and it's all about Liam. I wanted her to know the real truth because I wanted her to see the real me. The woman who's fallen in love with her son. Because no matter what happens between me and Liam, I want his mother to like me. To know me.

She sits on the stool next to me, her back straight and her hands on her polyester-covered knees. "Folks say you can look at someone's palm and tell about their life. Or read their future in tea leaves. Now, I don't know if that's true, but I do know that there's one surefire way to see a person's heart and future. Do you know what that is?"

"No, ma'am."

"You look at how much they've overcome and the people they keep close in their lives. What they've overcome shows their strength. And that strength is what paves their path. And what lights the path? That's the people they surround themselves with."

I blink, my eyes damp.

"You've overcome a lot, my girl. And you've got good people beside you. That singer. My boy." She reaches over and pats my hand. "I've lived in this house a long time, and I've seen a lot of horrible things. Great things, too. All that shit life throws at you. You know what to make of it?"

"Fertilizer?" I ask, and she bursts out laughing.

"Actually, yes. Not very original, I'll admit. But true." She's quiet for a moment, and I have the feeling she's searching for something in my face. "You love my boy."

My back straightens, the result of shock-induced good posture.

I start to answer, but she puts a finger over her lips. "You don't need to tell me," she says. "I have eyes, don't I?"

"I guess you do," I say.

"He loves you, too," she adds, tapping a finger under an eye.

"He hasn't said it." The words escape before I can stop

them, and I hate how insecure and needy I must sound to this woman.

"Does he have to?"

I start to reply, then close my mouth, unsure what to say.

"Love's a rare thing, my girl. And believe it or not, saying it aloud doesn't make it any more true. The words are just reassurance. And I think you already know he loves you."

"I think he's afraid that love isn't enough," I admit, wondering how much she knows about Dion and Franklin.

"Well, he had a hard time of it. But he's overcome it, hasn't he? He's got a well-paved, well-lit path. All he has to do is walk it."

With me, I think. I want him to walk it with me after he slays my demons, but I'm terribly afraid that he won't follow that path.

"And what about you," she asks. "Do you think love is enough?"

"Honestly? I don't know." If Liam loves me but leaves, then isn't it by definition not enough? And don't I already know that love is hardly a miracle cure?

"Don't you?"

A sharp stab of irritation gets me in the gut. "Well, I know that love can't save anybody," I snap, then immediately feel contrite. "I'm sorry. But love isn't a magic pill. My father loved me like everything, and it didn't save me."

"Didn't it? Maybe without that love you wouldn't have had the gumption to survive after you escaped. You might be like the real Susan Morgan now—dead in some unmarked grave—instead of a girl who fought her way free."

The damn tears are back. "I love a lot of qualities in your son," I say, sniffling a little. "Now, I think I know where he gets them."

25

LIAM SET the tray down on one of the accent tables in the great room as Dallas came down the stairs.

"How's she doing?"

"Frustrated that she's stuck in bed," Dallas said. "Also happy to stay there if that's best for the baby, and eager to see you and meet Xena." He nodded at the tray of cookies and milk. "I can take that up, why don't you wait for Xena, then bring her upstairs with you."

"Sounds good."

Dallas took a step toward the table, then hesitated before picking up the tray. "I like her, by the way. A girl who's been through that much shit should be pretty fucked up. But she doesn't seem fucked up at all."

"She's not."

Dallas watched Liam's face, as if his friend was seeing more than Liam's simple denial was meant to show. "So you're heading to your apartment tomorrow?"

"That's the plan."

"Why don't we have breakfast together before you go.

The four of us. I'll cook. And Jane can play hostess from her throne."

"I'm game," Liam said. "Although my mother might have something to say about it. She's very proprietary about her kitchen."

"Tomorrow's the farmers market. She's out by six and doesn't usually get back until at least eleven-thirty."

"Right. I forget. Well, I guess that's one perk of bed rest. You'll be doing the cooking, and not Jane."

Liam watched as Dallas stifled a chuckle. "Now you officially owe me one. Because I imagine you don't want me to tell Jane about that remark."

"I owe you for more than that," Liam admitted. "I owe you for pulling together this team. I couldn't bring anyone from the SSA—if any of Noyce's men were paying attention, they'd know we were here for more than research."

"Happy to help."

"How many have you lined up, and how many do I know?"

"Several, actually. I pulled from our support crew for Deliverance. I set up a video call for today, too. We'll head down to the basement when it's time."

Liam nodded. The basement used to be Deliverance's headquarters. Now it was home base for those times that Dallas—as he'd said—kept his hand in it.

"And, of course, I'm on deck, too."

"No," Liam said. "You're not."

Dallas's brows rose.

"I mean it." Liam was prepared to double-down on this. "These people are dangerous. And you're about to become a father. If you insist on coming with your team, then I just won't use your team."

"That would be a damn foolish decision. One that might get you killed."

"Maybe, but I'm not putting you in the hot zone. Not when Jane needs you. Not when your baby needs a father."

"Christ, Liam, you know—"

"I don't know anything except that's the way it is. So don't argue with me. This isn't Deliverance, Dallas. You don't have the last word."

"Fuck." Dallas ran his fingers through his hair. "Fine. You win."

"I like the sound of that," Liam admitted. "You want to take that up? I'll wait for Xena, like you said."

"Fine. Fine."

Liam laughed. "You're a terrible loser."

"Fuck you."

"Exhibit A, Your Honor."

"I was going to run something by you, but now I'll just leave you out in the cold. Don't blame me if you lose millions on the deal." Dallas let the words hang, his mouth clearly fighting a grin.

With anyone else—except Damien Stark—Liam would consider those words hyperbole. But Dallas has the Midas touch, and while Liam was doing just fine financially, if he ever wanted to start his own family—

He froze, suddenly aware of the direction of his thoughts.

"Liam? You still with me?"

"Sorry. Just remembered something. About work." He shook himself. "What did you want to run by me?"

"A real estate deal. What time are you two hitting the road tomorrow?"

"Between ten and eleven, most likely."

"Perfect. We can have breakfast at eight. I've got a

meeting here at nine. This developer I've been talking to—Norman Erickson—is looking for investors in a couple of refurbishment projects up and down the eastern seaboard."

"You've checked him out?"

"Just started that ball rolling. It's still early days, but the man's had his finger in real estate for years and has a large and varied portfolio. I've got more homework, but so far he passes the sniff test."

"Tomorrow's the handshake test."

"You got it. He's catching a plane at MacArthur around noon and offered to come by the house on his way so we could talk. Since you're here and it might be a good opportunity, I thought you should join us."

"Sounds good. I'll be your wing man."

"You've certainly done that before. Speaking of, tell me what's up with you and Xena."

To anyone else, the massive shift in topic might have seemed strange. But Liam and Dallas knew each other so well, it was nothing more than a conversational river taking a bend around a rocky protrusion.

"I'm protecting her," Liam said. "I already told you the whole story."

"The SSA story. I want to know what's really going on. And don't be an ass and tell me it's nothing. Tell me what she means to you."

Everything. "Dallas, listen, you know I can't—"

"Can't?" Dallas shook his head. "I know you *won't*. And I know that it fucked you up pretty bad after Dion was killed." He dragged his fingers through his thick hair. "I've spent years not talking about it—hell, not even thinking about it —because you asked me to never bring it up. But that was before."

"Before what?"

"Before I saw the way you look at that woman."

An invisible fist tightened around Liam's heart. "Dallas, I mean it. We're not going there."

"Goddammit, Liam. You're my best friend. My oldest friend, not counting my wife. And I'm here to tell you that you have got to move on."

His body was tense, fighting the urge to lash out. "Do you really think that's possible?"

"Look at who you're talking to, for Christ's sakes. Of course I do. You know what I've been through. You know everything I risked. And you also know that part of the reason I risked it was because of you."

Liam stumbled back, shocked by his friend's words. "Because of me? How the hell was I involved?"

"Don't you remember that day on the Island?"

That would be Barclay Island, a retreat that had been in the Sykes family for generations. And Liam knew which time Dallas was referring to. A trip to the island to celebrate Dallas's great-grandfather's hundredth birthday. And one night, Liam had been pretty damn blunt in his attempt to get Dallas to see reason with regard to Jane. "I remember it all," he said. "But that's not even close to the same."

"Don't you think?"

"I'm a risk to her safety, and we both know it. What I do? It can get her killed."

"You think Jane doesn't know that about me?"

"You're out of the game," Liam reminded his friend.

"We both know that's not entirely true. And so does Jane."

"And you're willing to accept the risk. I respect that. I don't know that I am."

Dallas looked into Liam's eyes, his more serious than Liam could remember since after the kidnapping. "If you don't remember exactly what you said to me that day, I do. Shall I remind you?"

"I remember," Liam said. "I told you that Jane was a hell of a woman, and that if it was me who was in love with her, there wasn't a power on earth that could make me stay away."

He'd meant the words, too. Dallas and Jane belonged together, and nothing, not even their familial relationship, should've kept them apart, no matter what stones and arrows they might have to endure.

That's what he'd told himself, but it was more than that. Because there was danger lurking in their lives, too. Dallas was doing then exactly what Liam did now. Helping people by sticking his nose in matters that could get him killed. Or could risk the wrath of some very nasty individuals.

"Are you telling me that Xena isn't a hell of a woman?" Dallas pressed. "I think she is."

The words washed over him; he was too lost in his head. Because unlike everything tangible that Dallas and Jane had faced because they were adopted siblings—the legal barriers, the social shaming, the family's reaction—all Liam was fighting against was love and fear.

He'd always thought that he was a brave man. But maybe he was pushing back on a relationship because deep in his heart, he was truly a coward.

And he damn sure didn't like the sound of that.

————

"Oh, thank goodness," Jane said as Liam, Xena, and Dallas entered the room. "Someone other than my husband to talk to." She grinned, her slightly angled eyebrows rising with her smile as she held her hand out to Xena. "I'm Jane, which you probably already figured out. And this," she added, laying a hand on her belly—prominent even under the covers—"is Mystery."

"Tell me that name's not going to stick," Liam said.

"It started as a joke," Dallas admitted. "Now it's growing on us."

"I think it's great," Xena said. "Then again, I chose my own name, and look what I picked out. So take my advice with a grain of salt."

"I like her," Jane said, with a smile aimed at him, followed by a wink to Xena. "Seriously, it's great to meet you. Sorry I'm not the world's most energetic hostess. Believe me when I say I want to be. And makeup and a hairbrush would have probably gone a long way, too."

"You're beautiful as always," Liam said, kissing her cheek. He meant what he said, too. Her dark brown hair hung in loose waves around her face, and her skin seemed to reflect the light.

"She glows," Dallas said, as if tracking Liam's thoughts. And sounding as proud as if he were the sunlight shooting out of her. In some ways, Liam supposed he was.

"I think you look great," Xena said. "And I love this room."

"Thanks. It was our parents, and then Dallas's, and now ours. Not much has changed. The wood paneling under the chair rail has been here since forever, but we did switch out the wallpaper above the rail. I have no idea what my mother was thinking," she added, shaking her head.

"Well, it's great now," Xena said, shifting her purse. It had her Ruger in it—easy enough to get to New York since they hadn't flown commercial—and he was glad she'd taken him seriously when he said she should keep it with her. Even in the house, it was good to maintain the habit.

"I'm so glad to be here," she continued. "Liam's told me so much about you—and I saw *The Price of Ransom*. I loved it."

Liam looked at her, surprised. He hadn't mentioned that Jane had written the book or the screenplay. She met his gaze and lifted a shoulder. "What? You didn't think I'd learn everything I could about your friends?"

Jane caught his eye, then gave one quick nod of approval. Not that Liam was surprised. As far as he was concerned, there wasn't a legitimate negative word that his friends could say about Xena. God knew he couldn't come up with one.

He was, in a word, besotted. An old-fashioned word, but it summed up his situation nicely. But why wouldn't he be? Xena Morgan was a hell of a woman, after all.

26

"I'M ABSOLUTELY in love with Jane," I tell Liam as we get into the queen-size bed that has replaced the bunk bed in what was once his room. Liam told me earlier that this whole wing is for guests now, and while I think that's a great and practical use of the space, I can't deny that I'm sad not to have seen Liam's real childhood home.

"She's amazing," Liam tells me. "And the three of us—we latched onto each other like superglue."

"That's why what happened to them hurt you so badly, too." Not that my statement is profound. He already knows that.

I wouldn't trade the hours laughing and chatting in Dallas and Jane's bedroom for anything, but the truth is that it's been a ridiculously long day, and I'm mentally and physically exhausted. I'm wearing a tank top and sleep shorts, which made Liam laugh since I've worn nothing in bed since that first night we were together. But this is someone else's house and it just seemed polite to wear clothes.

Now me and my excess layer of material are curled up

against him, my head tucked under his arm. In deference to what he says are my strange rules of propriety he's wearing boxer shorts. But his chest is bare, and I idly trace my finger over the ridges of his abs.

"Jane knows that I love you," I whisper, not sure what prompted me to speak.

"Does she?" I can't read his tone, so I just nod.

"I didn't tell her. After you guys left for that video call, we were talking, and she just … knew."

I stretch, then tell him about my time with Jane. We'd been talking about both the guys and about how Jane had learned about Deliverance, which Dallas had originally kept secret from her. "I guess that was sort of a pattern," she'd said. "Keeping things hidden. We didn't admit we loved each other for the longest time."

And then she'd looked at me and added, "I think he'll tell you soon. But you'll have the satisfaction of always knowing you said it first."

"How did you know I said it?" I'd asked her. "Did he tell you?"

She'd shrugged, one hand idly rubbing her belly. "I guess you told me. It's all over your face. You don't try to hide it at all. Which makes me think he must know, too, or you'd be trying to hide it from him."

"He knows," I'd told her. "But he hasn't said it back. Not out loud, anyway."

Jane had grinned. "Yeah, well, there's saying it and then there's *saying* it. Sounds to me like he's said it."

"Maybe," I'd admitted. "But I don't think love is the problem."

She'd nodded slowly, and even in such a short time I'd come to know her well enough that in that moment I'd thought I understood what was going on in her head. She knew about Dion and Franklin, but she didn't know if I did. And I was ninety percent sure I was right when she said, "Everybody has their issues. Things in their past that color their present. Just give him time."

As far as I'm concerned, Jane's suggestion of time was a good one. After all, I'm certainly not walking away from him —or letting him push me away. But I also don't have a magical toolkit with which to tweak the way he thinks. And even if I did, would I really use it? I love him the way he is, stupid, obstinate relationship phobias and all.

Which means time is the only ally I have. That and his friends.

I smile, realizing suddenly that as much as I love Ella and Rye, I'd been very alone. Now, I think about Jane, who seems to genuinely care, and all of the women from girls' night. I don't think it's an illusion that they like and care about me, and I know I care about them, and I feel tears prick my eyes at the thought that I could lose this small posse that has been growing around me if I lose Liam.

Except I won't lose him. I can't lose him.

I'd survive if I lost him, sure. Because survival seems to be one of my superpowers. I've been surviving for years.

But I've changed since that concert in LA. And surviving isn't enough for me anymore.

"Hey," Liam says gently. "Are you still with me?"

"Sorry." I'd been relaying my conversation with Jane to him when my mind had gone elsewhere. "I started to space out. Anyway, before I came down, I told her how strange it was that she'd seen it on my face. That I love you," I add, looking him straight in the eye because I want him to feel how real it is, and how it's not going to fade even if he shoves me aside. His eyes are steady, never wavering, but they are also entirely unreadable.

"Strange?"

"Yeah. Just weird that she could read me so well. I've spent years hiding my emotions. Any hint of anger or hatred or anything could have gotten me killed. But Jane and Helen both read me like a book."

His mouth turns down as he makes a *hmm* noise.

"Jane said it was because I wasn't safe before. But I am now. With you, I mean. In your world. So thank you," I add, propping myself up to kiss him gently. "It's nice to know I'm not a mannequin anymore. And it's nice that I can say that I love you and not be afraid." *Of anything except you not loving me back*, I add silently.

He says nothing, but reaches for me and rolls me on top of him before pulling my face down for a kiss. It's long and slow and full of the promise of things to come, and I lose myself in his touch, my body warm and ready as his hands slide down my back to cup my ass and push me closer to him.

"Now," I whisper, then immediately yelp when the sharp trill of his cell phone makes me jump.

"Fuck. That's Ryan."

I roll over as he grapples for his phone, then puts it on the bed between us. "What have you got for me?" Liam asks, the moment he pushes the button for the speaker.

"I've got Mario and Quince conferenced in," Ryan says, sounding a bit like he's down a well. "Still nothing at Weil's apartment, and none of our sources have tagged him in the last few days. He's not using his credit cards and hasn't pulled money from an ATM. He's in the wind. And we can't confirm that he ever even heard from Rye that you and Xena are in the city."

I exhale, frustrated. The whole idea is to trap Weil when he comes after me at the apartment. Or, better yet, when he's holed up at his place.

"We'll work with it," Liam says, though I can tell he's frustrated as well. "Worst case, Xena and I will just enjoy our time in the city."

"That's worst case?" I quip, just to lighten the mood.

"Yeah, well while you're enjoying yourself, don't forget to watch your backs," Ryan says. "We're operating on no information here, and that's not how I like to run things."

"Agree," Liam says. "Anything on Noyce?"

"A bit," Quince says. "He's bloody clever, I can tell you that much. Enrique Castille's given me full access to Corbu," he explains, "and he's being very cooperative. Can't blame him. He's in custody while his underling has gone to the wind."

"Does he have any information about his location?"

"No," Quince says. "But apparently Noyce has been collecting aliases for years. Corbu says he doesn't even know all of them, and I believe him."

"Why?" I ask.

There's a pause, then Quince says, "I'm very good at what I do."

I meet Liam's eyes, and he nods. I think about Quince, such a nice guy who's so sweet to Eliza, and try to imagine him in an interrogation room. It's not clicking for me, but I don't doubt his word.

"Have you learned any of his aliases?" Liam asks.

"Several. Emile Neely. Eric Nehu. Edgar Norton."

"Nice that he's predictable."

"Can't argue with that, but according to Corbu, he has such a stockpile, he could just disappear."

"But then I'd be safe, right? If he disappears, it would be

because he gave up on me and is just going to go live his life in Fiji or something."

"Maybe," Ryan says. "But how would you know? He's not going to send you a registered letter saying *Hey, not trying to kill you anymore. Going into hiding, they'll never find me, and you'll never have to testify.*"

"Which means I spend the rest of my life looking over my shoulder."

"I want this fucker," Liam says. "I want him for what he did to all of those women, not just Xena. And I want Xena to not just feel safe, I want her to be safe."

"So do we all," Ryan assures us. "And we're working through all of his aliases, hoping one of them pops. Seagrave's got the SOC on it, too, and Quince has pulled in MI6. I've got Ollie McKee working with the FBI, and we've reached out to other agencies and private entities, too. We'll find him. It just might take some time."

I nod, though Ryan can't see me. I want it over now, but at least the road to getting there is becoming clear.

"Which name is real?" Liam asks. "Edward Noyce?"

"We don't know," Mario says. "That's the name Corbu met him as, and the name he checked out back when he let Noyce into the inner circle. According to him, Noyce made wise investments and managed to turn a decent inheritance into a fortune. But who knows if that story is true, either. I can confirm that Edward Noyce—alias or not—did earn money in the market, but that doesn't prove that it's his primary, original name. Corbu also confirmed that Noyce procured the building that Xena was kept in, and he set up the various shell companies that owned it. Considering that didn't come out while he was in custody, we know the man has solid skills at becoming invisible."

Liam rubs the back of his neck, his expression frustrated. "Bottom line, the man is a chameleon who also knows how to be a ghost."

"At least he has a pattern," I say. "That's something, right?"

"That's something," Quince agrees. "But it's not much."

After a bit more housekeeping, Liam ends the call, his eyes hard on me. "What were you saying about safe?"

"Oh, no," I say, shaking my head. "If I'm not safe it's because of me. My past. Not because of what you do. You're the one who keeps me safe, and you know it."

"Maybe so, but we both know it will never end. Even when Noyce is behind bars—and we will catch him—you'll still be in danger. You'll be in danger because you're my Achilles' heel, and anyone who pays attention will know that."

"Liam, don't. You don't have to be alone because of what you do. Is Dallas? Quince? Ryan?"

He sits up, sighing deeply as he reaches up and rubs his temples with the thumb and middle finger of one large hand. "What I do ... it puts people at risk. And you've been at risk enough. But I'm not sure I care any more. I need you. And I will do whatever I can to protect you."

"I—" My heart is beating so loud I'm not even sure I really heard what he said. "Liam, are you saying—"

"I'm saying that maybe you and Dallas have managed to get through my thick skull. I'm saying I love you. And I'm saying that I couldn't stand it if something happened to you. So I either curl up in a ball and hide from reality, or I go all in and love you—and protect you."

My throat is thick with unshed tears.

"So I'm giving you one chance—just this one chance—to say no. Because if you say yes—if you stay—I'm not ever letting you go."

It's hard to talk, my tears are flowing so freely now, but I nod ferociously, and finally manage to find my voice. "I've never thought of myself as all that smart. And neither are you if you think you can get rid of me that easily."

"Thank God," Liam says, as he pulls me close. His lips brush over mine, soft and incredibly sweet and so full of love it makes me want to cry.

His touch is tender as he slowly peels off my tank and my shorts, then turns more demanding when I'm naked beside him. He undresses as well, then pulls me on top of him. I straddle his waist, my thighs tight against his torso as he reaches up to stroke my cheek.

"I'm sorry," he says.

"What for?"

"For ever thinking I could walk away from you."

Happiness swells inside me as I slide down his body, my sex stroking his erection. I meet his eyes, them slowly take him in, and neither of us look away as I slowly ride him.

One of his hands cups my rear, but he never steals control. The other plays with my breast, and I bite my lower lip, lost in the sweetness of his touch and the power of our connection.

"I want this to last," he says, and I can hear the strain in his voice. He's close and so am I, both of us right on the edge, but not wanting this moment to end.

I press my hands to his chest, feeling his heartbeat through my palms as I rock against him, the slow, easy motion of our lovemaking taking us both higher until, whether we want to or not, we're both forced over, crashing together as our bodies explode as one, pleasure careening through us until I have no choice but to collapse on top of him, our hearts beating as one as my body slowly recovers in his arms.

"That was incredible," I say, propping myself up enough to see his face. "You're incredible."

"I love you," he says, in a voice so full of emotion I feel tears prick my eyes. "And I'm never letting you go."

27

"So that's the proposal." The lean, fifty-something man with silver-streaked dark hair said, gesturing to the plat maps, blueprints, and colorful brochures that littered the formal dining table.

Norman Erickson had arrived less than an hour ago. And while Xena had stayed upstairs with Jane, the two deep in conversation about Jane's experience writing the *Price of Ransom* screenplay and her friendship with Lyle Tarpin, the now-A-list Hollywood star, Dallas and Liam had come down to hear Erickson's pitch.

The man was well-spoken and confident, a born sales-man, and Liam imagined that many a deal had closed as a result of his personality as much as his actual projects. As for that, Liam had to agree that in the moment, the develop-ment investment that Erickson proposed sounded sweet.

Of course, con men were skilled in making anything sound sweet, and despite Erickson's affable nature, there was something about him that rubbed Liam the wrong way.

Since Liam and Xena were heading into the city in about an hour, Erickson was stealing the last few minutes of their time with Jane and Dallas. So maybe he was just disposed to be irritated with the man.

"I've completed a similar project in Dallas," Erickson was saying. "Taking the decaying infrastructure of an under-utilized former industrial area and converting it into a community within a community, complete with high-end condos, a few single family homes, restaurants, theaters, day care, a variety of high-end but unique retail stores, and various other facilities such as spas, fitness centers, medical facilities. Plus plenty of greenspace, of course."

"It's definitely interesting," Dallas said, and Liam couldn't disagree.

"What kind of investors are you looking for, and how many?" Dallas asked.

"You're curious about how many slices of the pie I'm anticipating, and that depends entirely on the quality of the investors. With you involved, perhaps everyone takes a bigger slice. And if that's a factor that plays into your decision, I'm open to talk. Early stages, as I said."

"Are you already negotiating with specific retailers? And who's your architect?" Liam asked, only to say, "Sorry, I need to take this," when his ringtone signaled a call from Winston.

He stepped to the far side of the massive room, his back to Dallas and Erickson as he said, "What have you got for me?"

"Nothing good. Rye's admitted that he told Weil about Ella's cabin—that's how they found you in the mountains. And about your visit to Ellie Love's house the day you almost got run off the road."

"How? You swept for electronics."

"My fault," Winston said. "He had a burner phone, and I fucking missed it."

"Well, you ultimately found it."

"No," Winston said. "I had a come to Jesus with both of them this morning—Christ, they're early risers—and apparently Ellie had mentioned to him how terrified she was for the two of you, and he couldn't live with his conscience. I was right about one thing—he's head over heels for that girl. That's why he did it."

"They threatened her if he didn't help," Liam said, keeping his voice low.

"Got it in one."

"Fucking hell."

"His heart may have been in the right place, but his actions weren't. He should have come to us, not played their game. I'm not sure if Ella's going to forgive him for that."

"Right now, I don't have a lot of sympathy for the man."

"It gets worse," Winston said. "Yesterday, Ellie told Rye how worried she was about the sting at your apartment, and said she was glad they were going to Dallas's first. So at least you two would have a breather before shit hit the fan."

Shit.

With a sudden sense of trepidation, Liam glanced up and watched as the usually clear security disk turn blood red. "Sorry, buddy," he said. "It's too late for that."

———

Dallas was glancing at his phone when Liam casually approached. He nodded, just the hint of movement that let Liam know that Dallas was aware of the threat as well.

The corner indicator turned solid red—emergency services had been called—and then shut off completely.

"Mr. Erickson, if you could wait here, I just received a

text from the property caretaker. Apparently we have a small fire in one of the detached houses."

"Oh! I'm so sorry to hear that. I—well, of course I can wait."

"Liam, would you mind giving me a hand?"

"Not a problem."

They left the dining area, shutting the double doors behind them. "Noyce or Weil?" Liam asked as soon as he was certain Erickson wouldn't overhear them.

"Can't get a solid visual," Dallas said. "But the breach is in the guest wing. Someone broke a window and ninja'd their way in."

He passed Liam his phone, which displayed the security system's video feed. The intruder wore a black skin suit along with a hood, but the placement of his head made it impossible to see his face.

They hurried past the kitchen and into the wing where Liam had grown up—and where Liam knew there were only three routes to the rest of the house. A twisting passage that passed near the kitchen—their current location. The solarium walkway that led along the length of the house and terminated at the morning room. And the stairwell in the middle of the hall that led to the second floor and was slightly closer to their position than the intruder's entrance point.

"I remotely locked the stair door," Dallas said as they rounded the penultimate corner. "With luck, we'll get there before he breaks through. You armed?"

"These days, always."

"Good."

"You?"

Dallas shot him a wry look. "At home, not usually. With you two in the house, I decided to carry."

"Smart man."

They were close to the final turn, and Dallas held up a hand indicating silence, and they moved the rest of the distance more slowly, taking care not to let any sound give them away. Liam said a silent prayer that the perp was still there. From this position, once on the second floor, he was too damn close to Xena and Jane, and he hoped like hell that Jane had seen the alarm. Dallas would have locked them in remotely, but Liam wouldn't feel safe until he had Xena in his arms and saw with his own eyes that Jane and the baby were fine.

Slowly, they approached the corner, and when Liam sidled in front of Dallas, his friend let him, presumably understanding that Liam considered this his fight.

The bastard was there, and when he lifted his head, Liam saw it was Square Jaw, aka Weil. In one motion, Liam lifted his weapon, fired a warning shot, and told the fucker to drop his gun. He'd have preferred to put the bullet right between the bastard's eyes, but they needed him if they were going to have any chance of finding Noyce.

Weil, however, wasn't cooperating, and as Dallas approached on Liam's left, Weil lifted his gun, the sight on Dallas. A cold blast of fear and fury sliced through Liam, and he threw himself onto Dallas, knocking him out of the way a split second before the gun discharged.

His ears rang from the shot, and his left shoulder stung like a bitch.

He was on the ground on top of Dallas, and only barely realized it when Dallas shoved him off, pulled out his own gun, and fired.

Weil dropped, and Liam struggled to his feet as Dallas approached cautiously, his weapon trained on the fallen man.

"Dead," he said, turning back to Liam. "Shit, man."

"Clean entry and exit," Liam said, as Dallas scowled and hurried over. "I'll be okay." He was still in shock and his ears still rang, but his upper arm was numb, and that was a blessing. His fingers worked fine, and as far as he could tell, the bullet hadn't hit any major vessels.

He used his good hand to unfasten the buttons of his shirt, then handed it to Dallas. "Tight," he said, as he fumbled for his phone and the rarely used home security app for the Sykes house. Video surveillance was always unavailable unless there was a breach, and in that case, every room became visible. And even though he could see Weil's corpse, he wanted to confirm that the girls were safe.

They weren't. And what he saw made his blood run cold.

"Norman Erickson," he said, his voice raspy. "Initials N and E." He met Dallas's eyes and saw his own dark fear reflected right back at him. "He studied me. Realized we were friends. He knew I'd eventually come here."

"He's been positioning himself with me," Dallas said. "He set me up—he set both of us up. And now he's got Jane and Xena."

Liam forced down the fear and the pain, operating only on raw fury. That's what he needed. That's what would destroy the sick fuck.

He paused as they started to race up the stairs. "Go," he said. "I have an idea."

"What—?"

"Just *go*. I'll meet you. And hurry."

Dallas didn't argue, and Liam backtracked, hoping this would work, hoping he wasn't crazy. Because it *had* to work. He couldn't lose her.

He *wouldn't* lose her.

Not now that she was finally his.

28

"I'M SO HAPPY FOR YOU," Jane says after I tell her about last night. It's not the first thing we talked about, of course. We started out gossiping about movies, and even though I work with a rising pop star and have met several celebrities, I'm still in awe of the people Jane has worked with.

But the fact is, I simply couldn't hold it in any longer, and so it all spilled out in one gooey, mushy rush of happiness.

Well, not all. I didn't tell her about the entire night. Just the conversation with Liam, his confession of love, and, most importantly, his willingness to move forward together and not shove me aside out of fear.

"Didn't I tell you?"

"You did," I say happily. "I just wish all of this were over. I feel like I'm in a fairy tale and the prince has kissed me, but the curse still hasn't lifted."

"It will," Jane says. "Liam and Dallas make a good team, and with us beside them, how can they miss. I mean—"

She stops mid-sentence, and I slide off the edge of the

bed where I've been sitting, my pulse pounding. "Is it the baby? Jane? Jesus, Jane, what's going on?"

"Alarm," she says and I look up and see that the glass thingie is flashing red.

"What happened?" I ask, even as she reaches for her phone, and I remember what Liam said about an app.

I see her eyes widen, and one hand goes protectively to her belly. Above us, the alarm light goes out.

"Guest wing," Jane says. "Someone broke a window. The system alerted 911." I can tell that she's trying to stay calm, but the quiver in her voice gives her away, and I know that she's thinking what I'm thinking—Liam and Dallas.

"They have to be okay," Jane says, reading my thoughts. "Dallas locked us in."

"What?" My chest tightens with panic.

"Remote locks." She nods toward the door. "We're locked in. No one can get through from either side until it's disabled."

"Oh, God," I say, the panic rising. With Liam at my side, I haven't had an attack in days, not even that day in the car. But now, with him locked away from me...

My throat tightens, and I fight the sensation. I can't lose control. I have to fight.

I think of Liam. His touch. His love.

I have to fight so I can live.

I draw a deep breath. "The lock," I say to Jane, whose face looks as scared as I feel. "Can you disable it? I need to go help them." I glance wildly around for my purse, which has my tiny Ruger in it, and see it on the bedside table on the far side from Jane.

"No, never mind," I say, immediately contradicting myself. It's not like either of them need my meager skill set.

I'd only be in the way. But Jane is in no condition to fend for herself. All she has now is me.

I take a deep breath and tell myself that I've got this. We're safe in this room. Dallas and Liam have mad skills. And the cops are on the way. We're safe as houses, whatever the hell that means.

I take a step toward my purse, then freeze when a sharp crack just about shatters my eardrums. Jane's scream mingles with my own, and when I automatically look in her direction, I see that whoever is outside has shot the door lock. The doorjamb is shattered, too, and before I can even catch my breath, the door is kicked open and I find myself face to face with Edward Noyce, the man from my past and my nightmares.

And I'm staring straight down the barrel of his gun, cold fear icing my veins.

To my right, I see Jane slowly inching toward my purse. I hadn't told her I have a gun, but considering I was searching for my bag before my announcement that I had to go out and help the men, I'm guessing she assumes I have something more useful than lipstick in there.

"I wouldn't do that, Mommy. Not unless you and the little one want to be the next to die."

"You'll never get out of here alive," Jane says.

"She's right." That hard, cold voice belongs to Dallas, and as he speaks he moves into view behind Noyce, his gun aimed at the back of the bastard's head.

"I wouldn't be too sure of that. I'm a slippery mother-fucker. But even if I die, at least I'll have the satisfaction of taking her down with me."

I'm freezing cold. I've known fear, but this is different. Before, I'd half-wanted to die, believing it was the only way out of the nightmare that was my life. No, I had no life back then. Just an existence. And while I feared the pain, death would have been a relief.

Now, though...

Now, I have Liam, and the terror that this man can take that from me—from us—runs through me like ice. I can't think. I can't move. I can only pray for a miracle that I know won't come. After all, how many times had I made that plea in my past, only to wake up disappointed.

Now, though, another horrible thought comes to me. *Where's Liam?*

I try to swallow my fear. I force myself not to scream out the question to Dallas. He has to be okay.

He has to.

"We can work something out," Dallas is saying. "Testify against Corbu, and we can make a deal."

"And deny myself the pleasure of watching this bitch die?"

There is a dresser on the wall to his left with a mirror, and although he and Dallas can't see it, I can. And what I see brings both hope and dread. Because what I see is a panel of wood sliding slowly to the side, right across the room from Noyce.

Liam. It has to be Liam.

"Dallas is right," I say, trying to keep him engaged. Trying to buy a few minutes of life—a few minutes that might end up buying me a long and happy life with the man I love. "Testify and cut a deal and you can get everything erased. Do you think I care about pressing charges? I don't."

"She just wants her life back," Jane says, and I'm not sure if she's seen the moving panel, too, or if she's just trying to keep him talking.

"And what do I care about you?" Noyce asks, lifting his

gun as the panel moves enough to reveal the grate of the dumbwaiter.

I don't know what kind of gun he has, but I do know it's a revolver. And I do know he's just pulled back the hammer.

More than that, I know that I am directly between the gun and the dumbwaiter, and even though I'm terrified that by moving I'll reveal Liam before he's ready, the only thing I can think of to do is get the hell out of the way. And I do that by screaming, "Now!" and diving to the floor and rolling away just a split second before Noyce fires, his bullet boring into the opposite wall. Liam fires, too, his bullet passing through the dumbwaiter's grate to angle up and catch Noyce right between the eyes.

In almost the same instant, another shot rings out, and the force of the bullet from Dallas's gun knocks Noyce forward. He falls facedown onto the exceptionally nice carpet just as the sound of approaching sirens fill the room.

I ignore him, rushing across the room to Liam who is unfolding himself from the dumbwaiter. "Tight fit," he grumbles as he stands, then pulls me close to him, holding me so tight I can barely breathe.

On the bed, Dallas holds Jane, who sobs quietly in his arms, even more worked up than I am; thanks, I'm sure, to hormones.

For a moment, Liam and I just cling to each other. Then he puts me at arms-length, inspecting me for injuries. "I'm fine. I'm fine," I assure him, then freeze when I see his arm. "Oh my God."

"I'm fine, too," he says. "They'll stitch it up. No big deal. You're safe," he says. "It's over."

"Over? What about Weil?"

"Dead," he tells me, and that's when my knees really do collapse. Liam drops down beside me, pulling me close. I let him hold me, trying to adjust to this new reality. "I'm safe," I say, enjoying the taste of the words on my tongue. I look up at him, happier than I can ever remember being. "I told you I was safe with you."

"So you did," he says, then grins. "Looks like we've won. And our prize is each other."

"Tell me you love me," I say, just because I want to hear it.

"I love you. And I will happily spend the rest of my life proving it to you."

I grin, then squeeze his hand as the cops and EMT guys rush into the room. "In that case, let's get you stitched up so that you can take me home and start making your case."

"Um, guys," Jane says, as Dallas beams beside her. "I think that Liam may not be the only one who needs to go to the hospital."

EPILOGUE

"EVERYBODY, if I could have your attention, please." Liam stands on the edge of the hot tub in Damien Stark's back patio, his position giving him at least a foot of height over everyone else. It's a gorgeous space, with an infinity pool that looks out over his Malibu property and the Pacific ocean.

'Everyone' includes most of the staff at Stark Security, plus significant others and friends. Damien and Nikki are here, of course, along with Jackson and Sylvia, Cass, Emma, and several of the guys who used to work with Dallas at Deliverance.

And, most important, Dallas, Jane, and their three-month-old daughter, who is the star of this particular party.

"It is my very great pleasure to introduce to you Lisa Mystery Sykes. A toast," he says, then lifts his glass of champagne. Everyone else does the same, and we all sip our fizzy drink, mine a new raspberry and lime sparkling water.

I wait for Liam to come to my side, then twine my fingers with his. "Three months," he says. "It's our anniversary, too. Of being together, and of you being free."

I tilt my head up for his kiss. "We'll have to celebrate."

"Definitely." His brow furrows as if in thought. "But how best to do that..."

I flash what I hope is a wicked grin, making him laugh.

Eliza and Quince join us, waiting in what has become a cluster more than a line of people who want to see the baby. "So when are you two joining that club?" Liam asks Quince. It's become a running joke between them, and Eliza and I exchange amused glances.

"Probably about the time you finally pop the question to that one," Quince says, nodding toward me.

"Oh, soon then," Liam says, and I almost choke on my water.

Quince and Eliza exchange glances, too, but Liam only smiles, as if it was the most ordinary comment in the world. "I didn't say tomorrow," he whispers to me. "But soon is very much on my radar. If that's too fast for you, tell me now."

"No," I say, my heart tripping. "No, soon is just fine."

"Did you see Emma?" Eliza asks, her voice almost as giddy as I'm now feeling. "She was talking earlier to Damien and Ryan."

It took a few weeks after the drama in Southampton, but I finally met Damien Stark, and though he used to intimidate me—gorgeous, rich, very self-possessed—I finally realized he is simply a great guy in really awesome packaging.

"What were they talking about?" I ask.

"Emma is now officially with the SSA."

"I know," I say. "Isn't it great?"

Her face crumples. "You knew? But you didn't know," she says to Quince, her voice almost an accusation.

"Sorry to disappoint you, love, but I only catch the bad guys. As our office manager, Xena does the paperwork. And that would include setting up payroll."

"Well, hell," Eliza says, eyeing me. "Guess I'll start getting my gossip from you."

"Antonio is here," Quince tells Liam.

"He was in Deliverance with you, right?" I ask as we inch slightly forward.

Liam nods. "Great guy. I haven't seen much of him in the last couple of years."

"Neither have I," Quince says.

"Maybe he's joining Stark Security," Eliza says, looking at me.

I laugh. "I have no knowledge. Swear."

"I doubt it," Quince says. "He seemed relieved when we disbanded. I got the impression he had things of his own to work out."

From the look on Liam's face, I think he agrees, but I don't have time to ask because we've arrived at the baby. Dallas looks about to burst with pride as he holds his daughter and Jane looks exhausted but happy as she gives me a hug.

"I looked for you earlier," I tell her.

"I snuck away for a bit to change and feed her."

"I'm glad you kept Mystery," I tell her, my voice low.

"You inspired us," she says, and we both laugh.

"How's mommyhood?"

"Tiring," she says. "And absolutely freaking amazing."

"I'm so glad."

I feel a hand on my shoulder, then hear a soft whisper at my ear. "Someday."

I turn back, but Liam looks so innocent I can almost convince myself it was my imagination. I hope it wasn't. I want a family; I want it with Liam. And I've even started researching getting my tubal ligation reversed, even though I know I'm getting a little ahead of myself.

Behind us, Sylvia and Jackson come up to see the newest addition to the Sykes family, so Liam and I step aside after Jane promises to find me later to catch up. We're leaning against a stone wall, just holding hands and looking at the view, when Liam says, "There's Antonio."

He's clean-shaven in his mid-thirties with dark hair, warm brown skin, and a friendly, open face.

Liam starts to take a step toward him, but then pauses when Damien approaches, his hand outstretched. We watch as the two men shake. We're in the open, not intentionally eavesdropping, but I still feel like this is a private moment. At the same time, leaving would just call attention to ourselves.

Besides, Liam wants to talk to his friend, and lingering is the traditionally accepted cocktail party method of catching someone's attention.

All of which is to say that we can hear perfectly when Antonio says, "Thanks so much for inviting me. It's great to have the chance to see Dallas and Jane and the baby. And your house. It's exceptional."

"Thanks. Is that the only reason you accepted my invitation?"

Antonio grins. "I think you know it's not."

"What can I do for you?" Damien's hands are in the pockets of his khaki slacks, and the sun makes his raven-colored hair gleam.

"Do you remember what you said in Paris?"

"After you came to my wife's rescue? I'm not inclined to forget things like that. I said that if you ever need help, Stark Security is there for you. Anytime. Anything."

"Well," Antonio says, "it turns out I do need some help. Specifically, I need a woman."

———

I hoped you enjoyed Liam and Xena's story! And I hope you're excited to meet **ANTONIO** in *Wrecked With You!*

Be sure to visit my website at www.jkenner.com to subscribe to my newsletter or **Text JKenner to 21000** to subscribe to text alerts and be among the first to get all the news about new books, sales, free content, and other fun stuff!

The Stark Security books are set in a world that first came to life for me in *Release Me*, Damien Stark and Nikki Fairchild's story. Keep turning pages for the first chapter!

And did you know that you can find Jamie and Ryan's story in *Tame Me*?

And as for Dallas and Jane, their trilogy begins with *Dirtiest Secret*. Check it out! It's by far my most taboo book ... and I absolutely adore it!

Happy reading!

JK

RELEASE ME

CHAPTER ONE EXCERPT

From the author - The Stark Security series is part of my Stark World stories that began with Release Me, which introduced millions of readers to the world of Damien Stark. If you haven't read Nikki & Damien's story, I hope you enjoy this peek into their world!

A cool ocean breeze caresses my bare shoulders, and I shiver, wishing I'd taken my roommate's advice and brought a shawl with me tonight. I arrived in Los Angeles only four days ago, and I haven't yet adjusted to the concept of summer temperatures changing with the setting of the sun. In Dallas, June is hot, July is hotter, and August is hell.

Not so in California, at least not by the beach. LA Lesson Number One: Always carry a sweater if you'll be out after dark.

Of course, I could leave the balcony and go back inside to the party. Mingle with the millionaires. Chat up the celebrities. Gaze dutifully at the paintings. It is a gala art opening, after all, and my boss brought me here to meet and greet and charm and chat. Not to lust over the panorama that is coming alive in front of me. Bloodred clouds bursting against the pale orange sky. Blue-gray waves shimmering with dappled gold.

I press my hands against the balcony rail and lean forward, drawn to the intense, unreachable beauty of the setting sun. I regret that I didn't bring the battered Nikon I've had since high school. Not that it would have fit in my itty-bitty beaded purse. And a bulky camera bag paired with a little black dress is a big, fat fashion no-no.

But this is my very first Pacific Ocean sunset, and I'm determined to document the moment. I pull out my iPhone and snap a picture.

"Almost makes the paintings inside seem redundant, doesn't it?" I recognize the throaty, feminine voice and turn to face Evelyn Dodge, retired actress turned agent turned patron of the arts—and my hostess for the evening.

"I'm so sorry. I know I must look like a giddy tourist, but we don't have sunsets like this in Dallas."

"Don't apologize," she says. "I pay for that view every month when I write the mortgage check. It damn well better be spectacular."

I laugh, immediately more at ease.

"Hiding out?"

"Excuse me?"

"You're Carl's new assistant, right?" she asks, referring to my boss of three days.

"Nikki Fairchild."

"I remember now. Nikki from Texas." She looks me up and down, and I wonder if she's disappointed that I don't have big hair and cowboy boots. "So who does he want you to charm?"

Release Me | 755

"Charm?" I repeat, as if I don't know exactly what she means.

She cocks a single brow. "Honey, the man would rather walk on burning coals than come to an art show. He's fishing for investors and you're the bait." She makes a rough noise in the back of her throat. "Don't worry. I won't press you to tell me who. And I don't blame you for hiding out. Carl's brilliant, but he's a bit of a prick."

"It's the brilliant part I signed on for," I say, and she barks out a laugh.

The truth is that she's right about me being the bait. "Wear a cocktail dress," Carl had said. "Something flirty."

Seriously? I mean, *Seriously?*

I should have told him to wear his own damn cocktail dress. But I didn't. Because I want this job. I fought to get this job. Carl's company, C-Squared Technologies, successfully launched three web-based products in the last eighteen months. That track record had caught the industry's eye, and Carl had been hailed as a man to watch.

More important from my perspective, that meant he was a man to learn from, and I'd prepared for the job interview with an intensity bordering on obsession. Landing the position had been a huge coup for me. So what if he wanted me to wear something flirty? It was a small price to pay.

Shit.

"I need to get back to being the bait," I say.

"Oh, hell. Now I've gone and made you feel either guilty or self-conscious. Don't be. Let them get liquored up in there first. You catch more flies with alcohol anyway. Trust me. I know."

She's holding a pack of cigarettes, and now she taps one out, then extends the pack to me. I shake my head. I love the smell of tobacco—it reminds me of my grandfather—but actually inhaling the smoke does nothing for me.

"I'm too old and set in my ways to quit," she says. "But God forbid I smoke in my own damn house. I swear, the mob would burn me in effigy. You're not going to start lecturing me on the dangers of secondhand smoke, are you?"

"No," I promise.

"Then how about a light?"

I hold up the itty-bitty purse. "One lipstick, a credit card, my driver's license, and my phone."

"No condom?"

"I didn't think it was that kind of party," I say dryly.

"I knew I liked you." She glances around the balcony. "What the hell kind of party am I throwing if I don't even have one goddamn candle on one goddamn table? Well, fuck it." She puts the unlit cigarette to her mouth and inhales, her eyes closed and her expression rapturous. I can't help but like her. She wears hardly any makeup, in stark contrast to all the other women here tonight, myself included, and her dress is more of a caftan, the batik pattern as interesting as the woman herself.

She's what my mother would call a brassy broad—loud, large, opinionated, and self-confident. My mother would hate her. I think she's awesome.

She drops the unlit cigarette onto the tile and grinds it with the toe of her shoe. Then she signals to one of the catering staff, a girl dressed all in black and carrying a tray of champagne glasses.

The girl fumbles for a minute with the sliding door that opens onto the balcony, and I imagine those flutes tumbling off, breaking against the hard tile, the scattered shards glittering like a wash of diamonds.

I picture myself bending to snatch up a broken stem. I see the raw edge cutting into the soft flesh at the base of my thumb as I squeeze. I watch myself clutching it tighter, drawing strength from the pain, the way some people might try to extract luck from a rabbit's foot.

The fantasy blurs with memory, jarring me with its potency. It's fast and powerful, and a little disturbing because I haven't needed the pain in a long time, and I don't understand why I'm thinking about it now, when I feel steady and in control.

I am fine, I think. *I am fine, I am fine, I am fine.*

"Take one, honey," Evelyn says easily, holding a flute out to me.

I hesitate, searching her face for signs that my mask has slipped and she's caught a glimpse of my rawness. But her face is clear and genial.

"No, don't you argue," she adds, misinterpreting my hesitation. "I bought a dozen cases and I hate to see good alcohol go to waste. Hell no," she adds when the girl tries to hand her a flute. "I hate the stuff. Get me a vodka. Straight up. Chilled. Four olives. Hurry up, now. Do you want me to dry up like a leaf and float away?"

The girl shakes her head, looking a bit like a twitchy, frightened rabbit. Possibly one that had sacrificed his foot for someone else's good luck.

Evelyn's attention returns to me. "So how do you like LA? What have you seen? Where have you been? Have you bought a map of the stars yet? Dear God, tell me you're not getting sucked into all that tourist bullshit."

"Mostly I've seen miles of freeway and the inside of my apartment."

"Well, that's just sad. Makes me even more glad that Carl dragged your skinny ass all the way out here tonight."

I've put on fifteen welcome pounds since the years when my mother monitored every tiny thing that went in my mouth, and while I'm perfectly happy with my size-eight ass, I wouldn't describe it as skinny. I know Evelyn means it as a compliment, though, and so I smile. "I'm glad he brought me, too. The paintings really are amazing."

"Now don't do that—don't you go sliding into the polite-conversation routine. No, no," she says before I can protest. "I'm sure you mean it. Hell, the paintings are wonderful. But you're getting the flat-eyed look of a girl on her best behavior, and we can't have that. Not when I was getting to know the real you."

"Sorry," I say. "I swear I'm not fading away on you."

Because I genuinely like her, I don't tell her that she's wrong—she hasn't met the real Nikki Fairchild. She's met Social Nikki who, much like Malibu Barbie, comes with a complete set of accessories. In my case, it's not a bikini and a convertible. Instead, I have the *Elizabeth Fairchild Guide for Social Gatherings*.

My mother's big on rules. She claims it's her Southern upbringing. In my weaker moments, I agree. Mostly, I just think she's a controlling bitch. Since the first time she took me for tea at the Mansion at Turtle Creek in Dallas at age three, I have had the rules drilled into my head. How to walk, how to talk, how to dress. What to eat, how much to drink, what kinds of jokes to tell.

I have it all down, every trick, every nuance, and I wear my practiced pageant smile like armor against the world. The result being that I don't think I could truly be myself at a party even if my life depended on it.

This, however, is not something Evelyn needs to know.

"Where exactly are you living?" she asks.

"Studio City. I'm sharing a condo with my best friend from high school."

"Straight down the 101 for work and then back home again. No wonder you've only seen concrete. Didn't anyone tell you that you should have taken an apartment on the Westside?"

"Too pricey to go it alone," I admit, and I can tell that my admission surprises her. When I make the effort—like when I'm Social Nikki—I can't help but look like I come from money. Probably because I do. Come from it, that is. But that doesn't mean I brought it with me.

"How old are you?"

"Twenty-four."

Evelyn nods sagely, as if my age reveals some secret about me. "You'll be wanting a place of your own soon enough. You call me when you do and we'll find you some-place with a view. Not as good as this one, of course, but we can manage something better than a freeway on-ramp."

"It's not that bad, I promise."

"Of course it's not," she says in a tone that says the exact opposite. "As for views," she continues, gesturing toward the now-dark ocean and the sky that's starting to bloom with stars, "you're welcome to come back anytime and share mine."

"I might take you up on that," I admit. "I'd love to bring a decent camera back here and take a shot or two."

"It's an open invitation. I'll provide the wine and you can provide the entertainment. A young woman loose in the city. Will it be a drama? A rom-com? Not a tragedy, I hope. I love a good cry as much as the next woman, but I like you. You need a happy ending."

I tense, but Evelyn doesn't know she's hit a nerve. That's why I moved to LA, after all. New life. New story. New Nikki.

I ramp up the Social Nikki smile and lift my champagne flute. "To happy endings. And to this amazing party. I think I've kept you from it long enough."

"Bullshit," she says. "I'm the one monopolizing you, and we both know it."

We slip back inside, the buzz of alcohol-fueled conversation replacing the soft calm of the ocean.

"The truth is, I'm a terrible hostess. I do what I want, talk to whoever I want, and if my guests feel slighted they can damn well deal with it."

I gape. I can almost hear my mother's cries of horror all the way from Dallas.

"Besides," she continues, "this party isn't supposed to be about me. I put together this little shindig to introduce Blaine and his art to the community. He's the one who should be doing the mingling, not me. I may be fucking him, but I'm not going to baby him."

Evelyn has completely destroyed my image of how a hostess for the not-to-be-missed social event of the weekend is supposed to behave, and I think I'm a little in love with her for that.

"I haven't met Blaine yet. That's him, right?" I point to a tall reed of a man. He is bald, but sports a red goatee. I'm pretty sure it's not his natural color. A small crowd hums around him, like bees drawing nectar from a flower. His outfit is certainly as bright as one.

"That's my little center of attention, all right," Evelyn says. "The man of the hour. Talented, isn't he?" Her hand sweeps out to indicate her massive living room. Every wall is covered with paintings. Except for a few benches, whatever furniture was once in the room has been removed and replaced with easels on which more paintings stand.

I suppose technically they are portraits. The models are nudes, but these aren't like anything you would see in a classical art book. There's something edgy about them. Something provocative and raw. I can tell that they are expertly conceived and carried out, and yet they disturb me, as if they reveal more about the person viewing the portrait than about the painter or the model.

As far as I can tell, I'm the only one with that reaction. Certainly the crowd around Blaine is glowing. I can hear the gushing praise from here.

"I picked a winner with that one," Evelyn says. "But let's see. Who do you want to meet? Rip Carrington and Lyle Tarpin? Those two are guaranteed drama, that's for damn sure, and your roommate will be jealous as hell if you chat them up."

"She will?"

Evelyn's brows arch up. "Rip and Lyle? They've been feuding for weeks." She narrows her eyes at me. "The fiasco about the new season of their sitcom? It's all over the Internet? You really don't know them?"

"Sorry," I say, feeling the need to apologize. "My school schedule was pretty intense. And I'm sure you can imagine what working for Carl is like."

Speaking of ...

I glance around, but I don't see my boss anywhere.

"That is one serious gap in your education," Evelyn says. "Culture—and yes, pop culture counts—is just as important as—what did you say you studied?"

"I don't think I mentioned it. But I have a double major in electrical engineering and computer science."

"So you've got brains and beauty. See? That's something else we have in common. Gotta say, though, with an education like that, I don't see why you signed up to be Carl's secretary."

I laugh. "I'm not, I swear. Carl was looking for someone with tech experience to work with him on the business side of things, and I was looking for a job where I could learn the business side. Get my feet wet. I think he was a little hesitant to hire me at first—my skills definitely lean toward tech— but I convinced him I'm a fast learner."

She peers at me. "I smell ambition."

I lift a shoulder in a casual shrug. "It's Los Angeles. Isn't that what this town is all about?"

"Ha! Carl's lucky he's got you. It'll be interesting to see how long he keeps you. But let's see ... who here would intrigue you ...?"

She casts about the room, finally pointing to a fifty-something man holding court in a corner. "That's Charles Maynard," she says. "I've known Charlie for years. Intimidating as hell until you get to know him. But it's worth it. His clients are either celebrities with name recognition or power brokers with more money than God. Either way, he's got all the best stories."

"He's a lawyer?"

"With Bender, Twain & McGuire. Very prestigious firm."

"I know," I say, happy to show that I'm not entirely ignorant, despite not knowing Rip or Lyle. "One of my closest friends works for the firm. He started here but he's in their New York office now."

"Well, come on, then, Texas. I'll introduce you." We take one step in that direction, but then Evelyn stops me. Maynard has pulled out his phone, and is shouting instructions at someone. I catch a few well-placed curses and eye Evelyn sideways. She looks unconcerned "He's a pussycat at heart. Trust me, I've worked with him before.

Back in my agenting days, we put together more celebrity biopic deals for our clients than I can count. And we fought to keep a few tell-alls off the screen, too." She shakes her head, as if reliving those glory days, then pats my arm. "Still, we'll wait 'til he calms down a bit. In the meantime, though ..."

She trails off, and the corners of her mouth turn down in a frown as she scans the room again. "I don't think he's here yet, but—oh! Yes! Now *there's* someone you should meet. And if you want to talk views, the house he's building has one that makes my view look like, well, like yours." She points toward the entrance hall, but all I see are bobbing heads and haute couture. "He hardly ever accepts invitations, but we go way back," she says.

I still can't see who she's talking about, but then the crowd parts and I see the man in profile. Goose bumps rise on my arms, but I'm not cold. In fact, I'm suddenly very, very warm.

He's tall and so handsome that the word is almost an insult. But it's more than that. It's not his looks, it's his *presence.* He commands the room simply by being in it, and I realize that Evelyn and I aren't the only ones looking at him. The entire crowd has noticed his arrival. He must feel the weight of all those eyes, and yet the attention doesn't faze him at all. He smiles at the girl with the champagne, takes a glass, and begins to chat casually with a woman who approaches him, a simpering smile stretched across her face.

"Damn that girl," Evelyn says. "She never did bring me my vodka."

But I barely hear her. "Damien Stark," I say. My voice surprises me. It's little more than breath.

Evelyn's brows rise so high I notice the movement in my

peripheral vision. "Well, how about that?" she says knowingly. "Looks like I guessed right."

"You did," I admit. "Mr. Stark is just the man I want to see."

———

Meet Damien Stark in Release Me, *international bestselling sensation that started it all...*

ABOUT THE AUTHOR

J. Kenner (aka Julie Kenner) is the *New York Times, USA Today, Publishers Weekly, Wall Street Journal* and #1 International bestselling author of over one hundred novels, novellas and short stories in a variety of genres.

 JK has been praised by *Publishers Weekly* as an author with a "flair for dialogue and eccentric characterizations" and by *RT Bookclub* for having "cornered the market on sinfully attractive, dominant antiheroes and the women who swoon for them." A five-time finalist for Romance Writers of America's prestigious RITA award, JK took home the first RITA trophy awarded in the category of erotic romance in 2014 for her novel, *Claim Me* (book 2 of her Stark Trilogy) and the RITA trophy for *Wicked Dirty* in the same category in 2017.

In her previous career as an attorney, JK worked as a lawyer in Southern California and Texas. She currently lives in Central Texas, with her husband, two daughters, and two rather spastic cats.

Visit her website at www.juliekenner.com to learn more and to connect with JK through social media!

Lightning Source UK Ltd.
Milton Keynes UK
UKHW020929180522
403142UK00006B/569

9 781949 925944